#1 *New York Times* BESTSELLING AUTHOR JULIE GARWOOD "ATTRACTS READERS LIKE BEAUTIFUL HEROINES ATTRACT DASHING HEROES" *(USA Today)* AND WRITES "GRIPPING ESCAPISM OF THE TALLEST ORDER" ***(Kirkus Reviews).***

HER ENCHANTING BESTSELLERS ARE . . .

"Enthralling."

—*Romantic Times*

"Pure entertainment. . . . Truly unforgettable

—*Rendezvous*

"Riveting."

—*BookPage*

"Heartwarming . . . wonderful."

—*Abilene Reporter News* (TX)

THE LION'S LADY

"Outstanding . . . wonderfully unique in plot and characters, and beautifully told . . . delightful."

—Johanna Lindsey

"A beautiful love story. One of the best books I have read in a very long time."

—Judith McNaught

Books by Julie Garwood

Gentle Warrior
Rebellious Desire
Honor's Splendour
The Lion's Lady
The Bride
Guardian angel
The Gift
The Prize
The Secret
Castles
Saving Grace
Prince Charming
For the Roses
The Wedding
Come the Spring
Ransom
Heartbreaker
Mercy

The Clayborne Brides
One Pink Rose
One White Rose
One Red Rose

Published by Pocket Books

JULIE GARWOOD

CASTLES
THE LION'S LADY

POCKET BOOKS
New York London Toronto Sydney

This book is a work of fiction. Names, characters, places and incidents are products of the author's imagination or are used fictitiously. Any resemblance to actual events or locales or persons, living or dead, is entirely coincidental.

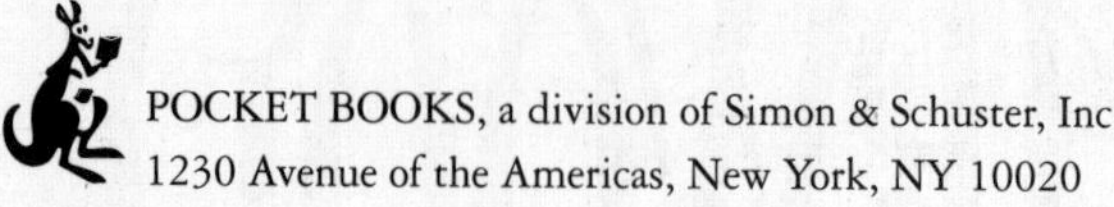

POCKET BOOKS, a division of Simon & Schuster, Inc.
1230 Avenue of the Americas, New York, NY 10020

ISBN-13: 978-1-4165-1712-2
ISBN-10: 1-4165-1712-X

This Pocket Books trade paperback edition January 2006

10 9 8 7 6 5 4 3 2 1

Manufactured in the United States of America

Castles and *The Lion's Lady* were previously published individually by Pocket Books

For Sharon Felice Murphy,
an easy listener, an inspiration,
a source of joy.
What would I do without you?

CASTLES

Prologue

England, 1819

He was a real lady killer.

The foolish woman never had a chance. She never knew she was being stalked, never guessed her secret admirer's real intent.

He believed he killed her with kindness. He was proud of that accomplishment. He could have been cruel. He wasn't. The craving eating away at him demanded to be appeased, and even though erotic thoughts of torture aroused him to a fever pitch, he hadn't given in to the base urge. He was a man, not an animal. He was after self-gratification, and the chit certainly deserved to die, yet he'd still shown true compassion. He had been very kind—considering.

She had, after all, died smiling. He deliberately caught her so by surprise he only glimpsed one quick spasm of terror in her cow brown eyes before it was over. He crooned to her then, like any good master would croon to his injured pet, letting her hear the sound of his compassion all the while he was strangling her, and he didn't stop his song of sympathy until the killing was finished and he knew she couldn't hear him.

He hadn't been without mercy. Even when he was certain she was dead, he gently turned her face away from him before he allowed himself to smile. He wanted to laugh, with relief because it was finally over, and with satisfaction because it had gone so very well, but he didn't dare make a sound now, for somewhere in the back of his mind lurked the thought that such undignified behavior would make him seem more monster than man, and he certainly wasn't a monster. No, no, he didn't hate women, he admired them—most anyway—and to those he considered redeemable, he was neither cruel nor heartless.

He was terribly clever though. There wasn't any shame in admitting that truth. The chase had been invigorating, but from start to finish he had been able to predict her every reaction. Granted, her own vanity had helped him immensely. She was a naive chit who thought of herself as worldly—a dangerous misconception—and he had proven to be far too cunning for the likes of her.

There had been sweet irony in his choice of weapons. He had planned to use his dagger to kill her. He wanted to feel the blade sink deep inside her, craved the feel of her hot blood as it poured over his hands each time he slammed the knife into her soft, smooth skin. Carve the fowl, carve the fowl. *The command echoed in his mind. He hadn't given in to his desire, however, for he was still stronger than his inner voice, and on the spur of the moment he decided not to use the dagger at all. The diamond necklace he'd given her was draped around her neck. He grabbed hold of the expensive trinket and used it to squeeze the life out of her. He thought the weapon was most appropriate. Women liked trinkets, this one more than most. He even considered burying the necklace with her, but just as he was about to pour the clumps of lime over her body he'd gathered from the cliffs to hurry the decay, he changed his inclination and put the necklace in his pocket.*

He walked away from the grave without a backward glance. He felt no remorse, no guilt. She'd served him well and now he was content.

A thick mist covered the ground. He didn't notice the lime powder on his boots until he had reached the main road. He wasn't bothered by the fact that his new Wellingtons were probably ruined. Nothing was going to blemish his glow of victory. He felt as though all his burdens had been lifted away. But there was more, too—the rush he'd felt again, that magnificent euphoria he'd experienced when he had his hands on her. . . . Oh, yes, this one was even better than the last.

She'd made him feel alive again. The world was once again rosy with choices for such a strong, virile man.

He knew he would feed on the memory of tonight for a long, long while. And then, when the glow began to ebb, he would go hunting again.

Chapter 1

Mother Superior Mary Felicity had always believed in miracles, but in all of her sixty-seven years on this sweet earth, she had never actually witnessed one until the frigid day in February of 1820 when the letter arrived from England.

At first the mother superior had been afraid to believe the blessed news, for she feared it was trickery on the devil's part to get her hopes up and then dash them later, but after she had dutifully answered the missive and received a second confirmation with the Duke of Williamshire's seal affixed, she accepted the gift for what it truly was.

A miracle.

They were finally going to get rid of the hellion. The mother superior shared her good news with the other nuns the following morning at matins. That evening they celebrated with duck soup and freshly baked black bread. Sister Rachael was positively giddy and had to be admonished twice for laughing out loud during evening vespers.

The hellion—or, rather, Princess Alesandra—was called into the mother superior's stark office the following afternoon. While she was being given the news of her departure from the convent, Sister Rachael was busy packing her bags.

The mother superior sat in a high-backed chair behind a

wide desk as scarred and old as she was. The nun absentmindedly fingered the heavy wooden beads of her rosary, hooked to the side of her black habit, while she waited for her charge to react to the announcement.

Princess Alesandra was stunned by the news. She gripped her hands together in a nervous gesture and kept her head bowed so the mother superior wouldn't see the tears in her eyes.

"Do sit down, Alesandra. I don't wish to talk to the top of your head."

"As you wish, Mother." She sat on the very edge of the hard chair, straightened her posture to please the superior, and then clasped her hands together in her lap.

"What do you think of this news?" the mother superior asked.

"It was the fire, wasn't it, Mother? You still haven't forgiven me that mishap."

"Nonsense," the mother superior replied. "I forgave you that thoughtlessness over a month ago."

"Was it Sister Rachael who convinced you to send me away? I did tell her how sorry I was, and her face isn't nearly as green anymore."

The mother superior shook her head. She frowned, too, for Alesandra was inadvertently getting her all riled up over the reminders of some of her antics.

"Why you believed that vile paste would remove freckles is beyond my understanding. However, Sister Rachael did agree to the experiment. She doesn't blame you . . . overly much," she hastened to add so the lie she was telling would only be considered a venial sin in God's eyes. "Alesandra, I didn't write to your guardian requesting your leave. He wrote to me. Here is the Duke of Williamshire's letter. Read it and then you'll see I'm telling you the truth."

Alesandra's hand shook when she reached for the missive. She quickly scanned the contents before handing the letter back to her superior.

"You can see the urgency, can't you? This General Ivan your guardian mentions sounds quite disreputable. Do you remember meeting him?"

Alesandra shook her head. "We visited father's homeland several times, but I was very young. I don't remember meeting him. Why in heaven's name would he want to marry me?"

"Your guardian understands the general's motives," the mother superior replied. She tapped the letter with her fingertips. "Your father's subjects haven't forgotten you. You're still their beloved princess. The general has a notion that if he marries you, he'll be able to take over the kingdom with the support of the masses. It's a clever plan."

"But I don't wish to marry him," Alesandra whispered.

"And neither does your guardian wish it," the superior said. "He believes the general won't take no for an answer, however, and will take you by force if necessary to insure his success. That is why the Duke of Williamshire wants guards to journey with you to England."

"I don't want to leave here, Mother. I really don't."

The anguish in Alesandra's voice tugged at the mother superior's heart. Forgotten for the moment were all the mischievous schemes Princess Alesandra had gotten involved in over the past years. The superior remembered the vulnerability and the fear in the little girl's eyes when she and her ailing mother had first arrived. Alesandra had been quite saintly while her mother lived. She had been so very young—only twelve—and had lost her dear father just six months before. Yet the child had shown tremendous strength. She took on the full responsibility of caring for her mother day and night. There was never any possibility her mother would recover. Her illness destroyed her body and her mind, and toward the end, when she had been crazed with her pain, Alesandra would climb into her mother's sickbed and take the frail woman into her arms. She would gently rock her back and forth and sing tender ballads to her, her voice that of an angel. Her love for her mother had been achingly beautiful to see. When at last the devil's torture was finished, her mother died in her daughter's arms.

Alesandra wouldn't allow anyone to comfort her. She wept during the dark hours of the night, alone in her cell, the white curtains surrounding her cubicle blocking out none of her sobs from the postulants.

Her mother was buried on the grounds behind the chapel in a lovely, flower-bordered grotto. Alesandra couldn't abide the thought of leaving her. The grounds of the convent were adjacent to the family's second home, Stone Haven, but Alesandra wouldn't even journey there for a visitation.

"I had thought I would stay here forever," Alesandra whispered.

"You must look upon this as your destiny unfolding," the mother superior advised. "One chapter of your life is closing and another is about to open up."

Alesandra lowered her head again. "I wish to have all my chapters here, Mother. You could deny the Duke of Williamshire's request if you wished, or stall him with endless correspondence until he forgot about me."

"And the general?"

Alesandra had already thought of an answer to that dilemma. "He wouldn't dare breach this sanctuary. I'm safe as long as I stay here."

"A man lusting for power will not care if he breaks the holy laws governing this convent, Alesandra. He certainly would breach our sanctuary. Do you realize you are also suggesting I deceive your dear guardian?"

The nun's voice held a note of reproach in it. "No, Mother," Alesandra answered with a little sigh, knowing full well that was the answer the nun wished to hear. "I suppose it would be wrong to deceive . . ."

The wistfulness in her voice made the mother superior shake her head. "I will not accommodate you. Even if there was a valid reason . . ."

Alesandra jumped on the possibility. "Oh, but there is," she blurted out. She took a deep breath, then announced, "I have decided to become a nun."

The mere thought of Alesandra joining their holy order sent chills down the mother superior's spine. "Heaven help us all," she muttered.

"It's because of the books, isn't it, Mother? You want to send me away because of that little . . . fabrication."

"Alesandra . . ."

"I only made the second set of books so the banker would give you the loan. You refused to use my funds, and I knew how much you needed the new chapel . . . what with the fire and all. And you did get the loan, didn't you? God has surely forgiven me my deception, and He must have wanted me to alter the numbers in the accounts or He never would have given me such a fine head for figures. Would he, Mother Superior? In my heart, I know He forgave me my bit of trickery."

"Trickery? I believe the correct word is *larceny,*" the mother superior snapped.

"Nay, Mother," Alesandra corrected. "*Larceny* means to pilfer and I didn't pilfer anything. I merely amended."

The fierce frown on the superior's face told Alesandra she shouldn't have contradicted her, or brought up the still tender topic of the bookkeeping.

"About the fire . . ."

"Mother, I have already confessed my sorrow over that unfortunate mishap," Alesandra rushed out. She hurried to change the subject before the superior could get all riled up again. "I was very serious when I said I would like to become a nun. I believe I have the calling."

"Alesandra, you aren't Catholic."

"I would convert," Alesandra fervently promised.

A long minute passed in silence. Then the mother superior leaned forward. The chair squeaked with her movement. "Look at me," she commanded.

She waited until the princess had complied with her order before speaking again. "I believe I understand what this is really all about. I'm going to give you a promise," she said, her voice a soothing whisper. "I'll take good care of your mother's grave. If anything should happen to me, then Sister Justina or Sister Rachael will tend to it. Your mother won't be forgotten. She'll continue to be in our prayers every day. That is my promise to you."

Alesandra burst into tears. "I cannot leave her."

The mother superior stood up and hurried over to Alesandra's side. She put her arm around her shoulders and patted her. "You won't be leaving her behind. She will always be in your heart. She would want you to get on with your life."

Tears streamed down Alesandra's face. She mopped them away with the backs of her hands. "I don't know the Duke of Williamshire, Mother. I only met him once and I barely recall what he looked like. What if I don't get along with him? What if he doesn't want me? I don't want to be a burden to anyone. Please let me stay here."

"Alesandra, you seem determined to believe I have a choice in the matter and that simply isn't true. I too must obey your guardian's request. You're going to do just fine in England. The Duke of Williamshire has six children of his own. One more isn't going to be a bother."

"I'm not a child any longer," Alesandra reminded the nun. "And my guardian is probably very old and weary by now."

The mother superior smiled. "The Duke of Williamshire was chosen and named guardian over you years ago by your father. He had good reason for naming the Englishman. Have faith in your father's judgment."

"Yes, Mother."

"You can lead a happy life, Alesandra," the mother superior continued. "As long as you remember to use a little restraint. Think before you act. That's the key. You have a sound mind. Use it."

"Thank you for saying so, Mother."

"Quit acting so submissive. It isn't like you at all. I have one more bit of advice to offer you and I want your full attention. Do sit up straight. A princess does not slump."

If she sat any straighter, she thought, her spine might snap. Alesandra thrust her shoulders back a bit more and knew she'd satisfied the nun when she nodded.

"As I was saying," the mother superior continued. "It never mattered here that you were a princess, but it will matter in England. Appearances must be kept up at all times. You simply cannot allow spontaneous actions to rule your life. Now tell me, Alesandra, what are the two words I've asked you again and again to take to heart?"

"Dignity and *decorum,* Mother."

"Yes."

"May I come back here . . . if I find I don't like my new life?"

"You will always be welcomed back here," the mother superior promised. "Go now and help Sister Rachael with the packing. You'll be leaving in the dead of night as a precautionary measure. I'll wait in the chapel to say my good-bye."

Alesandra stood up, made a quick curtsy, then left the room. The mother superior stood in the center of the small chamber and stared after her charge for a long while. She had believed it was a miracle the princess was leaving. The mother superior had always followed a rigid schedule. Then Alesandra came into her life, and schedules became nonexistent. The nun didn't like chaos, but chaos and Alesandra seemed to go hand in hand. Yet the minute the strong-willed princess walked out of the office, the mother superior's eyes filled with tears. It was as though the sun had just been covered with dark clouds.

Heaven help her, she was going to miss the imp and her antics.

Chapter 2

London, England, 1820

They'd called him the Dolphin. He'd called her the Brat. Princess Alesandra didn't know why her guardian's son Colin had been given the nickname of a sea mammal, but she was well aware of the reason behind his nickname for her. She'd earned it. She really had been a brat when she was a little girl, and the only time Colin and his older brother, Caine, had been in her company, she'd misbehaved shamefully. Granted, she had been very young—spoiled, too—a natural circumstance given the fact that she was an only child and was constantly being doted upon by relatives and servants alike. But her parents had both been gifted with patient natures, and they ignored her obnoxious behavior until she finally outgrew the temper tantrums and learned a little restraint.

Alesandra had been very young when her parents took her with them to England for a short visit. She had only a vague memory of the Duke and Duchess of Williamshire, didn't remember the daughters at all, and only had a hazy recollection of the two older sons. Caine and Colin. They were both giants in her mind, but then she had been very little and they had both been fully grown men. Her memory had probably exaggerated their size. She was certain she wouldn't be able to recognize either brother in a crowd today. She hoped

Colin had forgotten her past behavior as well as the fact that he'd called her a brat. Getting along with Colin would make everything so much easier to endure. The two duties she was about to undertake were going to be difficult, and having a safe haven at the end of each day was really quite imperative.

She had arrived in England on a dreary Monday morning and had immediately been taken to the Duke of Williamshire's country estate. Alesandra hadn't been feeling well, but believed her queasy stomach was due to anxiety. She was quick to recover, for she was welcomed into the family with sincerity and affection. Both the duke and duchess treated her as one of their own. Her awkwardness soon dissipated. She wasn't given special consideration, and was even allowed to speak her own mind every now and again. There was only one argument of substance between Alesandra and her guardian. He and his wife were going to escort her to London and open their town house for the season. Alesandra made over fifteen appointments, but just a few days before they were scheduled to leave for the city, both the duke and duchess became quite ill.

Alesandra wanted to go alone. She insisted she didn't want to be a bother to anyone and suggested that she rent her own town house for the season. The duchess had palpitations over the mere thought, but Alesandra held her ground. She reminded her guardian she was an adult, after all, and she could certainly take care of herself. The duke wouldn't hear of such talk. The debate raged for days. In the end it was decided that Alesandra would take up residence with Caine and his wife, Jade, while she was in London.

Unfortunately, just the day before she was supposed to arrive, both Caine and Jade came down with the same mysterious ailment currently afflicting the duke and duchess and their four daughters.

The only choice left was Colin. If Alesandra hadn't already scheduled so many appointments with her father's associates, she would have stayed in the country until her guardian had recovered. She didn't want to inconvenience

Colin, especially after hearing from his father about the terrible past two years he'd had. She imagined the last thing Colin needed now was chaos. Still, the Duke of Williamshire had been most insistent that she avail herself of his hospitality, and it wouldn't have been polite for her to refuse her guardian's wishes. Besides, living with Colin for a few days might make the request she was going to have to make of him easier.

She arrived on Colin's doorstep a little past the dinner hour. He had already gone out for the evening. Alesandra, her new lady's maid, and two trusted guards crowded into the narrow black and white tiled foyer to present her note from the Duke of Williamshire to the butler, a handsome young man named Flannaghan. The servant couldn't have been more than twenty-five years of age. The surprise of her arrival obviously rattled him, for he kept bowing to her, blushing to the roots of his white-blond hair, and she wasn't at all certain how to ease his discomfort.

"It is such an honor to have a princess in our home," he stammered out. He swallowed hard, then repeated the very same announcement.

"I hope your employer feels the way you do, sir," she replied. "I don't wish to be an inconvenience."

"No, no," Flannaghan blurted out, obviously appalled by the very idea. "You could never be an inconvenience."

"It's good of you to say so, sir."

Flannaghan swallowed hard again. In a worried tone he said, "But Princess Alesandra, I don't believe there's room for all of your staff." The butler's face was burning with embarrassment.

"We'll make do," she assured him with a smile, trying to put him at ease. The poor young man looked ill. "The Duke of Williamshire did insist I bring along my guards, and I couldn't travel anywhere without my new lady's maid. Her name's Valena. The duchess personally chose her for me. Valena has been living in London, you see, but she was born and raised in my father's homeland. Isn't it a wonderful coincidence she applied for the position? Yes, of course it is," she answered before Flannaghan could get a word in.

"Because she's only just been hired, I can't let her go. It wouldn't be at all polite, would it? You do understand. I can see you do."

Flannaghan had lost track of what was being explained to him, but he nodded agreement anyway just to please her. He was finally able to tear his gaze away from the beautiful princess. He bowed to her lady's maid, then ruined his first show of dignified behavior by blurting out, "She's just a child."

"Valena's a year older than I am," Alesandra explained. She turned to the fair-haired woman and spoke to her in a language Flannaghan had never heard before. It sounded a little like French to him, yet he knew it wasn't.

"Do any of your servants speak English?" he asked.

"When they wish to," she answered. She untied the cord at the top of her white fur-lined burgundy cloak. A tall, muscled guard with black hair and a menacing look about him stepped forward to take the garment from her. She thanked the man before turning back to Flannaghan. "I would like to get settled in for the night. The journey here took most of the day, sir, because of the rain, and I'm chilled to the bone. It was horrid outside," she added with a nod. "The rain felt like sleet, didn't it, Raymond?"

"Aye, it did, Princess," the guard agreed in a voice surprisingly gentle.

"We're all really quite exhausted," she told Flannaghan then.

"Of course you're exhausted," Flannaghan agreed. "If you'll follow me, please," he requested. He started up the stairs with the Princess at his side. "There are four chambers on the second level, Princess Alesandra, and three rooms on the floor above for the servants. If your guards will double up . . ."

"Raymond and Stefan will be happy to share quarters," she told him when he didn't continue. "Sir, this is really just a temporary arrangement until Colin's brother and his wife recover from their illness. I'll move in with them as soon as possible."

Flannaghan took hold of Alesandra's elbow to assist her

up the rest of the stairs. He seemed so eager to help that she didn't have the heart to tell him she didn't require his assistance. If it made him happy to treat her like an old woman, she would let him.

They had reached the landing before the servant noticed the guards weren't following. The two men had disappeared toward the back of the house. Alesandra explained that they were looking around the lower level to familiarize themselves with all of the entrances to the house and would come upstairs when they were finished.

"But why would they be interested . . ."

She didn't let him finish. "To make it safe for us, sir."

Flannaghan nodded, though in truth he still didn't have any idea what she was talking about.

"Would you mind taking over my employer's room tonight? The linens were freshly changed this morning and the other chambers aren't ready for company. There's only Cook and me on staff, you see, because of the difficult financial time my employer is suffering through, and I didn't see the need to put linens on the other beds because I didn't know we would . . ."

"You mustn't worry so," she interrupted. "We'll make do, I promise."

"It's good of you to be so understanding. I'll move your things into the larger guest room tomorrow."

"Aren't you forgetting Colin?" she asked. "I would think he'll be irritated to find me in his bed."

Flannaghan imagined just the opposite, and immediately blushed over his own shameful thoughts. He was still a bit shaken, he realized, and surely that was the reason he was acting like a dolt. The surprise of his guests' arrival was not the true cause of his sorry condition, however. No, it was Princess Alesandra. She was the most wonderful woman he'd ever met. Every time he looked at her, he forgot his own thoughts. Her eyes were such a wondrous shade of blue. She had the longest, and surely the darkest, eyelashes he'd ever noticed, too, and her complexion was exquisitely pure. Only a sprinkle of freckles across the bridge of her nose marred her skin, but Flannaghan found that flaw absolutely wonderful.

He cleared his throat in an attempt to unscramble his thoughts. "I'm certain my employer won't mind sleeping in one of the other chambers tonight. There is a good chance he won't even come home until tomorrow morning anyway. He went back to the Emerald Shipping Company to do some paperwork, and he often ends up spending the night there. The time, you see, gets away from him."

After giving her the explanation, Flannaghan began to tug her along the corridor. There were four rooms on the second level. The first door was wide open and both she and Flannaghan paused at the entrance.

"This is the study, Princess," Flannaghan announced. "It's a bit cluttered, but my employer won't allow me to touch anything."

Alesandra smiled. The study was more than cluttered, for there were stacks of paper everywhere. Yet it was still a warm, inviting room. A mahogany desk faced the door. There was a small hearth on the left, a brown leather chair with a matching foot rest on the right, and a beautiful burgundy and brown rug took up the space in between. Books lined the shelves on the walls, and ledgers were stacked high on the wooden file cabinet tucked in the corner.

The study was an extremely masculine room. The scents of brandy and leather filled the air. She found the aroma quite pleasant. She could even imagine herself curled up in front of a roaring fire in her robe and slippers reading the latest financial reports on her holdings.

Flannaghan tugged her along the hall. The second door was to Colin's bedroom. He hurried ahead of her to open it.

"Is your employer in the habit of working such long hours?" Alesandra asked.

"Yes, he is," Flannaghan answered. "He started the company several years ago with his good friend, the Marquess of St. James, and the gentlemen have had a struggle staying afloat. The competition is fierce."

Alesandra nodded. "The Emerald Shipping Company has an excellent reputation."

"It does?"

"Oh, yes. Colin's father wishes he could purchase shares. It would be a sure profit for investors, but the partners won't sell any stock."

"They want to maintain complete control," Flannaghan explained. He grinned then. "I heard him say just that to his father."

She nodded, then walked into the bedroom, dismissing the topic. Flannaghan noticed the chill in the air and hurried over to the hearth to start a fire. Valena skirted her way around her mistress to light the candles on the bedside table.

Colin's bedroom was every bit as masculine and appealing as his study. The bed faced the door. It was quite large in size and was covered with a dark chocolate brown quilt. The walls had been painted a rich beige color, an appropriate backdrop, she thought, for the beautiful pieces of mahogany wood furniture.

Two windows flanked the headboard posters and were draped with beige satin. Valena removed the ties holding the material away from the window panes so the room would be closeted from the street below.

There was a door on Alesandra's left that led into the study, and another door on her right, next to a tall, wooden privacy screen. She walked across the chamber, pulled the door wide, and found an adjoining bedroom. The colors were identical to those of the master suite, though the bed was much smaller in size.

"This is a wonderful house," she remarked. "Colin chose well."

"He doesn't own the property," Flannaghan told her. "His agent got him a good price on the rental. We'll have to move again at the end of the summer, when the owners return from the Americas."

Alesandra tried to hide her smile. She doubted Colin would appreciate his servant giving away all of his financial secrets. Flannaghan was the most enthusiastic servant she'd ever encountered. He was refreshingly honest, and Alesandra liked him immensely.

"I'll move your things into the adjoining room tomorrow," Flannaghan called out when he noticed she was looking into the other chamber. He turned back to the hearth, tossed another log on the budding fire, and then stood up. He brushed his hands on the sides of his pant legs. "These two rooms are the larger bed chambers," he explained. "The other two on this floor are quite small. There's a lock on the door," he added with a nod.

The dark-haired guard named Raymond knocked on the door. Alesandra hurried over to the entrance and listened to his whispered explanation.

"Raymond has just explained that one of the windows in the salon below has a broken latch. He would like your permission to repair it."

"Do you mean now?" Flannaghan asked.

"Yes," she answered. "Raymond's a worrier," she added. "He won't rest until the house is secure."

She didn't wait for the servant's permission but nodded to the guard, giving him her approval. Valena had already unpacked her mistress's sleeping gown and wrapper. Alesandra turned to help just as Valena let out a loud yawn.

"Valena, go and get your sleep. Tomorrow will be time enough to unpack the rest of my things."

The maid bowed low to her mistress. Flannaghan hurried forward. He suggested the maid take the last room along the corridor. It was the smallest of the chambers, he explained, but the bed was quite comfortable and the room was really rather cozy. He was certain Valena would find it suitable. After bidding Alesandra good night, he escorted the maid down the hall to help get her settled.

Alesandra fell asleep a scant thirty minutes later. As was her usual habit, she slept quite soundly for several hours, but promptly at two o'clock in the morning she awakened. She hadn't been able to sleep a full night through since returning to England, and she'd gotten used to the condition. She put on her robe, added another log to the fire, and then got back into bed with her satchel of papers. She would read her broker's report on the current financial status of Lloyd's of

London first, and if that didn't make her sleepy, she'd make a new chart of her own holdings.

A loud commotion coming from below the stairs interrupted her concentration. She recognized Flannaghan's voice and assumed from the frantic edge to his tone that he was trying to soothe his employer's temper.

Curiosity got the better of her. Alesandra put on her slippers, tightened the belt around her robe, and went to the landing. She stood in the darkness of the shadows, but the foyer below her was ablaze with candlelight. She let out a little sigh when she saw how Raymond and Stefan were blocking Colin's way. He was turned away from her, but Raymond happened to look up and spot her. She immediately motioned for him to leave. He nudged his companion back to his station, bowed to Colin, and then left the foyer.

Flannaghan didn't notice the guards' departure. He didn't notice Alesandra either. He never would have gone on and on if he'd known she was standing there listening to his every word.

"She's just what I imagined a real princess would be," he told his employer, his voice reeking with grating enthusiasm. "She has hair the color of midnight, and it's full of soft curls that seem to float around her shoulders. Her eyes are blue, but a shade of blue I've never seen before. They're so brilliant and clear. And you're certain to tower over her. Why even I find myself feeling like a giant, a bumbling one at that, when she's looking directly up at me. She has freckles, milord." Flannaghan paused long enough to take a breath. "She's really wonderful."

Colin wasn't paying much attention to the servant's remarks about the princess. He had been about to put his fist into one of the strangers blocking his way and then toss both men back into the street when Flannaghan had come running down the stairs to explain that the men came from the Duke of Williamshire. Colin had let go of the bigger of the two men and was now once again sorting through the stack of papers in his hands, looking for the report his partner had completed. He hoped to God he hadn't left the thing at the office, for he was determined to transfer the numbers into the ledgers before he went to bed.

Colin was in a foul mood. He was actually a little disappointed that his butler had interfered. A good fistfight might have helped him get rid of some of his frustration.

He finally found the missing sheet just as Flannaghan started in again.

"Princess Alesandra is on the thin side, yet I couldn't help but notice how shapely her figure is."

"Enough," Colin ordered, his voice soft, yet commanding.

The servant immediately stopped his litany of Princess Alesandra's considerable attributes. His disappointment was apparent in his crestfallen expression. He'd only just warmed to his topic and knew he could have gone on and on for at least another twenty minutes. Why, he hadn't even mentioned her smile yet, or the regal way she held herself. . . .

"All right, Flannaghan," Colin began, interrupting his servant's thoughts. "Let's try to get to the bottom of this. A princess just decided to take up residence with us? Is that correct?"

"Yes, milord."

"Why?"

"Why what, milord?"

Colin sighed. "Why do you suppose . . ."

"It isn't my place to suppose," Flannaghan interrupted.

"When has that ever stopped you?"

Flannaghan grinned. He acted as though he'd just been given a compliment.

Colin yawned. Lord, he was tired. He wasn't in the mood to put up with company tonight. He was exhausted from too many long hours working on the company books, frustrated because he couldn't make the damn numbers add up to enough of a profit and extremely weary fighting all the competition. It seemed to him that every other day a new shipping company opened its doors for business.

Added to his financial worries were his own aches and

pains. His left leg, injured in a sea mishap several years ago, was throbbing painfully now, and all he wanted to do was get into his bed with a hot brandy.

He wasn't going to give in to his fatigue. There was still work to be done before he went to bed. He tossed Flannaghan his cloak, placed his cane in the umbrella stand, and put the papers he'd been carrying on the side table.

"Milord, would you like me to fetch you something to drink?"

"I'll have a brandy in the study," he replied. "Why are you calling me your lord? You've been given permission to call me Colin."

"But that was before."

"Before what?"

"Before we had a real princess living with us," Flannaghan explained. "It wouldn't be proper for me to call you Colin now. Would you prefer I call you Sir Hallbrook?" he asked, using Colin's knighted title.

"I would prefer Colin."

"But I have explained, milord, it simply won't do."

Colin laughed. Flannaghan had sounded pompous. He was acting more and more like his brother's butler, Sterns, and Colin really shouldn't have been at all surprised. Sterns was Flannaghan's uncle and had installed the young man in Colin's household to begin his seasoning.

"You're becoming as arrogant as your uncle," Colin remarked.

"It's good of you to say so, milord."

Colin laughed again. Then he shook his head at his servant. "Let's get back to the princess, shall we? Why is she here?"

"She didn't confide in me," Flannaghan explained. "And I thought it would be improper for me to ask."

"So you just let her in?"

"She arrived with a note from your father."

They had finally gotten to the end of the maze. "Where is this note?"

"I put it in the salon . . . or was it the dining room?"

"Go and find the thing," Colin ordered. "Perhaps his note will explain why the woman has two thugs with her."

"They're her guards, milord," Flannaghan explained, his tone defensive. "Your father sent them with her," he added with a nod. "And a princess would not travel with thugs."

The expression on Flannaghan's face was almost comical in his awe of the woman. The princess had certainly dazzled the impressionable servant.

The butler went running into the salon in search of the note. Colin blew out the candles on the table, picked up his papers, and then turned to the steps.

He finally understood the reason for Princess Alesandra's arrival. His father was behind the scheme of course. His matchmaking attempts were becoming more outrageous, and Colin wasn't in the mood to put up with yet another one of his games.

He was halfway up the steps before he spotted her. The banister saved him from disgrace. Colin was certain he would have fallen backward if he hadn't had a firm grasp on the railing.

Flannaghan hadn't exaggerated. She did look like a princess. A beautiful one. Her hair floated around her shoulders and it really did look as dark as midnight. She was dressed in white, and, Lord, at first sight, she appeared to be a vision the gods had sent to test his determination.

He failed the test. Although he gave it his best effort, he was still powerless to control his own physical reaction to her.

His father had certainly outdone himself this time. Colin would have to remember to compliment him on his latest choice—after he'd sent her packing, of course.

They stood staring at each other for a long minute. She kept waiting for him to speak to her. He kept waiting for her to explain her presence to him.

Alesandra was the first to give in. She moved forward until she stood close to the top step, bowed her head, and then said, "Good evening, Colin. It's good to see you again."

Her voice was wonderfully appealing. Colin tried to

concentrate on what she had just said. It was ridiculously difficult.

"Again?" he asked. Lord, he sounded gruff.

"Yes, we met when I was just a little girl. You called me a brat."

That remark forced a reluctant smile from him. He had no memory of the encounter, however. "And were you a brat?"

"Oh, yes," she answered. "I'm told I kicked you—several times, in fact—but that was a very long time ago. I've grown up since then and I don't believe the nickname is appropriate now. I haven't kicked anyone in years."

Colin leaned against the banister so that he could take some of the weight off his injured leg. "Where did we meet?"

"At your father's home in the country," she explained. "My parents and I were visiting and you were home from Oxford at the time. Your brother had just graduated."

Colin still didn't remember her. That didn't surprise him. His parents were always entertaining houseguests and he'd barely paid any attention to any of them. Most, he recalled, were down on their luck, and his father, kindhearted to a fault, took anyone begging assistance into his home.

Her hands were demurely folded together and she appeared to be very relaxed. Yet Colin noticed how white her fingers were and knew she was actually gripping them together in either fear or nervousness. She wasn't quite as serene as she would have him believe. Her vulnerability was suddenly very apparent to him, and he found himself trying to find a way to put her at ease.

"Where are your parents now?" he asked.

"My father died when I was eleven years old," she answered. "Mother died the following summer. Sir, would you like me to help you collect your papers?" she added in a rush, hoping to change the subject.

"What papers?"

Her smile was enchanting. "The ones you dropped."

He looked down and saw his papers lining the steps. He felt like a complete idiot standing there with his hand grasping air. He grinned over his own preoccupation. He really wasn't any better than his butler, he thought to himself, and Flannaghan had an acceptable excuse for his besotted behavior. He was young, inexperienced, and simply didn't know better.

Colin should have known better, however. He was much older than his servant, in both years and experience. But he was overly weary tonight, he reminded himself, and surely that was the reason he was acting like a simpleton.

Besides, she was one hell of a beauty. He let out a sigh. "I'll get the papers later," he told her. "Exactly why are you here, Princess Alesandra?" he asked bluntly.

"Your brother and his wife are both ill," she explained. "I was to stay with them while in the city, but at the last minute they became indisposed and I was told to stay with you until they are feeling better."

"Who gave you these instructions?"

"Your father."

"Why would he take such an interest?"

"He's my guardian, Colin."

He couldn't contain his surprise over that little bit of news. His father had never mentioned a ward to him, although Colin guessed it wasn't any of his affair. His father held his own counsel and rarely confided in either one of his sons.

"Have you come to London for the season?"

"No," she answered. "Although I am looking forward to attending some of the parties and I do hope to see the sights."

Colin's curiosity intensified. He took another step toward her.

"I really didn't want to cause you any inconvenience," she said. "I suggested I rent my own town house or open your parents' London home, but your father simply wouldn't hear of it. He told me it wasn't done." She paused to sigh. "I did try to convince him. 'Tis the truth I couldn't outargue him."

Lord, she had a pretty smile. It was contagious too. He

found himself smiling back. "No one can outargue my father," he agreed. "You still haven't explained why you're here," he reminded her.

"I haven't, have I? It's most complicated," she added with a nod. "You see, it wasn't necessary for me to come to London before, but it is now."

He shook his head at her. "Half-given explanations make me crazed. I'm blunt to a fault—a trait I picked up from my partner, or so I'm told. I admire complete honesty because it's so rare, and for as long as you are a guest in my home, I would appreciate complete candor. Are we in agreement?"

"Yes, of course."

She was clutching her hands together again. He must have frightened her. He probably sounded like an ogre. God only knew he was suddenly feeling like one. He was sorry she was so obviously afraid of him, yet pleased, too, because he'd gotten his way. She hadn't argued with him over his dictate, or tried to act coy. He absolutely detested coyness in a woman.

He forced a mild tone of voice when he asked, "Would you mind answering a few pertinent questions now?"

"Certainly. What is it you wish to know?"

"Why are there two guards with you? Now that you've reached your destination, shouldn't they be dismissed? Or did you think I might withhold my hospitality?"

She answered the last of his question first. "Oh, I never considered you would deny me lodging, sir. Your father assured me you would be most gracious to me. Flannaghan has his note for you to read," she added with a nod. "Your father also insisted I retain my guards. Both Raymond and Stefan were hired by the mother superior of the convent where I used to live to travel with me to England, and your father insisted I keep them on. Neither guard has family back home to miss, and both are very well paid. You really shouldn't worry about them."

He held his exasperation. She was looking so earnest now. "I wasn't worried about them," he replied. He grinned then and shook his head again. "Do you know, trying to get answers out of you is proving to be very difficult."

She nodded. "Mother Superior used to say the very same thing to me. She considered it one of my greatest flaws. I am sorry if I confuse you. I don't mean to, sir."

"Alesandra, my father's behind this scheme, isn't he? He sent you to me."

"Yes and no."

She quickly held up her hand to waylay his frown. "I'm not hedging. You're father did send me to you, but only after he found out Caine and his wife were ill. I don't believe there was a scheme involved, however. As a matter of fact, your father and your mother wanted me to stay in the country until they were recovered enough to escort me to the city. I would have, too, if I hadn't made all of my appointments."

She sounded sincere. Colin still scoffed at the notion that his father wasn't behind this plan. He'd seen him at the club only a week before and he'd been perfectly healthy then. Colin remembered the inevitable argument too. His father had oh so casually brought up the topic of marriage, then become relentless as he once again nagged Colin about taking a wife. Colin had pretended to listen, and once his father had wound down, he told him he was determined to remain alone.

Alesandra didn't have any idea what was going through Colin's mind. His frown was making her nervous, however. He certainly seemed to be a suspicious sort. He was a handsome man, she thought to herself, with rich, auburn-colored hair and more green- than hazel-colored eyes. They had fairly sparkled when he smiled. He had an adorable little dimple, too, in the left side of his cheek. But, heavens, his frown was fierce. He was even more intimidating than the mother superior, and Alesandra considered that an impressive feat.

She couldn't stand the silence long. "Your father planned to speak to you about my unusual circumstances," she whispered. "He was going to be very straightforward about the matter."

"When it comes to my father and his plans, nothing's ever straightforward."

She arched her shoulders back and frowned at him. "Your father is one of the most honorable men I've ever had the pleasure to know. He's been extremely kind to me, and he only has my best interests at heart."

She was sounding incensed by the time she finished her defense of his father. Colin grinned. "You don't have to defend him to me. I know my father's honorable. It's one of the hundred or so reasons why I love him."

Her stance relaxed. "You're very fortunate to have such a fine man for a father."

"Were you as fortunate?"

"Oh, yes," she answered. "My father was a wonderful man."

She started backing away when Colin came up the rest of the steps. She bumped into the wall, then turned and slowly walked down the hall to her room.

Colin clasped his hands behind his back and fell into step beside her. Flannaghan was right, he thought to himself. He did tower over Alesandra. Perhaps his size intimidated her.

"You don't have to be afraid of me."

She came to a quick stop and turned to look up at him. "Afraid? Why in heaven's name would you think I was afraid of you?"

She'd sounded incredulous. Colin shrugged. "You backed away rather hastily when I reached the landing," he pointed out. He didn't mention the fear he'd glimpsed in her eyes or the fact that she'd been wringing her hands together. If she wanted to pretend she wasn't afraid, he'd let her have her way.

"Well, I'm not very afraid," she announced. "I'm not used to . . . visiting while in my nightgown and wrapper. In fact, Colin, I'm feeling quite safe here. It's a nice feeling. I have been a little jumpy lately."

She blushed, acting as though her confession was embarrassing her.

"Why have you been jumpy?" he asked.

Instead of answering his question, she turned the topic. "Would you like to know why I've come to London?"

He almost laughed then and there. Hadn't he been

diligently trying to find out just that for the past ten minutes? "If you want to tell me," he said.

"I really have two reasons for my journey," she began. "They're both equally important to me. The first involves a mystery I'm determined to solve. I met a young lady by the name of Victoria Perry over a year ago. She stayed at the Holy Cross convent for a spell. She was touring Austria with her family, you see, and she became quite ill. The sisters at Holy Cross are well known for their nursing skills, and once it was determined that Victoria would recover, her family felt it safe to leave her there to recuperate. She and I became fast friends, and after she returned to England, she wrote to me at least once a month, sometimes more. I do wish I'd saved the letters, because in two or three of them she made references to a secret admirer who was courting her. She thought it was all very romantic."

"Perry . . . where have I heard that name?" Colin wondered aloud.

"I don't know, sir."

He smiled. "I shouldn't have interrupted you. Please continue."

She nodded. "The last letter I received was dated the first of September. I immediately wrote back, but I didn't hear another word. I was concerned, of course. When I reached your father's home, I told him I was going to send a messenger to Victoria to request an audience. I wanted to catch up on all the latest happenings. Victoria led such an exciting life and I so enjoyed her correspondence."

"And did you get your audience?"

"No," Alesandra answered. She stopped and turned to look up at Colin. "Your father told me about the scandal. Victoria was supposed to have run off with a man from a lower station. They were married in Gretna Green. Can you imagine such a tale? Her family certainly believes it. Your father told me they've disowned her."

"Now I remember. I did hear about the scandal."

"None of it's true."

He raised an eyebrow over the vehemence in her voice. "It isn't?" he asked.

"No, it isn't," she said. "I'm a good judge of character, Colin, and I assure you Victoria wouldn't have eloped. She simply isn't the sort. I'm going to find out what really happened to her. She may be in trouble and need my help," she added. "Tomorrow I shall send a note to her brother, Neil, begging an audience."

"I don't think the family will want their daughter's embarrassment drudged up again."

"I shall be most discreet."

Her voice reeked with sincerity. She was a dramatic thing, and so damned beautiful it was difficult to pay attention to anything she said. Her eyes mesmerized him. He happened to notice she had her hand on the doorknob to his room. He was further distracted by her wonderful scent. The faint smell of roses floated in the air between them. Colin immediately took a step back to put some distance between them.

"Do you mind that I'm sleeping in your bed?"

"I didn't know you were."

"Flannaghan's going to move my things into the adjoining chamber tomorrow. He didn't think you would be coming home tonight. It's just for one night, sir, but now that he's had time to put linens on the bed next door, I'll be happy to give you your bed back."

"We'll change in the morning."

"You're being very kind to me. Thank you."

Colin finally noticed the dark smudges under her eyes. The woman was clearly exhausted and he'd kept her from her sleep by grilling her.

"You need your rest, Alesandra. It's the middle of the night."

She nodded, then opened the door to his bedroom. "Good night, Colin. Thank you again for being so hospitable."

"I couldn't turn my back on a princess when she's down on her luck," he said.

"I beg your pardon?" She didn't have the faintest idea what he meant by that remark. Where had he gotten the idea she was down on her luck?

"Alesandra, what was the other reason for coming to London?"

She looked confused by the question. The second reason must not have been very important, he decided. "I was merely curious," he admitted with a shrug. "You mentioned you had two reasons and I wondered . . . never mind. Go to bed now. I'll see you in the morning. Sleep well, Princess."

"I remember the reason now," she blurted out.

He turned back to her. "Yes?"

"Would you like me to tell you?"

"Yes, I would."

She stared up at him a long minute. Her hesitation was obvious. So was her vulnerability. "Do you want me to be honest with you?"

He nodded. "Of course I do."

"Very well then. I'll be honest. Your father suggested I not confide in you, but since you have insisted upon knowing and I did promise I would be honest . . ."

"Yes?" he prodded.

"I've come to London to marry you."

He was suddenly hungry again. It was peculiar to him the way the craving burst upon him all at once. There was never any warning. He hadn't thought about a hunt in a long, long while, and now, at the midnight hour, while he was standing in the doorway of Sir Johnston's library listening to the latest gossip about the prince regent, sipping his brandy with several other titled gentlemen of the ton, he was nearly overwhelmed with his need.

He could feel the power draining away from him. His eyes burned. His stomach ached. He was empty, empty, empty.

He needed to feed again.

Chapter 3

Alesandra didn't get much sleep the rest of the night. The expression on Colin's face when she had blurted out her second reason for coming to London had made her breath catch in the back of her throat. Lord, he'd been furious. No matter how hard she tried, she couldn't seem to block the image of his anger long enough to fall back to sleep.

So much for honesty, she thought to herself. Telling the truth hadn't served her well at all. She should have kept silent. Alesandra let out a loud sigh. No, she had to tell the truth. Mother Superior had drummed that fact into her.

Her thoughts immediately returned to Colin's expression of fury. How could a man with such an adorable dimple in his cheek have eyes so frigid? Colin could be dangerous when he was riled. She really wished his papa had mentioned that important fact to her before she had embarrassed herself so thoroughly and infuriated Colin so completely.

She dreaded her next encounter with him. She took her time getting dressed. Valena assisted her. The maid kept up a constant chatter while she brushed Alesandra's hair. She wished to know all the details of her princess's day. Was she going out? Would she wish her maid to accompany her? Alesandra answered her questions as best she could.

"We may have to find another lodging after today," she remarked. "I shall share my plans with you as soon as I've formulated them, Valena."

The maid finished buttoning the back of Alesandra's royal blue walking dress just as a knock sounded at the door.

Flannaghan requested the princess join his employer in the salon as soon as possible.

Alesandra didn't think it would be a good idea to keep him waiting. There wasn't time to braid her hair, and she didn't want the bother anyway. She didn't have a lady's maid while living at the convent and found the formality a nuisance. She had learned to do for herself.

She dismissed Valena, told Flannaghan she would be downstairs in just a moment, and then hurried over to her valise. She pulled out the notecard her guardian had given her, brushed her hair back over her shoulders, and then left the room.

She was ready to take on the dragon. Colin was waiting for her in the salon. He stood in front of the hearth, facing the door, with his hands clasped behind his back. She was relieved to notice he wasn't scowling. He looked only mildly irritated with her now.

She stood in the entrance, waiting for him to invite her to join him. He didn't say a word for a long while. He simply stood there staring at her. She thought he might be trying to get his thoughts under control. Or his temper. She could feel herself blushing over his close scrutiny, then realized she was being just as rude scrutinizing him.

He was a difficult man not to notice. He was so attractive. He had a hard, fit body. He was dressed in fawn-colored riding buckskins, polished brown high boots, and a sparkling white shirt. His personality came through in the way he wore his apparel, she decided, because Colin had left the top button of his shirt undone, and he wasn't wearing one of those awful starched cravats. He was obviously a bit of a rebel who lived in a society of conservatives. His hair wasn't at all fashionable. It was quite long—shoulder length at least, she guessed—although she couldn't tell the exact length because he had it secured behind his neck with a leather thong. Colin was definitely an independent man. He was tall, muscular in both shoulders and thighs, and he reminded Alesandra of one of those fierce-looking frontiersmen she'd seen charcoal sketches of in the dailies. Colin was wonderfully handsome, yes, but weathered-looking too. What saved him from being unapproachable, she decided, was the warmth of his smile when he was amused.

He wasn't amused now.

"Come in and sit down, Alesandra. We have to talk."

"Certainly," she immediately replied.

Flannaghan suddenly appeared at her side. He took hold of her elbow to assist her across the room. "That isn't necessary," Colin called out. "Alesandra can walk without assistance."

"But she's a princess," Flannaghan reminded his employer. "We must show her every courtesy."

Colin's glare told the butler to cease his comments. Flannaghan reluctantly let go of Alesandra.

He looked crushed. Alesandra immediately tried to soothe his injured feelings. "You're a very thoughtful man, Flannaghan," she praised.

The butler immediately latched on to her elbow again. She let him guide her over to the brocaded settee. Once she was seated, Flannaghan knelt down and tried to smooth her skirts for her. She wouldn't allow his help.

"Is there anything more you require, Princess?" he asked. "Cook will have your breakfast ready in just a few more minutes," he added with a nod. "Would you care for a cup of chocolate while you wait?"

"No, thank you," she replied. "I do need a pen and inkwell," she added. "Would you be kind enough to fetch them for me?"

Flannaghan ran out of the salon to see to the errand.

"I'm surprised he didn't genuflect," Colin drawled out.

His jest made her smile. "You're fortunate to have such a kindhearted servant, Colin."

He didn't reply. Flannaghan came rushing back inside with the items she requested. He placed the pen and inkwell on a narrow side table, then picked up the table and carried it over to her.

She thanked him, of course, and that bit of praise made him blush with pleasure.

"Close the doors behind you, Flannaghan," Colin ordered. "I don't want to be interrupted."

He was sounding irritated again. Alesandra let out a little sigh. Colin wasn't a very accommodating man.

She turned her full attention to her host. "I've upset you. I really am sorry . . ."

He wouldn't let her finish her apology. "You haven't upset me," he snapped.

She would have laughed if she'd been alone. The man was upset, and that was that. His jaw was clenched, and if that wasn't a giveaway to his true feelings, she didn't know what was.

"I see," she agreed just to placate him.

"However," he began in a clipped, no-nonsense tone of voice, "I believe we should settle a few pertinent issues here and now. Why in heaven's name did you think I would marry you?"

"Your father said you would."

He didn't even try to hide his exasperation. "I'm a grown man, Alesandra. I make my own decisions."

"Yes, of course you're a grown man," she agreed. "But you'll always be his son, Colin. It's your duty to do whatever he wants you to do. Sons must obey their fathers, no matter how old they are."

"That's ridiculous."

She lifted her shoulders in a dainty shrug. Colin held on to his patience. "I don't know what kind of bargain you struck with my father, and I'm sorry if he made promises on my behalf, but I want you to understand I have no intention of marrying you."

She lowered her gaze to the notecard she held in her hands. "All right," she agreed.

Her quick agreement, given in such a casual tone of voice, made him suspicious. "You aren't angry over my refusal?"

"No, of course not."

She glanced up and smiled. Colin looked confused. "I'm disappointed," she admitted. "But certainly not angry. I barely know you. It would be unreasonable for me to be angry."

"Exactly," he agreed with a quick nod. "You don't know me. Why would you wish to marry me if you . . ."

"I believe I've already explained, sir. Your father instructed me to marry you."

"Alesandra, I want you to understand . . ."

She wouldn't let him finish. "I accept your decision, sir."

He smiled in spite of himself. Princess Alesandra looked so forlorn.

"You won't have any trouble finding someone suitable. You're a very beautiful woman, Princess."

She shrugged. She was obviously unaffected by his compliment.

"I imagine it was difficult for you to ask me," he began then.

She straightened her shoulders. "I didn't ask," she announced. "I simply explained to you what your father's primary objective was."

"His primary objective?"

He sounded as though he was laughing at her. She could feel herself blushing with embarrassment. "Do not mock me, sir. This discussion is difficult enough without having you ridicule me."

Colin shook his head. His voice was gentle when he spoke again. "I wasn't mocking you," he said. "I realize this is difficult for you. I hold my father responsible for both your discomfort and mine. He will not give up on trying to find a wife for me."

"He suggested I not say anything at all about marriage to you. He said you tend to develop a rash whenever that word is used in your presence. He wanted me to give you time to get to know me before he explained what he wanted. He thought . . . you might learn to like me."

"Look, I already like you," he said. "But I'm not in a position to marry anyone right now. In five years, according to my schedule, I'll be in a strong financial position and will be able to take a wife."

"Mother Superior would like you, Colin," Alesandra announced. "She loves schedules. She believes life would be chaotic without them."

"How long did you live in this convent?" he asked, anxious to turn the topic away from marriage.

"Quite a while," she answered. "Colin, I'm sorry, but I can't wait for you. I really must get married right away. It's unfortunate," she added with a sigh. "I believe you would make an acceptable husband."

"And how would you know that?"

"Your father told me so."

He did laugh then. He couldn't help himself. Lord, she was an innocent. He noticed she was clutching the notecard in her hands then and immediately forced himself to stop. She was already embarrassed. His laughter was only adding to her discomfort.

"I'll talk to my father and save you that ordeal," he promised. "I know he put these ideas into your head. He can be very convincing, can't he?"

She didn't answer him. She kept her gaze on her lap. Colin suddenly felt like a cad because he had disappointed her. Hell, he thought to himself. He wasn't making any sense.

"Alesandra, this bargain you made with my father surely involved a profit. How much was it?"

He let out a low whistle after she told him the exact amount. He leaned back against the mantel and shook his head. He was furious with his father now. "Well, by God, you aren't going to be disappointed. If he promised you a near fortune, then he's going to pay. You kept your part of the bargain . . ."

She raised one hand for silence, unconsciously mimicking the mother superior's behavior.

Colin obeyed without even realizing it. "You misunderstand, sir. Your father didn't promise me anything. I promised him. He wouldn't accept my bargain, however, and was in fact appalled I even suggested paying for a husband."

Colin laughed again. He was certain she was jesting with him.

"This isn't at all humorous, Colin. I must get married in three weeks' time, and your father is simply helping me. He's my guardian, after all."

Colin needed to sit down. He walked over to the leather chair facing the settee and sprawled out.

"You're going to get married in three weeks?"

"Yes," she replied. "And that is why I asked your father's assistance."

"Alesandra . . ."

She waved the notecard in the air. "I asked for assistance in preparing a list."

"A list of what?"

"Suitable candidates."

"And?" he prodded.

"He told me to marry you."

Colin leaned forward, braced his elbows on his knees, and frowned at her. "Listen carefully," he ordered. "I'm not marrying you."

She immediately reached for the pen. She dipped it into the inkwell, then drew a line across the top of her notecard.

"What did you just do?"

"I crossed you off."

"Off what?"

She looked exasperated. "My list. Do you happen to know the Earl of Templeton?"

"Yes."

"Is he a good man?"

"Hell, no," he muttered. "He's a rake. He used his sister's dowry to pay off a few of his gambling debts, but he still haunts the tables every night."

Alesandra immediately dipped the pen into the inkwell again and scratched through the second name on her list. "It's peculiar your father didn't know about the earl's gambling vice."

"Father doesn't go to the clubs anymore."

"That would explain it," she replied. "Heavens, this is turning out to be more difficult than I anticipated."

"Alesandra, why are you in such a hurry to get married?"

Her pen was poised in the air. "I beg your pardon?" she asked, her concentration directed on her notecard.

He repeated his question. "You told me you had to get married in three weeks' time. I wondered why."

"The church," she explained with a quick nod. "Colin, do you know the Marquess of Townsend perchance? Does *he* have any horrible vices?"

His patience was gone. "Put the list down, Alesandra, and start answering my questions. What in God's name does the church have to do with . . ."

She interrupted him. "Your mother already reserved it. She made all the other arrangements, too. She's the most wonderful lady, and heavens, she's so organized. It's going to be a beautiful wedding. I do hope you can attend. I've decided against a large wedding, much to your parents' frustration, and settled instead on small and intimate."

Colin wondered if his father realized his ward was out of her mind. "Let me get this straight," he began. "You've taken care of all the arrangements without a man to . . ."

"I can't take the credit," she interrupted. "As I just explained, your mother did all the work."

"Aren't you approaching this from the wrong angle? It's usual to find a groom first, Alesandra."

"I agree with you, but this isn't a usual circumstance. I simply must get married right away."

"Why?"

"Please don't think me rude, but since you've decided against marrying me, I think it's best you not know anything more. I would still appreciate your help, however, if you're inclined to give it."

Colin didn't have any intention of letting the matter drop. He would find out the real reason why she needed to get married, and he'd find out before the day was over. He decided to use a little trickery now and ease back to his question later.

"I would be happy to assist you," he said. "What is it you need?"

"Would you please give me the names of five—no, make

that six—suitable men? I'll interview them this week. By Monday next, I should have settled on someone."

God, she was exasperating. "What are your requirements?" he inquired mildly.

"First, he must be honorable," she began. "Second, he must be titled. My father would twist in his grave if I married a commoner."

"I'm not titled," he reminded her.

"You were knighted. That qualifies."

He laughed. "You've left out the most important requirement, haven't you? He'll have to be wealthy."

She frowned at him. "I believe you've just insulted me," she announced. "Still, you don't know me at all well and for that reason I'll forgive you your cynicism."

"Alesandra, most women looking for husbands want to live a comfortable life," he countered.

"Rich isn't important to me," she replied. "You're as poor as a serf and I was willing to marry you, remember?"

He chafed over her bit of honesty. "How would you know if I'm rich or poor?"

"Your father told me. Do you know, Colin, when you frown, you remind me of a dragon. I used to call Sister Mary Felicity a dragon, though I was too cowardly to say it to her face. Your frown is every bit as fierce, and I do believe the nickname is more appropriate for you."

Colin refused to let her bait him. He wasn't going to let her switch topics either. "What else do you require in a husband?"

"He'll have to leave me alone," she replied after a moment's consideration. "I don't want a man who . . . hovers."

He laughed again. He immediately regretted that action when he saw her expression. Hell, he'd hurt her feelings. Her eyes got all teary, too.

"I don't particularly want a wife who would hover either," he admitted, thinking his agreement would ease her hurt.

She wouldn't look at him. "Would a rich woman appeal to you?" she asked.

"No," he answered. "I determined a long time ago to make my own fortune without any outside help, and I mean to keep that promise to myself. My brother has offered to lend my partner and me funds and of course my father has also offered to help."

"But you refused them," she countered. "Your father believes you're too independent."

Colin decided to change the subject. "Will your husband share your bed?"

She refused to answer him. She lifted her pen again. "Begin your list, please."

"No."

"But you said you would help me."

"That was before I realized you were out of your mind."

She put the pen back on the table and stood up. "Please excuse me."

"Where are you going?"

"To pack."

He chased her to the door. He took hold of her arm and turned her around to face him. Damn, he really had upset her. He hated to see the tears in her eyes, especially since he knew he was the cause of her distress.

"You're going to stay here until I decide what to do with you," he said, his voice gruff.

"I decide my future, Colin, not you. Let go of me. I won't stay where I'm not wanted."

"You're staying here."

He added a glare to his order so she would back down. It didn't work. She wouldn't be intimidated. In truth, she glared back. "You don't want me, remember?" she challenged.

He smiled. "Oh, I want you all right. I'm just not willing to marry you. I'm being completely honest with you and I can see from your blush I've embarrassed you. You're too damn young and innocent for this ridiculous game you've taken on. Let my father . . ."

"Your father is too ill to help me," she interrupted. She jerked her arm away from his hold. "But there are others who will come to my aid. You needn't be concerned."

He couldn't explain why he felt insulted, but he did. "Since my father is too ill to see to his duty of looking out for you, the task falls on my shoulders."

"No, it doesn't," she argued. "Your brother, Caine, will act as my guardian. He's next in line."

"But Caine's conveniently ill too, isn't he?"

"I don't believe there is anything convenient about his illness, Colin."

He didn't argue the point with her, and in fact pretended he hadn't heard her. "And as your guardian during this period of family illness, I will decide where you go and when. Don't give me that defiant look, young lady," he ordered. "I always get my way. By nightfall I'll know why you think you have to get married so quickly."

She shook her head. He grabbed hold of her chin and held her steady. "God, but you're stubborn." He tweaked her nose, then let go of her. "I'll be back in a few hours. Stay put, Alesandra. If you leave, I'll come after you."

Raymond and Stefan were both waiting in the foyer. Colin walked past the two guards, then stopped. "Don't let her leave," he ordered.

Raymond immediately nodded. Alesandra's eyes widened. "They're my guards, Colin," she called out. Damn, he'd treated her like a child when he'd tweaked her nose and talked so condescendingly to her, and now she was behaving like one.

"Yes, they are your guards," Colin agreed. He opened the front door, then turned back to her. "But they answer to me. Isn't that right, boys?"

Both Raymond and Stefan immediately nodded. She was a bit piqued, and almost blurted out her opinion of his high-handed methods.

Dignity and *decorum.* The words echoed in her mind. She could feel the mother superior standing behind her, looking over her shoulder. It was a ridiculous feeling, of course, for the nun was an ocean away. Still, her lectures had taken root. Alesandra forced a serene expression and simply nodded agreement.

"Will you be gone long, Colin?" she inquired, her voice quite calm.

He thought she sounded hoarse. She looked like she wanted to shout at him. Colin smiled. "Probably," he answered. "Will you miss me?"

She matched his smile. "Probably not."

The door closed on his laughter.

Chapter 4

She didn't miss him at all. Colin didn't come home until well after the dinner hour. Alesandra was thankful he stayed away because she didn't want his interference, and the man certainly did seem to interfere.

She was kept busy with her appointments. She spent the remainder of the morning and all afternoon entertaining her father's old friends. They called, one after another, to pay their respects and to offer her assistance while she was in London. Most of the visitors were titled members of the ton, but there were also artists and laborers as well. Alesandra's father had had a wide range of friends. He had been an excellent judge of character, a trait she believed she had inherited, and she found she liked every one of his friends.

Matthew Andrew Dreyson was her last appointment. The elderly, potbellied man had been her father's trusted agent in England, and he still handled some of Alesandra's assets. Dreyson had held the coveted position of subscriber on the rolls of Lloyd's of London for over twenty-three years. His standards as a broker were of the very highest. He wasn't just ethical; he was also clever. Alesandra's father had instructed his wife, who in turn had instructed his daughter, that in the event of his death Dreyson should be leaned upon for financial advice.

Alesandra invited him to stay for dinner. Flannaghan and Valena served the meal. The lady's maid did most of the work, however, as Flannaghan was busy listening to the financial discussion at the table. He was astonished that a woman would have extensive knowledge of the marketplace, and made a mental note to tell his employer what he had overheard.

Dreyson spent a good two hours going over various recommendations. Alesandra added one of her own, then completed her transactions. The broker used only her initials when placing his slips before the underwriters at Lloyd's, because it was simply unthinkable for a woman to invest in any venture. Even Dreyson would have been appalled if he'd known the suggestions she gave him actually came from her, but she understood the man's prejudice against women. She'd gotten around that obstacle by inventing an old friend of the family she called her Uncle Albert. She told Dreyson the man wasn't really related to her, but she held such great affection for him she'd begun to think of him as her relative years ago. To ensure Dreyson wouldn't try to investigate the man, she added the mention that Albert had been a close personal friend of her father's.

Dreyson's curiosity had been appeased by her explanation. He didn't have any qualms about taking stock orders from a man, although he did comment more than once how odd it was that Albert allowed her to sign her initials as his ambassador. He wanted to meet her adviser and honorary relative, but Alesandra quickly explained that Albert was a recluse these days and wouldn't allow company. Since he'd moved to England, he found visitors a distraction to his peaceful daily routine, she lied. Because Dreyson was making a handsome commission on each order he placed with the underwriters, and because Uncle Albert's advice to date had been quite on the mark, he didn't argue with the princess. If Albert didn't wish to meet him, so be it. The last thing he wanted to do was alienate his client. Albert, he decided, was simply eccentric.

After dinner they returned to the salon, where Flannaghan served Dreyson a glass of port. Alesandra sat on the settee across from her guest and listened to several amusing stories about the subscribers who haunted the floors of the Royal Exchange. She would have loved to see for herself the gleaming hardwood floors cluttered with wooden stalls they called boxes where the underwriters conducted their business. Dreyson told her about a quaint custom that had begun way back in 1710, referred to as the Caller in the Room. A waiter, he explained, known as the Kidney, would step up into what looked very like a pulpit and read the newspapers in a loud, clear voice while the audience of gentlemen sat at their tables and sipped their drinks. Alesandra had to be content to picture the events in her mind, however, as women were not allowed in the Royal Exchange.

Colin came home just as Dreyson was finishing his drink. He tossed his cloak in Flannaghan's direction, then strode into the salon. He came to a quick stop when he spotted the visitor.

Both Alesandra and Dreyson stood up. She introduced the agent to her host. Colin already knew who Dreyson was. He was impressed, too, for Dreyson's reputation was well known in the shipping community. The broker was considered by many to be a financial genius. Colin admired the man. In the cutthroat business of the market, Dreyson was one of the very few who put his clients' affairs above his own profits. He was actually honorable, and Colin considered that a remarkable quality in an agent.

"Have I interrupted an important meeting?" he asked.

"We were finished with our business," Dreyson replied. "It's a pleasure to meet you, sir," the broker continued. "I've been following the progress of your company and I must compliment you. From ownership of three ships to over twenty in just five years' time is quite impressive, sir."

Colin nodded. "My partner and I try to stay competitive," he said.

"Have you considered offering shares to outsiders, sir? Why, I myself would be interested in investing in such a sound venture."

Colin's leg was throbbing painfully. He shifted positions, winced, and then shook his head. He wanted to sit down, prop his injured leg up, and drink until the ache went away. He wasn't about to pamper himself, however, and shifted positions again until he was leaning against the side of the settee, then forced himself to think about the conversation he was engaged in with the agent.

"No," he announced. "The shares in the Emerald Shipping Company are fifty-fifty between Nathan and me. We aren't interested in outsiders gaining possession."

"If you ever change your mind . . ."

"I won't."

Dreyson nodded. "Princess Alesandra has explained you are acting as her temporary guardian during the family illness."

"That is correct."

"You've been given quite an honor," Dreyson said. He paused to smile at Alesandra. "Protect her well, sir. She's a rare treasure."

Alesandra was embarrassed by Dreyson's praise. Her attention was turned, however, when the broker asked Colin how his father was doing.

"I've just seen him," Colin replied. "He's really been quite ill, but he's on the mend now."

Alesandra couldn't hide her surprise. She turned to Colin. "You didn't . . ." She stopped herself just in time. She was about to blurt out the obvious fact that Colin hadn't believed her and had in fact tried to catch his father in a lie. She found his behavior shameful. Private affairs, however, should never be discussed in front of business associates. She wasn't about to break that sacred rule, no matter how pricked she was.

"I didn't what?" Colin asked. His grin suggested he knew what she was about to say.

She kept her expression serene, but the look in her eyes had turned frigid.

"You didn't get too close to your father or your mother, did you?" she asked. "I believe the illness might be the catching kind," she explained to Dreyson.

"Might be?" Colin was choking on his laughter.

Alesandra ignored him. She kept her gaze directed on the agent. "Colin's older brother visited his father for just an hour or two several days ago, and now he and his dear wife are both ill. I would have warned the man, of course, but I had gone out riding, and by the time I returned, Caine had come and gone."

Dreyson expressed his sympathy over the family's plight. Both Alesandra and Colin walked with the agent to the entrance. "I'll return in three days, if that fits your schedule, Princess Alesandra, with the papers ready for your signature initials."

The broker left a moment later. Colin closed the door after him. He turned around and found Alesandra just a foot away, glaring up at him. Her hands were settled on her hips.

"You owe me an apology," she announced.

"Yes, I do."

"When I think how you . . . you do?"

The bluster went out of her anger. Colin smiled. "Yes, I do," he said again. "I didn't believe you when you said my brother and my father were both too ill to watch out for you."

"You had to find out for yourself, didn't you?"

He ignored the anger in her voice. "I admit I believed it was all a scheme," he told her. "And I really thought I'd be bringing my father back with me."

"For what purpose?"

He decided to be completely honest. "To take you off my hands, Alesandra."

She tried to hide her hurt feelings from him. "I'm sorry my staying here is such an inconvenience for you."

He let out a sigh. "You shouldn't take this personally. It's just that I'm swamped with business matters now and I don't have time to play guardian."

Colin turned to his butler before she could tell him she most certainly did take his remarks personally.

"Flannaghan, get me a drink. Something hot. It was damned cold riding today."

"Serves you right," Alesandra interjected. "Your suspicious nature is going to get you into trouble someday."

He leaned down until his face was just inches away from hers. "My suspicious nature has kept me alive, Princess."

She didn't know what he meant by that remark. She didn't like the way he was frowning at her either, and decided to leave him alone. She turned to go up the stairs. Colin followed her. He could hear her muttering something under her breath, but he couldn't catch any clear words. His concentration was too scattered to pay much attention to her remarks anyway. He was thoroughly occupied trying not to notice the gentle sway of her hips or acknowledge how enticing he found her sexy little backside.

She heard a loud sigh behind her and knew he was following her up the stairs. She didn't turn around when she asked, "Did you look in on Caine, too, or did you accept your father's word that your brother was also ill?"

"I looked in on him."

She whirled around to frown at him. She almost bumped into him. Since she was on the step above, they were now eye to eye.

She noticed how tanned his face was, how hard his mouth looked, how his eyes sparkled green with his incredible smile.

He noticed the sexy freckles on the bridge of her nose.

Alesandra didn't like the path her thoughts were taking. "You're covered with dust, Colin, and probably smell like your horse. You need a bath."

He didn't like her tone of voice. "You need to quit glaring at me," he ordered, his voice every bit as curt as hers had been. "A ward shouldn't treat her guardian with such disrespect."

She didn't have a ready comeback for that statement of fact. Colin was her guardian for the time being, and she probably should be respectful. She didn't want to agree with him, however, and all because he had made it perfectly clear he didn't want her there.

"Is your brother feeling better?"

"He's half dead," he told her quite cheerfully.

"You don't like Caine?"

He laughed. "Of course I like my brother."

"Then why did you sound so happy when you said he was half dead?"

"Because he really is sick and isn't in league with my father and his schemes."

She shook her head at him, turned around again, and ran up the rest of the steps. "Is his wife feeling any better?" she called over her shoulder.

"She isn't as green as Caine is," Colin answered. "Thankfully their little girl wasn't exposed. She and Sterns stayed on in the country."

"Who is Sterns?"

"Their butler-turned-nanny," he explained. "Caine and Jade will remain in London until they're recovered. My mother's feeling better, but my sisters still can't keep anything in their stomachs. Isn't it odd, Alesandra, that you didn't get sick?"

She wouldn't look at him. She knew she was responsible and hated having to admit it. "Actually, now that I think about it, I was a little bit ill on the journey to England," she remarked casually.

He laughed. "Caine's calling you The Plague."

She turned around to look at him again. "I didn't deliberately make everyone sick. Does he really blame me?"

"Yes." He deliberately lied just to tease her.

Her shoulders slumped. "I had hoped to move in with your brother and his wife tomorrow."

"You can't."

"Now you think you're going to be stuck with me, don't you?"

She waited for his denial. A gentleman, after all, would have said something gallant, even if it was a lie, just to be polite.

"Alesandra, I am stuck with you."

She glared at him for being so honest. "You might as well accept the situation and try to be pleasant."

She hurried down the hallway and went into his study. He

leaned against the door frame and watched her collect her papers from the table by the hearth.

"You aren't really upset because I didn't believe my family was ill, are you?"

She didn't answer him. "Did your father talk to you about my circumstances?"

The fear in her eyes surprised him. "He wasn't up to a long talk."

She visibly relaxed.

"But you're going to tell me about your circumstances, aren't you?"

He kept his voice low, soothing. She still reacted as though he'd just shouted at her. "I would prefer your father explain."

"He can't. You will."

"Yes," she finally agreed. "I will have to be the one to tell you. You're blocking Flannaghan's way," she added, her relief obvious over the interruption.

"Princess Alesandra, you have a visitor. Neil Perry, the Earl of Hargrave, is waiting in the salon to speak to you."

"What does he want?" Colin asked.

"Neil is Victoria's older brother," she explained. "I sent a note this morning requesting him to call."

Colin walked over to his desk and leaned against it. "Does he know you want to question him about his sister?"

Alesandra handed Flannaghan her papers, asked him to please put them in her room, and then turned back to Colin. "I didn't exactly explain the purpose of the meeting."

She hurried out of the room so Colin wouldn't have time to berate her for using trickery. She ignored his summons to come back inside and went down the hallway to her room. She had made a list of questions to ask Neil and she didn't want to forget any of them. The sheet of paper was on her nightstand. She folded it, smiled at Flannaghan, who was straightening her bed covers, and hurried downstairs.

Flannaghan wanted to announce her. She wouldn't let him. Neil was standing just inside the salon. He turned when Alesandra reached the foyer and bowed low in greeting.

"I do appreciate you coming so soon," she began as soon as she had finished with her curtsy.

"You mentioned the matter you wished to discuss was quite important, Princess. Have we met before? I feel sure that if we had met, I certainly would have remembered."

Victoria's brother was trying to be charming, Alesandra supposed, but the smile he gave her looked more like a sneer. The Earl of Hargrave was only an inch or two taller than she was and he held himself so rigid it appeared his clothing had been starched stiff. Alesandra couldn't see any resemblance in his thin face to Victoria other than the color of his eyes. They were the same shade of brown. Victoria had gotten the pleasing features in the family, however. Her nose was short, straight. Neil's was long, very like a hawk's, and extremely narrow. Alesandra thought he was a thoroughly unattractive man and she found his nasal voice to be grating.

Appearances, she reminded herself, meant nothing. She prayed Neil had a sweet disposition like his sister. He looked persnickety. She hoped he wasn't.

"Please come inside and sit down. I wanted to talk to you about a matter that concerns me and beg your indulgence with a few questions."

Neil nodded agreement before turning to walk across the room. He waited until she had taken her place on the settee and then sat down in the adjacent chair. He folded one leg over the other, stacked his hands on top of one knee. His nails, she noticed, were quite long for a man and immaculately manicured.

"I've never been inside this town house," Neil remarked. He looked around the room. There was scorn in his voice when he added, "The location is marvelous, of course, but I understand it's just a rental."

"Yes, it is," she agreed.

"It's terribly small, isn't it? I would think a princess would require more suitable quarters."

Neil was a snob. Alesandra was trying not to dislike the man, but his remarks were making it difficult. He was

Victoria's brother, however, and Alesandra needed his assistance in locating her friend.

"I'm very happy here," she remarked, forcing a pleasant tone of voice. "Now then, sir, I wanted to talk to you about your sister."

He didn't like hearing that announcement. His smile faded immediately. "My sister is not a topic for discussion, Princess Alesandra."

"I hope to change your mind," she countered. "I met Victoria last year," she added with a nod. "She stayed at the Holy Cross convent with me when she became ill on her journey. Did she by chance mention me?"

Neil shook his head. "My sister and I rarely spoke to one another."

"Really?" Alesandra couldn't hide her surprise.

Neil let out a loud, exaggerated sigh. "Victoria lived with our mother. I have my own estate," he added, a hint of a boast in his voice. "Of course, now that she's gone to God knows where, mother has moved in with me."

He started tapping his fingers on his knee, his impatience apparent.

"I apologize if this is difficult for you to talk about, but I'm concerned about Victoria. I don't believe she would ever run off and get married."

"Don't be concerned," he countered. "She isn't worth anyone's concern. She made her bed . . ."

"I don't understand your callous attitude. Victoria could be in trouble."

"And I don't understand your attitude, Princess," Neil retaliated. "You haven't been in England long and you therefore don't understand what a scandal can do to one's social standing. My mother was almost destroyed by Victoria's thoughtless actions. Why, for the first time in fifteen years, she wasn't invited to Ashford's bash. The humiliation sent her to bed for a month. My sister threw it all away. She is and always has been a fool. She could have married anyone she wanted. I know of at least three titled gentlemen she turned down. Victoria only thought about herself, of course. While our mother was worrying and fretting over a good match, she was sneaking out the back door to meet her lover."

Alesandra struggled to hold on to her temper. "You can't know that for certain," she argued. "As for the scandal . . ."

She never got to finish her argument. "You obviously don't care about a scandal either," Neil muttered. "No wonder you and my sister got along so well."

"Exactly what are you implying?" she asked.

"You're living in the same house with an unattached man," he said. "There're whispers going around already."

Alesandra took a deep breath in an attempt to control her temper. "Exactly what are these whispers?"

"Some are saying Sir Colin Hallbrook is your cousin. Others believe he's your lover."

She dropped her list in her lap, then stood up. "Your sister rarely mentioned you to me and now I understand why. You're a despicable man, Neil Perry. If I weren't so concerned about Victoria's welfare, I would throw you out this minute."

"I'll take care of that chore for you."

Colin made the announcement from the entrance. He was leaning against the door frame, his arms folded casually across his chest. He looked relaxed, but his eyes . . . oh, Lord, his eyes showed his fury. Alesandra had never seen Colin so angry. She shivered in reaction.

Neil looked startled by the interruption. He quickly recovered, awkwardly unfolded his legs, and stood up.

"Had I known the true reason you wished to see me, I never would have come here. Good day, Princess Alesandra."

She couldn't take her gaze off Colin long enough to speak to Neil. She had the oddest notion Colin was getting ready to pounce.

The notion proved true. Flannaghan held the door open for their guest. Colin moved to stand next to his butler. His expression was masked, and for that reason Neil had no idea that he really meant to throw him outside.

If she'd blinked, she would have missed it. Neil only had time to let out a squeal of indignation that sounded very like a pig's howl of distress. Colin grabbed him by the back of his neck and the back of the waistband to his trousers, lifted him up, and threw him outside. Neil landed in the gutter.

Alesandra let out a little gasp, picked up her skirts, and went running to the front door. Flannaghan let her see the Earl of Hargrave sprawled out on the street before he shut the door.

She whirled around to confront Colin. "Now what am I going to do? I doubt he'll come back here after the way you tossed him out, Colin."

"The man insulted you. I can't allow that."

"But I need him to answer my questions."

He shrugged. She threaded her fingers through her hair in an agitated action. She couldn't decide if she was pleased or pricked at Colin. "What did I do with my list?"

"Which list, Princess?" Flannaghan asked.

"The list of questions I was going to ask Neil."

She went hurrying back into the salon, bent down, and found the sheet of paper under the settee.

Flannaghan and Colin watched her. "Princess Alesandra is a firm believer in lists, milord," Flannaghan said.

Colin didn't make any remark on that bit of information. He frowned at Alesandra when she passed him and went up the steps.

"I won't allow you to invite Perry back here, Alesandra," he called out, still burning with irritation over the pompous man's snide remarks.

"I certainly will invite him back," she called over her shoulder. "This is as much my home as it is yours while you're acting as my guardian. I'm determined to find out if Victoria is all right, Colin, and if that means putting up with her horrid brother, then put up with him I will."

Colin turned to his butler. "Don't let him in. Understand?"

"Perfectly, milord. It is our duty to protect our princess from slanderers."

Alesandra had already turned the corner above the stairs and therefore didn't hear Colin's order or Flannaghan's agreement. She was thoroughly weary of men in general and Neil Perry in particular. She decided to put Victoria's brother out of her mind for the time being. Tomorrow would be soon enough to decide what to do next.

Valena was waiting for her mistress in her bedroom. She and Flannaghan had already moved Alesandra's things from Colin's room into the adjoining chamber.

Alesandra sat down on the side of the bed and kicked her shoes off. "It looks as though we're going to have to stay here a few more days, Valena."

"Your trunks arrived, Princess. Shall I begin unpacking?"

"Tomorrow's soon enough. I know it's still early, but I believe I'll go to bed now. You needn't stay to help me."

Valena left her alone. Alesandra took her time getting ready for bed. She felt quite drained from today's meetings. Speaking to so many of her father's friends and hearing the wonderful stories about him made her miss both her father and her mother. Alesandra might have been able to control her mood if Neil hadn't proven to be such a self-serving, cruel-hearted man. She wanted to shout at the man and tell him he should be thankful he had a mother and a sister to love. Perry wouldn't understand, or care, she imagined, for he was like so many other people she'd met who took their families for granted.

Alesandra gave in to self-pity within minutes. She didn't have anyone who truly cared about her. Colin had let it be known she was just a nuisance, and her real guardian, though far more gentle and understanding than his son, probably considered her a nuisance, too.

She wanted her mama. Her memories of family life didn't comfort her now. They made her ache with her loneliness. She went to bed a few minutes later, hid under the covers, and cried herself to sleep. She awakened in the middle of the night, didn't feel any better about herself or her circumstances, and, heaven help her, she started weeping again.

Colin heard her. He was also in bed. He couldn't get to sleep, however. The throbbing in his leg kept him wide awake. Alesandra wasn't making much noise, but Colin was attuned to every sound in the house. He immediately tossed the covers aside and got out of bed. He was halfway across the chamber before he realized he was stark naked. He put on a pair of pants, reached for the doorknob, and then stopped.

He wanted to comfort her, yet at the same time he knew he would probably be embarrassed because he'd heard her crying. The sounds were muffled, indicating to him she was trying to be as quiet as possible. She didn't want to be overheard, and he knew he should respect her privacy.

"Hell," he muttered to himself. He didn't know his own mind anymore. He wasn't usually so indecisive. His instincts were telling him to distance himself from Alesandra. She was a complication he wasn't ready to take on.

He turned around and went back to his own bed. He finally admitted the real truth to himself. He wasn't just protecting Alesandra from embarrassment. No, he was also protecting her from his own lecherous ideas. She was in bed, probably only wearing a thin nightgown, and, damn it all, if he got close, he knew he would touch her.

Colin gritted his teeth and closed his eyes. If the little innocent next door had any idea what he was thinking, she would have her guards doing sentry duty around her bed.

Lord, he wanted her.

He killed a whore. It had been a mistake. It hadn't been at all satisfying. The rush of absolute power and excitement were missing. It took him days of reflecting upon the problem before he came up with a suitable explanation. The surge came only after a satisfying hunt. The whore had been too easy, and although her screams excited him, it still wasn't the same. No, no, it was the cleverness he had to call upon to lure the bait. It was the seduction of the innocent by the master. Those were the key elements that made all the difference. The whore had been dirty. She didn't deserve to sleep with the others. He tossed her into a ravine and left her for the wild animals.

He needed a lady.

Colin was gone by the time Alesandra came downstairs the following morning. Flannaghan and Raymond sat with her at the dining room table while she sorted through the huge stack of invitations that had arrived that morning. Stefan was sleeping now because he'd taken the night watch. Alesandra didn't believe it was necessary for anyone to stay up all night, but Raymond, the senior of the two guards, wouldn't listen to her. Someone always had to be on the alert in case of trouble, Raymond argued, and since she had placed him in charge, she really should let him do things his way.

"But we are in England now," she reminded the guard again.

"The general isn't to be taken lightly," Raymond countered. "We got here, didn't we? He could have sent men on the next available ship."

Alesandra quit arguing with him then and turned her attention to the mound of invitations.

"It's astonishing to me that so many found out so soon I was in London," she remarked.

"I'm not surprised," Flannaghan replied. "I already heard from Cook who heard from the butcher that you're causing quite a stir. I'm afraid there's a bit of gossip attached to your name because you're staying here, but the fact that you have a lady's maid and two guards with you has taken the sting out of the remarks. There's also a rather amusing bit of talk . . . nonsense really . . ."

Alesandra was in the process of pulling a note out of an envelope. She paused to look up at Flannaghan. "What bit of nonsense?"

"It's believed by some that you and my employer are related," he explained. "They think Colin's your cousin."

"Neil Perry mentioned that," she said. "He also said that there are others who believe Colin's my lover."

Flannaghan was properly appalled. She reached out and

patted his hand. "It's all right. People will believe what they want to believe. Poor Colin. He can barely stand to have me around as it is, and if anyone refers to me as his cousin, heaven only knows what he'll do."

"How can you say such a thing?" Flannaghan asked. "Milord adores having you here."

"I'm impressed, Flannaghan."

"Why is that, Princess?"

"You've just told the most outrageous lie with a straight face."

Flannaghan didn't laugh until she smiled. "Well, he would adore having you here if he wasn't so busy worrying about his ledgers," he remarked.

He was trying to save face, Alesandra supposed. She nodded, pretending agreement, and then turned her attention back to her task. Flannaghan begged to help. She gave him the duty of affixing her seal to the envelopes. Her crest was most unusual. Flannaghan had never seen anything like it. There was a clear outline of a castle and what appeared to be an eagle or falcon atop one turret.

"Does the castle have a name, Princess?" Flannaghan asked, intrigued by the amazing detail.

"It's called Stone Haven. My father and mother were married there."

She answered every question put to her. Flannaghan's jovial mood lightened her own. He was incredulous when he heard she owned not one but two castles, and his expression made her laugh. He really was a delightful man.

They worked together all morning long, but when the bell chimed one o'clock Alesandra went upstairs to change her gown. She told Flannaghan only that she was expecting more company and wanted to look her best.

Flannaghan didn't think the princess needed to change a thing. It simply wasn't possible for her to become any more beautiful than she already was.

Colin came home around seven that evening. He was stiff and irritable from sitting at his desk at the shipping offices for such long hours. He carried his heavy ledgers under his arm.

He found his butler sprawled out on the steps leading upstairs. It was Raymond who opened the front door for him.

Flannaghan looked done in. "What happened to you?" Colin asked.

The butler roused himself from his stupor and stood up. "We had company again today. The princess didn't give me any warning. I'm not faulting her, of course, and she did tell me she was going to have callers, but I didn't realize who, and then he was here with his attendants and I spilled the tea Cook prepared. After he left, a dock worker appeared at the door. I thought he was after begging, but Princess Alesandra heard me tell him to go around to the back door and Cook would give him something to eat. She intervened. Why, she was expecting the man, and do you know, milord, she treated him with the same respect as the other."

"What other?" Colin asked, trying to sort through the servant's bizarre explanation.

"The prince regent."

"He was here? I'll be damned."

Flannaghan sat back down on the steps. "If my uncle Sterns gets wind of my disgrace, he'll box my ears."

"What disgrace?"

"I spilled tea on the prince regent's jacket."

"Good for you," Colin replied. "When I can afford it, you're getting a raise."

Flannaghan smiled. He'd forgotten how much his employer disliked the prince regent. "I was quite rattled by his presence, but Princess Alesandra acted as though nothing out of the ordinary was happening. She was very dignified. The prince regent wasn't his usual pompous self either. He acted like a besotted schoolboy. It was apparent to me he has great affection for the princess."

Alesandra appeared at the landing above. Colin looked up and immediately frowned. A tightness in his chest made him realize he'd quit breathing.

She looked absolutely beautiful. She was dressed in a silver and white gown that shimmered in the light when she moved. The cut of the dress wasn't overly revealing, but there was still a hint of flesh visible at the top of her neckline.

Her hair was pinned up with a thin white ribbon threaded through her curls. Wisps of hair curled at the base of her neck.

She looked breathtakingly beautiful. Every nerve in Colin's body reacted to the sight of her. He wanted to take her into his arms, kiss her, taste her. . . .

"Where the hell do you think you're going?" He snapped out the question in a general's tone of voice. Anger hid his lust—or so he hoped.

Her eyes widened over the hostility in his demand. "To the opera," she answered. "The prince regent insisted I take his box tonight. I'm taking Raymond with me."

"You're staying home, Alesandra," Colin stated.

"Princess, you cannot expect me to go inside the opera and sit near the prince regent," Raymond said, somewhat plaintively for such a large, fearsome man.

"He won't be there, Raymond," she explained.

"I still can't go inside. It wouldn't be proper. I'll wait by the carriage."

"You aren't going anywhere without me," Colin announced. He added a hard glare so she would understand he meant what he said.

Her smile was radiant. He realized then she'd had no intention of dragging Raymond into the opera house. She'd cleverly tricked him into accommodating her.

"Do hurry and change, Colin. We don't want to be late."

"I hate the opera."

He sounded like a little boy complaining about having to eat his vegetables. She didn't have a bit of sympathy for him. She didn't particularly like the opera either, but she wasn't going to admit that fact to him. He'd want to stay home then, and she really couldn't insult the prince regent by not using his box.

"Too bad, Colin. You already gave me your promise to go. Do hurry."

Alesandra lifted the hem of her gown and came down the stairs. Flannaghan watched her with his mouth gaping open. She smiled when she passed him.

"She moves like a princess," Flannaghan whispered to his employer.

Colin smiled. "She is a princess, Flannaghan."

Colin suddenly quit smiling. Alesandra's dress was a little lower on top than he'd realized. Up close he could see the swell of her bosom.

"You're going to have to change your gown before we go anywhere," he announced.

"Why would I want to change?"

He muttered something under his breath. "This gown is too . . . enticing. Do you want every man there boldly staring at you?"

"Do you think they will?"

"Hell, yes."

She smiled. "Good."

"You want to attract their notice?" He sounded incredulous.

She looked exasperated. "Of course I want to attract their notice. I'm trying to find a husband, remember?"

"You're changing your gown."

"I'll keep my cloak on."

"Change."

Flannaghan's neck was beginning to ache from turning his head back and forth during the heated debate.

"You're being ridiculous," she announced. "And acting terribly old-fashioned."

"I'm your guardian. I'll act any damned way I want to act."

"Colin, be reasonable about this. Valena went to a great deal of trouble and time to get all the wrinkles out."

He didn't let her finish. "You're wasting time."

She shook her head at him. She wasn't going to give in, no matter how intimidating his scowl became.

He walked over to her. Before she knew what he was going to do, he grabbed hold of the bodice of her dress and tried to pull the material up to her chin.

"Every time I think your dress needs some adjustment, I'm going to haul it up, just like this, no matter where we are."

"I'll change."

"I thought you might."

As soon as he let go of her, she turned and ran up the steps. "You're a horrible man, Colin."

He didn't mind her insult. He'd gotten his way, and that was all that mattered. He'd be damned if he'd let the unattached predators ogle her.

It didn't take him long to wash and dress in formal attire. He was back downstairs in less than fifteen minutes.

She took much longer. She was coming down the stairs again when Colin sauntered in from the dining room. He was eating a green apple. He stopped when he saw her on the staircase. His gaze lingered on the bodice of her gown for a long minute, then he nodded his approval. He smiled with satisfaction. She thought he might very well be gloating over his victory. It was apparent he found the forest green gown suitable. It wasn't, though. The cut of the bodice was a deep V, but she'd cleverly stuffed a piece of lace down the middle to appease her guardian.

She didn't choose the gown to deliberately provoke Colin. The dress was the only other option left to her. The other gowns were too wrinkled to wear, and Valena had only just finished getting the creases out of this one.

Colin certainly looked dashing. Black suited him. He tugged on his starched white cravat and devoured his apple at the same time.

He still looked incredibly sexy. The fabric of his jacket was stretched tight across his broad shoulders. His pants were indecently snug, and Alesandra couldn't help but notice the bulge of muscle in his thighs.

Colin seemed preoccupied for most of the ride to their destination. Alesandra sat across from him in the small carriage with her hands folded together in her lap. His legs crowded her into one corner, and in the darkness his size was far more intimidating. So was his silence.

"I didn't realize you were friends with the prince regent," he remarked.

"He isn't my friend. I only just met him today."

"Flannaghan told me the prince was taken with you."

She shook her head. "He was taken with what I am, not who I am."

"Meaning?"

She let out a little sigh before answering. "It was an official call, Colin. The prince came because I'm a princess. He doesn't know me personally at all. Now do you understand?"

He nodded. "Most of society will embrace you because of what you are, Alesandra. I'm pleased you understand the shallowness that may exist in the friendships offered to you. It shows you have maturity."

"Maturity? No, it shows cynicism."

He smiled. "That too."

Several minutes passed in silence. Then Colin spoke again. "Did you like him?"

"Who?"

"The prince."

"I don't know him well enough to form an opinion."

"You're hedging, Alesandra. Tell me the truth."

"I was being diplomatic," she replied. "But I'll give you an honest answer. No, I didn't particularly like him. There, are you happy now?"

"Yes. Your answer proves you're a good judge of character."

"Perhaps the prince has a kind heart," she remarked, feeling guilty because she'd admitted she hadn't liked him.

"He doesn't."

"Why don't *you* like him?"

"He broke his word—a promise made to my partner," Colin explained. "The prince regent held a large treasury belonging to Nathan's wife, Sara, and after a time he decided to keep it for himself. It was dishonorable."

"That is shameful," she agreed.

"Why didn't you like him?"

"He seemed . . . full of himself," she admitted.

Colin snorted. "He's full of . . ." He stopped himself from using the crude word he was thinking of and substituted another. "Vinegar."

The carriage came to a rocking stop in front of the Royal Opera House. Alesandra adjusted her white gloves, her attention fully on Colin. "I never would have allowed him entrance into your home if I'd known what he'd done to your partner. I apologize to you, Colin. Your home is your castle, where only friends should be invited."

"You would have refused him?"

She nodded. He winked at her. Her heart immediately started pounding a wild beat. Dear God, he was a charmer.

Raymond had ridden with the driver in front of the carriage. He jumped down from his perch and opened the door for them.

Colin got out first, then turned to assist Alesandra. Her cloak opened when she reached for his hand. The handkerchief she'd stuffed into the bodice shifted, and when she stepped to the pavement, the lace fell out.

He caught it. He took one look at her provocative neckline and started glaring at her.

He was furious with her. She tried to back away from his frown and almost fell over the curb. Colin grabbed her, then turned her around until she was facing the carriage door. He stuffed the bit of lace back into her dress.

She suffered through the humiliation, matching him frown for frown. Their gazes held for a long minute before she finally gave in and turned away.

Colin adjusted her cloak over her shoulders, hauled her into his side, and turned back to the steps. She guessed she should be thankful he hadn't made a scene, and she didn't think anyone had noticed their little confrontation. He had blocked her from the view of the crowd going inside the opera house. Yes, she should have been thankful. She wasn't, though. Colin was acting like an old man.

"You've spent too much time with your ledgers, sir. You really need to get out more often. Then you'd notice my gown isn't at all inappropriate. It's actually quite prim."

She didn't appreciate his snort of disbelief. She felt like

kicking him. "You've taken this duty as guardian to heart, haven't you?"

He kept his arm anchored on her shoulders as they went up the steps. She kept trying to shrug him away from her. Colin was determined to be possessive, however, and she finally gave up.

"Alesandra, my father entrusted me with your care. It doesn't matter if I like this duty or not. I'm your guardian and you'll do as I order."

"It's a pity you aren't more like your father. He's such a sweet, understanding man. You could learn a lesson or two from him."

"When you quit dressing like a trollop, I'll be more understanding," he promised.

Her gasp sounded like a hiccup. "No one has ever dared to call me a trollop."

Colin didn't remark on that outraged statement. He did smile, though.

Neither one said another word to the other for a long, long while. They were escorted to the prince regent's box and took their seats side by side.

The opera house was filled to capacity, but Colin was certain only Alesandra watched the performance. Everyone else watched her.

She pretended not to be aware of their stares. She impressed the hell out of Colin, too. She looked so beautifully composed. Her posture was ramrod straight, and she never once turned her attention from the stage. He could see her hands, however. They were clenched tight in her lap.

He moved a little closer to her. Then he reached over and covered her hands with one of his. She didn't turn her gaze to him, but she latched on to his hand and held tight. They stayed like that through the rest of the performance.

The white starched cravat around his neck was driving him crazy. He wanted to tear the thing off, prop his feet up on the railing overlooking the stage, and close his eyes. Alesandra would probably have heart palpitations if he dared to behave so shamefully. He wouldn't embarrass her, of course, but, God, how he hated all the pretense associated with the ton's affairs.

He hated having to sit in the prince regent's box, too. Nathan would bellow for a week if he found out. His partner disliked their ruler even more than Colin did, for it was his wife who had been cheated out of her inheritance by the not-so-noble prince.

The god-awful opera he was being subjected to didn't improve his cranky disposition. He did close his eyes then, and tried to block out the sounds of screeching coming from the stage.

Alesandra didn't realize until the performance was over that Colin had fallen asleep. She turned to ask him if he had enjoyed the opera as much as she had, but just as she was about to speak, he started to snore. She almost laughed. It took all she had to keep her expression composed. The opera really had been dreadful, and in her heart she wished *she* could have slept through the ordeal. She would never admit such a thing to Colin, however, for the simple reason that she knew he would gloat.

She nudged him hard with her elbow. Colin came awake with a start.

"You really are impossible," she told him in a whisper.

He gave her a sleepy-eyed grin. "I like to think I am."

It simply wasn't possible to offend him. She gave up trying. She stood up, took hold of her cloak, and turned to leave the box. Colin followed her.

There was a crush of people in the foyer below. Most were waiting to get a closer look at her. Alesandra found herself surrounded by gentlemen begging an introduction. She lost Colin in the shuffle, and when she finally located him again, she saw he was surrounded by ladies. One, a gaudy redheaded woman with exposed bosoms down to her knees, was hanging on Colin's arm. The woman kept licking her upper lip, and Alesandra was reminded of a hungry alley cat that had just spotted a bowl of cream.

Colin appeared to be the woman's snack. Alesandra tried to pay attention to what was being said to her by a gentleman who'd introduced himself as the Earl of something or other, but her gaze kept returning to Colin. He looked very happy with all the attention he was getting, and for some strange reason that notice infuriated Alesandra.

It hit her all at once, this unreasonable burst of jealousy. And, Lord, it was the most horrible feeling. She simply couldn't stand to see the woman's hand on Colin's arm.

She was more disgusted with herself than with Colin. Since the moment she'd arrived in England, she'd been trying to behave the way she thought a princess should behave. The mother superior's two sainted words, *dignity* and *decorum* echoed in her mind. Alesandra remembered the nun's warning to avoid spontaneous actions. She'd pointed out over ten examples of trouble that had resulted because of her spur-of-the-moment ideas.

Alesandra let out a sigh. She guessed marching over to Colin's side and ripping that horrible woman's hand off his arm would qualify as a spontaneous action. Further, she knew the gossip tomorrow would make her sorry for her action.

It felt as though the foyer was closing in on her. No one appeared to be in a hurry to leave. More and more people crowded into the tiny area to see who was there and to be seen.

She desperately needed fresh air. She excused herself from the gentleman requesting an audience with her by giving him permission to send her a note, then slowly made her way through the throng of people to the front doors.

She didn't care if Colin followed her or not. She went outside. She paused on the front step, took a deep breath of the not-so-fresh city air, and put on her cloak. Colin's carriage was directly below her. Raymond spotted her right away. He jumped down from his perch, where he'd been waiting with the driver.

Alesandra lifted the hem of her gown and started down the steps. Someone grabbed hold of her arm. She thought it was Colin finally catching up with her. His grip stung. She tried to pull her arm away, then turned to tell him to lessen his hold.

It wasn't Colin. The stranger holding on to her was dressed in black from head to foot. He wore a cap that covered most of his brow. She could barely see his face.

"Let go of me," she commanded.

"You must come home with us now, Princess Alesandra."

A chill settled around her heart. The man had spoken to her in the language of her father's homeland. She understood what was happening then. She tried not to panic. She pulled back and tried to run, but she was captured by another man from behind. He was hurting her with his fierce hold. Alesandra was suddenly too furious to think about the pain. With his friend's assistance, the man started to drag her back toward the side of the building. A third man appeared out of the shadows of the stone columns in front of the opera house and ran down the steps to stop Raymond from interfering. Her guard was charging up the steps to protect her. Raymond landed the first punch, but the man he'd struck only staggered backward. Then he lashed out at her guard with something sharp. Alesandra saw the blood spurting down the side of Raymond's face and started screaming.

A hand clamped down over her mouth, cutting off the sound. She bit her attacker as hard as she could. He let out a howl of pain while he shifted his hold on her.

He was strangling her now. He kept telling her to quit her struggles or he would have to hurt her.

Alesandra was terrified. She couldn't breathe. She kept up her struggle, determined to get away from the horrible men and run to Raymond. She had to help him. He could be bleeding to death, and, dear God, this was all her fault. She should have listened to Raymond when he insisted the general's men would come after her. She should have stayed home . . . she should have . . .

She heard Colin before she saw him. A roar of fury unlike anything she'd ever heard before sounded in the darkness. The man anchoring her from behind was suddenly ripped away from her and tossed headfirst into one of the stone pillars. He collapsed to the ground like a discarded apple core.

Alesandra was coughing and gasping for air. The stranger holding on to her arm tried to pull her in front of him to use as a shield against Colin. He wouldn't allow that. He moved so quickly, Alesandra didn't have time to help. Colin's fist slammed into the man's face. Her attacker's cap went flying in one direction, and he went flying down the steps. He landed with a thud at Raymond's feet. Alesandra's guard was fully occupied circling his adversary, his concentration totally centered on the gleaming knife he held in his hand.

Colin moved in from behind. The man turned to lash out at him. Colin kicked the blade out of his hand, moved forward again, and grabbed hold of his arm. He twisted it into an unnatural position. The bone snapped, and that horrid sound was followed by a scream of pain. Colin was not finished with his victim, however. He shoved him headfirst into the back of the carriage.

Alesandra came running down the steps. She used the handkerchief from the bodice of her gown to stem the flow of blood pouring from the deep cut in Raymond's right cheek.

Colin didn't know if there were others ready to strike or not, and in his mind Alesandra wasn't going to be safe until she was home.

"Get inside the carriage, Alesandra. Now."

His voice was harsh with anger. She thought he was furious with her. She hurried to do as he commanded, but tried to take Raymond with her. She put his arm around her shoulder, braced herself for his weight, and whispered for him to lean on her.

"I'll be all right, Princess," Raymond told her. "Get inside. It isn't safe for you here."

Colin pulled her away from the guard. He half lifted, half tossed her into the carriage, then turned to help Raymond.

If the guard had been in any condition to look after Alesandra, Colin would have stayed behind to get some answers out of the bastards who'd dared to touch her. Raymond had lost quite a bit of blood, however, and now looked close to collapse.

Colin let out a low expletive, then got inside. The driver immediately whistled the horses into a full trot.

Alesandra sat next to the guard. "I don't understand why no one helped us," she whispered. "Couldn't they see we were in trouble?"

"You were the only one outside, Princess," Raymond answered. He slumped into the corner of the carriage. "It happened too fast. Why wasn't your escort with you?"

Raymond turned his head to glare at Colin when he asked his question. The handkerchief he held to his cheek was turning bright red. He adjusted the cloth against the cut, then turned to look at her.

She folded her hands together in her lap and lowered her gaze. "This is all my fault," she said. "I was impatient and there was such a crowd inside. I wanted some fresh air. I should have waited."

"Damn right you should have waited."

"Please don't be angry with me, Colin."

"Where the hell was Hillman?"

"The earl you introduced me to before you left me?"

"I didn't leave you," he muttered. "Hillman was introducing you to some of his friends and I turned my back for one minute to say hello to a couple of business associates. Damn it, Alesandra, if you wanted to leave why didn't you tell Hillman to come and get me?"

"Nothing will be served by raising your voice to me. I accept full responsibility for what happened."

She turned to her guard. "Raymond, can you ever forgive me? I should have stayed home. I put you in danger . . ."

Colin interrupted. "You don't have to hide behind lock and key, Alesandra. You just shouldn't have gone outside without me."

"They would have attacked even if you'd been with me," she countered.

He gave her a speculative look. "Start explaining," he ordered.

"I will explain when you quit shouting at me."

He hadn't been shouting, but she was obviously too upset

to notice. She'd taken her white gloves off. He watched as she folded the pair into a square and turned back to Raymond. She ordered Raymond to use the gloves for his bandage now that the handkerchief was saturated with blood.

"Damn it, Alesandra, you could have been hurt."

"And so could you, Colin," she responded. "Raymond needs a physician."

"I'll send Flannaghan over to fetch Winters as soon as we get home."

"Is Winters your personal physician?"

"Yes. Alesandra, did you know the men who attacked?"

"No," she answered. "At least, not by name. I know where they came from, though."

"They're fanatics," Raymond interjected.

Alesandra couldn't bear to look at Colin's frown. She leaned back against the cushion of the seat and closed her eyes. "The men are from my homeland. They want to take me back."

"For what purpose?"

"To marry their bastard general," Raymond answered. "Begging your pardon, Princess, for using that word in your presence, but Ivan is a bastard to be sure."

Colin had to wait to ask additional questions because they'd reached his town house. He wouldn't let Alesandra leave the safety of the carriage until he had the front door opened and had shouted for Stefan. Stefan came outside to assist Raymond, and Colin took hold of Alesandra.

A good hour was spent seeing to Raymond's care. Colin's physician lived just three blocks away and was thankfully home for the evening. Flannaghan brought him back in Colin's carriage.

Sir Winters was a white-haired man with brown eyes, a gentle voice, and an efficient matter.

He believed thugs were responsible for the attack. No one set him straight on that misconception.

"It isn't safe to go anywhere in London anymore, what with the mob of ruffians roaming the streets. Something has got to be done, and soon, before every decent man and woman is killed."

The physician stood in the center of the foyer, his hand on Raymond's jaw as he studied the damage done to his cheek and lamented the condition of London's streets.

Colin suggested Raymond sit at the dining room table. Flannaghan carried in extra candles so the physician would have enough light.

The cut was cleaned with a foul-smelling liquid, then stitched together with black thread. Raymond never once flinched during the painful ordeal. Alesandra flinched for him. She sat next to the guard, and when Winters applied the needle to his flesh, she reached over and took hold of Raymond's hand.

Colin stood in the doorway, watching. His attention was centered on Alesandra. He could see how upset she was. There were tears in her eyes and her shoulders were shaking. Colin fought the urge to go and comfort her.

Alesandra was such a gentle, compassionate woman, and Colin could well see her vulnerability, too. She was whispering something to the guard but he couldn't make out the words. He walked forward, then came to an abrupt stop when he understood what she was saying.

Alesandra was giving her promise that nothing further would happen to the guard. Ivan, she said, would not make such a terrible husband, after all. She told the guard she'd given the matter considerable consideration and had decided to return to her homeland.

Raymond didn't look too happy with her promises. Colin was furious. "You will not decide anything tonight, Alesandra," he commanded.

She turned to look up at him. The anger in his voice surprised her. Why did he care what she decided?

"Yes, Princess," Raymond said, drawing her attention. "Tomorrow will be soon enough to decide what should be done."

Alesandra pretended agreement. She had already made up her mind, however. She wasn't going to let anyone else get hurt because of her. Until tonight she hadn't realized the lengths the general's supporters would go to in order to accomplish their goal. And if Colin hadn't intervened, Raymond might have been killed.

Colin could have been injured, too. Oh, yes, she had made up her mind on the matter.

Winters finished his work, gave instructions, and then took his leave. Colin poured Raymond a goblet full of brandy. The guard downed the contents in one long swallow.

As soon as Raymond went upstairs to bed, Flannaghan took over his nightly ritual of checking all the locks on the windows and doors to make certain the house was secure.

Alesandra tried to go to her bedroom, but Colin intercepted her just as she was reaching for her doorknob. He took hold of her hand and pulled her along with him back to the study. He didn't say a word to her, just nudged her inside and then pulled the door closed behind him.

The time had come to explain in full her unusual circumstances, she supposed. She walked over to the hearth and stood there warming her hands with the heat of the fire Flannaghan had thoughtfully prepared.

Colin watched her, but he didn't say a word. She finally turned around to look at him. He was leaning against the door with his arms folded across his chest. He wasn't frowning and he didn't look at all angry—just thoughtful.

"I put you in danger tonight," she whispered. "I should have explained everything right away."

She waited for him to agree with that statement of fact. He surprised her by shaking his head. "This is as much my fault as yours, Alesandra. I could have insisted you explain your circumstances. I was too caught up in my own affairs to pay much attention to you. I've been remiss as your guardian. That, however, has changed. You're going to tell me everything, aren't you?"

She gripped her hands together. "None of this is your fault, sir. I didn't believe I would be staying here long enough to bother you with my problems, especially after you explained you had no intention of getting married for a long while. I also believed the general would send an ambassador to request my return. I misjudged, you see. I thought he would be civilized. He isn't. He's obviously determined . . . and desperate."

Tears came into her eyes. She took a deep breath to try to gain control of her emotions. "I'm so sorry for what happened tonight."

Colin took mercy on her. "You weren't responsible."

"They were after me," she argued. "Not Raymond or you."

Colin finally moved. He walked over to the chair behind his desk, sat down, and propped his feet up on the nearby footrest.

"Why does this general want you to come home?"

"It isn't my home," she corrected. "I wasn't even born there. My father was king, you see, until he married my mother. She was English and considered an outsider. Father stepped down so he could marry her and his younger brother, Edward, became ruler. It was all very polite."

Colin didn't remark on her explanation and she didn't have any idea what he was thinking. "Would you like me to continue?" she asked, her worry obvious.

"I want you to explain why the general wants you to come home," he repeated.

"My father was loved by his subjects. They didn't condemn him because he married my mother. In fact, they found it all very romantic. He did give up his kingdom for her, after all, and everyone who met my mother adored her. She was a dear, kindhearted woman."

"Do you resemble your mother in appearance?"

"Yes."

"Then she was also a beautiful woman, wasn't she?"

He had just given her a compliment, but she had difficulty accepting it. Her mother had been so much more than simply beautiful.

"A compliment shouldn't make you frown," Colin remarked.

"My mother was beautiful," she said. "But she also had a pure heart. I wish I was more like her, Colin. My thoughts are rarely pure. I was so angry tonight I wanted to hurt those men."

He found his first smile. "I did hurt them," he reminded her. "Now please continue with your explanation. I'm anxious to hear the rest of this."

"My father's brother died just last year and the country was once again thrown into turmoil. There seems to be a notion held by some that I should come home. The general wants marriage and believes he'll be able to secure the throne if I become his wife."

"Why does he believe that?"

She let out a sigh. "Because I'm the only surviving heir to the throne. Everyone has conveniently forgotten my father abdicated. As I said before, he was well loved by his subjects and that love . . ."

She didn't go on. Colin was intrigued by the faint blush on her cheeks. "And that love what?" he asked.

"Has been transferred to me," she blurted out. "At least, that is what Sir Richards of your War Department explained to me, and all the letters I've received over the years from the loyalists would confirm his supposition."

Colin straightened in his chair. "You know Sir Richards?" he asked.

"Yes," she answered. "He has been quite helpful to me. Why do you look so surprised? Is something wrong? You reacted with quite a startle at the mention of his name."

He shook his head. "How is the head of England's security section involved in this?"

"Then you know Sir Richards too?"

"I work for him."

It was her turn to look startled. And appalled. "But he runs the secret . . . Colin, if you work for him you must be involved in dangerous work. What do your parents think of this double life you lead? Oh, sir, no wonder you have no wish to marry. Your wife would worry all the time. Yes, she would."

Colin regretted telling her the truth. "I used to work for him," he qualified.

She could tell he was lying to her. The proof was in his eyes. They'd gone . . . cold, hard. She decided not to argue with him. If he wanted her to think he wasn't involved with the Security Section, she would pretend to believe him.

"How and why did Sir Richards get involved?"

His irritated tone of voice pulled her back to the primary topic. "He came to see me just the day before your father became ill. He and his associates—or superiors, as he referred to them—wish me to marry General Ivan."

"Then he knows the general?"

She shook her head. "He knows of him," she explained. "Sir Richards considers Ivan the lesser of two evils."

Colin let out a low expletive. She pretended she didn't hear it. "Sir Richards told your father the general would be easier to control. England wants the continuation of imports and the general would certainly look upon your country as a friend if I had been convinced by your leaders to marry Ivan. There is another man eager to snatch the throne and Sir Richards believes he's more ruthless. He also believes he wouldn't cooperate with trade agreements."

"So you're the sacrificial lamb, is that right?"

She didn't answer him.

"What did my father say to Sir Richards?"

She started twisting her hands together. "The director can be very persuasive. Your father listened to his argument and then promised to consider the matter. After Richards left, he decided against the marriage."

"Why?"

She lowered her gaze to her hands, saw how red her skin had become, and immediately relaxed her grip. "I cried," she confessed. "I'm ashamed to admit that, but I did cry. I was very upset. Your mother became furious with your father and I was the cause of a heated argument. That made me feel even more miserable. I felt I was disappointing everyone by being selfish. My only excuse is that my parents had such a happy marriage and I wanted to find that same kind of joy. I didn't believe I would ever find love or happiness married to a man who only wanted me for political gain. I've never met the general, but Raymond and Stefan have told me stories about him. If half of what they said is true, he's a very self-indulgent man."

Alesandra paused to take a deep breath. "Your father has a soft heart. He couldn't stand to see me upset. And he had made a promise to my father to take care of me."

"So he decided you should marry me."

"Yes," she answered. "It was his hope, but he wasn't counting on it. Otherwise your mother would have had your name written down on the invitations. Understand, sir, I was being fanciful when I told your father I wanted to marry for love. I realize that isn't possible now, given the urgency of finding a husband, and so I decided I would consider the marriage a business arrangement. In return for the use of my considerable inheritance, my husband would go his way and I would go mine. I thought I would travel . . . and in time, perhaps, go back to Holy Cross. It was very peaceful there."

"Hell."

She didn't know what to make of that muttered blasphemy. She frowned in reaction and then said, "I also hoped that eventually my husband and I would become friends."

"And lovers?" he asked.

She lifted her shoulders in a shrug. "Anything is possible, Colin, given time and patience. However, I have had time to reevaluate my position. Granted, the gentlemen in England seem to be more civilized, and I had hoped to find one who was at least ethical, but tonight I realized none of it matters anymore. I'm going to cooperate. I'll marry the general. I've caused quite enough trouble. Perhaps in time this man will learn to . . . soften in his attitudes."

Colin snorted. "A snake doesn't ever stop slithering. He won't change, and you aren't going to marry him. Got that?"

She shivered over the harshness in his voice. "I want your agreement, Alesandra."

She wouldn't give it. She kept picturing the blood pouring down Raymond's face. "I won't be the cause of any more . . ."

"Come here."

Alesandra walked over to stand in front of his desk. He motioned her closer with the crook of his finger. She edged her way around the side and stopped when she was just a foot away from him.

"The general would give up his plan and leave me alone if I had a husband . . . wouldn't he?"

The combination of fear and hope in her voice bothered the hell out of him. She was too young to have such worries. Alesandra should be as scatterbrained and as giddy as his younger sisters.

Damn it all, she was in need of a champion. He reached out and took hold of her hands. She realized she was gripping them together again. She tried to relax. She couldn't.

"Marriage to the general is out of the question. Are we agreed on that?"

He squeezed her hands until she nodded. "Good," he remarked then. "Have you left anything out in your explanation?"

"No."

Colin smiled. "No one bucks the head of security," he remarked then, referring to Sir Richards.

"Your father did."

"Yes, he did, didn't he?" He was inordinately pleased with his father. "I'll talk to Richards tomorrow and see if we can't get his support."

"Thank you."

His nod was quick. "Since my family is responsible for you, I'll set up a meeting with my father and my brother as soon as they're feeling well again."

"For what purpose?"

"To figure out what the hell to do with you."

He'd meant the remark as a jest of sorts. She took it to heart. She jerked her hands away from his. His bluntness had offended her. Alesandra had an extremely tender nature. He considered suggesting she learn to toughen her emotional hide, then decided not to offer that advice because she would probably take that as an insult too.

"I will not become a burden."

"I didn't say you were."

"You implied it."

"I don't ever imply. I always tell it the way it is."

She turned and walked toward the door. "I believe it's time to reevaluate."

"You've already done that."

"I'm going to again," she announced.

A wave of nausea caught Colin by surprise. He closed his eyes and took a deep breath. His stomach growled, too, and he assumed his sudden weak condition was due to the fact that he had skipped dinner.

He forced himself to think about her last remark. "What are you going to reevaluate now?"

"Our arrangement," she explained. "It isn't working out. I really believe I should find other lodgings tomorrow."

"Alesandra."

He hadn't raised his voice but the bite was still there in his hard tone. She stopped at the entrance and turned to look at him. She braced herself for his next hurtful bit of honesty.

He felt like hell when he saw the tears in her eyes. "I'm sorry," he muttered. "You aren't a burden. Your current situation, however, is a mess. Wouldn't you agree with that evaluation?" he asked.

"Yes, I would agree."

Colin rubbed his brow in an absentminded action and was surprised to feel the perspiration there. He tugged on his cravat next. Damn, it was hot in the study. The fire from the hearth was putting out more heat than was necessary, he supposed. He thought about taking off his jacket but was too weary to go to the trouble now.

"It's a very serious situation, Colin," she added when he didn't respond to her earlier agreement.

"But it isn't the end of the world, is it? You're looking overwhelmed by it all."

"I am overwhelmed," she cried out. "Raymond was injured tonight. Have you already forgotten? He could have been killed. And you . . . you could have been hurt too."

He was frowning again. She was almost sorry she'd

reminded him of the incident. She decided not to end the evening on such a sour note.

"I've forgotten my manners," she blurted out. "I should say thank you now."

"You should? Why?"

"Because you apologized," she explained. "I know it was difficult for you."

"And how would you know that?"

"Your voice got all gruff, and you were glaring at me. Yes, it was difficult. Yet you did say you were sorry. That makes your apology all the more pleasing to me."

She walked back over to his side. Before she lost her courage, she leaned forward and kissed him on his cheek. "I still prefer your father for my guardian," she told him, hoping to gain a smile. "He's much easier to . . ."

She was searching for the right word. He gave it to her. "Manipulate?"

She laughed. "Yes."

"My four little sisters have worn him down. He's been turned into milk toast by all those women."

Colin let out a weary sigh and rubbed his brow again. He'd developed a pounding headache in the last few minutes, and he could barely concentrate on the topic at hand. "Go to bed, Alesandra. It's late and you've had quite a day."

She started to leave, then paused. "Are you feeling all right? Your face looks terribly pale to me."

"I feel fine," he told her. "Go to bed."

He told the lie easily. He didn't feel at all fine, however. He felt like hell. His insides were on fire. His stomach was reacting as though he'd just swallowed a hot piece of coal. His skin was clammy and hot, and he found himself thanking God he hadn't had much to eat tonight. The mere thought of food made him want to gag.

Colin was certain he would feel better once he had gotten some sleep. At one o'clock in the morning he was wishing he could close his eyes and die.

By three o'clock, he thought he had.

He was burning up with fever, and damn if he hadn't

thrown up at least twenty times the paltry little apple he'd eaten before he left for the opera.

His stomach finally accepted the fact that there wasn't anything more to get rid of and settled down into a tight knot. Colin sprawled out on the bed, face down, with his arms spread wide.

Oh, yes, death would have been a treat.

Chapter 5

She wouldn't let him die. She wouldn't leave him alone either. The minute she was awakened by the sounds of retching coming from Colin's bedroom, she threw off her covers and got out of bed.

Alesandra didn't care about appearances. It didn't matter to her if going into his bedroom would be looked upon as inappropriate behavior; Colin needed her help, and he was going to get it.

By the time she put on her robe and went next door, Colin was back in his bed. He was sprawled out on his stomach on top of the covers. He was stark naked. She tried not to notice. Colin had opened both windows and the room was now so frigid with cold she could see her breath. The drapes billowed out like inflated balloons from the hard, spitting wind and rain coming through the windows.

"Dear God, are you trying to kill yourself?" she asked.

Colin didn't answer her. She hurried over to shut the windows before turning to the bed. Only one side of Colin's face was visible to her, yet that was quite enough for her to surmise from his tortured expression how miserable he was feeling.

It was a struggle, but she finally was able to tug the covers out from under him and then cover him up and properly tuck him in. He told her to leave him the hell alone. She ignored that order. She put the back of her hand to his forehead, felt the heat there, and immediately went to fetch a cold, wet cloth.

Colin was too weak to fight her. She spent the rest of the night with him, mopping his brow every five minutes or so and holding the chamber pot for him just as often. He wasn't able to throw up anything more, for his stomach was empty now, but he still made the most horrible gagging sounds trying.

He wanted water. She wouldn't let him have any. She tried reasoning with him, but he wasn't in the mood to listen to her. Thankfully he was too exhausted to get the water by himself.

"If you swallow anything, it's going to come right back up. I've had this illness, Colin. I know what I'm talking about. Now close your eyes and try to get some rest. You're going to feel better tomorrow."

She wanted to give him a bit of hope, and for that reason she deliberately lied. If Colin followed the same course as everyone else, he was going to be miserable for a good week.

Her prediction proved accurate. He wasn't feeling any better the following day, or the day after that. She personally tended to him. She wouldn't let Flannaghan or Valena into the chamber, fearing they would also catch the illness if they got too close to Colin. Flannaghan tried to argue with her. Colin was his responsibility, after all, and he should be the one to tend to him. It was his noble duty, he explained, to put himself at risk.

Alesandra countered with the explanation that she had already suffered with the illness and was therefore the only one suited to see to Colin's needs. It was highly doubtful she would get sick again. Flannaghan, however, would be taking a much greater gamble, and how would they all ever get along if he became too sick to take care of them?

Flannaghan was finally convinced. He was kept busy with the running of the household, and even took on the added duty of answering all of her correspondence. The town house was off-limits to all callers. The physician, Sir Winters, returned to look at Raymond's injury, and while he was there Alesandra consulted him about Colin's illness. The physician didn't go into Colin's bedroom, for he had no wish to contract the illness, but he left a tonic he thought might settle the patient's irritable stomach and suggested sponge baths to cool the fever.

Colin was a difficult patient. Alesandra tried to follow the physician's advice by giving Colin a sponge bath late that night when his temperature increased. She stroked his chest and arms with the cooling cloth first, then turned to his legs. He seemed to be asleep, but when she touched his scarred leg, he almost came off the bed.

"I would like to die in peace, Alesandra. Now get the hell out of here."

His hoarse bellow didn't affect her, for she was still reeling from the sight of his injured leg. The calf was a mass of scar tissue from the back of his knee to the edge of his heel. Alesandra didn't know how he'd come by the injury, but the agony he must have endured tore at her heart.

She thought it a miracle he could walk at all. Colin jerked the covers over his legs and told her again, though in a much more weary tone of voice, to leave his room.

There were tears in her eyes. She thought he might have seen them. She didn't want him to know the brief glimpse at his leg had caused that reaction. Colin was a proud, unbending man. He didn't want her pity, she knew, and he was obviously prickly about the scar.

Alesandra decided to turn his attention. "Your shouts are most upsetting to me, Colin, and if you continue to give me such harsh commands, I'll probably cry like a child. I won't leave, however, no matter how mean hearted you become. Now kindly give me your leg. I'm going to wash it."

"Alesandra, I swear to God, I'm going to toss you out the window if you don't leave me alone."

"Colin, the sponge bath didn't bother you at all last night. Why are you so irritable now? Is the fever higher tonight?"

"You washed my legs last night?"

"I did," she blatantly lied.

"What the hell else did you wash?"

She knew what he was asking. She tried not to blush when she answered him. "Your arms and chest and legs," she told him. "I left the middle alone. Do quit fighting me, sir," she ordered as she snatched his leg from under the cover.

Colin gave up. He muttered something atrocious under his breath and closed his eyes. Alesandra dipped the cloth into the cold water, then gently washed both legs.

Her composure never faltered, and it was only after she'd covered him up again that she realized he'd been watching her.

"Now then," she said with a sigh. "Don't you feel better?"

His glare was his answer. She stood up and turned away from him so he wouldn't see her smile. She put the bowl of water back on the washstand, then carried a goblet only half filled with water back over to her patient.

She handed him the drink, told him she would leave him alone for a little while, and then tried to do just that. He grabbed hold of her hand and held tight.

"Are you sleepy?" he asked her, his voice still gruff with irritation.

"Not particularly."

"Then stay and talk to me."

He moved his legs out of the way and patted the side of the bed. Alesandra sat down. She folded her hands together in her lap and desperately tried not to stare at his chest.

"Don't you own any nightshirts?" she asked.

"No."

"Cover yourself, Colin," she suggested then. She didn't wait for him to do as she ordered, but saw to the duty herself.

He immediately shoved the quilt back. He sat up, propped his back against the headboard, and let out a loud yawn.

"God, I feel like hell."

"Why do you wear your hair so long? It reaches your shoulders now. It looks quite barbaric," she added with a smile so he wouldn't think she was insulting him. "'Tis the truth, it makes you look like a pirate."

He shrugged. "It's a reminder to me," he said.

"A reminder of what?"

"Being free."

She didn't know what he was talking about, but he didn't look inclined to explain further. He turned the topic then by asking her to catch him up on business matters.

"Did Flannaghan remember to send a note to Borders?"

"Do you mean your associate?"

"Borders isn't an associate. He's retired from the shipping business these days, but he helps out when I need him."

"Yes," she answered. "Flannaghan did send a messenger and Mister Borders is taking care of business. Each evening he sends the daily report, and they're all stacked up on your desk for you to look over when you're feeling better. You also received another letter from your partner," she added with a nod. "I didn't realize the two of you had opened a second office across the sea. You'll soon be worldwide, won't you?"

"Perhaps. Now tell me what you've been doing. You haven't gone out, have you?"

She shook her head. "I've been taking care of you. I did write another note to Victoria's brother begging a second audience. Neil responded with a terse note, denying my request. I do wish you hadn't tossed him out."

"I don't want him coming back here, Alesandra."

She let out a sigh. He gave her a good frown. "You're stirring up unnecessary trouble."

"I promised to be discreet. I'm worried about Victoria," she added with a nod.

"No one else is," he countered.

"Yes, I know," she whispered. "Colin, if you were in trouble, I would do whatever it took to help you."

He was pleased with her fervent promise. "You would?"

She nodded. "We are like family now, aren't we? Your father is my guardian, and I try to think of you as a brother . . ."

"The hell with that."

Her eyes widened. Colin looked furious with her. "You don't want me to think of you as a brother?"

"Damned right I don't."

She looked crushed.

Colin stared at her with an incredulous expression on his face. The fever hadn't diminished his desire for her at all. Hell, he'd have to be dead and buried before he could rid himself of his growing need to touch her.

She didn't have a clue as to her own appeal. She sat so prim and proper next to him, wearing that virginal white gown that wasn't suppose to be the least bit provocative but still damn well was. The dress was buttoned up to her chin. He thought it was extremely sexy. So was her hair. It wasn't bound up behind her head tonight but fell in wild curls around her shoulders. She kept brushing the locks back over her shoulders in a motion he found utterly appealing.

Damned if he would let her think of him as her brother.

"Less than a week ago you were thinking of me as your future husband, remember?"

His unreasonable anger fueled her own. "But you declined, remember that?"

"Don't take that tone of voice with me, Alesandra."

"Don't raise your voice to me, Colin."

He let out a long sigh. They were both exhausted, he told himself, and surely that was the reason their tempers were so fragile tonight.

"You're a princess," he said then. "And I'm . . ."

She finished his sentence for him. "A dragon."

"Fine," he snapped. "A dragon then. And princesses don't marry dragons."

"Lord, but you're irritable tonight."

"I'm always irritable."

"Then it's a blessing we aren't going to marry each other. You would make me quite miserable."

Colin yawned again. "Probably," he drawled out.

She stood up. "You need to go to sleep now," she announced. She leaned over him and touched his forehead with her hand. "You've still got a fever, though it isn't as high as last night. Colin, do you dislike women who say I told you so?"

"Hell, yes."

She smiled. "Good. I remember telling you your suspicious nature would get you into trouble, and I was right, wasn't I?"

He didn't answer her. She didn't mind. She was too busy gloating. She turned and walked over to the door connecting the bedrooms. She wasn't quite finished goading him, however. "You just had to find out for yourself that Caine was really sick, and now look at you."

She pulled the door wide. "Good night, dragon."

"Alesandra?"

"Yes?"

"I was wrong."

"You were?" She was thrilled by his admission and waited to hear the rest of his apology. The man wasn't quite an ogre after all. "And?" she prodded when he didn't go on.

"You're still a brat."

Colin's fever continued to plague him for seven long days and nights. He awakened during the eighth night feeling human again and knew the fever was gone. He was surprised to find Alesandra in his bed. She was fully clothed and slept sitting up with her shoulders propped against the headboard. Her hair hung over her face, and she didn't move at all when he got out of bed. Colin washed, changed into a clean pair of britches, and then went back to the bed. He lifted Alesandra into his arms, and even in his weakened condition, it didn't take any effort at all. She was as light as air to him. He smiled when she snuggled up against his shoulder and let out a feminine little sigh. Colin carried her back to her own room, put her in bed, and covered her with a satin quilt.

He stood there staring down at her for a long while. She never opened her eyes. She was clearly exhausted from lack of sleep. He knew she had stayed by his side throughout most of the god-awful ordeal. Alesandra had taken good care of him, and, Lord, he didn't know how he felt about that.

He accepted that he was in her debt, but, damn it all, his feelings went far beyond gratitude. She was beginning to matter to him. As soon as he acknowledged that truth, he tried to think of a way to soften her impact on him. Now wasn't the time to get involved with any woman. Yes, the timing was all wrong, and he sure as certain wasn't going to push his own goals and dreams aside now for any woman.

Alesandra wasn't just any woman, though, and he knew, if he didn't get away from her soon, it would be too late. Hell, it was complicated. His mind was filled with such conflicting emotions. He didn't want her, he told himself again and again, and yet the thought of anyone else having her made his stomach turn.

He wasn't making any sense. Colin finally forced himself to move away from the side of her bed. He went back through his bedroom and continued on into his study. He had at least a month's work piled up now and it would surely take him that long just to transfer all the numbers into the ledgers. Burying himself in his work was just what he needed to take his mind off Alesandra.

Someone had done all the work. Colin was incredulous when he saw the ledgers. The entries were completely up-to-date, ending with today's shipping numbers. He spent an hour double-checking to make certain the totals were accurate, then leaned back in his chair to go through the stack of notes left for him to read.

Caine had obviously taken charge, Colin decided. He would have to remember to thank his brother for his help. It had to have taken him the full week, for there were over fifty pages of transfers added, and Colin hadn't been this current in over a year.

He turned his attention to his messages. Colin worked in his study from dawn until late afternoon. Flannaghan was pleased to see his employer was looking so much better. He carried up a breakfast tray and another tray of food at the noon hour. Colin had bathed and dressed in a white shirt and black britches, and Flannaghan remarked that the color was coming back to his lord's complexion. The servant hovered like a mother hen and soon drove Colin to distraction.

Flannaghan again interrupted him around three that afternoon to give him messages from both his father and his brother.

The note from the Duke of Williamshire was filled with concern for Princess Alesandra's safety. He'd obviously heard about the attack outside the Opera House. He requested a family meeting be set to settle Alesandra's future and asked that Colin let him know the minute he was feeling well enough to bring the princess to their London town house.

Caine's note was similar—confusing, too, for he made no mention of helping with the books. Colin thought Caine was simply being humble.

"It's good news, isn't it?" Flannaghan asked. "Your family has fully recovered. Cook talked to your father's gardener and he said everyone was feeling fit again. Your father has already ordered his town house opened and should be settled in by nightfall. The duchess is with him, but your sisters have been ordered to stay in the country for another week or two. Do you wish for me to send a messenger with the news of your recovery?"

Colin wasn't surprised by his servant's information. The grapevine between the households was always up to the minute with the latest happenings. "My father wants a family council, or did you already find that out from the gardener?" he asked dryly.

Flannaghan nodded. "I had heard, but I wasn't given a specific time."

Colin shook his head in vexation. "Set the meeting for tomorrow afternoon."

"At what time?"

"Two."

"And your brother?" Flannaghan asked. "Should I send a messenger to him as well?"

"Yes," Colin agreed. "I'm certain he'll want to be there."

Flannaghan hurried toward the door to see to his duties. He reached the entrance, then paused again. "Milord, is our home open to visitors yet? Princess Alesandra's suitors have been begging entrance all week."

Colin frowned. "Are you telling me the rakes are already camping out on my doorstep?"

Flannaghan flinched over the outrage in his employer's

voice. "Word has spread like fire that we have a beautiful, unattached princess residing with us."

"Hell."

"Precisely, milord."

"No one is allowed entrance until after the meeting," Colin announced. He smiled then. "You seem as irritated as I am about Alesandra's suitors. Why is that, Flannaghan?"

The servant didn't pretend indifference. "I am as irritated," he confessed. "She belongs to us, Colin," he blurted out, slipping back to their casual relationship of using first names. "And it is our duty to keep those lechers away from her."

Colin nodded agreement. Flannaghan turned the topic just a little then. "What should I do about her father's business associate? Dreyson has sent a note each and every morning begging an audience. He has papers for her signature," he added. "But in one of the notes I chanced to read over Princess Alesandra's shoulder, Dreyson also insisted he had alarming news to give her."

Colin leaned further back in his chair. "How did Alesandra react to this note?"

"She wasn't at all upset," Flannaghan replied. "I questioned her, of course, and asked her if she shouldn't be a little concerned. She said Dreyson's alarm probably had something to do with a market downswing. I didn't know what she was talking about."

"She was talking about financial losses," he explained. "Send a note to Dreyson, too, telling him that he is invited to call on Alesandra at my father's town house. Set the time for three o'clock, Flannaghan. We should be through with family business by then."

The servant still didn't leave. "Was there something more you wanted?"

"Will Princess Alesandra be leaving us?" The worry in the servant's tone was evident.

"There is a good chance she'll move in with my father and mother."

"But, milord . . ."

"My father is her guardian, Flannaghan."

"That may be," the servant countered. "But you're the only one fit enough to watch out for her. Begging your pardon for being so blunt, but your father is getting along in years and your brother has his wife and child to look after. That leaves you, milord. 'Tis the truth, I would be very distressed if anything happened to our princess."

"Nothing's going to happen to her."

The conviction in his employer's voice appeased Flannaghan's worry. Colin was acting like a protector now. He was a possessive man by nature, stubborn, and just a little bit obtuse, in Flannaghan's estimation, because Colin was taking forever to come to the realization that he and Princess Alesandra were meant for each other.

Colin turned his attention back to his ledgers. Flannaghan coughed to let him know he wasn't quite finished bothering him.

"What else is on your mind?"

"I just thought I would mention . . . that is, the incident in front of the Opera . . ."

Colin shut his book. "Yes?" he prodded.

"It's affected her. She hasn't said anything to me, but I know she hasn't gotten over the incident. She's still blaming herself for Raymond's injury."

"That's ridiculous."

Flannaghan nodded. "She keeps apologizing to her guard and this morning, when she came downstairs, I could tell she'd been weeping. I believe you should have a talk with her, milord. A princess should not cry."

Flannaghan sounded like an authority on the topic of royalty. Colin nodded. "All right, I'll have a talk with her later. Now leave me alone. For the first time in months, I'm actually close to being caught up and I want to get today's totals entered. I don't wish to be disturbed until dinner."

Flannaghan didn't mind his employer's gruffness. Colin would take care of the princess, and that was all that really mattered.

The butler's cheerful mood was sorely tested the rest of

the afternoon. He spent most of his time answering the front door and turning away potential suitors. It was a damn nuisance.

At seven o'clock that evening, Sir Richards arrived on their doorstep. He didn't request admission. The head of England's Security Section demanded to be let in.

Flannaghan ushered Sir Richards up the stairs and into Colin's study. The distinguished-looking gray-haired gentleman waited until the butler had taken his leave before speaking to Colin.

"You're looking none the worse for wear," he announced. "I wanted to look in on you to see how you're doing, of course, and also compliment you on a job well done. The Wellingham business could have gotten sticky. You handled it well."

Colin leaned back in his chair. "It did get sticky," he reminded the director.

"Yes, but you handled it with your usual tact."

Colin caught himself before he snorted with laughter. Handled with tact? How like the director to summarize in gentlemen's terms the necessary killing of one of England's enemies.

"Why are you really here, Richards?"

"To compliment you, of course."

Colin did laugh then. Richards smiled. "I could use a spot of brandy," he announced with a wave of his hand in the direction of the side bar against the wall. "Will you join me?"

Colin declined the offer. He started to get up to see to the director's request, but Richards waved him back to his seat. "I can fetch it."

The director poured himself a drink, then went over to sit in the leather-backed chair facing the desk. "Morgan's going to be joining us in just a few minutes. I wanted to talk to you first, however. Another little problem has developed and I thought it might be just the task for Morgan to handle. An opportunity, you see, for him to get his feet wet."

"He's joining the ranks then?"

"He would like to be of service to his country," the director told him. "What do you think of him, Colin? Forget diplomacy and give me your gut reaction to the man."

Colin shrugged. His neck was stiff from leaning over the ledgers for so long and he rolled his shoulders, trying to work the knots out. "I understand he inherited title and land from his father a few years back. He's the Earl of Oakmount now, isn't he?"

"Yes," Sir Richards replied. "But you're only half right. The title and land came from an uncle. Morgan's father ran tail years ago. The boy was shuffled from one relative to another during the growing years. There was talk of illegitimacy and some think that was the reason the father abandoned the boy. Morgan's mother died when he was four or five."

"A difficult childhood," Colin remarked.

The director agreed. "It made him the man he is today. He learned to be clever early on, you see."

"You know more about his background than I do," Colin said. "All I can add is superficial. I've seen him at various functions. He's well liked by the ton."

The director took a long swallow of the brandy before speaking again. "You still haven't given me your opinion," he reminded Colin.

"I'm not hedging," Colin replied. "I honestly don't know him well enough to form an opinion. He seems likable enough. Nathan doesn't particularly like him, though. I do remember him making that remark."

The director smiled. "Your partner doesn't like anyone."

"That's true, he doesn't."

"Did he have specific reasons for disliking Morgan?"

"No. He referred to him as one of the pretty boys. Morgan's a handsome man, or so I'm told by the women."

"Nathan doesn't like him because of his appearance?"

Colin laughed. Sir Richards sounded incredulous. "My partner doesn't like charmers. He says he never knows what they're thinking."

The director filed that information away in the back of his

mind. "Morgan has almost as many contacts as you have, and he would be a tremendous asset to the department. Still, I'm determined to take it slow. I still don't know how he'll handle himself in a crisis. I've invited him here to talk to you, Colin. There's another delicate matter you might want to consider handling for us. If you decide in favor of taking on the assignment, I'd like Morgan to get involved. He could do well to learn from you."

"I'm retired, remember?"

The director smiled. "So am I," he drawled out. "I've been trying to hand the reins over for a good four years now. I'm getting too old for this business."

"You'll never quit."

"And neither will you," Richards predicted. "At least not until your company can survive without your added income. Tell me this, son. Has your partner wondered yet where the additional funds are coming from? I know you didn't want him to know you've started helping the department out again."

Colin stacked his hands behind his neck. "He isn't aware," he explained. "Nathan's been occupied opening the second office. His wife, Sara, is due to have their first baby any day now. I doubt Nathan has had time to notice."

"And when he does notice?"

"I'll tell him the truth."

"We could use Nathan again," the director said.

"That's out of the question. He has a family now."

Sir Richards reluctantly agreed. He turned the topic back to the task he wanted Colin to accept. "About this assignment," he began. "It's no more dangerous than the last, but . . . ah, good evening, Princess Alesandra. It's a pleasure to see you again."

She stood just outside the entrance. Colin wondered how much she had overheard.

She smiled at the director. "It's good to see you again, sir," she replied in a soft whisper. "I hope I haven't intruded. The door was ajar, but if you're in the middle of a conference, I'll come back later."

Sir Richards hastily stood up and walked over to her. He took hold of her hand and bowed low. "You haven't intruded," he assured her. "Come and sit down. I wanted to talk to you before I left."

He latched on to her elbow and ushered her over to a chair. She sat down and smoothed her skirts while she waited for him to take his seat as well.

"I heard about the unfortunate incident outside the Royal Opera House," the director remarked with a frown. He sat down, nodded to Colin, and then turned his attention back to her. "Have you recovered from your upset?"

"There wasn't anything for me to recover from, Sir Richards. My guard was injured. Raymond required eight stitches in all, but they were removed yesterday. He's feeling much better now. Isn't that right, Colin?"

She kept her gaze fully directed on Sir Richards when she included Colin in the conversation. He didn't mind her lack of attention. He was fully occupied trying to hide his amusement. Sir Richards was blushing. Colin couldn't believe it. The hard-nosed, steel-hearted director of covert operations was blushing like a schoolboy.

Alesandra was mesmerizing the man. Colin wondered if she had any idea of her effect or if it was deliberate. Her smile was innocently sweet, her gaze direct, unwavering, and if she started in batting her eyelashes, then Colin would know the seduction wasn't quite so innocent after all.

"Have you had an opportunity to look into the other matter we discussed?" she asked. "I realize it was bold of me to ask anything of such an important man, Sir Richards, and I want you to know how grateful I am for your offer to send someone to Gretna Green."

"I've already taken care of that duty," the director replied. "My man, Simpson, only just returned last evening. You were correct, Princess. There isn't a record with either Robert Elliott or his rival, David Laing."

"I knew it," Alesandra cried out. She clasped her hands together as though in prayer and turned to frown at Colin. "Didn't I tell you so?"

Her enthusiasm made him smile. "Tell me what?"

"That Lady Victoria wouldn't elope. Your director has just confirmed my suspicions."

"Now, Princess, it's still a possibility—remote, of course—that she did marry there. Both Elliott and Laing keep accurate records so each can boast the number of weddings performed. It's a competitive thing, you see. However, they aren't the only men in Gretna Green who can marry a couple. Some less reputable gents just don't bother with records. They would fill out the certificate and hand it over to the husband. So you see, my dear, she still could have eloped after all."

"She didn't."

Alesandra was emphatic in that belief. Colin shook his head. "She's stirring up a hornet's nest, Richards. I've told her to leave it alone but she won't listen to me."

She frowned at Colin. "I am not stirring anything up."

"Yes, you are," Colin replied. "You're going to cause Victoria's family additional heartache if you pester them with questions."

His criticism stung. She bowed her head. "You must have a low opinion of me if you believe I would deliberately set out to hurt anyone."

"You didn't have to be so harsh with her, son."

Colin was exasperated. "I wasn't being harsh, just honest."

Sir Richards shook his head. Alesandra smiled at the director. She was pleased he'd taken her side.

"If he would only listen to my reasons for being worried, Sir Richards, he wouldn't be so quick to call my concern interference."

The director glared at Colin. "You wouldn't listen to her reasons? She makes a sound argument, Colin. You shouldn't judge without knowing all the facts."

"Thank you, Sir Richards." Colin snorted.

Alesandra decided to ignore the rude man. "What is our next step in this investigation?" she asked the director.

Sir Richards looked a bit confused. "Investigation? I hadn't thought of the problem in that light. . . ."

"You said you would help me," she reminded the director. "You mustn't become discouraged so quickly."

Sir Richards looked to Colin for assistance. Colin grinned.

"It isn't a matter of giving up," Sir Richards said. "I'm just not certain what it is I'm investigating. It's a plain fact your friend did run off with someone and I believe Colin's correct when he suggests you let the matter go."

"Why is it a plain fact?"

"Victoria left a note," Sir Richards explained.

She shook her head. "Anyone could have written a note."

"Yes, but . . ."

"I had so hoped you would help me, Sir Richards," she interrupted. Her tone of voice sounded forlorn. "You were my last hope. Victoria could be in danger and she only has you and me to help her. If anyone can ferret out the truth, it's you. You're so intelligent and clever."

Sir Richards puffed up like a rooster. Colin had to shake his head. One compliment had turned the man into mush.

"Will you be satisfied if I can find a record of the marriage?"

"You won't find one."

"But if I do . . ."

"I'll let the matter rest."

Sir Richards nodded. "Very well," he agreed. "I'll start with her family. I'll send a man around tomorrow to talk to the brother. One way or another, I'll find out what happened."

Her smile was radiant. "Thank you so much," she whispered. "I should warn you, though. I sent a note to Victoria's brother and he refused to grant me another audience. Colin, you see, was rude to him and he obviously hasn't forgiven him."

"He won't refuse me," Sir Richards announced with a hard nod.

Colin had heard enough of what he considered a ridiculous topic. He didn't like the idea that the director of England's Security Section was lowering himself to snoop into another family's private affairs.

He was about to change the subject when Sir Richards's next remark caught his attention. "Princess Alesandra, after the cooperation you've given, looking into this delicate matter is the very least I can do for you. Rest easy, my dear. I'll have some answers for you before you leave England."

Colin leaned forward. "Back up, Richards," he demanded, his voice hard. "Exactly how has Alesandra cooperated?"

The director looked surprised by the question. "She didn't explain to you . . ."

"I didn't believe it was necessary," Alesandra blurted out. She hastily stood up. "If you'll excuse me now, I'll leave you two gentlemen alone to discuss your business."

"Alesandra, sit down."

Colin's tone suggested she not argue with him. She let out a little sigh and did as he ordered. She refused to look at him, however, and kept her gaze directed on her lap. She wanted to run and hide rather than talk about her decision, but that would be cowardly and irresponsible, and Colin deserved to know what had been decided.

Dignity and decorum, she thought to herself. Colin would never know how upset she was, and there was a bit of victory in that, wasn't there?

"Explain to me why Richards is so pleased with your cooperation."

"I've decided to return to my father's homeland," she explained in a bare whisper. "I'm going to marry the general. Your father has given his approval."

Colin didn't say anything for a long while. He stared at Alesandra. She stared at her lap.

"All of this was decided while I was sick?"

"Yes."

"Look at me," he commanded.

She was close to bursting into tears. She took a deep breath and finally turned to look at him.

Colin knew she was upset. She was twisting her hands together and trying not to cry.

"She wasn't coerced," Sir Richards interjected.

"The hell she wasn't."

"It was my decision," she insisted.

Colin shook his head. "Richards, nothing has been decided. Understand? Alesandra is still reacting to the incident last week. Her guard was injured and she feels responsible."

"I am responsible," she cried out.

"No," he countered, his voice emphatic. "You were frightened."

"Does it matter what my reasons were?"

"Hell, yes, it matters," he snapped. He turned his attention back to the director. "Alesandra has obviously forgotten her promise to me last week."

"Colin . . ."

"Be silent."

Her eyes widened in disbelief. "Be silent? This is my future under discussion, not yours."

"I'm your guardian," he countered. "I decide your future. You seem to have forgotten that fact."

His scowl was as hot as the fire from a dragon's nostrils. She decided not to argue with him. He wasn't being at all reasonable, and if he didn't quit glaring at her she was definitely going to get up and leave the room.

Colin turned his attention back to the director. "Alesandra and I talked about this problem last week," he explained. "We decided she wouldn't marry the general. You can tell your associates in finance the deal's off."

Colin was so furious he barely noticed the director's nod of agreement as he continued on. "She isn't going to marry him. The general sounds like a real sweetheart, doesn't he? He sent a gang of cutthroats to kidnap his bride for him. A hell of a courtship, wouldn't you say? How I wish he'd come to England. I'd like to have a few minutes alone with the bastard."

Alesandra couldn't understand why Colin was getting so worked up. She had never seen him this angry. She was too astonished to be frightened. She didn't know what to say or do to calm him.

"He won't give up, Colin," she whispered, grimacing over the shiver in her voice. "He'll send others."

"That's my problem, not yours."

"It is?"

The fear he glimpsed in her eyes took away some of his anger. He didn't want her to be afraid of him. He deliberately softened his voice when he answered her. "Yes, it is."

They stared at each other a long minute. The tenderness in his expression made her want to weep with relief. He wasn't going to let her leave England.

She had to force herself to turn her gaze away from him so he wouldn't see the tears in her eyes. She stared at her lap, took a deep breath in an attempt to control her emotions, and then said, "I was trying to be noble. I didn't want anyone else to get hurt and Sir Richards said there was a chance for better trade agreements . . ."

"My associates believe the general would cooperate," Sir Richards interjected. "I personally don't hold with that nonsense. I'm of the same mind as Colin," he added with a nod. "The general isn't a man to be trusted. So you see, my dear, you don't have to be noble."

"And if Colin gets hurt?" she blurted out.

Both Sir Richards and Colin were astonished by that question. The fear was back in Alesandra's expression. Colin leaned back in his chair and stared at her. She wasn't afraid for her own safety; no, she was worried about him. He probably should have been irritated with her. He could take care of himself, and it was a bit insulting to know she was worried about him.

It was damned flattering, too.

Sir Richards raised an eyebrow and looked at Colin, waiting for him to answer her.

"I can take care of myself," Colin said. "I don't want you to worry, understand?"

"Yes, Colin."

Her immediate agreement pleased him. "Leave us now, Alesandra. Richards and I have other matters to discuss."

She couldn't get out of the room fast enough. She didn't even say good-bye to the director. Her conduct was most unladylike, but she didn't care. She was shaking so violently she could barely get the door closed behind her.

Relief made her knees weak. She sagged against the wall and closed her eyes. A tear slipped down her cheek. She took a deep breath in an attempt to calm herself.

She wasn't going to have to be noble and marry that horrible man after all. Colin had taken the decision out of her hands and she was so grateful she didn't mind at all that he'd been so angry. For some reason she couldn't define, Colin had decided to take the duty of guardian to heart. He had acted like a protector, and Alesandra was so thankful to have someone on her side she said a prayer of thanksgiving.

"Princess Alesandra, are you all right?"

She jumped a good foot. Then she burst into laughter. Flannaghan and another man she'd never met before stood just a few feet away from her. She'd not even heard their approach.

She could feel herself blushing. The stranger standing just behind the butler was smiling at her. She decided he probably thought she'd lost her mind. Alesandra moved away from the wall, forced herself to quit laughing, and then said, "I'm quite all right."

"What were you doing?"

"Reflecting," she replied. And praying, she silently added.

Flannaghan didn't know what she meant by that remark. He continued to stare at her with a perplexed look on his face. She turned to their guest. "Good evening, sir."

The butler finally remembered his manners. "Princess Alesandra, may I present Morgan Atkins, the Earl of Oakmount."

Alesandra smiled in greeting. "It is a pleasure to meet you."

He moved forward and took hold of her hand. "The pleasure is all mine, Princess. I've been most eager to meet you."

"You have?"

He smiled over the surprise in her eyes. "Yes, I have," he assured her. "You're the talk of London, but I imagine you realize that."

She shook her head. "No, I didn't realize," she admitted.

"The prince regent has been singing your praises," Morgan explained. "You mustn't frown, Princess. I've only heard wonderful things about you."

"What wonderful things?" Flannaghan dared to ask.

Morgan didn't take his gaze away from Alesandra when he answered the butler. "I was told she was very beautiful and now I know that story is true. She is beautiful—exquisite, in fact."

She was embarrassed by his flattery. She tried to pull her hand away from his, but he wouldn't let go.

"You have a delightful blush, Princess," he told her. He moved closer, and in the candlelight she could see the handsome silver threads streaking his dark brown hair. His eyes, a deep black brown color, sparkled with his smile. Morgan wasn't much taller than Flannaghan, but he seemed to overwhelm the butler. The aura of power surrounding him was probably due to his important position in society, she guessed. His title allowed him to be arrogant and self-assured.

The man was a charmer, however, who understood his own appeal. He knew he was making her uncomfortable under his close scrutiny, too.

"Are you enjoying your stay in England?" he asked.

"Yes, thank you."

Colin opened the door just as Morgan was asking Alesandra if he might be permitted to call on her the following afternoon. He immediately noticed Alesandra's blush. He noticed Morgan was holding her hand, too.

He reacted before he could stop himself. He reached out, grabbed hold of Alesandra's arm, and jerked her into his side. Then he draped his arm around her shoulders in an action she found terribly possessive and frowned at their guest.

"Alesandra's going to be busy tomorrow," he announced. "Go on inside, Morgan. The director's waiting to talk to you."

Morgan didn't seem to notice the irritation in Colin's tone of voice, or if he did notice, he chose to ignore it. He nodded his agreement, then turned his attention back to her.

"With your permission, Princess, I'll continue to try to convince your cousin to let me call on you."

As soon as she nodded agreement, he bowed to her and walked into the study.

"Do quit squeezing me, Cousin," Alesandra whispered.

He heard the laughter in her voice and looked down at her. "Where the hell did he get that idea? Did you tell him I was your cousin?"

"No, of course I didn't," she replied. "Will you unhand me now? I have to go back to my room to fetch my notecard."

He wouldn't let go of her. "Alesandra, why are you so damned happy?"

"I'm happy because it appears as though I won't have to marry the general," she said. She squirmed her way out of his grasp and went hurrying down the hallway. "And," she called over her shoulder, "I have a new name to put on my list."

As she ran down the hall, Morgan stepped out of the study and watched her—a devil-may-care smile upon his lips—until Colin's curt reminder called him back into the study.

All married women were unhappy creatures. The bitches all felt neglected by their husbands. They whined and complained, and nothing ever pleased them. Oh, he'd watched, he'd observed. The husbands usually ignored their wives, too, but he didn't fault them. Everyone knew mistresses were reserved for affection and attention; wives were simply necessary leeches to be used for the reproduction of heirs. One put up with a wife when one had to, rutted with her as often as necessary until she was carrying one's child, and then forgot about her.

He had deliberately ignored married women because he believed the hunt wouldn't amount to much. There wouldn't be any satisfaction gained in chasing a dog who wouldn't run. Still, this one intrigued him. She looked so miserable. He'd watched her for over an hour now. She was clinging to her husband's arm, and trying every now and then to say or do something to draw his attention. It was wasted effort. The gallant husband was thoroughly occupied talking to his friends from the clubs. He wasn't giving his pretty little wife any attention.

The poor little chit. It was obvious to anyone watching she loved the man. She was pitifully unhappy. He was about to change all that. He smiled then, his mind made up. The hunt was on again. Soon, very soon, he would put his new pet out of her misery.

Chapter 6

Colin stayed in conference with Sir Richards and Morgan for several hours. Alesandra ate her supper alone in the dining room. She stayed downstairs as long as she could manage without falling asleep, hoping Colin would join her. She wanted to thank him for showing such an interest in her future and ask him a few questions about the Earl of Oakmount.

She gave up the wait around midnight and went up to bed. Valena knocked on her door fifteen minutes later.

"You are requested to be ready to go out tomorrow morning, Princess. You must be ready to leave at ten o'clock."

Alesandra got into her bed and pulled the covers up. "Did Colin explain where we're going?"

The lady's maid nodded. "To Sir Richards's home," she answered. "On Bowers Street at number twelve."

Alesandra smiled. "He gave you the address?"

"Yes, Princess. He was very thorough in his instructions to me. He wanted me to tell you he doesn't wish to be kept waiting," she said with a frown. "There was something more he wanted me to . . . oh, yes, now I remember. The meeting scheduled for the afternoon with the Duke and Duchess of Williamshire has been canceled."

"Did Colin tell you why it was canceled?"

"No, Princess, he didn't."

Valena let out a dramatic yawn and immediately begged her mistress's pardon. "I'm very weary tonight," she whispered.

"Of course you're weary," Alesandra said. "It's quite late and you've put in a full day's work, Valena. Go to bed now. Sleep well," she called out when the maid went hurrying out the doorway.

Alesandra fell asleep a few minutes later. She was so exhausted from the long week of taking care of Colin, she slept the night through. She awakened a little after eight the next morning and hurried to get ready. She wore a pale pink walking dress. Colin would approve of the garment for the square-cut neckline was very prim and proper.

Alesandra was downstairs a good twenty minutes before they were scheduled to leave. Colin didn't join her until a few minutes after ten. As soon as she spotted him coming down the stairs, she called out to him. "We're already late, Colin. Do hurry."

"There's been a change in plans, Alesandra," Colin explained. He winked at her when he passed her on his way into the dining room.

She chased after him. "What change in plans?"

"The meeting's been canceled."

"The meeting with Sir Richards or the meeting this afternoon? Valena said . . ."

Colin pulled the chair out and motioned for her to sit down at the dining room table. "Both meetings were canceled," he said.

"Would you care for chocolate or hot tea, Princess?" Flannaghan called out from the entrance.

"Tea, thank you. Colin, how did you find out the meeting was canceled? I've been waiting in the foyer and no messenger came to the door."

Colin didn't answer her. He sat down, picked up the newspaper, and started reading. Flannaghan appeared at his side with a basket of biscuits, which he placed in front of him.

Alesandra was both irritated and confused. "Exactly why did Sir Richards want a meeting? We both spoke to him last evening."

"Eat your breakfast, Alesandra."

"You aren't going to explain, are you?"

"No."

"Colin, it's impolite to be rude first thing in the morning."

He lowered the paper to grin at her. She realized then her statement had been foolish. "I mean to say, it's always impolite to be rude."

He disappeared behind his paper again. She drummed her fingertips on the tabletop. Raymond walked into the dining room then. Alesandra immediately motioned him to her side. "Did a messenger . . ."

Colin interrupted her. "Alesandra, are you challenging my word?"

"No," she answered. "I'm just trying to understand. Will you quit hiding behind that paper?"

"Are you always in such a foul mood in the morning?"

Alesandra gave up trying to have a decent conversation with the man. She ate half a biscuit and then excused herself from the table. Raymond gave her a sympathetic look when she walked past him.

Alesandra went back upstairs and worked on her correspondence the rest of the morning. She wrote a long letter to the mother superior, telling her all about her journey to England. She described her guardian and his family, and spent three full pages explaining how she had ended up living with Colin.

She was sealing the envelope closed when Stefan knocked on the door. "You're wanted downstairs, Princess Alesandra."

"Do we have company, Stefan?"

The guard shook his head. "We're going out. You'll need your cloak. The wind's up today."

"Where are we going?"

"To a meeting, Princess."

"On again, off again, on again," she remarked.

"Begging your pardon, Princess?"

Alesandra closed the lid to the inkwell, straightened the desk, and then stood up. "I was just complaining to myself," she admitted with a smile. "Is this meeting with Colin's father or with Sir Richards?"

"I'm not certain," Stefan admitted. "But Colin's waiting in the foyer and he seems impatient to get going."

Alesandra promised the guard she would be right down. Stefan bowed to her and then left the room. She hurried to brush her hair, then went to the wardrobe to fetch her cloak. She was walking out the doorway when she remembered her list. If they were going to the Duke of Williamshire's town house, she would certainly need the notecard, she decided, so that she could go over the names with her guardian and his wife. She hurried back over to the desk to get the list and tucked it into the pocket of her cloak.

Colin was waiting in the foyer. She paused at the landing to put her cloak over her arm.

"Colin? Are we going to see your father or Sir Richards?"

He didn't answer her. She hurried down the steps and then repeated her question.

"We're going to see Sir Richards," he explained.

"Why does he want to see us again so soon? He was just here last evening," she reminded him.

"He has his reasons."

Valena was standing with Stefan and Raymond near the entrance to the salon. She hurried forward to assist her mistress with her cloak.

Colin beat her to the task. He put the cloak around Alesandra's shoulders, took hold of her hand, and then walked outside, dragging her behind him. She had to run to keep up with his long-legged stride.

Raymond and Stefan followed behind. The two guards climbed up the rack to sit with the driver. Colin and Alesandra sat across from each other inside the carriage.

He locked the doors, then leaned back against the cushions and smiled at her.

"Why are you frowning?" he asked.

"Why are you acting so peculiar?"

"I don't like surprises."

"Do you see? That was a peculiar answer."

Colin stretched out his long legs. She adjusted her skirts and moved closer to the corner to give him more room.

"Do you know what Sir Richards wants to talk to us about?" she asked.

"We aren't going to see him," Colin explained.

"But you said . . ."

"I lied."

Her gasp made him smile. "You lied to me?"

She looked incredulous. He slowly nodded. "Yes, I lied to you."

"Why?"

Her outrage made him want to laugh. She was such a delight when she was riled. And, Lord, she was certainly riled now. Her cheeks were flushed with a blush, and if her shoulders got any straighter, he thought, her spine might snap.

"I'll explain later," he told her. "Quit your frown, brat. It's too fine a day to get upset."

She finally noticed how cheerful he was. "Why are you so happy?"

He shrugged his answer. She let out a sigh. The man was deliberately trying to confuse her, she decided. "Exactly where are we going, Colin?"

"To a meeting with the family to decide what to do . . ."

She finished his explanation for him. "With me?"

He nodded. Alesandra lowered her gaze to her lap, but not before Colin saw her expression. She looked crushed. Her feelings had been hurt, he knew, but he didn't know what he'd said to cause that reaction.

His voice was gruff when he said, "Now what's the matter with you?"

"Nothing's the matter."

"Don't lie to me."

"You lied to me."

"I said I'd explain later," he countered. He tried to keep the irritation out of his voice when he added, "Now explain why you're looking ready to weep."

"I'll explain later."

Colin leaned forward. He grabbed hold of her chin and forced her to look at him. "Don't turn my words back on me," he ordered.

She pushed his hand away. "Very well," she announced. "I was a little upset when I realized why you're so happy."

"Make sense, damn it."

The carriage came to a stop in front of the Duke of Williamshire's town house. Colin unlatched the door but kept his gaze on her. "Well?" he demanded.

She adjusted her cloak around her shoulders. "It makes perfect sense to me," she told him with a nod.

Raymond opened the door and held his hand out to assist her. She immediately stepped outside, then turned to frown at Colin. "You're happy because you're finally getting rid of me."

He opened his mouth to argue with her. She raised her hand in an unspoken command to keep silent. "You needn't worry, sir. I'm over my upset. Shall we go inside now?"

She was trying to be dignified. Colin wouldn't let her. He started laughing. She turned and hurried up the steps. Raymond and Stefan flanked her sides.

"You still look upset, brat."

The door was opened by the butler just as she whirled around to tell Colin what she thought of that rude remark. "If you call me a brat again, I swear I'll do something most undignified. I am not upset," she added in a voice that mocked that lie. "I just thought you and I had become friends. Yes, I did. You were becoming like a cousin to me and I . . ."

Colin leaned down until he was just an inch or so from her face. "I'm not your cousin," he snapped.

Colin's brother, Caine, took over the butler's duty and stood in the doorway, waiting for someone to notice him. He could only see the back of Princess Alesandra. She was a little thing and, he judged, quite courageous. Colin was towering over her, giving her his best glare, but she wasn't cowering away. She didn't seem to be at all intimidated.

"Everyone believes we're cousins," she snapped.

"I don't give a damn what everyone else thinks."

She took a deep breath. "This conversation is ridiculous. If you don't wish to be related to me, that's just fine."

"I'm not related to you."

"You don't have to shout, Colin."

"You're making me crazed, Alesandra."

"Good afternoon."

Caine fairly bellowed his greeting so he'd be heard. Alesandra was so startled by the interruption, she grabbed hold of Colin.

She was quick to recover. She pushed herself out of his arms and turned around. She tried to force a serene, dignified expression. The incredibly handsome man standing in the doorway had to be Colin's brother. Their smiles were almost identical. Caine's hair was a bit lighter in shade, however, and his eyes were an altogether different color. They were gray, and in her estimation not nearly as attractive as Colin's more-green-than-hazel color.

Alesandra tried to curtsy. Colin wouldn't let her. He grabbed hold of her arm and nudged her through the opening.

She pinched him to make him let go of her. A tug of war resulted when Colin tried to take her cloak. She kept slapping his hand away so she could retrieve her notecard from the pocket of the garment.

Caine stood behind his brother. His hands were clasped behind his back and he was desperately trying not to laugh. He hadn't seen his brother this rattled in a good long while.

Alesandra finally pulled the notecard free. "Now you may take my cloak, thank you."

Colin rolled his eyes heavenward. He tossed her cloak in Caine's direction. His brother caught the garment in midair just as Colin spotted the notecard clutched in Alesandra's hand. "Why in God's name did you bring that thing along?"

"I'm going to need it," she explained. "I simply don't understand your aversion to this list, Colin. Your hostility is most unreasonable."

She turned her attention to his brother. "You'll have to excuse your brother's rudeness. He's been ill."

Caine smiled. Colin shook his head. "You don't have to

make excuses for me," he stated. "Caine, this is the woman you've been referring to as The Plague. Alesandra, meet my brother."

She again tried to curtsy and Colin again ruined it. She was just leaning forward to catch hold of her gown when Colin grabbed hold of her hand and started dragging her into the salon.

"Where's your wife, Caine?" Colin called over his shoulder.

"Upstairs with Mother," he answered.

Alesandra was tugging on Colin's hand, trying to get loose. "Why don't you just toss me on a chair and leave. You're obviously in a hurry to get rid of me."

"Which chair do you prefer?"

He finally let go of her. She took a step back and immediately bumped into Caine. She turned around, begged his forgiveness for her clumsiness, and then asked where his father was. She really wanted to speak to him as soon as possible, she explained.

Because she was looking so serious and worried, Caine didn't dare smile. Princess Alesandra was a pretty thing, he thought to himself. Her eyes were a brilliant shade of blue and the freckles on the bridge of her nose reminded him of his wife, Jade. She was actually very beautiful, he realized.

"Jenkins went upstairs to tell my father you're here, Princess Alesandra. Why don't you make yourself comfortable while you wait?"

She thought that was a splendid idea. Caine had obviously been given all the manners in the family. He was very solicitous and polite. It was a nice change from his brother.

Colin stood near the fireplace watching her. She ignored him. She hadn't paid any attention to the exterior of her guardian's town house, but she imagined it was just as grand as the interior. The salon was at least four times the size of Colin's. There were three settees placed in a half circle around the ivory-colored marble hearth. It was a lovely room filled with treasures the Duke of Williamshire had collected from around the world. Her gaze scanned the room, then came to rest on the gleaming object in the center of the mantel. She let out a gasp of pleasure. The replica in gold of her father's castle hadn't been misplaced after all. The reproduction of her childhood home was the size of a small brandy decanter and was exact in every detail to the real castle.

The look of joy on Alesandra's face took Colin's breath away. "Alesandra?" he asked, wondering what had caused that reaction.

She turned to smile at him. Then she hurried over to the mantel. Her hand trembled when she reached up and gently touched the side of one golden turret. "This is a replica of my home, Colin. It's called Stone Haven. I lived there with my mother and father."

"I thought your father gave up his kingdom when he married your mother," Colin remarked.

She nodded. "Yes, he did. He purchased Stone Haven before he married her. The general can't touch it, either. It's located in Austria and he won't have any jurisdiction there, even if he is able to take over the throne. The castle will continue to be safe."

"Who owns it now?" Caine asked.

She didn't answer him. He assumed she hadn't heard his question. He was as intrigued by the castle as Colin appeared to be. The two brothers flanked Alesandra's sides as they stared at the reproduction. "The detail is quite impressive," Caine remarked.

"My father gave it as a gift to your father," she explained. "He was playing a bit of trickery—good-hearted, of course—and I looked for the castle when I was staying at his country home, but I couldn't find it. I thought it had been lost. It pleases me to see it has a place of honor."

Colin was about to ask her what she'd meant by her remark that trickery had been involved when they were interrupted.

"Of course it has a place of honor," the Duke of Williamshire called out from the entrance. "Your father was my friend, Alesandra."

She turned at the sound of her guardian's voice and smiled in greeting. The Duke of Williamshire was a distinguished-looking man with silver-tipped hair and dark gray eyes. The sons had gotten their good looks from him, of course, and their height as well.

"Good afternoon, Father," Colin called out.

His father returned the greeting, then walked into the salon. He stopped in the center and opened his arms to Alesandra.

She didn't hesitate. She ran to him and threw herself into his arms. He hugged her tight and kissed the top of her head.

Colin and Caine shared a look of disbelief. They were astonished by their father's show of affection to his ward. The elderly man was usually very reserved, but he was treating Alesandra as though she were his long-lost daughter.

"Has Colin been treating you well?"

"Yes, Uncle Henry."

"Uncle Henry?" Caine and Colin repeated the name at the same time.

Alesandra pulled away from her guardian and turned to glare at Colin. "Uncle Henry doesn't mind being related to me."

"But he isn't related to you," Colin stubbornly reminded her.

His father smiled. "I've asked her to call me Uncle," he explained. "Alesandra's part of our family now, son."

He turned to his ward then. "Sit down and we'll talk about this marriage business."

She hurried to do as he requested. She spotted her notecard on the floor and immediately went to fetch it. Colin waited until she was settled in the center of the brocaded settee and then went over and sat down next to her.

His bulk crowded her into the corner. Alesandra nudged his hard thigh away so she could collect her skirts from underneath him. "There are plenty of other seats available," she whispered so her Uncle Henry wouldn't hear her criticizing his son. "Do sit somewhere else, Cousin."

"If you call me cousin one more time I swear I'm going to

throttle you," Colin threatened in a low growl. "And quit squirming."

"You're crowding her, son. Move over."

Colin didn't budge. His father frowned, then took his seat next to Caine on the larger settee facing Alesandra.

"How have you two been getting along?" his father asked.

"Colin was sick all week," Alesandra announced. "Am I moving in with you today, Uncle?"

"No." Colin's denial was abrupt—harsh, too.

His father frowned at his son before turning his gaze back to Alesandra. "Would you like to move in here?" he asked.

"I thought Colin wanted me to," she answered. Her confusion was apparent in her expression. "It seemed an imposition, having to look out for me. He's been acting very irritable today. I believe the cause is anxiety."

Colin rolled his eyes heavenward. "Let's get back to the main topic," he muttered.

His father ignored that command. "Colin's anxious?" he asked Alesandra.

"Yes, Uncle," she answered. She folded her hands together in her lap while she added, "He's anxious to get rid of me. So you can understand my confusion, can't you? A few minutes ago he was ready to toss me on the settee and leave, and now he's telling you I should stay with him."

"That is a contradiction," Caine interjected.

Colin leaned forward. He braced his elbows on his knees and stared at his father. "I don't believe it's a good idea to have her move anywhere just now. There was an incident outside the Opera House," he added with a nod.

Alesandra interrupted him by nudging him in his side. He turned back to look at her.

"You don't need to go into that," she whispered. "You'll only worry him."

"He needs to be worried," Colin told her. "If he's going to take over the responsibility of looking out for you, he'll have to understand what he's up against."

Colin didn't give her time to argue with him, but turned back to his father. He quickly explained what had happened, added a few pertinent details he'd gathered from his talk with Sir Richards, and ended with his opinion that the threats weren't going to stop until Alesandra was married.

"Or until the general has either won or lost his campaign for the throne," Caine interjected.

"Hell, that could take a year," Colin predicted with a scowl.

"Perhaps," his brother agreed. He turned to his father then and said, "I think Colin's right. Alesandra should continue to stay with him. He's more experienced in these matters and it would be less dangerous for you and Mother."

"Nonsense," his father countered. "I know a thing or two about protecting my family. I can handle any danger that comes my way. The gossip, however, is something we must address. Now that your mother and I are feeling fit again, Alesandra will have to move in with us. It isn't acceptable for an unattached man and woman to live together."

"It was the thing last week," Caine reminded his father.

"Because of our illness," his father replied. "Surely people will understand."

Colin was incredulous. He didn't know what to say to his father's naive belief. He turned to his brother for help in arguing his point against Alesandra moving and saw that Caine was just as incredulous.

"Have you heard any gossip?" his father asked Caine, frowning now over that worry.

Caine shook his head. Colin tried to hold on to his patience. "Father, gossip isn't the important issue here," he said. "You cannot equate the danger you would be placing your family in with a few whispered remarks. Of course people are talking. Alesandra and I don't care."

"I won't let you argue me out of my decision," his father stubbornly insisted. "You insult me if you believe I can't look out for my ward. I've taken care of a wife and six children all these years without a problem and I'm not about to stop now."

"But no one has wanted to kidnap Mother or . . ." Caine began.

"Enough," his father ordered. "The topic is closed." He softened his tone when he added, "Your mother was right when she said Alesandra should get married as soon as possible. That would put an end to all this nonsense."

Colin looked at Caine. "She has this damned list."

"I gave her that list, son."

Colin didn't know what to say to that.

"A list of what?" Caine asked.

"Must you explain to Caine?" she whispered. Her cheeks were turning pink with embarrassment. "He's already married."

"I know he's married," Colin replied with a grin.

Caine pretended he hadn't heard Alesandra's protest. "A list of what?" he asked his brother again.

"Men," Colin answered. "She and Father have made a list of suitable men to marry."

Caine didn't show any outward reaction to that explanation. He could tell from Alesandra's expression she was uncomfortable with the topic they were discussing. He decided to try to make her feel more at ease. "That sounds reasonable to me," he announced.

"Reasonable? It's barbaric," Colin told him.

Caine couldn't suppress his grin.

"This isn't amusing," Colin snapped.

"No," Caine agreed. "It isn't amusing."

"It's most serious, sir," Alesandra interjected with a nod.

Caine sat up a little straighter. "So the purpose of this meeting is to select a husband from the list? Have I got it straight in my mind?"

"Yes," Alesandra answered. "I wanted to interview the candidates last week, but Colin became ill and I was occupied nursing him back to health."

"You nursed him?" Caine asked with a smile.

She nodded. "Night and day," she said. "He needed me."

Colin was exasperated. "I did not need you."

She took exception to his gruff tone of voice. She leaned back against the settee. "You're a very unappreciative man," she whispered.

Colin ignored her remark. He nodded to Caine. "That reminds me," he said. "I wanted to thank you for your help. The ledgers haven't looked so organized in over a year."

"What ledgers?"

"The shipping ledgers," Colin explained. "I appreciated your help."

Caine shook his head. Alesandra nudged Colin to get his attention. "Couldn't we get back to the topic at hand? I would like to get this settled as soon as possible."

"I didn't touch your ledgers," Caine told his brother.

"Then who . . . ?"

No one said a word for a long minute. Alesandra turned her attention to straightening the folds in her gown. Colin slowly turned to look at her.

"Did you hire Dreyson or someone else to work on my books?"

"Of course not. Your books are private. I wouldn't let an outsider look at them. Besides, no one was admitted while you were sick."

"Then who the hell did the work?"

"I did."

He shook his head. She nodded. "Don't jest with me, Alesandra. I'm not in the mood for it."

"I'm not jesting. I did do the work. I organized all of your logs, too, and filed them away."

"Who helped you?"

She was highly insulted by that question. "No one helped me. I'm very good with figures," she told him. "You have my permission to write to Mother Superior if you don't believe me. I made a second set of books for her so the banker would give her . . . Oh, dear, I probably shouldn't have mentioned that. Mother Superior called it a sin, but I didn't believe it was. It wasn't larceny, either. I only changed the numbers so she could get the loan."

Colin had an astonished expression on his face. She guessed he found her confession shameful. She quit trying to explain herself and took a deep breath. "As for your ledgers," she continued. "Transferring numbers and totaling your columns didn't require special training. It wasn't difficult, just tedius."

"And the percentages?" Colin asked, still not certain he believed her.

She shrugged. "Anyone with half a mind could figure out percentages."

He shook his head. "But you're a woman . . ."

He was going to add that he couldn't imagine where she'd gotten the training for book work, but she wouldn't let him finish.

"I knew that would come up," she cried out. "Just because I'm a woman, you assume I couldn't possibly understand anything but the latest fashions, isn't that right? Well, sir, you're in for a surprise. I don't give a twit about fashions."

Colin had never seen her this riled. Her eyes had turned into blue fire. He thought he might like to strangle her. But he'd kiss her first, he decided.

Caine came to her rescue. "And did the mother superior get her loan, Alesandra?"

"Yes, she did," Alesandra answered, her voice tinged with pride. "Mother didn't know the banker was looking at the second set of books, of course, or her vows would have forced her to confess. The nuns all follow very strict rules. She didn't find out until it was too late. She'd already spent the money on a new chapel. So it all worked out quite nicely."

Colin let out a snort. "I'll wager she was sorry to see you leave," he said dryly.

"Shall we get back to our reason for being here?" Caine suggested. He stood up and walked over to Alesandra. "May I have a look at your list, please?"

"Yes, of course."

Caine took the notecard and went back to his seat. "It isn't complete," Alesandra explained. "There are ten names on the list now, but if you want to add another one or two, please do so."

"I believe we should go ahead and start without Gweneth," her guardian announced. "Caine, read the first name and we'll put the man under discussion."

Caine unfolded the sheet of paper, scanned the contents, and then looked at his brother.

"Get started, son," his father insisted.

"The first name on the list is Colin," Caine announced, his gaze directed on his brother.

"Yes, but I've scratched him off," Alesandra explained. "Do you see the line through his name? Please go on to the names I haven't scratched through."

"Hold on," Caine said. "I want to know why he was marked off, Alesandra. Did you put his name on the list or did my father suggest Colin?"

"I gave her his name," his father answered. "She hadn't even met Colin when we started the list. I believed it would be a sound match, but now I can see it wouldn't wash. They aren't suitable for each other."

Caine was of the opposite opinion. The sparks flying between Alesandra and Colin were close to igniting, and each was desperately trying not to acknowledge the reason behind his or her frustration.

"How did you come to the conclusion they weren't suited?" Caine asked his father.

"Just look at the two of them together, son. It's plain for anyone to see. Alesandra's looking terribly uncomfortable and Colin hasn't quit frowning since he sat down. It's apparent they don't get along. And that, you see, is an important ingredient for a sound marriage."

"Could we get on with it, Caine?" asked Colin.

"Colin, do you have to be so irritable?" Alesandra asked.

He didn't answer her. She turned her attention to Caine. "He's been ill," she reminded his brother, using that as her excuse for Colin's surly mood.

"It's this topic," his father interjected with a frown in Colin's direction.

"If Colin agreed to marry you, Alesandra, would you have him?" Caine wanted to know.

"He has already declined," Alesandra explained. "And he wouldn't be acceptable anyway."

"Why not?" Caine asked.

"Will you let it go?" Colin demanded.

Caine ignored his brother's protest. So did Alesandra. She frowned while she thought about her answer. She didn't want to confuse Caine but she didn't want to have to go into a lengthy explanation either. "He isn't acceptable because he wouldn't touch my inheritance."

"Damned right I wouldn't touch it."

"There, do you understand now?"

Caine didn't understand anything. The look on his brother's face told him not to prod further, however. Colin looked ready to grab somebody's throat and Caine didn't want to be his victim.

"Isn't there a better way to handle this situation?" Caine asked then. "Alesandra should be allowed to take her time . . ."

"But there isn't time," his father interjected.

"I do thank you for your concern, Caine," Alesandra added.

"Go ahead, son. Read the second name on the list."

Caine gave up. The second name had also been crossed through. Caine moved to the third name. "Horton," he read. "The Earl of Wheaton."

"I met him once," his father announced. "He seemed like a decent chap to me."

Caine was nodding agreement when Colin started shaking his head. "What's wrong with him, Colin?" his brother asked.

"He's a drunk. He won't do."

"He's a drunk?" his father asked. "I never realized that about Horton. Cross him off, Caine," he added with a scowl. "I won't have her wed to a drunk."

"Thank you, Uncle Henry."

Colin could feel himself getting ready to explode. It took all he had to keep his temper under control. In truth, he didn't understand why he was so agitated. He had made the decision not to marry Alesandra, but, damn it all, the thought of anyone else touching her didn't sit well with him.

As though it were the most natural thing in the world to do, Colin leaned back against the cushions and put his arm around Alesandra's shoulders. She instinctively moved closer to him. He could feel her trembling, knew then she hated having to go through this ordeal as much as he did.

Caine was right. There had to be a better way.

His brother drew his attention when he read the next name. "Kingsford, the Earl of Lockwood."

"Gweneth suggested Kingsford," his father announced. "She was taken with his polite ways."

Colin shook his head. "He might be polite, but he's also got a reputation for his sadistic pleasures."

"Good God," his father muttered. "Sadistic pleasures, you say? Mark him off, Caine."

"Yes, Father," Caine agreed. He read the next name. "Williams, the Marquess of Coringham."

"I suggested him," his father explained. His voice reeked with fresh enthusiasm. "He's a fine fellow. I've known the family for years. Comes from good blood, Harry does."

Caine was having difficulty maintaining his serious expression. Colin was already shaking his head.

"Harry's a womanizer," Colin announced.

"I never realized that about Harry," his father muttered. "Gweneth and I need to get out more often. I'd pick up on these things if we mingled more with society. All right, then, he won't do. We aren't marrying her to a future adulterer."

Caine stared at Colin when he called out the next name on the list. "Johnson, the Earl of Wentzhill."

He hadn't gotten the man's full title out of his mouth before Colin started shaking his head.

And so it continued. Colin found something wrong with every man mentioned. By the time Caine had gotten to the last name on the list, the Duke of Williamshire was slumped in the corner of the settee, his hand to his forehead, looking thoroughly defeated. Caine could barely contain his amusement. His brother was having difficulty coming up with a suitable vice after Caine had read the last name, Morgan Atkins, the Earl of Oakmount, and Caine was dying to hear what he had to say about him.

"I've met Morgan," Alesandra announced. "He came to Colin's house to discuss a business matter. He seemed very nice."

Alesandra's voice lacked conviction. She was having trouble hiding her unhappiness now. She hated what was happening. She felt out of control of her future and her destiny. Just as horrible to her, she was beginning to feel like a charity case.

"I can't give you an opinion of Morgan," Caine remarked. "I've never met him."

"I've met him," his father said. "I liked him well enough. Perhaps we could invite him over for . . . Why in God's name are you shaking your head now, Colin?"

"Yes, brother," Caine interjected. "What's wrong with Morgan?"

Colin let out a sigh. He was having difficulty finding anything wrong with the man. Caine wasn't helping him concentrate. He started laughing.

"This isn't amusing," Colin snapped.

"Yes, it is," Caine contradicted. "Let's see now," he drawled out. "So far we've discarded nine possible candidates because of drunkenness, averice, gluttony, jealousy, perversion, greed, lust, and so on, and I'd really love to hear your reason for finding Morgan unsuitable. I believe you've used up all the seven deadly sins, Colin."

"What are you suggesting, Caine?" Colin demanded.

"You don't like any of them."

"Damned right I don't. I'm thinking of Alesandra's happiness. She's a princess. She deserves better."

That last remark told Caine everything he needed to know. He now understood why Colin was in such a foul mood. It was obvious to Caine that his brother wanted Alesandra, but in his mind he had decided he wasn't worthy enough. Oh, yes, that was it, Caine decided. Colin was the second son and therefore hadn't inherited land or title. His obsession with building an empire was all part of his quest to achieve recognition on his own. Caine was proud that his brother was an independent man, but, damn it all, that pride would force him to let Alesandra slip away.

Unless he was forced into marriage, of course.

"But what about Morgan?" his father asked again. "What's wrong with him?"

"Nothing," Colin snapped.

His father was beginning to smile when Colin added, "If Alesandra doesn't mind bowlegged children."

"For the love of . . ." His father slumped back against the cushions in defeat.

"Is Morgan bowlegged?" Caine asked Alesandra. He was feeling quite proud of himself. He'd been able to ask that question without even cracking a smile.

"I must confess I didn't notice his legs, but if Colin says he's bowlegged, then he must be. Will I have to have children?"

"Yes," Colin told her.

"He won't do then. I don't wish to have bowlegged children."

She turned to look up at Colin. "Is it a painful condition?" she asked him in a whisper.

"Yes," Colin lied.

The discussion continued for another hour. Caine and his father both took turns tossing out names of possible husbands and Colin found something wrong with every one of them.

Caine was thoroughly enjoying himself. He pulled the footrest over, stretched out, and propped his feet up so that he'd be more comfortable.

Colin was becoming more and more agitated. He'd removed his arm from Alesandra's shoulders and was now leaning forward with his elbows on his knees while he waited for his father to think of another candidate.

The longer the talk continued, the more upset Alesandra became. She hid behind her mask of serenity, but her hands were clutched into fists in her lap.

Just when she thought she couldn't stand to hear another name offered, Colin leaned back and covered her hands with one of his.

She didn't want his comfort, yet she clung to his hand.

"Alesandra, what do you want to do?"

Caine asked her that question. She was too embarrassed to tell him the truth, to admit that more than anything she wished she could marry a man she loved. She wanted the kind of marriage her parents had had, but that wasn't possible.

"I thought I wanted to become a nun, but Mother Superior wouldn't let me."

There were tears in her eyes and for that reason no one laughed. "And why wouldn't she let you?" Caine asked.

"I'm not Catholic," Alesandra explained. "It's an important requirement."

He did smile then. He simply couldn't help it. "You wouldn't have been happy as a nun," he predicted.

She wasn't particularly happy now, but she didn't believe it would be polite to mention that.

"Alesandra, why don't you go and find Gweneth," her guardian suggested. "You haven't met Jade yet, now have you? Go and introduce yourself to Caine's lovely wife."

She acted as though she'd just been given a reprieve. The look of relief on her face was there for all of them to see.

Alesandra had stood up before she realized she hadn't let go of Colin's hand yet. She quickly pulled away, and then left the room.

The three men stood up until she'd left the salon, then resumed their seats. Colin dragged the footrest over, propped his feet up, and leaned back.

"This is damned difficult for her," he muttered.

"Yes," his father agreed. "I wish there was time for her to adjust to her circumstances, but there isn't, Colin."

Caine decided to turn the topic. "I'm curious, Father," he remarked. "How did you meet Alesandra's father?"

"It was at Ashford's annual bash," his father explained. "Nathaniel and I took to one another right away. He was quite a man," he added with a nod.

"And so are you to take on responsibility for his daughter," Colin remarked.

His father's expression underwent a dramatic change. He looked terribly sad now. "No, you've got it all wrong," he said. "There is something neither one of you knows and I imagine now is the time for me to confess my sins. You're going to find out sooner or later."

The seriousness in their father's voice told both sons the matter was of grave importance. They gave him their full attention and waited for him to compose his thoughts.

Long minutes passed before he spoke again. "I got into trouble just after your mother died, Caine," he explained. "I hadn't met Gweneth yet and I had started drinking—quite heavily, as a matter of fact."

"You? But you never drink," Colin argued.

"I don't drink now," his father agreed. "I did back then. I gambled too. The debts, they piled up, of course, and I kept fooling myself into believing I would win back enough to cover my losses."

Colin and Caine were too astonished to say anything. They stared at their father as though he'd suddenly turned into a complete stranger.

"This is a difficult confession for me to make," he continued. "No father likes parading his sins in front of his sons."

"The past is over," Colin told him. "Let it go."

His father shook his head. "It isn't as simple as all that," he explained. "I want you to understand. I was almost ruined, you see, and would have been if it hadn't been for Alesandra's father. Everything I'd inherited and worked so hard to build was in the hands of the moneylenders as collateral against the loans. Yes, I would have been ruined."

"What happened then?" Caine asked when his father didn't continue.

"Nathaniel came to my rescue. I was at White's one minute and the next I remember I was back home. I was told I blacked out at the tables from too much drink. When I next opened my eyes, Nathaniel was standing over me, and, Lord, was he angry. I was so hung over all I wanted was to be left alone. He wouldn't leave, however. He threatened me, too."

"What was his threat?" Caine asked. He was so surprised by his father's confession he leaned forward and clasped his hands together in expectation.

"He told me you were downstairs," his father said. "You

were so young and impressionable and Nathaniel threatened to bring you up so you could see what your father had become. Needless to say, the threat sobered me up. I would rather have died than let you see me in such a humiliating condition."

No one said a word for several minutes. Caine didn't have any memory of his father's drinking days. "How old was I?" he asked.

"Almost five."

"If I was that young, I probably wouldn't have remembered if I had seen you drunk," he remarked.

"Nathaniel knew how much I loved you," his father said. "Oh, he was clever, all right. It was my darkest hour, my turning point as well."

"What was done about the debts?" Colin asked.

His father smiled. How like Colin to be the one to ask that question. His younger son was the most practical member of the family—the most disciplined, too.

"Nathaniel went to all the moneylenders. He purchased the notes. In less than one day, I was completely out of debt. He tried to give me the notes, but I refused his charity. I wouldn't let him tear them up either. I wanted him to hold on to them until I could repay. I even insisted he add interest."

"And has the debt been repaid?" Caine asked.

"No, it hasn't. Nathaniel took his wife back to Stone Haven. He gave me that beautiful treasure before he left," he said with a nod toward the castle perched on the mantel. "Imagine that, giving me a gift after all he'd done. We kept current through letters, of course, and the next time he and his wife came to England, they had Alesandra with them. I tried to give him half of what I owed, but he wouldn't take it. It was damned awkward. Because he had acted so honorably with me, I couldn't ask him where the notes were. He died the following winter. Lord, I still mourn his passing. He was my dearest friend."

Both sons agreed. Nathaniel had been a good friend.

"Who holds the notes now?" Caine asked.

"That's the dilemma, son. I don't know."

"Have you asked Alesandra?" Colin wanted to know.

"No," his father answered. "I doubt she knows anything about the transaction. As her guardian, I have access to some of her accounts. Dreyson, her agent, takes care of investments, but I don't believe he knows anything about the notes either."

"Would you be able to repay the full amount if the notes and interest were called today?" Caine asked.

"Not all of it," his father replied. "But I'm in a strong financial position now. If the notes were called, I could borrow what I need. I don't want to give either one of you the impression I'm worried. Nathaniel was a methodical, careful man. He put the notes in a safe place. I'm just curious to know where they are."

"I'm curious, too," Caine agreed.

"The purpose of my confession is twofold," their father continued. "First, I want both of you to know the kind of man Alesandra's father was, and to understand the debt I owe him. Second, I want you to understand how I feel about his daughter. She's all alone in this world now and it is my duty to see she's protected from harm."

"It is our duty as well," Caine interjected.

Colin nodded agreement. The three men lapsed into silence again, each caught up in his own thoughts.

Colin tried to consider all the ramifications.

He had nothing to offer her. He had an empire to build, damn it, and there simply wasn't room or time for a wife.

She would drive him to distraction.

But there was the debt to be repaid, and all three of them were bound by honor to look out for Princess Alesandra.

His father was too old to take on the duty of keeping her safe. He didn't have the experience dealing with bastards either, Colin decided.

And then there was Caine. His older brother was busy running his own estates. He was married, too, and had his own family to consider.

There was only one son left.

Colin glanced up and noticed both his father and his brother were staring at him. He let out a loud sigh. They had known all along, of course, and were only waiting for him to come to the same conclusion.

"Hell, I'm going to have to marry her, aren't I?"

Chapter 7

Colin's father wanted to be the one to break the good news to Alesandra. Colin wouldn't let him. He thought he should be the one to tell her what had been decided.

"May I offer a word of advice, brother?" Caine asked.

He waited for Colin's nod, then said, "I don't believe you should tell her anything . . ."

His father wouldn't let him finish. "She'll have to know, Caine."

His son smiled. "Yes, of course she'll have to know," he agreed. "However, from my rather limited experience with women I've still been able to surmise that they don't like being told anything. Colin should ask her to marry him."

"Do it at the dinner table then," his father suggested.

Colin smiled. "I'll decide when and where," he announced.

"Will you promise me you'll have it settled before the night is over?" his father demanded. "I can't say a word until you've asked. And Gweneth will have to start work on the arrangements."

"Mother has already seen to everything," Colin replied.

His father stood up and rubbed his hands together. "I can't tell you how pleased I am, and I'm certain Alesandra's going to be thrilled."

Because his father was looking so proud of himself, neither Colin nor Caine reminded him that less than an hour ago he'd been against a marriage between his ward and his son. He'd believed they were completely unsuited to each other.

Caine wanted to have a private discussion with Colin but their mother came hurrying into the salon then, demanding everyone's attention.

The Duchess of Williamshire was a petite woman with blond curls and hazel-colored eyes. Her husband and sons towered over her. The years had been very kind to the lovely woman. She had very few wrinkles and only a hint of gray in her hair.

Gweneth was actually Caine's stepmother, but no one paid any attention to that distinction. She treated him as one of her own, and Caine had long ago accepted her as his mother.

"Jade and Alesandra will be down in just a moment. Do come into the dining room. Supper will get cold. Boys, give your mother a kiss. Heavens, you've lost some weight, Caine, haven't you? Colin, dear, how is your leg? Is it paining you?"

Her sons understood that their mother didn't really expect answers to her questions. They understood she liked to coddle, too, and put up with the show of motherly concern without even a hint of a reminder that they were both fully grown men now.

Gweneth was the only one who dared inquire about Colin's leg. Everyone else understood they were to ignore the affliction.

"Caine, Princess Alesandra is the most delightful young woman."

His wife made that remark as she came strolling into the salon. She paused on her way to her husband's side to give his father a kiss in greeting, then stopped again to kiss Colin on his cheek.

"Are you enchanted by Alesandra, Dolphin?" she asked Colin, using the nickname he'd earned from his days on the seas.

"Where is she?" Colin asked.

"In your father's library," Jade answered. Her green eyes sparkled with amusement. "She caught sight of all his books and almost swooned with joy. When I left her, she was looking through his journal on the latest shipping innovations."

Gweneth immediately turned to the butler and requested that he go upstairs and tell Alesandra dinner was waiting.

Jade linked her arm through her husband's. She was dying to ask him what had been decided at the family conference, but couldn't because Colin and their parents were standing so close.

Caine brushed his wife's deep red hair back over her shoulder and leaned down to kiss her.

"I believe we should go on in," Gweneth announced. She took her husband's arm and walked by his side out of the salon. Colin followed until Caine called out to him. "I want to talk to you in private later," he requested.

"There isn't anything to talk about," Colin countered. He could tell from his brother's expression he wanted to discuss Alesandra again.

"I believe there is," Caine countered.

"Do forgive me for interrupting," Jade said then. "But I've just come up with a wonderful suggestion for a suitable husband. Have you considered Johnson? You remember him, Colin. He's Lyon's good friend," she reminded her brother-in-law.

"I remember him," Colin agreed.

"And?" Jade prodded when he didn't continue.

"I can tell you right now he won't do," Caine drawled out.

"Why not?" Jade asked. "I like him."

"So do I," Caine agreed. "But Colin will find something wrong with him. Besides, the matter has already been settled."

Caine shook his head at his wife when she started to protest, added a wink so her feelings wouldn't be injured, and then whispered, "Later," to let her know he would explain everything when they were alone.

Colin turned around and walked out of the salon. He

didn't go into the dining room however, but started up the steps.

"Go ahead without us," he called down to Caine. "I must speak to Alesandra for a few minutes."

Colin didn't think it would take him any time at all to explain to Alesandra he was going to marry her. No, that announcement wouldn't take more than a minute. The rest of the time would be spent on expectations. His.

The library was down at the end of the long corridor. Alesandra was standing in front of the window, looking out. She held a thick book in her hands. She turned when Colin walked inside.

He shut the door behind him and then leaned against it. He frowned at her. She smiled at him.

"You are finished with your conference?" she asked.

"Yes."

"I see," she whispered when he didn't continue. She walked over to the desk and put the book down on the ink blotter. "What was decided?" she asked then, trying desperately to sound only mildly interested.

He started to tell her he was going to marry her, then took Caine's advice and put the decision into a question.

"Will you marry me, Alesandra?"

"No," she answered in a whisper. "But I do thank you for offering."

"After the wedding, you and I . . . what do you mean, no? I'm going to marry you, Alesandra. It's all been decided."

"No, you aren't going to marry me," she countered. "Quit frowning, Colin. You're off the hook. You asked and I turned you down. You can start breathing again."

"Alesandra . . ." he began in a warning tone of voice she completely ignored.

"I know exactly what happened downstairs after I left," she boasted. "Your father cleverly manipulated you into agreeing to have me. He told you about the gift my father gave him, didn't he?"

Colin smiled. Alesandra was really very astute. "Yes," he answered. "It wasn't a gift, however. It was a loan."

He moved away from the door and walked toward her. She immediately started backing away.

"It was a loan only in your father's eyes," she argued.

He shook his head. "Forget the loan," he ordered. "And start making sense. You need to get married, damn it, and I've agreed to become your husband. Why are you being so difficult?"

"Because you don't love me."

She'd blurted out that truth before she could stop herself. Colin looked astonished. She was so embarrassed now she wished she could open the window and leap out. That ridiculous notion made her want to scream. She really needed to get a better hold on her emotions, she told herself.

"What does love have to do with anything? Do you honestly believe any of the men on your list would love you? Hell, whomever you chose wouldn't even know you well enough to form an opinion . . ."

She interrupted him. "No, of course he wouldn't love me. I wouldn't want him to. It was going to be a purely financial arrangement. You, however, have made it perfectly clear you won't touch my funds. You told me you were determined to make it on your own, remember?"

"I remember."

"And have you changed your mind in the last five minutes?"

"No."

"There, do you finally understand? Since you have nothing to gain from marrying me, and since you don't love me, which would be the only other reason for marriage, then there really isn't any point to your noble sacrifice."

Colin leaned on the edge of the desk and stared at her. "Let me get this straight," he muttered. "You actually believed you could buy a husband?"

"Of course," she cried out in exasperation. "Women do it all the time."

"You aren't buying me."

He sounded furious. She let out a sigh and tried to hold on to her patience. "I know I'm not buying you," she agreed.

"And that puts me in a weaker bargaining position. I can't allow that."

Colin felt like shaking some sense into her. "We're talking about marriage, not contracts for hire," he snapped. "Were you planning to sleep with your husband? What about children, Alesandra?"

He was asking her questions she didn't want to answer. "Perhaps . . . in time. Oh, I don't know," she whispered. "It doesn't concern you."

Colin suddenly moved. Before Alesandra had time to guess his intent, he pulled her into his arms.

He held her around her waist with one arm and forced her chin up with his other hand so she would look at him.

He thought he might want to shout at her, but then he saw the tears in her eyes and he forgot all about arguing with her.

"I'm going to be touching you all the time," he announced in a gruff whisper.

"Why?"

He took exception to the fact that she looked so surprised. "Call it a benefit," he drawled out.

He probably would have only given her a chaste kiss to seal his commitment to wed her, but she goaded his temper again when she whispered her denial.

"Yes," he whispered back just seconds before his mouth descended to hers. The kiss was meant to gain her submission. It was hard, demanding, thorough. He felt her try to pull away with the first touch of his mouth on hers, but he ignored her struggle to get free by tightening his hold on her. He forced her mouth open by applying pressure on her chin with his hand, and then his tongue swept inside to rid her of her resistance.

The kiss wasn't at all gentle. But, Lord, it was hot. Alesandra didn't know if she struggled or not. She was having trouble thinking at all. Colin's mouth was so wonderfully thorough, she never wanted him to stop. Alesandra had never been kissed before and had therefore never experienced passion. She was overwhelmed by it now. Colin was certainly experienced, though. His mouth slanted over hers again and again while his tongue rubbed against hers in intimate love play.

Colin realized he should stop when he heard her sexy little whimper. He growled low in his throat and kissed her again. Damn, he wanted her. His hand brushed against the swell of her breast and the heat and fullness he felt under his hand through the material of her gown made him ache to make love to her.

He forced himself to pull away from her. Alesandra collapsed against him. She didn't realize she had her arms around his waist until he told her to let go.

She was so confused by what had just happened to her, she didn't know what to say or do. She tried to back away from him, but she was trembling so much she could barely get her legs to support her.

He knew he'd rattled her. The grin on his face was extremely telling—arrogant, too.

"That was my first kiss," she stammered out as an excuse for her sorry condition.

Colin couldn't resist. He pulled her back into his arms and kissed her again. "And that was your second," he whispered.

"Begging your pardon," Jenkins called out from the doorway. "The duchess is most insistent you join her in the dining room."

Alesandra jerked away from Colin. She acted as though she'd just been scorched by the sun. Her cheeks turned pink with embarrassment. She peeked around Colin to look at the butler. He smiled at her.

"We're coming, Jenkins," Colin called out. He kept his gaze on Alesandra, smiling over her embarrassment.

She tried to skirt her way around him. He took hold of her hand and wouldn't let go. "I'll make the announcement during dinner," he told her as he pulled her through the doorway.

"No," she countered. "Colin, your kisses haven't changed anything. I'm not going to marry you and ruin all your carefully laid plans."

"Alesandra, I always win. Understand me?"

She let out an unladylike snort. He squeezed her hand and started down the steps. She had to run to keep up with him.

"I dislike arrogant, think-they're-always-right men," she muttered.

"I do too," he agreed.

"I was referring to you." Lord, she felt like screaming. "I'm not marrying you."

"We'll see."

He wasn't going to give up. The man was sinfully stubborn. But then so was she, she reminded herself. Her guardian had given her his word she could choose her own husband and Colin's intimidating tactics didn't matter.

Dinner was a nerve-racking affair. Alesandra's stomach was tied in knots and she could barely swallow anything. She should have been hungry, but she wasn't. She kept waiting for Colin to say something, and was praying at the same time that he wouldn't open his mouth.

Jade drew her into conversation. "I understand the prince regent called on you," she remarked.

"Yes," Alesandra answered. "I wouldn't have allowed him entrance into Colin's home if I'd known he'd cheated Colin's partner out of an inheritance, however."

Jade smiled. "His partner is my brother," she said. She turned to the duchess to explain what they'd been talking about. "The prince regent was holding my brother's wife's inheritance while the fighting was going on between the families, but once it was all resolved, he decided to keep the gift for himself. It was a sizable sum."

"You really wouldn't have let the prince regent in?" Caine asked.

"No, I wouldn't have," Alesandra said again. "Why do you look so surprised? Colin's home is his castle. Only friends should be allowed inside."

Alesandra turned her attention to Jade and therefore missed the grin the two brothers shared.

"Do you happen to know a lady named Victoria Perry?" she asked.

Jade shook her head. "The name isn't familiar to me. Why do you ask?"

"I'm worried about her," Alesandra confessed. She explained how she'd met Victoria and what she had learned since she'd last received a letter from her.

"My dear, I don't believe it's a good idea to pursue this further," the duchess announced. "Her mother must be heartbroken. It's cruel to dredge it all up again."

"Colin said the very same thing to me," Alesandra said. "Perhaps you are right. I should let the matter rest. I wish I could quit worrying about her."

The duchess turned the conversation then to the topic of her eldest daughter. This was Catherine's year for coming out and she was full of plans for her first ball.

Caine didn't say a word throughout the rest of the meal. He kept his gaze on his brother.

Colin wasn't giving anything away. His expression could have been carved in stone.

Alesandra actually began to relax a little when dessert was served and Colin still hadn't brought up the topic of marriage. She thought he'd probably had enough time to think the matter through. Yes, he'd come to his senses.

"Have you had time to talk to Alesandra, son?" the Duke of Williamshire asked.

"Yes," Colin replied. "We've decided . . ."

"Not to marry," she blurted out.

"What's this? Colin, I thought it had all been decided," his father protested.

"It has been decided," Colin agreed. He reached over and covered Alesandra's hand with his. "We're getting married. Alesandra has agreed to become my wife."

She started shaking her head in denial but no one seemed to be paying any attention to her.

"Congratulations," her guardian announced. "Gweneth, this calls for a toast."

"Don't you think Alesandra should agree first?" Jade asked just as her father-in-law started to stand up with his water glass in hand.

He sat back down. "Yes, of course," he replied.

"She'll marry me," Colin said, his voice hard, unbending.

She turned to him. "I won't let you make this noble sacrifice. You don't want to get married for another five years, remember? What about your schedule?"

She didn't wait for Colin to answer her question but turned her attention back to Uncle Henry. "I don't want to marry him, Uncle, and you did promise me I could choose."

Her guardian slowly nodded. "I did agree to let you select your husband. Was there a specific reason why you refused Colin?"

"He won't agree to a financial arrangement," she explained. "He wants other benefits."

"Benefits?" Caine asked, his curiosity pricked. "Such as?"

She started blushing. She looked at Colin, hoping he'd explain. He shook his head at her. "You started this, you finish it," he ordered.

The sparkle in his eyes indicated his amusement. She straightened her shoulders. "Very well," she announced. She couldn't quite look at Caine when she gave him her answer, however, and stared at the wall behind him. "Colin would demand . . . intimacy."

No one knew what to say to that confession. Her guardian looked thoroughly confused. He started to open his mouth to say something, then changed his mind.

"Aren't most marriages intimate?" Caine asked. "You are referring to the marriage bed, aren't you, Alesandra?"

"Yes."

"And?" he prodded.

"My marriage will not be intimate," she announced, her voice emphatic. She tried to change the subject by adding, "Colin didn't want to marry me until after he'd talked to his father. Now he's feeling honor bound. Clearly, he's marrying me out of duty."

Her guardian let out a sigh. "I did give you my word," he admitted. "If you don't want to marry Colin, I won't force you."

The duchess was fanning herself with her napkin. "Jade, dear, I believe you should be the one to have a private talk with Alesandra. You're younger and not as set in your ways as I am, and it should be a woman to discuss this topic I have in mind. Alesandra seems to harbor some fears about the . . . marriage bed . . . and I don't feel qualified to explain . . . that is . . ."

She couldn't finish her request. The duchess was violently fanning herself now and her face looked like it was on fire.

"Mother, you've had children. I believe that makes you very qualified," Colin told her.

Jade poked her husband in his side in a bid to get him to quit laughing.

"I believe Morgan Atkins will be suitable," Alesandra blurted out. "If he needs my inheritance, he'll agree to my terms, and I don't mind bowlegged children. No, I don't mind at all."

"If you aren't going to be intimate with your husband, how the hell are you going to have children?" Colin asked.

"I was thinking into the future," Alesandra stammered. She realized the contradictions in her argument but couldn't seem to think of a way to straighten it all out. Why would she want to be intimate with a man she didn't know? The very thought made her stomach twist.

"Jade, I believe you should have that talk with Alesandra directly after dinner," the duchess interjected.

"Yes, Mother," Jade agreed.

"Has anyone ever discussed the facts of marriage to you?" Caine asked.

Alesandra's blush was hot enough to scorch the tablecloth. "Yes, of course. Mother Superior told me everything I need to know. Could we please change this topic now?"

Her guardian took mercy on her. "So it's Morgan you've chosen?" he asked. He waited for her nod, then continued. "Very well. We'll invite him over for supper and take his measure."

"I'll want to talk to him too," Colin announced. "He'll need to know, of course."

"Know what?" his father inquired.

Caine was already grinning. He knew his brother was up

to something, but he couldn't imagine what it was. Only one thing was certain in Caine's mind. Colin had made the decision to marry Alesandra, and he wasn't going to let her get away now.

"Yes, son," his mother said. "What is it Morgan needs to know?"

"That Alesandra and I slept together."

The duchess dropped her napkin and let out a little screech. Jade's mouth dropped open. Caine started laughing. The Duke of Williamshire had just taken a swallow of water when Colin made his announcement. He started choking.

Alesandra closed her eyes and fought the urge to scream.

"You slept with her?" his father demanded in a strangled roar.

"Yes, sir," Colin answered. His voice was very pleasant, cheerful in fact. He seemed completely unaffected by his father's wrath. "Several times in fact."

"How could you deliberately . . ." Alesandra couldn't go on. She was so mortified, she couldn't seem to catch a thought long enough to speak it.

"How could I lie?" Colin asked her. "You know better. I never lie. We did sleep together, didn't we?"

Everyone was staring at her now, waiting for her denial.

"Yes," she whispered. "But we . . ."

"For the love of God," her guardian shouted.

"Henry, calm yourself. You're going to make yourself ill," his wife advised when she saw how mottled his complexion was becoming. The duchess was once again frantically fanning herself with her napkin in an effort to remain composed.

Colin leaned back in his chair and let the sparks fly around him. He looked bored. Caine was thoroughly enjoying himself. Jade kept trying to make her husband take the matter more seriously by poking him in his ribs.

"Colin, have you nothing to say to straighten out this misconception?" Alesandra demanded in a near shout so she would be heard above Caine's laughter.

"Yes," Colin answered.

She sagged with relief and gratitude. The feeling was short-lived, however.

"If Morgan still wants you after I've explained how we spent the last week, he's a better man than I am."

"You don't have to tell him anything." Alesandra tried to control the anger in her voice. She didn't want to lose her dignity, but, Lord, Colin was making that difficult. Her composure was in shreds and her throat was aching with the need to shout.

"Oh, but I do have to explain the situation to Morgan," Colin said. "It's the only honorable thing to do. Isn't that right, Caine?"

"Absolutely right," Caine agreed. "It's the only honorable thing to do."

Caine turned to his wife then. "Sweetheart, I don't believe you'll need to have that private talk about the marriage bed with Alesandra after all."

Alesandra glared at Caine for that comment, because she could tell from his grin he was jesting.

"Dear God, what must Nathaniel be thinking? He's looking down from heaven and probably shaking his head in regret for leaving his daughter in my hands."

"Uncle Henry, my father wouldn't have any regrets," Alesandra announced. She was so furious with Colin for getting his own papa upset her voice crackled with tension. "Nothing sinful happened. I did go into his room and I did sleep with him, but only because he was so demanding and I became so weary . . ."

The Duke of Williamshire covered his forehead with his hands and let out a low groan. Alesandra knew she was making a mess out of her explanation and tried to start over. "I kept my clothes on," she blurted out. "And he . . ."

She was going to explain that Colin had been ill and had needed her help, but she was interrupted before she could finish.

"I wasn't wearing anything," Colin cheerfully informed his family.

"That's it," his father bellowed. His fist came down hard on the tabletop. The crystal goblets clattered together in reaction.

Alesandra jumped, then turned to glare at Colin. She'd never been this angry in all her life. Colin had deliberately twisted the truth to his advantage and now her guardian thought she was a trollop. She decided she wasn't going to sit there another second. She threw her napkin on the table and tried to leave. Colin caught her before she'd even pushed her chair back. He put his arm around her shoulders and hauled her into his side.

"You two are going to be married in exactly three days' time. Caine, you see to the special license. Colin, you keep silent about what happened. I won't have Alesandra's reputation in tatters because of your lust."

"Three days, Henry?" Gweneth asked. "The church is reserved for the Saturday after next. Couldn't you reconsider?"

Her husband shook his head. "Three days," he repeated. He noticed Colin had his arm around Alesandra's shoulders and added, "He can't keep his hands off her as it is."

"But, Henry . . ." his wife pleaded.

"My mind's set, Gweneth. You may invite a few close friends if you're wanting to, but that is the only concession I'll allow."

"No, Father," Colin said. "I don't want the news of the marriage to get out until it's over. It's safer for Alesandra that way."

His father nodded. "I'd forgotten," he admitted. "Yes, it would be safer. All right then, only the immediate family will be here."

He turned his full attention to Alesandra. "I want your agreement to wed Colin," he commanded. "And I want it now."

"Do you agree?" Colin asked.

He'd won and he knew it. She slowly nodded. Colin leaned down and kissed her. She was so startled by the show of affection she didn't pull away.

"That's quite enough of that," Henry snapped. "You won't be touching her again until you're married."

Alesandra turned to Colin. "You're going to regret marrying me."

He didn't seem overly worried about that possibility. He wouldn't have winked at her if he'd really been concerned.

Jenkins appeared in the doorway. "Begging your pardon, your grace, but we have a visitor at the door. Sir Richards is requesting an immediate audience with your son, Colin."

"Show him into the salon, Jenkins," Colin called out.

"Why would the director of security be wanting to see you?" his father demanded to know. "You told me you'd quit the department."

The worry in his voice confused Alesandra. She started to ask her guardian why he was so concerned, but just as she opened her mouth to say something, Colin tightened his hold on her shoulders. She turned to look at him. His expression didn't give anything away and she knew no one else at the table realized he was silently ordering her to remain quiet.

"After what happened to your leg, I can't imagine why you would continue working for the director," his mother interjected.

Colin tried to hold on to his patience. "The director had nothing to do with my injury."

"It was a long time ago," Jade reminded the duchess.

"By God, he's finished with that cloak-and-dagger business," his father announced.

Caine leaned forward, drawing Colin's attention. "Why exactly is Richards here?" he asked.

"I requested his help," Colin answered. "And he was also going to gather some information for me."

"Regarding?" Caine asked.

"Alesandra."

Their father looked relieved. "Well, then, that's quite all right. Yes, Richards is just the man to ask about the general. Shall we go into the salon and hear what he has to tell us?"

"We aren't going to be left out, Henry," his wife announced. She stood up to face her husband. "Come along, Jade. You, too, Alesandra. If the matter concerns one of us, it concerns all of us. Isn't that right, Henry?" Then she and the others left the room.

Colin let go of Alesandra. She stood up when he did. She caught hold of his hand before he could leave.

"Your father now believes I'm a trollop," she whispered. "I would appreciate it if you would set him straight."

Colin leaned down close to her ear. "I'll explain everything after we're married."

His warm breath sent a shiver of pleasure down her neck, making it difficult for her to concentrate. Up until an hour ago, when Colin had kissed her so passionately, she'd been desperately trying to think of him as a friend . . . or a cousin. She'd been lying to herself, of course, but, damn it all, it was working. Colin had turned the tables on her, though, when he'd touched her. Now, just standing so close to him made her heartbeat race. He smelled so wonderful, so masculine, and . . . Oh, Lord, she really needed to get hold of her thoughts.

"You're a scoundrel, Colin."

"I like to think I am."

She gave up trying to make him angry. "Why don't you want your family to know you're working for . . ."

He wouldn't let her finish. His mouth covered hers in a quick, hard kiss. She let out a little sigh when he pulled back, then repeated her question. He kissed her again.

She finally got his message and quit her questions. "Will you explain after we're married?"

"Yes."

Jade walked back into the dining room. "Colin, I would like to speak to Alesandra in private. We'll be along in a minute."

Alesandra waited until Colin had left the dining room, then went around the table to stand next to Jade.

"Do you really dislike the idea of marrying Colin?"

"No," Alesandra answered. "And that, you see, is the problem."

"How is it a problem?"

"Colin's being forced into marrying me. He's acting out of duty. I can't control that."

"I don't understand," Jade remarked.

Alesandra brushed her hair back over her shoulder in a nervous gesture. "I wanted to control the situation," she whispered. When it first became apparent I would have to get married, I was very angry inside. I felt so . . . powerless. It didn't seem fair. I finally came to terms with my circumstances, however, as soon as I began to think of the marriage as a business transaction and not a personal relationship. I decided that if I chose my husband and set my own terms, then it wouldn't matter if he loved me or not. It would be a business arrangement, nothing more."

"Colin won't agree to your terms, though, will he? I'm not surprised," Jade remarked. "He's an independent man. He's proud of the fact that he's making it on his own, without help from family or friends. He isn't going to be easy to control, but in time I believe you'll be happy about that. Have some faith in him, Alesandra. He'll take care of you."

Yes, Alesandra thought to herself. Colin would take care of her.

And she would become a burden to him.

He wasn't interested in her inheritance and in fact had made it perfectly clear he wouldn't touch it.

He wasn't impressed with her title, either. Being married to a princess was going to be a nuisance because he would have to suffer going to several important functions during the year. He'd have to mingle with the prince regent, and, Lord, she knew he'd hate that.

Colin had rejected everything she had to offer.

No, it wasn't a fair exchange.

Chapter 8

Sir Richards had just finished greeting everyone when Jade and Alesandra walked into the salon. The director turned to both ladies. He knew Jade, and after telling her how wonderful it was to see her again, he turned his full attention to Alesandra.

"Henry told me the good news. Congratulations, Princess. You've chosen a fine man."

Alesandra forced a smile. She thanked the director, agreed Colin was indeed a fine man, and asked him if he would be attending the wedding.

"Yes," Sir Richards replied. "I wouldn't miss it. It's a pity it has to be kept a secret, but you understand well enough the reasons. Come and sit down now. I've some information you'll be interested in hearing."

Sir Richards ushered her over to one of the settees. Jade and Caine were seated across from her, and the duke and duchess took the third settee.

Colin stood alone in front of the hearth. He wasn't paying any attention to the director or his family. His back was turned to the gathering and he was intently studying the miniature on the mantel. Alesandra watched Colin as he lifted the castle to get a better look at it. The expression on

Colin's face was masked, and she wondered what he was thinking.

The duchess was explaining her plans for the wedding. She was determined to make the intimate affair as lovely as possible. She was interrupted by her husband when he called out to Colin.

"Be careful with that, son. It's priceless to me."

Colin nodded but he didn't turn around. He had just noticed the tiny drawbridge latched with a delicate-looking chain. "This really is a piece of workmanship," he remarked as he gently pried the drawbridge away from the hook. The door immediately dropped down. Colin lifted the castle higher so that he could look inside.

Alesandra saw the surprised look in his eyes. He smiled, too. She smiled in reaction. He had just figured out the bit of trickery her father had played on his friend so many years ago.

Colin turned to Caine and motioned to him with a quick tilt of his head. Caine stood up and walked over to the mantel. Colin didn't say a word to his brother. He simply handed him the castle, then turned and walked over to sit next to Alesandra.

The duchess had only just warmed to her topic of the wedding plans. Both her husband and the director were patiently listening to her.

Caine suddenly let out a hoot of laughter. He drew everyone's attention, of course.

Caine turned to Alesandra. "Did you know about this?"

She nodded. "My mother told me the story."

"Later, when you're alone with Father, would you show him?" Caine asked.

"Yes, of course."

"Put that down," his father ordered. "It makes me nervous to see it handled. Do you have any idea of its value, Caine?"

His son laughed. "Yes, father, I understand its value." He closed the drawbridge and put the castle back where it belonged.

"Mother, I don't believe Sir Richards is interested in your

plans for the wedding," Colin said. "He's been polite long enough. Let him get to his reason for calling."

Gweneth turned to the director. "Were you just being polite?"

"Of course he was, Gweneth," her husband told her. He softened his bluntness by patting his wife's hand.

Caine had returned to his seat next to his wife. He put his arm around her shoulders and pulled her close to his side.

Alesandra noticed that both her guardian and his eldest son were very open in showing their affection for their wives. Caine was stroking his wife's arm in an absent-minded way and her uncle Henry hadn't let go of his wife's hand. Alesandra envied the loving couples. She knew it had been a true love match between her guardian and his wife, and from the way Jade and Caine looked at each other, she assumed they had also fallen in love before they were married.

She and Colin were another matter altogether. She wondered if he realized what he was giving up to marry her and almost asked him that question then and there.

Sir Richards saved her from embarrassing herself when he took the floor. "Colin asked me to assist him with a little experiment. He had reason to believe the lady's maid, Valena, was in a league with the ruffians trying to snatch the princess."

Alesandra was stunned by the director's explanation. She turned to Colin. "What reason would you have to distrust that sweet . . ."

He interrupted her. "Let him finish, Alesandra."

"Colin was correct," Sir Richards announced. He smiled at his host. "Both your sons have the best instincts I've ever come across in all my days working for the department."

Henry beamed with pleasure. "It's a trait I like to think they inherited from me," he remarked.

"Yes," Gweneth agreed. Her loyalty to her husband was absolute. "Henry's always been as cunning as a lion."

Colin tried not to smile. He believed his father was more like a lamb than a lion, but he didn't see that as a flaw. In truth, he envied his innocence. He'd lost his own years ago.

His father was a rare man indeed. He seemed to be immune to the darker side of life. Having heard his father's confession of the dark period he went through when he was a younger man made him all the more remarkable. The experience hadn't made him cynical. He wore his heart on his sleeve most of the time, and Colin knew that if there was any softness at all left in his own nature, it had come from his father.

"Now, then, as I was saying," the director continued. "Colin told the maid to inform the princess that there would be a meeting at my town house. He set the time for ten the following morning. Valena slipped out during the night to tell her companions. Colin had one of Alesandra's guards follow her. Right as rain the following morning, there they were, four in all, hiding in wait near my home to nab the princess."

"So there were four in all?" Colin asked. He wasn't at all surprised by the news. Alesandra was speechless. She had always believed she was a good judge of character but now admitted she'd certainly been off the mark with Valena. Alesandra's thoughts immediately turned to Victoria and she wondered if she'd been wrong about her, too.

"Good heavens, I hired Valena," the duchess blurted out. "She came to me and I should have thought that odd, but I was so pleased with her because she was born near Alesandra's father's home. I thought it would make our ward feel more comfortable to have a reminder of her past. Valena spoke the language, you see. I looked into her references, Henry. Yes, I did, but now I realize I should have been more thorough."

"No one's blaming you, Mother," Colin told her.

"Why didn't you tell me about your suspicions?" Alesandra asked Colin.

He was surprised by the question. "Because it was my problem to solve, not yours."

He looked like he believed what he'd just told her. Alesandra didn't know how to respond to that arrogant belief. "But how did you know? What made you suspicious?"

"The latch on one of the windows was unlocked an hour after Raymond had checked," he explained. "And someone had to alert the men that we would be attending the opera."

"The prince regent could have mentioned it to . . ."

Colin cut her off. "Yes, he could have," he agreed. "But he wouldn't have unlocked the window."

"Did you catch all of them?" Henry asked the director then.

"Yes, we did," Richards answered. "They're safely tucked away."

"I'll talk to them first thing tomorrow," Colin announced.

"May I go with you?" Alesandra asked.

"No."

Colin's voice suggested she not argue. His father supported his son's decision, too. "It's out of the question, Alesandra."

The discussion was over. Sir Richards took his leave a few minutes later. Colin accompanied the director to the door. Jade and Caine said their farewells at the same time. Both the duke and duchess walked to the door with them. Alesandra stood by the hearth, watching the way the family members talked and laughed with one another, and the sudden yearning to be a part of the loving, close-knit family fairly overwhelmed her. She shook her head against the possibility. Colin wasn't marrying her because he loved her. She mustn't forget that, she told herself.

The door closed behind Jade and Caine, and she realized then that Colin had already taken his leave.

He hadn't even bothered to say good-bye. Alesandra was so hurt by his rudeness, she turned around to stare at the mantel so her guardian wouldn't see the tears in her eyes.

Dignity and decorum, she silently chanted to herself. She would get through the wedding with her cloak of serenity tightly wrapped around her. If Colin was determined to be stupidly noble, then so be it.

The castle caught her attention and the anger she was trying to stir up over Colin's high-handed methods in gaining her agreement was all but forgotten. A wave of homesickness for her mother and father made her ache inside.

Dear God, she was miserable. She never should have left the convent—she realized that mistake now. She'd been safe there, and the memories of her mother were somehow far more comforting.

Alesandra took a deep breath in an attempt to stop the panic she could feel catching hold. She understood why she was so afraid. God help her, she was falling in love with the Dragon.

It was unacceptable to her. Colin would never know how she felt about him. She wasn't about to end up like a vine of ivy clinging to a man who didn't love her. She wouldn't hover, either, no matter how much she wanted to, and she would force herself to think of the marriage as nothing but an arrangement. Colin had his reasons for marrying her, foolish though they were, and in return for his name and protection she would leave him to his own agenda. She wouldn't interfere in any way with his schedule, and in return for her consideration he would leave her alone to follow her own destiny.

Alesandra mopped the tears from her eyes. She was feeling better now that she'd come up with a viable plan of action. She would request an audience with Colin tomorrow and tell him how she had worked it all out in her mind.

She would even allow for negotiating, but only on minor points, of course.

"Alesandra, your guards will bring your things over in just a little while."

Her guardian made that announcement as he walked back into the salon. She turned to thank him. Uncle Henry frowned when he saw the tears in her eyes.

"What's this?" he demanded. "Are you so unhappy over my choice for your husband that you . . ."

She shook her head. "I was looking at the castle and it made me a bit homesick."

He looked relieved. He walked over to stand next to her. "I believe I'll take that back to our country house. I don't like seeing it touched. Colin and Caine couldn't keep their hands off it, could they?" he added with a grin. "They can both be like bulls in a pen at times. I wouldn't want this treasure broken."

He turned to look at the miniature. "Do you know the story behind this gift?" he asked.

"My mother told me Father gave it to you," Alesandra answered.

"The castle was a gift," Uncle Henry explained. "But I was asking you if you'd been told about the loan your father gave me? You have every right to hear it, and to know how your father came to my aid."

His voice had gotten gruff with emotion. Alesandra shook her head. "It wasn't a loan, Uncle, and, yes, I did know what happened. Mother told me the story because she thought it clever and amusing the way he tricked you."

"Nathaniel tricked me? How?"

Alesandra turned and lifted the castle from the mantel, nodding when her guardian instinctively warned her to be careful. While he watched, she pried the drawbridge away from the latch, then handed the castle to him.

"They've been inside all the while," she explained, her voice a gentle whisper. "Have a look, Uncle Henry. The notes are there."

He couldn't seem to comprehend what she was telling him. He stared at her with a look of astonishment on his face.

"All these years . . ." His voice cracked with tension and his eyes turned quite misty.

"Father liked to get his way," Alesandra explained. "He insisted it was a gift and you insisted it was a loan. Mother told me you demanded notes be signed and father accommodated you. But he had the last laugh, Uncle, when he gave you the castle as a gift."

"With the notes."

She put her hand on his arm. "You hold the notes," she said. "And you must therefore accept that the debt has been repaid."

Her guardian held the castle up and looked inside. He spotted the folded pieces of paper immediately. "The debt will be repaid when you marry my son," he said.

He didn't have any idea how his words affected her. His attention was on the castle now, and he therefore missed the look on her face.

She turned around and walked out of the salon. She passed Aunt Gweneth in the foyer but didn't trust her voice enough to speak.

Gweneth hurried into the salon just as Alesandra ran up the steps. "Henry, what did you say to that child?" she demanded.

Henry motioned her over to his side. "Alesandra's fine, Gweneth. She's just feeling a little homesick, that's all. Let her have a few minutes alone. Look at this," he ordered then, his concentration turned back to the notes hidden inside the treasure.

Alesandra was forgotten for the moment. She was thankful no one followed her up the stairs. She went into her uncle Henry's study, closed the door behind her, and promptly burst into tears. She cried for at least twenty minutes and all because she was feeling so horribly sorry for herself. She knew she was being childish—pitiful, too—but she didn't care.

She didn't feel any better when she'd finished weeping. Her nerves were still frazzled with worry and confusion.

Dreyson arrived on the doorstep an hour later. She signed the papers he'd prepared and then listened to his long explanation regarding the transfer of her funds from her father's homeland to the Bank of England. The agent Dreyson had hired to make the transaction was having difficulty getting the money released, but Dreyson assured her it wasn't anything to worry about. It would just take time and patience.

Alesandra could barely concentrate on financial matters. She went to bed early that night and prayed for strength to get through the next three days.

Time didn't drag, however. Aunt Gweneth kept her busy with the preparations for the wedding. Unbeknownst to her husband or her family, Gweneth invited a few close friends to join in the celebration—thirty-eight, in fact—and there was so much to be done before the wedding she could barely keep up with her lists of duties. There were fresh flowers to be ordered for the tables inside, food to be prepared for the formal sit-down dinner she planned on serving everyone, and a gown to be sewn by the sour-dispositioned but incredibly creative Millicent Norton. The dressmaker and her three assistants had taken over one of the larger rooms on the third floor and were working around the clock with their needles and threads on the yards and yards of imported lace Millicent Norton had been hoarding for just such an occasion.

When Alesandra wasn't needed for fittings, she worked on the task Gweneth had assigned her—writing out the announcements. There were over two hundred names on her list. The envelopes had to be addressed too, of course, and Gweneth insisted they be ready to be sent out by messenger as soon as Colin and Alesandra were married.

Alesandra didn't understand the need for all the fuss. She believed only the immediate family, the minister, and Sir Richards would be attending. She asked her aunt why she was going to all the trouble and was told that it was the very least she could do to repay the goodness Alesandra's father had shown her family.

The day of the wedding finally arrived. The weather proved accommodating, much to Gweneth's delight. The garden could be used after all. The sun was bright and the temperature quite warm for spring. The guests wouldn't even need to wear cloaks, the duchess decided. She ordered the French doors opened and put the servants to work sweeping the stones clean.

The ceremony was scheduled for four o'clock in the afternoon. The flowers began arriving at noon. The parade of messengers seemed endless. Alesandra stayed in the dining room and out of everyone's way. Her Aunt Gweneth had really gone all out, she decided when she saw two huge vases of flowers being carried upstairs. She imagined the library was also going to be decorated. Perhaps Gweneth thought her husband might decide to entertain Sir Richards in the library.

Alesandra was just about to go up to her room to get ready for the ceremony, but she was waylaid from that duty when Colin's sisters arrived. The youngest, Marian Rose, was only ten years old, and so thrilled to be included in the party she could barely stand still. Marian had been a happy surprise to her parents for, almost four years after their third daughter had been born, they had believed Gweneth's childbearing years were over. The youngest was doted upon by her parents and her older brothers, of course, but she was kept from being completely spoiled by her sisters. Alison was fourteen years old, Jennifer was fifteen, and Catherine had just turned sixteen.

Alesandra liked all of Colin's sisters, but her favorite was Catherine. She was careful not to let the others know how she felt, fearing she would cause hurt feelings.

Catherine was such a delight. She was the complete opposite of Alesandra, and perhaps that was the reason she liked her so much. She admitted she envied Colin's sister. Catherine was outrageously outspoken. One never had to guess what she might be thinking. She told her every thought. She was very dramatic, too, and was constantly getting into mischief with her dearest friend, Lady Michelle Marie. Catherine never worried about restraint. Alesandra doubted she fully understood what dignity and decorum were, and she was the most wonderfully honest person Alesandra had ever known.

She was becoming a very pretty young lady, too. Catherine had dark blond hair and hazel-colored eyes. She was taller than Alesandra by a good two inches.

None of Colin's sisters had been given the reason why they were being called to London, and when their mother gathered them together and explained about the wedding, Catherine was the first to screech with delight. She threw herself into Alesandra's arms and hugged her tight.

"Michelle Marie will probably try to kill you for ruining her plans," she cheerfully informed Alesandra. "She thinks she's going to marry Colin. She's planned it for years and years."

Gweneth shook her head in exasperation. "Colin's never even met your friend. Why in heaven's name would she believe he would marry her? She's your age, Catherine, and Colin's much too old for her. Why, he's almost twice her age."

Alison and Jennifer rushed forward to hug Alesandra, too. All three sisters clung to her and it was all Alesandra could do to keep her balance. They were all talking at once, of course. It was chaotic, and a little overwhelming for Alesandra.

There wasn't room for Marian Rose. She hung back, but not for long. She stomped her foot in a bid to get attention, and when that didn't work, she let out a bloodcurdling scream. Everyone immediately turned to see what was wrong, and Marian Rose used that opportunity to hurl herself at Alesandra.

Raymond and Stefan heard the scream and came running. Gweneth apologized for her daughter's behavior, told Marian Rose to hush, and then put the guards to work carrying up the extra crates of wineglasses from the cellar.

Raymond motioned to Alesandra. She excused herself from Colin's family and went over to him.

"The duchess keeps opening the French doors, Princess. We keep closing them. It isn't safe to have the back of the house unlocked. Could you please talk to her? Colin's going to be furious when he gets here and sees all the doors and windows open."

"I'll try to talk to her," Alesandra promised. "I doubt she'll listen. I guess we're going to have to have faith it will all go well. Just a few more hours and the worry will be over."

Raymond bowed to the princess. He wasn't about to sit back and hope things would go well. Both he and Stefan were ready to pull their hair out over the number of strangers stomping into the town house with flowers and trays and gifts. It had been almost impossible to keep count of who everyone was. Raymond went into the kitchen. He grabbed hold of a servant and ordered him to take a message to Colin. The duchess wouldn't listen to a guard, but she would certainly listen to her son.

Raymond didn't stop there. He went upstairs next to look for the Duke of Williamshire and alert him to the possible danger.

The time got away from Alesandra. Millicent Norton and her assistants came downstairs and waylaid her just as she was about to go up. The dressmaker explained that the wedding gown was hanging in front of the wardrobe in Alesandra's bedroom and that it was without a doubt the most exquisite dress she'd ever created. Alesandra was in full agreement. She spent a long while complimenting the dressmaker and longer still promising to take every care when she put on the delicate gown.

Gweneth came rushing into the foyer just as Millicent and her assistants left. "Good heavens, Alesandra. It's already three and you haven't begun to get ready. Have you had your bath yet?"

"Yes, Aunt."

"The girls are getting ready now," Gweneth told her. She took hold of Alesandra's hand and started up the steps. "Janet will be in to help you just as soon as she finishes braiding Marian Rose's hair. Is your stomach full of butterflies, Alesandra? I know you must be excited. You mustn't worry though. Everything's ready. It's going to be a beautiful wedding. Hurry now or you'll miss it."

The duchess laughed over her own jest. She gave Alesandra's hand an affectionate squeeze when she reached her bed chamber, then opened the door and went inside. Alesandra could hear Marian Rose begging the maid to let her hair loose and then Gweneth's command to sit still.

Alesandra's bedroom was the last along the corridor. She opened the door and went inside. She was in such a hurry now, she didn't pay attention to anything but getting out of her dress. The buttons were in the front, and she had them undone before she'd even pushed the door shut behind her. She stripped out of her clothes, washed from top to bottom again, and then put on her white cotton robe. She was just securing the belt around her waist when the door opened behind her. Alesandra assumed it was the maid coming in to assist her. She started to turn around, but was suddenly grabbed from behind. A hand clamped down over her mouth to silence the instinctive scream already gathering in her throat.

She heard the sound of the door being bolted and knew then that there were at least two men in the room with her.

It took all of her determination to remain calm. She forced herself not to struggle. She was terrified inside, but she wasn't going to let that interfere with her ability to think. She could become hysterical later, after she'd gotten away from the horrible men.

She would have to be patient, she told herself, and wait for her opportunity to get free. She wouldn't scream, no matter how strong the urge became. Colin's sisters would come running and, dear God, she didn't want any of them to get hurt.

Alesandra calmed down as soon as she settled on a plan of action. She would cooperate until she was well away from the town house. It would be safer for the family that way. Then she would fight, scream, and bite, to make them sorry they'd dared to touch her.

A knock sounded at the door. The infidel behind her tightened his hold. He ordered her in a whisper to tell whoever it was begging entrance to go away.

She nodded agreement before he removed his hand from her mouth. The second man unbolted the door. Alesandra got a good look at his face. He was a dark-haired man with heavy eyebrows and oily skin. The sinister expression on his face made her shiver with fear. From the look of him, she knew he wouldn't suffer any remorse about hurting anyone.

The man behind her waved a knife in front of her face and told her that if she called out a warning he would kill her.

She wasn't worried about that possibility, for she knew he was bluffing. The general needed a live bride, not a dead one. She thought about telling the horrid man she wasn't afraid about her own safety, then changed her mind. It would be more cunning not to argue. If they believed she was going to cooperate, they might let their guard down just a little.

Alesandra was allowed to open the door a few inches. Jade stood in the hallway, smiling at her.

"Goodness, Alesandra, you're not even dressed. Would you like me to help you?"

Alesandra shook her head. "I don't need any help, Catherine, but I thank you for offering. Why don't you go back downstairs and wait with your husband? I'm sure your Henry would like you to stand by his side while he greets the guests."

Jade's expression didn't change. She kept right on smiling until the door closed again. She heard the sound of the bolt sliding into place as she turned and ran down the hallway.

Colin had just walked into the foyer when Jade reached the landing above. Marian Rose came running in from the salon and threw herself at her older brother. He lifted her up, kissed her on the cheek, and then bent down to take Caine's daughter, Olivia, into his other arm. The four-year-old gave her uncle a wet kiss.

Jade came rushing down the stairs. Caine caught her at the bottom. "Slow down, sweetheart. You're going to break . . ."

The fear he saw in her eyes stopped him cold. "What's wrong?" he demanded.

"Alesandra called me Catherine."

Colin heard his sister-in-law's worried remark. He put the little girls down and walked forward. He noticed then that the French doors leading to the garden were wide open and scowled in reaction. Didn't his parents understand the need for caution?

"She was just confused," Caine suggested to his wife. "It's her wedding day and she's bound to be a little nervous."

Jade shook her head. She turned to explain to Colin. "Alesandra told me to go downstairs and stand with my husband, Henry. Someone's in that room with her. I'm sure of it. She was trying to warn me."

Colin was already moving toward the steps. "Have Raymond and Stefan stand guard below Alesandra's window outside," he ordered. "Caine, you take the back steps. They'll probably try to take her out that way."

He'd reached the landing before he'd finished his instructions, passed his mother and father as they started down the staircase, and continued on down the corridor.

He was deadly calm about what he was going to do. Rage burned inside him, but he wouldn't let that emotion overwhelm his judgment. Only after Alesandra was safe would he unleash his fury.

He reached her bedroom, quietly tested the door to make certain it was locked, then slammed his shoulder against the wood with all his might. The door splintered off its hinges, the bolt snapped, and what was left of the door flew into the bedroom.

Alesandra tried to shout a warning to Colin but she was silenced by her captor's hand over her mouth again.

The second man charged Colin with his knife in his hand. Colin moved so swiftly, his enemy didn't understand until it was too late that his knife had been snatched away. Colin didn't let go of his hand, however. He twisted it behind his back, then upward, until the shoulder bone had popped out of its socket. The man howled with pain. Colin didn't show him any mercy. He threw him headfirst into the wall next to the doorway.

Fury gave him the strength of four men. He was almost blind with his anger now, for Alesandra looked so damned frightened and the bastard had his hands all over her. The robe she wore had opened enough for him to realize she wasn't wearing anything underneath.

"Get your hands off my bride."

Colin roared that command and started forward. Alesandra's captor knew he was trapped. He waited until Colin was almost upon him, then threw Alesandra forward and tried to run out of the room.

In one quick motion Colin tossed Alesandra onto the bed and out of harm's way, then turned and grabbed her captor by his neck.

He thought about breaking the son-of-a-bitch's neck then and there, but Alesandra was watching him and, damn it all, he didn't want her any more frightened than she already was.

"There's a quicker way out than taking the steps," he announced.

Because his voice had sounded so calm and reasonable, Alesandra wasn't at all prepared for his next action. Colin literally picked up the man by the seat of his britches and threw him headfirst out the window.

It wasn't open. Glass sprayed the walls and floor, and a few of the wooden panes that weren't imbedded in the man's shoulders fell to the ledge.

Colin didn't even look winded. He muttered, "Hell," when he noticed the dust on his trousers, let out a sigh, and then turned back to her.

Alesandra didn't know what to think. Colin had been quite terrifying just a minute before, and now he was acting like nothing out of the ordinary had taken place.

Didn't he realize that he might have killed that man? Or did he realize and simply not care?

Alesandra was determined to find out for herself. She jumped off the bed and went running toward the window. Colin intercepted her before she could step on the broken glass with her bare feet. He dragged her back toward the bed, then roughly pulled her into his arms.

"Dear God, Colin, do you think you killed him?"

The raw fear in her voice made him regret the fact that she had witnessed the fight. She was too young and innocent to understand that some men were really better off in hell. The way she trembled in his arms told him she was afraid of him.

"No, I didn't kill him," he told her, his voice a gruff whisper. "I'm sure Raymond caught him."

Colin was proud of himself. He'd told the outrageous lie without laughing.

She couldn't believe he would think she would believe such nonsense. She could feel him shaking, knew he was still reacting to the upsetting fight, and decided to placate him.

"If you say so," she agreed. She let out a pent-up sigh and relaxed against him. "You forgot to open the window, didn't you?"

"Yes," he lied. "I forgot."

She peeked up to look over his shoulder. "You're certain Raymond caught him?"

He didn't hear the amusement in her voice. "Absolutely certain."

He tightened his hold on her and leaned down to kiss the top of her head.

"Did they hurt you?" he asked, his voice harsh with worry over that possibility.

She found comfort in his concern. "No," she whispered against his chest.

She caught a movement out of the corner of her eye and looked around Colin again. "The other one's crawling away."

"Caine's waiting for him," he answered. He leaned down to kiss her again. She turned her face up at the same time. The temptation was too great to resist. His mouth covered hers in a gentle caress, but it wasn't enough for him. He deepened the kiss, pleased he didn't have to force her mouth open for him. His tongue swept inside to mate with hers and a low, primitive growl sounded in the back of his throat.

The kiss consumed her. Because she was so inexperienced, she couldn't control her response to his magical touch. She couldn't get enough of the taste of him either, and, dear God, his scent—so clean, so wonderfully masculine—was extremely arousing.

Her uninhibited response was almost shattering to his own control. Colin knew it was time to stop. He tried to pull back, but Alesandra wouldn't cooperate with his noble plan. She wound her arms around his neck and tugged on his hair to get him to deepen the kiss again.

He let her have her way. She sighed into his mouth seconds before her tongue timidly rubbed against his. Colin felt his discipline slipping away. His mouth slanted over hers again and again with hard demand.

"Is everything . . . for the love of . . . save that for after the ceremony, Colin."

Caine's voice cut through the passionate haze surrounding Colin and Alesandra. He slowly pulled back. She took a little longer to recover her wits. Colin had to help her take her hands away from the back of his neck. He tightened the belt on her robe, too. She didn't take over the task, but watched as he adjusted her robe to hide every inch of her neck.

"You should get dressed now," he suggested in a whisper, smiling over the look of bemusement on her face. She still hadn't recovered from his touch, and that fact pleased the hell out of him.

"Didn't you hear me?" he asked when she didn't move.

She knew she had to get hold of herself. She took a step back, away from the cause of her befuddled condition. "Yes, I should get dressed," she agreed with a nod. She immediately contradicted herself by shaking her head. "I can't get dressed. They . . ."

"I'll be happy to help you," Jade volunteered. Colin's sister-in-law was frowning with worry and sympathy. "It won't take any time at all," she promised.

Alesandra turned and forced a smile. She was surprised to find both Caine and Jade standing only a few feet away. She hadn't heard either one of them come into the room.

Colin's kiss had blocked out the world, she decided, and, Lord, had they seen the way she'd been clinging to him? She blushed just thinking about that possibility.

She was suddenly so rattled she couldn't seem to think. There was something she wanted to say, but she couldn't remember what it was. She threaded her fingers through her hair in an absentminded gesture. The robe parted just a little with her movement. Colin immediately stepped forward to tug it back into place. He was acting like a possessive husband now. She might have thought that was an endearing action if he hadn't started frowning at her.

"You shouldn't be entertaining in your robe," he told her. "Didn't the nuns teach you anything?"

He wasn't jesting. She slapped his hand away from her throat and backed up another space. "Did you catch the man crawling down the steps?" she asked Caine.

"Yes."

"Good," she whispered. "They came in with the flowers," she added with a nod. "I should have realized . . . when they carried the vases upstairs, but I . . ."

Everyone waited for her to finish her explanation. After a minute or two they realized she wasn't going to say anything more.

"What happened to the other one?" Caine asked.

"Colin threw him out the window."

"Raymond caught him," Colin said.

Caine almost laughed until his brother tilted his head toward Alesandra. He immediately nodded agreement over the ridiculous lie. "That's good to know."

"Could there be more waiting in one of the other rooms?" Alesandra asked.

Colin answered her. "No."

"Your guards have made a thorough check of the house." Caine made that comment in an attempt to ease her fear. "There aren't any others."

Jade drew her husband's attention when she let out a little gasp. He turned to her and saw the tears in her eyes. "What is it, sweetheart?" he asked in a whisper.

Jade pointed to the floor in front of the wardrobe. Caine turned, saw the wedding gown, and let out a low expletive.

Alesandra wasn't paying any attention to anyone but Colin. She'd only just decided that there was something different about him, but she couldn't seem to put her finger on what that might be.

"We're getting married in ten minutes, Alesandra. If you're still wearing that robe, you'll be wed in it. Caine, change jackets with me. I tore mine."

"I don't think it's a good idea to get married today," Alesandra whispered.

"Ten minutes," Colin repeated.

The set of his jaw told her he wasn't going to listen to reason. She still gave it one last try. "No," she announced, her expression mutinous.

He leaned down until he was just inches from her face. "Yes."

She let out a sigh. Then she nodded. Colin was so pleased she had finally decided to cooperate, he gave her a hard kiss. Then he turned and walked toward the doorway.

"They destroyed her wedding dress, Colin."

Jade gave him that news. Alesandra burst into tears. Everyone believed she was upset about the dress, of course, but that wasn't the real reason she was so distraught. She had just noticed what was different about Colin.

"You cut your hair."

The fury in her voice stunned Colin. He turned around, saw the tears streaming down her face, and immediately wanted to comfort her. As soon as he started toward her, she started backing away. He stopped so she would stand still. He didn't want her to accidentally step on a piece of glass. He didn't want her to panic, either, and she appeared ready to do just that.

Alesandra had gone through a hell of an ordeal and that, added to the usual wedding day jitters he assumed most brides experienced, was making her act unreasonable now.

Colin knew he would never get her downstairs and married until he helped her calm down first. He decided that if she wanted to talk about his hair now instead of focusing on the real issue upsetting her, he would let her.

"Yes," he said, his voice as soothing as he could manage. "I cut my hair. Does that displease you?"

She nodded. "Oh, yes, it does displease me," she said, her voice shaking with her anger. "As a matter of fact, it makes me furious."

She could tell from his expression he didn't understand why she was so angry with him. He obviously didn't remember what he'd told her when she'd asked him why he wore his hair so long.

Freedom. Yes, that's what he'd told her. She remembered every word of his explanation. The shoulder-length hair reminded him that he was a free man.

Alesandra turned her attention to his feet. "Why aren't you wearing shackles, Colin?"

"What are you talking about?" Colin hadn't been able to keep his exasperation out of his voice.

"She's upset about the dress," Caine decided.

"Do stay out of this," Alesandra ordered.

Caine raised an eyebrow over that command. Alesandra was acting very like a princess now, and she was treating Caine like one of her subjects. He didn't dare smile, fearing his amusement would push her temper right over the edge. She looked furious, and miserable.

"Oh, Lord, look what you've made me do," she told Colin. She folded her arms in front of her and glared at him before turning to his brother. "Pray forgive me for snapping at you. I don't usually let anyone notice when I'm upset, but that man makes me forget Mother Superior's golden rules. I wouldn't be in such a state if he hadn't cut his hair."

"That man?" Caine repeated with a grin.

"What golden rules?" Jade asked, curious over that remark.

"Isn't the wedding dress the reason you're so upset?"

"Dignity and decorum," Alesandra explained to Jade before turning back to Colin. "No, it isn't really the dress," she announced. She took a deep breath and ordered herself to calm down. Colin couldn't help being such an insensitive clout, she supposed, and he was giving up his freedom. "Oh, never mind. Yes, of course I'm upset about the dress. Your mother's going to be most upset. She paid a fortune for that lace. It will break her heart if she finds out it was destroyed."

"Then you're worried about my mother's feelings?" Colin asked, trying to get to the heart of the issue.

"Didn't I just say I was? Colin, how can you smile at a time like this? I don't have anything to wear."

"Surely . . ."

She wouldn't let him finish. "Promise me you won't tell your mother," Alesandra demanded. "I want your word, Colin. It would ruin her wedding if she finds out."

"It's your wedding, Alesandra, not hers."

She didn't want to listen to reason. "Promise me."

Colin let out a sigh. "I won't tell her." He didn't add that his mother was damn well going to notice Alesandra wasn't wearing the gown. She was still too rattled to think about that, and he wasn't going to remind her.

She made Jade and Caine promise, too. Everyone's quick agreement calmed Alesandra. Colin had to shake his head over her bizarre behavior. He grabbed her by her shoulders, pulled her close, and kissed her. Then he let go of her and walked out of the room. His brother followed him.

"She seems a little nervous, doesn't she?" Colin remarked to Caine.

His brother burst into laughter. "I can't imagine why," he replied dryly. "Your bride has been mauled, nearly kidnapped by two of the ugliest bastards I've ever laid eyes on, and certainly terrorized. She has also made it perfectly clear she doesn't want to marry you, and her wedding dress was torn into shreds. No, I can't imagine why she would be nervous."

Colin's shoulders slumped. "It has been a difficult day," he muttered.

"It can only get better," Caine predicted. He hoped to God he was right.

Neither brother said another word until they reached the foyer. They exchanged jackets on the way down the stairs. The fit was almost exact, for Colin had filled out through his shoulders over the past few years and was now every bit as muscular as his brother.

Colin noticed the crowd gathered in the salon, started to go inside, then suddenly stopped and turned to Caine.

"You're wrong."

"It won't get better?"

Colin shook his head. "You said Alesandra didn't want to marry me. You're wrong. She does."

Caine smiled. "So you realize she's in love with you?"

He'd made that remark as a statement of fact, but Colin treated it as though it were a question. "No, she doesn't love me yet, but she will. In five years, after I've made my fortune, then she'll realize she didn't make a mistake."

Caine couldn't believe his brother could be so obtuse. "She already has a fortune, Colin. She needs . . ."

"To get married," Colin finished for him. "What are all those people doing here?"

The switch in topics was deliberate, of course. Colin

didn't want to get into a heated discussion about Alesandra's motives now. He didn't particularly want to think about his own reasons for marrying her, either.

The ceremony took place an hour later. Colin stood with his brother in front of the minister. The wait for his bride was taking its toll on him, and it was a struggle to hold on to his composure. His own agitation was appalling to him, for he liked to believe that he was a man who was always in control. Nothing ever rattled him, he reminded himself. Hell, he admitted with a sigh, he was rattled now, and the feeling was so foreign to his nature he didn't know how to fight it. He blamed his lack of discipline on Alesandra. Until the day she came into his life, the mere idea of marrying made him blanch. Now, however, his agitation was for the opposite reason. He wanted to get the deed done before anything else could go wrong.

He could still lose her.

"For the love of God, Colin. This is a wedding, not a burial. Quit scowling."

Colin wasn't in the mood to accommodate his brother. His mind was occupied thinking about all the things that could still go wrong.

And then the Duke of Williamshire escorted Alesandra into the salon. She held on to his father, but Colin didn't give him any notice. His gaze was centered on his bride. The closer she came, the more his composure returned. A feeling of contentment rid him of his need to worry, and by the time she reached his side he wasn't scowling at all.

She was going to belong to him.

Alesandra was so nervous she was shaking. She wore an ivory-colored satin gown. The cut was simple, yet elegant. The neckline wasn't overly revealing, but it was still provocative. Alesandra wasn't wearing any jewels. She didn't carry flowers in her hands, and her hair wasn't confined with pins. The dark curls that gently swayed around her shoulders when she moved were all the adornment she needed.

Dear God, she pleased him. He smiled over her shyness. She wouldn't look at him, but kept her gaze downcast, even when her guardian kissed her cheek. She didn't want to let go of him, either. He had to pry her hand away and place it on Colin's arm.

The crowd of family and friends gathered around them. Alesandra almost bolted then and there. She felt trapped, overwhelmed, and terrified that both she and Colin were making a mistake. Her trembling increased until she could barely stand still, and she couldn't seem to catch a proper breath. Then Colin took her hand in his and tightened his hold on her. Odd, but his touch made her trembling ease a little.

Caine's four-year-old daughter helped Alesandra get rid of the rest of her fear. The little girl couldn't see what was going on and squirmed her way through the crowd to stand next to Alesandra. She pretended she didn't see her mother frantically shaking her head at her and reached up to take hold of Alesandra's hand.

The minister had just opened his book of prayers when he happened to glance down and see the child. He immediately coughed to cover his amusement.

Alesandra wasn't as disciplined. She took one look at the dark-haired, green-eyed imp and burst into laughter. Olivia had obviously been having the time of her life and whoever was suppose to be watching her hadn't done his duty. The child was a disaster. The lower part of her skirt was smudged with dirt, indicating she'd spent some of her time running in the garden, and there was another spot the color of the red punch the duchess planned to serve after the ceremony, indicating she'd gotten into the kitchen too. The sash was hanging down around her hips, but what made Alesandra completely lose her composure was Olivia's fat pink bow. It was precariously perched over her right eye, and while she smiled up at Alesandra, she kept trying to bat the thing back on top of her head.

Jade was probably having heart palpitations over Olivia's appearance. Caine bent down and tried to reach behind both Colin and Alesandra to grab hold of his daughter. She wiggled back and giggled with delight.

Alesandra took charge. She couldn't do anything about the smudges on Olivia's dress, but she could straighten her appearance. She pulled away from Colin's hold, retied Olivia's sash, then repinned the bow on top of her head. Olivia suffered through the minute of fussing, and when Alesandra finished, she took hold of her hand again.

She straightened back up and turned to the minister. She still wouldn't look at Colin, but she reached over and brushed her fingers against his. He took the hint and held her hand again.

She was in control now. Her voice barely shivered when she answered the minister's questions. She noticed that as soon as she agreed to become Colin's wife, he visibly relaxed. She looked up at him then and found him smiling at her. The sparkle in his eyes made her heart pound a bit quicker.

It was finally over. Colin gently turned her to face him and leaned down to kiss her. Everyone cheered, and Colin had only just brushed his mouth over hers when he was pounded on his back and pulled away to be congratulated.

He took Alesandra with him. He wasn't going to let her out of his sight . . . or his touch. He put his arm around her waist and pulled her up against his side.

Alesandra didn't remember much of the celebration that followed the ceremony. She felt as though she were walking around in a fog. Toasts were given before, during, and after the supper, but she couldn't remember anything that was said. She was surrounded by Colin's family and friends, and their immediate acceptance of her was both pleasing and overwhelming.

Sir Richards insisted on having a word with Colin and his brother in the library, but Colin kept putting him off. The director wouldn't be denied, however, and finally, after Alesandra promised to stay within sight of her guards, Colin agreed. He and Caine followed the director up the stairs. They had their conference and were back downstairs less than fifteen minutes later.

Colin found his bride in the salon. She was trying to listen to three different conversations at the same time. Marian Rose was demanding permission to go home with her, Catherine was asking her when she would see her again, and

Colin's father was telling anyone who would listen an amusing childhood story involving his sons.

Alesandra looked overwhelmed by it all. Colin decided it was time to take her home. She didn't argue with his decision and, in fact, seemed relieved.

It took twenty minutes to say thank you and farewell, and just when Colin's patience was all used up, they were in the carriage and on their way back to his town house.

The silence inside the carriage was a stark contrast to the chaos they'd just left. Colin stretched out his long legs, closed his eyes, and grinned.

He was thinking about the wedding night.

Alesandra sat across from him. Her posture was rigid and her hands were tightly folded together in her lap.

She was also thinking about their wedding night.

Colin opened his eyes and saw her frown. He noticed she was wringing her hands together, too.

"Is something wrong?" he asked, already guessing what that might be.

"Tonight . . ."

"Yes?"

"Are you going to insist I share your bed?"

"Yes."

Her shoulders slumped. The color left her face and, damn, she looked forlorn. He almost laughed. He caught himself in time, and he felt like a cad for finding any amusement at all in her distress. She was innocent, obviously frightened of the unknown, and it was his duty to help her get over her fear, not increase it.

He leaned forward and captured her hands in his. "It's going to be all right," he told her, his voice a husky whisper.

The look she gave him told him she didn't believe him. "Then you aren't interested in renegotiating?"

"Renegotiating what?"

"Your benefits."

He slowly shook his head. She pulled her hands away from him. "Alesandra, everything will be fine," he told her again.

"So you say," she countered in a bare whisper. "But I don't have any information to prove you're right. Do you happen to have any material on the subject I could read before going to bed?"

He leaned back, propped his leg against the opposite seat, and stared at her. To his credit, he didn't smile. "What kind of material?"

"I thought you might have a manual . . . or something," she explained. She was trying to stop herself from twisting her hands together so he wouldn't notice how nervous she was. "Just something that would explain what's going to happen," she added with a deliberate shrug. "I'm only mildly curious, you understand."

He understood she was completely terrified. He nodded so she would think he believed her lie, then asked in a casual tone of voice, "Didn't you say that the mother superior told you everything you needed to know?"

She didn't answer him for a long while. Colin patiently waited. Alesandra turned to look out the window. It was dark outside, but the moon was bright enough for her to recognize the street they were on and to realize they were almost home. She wasn't going to panic, she told herself. She was a fully grown woman and it was ridiculous to get so upset.

"Alesandra, answer me," Colin ordered.

She tried to hide her embarrassment and sound nonchalant when she finally explained. "Mother Superior did have a private talk with me, but now I realize she didn't give me sufficient information."

"Exactly what did she tell you?"

She didn't want to continue with this topic and was sorry she'd ever brought it up. "Oh, this and that," she whispered with a shrug.

Colin wouldn't let it go. "Exactly what this and that?"

The carriage came to a stop in front of his town house. She all but lunged for the latch. Colin grabbed her hand and held it. "You haven't answered me yet," he reminded her.

She stared at his hand on top of hers. It was at least twice the size of her own and, dear God, why hadn't she paid attention to his size before? She hadn't thought she'd be sharing his bed, she reminded herself. At least not for years and years, until she'd grown comfortable with the idea . . . and, Lord, how naive that ignorant belief was. Alesandra suddenly felt like a complete fool.

She really should have insisted on becoming a nun after all, she decided.

"Mother Superior said I wasn't suited for the holy order." She blurted that thought aloud, then let out a sigh. "I'm not humble enough. She told me so."

She was deliberately trying to turn the topic. Colin knew exactly what she was up to, of course. "And what did she tell you about the marriage bed?"

She turned her gaze back to his hand when she finally answered. "She said that a woman's body is like a temple. There, I've told it. Now will you let go of me? I wish to get out."

"Not yet," he countered. The tenderness in his voice cut through some of her embarrassment.

"You're going to make me tell it all, aren't you?"

He smiled over the disgruntled look on her face. "Yes," he agreed. "I'm going to make you tell it all."

"Colin, you probably haven't noticed, but this topic embarrasses me."

"I noticed."

She heard the thread of amusement in his voice but refused to look up at him, for she knew that if she saw him smiling, she would probably start in screaming.

"Are you embarrassed?" she asked.

"No."

She tried to pull her hand away from his again. He held tight. Lord, he was stubborn. She knew he wasn't going to let her out of the carriage until she explained.

"Men will want to worship there," she blurted out.

"Where?" he asked, his confusion obvious.

"At the temple," she told him in a near shout.

He didn't laugh. He let go of her hand and leaned back. His leg effectively blocked her exit in the event she still wanted to bolt. "I see," he replied. He kept his voice as neutral as possible, hoping his casual attitude would ease her distress.

The color had come back into her face with a vengeance. She looked like she was suffering from sunburn now. Colin found her innocence incredibly pleasing.

"What else did she tell you?" he asked.

"I mustn't let them."

"Worship?"

She nodded. "I mustn't let anyone touch me until I married. Then Mother Superior assured me it was all right because the result of the union was worthy and noble."

She glanced up to see how he was reacting to her explanation, noticed his incredulous expression, and thought he didn't quite understand. "A child is the worthy result."

"I gathered as much."

Alesandra sat back and turned her attention to straightening the folds in her gown. A long minute passed in silence before Colin spoke again. "She left out a few details, didn't she?"

"Yes," Alesandra whispered. She was relieved Colin finally understood her lack of knowledge. "If there was a book or a manual I could read . . ."

"I don't have anything on the topic in my study," he told her. "I don't even know if there is such a thing in print."

"But surely . . ."

"Oh, there are books around, but not the kind I would ever allow you to read," he said with a nod. "They aren't sold on the open market, either."

Colin reached over, flipped the latch up, and pushed the door open. He kept his gaze on his blushing bride all the while.

"What do you suggest I do?"

She asked her lap that question. He nudged her chin up and forced her to look at him. Her blue eyes were cloudy with worry. "I suggest you trust me."

It sounded more like an order than a suggestion to her. She decided she was going to have to trust him, however, for the simple reason that she didn't have any other options available to her. She gave him a quick nod. "All right then. I'll trust you."

Her immediate agreement pleased him. Colin understood why she wanted to know beforehand exactly what was going to happen. It was a way for Alesandra to gain control. The more she knew, the less afraid she would be.

It was usual and customary for a young lady to get the needed information from her mother, of course. At least, Colin thought that was how it worked. He assumed his mother had spoken to his sister Catherine about the marriage act. Regardless, Alesandra's mother had died before her daughter was old enough to need such knowledge.

And so one of the nuns had tried to take over the duty. "Exactly how old is this mother superior?" he asked.

"She looks eighty, but I imagine she's probably younger," Alesandra replied. "I never dared ask her. Why do you ask?"

"Never mind," he said. He turned the topic back to her worry. "Alesandra, I'm going to explain everything you need to know."

The tenderness in his voice felt like a soothing stroke against her cheek. "You will?"

"Yes," he promised almost absentmindedly. His mind was occupied trying to picture the ancient nun explaining the facts of life to Alesandra, using such descriptive words as *temple* and *worship.* Lord, he wished he'd been there to hear the private discussion.

Alesandra saw the sparkle in Colin's eyes and immediately jumped to the conclusion that her naïveté amused him.

"I'm sorry I'm acting so . . . inexperienced."

"You are inexperienced," he gently reminded her.

"Yes, and I'm sorry."

Colin laughed. "I'm not," he told her.

"You'll really answer all my questions?" she asked, still not certain she believed him. "You won't leave anything out? I don't like surprises."

"I won't leave anything out."

She let out a sigh. She quit twisting the wrinkles in her gown, too. Colin's promise had just helped her regain control of her fear. She didn't even mind that he found her embarrassment amusing. He was going to give her the necessary information and that was all that counted. Her relief made her weak with gratitude.

"Well, then, it's going to be all right," she announced. "Shouldn't we get out of the carriage now?"

Colin agreed. He jumped out first, then turned to assist Alesandra. Both the guards were frowning with obvious concern for their princess. They wanted her under lock and key.

Flannaghan hovered in the doorway, waiting to greet his new mistress. He took her cloak from her, draped it over his arm, and then gave her his heartfelt congratulations.

"If you would like to go upstairs now I'll prepare your bathwater, Princess," he suggested.

The idea of a long hot bath after the stress-filled day appealed to her. It would be her second today, but Mother Superior had told her that cleanliness was next to godliness, so she didn't feel at all decadent.

"Colin's going to have a talk with me in the study," she told Flannaghan. "I'll have my bath after."

"Have your bath first," Colin suggested. "I have some papers to look over."

It was a lie, of course. Colin didn't have any intention of working on his wedding night, but he thought a bath might help relax Alesandra, and she looked in need of the diversion.

It had been one hell of a wedding day for her, and even though she appeared to be a little less worried and a little more in control of her emotions now, he knew her nerves were still frayed.

"As you wish," Alesandra agreed. She turned to follow the butler up the steps. Colin was right behind her.

"Was it a beautiful wedding?" Flannaghan asked.

"Oh, yes," Alesandra answered, her voice filled with enthusiasm. "Everything went quite well. Didn't it, Colin?"

"You were almost kidnapped," he reminded her.

"Yes, but other than that, it was wonderful, wasn't it?"

"And terrorized."

"Yes, but . . ."

"They destroyed your wedding dress."

She stopped on the top step and whirled around to glare at him. She obviously didn't want to be reminded of those incidents.

"Every bride wishes to believe her wedding was perfect," she announced.

He winked at her. "Then it was perfect," he announced.

She smiled, satisfied.

Flannaghan waited until he and Alesandra were alone in her bedroom to nag the details out of her. Raymond and Stefan carried in additional buckets of hot, steaming water to fill the oval tub. The butler had thoughtfully unpacked her clothes and had placed a white gown and wrapper on her bed.

She took her time in the bath. The hot water relaxed her and helped ease the tension out of her shoulders. She washed her hair with the rose-scented soap, then sat by the hearth to dry it. Alesandra didn't worry about hurrying because she knew Colin was busy working and had probably already lost track of the time.

At least an hour had passed before she decided to interrupt him. Her hair was completely dry, but after she put on her robe, she took another ten minutes or so brushing the curls again. She was yawning every other minute. The hot bath, added to the heat radiating from the fire in the hearth, made her drowsy, and she didn't want to fall asleep during Colin's explanation.

She went down the hallway to the study. She knocked on the door, then walked inside. Colin wasn't at his desk. Alesandra wasn't certain if he'd gone into his bedroom or downstairs. She decided to wait in the study for him, assuming he would want to have his talk with her there, and went over to the desk to collect a sheet of paper. She was just reaching for the pen and inkwell when Colin appeared in the doorway to his bedroom.

The sight of him took her breath away. Colin had obviously just had a bath too, for his hair was still damp. He wasn't dressed, but wore only a pair of black pants. They weren't buttoned.

He had a powerful build. His skin was beautifully bronzed and the bulge of sinewy strength hiding under the sleek exterior reminded her of a panther. The roped muscles rolled ever so slightly when he moved. His chest was covered with a thick mat of dark curly hair that tapered to a **V** at his waist.

She didn't look any lower.

Colin leaned against the doorframe, folded his arms across his chest, and smiled at her. A faint blush stained her cheeks. She was folding and refolding the sheet of paper in her hands and desperately trying to act nonchalant, and he knew he was going to have to take it slow and easy with her in order to help her keep her fear at bay. It was going to be a difficult undertaking, because Colin had never taken a virgin to his bed before and the sight of Alesandra in her white gown and robe was already sending heat coursing through his body. He was getting aroused just looking at her. His gaze was centered on her mouth and he was thinking what he would like her to do to him with those sweet, full, pouting lips.

"Colin, what are you thinking?"

He didn't believe it would be a good idea to tell her the truth. "I was wondering what you're doing with that paper," he lied instead.

Her concentration had become so scattered from her nervousness she had to look down at her hands before she understood what he was asking her. "Notes," she blurted out with a quick nod.

He raised an eyebrow. "Notes?"

"Yes. I thought I would take notes during your explanation so I won't forget anything important. Is that all right, Colin?"

The worry in her voice cut through his amusement. "How very organized of you," he said.

She smiled. "Thank you. My father was the first to teach me how important it is to be organized. Then Mother Superior took over my training."

Dear God, she wished she could quit rambling.

"How old were you when your father died?"

"Eleven."

"Yet you remember . . ."

"Oh, yes, I remember everything he taught me," she replied. "It was my way of pleasing him, Colin, and I thoroughly enjoyed the time we spent together. It made him happy to talk about his business transactions and it made me happy to be included."

She'd turned the sheet of paper into a wrinkled ball. Colin doubted she was aware of what she'd just done. "I'll only write down key words," she promised.

He slowly shook his head. "You won't need to take notes," he assured her. "You're going to remember everything I tell you."

He was feeling damn proud of himself. The urge to laugh had almost overwhelmed him, but he'd been able to contain himself.

"All right then." She turned back to the desk, started to put the sheet of paper back, and only then realized the mess she'd made. She tossed it into the trash basket, then turned back to stare at him.

The warm glint in his eyes made her shiver with pleasure and that wonderful lopsided grin of his made her heartbeat become quite frantic. She took a deep breath and ordered herself to calm down.

Dear God, he was beautiful. Without realizing what she was doing, she blurted that thought aloud.

He laughed in reaction to her praise. His amusement didn't upset her, though, and she found herself smiling back. "For a dragon," she teased.

The way he was looking at her made her feel as though butterflies were gathering inside her stomach. She needed to give her hands something to do, she decided, and immediately folded them together. "Are we going to have our talk now?"

"First things first," he announced. "I just realized I didn't give you a proper wedding kiss."

"You didn't?"

He shook his head. Then he crooked his finger at her. She

slowly walked across the room to stand directly in front of him.

"Are you going to kiss me now?" she asked, her voice a breathless whisper.

"Yeah."

He'd drawled out that admission. He slowly unfolded himself from the doorway to tower over her. She took an instinctive step back. She immediately stopped herself. She wasn't afraid of Colin, she reminded herself, and she really did want him to kiss her. She moved forward again. "I like the way you kiss me," she whispered.

"I know."

His grin was arrogant. He knew she was nervous, too. She didn't have any doubt about that. And he was enjoying her embarrassment, too.

"How do you know?" she asked, thinking to give him some clever reply once he answered.

"The way you respond to me tells me you like me to touch you."

She couldn't think of anything clever to say to that fact. In truth she was having trouble holding on to any thought. Colin was fully responsible for her condition, of course. The warmth in his gaze was making her stomach quiver.

She felt his hands on her waist, looked down, and watched him untie the belt to her robe. She tried to stop him, but before she'd even placed her hands on top of his, he was easing her robe off her shoulders.

"Why did you do that?"

"You look warm."

"Oh."

The robe dropped to the floor. Her gown was transparent enough for him to see the soft curves of her body. She tried to pull the folds of the garment close around the front of her. Colin didn't give her time to shield herself. He pulled her tight against him. "Put your arms around me, Alesandra. Hold me while I kiss you."

She wound her arms around his neck just as he leaned down and began to nibble on her lips. His tongue traced the inside of her lower lip, sending shivers down her spine. She tightened her hold and leaned up on tiptoes to try to deepen the kiss. Her breasts rubbed against his chest and she let out a broken sigh over the strange feeling of his skin against her. Her breasts suddenly felt heavy, tight, and her nipples hardened. It wasn't an unpleasant feeling, just strange and wonderful. She deliberately rubbed against him again, but ever so slightly so he wouldn't know what she was doing. She didn't want him to think she was bold. She wanted to be bold, though, for the heat from his hard body affected her like an aphrodisiac and she couldn't seem to get close enough to him.

He was driving her crazy teasing her lips with his tongue, his teeth. She couldn't put up with the gentle torment long. She tugged impatiently on his hair, telling him without words that she wanted more.

His mouth finally settled on top of hers in a gentle caress and his tongue eased inside to stroke hers. He acted as though he had all the time in the world. He was slow, deliberate, exerting only scant pressure as he nudged the fires of passion inside her.

Her soft moan told him how much she liked what he was doing to her. He pulled back, saw the passion in her eyes, knew it was mirrored in his own, and let out a low groan of his own. "So sweet," he whispered against her mouth. "Open up for me," he commanded in a rough whisper.

He didn't give her time to comply with that order but used his thumb to force her chin down. His tongue thrust inside, then retreated before penetrating again. She went all soft and willing on him, and that innocent response made him forget about going slow. He was suddenly so hungry for her he couldn't control his pace. His mouth became hard, demanding. The love play between their tongues—his bold, hers timid—made both of them shake with desire. She was too overwhelmed by the fire Colin was spreading inside her to be afraid of what was to come. She couldn't think, only react. She moved against him restlessly, unaware of what she was doing now, or what she was doing to him. Her fingers threaded through his hair, and his control almost snapped when she began to whimper and move so enticingly against his hard arousal. The kiss turned carnal, ravenous. Passion ignited into raw desire as his mouth slanted over hers with primal ownership. His hunger stroked her own.

The kiss seemed unending and yet over all too soon. When Colin pulled back, her mouth was rosy and wet from his touch. The taste of her was on his mouth now, but it wasn't enough for him.

She collapsed against his chest and tucked her face under his chin. Her breathing was choppy against his collarbone.

Colin lifted her into his arms and carried her into his room. He gently placed her in the center of his bed and then stood by the side, staring down at her. His hot gaze warmed her and made her shiver at the same time.

She felt drowsy from his kisses. Her mind cleared when he hooked his thumbs into the waistband of his pants and began to pull them off. She closed her eyes and tried to turn away from him. Colin was quicker than she was, however. He'd stripped out of his pants and joined her in the bed before she'd even made it to the other side.

He caught her by her nightgown. The fabric ripped when he pulled her back to him. She only had enough time to gasp before the gown was completely discarded and Colin was covering her with his body.

She became as rigid as a board. He gently pried her legs apart with his knee and then completely stretched out on top of her just the way he'd fantasized in his dreams since the moment he met her. His hard arousal pressed against the soft curls at the junction of her thighs, and it felt so damn good to him he let out a low growl of satisfaction.

Reality was better than fantasy, however, for he hadn't been able to imagine how incredibly soft and smooth her skin would feel against him. Her breasts were much fuller than he'd fantasized, and he hadn't been able to capture the intensity of his reaction to having her trembling underneath him. It was as close to heaven as he thought he'd ever be.

"Colin, shouldn't we have our talk now?"

He leaned up on his elbows to look at her. Worry was evident in her eyes; victory was evident in his.

"Absolutely." He cupped the sides of her face to hold her still, then kissed her long and hard.

He made her shiver with desire. She couldn't resist putting her arms around his waist to draw more of his warmth. Her toes curled against his legs and it suddenly wasn't enough to simply hold on to him. She needed to touch him, stroke him. Her hands moved up his back, then down the sides of his arms.

Her touch was as light as a butterfly's wings against his skin and yet it was the most erotic caress he'd ever received. He turned his attention to her neck. She turned her head ever so slightly to give him better access. His teeth gently tugged on her earlobe, sending jolts of pleasure cascading all the way down to her toes, and, dear God, his tongue was making it impossible to think.

She started moving with silent demand for more. Colin shifted his position and kissed a line down her throat. He moved lower and kissed the valley between her breasts. She smelled like roses and woman. It was a heady combination. Colin inhaled her sweet scent, then used his tongue to taste her.

He was taking entirely too many liberties with her body. She thought she would die if he stopped. His hands cupped her breasts and they immediately began to ache for more. She didn't understand the frustration building inside her. She felt as though she was made of seams and they were all splitting apart on her. Then Colin's tongue brushed across her nipple. She almost came off the bed. She cried out in fear and pleasure. The feeling was almost too intense to endure, yet it was exquisitely wonderful, too. Her hands dropped back to her sides and she grabbed fistfuls of the sheets in an attempt to anchor herself against the storm of emotions flooding her.

"Colin!"

His name came out with a sob and she began to writhe against him when he took her nipple into his mouth and began to suckle. He was driving her beyond control. His hands stroked her everywhere. She drew a deep, ragged breath and began to whimper. His mouth captured hers again just as his hand slid into the soft curls shielding her virginity. She tried to stop him, but he wouldn't be denied. His fingers slowly penetrated the tight, slick opening, then withdrew. The pad of his thumb rubbed against the very spot he knew would drive her wild.

He made love to her with his fingers until she was mindless to everything but finding fulfillment. Colin had never had a woman respond to him with such honesty. It made it impossible for him to hold on to his own discipline.

"Baby, you're so tight," he whispered, his own voice a harsh whisper.

She could barely concentrate on what he was telling her. "You're making me ache. Please . . ."

She didn't know what she wanted from him, only knew she would go mad if he didn't do something to ease the sweet torment.

He hoped to God she was ready for him. He pulled her hands away from the sheets and wrapped them around his neck. His knee nudged her thighs wider and then his hands slid under her hips to hold her close. The tip of his arousal was surrounded by her liquid heat. He slowly pressed inside her, paused when he felt the barrier of her virginity, and then tried to gently push past the obstacle. The barrier wouldn't give. Colin's jaw was clenched tight and his breathing was as ragged as though he'd just run a mile, for the pleasure was already so intense he could barely hold on to what little control he had left. He knew he was hurting her. She cried out against his mouth and tried to push him away at the same time.

He soothed her with honeyed words. "Sweetheart, it's going to be all right. The pain won't last long. Hold on to me. Oh, baby, don't move like that . . . not yet."

Trying to be gentle was only prolonging the pain for her . . . and it was killing him. His forehead was covered with perspiration and he knew he would go completely out of his mind if he didn't bury himself deep inside her.

He shifted his hold on her, lifted her hips, then thrust deep with one powerful surge. She cried out, her pain as intense now as his pleasure, and tried to push away from him again. His weight wouldn't allow any movement. His possession was complete and, dear God, she fit him like a second skin. He fought the urge to partially withdraw and then thrust back into her, for he wanted to give her time to adjust to him. Her nails scored his shoulderblades and he knew she was trying to get him to let her go. Colin tried to capture her mouth for another searing kiss, but she turned her head away from him. He kissed her ear instead, then her cheek, trying his damnedest to hold on to the remnants of his control long enough to rekindle the passion inside her. Tears streamed down her face and she let out a little broken sob.

"Sweetheart, don't cry. I'm sorry. God, I had to hurt you. It's going to get better in just a few minutes. You feel so damned good. Hold me, baby. Hold me."

The worry in his voice soothed her far more than his words. Pleasure warred with pain. She was so confused by the conflicting feelings, she didn't know what to do. She wanted him to stop and yet she wanted him to stay joined with her too. His breath was hot against her ear. Harsh, too. The sound excited her. She didn't understand what was happening to her. Her body was demanding release, but release from what? She didn't know. The urge to move was suddenly there, and every nerve inside her clamored in anticipation.

"I want to move." Her voice was a bare whisper of confusion.

Colin leaned up on his elbows to look at her. Her eyes shimmered with passion, but more important to him, she'd quit crying.

"I want to move, too. I want to pull out, then sink deep inside you again."

His voice was rough with emotion. She instinctively squeezed him tight. She decided to test just to make certain it really had gotten better. She'd felt as though he'd torn her apart a minute ago, but now the throbbing wasn't as intense, and when she moved restlessly against him, pain didn't result. The touch of splendor caught her by surprise.

"It's starting to feel . . . nice."

It was all the permission he needed. His control snapped. His mouth covered hers in a ravenous kiss. The hunger inside him raged out of control. He slowly withdrew from her, then thrust deep inside. The mating ritual consumed him, and when she tightened around him again and lifted her hips up to meet his thrusts, he buried his face against the side of her neck and let out a raw groan. The pressure building inside him was excruciatingly beautiful. Colin had never experienced anything like this before. Alesandra was like fire in his arms, and her wild, uninhibited response shook him to his very soul. She held nothing back, and that selfless act forced him to do the same. The bed squeaked in protest as he thrust inside her again and again. He was mindless to everything but giving both of them fulfillment.

It came upon them in a rush. She found her release first and when she instinctively squeezed him tight and arched against him, he gave in to his own orgasm.

It took her a long while to come back to reality. She clung to her husband and let the waves of blissful surrender wash over her. A part of her mind understood that as long as she was holding Colin, she was safe. She didn't have to worry about control. He would take care of her. Alesandra closed her eyes and let the wonder of their lovemaking consume her every thought.

She had never felt this safe, this free.

Colin was experiencing the opposite reaction. He was shaken by what had just happened to him, for he'd never allowed himself to completely abandon his control. Never. It scared the hell out of him. Her silky thighs had squeezed every thought out of his mind. She was the innocent, he experienced, and yet she'd been able to strip him of all his defenses. He hadn't been able to hold a part of himself back and toward the end, when they were both reaching for their fulfillment, he had been as much at her mercy as she at his—and, God help him, it had never been this good before. It scared the hell out of him.

For the first time in his life he felt vulnerable, trapped.

They were still joined together. Colin slowly withdrew before the feel of her made him hard again. He gritted his teeth against the pleasure that movement caused. He didn't have the strength to move away from her yet, but he knew his weight was probably crushing her. Her arms were wrapped around his neck. He reached up and gently pulled them away. He leaned down to kiss the base of her throat, felt her frantic heartbeat, and found arrogant male satisfaction then, for he realized she hadn't completely recovered either.

A minute later he rolled onto his back, away from her. He took a deep, shuddering breath and closed his eyes. The scent of their lovemaking permeated the air around them. The taste of her was still in his mouth and, God help him, he could feel himself getting hard again.

Alesandra finally roused herself from her thoughts and turned to him. She propped herself up on one elbow to look at him.

His scowl stunned her. "Colin?" she whispered. "Are you all right?"

He turned his head to look at her. Within a bare second, his expression changed. Colin wasn't about to let her see his vulnerability. He smiled at her and then reached over to brush the back of his hand against the side of her face. She leaned into his caress.

"I'm supposed to ask you if *you're* all right," he explained.

She looked more than all right to him. Her eyes were still shimmering with passion, her mouth looked swollen from his kisses, her hair was draped over one shoulder, and Colin thought she was the sexiest woman in the world.

"I hurt you, didn't I?"

She slowly nodded. She noticed he didn't seem overly worried about that fact. "I was . . ."

"Hot?"

She blushed. He laughed. Then he pulled her into his arms and let her hide her face against his chest. "It's a little late to become embarrassed, isn't it? Or have you forgotten how wild you were a few minutes ago?"

She hadn't forgotten. She blushed to the roots of her hair just thinking about her wanton reaction. His chest rumbled with amusement. She didn't mind that he was laughing at her. The most wonderful thing in the world had just happened to her and she wasn't going to let anything ruin it. A warm glow still surrounded her, making her feel both blissful and sleepy.

"I wasn't very dignified, was I?"

"Do you mean you weren't dignified when you begged me not to stop?"

He rubbed her backside in a lazy fashion while he waited for her answer.

"I did do that, didn't I?"

The wonder in her voice made him smile. "Yes," he drawled out. "You did."

She sighed. "It was nice, wasn't it?"

He laughed. "It was a whole lot better than nice."

Long minutes passed in silence. He broke the peaceful interlude when he let out a loud yawn.

"Colin? Did I . . . was I . . ."

She couldn't seem to finish her question. Her own vulnerability made her too timid to find out if she had been satisfactory.

He knew what she needed from him now. "Alesandra?"

The way he whispered her name felt like a caress. "Yes?"

"You were perfect."

"It's good of you to say so."

She relaxed against him and closed her eyes. The sound of his heartbeat mingled with his soft laughter soothed her. His one hand stroked her back and his other gently rubbed her neck. She was just drifting off to sleep when he called her name again.

"Hmm?"

"Would you like me to begin explaining now?"

He waited several minutes before he realized she'd fallen asleep. His fingers threaded through her hair and he shifted positions just a little so he could kiss the top of her head. "A woman's body is like a temple," he whispered.

He didn't expect an answer and didn't get one. He pulled the covers up, wrapped his arms around his bride, and closed his eyes.

His last thought before he drifted off to sleep made him

smile. The nun really had been right when she'd told Alesandra men would want to worship.

He sure as certain had.

He was neither mad nor out of control. He still had a conscience. He simply chose not to listen to it. Yes, he knew what he was doing was wrong. It still mattered to him, or at least it had mattered that first time. She had rejected him and had deserved to die. Rage had guided his hands, his dagger. He'd only wanted to kill her. He hadn't expected the rush, hadn't known how powerful he would feel, how invincible.

He could stop. He raised his glass and took a long drink. He would stop, he vowed.

His scarred boots were in the corner. He stared at them a long minute before making up his mind to throw them away tomorrow. There were flowers on the table . . . waiting . . . ready . . . taunting him.

He hurled the glass at the hearth. Glass splintered to the ground. He reached for the bottle while he chanted his promise.

He would stop.

Chapter 9

Alesandra awoke late the next morning. Colin had already left the bedroom. It was just as well because she didn't want him to see her pitiful condition. She was so stiff and sore, she groaned like an old woman when she got out of bed. And no wonder, she thought to herself when she saw the stains of blood on the sheets. No one had warned her that making love would cause her to bleed. She frowned with worry and irritation then, for it was a fact that no one had told her anything. Was it a usual occurrence to bleed? What if it wasn't usual at all? What if Colin had accidentally torn something that couldn't be repaired?

She tried not to panic and succeeded until she bathed. The tenderness and the additional blood on the washcloth frightened her, though. She was embarrassed, too. She didn't want Flannaghan to see the stains when he changed the sheets, so she stripped the bed herself.

Alesandra continued to fret while she dressed. She put on a pale blue dress and matching soft leather shoes. The gown had a white border along the square neckline and around the cuffs of the long sleeves. It was a very feminine dress and one of Alesandra's favorites. She brushed her hair until it crackled with curl, then went in search of her husband.

Their first encounter in the light of day after the intimacy they had shared the night before was going to be awkward for her and she wanted to get it over with as soon as possible. If she tried, she was certain she would be able to hide her embarrassment.

Colin was sitting at his desk in the study. The door facing the corridor was open. She stood in the entrance, debating whether she should interrupt him or not. He must have felt her gaze on him, however, because he suddenly looked up. He was still frowning with concentration over the letter he was reading, but his expression quickly changed. Tenderness came into his eyes when he smiled at her.

She thought she might have smiled back. She couldn't be certain. Dear Lord, was she ever going to become accustomed to having him around? He was such a handsome man. His shoulders seemed wider to her today, his hair appeared darker, his skin more bronzed. The white shirt he wore accentuated his appeal. It was a stark contrast to his coloring. Her gaze turned to his mouth and she was suddenly flooded with memories of how it had felt to be kissed by him . . . everywhere.

Alesandra hastily lowered her gaze to his chin. She wasn't about to let him know how embarrassed she was feeling. She would be dignified and sophisticated.

"Good morning, Colin." Her voice croaked like a frog. Her face felt as though it was on fire. Retreat seemed the only choice. She would try to face him later, when she was more in control. "I can see you're busy," she told him in a rush as she backed away. "I'll go on downstairs."

She turned and started to walk away. "Alesandra."

"Yes?"

"Come here."

She walked back to the entrance. Colin leaned back in his chair and crooked his finger at her. She straightened her shoulders, forced a smile, and walked inside. She stopped when she reached his desk. That wasn't good enough for him. He motioned her over to his side. She maintained her nonchalant attitude as she circled the desk. Colin was never going to know how awkward she was feeling.

He looked at her for a long minute. "Are you going to tell me what's the matter with you?"

Her shoulders slumped a little. "You're a difficult man to fool," she remarked.

He frowned. "Since you're never going to try to fool me, that fact isn't significant, is it?"

"No."

He waited another minute or two, and when she didn't explain, he asked her again. "Tell me what's bothering you."

She turned her gaze to the floor. "This is . . . awkward for me, seeing you after . . ."

"After what?"

"Last night."

A faint blush turned her cheeks pink. Colin found her reaction delightful—arousing, too. He pulled her onto his lap, then nudged her chin up and smiled at her. "And?" he prodded.

"In the light of day, the memory of what we did together makes me feel a little embarrassed."

"The memory makes me want you again."

Her eyes widened over his gruff confession. "But you can't."

"Sure I can," he told her cheerfully.

She shook her head. "I can't," she whispered.

He frowned. "Why can't you?"

Her blush felt as though it was burning her skin. "Isn't it enough that I tell you I can't?"

"Hell, no, it isn't enough."

She turned her gaze to her lap. "You're making this difficult," she remarked. "If my mother was here I could talk to her, but . . ."

She didn't continue. The sadness in her voice made him forget his irritation. She was worrying about something and he was determined to find out what it was. "You can talk to me," he said. "I'm your husband, remember? We shouldn't have any secrets between us. You liked making love," he added with a nod.

He sounded terribly arrogant to her. "Perhaps," she replied, just to prick his temper.

He let her see his exasperation. "Perhaps? You came apart in my arms," he whispered. The memory made his own voice harsh. "Have you forgotten so soon?"

"No. I haven't forgotten. Colin, you hurt me."

She blurted out that truth and waited for him to apologize. She would tell him about her injury then and he would understand why he couldn't touch her again.

"Baby, I know I hurt you."

The heat in his voice, so rough, so masculine, made her shiver. She shifted in his lap. He immediately grabbed hold of her hips to hold her still. She didn't have any idea what the conversation was doing to him, of course—having her sweet bottom rubbing so intimately against him made him hard with desire.

Alesandra wasn't embarrassed any longer. She was irritated because she had just realized her husband was callous in his attitudes. He didn't seem at all contrite.

The disgruntled look on her face made him smile. "Sweetheart," he began, his voice soothing now. "It won't hurt like that again."

She shook her head. She wouldn't look into his eyes and turned her gaze to his chin. "You don't understand," she whispered. "Something . . . happened."

"What happened?" he asked, holding on to his patience.

"I bled. It was on the sheets and I . . ."

He finally understood. Colin wrapped his arms around her and pulled her against his chest. He had two purposes in mind. One, he wanted to hold her, and two, he didn't want her to see his smile. She might think he was laughing at her.

She didn't want his embrace at all, but he was much stronger than she was and much more determined. He was going to soothe her whether she wanted him to or not. When she finally gave in and relaxed against him, he let out a sigh and rubbed his chin against the top of her head. "And you thought something was wrong, didn't you? I should have explained. I'm sorry. You've been worrying for no reason."

The tenderness in his voice calmed her fear just a little. She still wasn't certain she believed him, though. "Are you telling me I was supposed to bleed?"

She sounded suspicious—and appalled at the very idea. Colin didn't laugh. "Yes," he announced. "You were supposed to bleed."

"But that's . . . barbaric."

He disagreed with that opinion. He told her he found it both pleasing and arousing, and she immediately announced that he was barbaric, too.

Alesandra had lived in a cocoon with the nuns. She'd arrived as a little girl and left as a woman. She hadn't been allowed to talk to anyone about the changes taking place in her body or talk about the feelings those changes evoked, and Colin counted himself blessed because her sensuality hadn't been destroyed or marred. The mother superior might not have wanted to talk about sex, but she hadn't filled Alesandra's head with a lot of frightening nonsense. The nun had elevated the marriage act, too, by using such euphemisms as *temple* and *worship,* and even *noble* and *worthy,* and because of her attitude, Alesandra hadn't believed it was degrading or foul.

His sweet bride was like a butterfly emerging from her isolated shelter. Her own sensuality and her passionate response probably scared the hell out of her.

"I'm fortunate the nuns didn't warp you by planting fears in your head," he remarked.

"Why would they?" she asked, clearly puzzled. "The wedding vows we took are sacred. It would have been a sin to mock the sacrament."

Colin was so pleased with her, he hugged her. He apologized again because she had fretted needlessly, and then explained in detail exactly why she was supposed to bleed. He didn't stop there. The mother superior had told Alesandra that a child was the noble and worthy result of the union. Colin explained exactly how conception occurred. He talked about the differences in their bodies while he rubbed her back in a lazy fashion. The spontaneous lecture lasted nearly twenty minutes. She'd been embarrassed when he began his explanation, but his matter-of-fact attitude soon helped her get over her shyness. She was extremely curious about his body and plied him with questions. He answered all of them.

She was vastly relieved when he'd finished. She leaned away from him, thinking to give him her thank you for explaining, but the warm glint in his eyes made her forget what she was about to say. She kissed him instead.

"Did you honestly believe we would never . . ."

She wouldn't let him finish. "I worried we couldn't."

"I want you now."

"I'm too tender," she whispered. "And you did just say it would take a few days to feel better."

"There are other ways to find fulfillment."

Her curiosity was pricked. "There are?" she asked in a breathless whisper.

He nodded. "Lots of ways."

The way he was staring at her made her restless with desire. A warm glow was forming in the pit of her stomach and she suddenly wanted to get a little closer to him. She put her arms around his neck, threaded her fingers through his hair, and smiled at him. "How many ways?"

"Hundreds," he exaggerated.

The way he was smiling at her told her he was teasing. She responded in kind. "Then I should probably take notes while you explain them to me. I wouldn't want to forget one or two."

He laughed. "Demonstration is more fun than taking notes."

"Begging your pardon, milord, but you have a visitor downstairs."

Alesandra almost jumped off Colin's lap when the sound of Flannaghan's voice reached her. Colin wouldn't let her go. He continued to look at his bride when he spoke to his servant. "Who is it?"

"Sir Richards."

"Damn."

"Don't you like him?" asked Alesandra.

Colin let out a sigh. He lifted Alesandra off his lap and stood up. "Sure I like him," he replied. "The damn was because I know he won't be put off. I'll have to see him. Flannaghan, send him up."

The butler immediately left to fetch the director. Alesandra turned to leave. Colin grabbed her hand and pulled her back. He put his arms around her, leaned down, and gave her a long kiss. His mouth was hot, wet, demanding, and when he pulled back, she was trembling with desire. Her uninhibited response pleased him. "Later," he whispered before he let her go.

The dark promise in his eyes left no doubt as to what he was talking about. Alesandra didn't trust her voice yet, so she simply nodded her agreement. She turned and walked out of the study. Her hands shook when she brushed her hair back over her shoulders and she bumped into the wall when she turned to go back down the hallway. She let out a little sigh over her own sorry condition. All the man had to do was look at her and her mind turned into lettuce. One kiss and she wilted in his arms.

It was a fanciful thought, she admitted, yet all too true. Perhaps, once the newness of having a husband had worn off, she would become accustomed to Colin. She certainly hoped so, for she didn't want to spend the rest of her life bumping into walls and walking around in a daze.

She didn't want to ever take him for granted either. That thought made her smile. Colin would never let her become lax. He was a demanding, lustful man, and if last night was any indication, she also had those same qualities.

Alesandra went back into Colin's bedroom and stood by one of the windows looking out. It was a glorious day and all because Colin wanted her. She must have been perfect last night, she thought to herself. It hadn't been idle praise on his part, or he wouldn't have wanted her so soon again today, would he?

Wanting and loving weren't the same. Alesandra understood that truth well enough. She thought of herself as a realist. Yes, Colin had married her because of duty. She couldn't change that fact. She couldn't make him love her either, of course, but she believed that in time his heart would belong to her. She had already become his friend, hadn't she?

It was going to be a good, strong marriage. Both of them had taken a vow in front of God and witnesses to live as husband and wife until death did they part. Colin was too honorable to break his commitment to her, and surely in the years to come he would learn to love her.

She was already falling in love with him. Alesandra immediately shook her head in denial. She wasn't ready to think about her own feelings.

Alesandra's own vulnerability frightened her. Marriage, she decided, was far more complex than she'd ever imagined.

"Princess Alesandra, will I disturb you if I put fresh sheets on the bed?"

She turned and smiled at Flannaghan. "I would be happy to help you."

He reacted as though she'd just called him a foul word. He looked appalled. She laughed. "I do know how to change sheets, Flannaghan."

"You've actually . . ."

He was too flabbergasted to continue. She found his behavior puzzling. "Where I lived before I came to England I was fully responsible for my clothes and my bedroom. If I wanted the luxury of clean sheets, I changed them."

"Who would demand such a thing from a princess?"

"The mother superior," she answered. "I lived in a convent," she explained. "And I wasn't given special treatment. I was happy not to be thought of as different."

Flannaghan nodded. "Now I understand why you're so unspoiled," he blurted out. "I—I meant that as a compliment," he added in a stammer.

"Thank you," she answered.

The butler hurried over to the bed and began to unfold the linens. "I've already put fresh sheets on your bed, Princess. I'll turn the covers down for you directly after dinner."

His explanation confused her. "Why would you go to the trouble? I thought I would sleep with my husband in his bed."

Flannaghan didn't notice the worry in her voice. He was busy with his task of tucking the bottom sheet into a perfect corner fold. "Milord told me you would be sleeping in your own room," he told her.

The half-given explanation confused her even more. She turned around and pretended to look out the window so Flannaghan wouldn't see her expression. She doubted she could keep the hurt from showing in her eyes.

"I see," she replied for lack of anything better to say. "Did Colin explain why?"

"No," Flannaghan answered. He straightened up and walked around to the other side of the bed. "In England, most of the husbands and wives sleep in separate quarters. It's just the way it's done here."

Alesandra started to feel a little better. Then Flannaghan continued with his explanation. "Of course, Colin's brother, Caine, doesn't follow that dictate. Sterns is the marquess's man. He's my uncle, too," he added with a note of pride in his voice. "He let it slip once that his employer and his wife never sleep apart."

She was instantly miserable again. Of course Caine and Jade slept in the same bed. They happened to love each other. She wagered the duke and duchess only shared one bedroom, too, for they, too, held great affection for each other.

Alesandra straightened her shoulders. She wasn't going to ask Colin why he didn't want her in his bed. She did have her pride, after all. The man was making it perfectly clear how he felt about their marriage. First he cut his hair and now he was going to make her sleep alone. So be it, she decided. She certainly wasn't going to have hurt feelings. No, of course not. It would be a bother having to share a bed. She didn't need his warmth during the night and she certainly wouldn't miss being held in his arms.

The lies weren't working. Alesandra finally quit trying to make herself feel better. She decided she needed to get busy so her mind would be better occupied.

Flannaghan finished making the bed. She followed him down the hall. The door to the study was closed. Alesandra waited until she was well past the entrance to ask the butler how long she thought Colin would be in conference.

"The director had a stack of papers with him," Flannaghan said. "I'd wager it will take a good hour before they're finished."

Flannaghan had miscalculated by several hours. It was well after two that afternoon when he carried the tray of food Cook had prepared up the stairs. He came back down and told Alesandra that the men were still pouring over the documents.

Dreyson was scheduled to call at three, and Alesandra was trying to hurry through the correspondence she and her husband had received that morning. There were over fifty letters of congratulations and almost as many invitations to sort through. Alesandra had divided the papers into stacks, then made lists for each. She gave Flannaghan the stack of invitations to decline while she penned another note to Neil Perry, pleading for him to give her just one hour of his time to discuss his sister.

"I must speak to milord about hiring you both a lady's maid and a full-time secretary," Flannaghan remarked.

"No," Alesandra countered. "I don't have need for either, unless you dislike helping me out now and again, Flannaghan, and your employer is busy building his company. He doesn't need the added expense."

The vehemence in her tone told the butler she would be pricked if he went behind her back. He nodded acceptance. "It is good of you to be so understanding about your husband's financial affairs. We won't be poor for long," he added with a smile.

They weren't poor now, Alesandra thought to herself. If Colin would take advantage of her own funds, of course, she qualified to herself. "Your employer is very stubborn," she whispered.

Flannaghan didn't know what had caused that remark. The knocker sounded at the door and he excused himself from the table immediately.

Morgan Atkins walked into the foyer. He spotted

Alesandra in the dining room and turned to smile at her. "Congratulations, Princess. I just heard the news of your wedding. I hope you'll be very happy."

Alesandra started to stand up but Morgan motioned her to stay seated. He explained he was already late for a meeting with Colin and the director.

He really was a charming gentleman. He bowed low before turning to follow Flannaghan up the steps. She watched him until he disappeared from view, then shook her head. Colin had been wrong. Morgan Atkins wasn't the least bit bowlegged.

Another twenty minutes passed before Sir Richards and Morgan came downstairs together. They exchanged pleasantries with Alesandra and took their leave. Dreyson was given entrance just as the director and his new recruit left.

"I'm most alarmed, Princess," Dreyson announced as soon as he'd finished his greeting. "Is there someplace where we might have a bit of privacy?"

Raymond and Stefan were both standing in the foyer with Flannaghan. The guards always came running whenever a visitor wished entrance. Alesandra didn't believe their protection was necessary any longer, as she was married now and surely out of the general's reach, but she knew both guards would continue to do their duty until they were dismissed. She wasn't going to let them go, however, until she'd found suitable positions for them in London. Raymond and Stefan had let it be known they wanted to stay on in England, and she was determined to find a way to accommodate them. It was the very least she could do for such loyal men.

"Shall we go into the salon?" Alesandra suggested to the agent.

Dreyson nodded. He waited until the princess had walked past him, then turned to Flannaghan. "Is Sir Hallbrook at home today?" he asked.

Flannaghan nodded. Dreyson looked relieved. "Would you mind getting him for me? I believe he'll want to hear this distressing news."

The butler turned and hurried up the steps to see the task completed. Dreyson went inside the salon and sat down across from Alesandra.

"Your frown is very fierce," she said. She folded her hands in her lap and smiled at the agent. "Could the news be that terrible, sir?"

"I've come with two bits of bad news," Dreyson admitted. His voice sounded weary. "I'm sorry to have to bother you at all on your second day of marriage." He let out a sigh before continuing. "My contact has just informed me a substantial amount of your funds—in fact, all of the funds in the account back home—won't be released, Princess. It seems a general named Ivan has cleverly found a way to confiscate the near fortune."

Alesandra showed very little reaction to the news. She was mildly confused by his explanation. "I understood the money had already been transferred to the bank in Austria," she said. "Is that not correct?"

"Yes, it was transferred," Dreyson replied.

"General Ivan has no jurisdiction there."

"His tentacles are far-reaching, Princess."

"Has he actually taken the money out of the bank or frozen the account?"

"What difference does it make?"

"Please answer me and then I'll explain the reason behind my question."

"It was frozen. The bank won't let Ivan touch the money, but the officers have been intimidated by the unethical man and won't release the funds to England's bank."

"That is a dilemma," Alesandra agreed.

"Dilemma? Princess, I would call it a disaster. Have you no idea how much money sits idle in that bank? Why, it's most of your fortune."

Dreyson looked in jeopardy of weeping. She tried to soothe him. "I still have quite enough to live a comfortable life," she reminded him. "Thanks to your sound investments, I'll never become a burden to anyone, least of all my husband. I am confused by this news, however. If the general believed I would marry him, why would he . . ."

"He knew you'd left the convent," Dreyson explained. "And I imagine he knew you were running away from him. He's out to punish you, Princess, for defying him."

"Revenge is always a nice motive."

Colin made that announcement from the entrance. Both Alesandra and Dreyson turned to look at him. The agent stood up. Colin turned, closed the doors behind him, and then walked over to take his place on the settee next to Alesandra. He motioned to Dreyson to sit down again.

"There isn't anything nice about revenge, Colin," Alesandra announced.

She turned her gaze back to the agent. "I believe I know how we might get the funds released. I shall write to Mother Superior and give her a note for the full amount. The bankers might very well be intimidated by the general, but they'll be quite terrified of the superior when she calls on them to collect. Oh, yes, I do believe that's just the ticket, Dreyson. Holy Cross needs the money. I don't."

Colin shook his head. "Your father worked hard to build up his estate. I don't want you to give it away."

"Why do I need it?" she countered.

Dreyson interjected the sum of money under discussion. Colin visibly blanched. Alesandra shrugged. "It will go to a worthy cause. My father would approve. Mother Superior and the other nuns took care of my mother while she was ill. They were very loving to her. Yes, father would approve. I'll write the letter and sign the note before you leave, Matthew."

Alesandra turned back to her husband. He still didn't look pleased by her decision, and she was thankful he wasn't going to argue about it.

"About the ship, Princess," Dreyson interjected. "They have agreed to your terms and arrival date."

"What ship?" Colin asked.

Alesandra hastened to turn the topic. "You said there was another bit of bad news, Matthew. What was it?"

"First he's going to explain about the ship," Colin insisted.

"It was supposed to be a surprise," she whispered.

"Alesandra?" Colin wouldn't be put off.

"When I was in your father's library, I happened to read about a wonderful new invention. It's called a steam vessel, Colin, and it can cross the Atlantic in just twenty-six days. Isn't that amazing," she added in a rush. "Why, my letter to the mother superior will take at least three months to reach her, perhaps longer."

Colin nodded. He was well aware of the new invention, of course. He and his partner had already discussed the possibility of purchasing one to add to their fleet. The cost was prohibitive, however, and the idea was put on hold.

"And you purchased one, is that it?" Colin's voice shook with anger. He didn't give his wife time to answer his question but turned his attention, and his scowl, to her agent. "Cancel the order," he commanded.

"You cannot mean it," Alesandra cried out, her distress apparent. She was suddenly so angry with Colin she wanted to kick him. The steam vessel would increase revenues considerably and he was just being stubborn because the money came from her inheritance.

"I do mean it," he snapped. He was furious with her now because he had been quite explicit when he'd told her he wouldn't touch her money and she had blatantly disregarded his decision.

The set of his jaw told her he wasn't going to listen to reason. She was about to tell Dreyson to cancel the order when the agent intervened.

"I'm having trouble understanding," he remarked. "Sir Hallbrook, are you telling me you're going to refuse her uncle Albert's wedding gift? I believe it is customary to receive gifts."

"Who is Uncle Albert?"

Colin asked Alesandra that question. She didn't know what to do. If she told him the truth, that Albert didn't exist, Dreyson would be insulted. He would probably refuse to do further business with her, too, and she certainly didn't want to jeopardize that relationship.

She didn't want to lie to her husband either.

Truth won out. "He isn't my uncle," she began.

Dreyson enthusiastically cut her off. "But he likes to believe he is," he interjected. "He's a friend of the family. Why, I've known him for years," he added as a boast. "And made a pretty profit from his investments, I might add. Albert handles some of your wife's funds, you see, and I believe he would be very offended if you didn't accept his gift."

Colin's gaze stayed on Alesandra. Her expression didn't tell him anything. She looked very serene. Her hands told a different story, however. They were clenched tight in her lap. Something wasn't quite right, but Colin couldn't put his finger on what that might be.

"Why haven't you mentioned this uncle Albert to me? And why wasn't he invited to the wedding?"

She was going to have to lie after all. The truth wasn't going to do anyone any good.

Alesandra could also see the mother superior shaking her head with displeasure. She forced herself to block the image. She would have plenty of time to feel guilty later.

"I thought I had mentioned Albert to you," she said. She looked at his chin while she gave that lie. "Albert wouldn't have come to the wedding. He never goes anywhere. He won't receive visitors either," she added with a nod.

"He's a recluse, you see," Dreyson interjected. "Alesandra's his only connection to the outside world. He doesn't have any family. Isn't that right, Princess? If your hesitation stems from the cost of his gift, rest assured. He can well afford it, Sir Hallbrook."

"You've known this man for years?" Colin asked Dreyson.

"Yes, of course."

Colin leaned back against the cushions. He knew he probably owed Alesandra an apology for jumping to the wrong conclusion. He decided he would get to that later, when they were alone.

"Convey my appreciation in your next letter," Colin told Alesandra.

"Then you accept . . ."

She stopped her question when Colin shook his head. "It

was thoughtful of him, but much too extravagant. I—or, rather, we—cannot accept it. Suggest something else to him."

"Such as?"

Colin shrugged. "You'll think of something," he told her. "What was the other matter you wished to discuss?"

Dreyson became agitated. He started to explain, then suddenly stopped. While he threaded his fingers through his thinning gray hair, he cleared his throat. Then he started again. "A delicate situation has developed," he announced. "A nasty piece of business, I warn you."

"Yes?" Colin urged when the broker didn't immediately continue.

"Is either of you familiar with the Life Assurance Act of 1774?"

He didn't give Colin or Alesandra time to answer. "No one pays much attention to the ruling these days. It was passed such a long time ago."

"For what purpose?" Alesandra asked, wondering where in heaven's name this discussion was leading.

"A shameful practice was found out," Dreyson explained. "There were immoral men who would insure a life and then hire out the murder so they could collect the profit. Yes, it's shameful, but true, Princess."

"But what does this have—"

Colin interrupted her. "Give him time to explain, Alesandra."

She nodded. "Yes, of course," she whispered.

Dreyson turned his attention to Colin. "Not too many of the firms pay any attention to the Act anymore. It served its purpose, you see . . . for a time. However, it has just come to my attention that an insurance policy was taken out on your wife. The date was set at noon yesterday, and the sum is quite high."

Colin let out a low expletive. Alesandra leaned into his side. "Who would do such a thing? And why?"

"There are stipulations," Dreyson added with a nod. "And a time allowance as well."

"I heard that Napoleon's life was insured, but only for one month's time," Alesandra whispered. "And the Duke of Westminster insured his horse. Is that what you mean when you speak of a time allowance, Matthew?"

The broker nodded. "Yes, Princess. That is what I mean."

"Who underwrote this policy?" Colin demanded. The anger in his voice was barely controlled.

"Was it Lloyd's of London?" Alesandra asked.

"No," Matthew answered. "They're too reputable to become involved in a common wager. Morton and Sons underwrote the policy. They're the culprits, all right. They'll take any contract if the sum is high enough. I certainly don't deal with them," he added with a nod. "But a friend of mine does and he's the one who gave me the news. Thank the Lord I happened to run into him."

"Give me the particulars," Colin commanded. "What is the time limit?"

"One month."

"Who benefits if she dies?"

"The man who purchased the contract wishes anonymity" he answered.

"Can he do that?" Alesandra asked.

"Yes," Dreyson answered. "Your uncle Albert does the very same by using his initials and he wouldn't have to put those down if he didn't want to, Princess. The underwriters are sworn to secrecy."

The agent turned his attention back to Colin. "Thus far my friend and I haven't been able to find out who is behind this foul scheme. I'd wager, however, that it is the same scoundrel who blocked your wife's funds."

"General Ivan? It can't be," Alesandra argued. "Colin and I have been married only one day. He can't know yet."

"Precautions," Dreyson speculated.

Colin understood what the broker was trying to tell Alesandra. He put his arm around his wife, gave her an affectionate squeeze, and then said, "He probably gave orders to one of the men he sent after you. He's just having his fun, wife. He's a damned poor loser. He obviously knew you didn't want to marry him. You did run away in the dead of night."

"He's cruel-hearted, isn't he?"

Colin could think of at least a hundred better descriptions. "Yes, he is cruel," he agreed, just to please her.

"Matthew, did you mean it when you said Morton and Sons will issue any sort of policy?"

"Not policy, Princess, but contract," Dreyson corrected.

"What is the difference?"

"Your husband would insure his ship," he answered. "He would take out a policy to protect against disaster. A contract is another matter altogether. At least the type of voucher Morton and Sons issues is different," he added in a mutter. "It's nothing but a wager, but cloaked as insurance protection so it doesn't violate the Act of 1774. Now then, in answer to your question, yes, they will issue any sort of wager. I remember one in particular. Everyone in London was talking about it. The Marquess of Covingham's wife delivered him a son, and a contract was immediately taken out on the infant's life for one year. The amount was high and payable only if the infant died."

"Do you mean to say the contract could have been issued for the opposite? To pay if the infant lived?"

"Yes, Princess," Dreyson agreed. "Everyone was appalled, of course. The Marquess was in a rage. Speculation grew during the course of the year, for you see, although the buyer of the contract can remain unknown at the time of purchase, his identity will be found out when he collects the sum due him. He must present himself at Morton and Sons and personally sign the voucher. He cannot send a representative."

"So we will know, in one month's time, if General Ivan was behind the purchase," Alesandra said.

Colin shook his head. "It will only pay if you die, remember? And since you're going to stay fit, the general won't have anything to collect. He'll have no reason to come to England."

She nodded. "Yes, of course. Matthew? Did the son live or

die?" she asked, her mind still centered on the story about the Marquess of Covingham.

"He lived."

"Who took the contract out?"

"To this day no one knows," he answered. "Princess, I'm pleased to see you're taking this news calmly," he added.

Colin almost smiled. Alesandra really was very good at hiding her reactions. He could feel her trembling in his arms, but the expression on her face never faltered. She looked quite serene.

He knew better. "She has no reason to worry," he said. "She knows I'll protect her. Matthew, I want you to continue to try to find out who is behind this," he ordered then. "We can assume it's the general, but I want actual proof."

"Yes, of course. I won't give up."

"I wonder if everyone in London knows about this contract yet," Alesandra said. "If so, someone might have heard of a boast . . ."

"If a boast's been made, I'll hear about it," Dreyson assured her. "I wouldn't hold out hope that it's getting much notice, however, what with the fresh scandal making the rounds."

"What scandal?" Alesandra asked, her curiosity pricked.

"Why the Viscount of Talbolt's trouble, of course. His wife has caused the scandal. She left her husband. Astonishing, isn't it?"

Colin had never heard of anything so preposterous. Husbands and wives stayed together no matter how difficult the marriage became. "There has to be another explanation," he said.

"Do you know the viscount?" Alesandra asked her husband.

"Yes. He went to Oxford with my brother. He's a good man. Lady Roberta probably just went back to their country estate for a few days. The *ton* is always looking for reasons to gossip."

Dreyson nodded his agreement. "I heard the rumor from

Lord Thorton and I'll be the first to admit he's one to gossip. Still, the facts tell. Lady Roberta seems to have vanished into thin air. The viscount is beside himself with worry."

A shiver rushed down Alesandra's arms. "Vanished?" she whispered.

"She'll turn up," Dreyson rushed out as soon as he saw how worried the princess was becoming. "I'll wager they had a little marital spat and she's punishing him. She'll come out of hiding in a day or two."

The broker stood up. Colin walked by his side to the foyer. Alesandra stopped the two of them when she called out, "Matthew, no matter how outrageous the contract, if the sum is high enough Morton and Sons will agree?"

"Yes, Princess."

Alesandra smiled at Colin. "Husband, I would like for you to prove to me you mean to protect me."

His wife dared to keep right on smiling at him after she'd given him that insult. He knew she was up to something but he didn't have the faintest notion what it was.

"What do you have in mind?" he asked.

She walked over to Colin's side. "Take a contract out on me, naming yourself as beneficiary, for the exact sum and the exact time limit."

Colin was already shaking his head before she'd finished her request.

"It's a clever plan," she argued. "Do quit shaking your head at me."

"And will the policy pay if you live or die, Alesandra?"

She gave him a disgruntled look. "If I live, of course."

She turned her attention to Dreyson. "I know you dislike doing business with Morton and Sons, but couldn't you see to this little transaction?"

"I haven't agreed to this—"

"Please, Matthew," she interrupted, ignoring her husband's protest.

"Then you want his name on the voucher for everyone to read?" Dreyson asked.

"Yes, of course," she answered.

"You'll have to pay a high premium, and I'm not at all certain there's an underwriter willing to sign his initials alongside yours," he told Colin.

"You told me once that Lloyd's of London would insure a sinking ship if the price was high enough," Alesandra reminded the broker. "I'm certain Morton and Sons, with its tainted reputation for common wagering, would leap at the chance to make a profit."

"Perhaps . . . if you were married to anyone but Sir Hallbrook, that would be true. However, your husband's reputation will defeat your plan, Princess. No one's going to wager against him."

"Why is that?" she asked.

Dreyson smiled. "Your husband has become a legend of sorts. He's feared in most circles. His work, you see, for the War Department—"

"That's enough, Dreyson," Colin interrupted. "You're worrying my wife."

The agent immediately apologized. "Do I try to find someone to underwrite the voucher, Sir Hallbrook?"

"Call it what it is," Colin said. "A wager."

"If you have any doubts about your ability to keep me safe, then I would of course understand your reluctance to put your hard-earned money—"

"You know damned good and well I'm going to protect you," he snapped. "Honest to God, Alesandra, most women would be weeping with fear after finding out someone has taken a contract out on them, but you . . ."

"Yes?"

He shook his head. He finally accepted defeat, though not at all gracefully. "Do it then," he grumbled. "If my wife wants everyone in London to know there are two vouchers in effect, we'll let her have her way."

Alesandra smiled. "Do you know, Colin, you're actually wagering on your own ability. It's quite sporting, really," she added. "And in my opinion, a certain profit for you. You really shouldn't act so surly about this. I have ultimate faith in you. I therefore see no reason to fret."

Alesandra didn't wait to hear what Colin had to say about her opinions. She bid the agent good-bye and then went upstairs.

Flannaghan appeared out of the shadows. He let Dreyson out the front door and then hurried over to his employer.

"She isn't at all worried, is she, milord?"

"How much did you overhear?"

"All of it."

Colin shook his head. "Your uncle would be pleased. You're picking up all of his unsavory habits."

"Thank you, milord. Your princess's loyalty must please you."

Colin smiled. He didn't answer his servant but went up the stairs to his study. Flannaghan's words echoed in his mind.

My princess, he thought to himself. Yes, she was his princess now, and, oh, how she pleased him.

Chapter 10

He infuriated her. They had their first argument late that night. Alesandra had already gone to bed, but she couldn't sleep, so she worked on the list of duties she wanted to accomplish the following day. She was in her own bedroom, of course, because that was where Flannaghan had told her Colin wanted her to sleep, and she was desperately trying not to become upset with her husband because he happened to be such an unfeeling clout. He couldn't help the way he was, could he? Their marriage wasn't a love match either, and if Colin wanted to sleep apart from her, she shouldn't take exception. She did, though. She felt vulnerable—frightened, too—and she couldn't understand why she would be plagued by either emotion.

She tried to understand what was happening to her. She decided she was feeling so insecure because Colin had put her in a much weaker bargaining position. Then she shook her head over that fanciful thought. What did she have to bargain? Her husband had rejected everything she had to give.

Heaven help her, she was beginning to feel sorry for herself. Mother Superior, in one of her daily lectures, had told her that men and women often wanted things they could never have. Envy, she explained, soon turned into jealousy, and once the tentacles of that sinful emotion had taken hold, misery soon followed. Jealousy burned, consumed, until there wasn't room for joy or love or happiness of any sort.

"But I'm not jealous," she whispered to herself. She was envious, though, and let out a little worried sigh over that admission. She was already envious of Colin's brother's happy marriage, and, Lord, did that mean she would soon turn into a jealous shrew and be miserable for the rest of her days?

Marriage, she decided, was a complicated business.

Colin didn't have time for it. He had disappeared into his study directly after dinner to work on his accounts. Having a wife wasn't going to change his habits. He was building an empire, and no one, especially an unwanted bride, was going to interfere with his plans. Colin hadn't had to sit her down and explain his views to her. His actions spoke for him.

Alesandra wasn't upset by his attitude. In truth, she approved of his dedication. She didn't have any doubts, either. Colin would achieve any goal he set. He was strong, terribly clever, and wonderfully disciplined.

She didn't have any intention of getting in his way. She wouldn't distract him, either. The last thing Colin needed was a clinging wife. Still . . . at night, when the work was done, she wished he wanted to be with her then. It would be nice to fall asleep in his arms, to feel him pressed against her during the dark hours of the night. She liked the way he touched her, kissed her . . .

She let out a groan. She was never going to be able to concentrate on her lists if she didn't quit daydreaming about her husband. She shook herself out of her daze and forced herself back to work.

It was almost midnight when Colin walked into her room through the connecting doorway to his own chamber. He wore only a pair of black pants, but he had those stripped off before he reached the side of the bed.

He was very casual about his nudity. She tried to be casual

about it, too. "Have you finished working on your accounts?"

She asked the bed that question. Color flooded her face and her voice sounded as though she were being strangled.

Colin grinned. "Yes," he answered. "I'm completely caught up now."

"Caught up on what?"

He tried not to laugh. "Alesandra, there isn't anything to be embarrassed about."

"I'm not embarrassed."

She was actually able to look directly into his eyes when she told that blatant lie. Colin thought it was an improvement. He pulled the covers back and got into bed. She hurried to move her papers out of his way.

He propped his back against the headboard and let out a loud sigh. He was deliberately giving her time to calm down. If she turned any redder, he thought she might ignite. Her hands shook when she reached for her papers. He didn't understand why she was acting so nervous with him, but he decided he'd have to wait to ask her. Questions now would only make her condition worse.

"Are you cold?"

"No."

"Your hands are shaking."

"Perhaps I am a little cold. My hair was still damp after my bath and I didn't take time to dry it."

He reached over and cupped the back of her neck with his hand. He could feel the tension and began to massage the knots away. She closed her eyes and let out a sigh of pleasure.

"What are you working on?" he asked.

"My list of duties for everyone. I made a list for Flannaghan, another one for Cook, one each for Raymond and Stefan, and several lists for myself. Oh, and the master list, of course. I just finished that one."

She made the mistake of turning to look at him. Her train of thought went flying out the window then. She couldn't even remember if she'd finished her explanation or not.

It was all his doing. If he hadn't had such beautiful eyes, and if he hadn't had such a wonderful smile, and if his teeth hadn't been as white as God's surely were, she wouldn't have taken the time to notice and forget every other thought. Closing her eyes wouldn't help. She would still be able to feel the heat from his body, still inhale his clean male scent, still . . .

"What is a master list?"

"I beg your pardon?"

He grinned. "A master list," he repeated.

He knew she was rattled. He was enjoying her discomfort, too, if his smile was any indication. That realization helped her regain a little of her composure.

"It's a list of my lists," she explained.

"You made a list of your lists?"

"Yes, of course."

He burst into laughter. The bed shook with the force of his amusement. She took immediate exception to his attitude. "Colin, lists are the keys to true organization."

Her voice reeked with authority. Because she was acting so sincere, he tried to control his laughter. "I see," he drawled out. "And where did you learn this important fact?"

"Mother Superior taught me everything I needed to know about organization."

"Was she as thorough as she was when she explained the intimate . . ."

She didn't let him finish. "She was much more thorough. It was very difficult for her to talk about . . . the other. She's a nun, after all, and had taken the vow of chastity years ago. You can understand her reticence, can't you? She didn't have much experience."

"No, I don't imagine she did have much experience," he agreed.

Colin was swallowing up the bed. She kept edging closer to the side to give his legs more room and he kept . . . expanding until he was comfortable. He stretched and yawned and soon took up all the space.

He took her papers, too. He put them on the table next to

his side of the bed, then blew out the two candles and turned back to her.

She folded her hands in her lap and ordered herself to quit being so nervous.

"Without organization we would have anarchy."

It was a stupid thing to say, but she couldn't think of anything better. She was dying to ask him why he was in her bed. Was he going to sleep with her in her chamber every night? No, she thought to herself. That didn't make any sense. His bed was much larger—much more comfortable, too.

Alesandra decided to ease into the topic of their sleeping arrangement. She was calm now, and in total control. He was her husband, after all, and she should be able to ask him any questions, no matter how personal the topic.

A clap of thunder sounded in the distance. She almost fell out of bed. He grabbed her before she went over the side and hauled her up close to him.

"Does thunder make you nervous?"

"No," she answered. "Colin, I was wondering . . ."

"Take your nightgown off, sweetheart," he ordered at the very same time.

His command gained her full attention. "Why?"

"I want to touch you."

"Oh."

She didn't move. "Alesandra? What's wrong?"

"You confuse me," she whispered. "I thought you did like to . . . and then when Flannaghan told me to . . . well, I didn't."

She knew she wasn't making any sense. She quit trying to explain and considered his order instead. She wished he wasn't watching her. She wished it was darker inside the chamber, too. The fire burning in the hearth was still bright enough to cast a golden glow on the bed. She knew she shouldn't be embarrassed. Colin was her husband, and he'd already seen every inch of her body. She hated being shy and wished she could be as uninhibited as he was.

Still, they'd only been married less than two full days. Alesandra decided to tell him how awkward she was feeling and perhaps gain a few pointers on how to get past her shyness.

He turned her attention, then, when he tugged her nightgown up over her hips. She had to force herself not to slap his hands away.

"What are you doing?" She sounded breathless, felt like a complete fool. She knew exactly what he was doing.

"I'm helping you."

"Do you notice how nervous I seem to be tonight?"

"Yes, I noticed," he replied. The laughter was in his voice, but there was heat there, too. The craving to touch her had been plaguing him all day, breaking through his concentration at the oddest moments, and now, finally, he was going to satisfy the intense desire building inside him.

"You're still a little shy with me, aren't you, Alesandra?"

She rolled her eyes heavenward. A little shy? She felt as though she was about to explode with her embarrassment.

Colin pulled the gown up over her head and tossed it over the side of the bed. She immediately tried to cover herself with the blankets. He wouldn't let her shield herself from his gaze, however, and gently tugged the covers down to her waist.

She was perfectly formed. Her breasts were full, lush, beautiful. The pink nipples were already hard, ready, and he arrogantly believed it was his nearness that caused that reaction. He didn't think the goose bumps on her arms were due to the chill in the room, either. Her body was already responding to him, and he hadn't even touched her yet.

He took his time looking at her. She stared at the covers. "I'm not used to sleeping without a gown."

"We aren't going to sleep, sweetheart."

She found her first smile. "I know," she whispered. She decided she had had quite enough of her own awkwardness, and although it took every bit of determination inside her, she turned to him. The look in his eyes—so warm, so caring—made her boldness easier. She wrapped her arms around his neck and pressed herself against him.

It felt wonderful to hold him so close, so intimately. The

hair on his chest tickled her breasts. She let out a little sigh of pleasure and deliberately rubbed against him again. He grunted in reaction. His hands cupped her backside and he pulled her tight against his hard arousal. Her face was tucked under his chin. He nudged her chin up, then lowered his head to hers.

He kissed her forehead first, the bridge of her nose next, and then teased her mouth open by pulling on her lower lip with his teeth. His mouth settled over her parted lips. Her mouth felt so wondrously soft against his own, and the sweet taste of her made him ravenous for more. The slow penetration of his tongue made her shiver. She let out a tiny whimper when he withdrew and then his tongue penetrated deeper inside again. The lazy love play went on and on, for the kiss seemed endless as his mouth slanted over hers again and again. The broken sighs of her pleasure intensified his own. He'd never had a woman respond with such abandon. Her sensuality intoxicated him, and, dear God, he hadn't understood until last night, when he'd first taken her, that such passion was possible between a man and a woman. She held nothing back, and that honest response forced him to let go of his own shields, his own barriers.

He rolled her onto her back, kissed her again, then turned his attention to the side of her neck. His breathing was ragged against her ear. "You make me burn," he whispered, his voice rough with need. "You get so hot so fast it makes me a little crazy."

He sounded almost angry when he told her how she made him feel, but she still took his confession as a compliment. "It's the way you touch me, Colin," she whispered back. "I can't help how I . . ."

The last of her words ended in a low whimper, for Colin had just taken one straining nipple into his mouth and began to suck it. His hand slid between her thighs and he began to stroke the fire inside her. His fingers slowly penetrated her tight sheath. She cried out, in pain and pleasure, and reached down to take hold of his hand. She wanted to push him away, for she was still terribly tender, but she couldn't seem to make herself do that. She couldn't quit twisting in his arms either. The pad of his thumb made circles around and around the soft curls at the junction of her thighs. He delved deeper and brushed against the hot nub of flesh hidden between the sleek folds of skin. She moaned his name.

"Colin, we shouldn't . . . I can't . . . Don't do that," she cried out when his fingers penetrated her again. "It hurts. Oh, God, don't stop."

She clung to her husband while she gave him her contradictory orders. She knew she wasn't making any sense, but she couldn't seem to find the right words to explain how he made her feel. Colin stopped her protest by covering her mouth with his. The kiss was ravenous, unending, consuming. When he next pulled back, she was so overwhelmed by her own desire, she couldn't think about the pain.

She could barely think at all.

Colin stared down at the beautiful woman in his arms and was almost undone by the passion in her eyes. Her lips, swollen and rosy from his kisses, beckoned him again. He gave into the need and kissed her once again.

"Do you remember I told you there was more than one way to make love?" he asked her, his voice thick with emotion.

She tried to concentrate on what he was asking her, but it was terribly difficult. Everything about Colin overwhelmed her. His skin was so hot against hers and she moved restlessly against him, trying to get closer and closer. His scent, an erotic mixture of male and sex, aroused her as much as his magical touch. Her toes curled into the hair on his muscular legs and her breasts rubbed against the crisp hair on his chest. Her hands stroked the bulge of muscle along his upper arms. He felt like hot steel and the sheer power she felt beneath her fingertips was an intoxication all its own. He was such a strong man, yet he was being terribly gentle with her.

Colin didn't wait for an answer to his question. The need to know all of her overwhelmed his every other thought. He kissed the flat of her stomach, traced her navel with his wet tongue, and then, before she could understand his intent, he pushed her thighs apart with his hands and moved lower to taste the liquid heat of her.

"No, you mustn't." She whimpered the denial, for what he was doing to her was surely forbidden. It was appalling . . . and wonderful. Her control slipped further and further away with each erotic stroke of his tongue against the most private part of her. White-hot pleasure spiraled through her. She knew she was going to die from the sweet agony. The intimate sparing of his rough tongue against the sensitive nub of her desire drove her wild. She tried to tell him to stop even as she held him there and arched up against him for more of his erotic touch.

Her response drove him crazy. He wanted to give her fulfillment first, then teach her how to pleasure him, but the uninhibited way she moved beneath him made his own control snap. Her sexy moans made him wild to be inside her. He barely knew what he was doing now. The need overwhelmed him, ruled his every thought. His movements became rough, forceful, as he knelt between her silken thighs, dragged her arms around his neck, and plunged deep inside her. Perspiration beaded his brow, his breathing became choppy, and he clenched his jaw tight against the incredible feeling of her tight sheath squeezing every inch of his arousal. She fit him completely and the wet heat surrounding him made him shudder with raw pleasure. He heard her cry out. He stilled his movements, grimacing over that sweet torture.

"Am I hurting you, baby?"

She couldn't have answered him if she'd wanted to, for his mouth covered hers again, cutting off words and thoughts. The worry in his voice cut through the sensual haze of passion and she wanted to tell him yes, he was hurting her, but it didn't matter. The pleasure he gave her was far more intense—more demanding, too. She throbbed for release now. He wasn't moving quickly enough to suit her. She wrapped her legs around his thighs and arched up against him, telling him without words that she wanted more, and more, and more.

Colin understood. He buried his face in the crook of her

neck and began to move within her. His thrusts weren't measured but hard, fast, because it was impossible for him to control anything now. The fire inside her beckoned him, burned him, and he wanted and needed to get closer.

He never wanted the agony and the ecstasy to end. He sank into her again and again. And yet, when he felt her tighten around him even more, heard her cry out his name, and knew then she was finding her own release, he thrust deep one last time and let out a low grunt of acceptance as he poured his seed into her.

He thought he had died. And gone to paradise. He collapsed against her, took a long gulp of air, and groaned again. He was so damned satisfied, he felt like smiling. He couldn't, though. He didn't have the strength.

It took Alesandra long minutes to recover. She felt safe and warm held so tenderly in her husband's arms. The terror she'd felt seconds before subsided with each ragged breath Colin took.

"Damn, you're good," he said and rolled onto his back. The man wasn't much for flowery speech, Alesandra thought with a smile. It didn't matter. She was arrogantly proud of herself because she'd pleased him. Perhaps she should give him a little praise too. She rolled onto her side to face him, put her hand on his chest directly over his pounding heart, and whispered, "You're good, too. 'Tis the truth, you're the best I've ever had."

He opened his eyes to look at her. "I'm the *only* one you've ever had, remember?" His voice was gruff with affection.

"I remember," she said.

"No other man is ever going to touch you, Alesandra. You're mine."

She wasn't bothered by his possessiveness. In truth, she found comfort in his attitude, for it made her think he must care for her. She belonged to him now, and the thought of doing what she had just done with any other man repelled her. There was only one Colin, and he belonged to her.

She rested the side of her face on his shoulder. "I wouldn't want anyone but you."

He liked hearing her fervent admission and leaned up to kiss the top of her forehead to let her know how pleased he was.

Long minutes passed in silence. Alesandra thought about what had just happened to her and tried to make logical sense out of her behavior. It proved to be an impossible task, however, for her response to her husband was most illogical.

"Colin?"

"Yes?"

"When you touch me, my control seems to vanish. It felt as though my mind had become separated from my body. That doesn't make sense, does it?"

She didn't wait for his answer. "It was frightening—overwhelming, too—but it was also . . . splendid."

Colin smiled in the darkness. His wife sounded thoroughly confused—worried, too. "It's supposed to feel good, sweetheart," he whispered.

"Mother Superior didn't mention that fact."

"No, I don't imagine she would," he countered.

"I would like to make sense out of this bizarre mating ritual," she announced.

"Why?"

"So that I can understand," she replied. She leaned up to look at him. His eyes were closed and he looked very peaceful. She thought he was about to fall asleep. Alesandra decided to let the matter drop. She cuddled up against her husband and closed her eyes. Her mind wouldn't cooperate, however, and one question after another raced through her thoughts.

"Colin?"

He grunted his reply.

"Have you taken other women to your bed?"

He didn't immediately answer her. She nudged him in his side. He let out a sigh. "Yes."

"Very many?"

He almost shrugged her off his shoulder. "Depends on who's doing the counting."

She disliked that answer intensely. Was it two others, or twenty? The thought of Colin being intimate with even one other woman made her stomach tighten. Her reaction wasn't at all reasonable. His past shouldn't concern her. It did, though. "Was it lust or love that made you want them?"

"Alesandra, why are you asking me all these questions?"

He sounded irritated now. Realizing that made her annoyed as well. She was feeling vulnerable, but her insensitive husband was too obtuse to understand.

Her burst of anger vanished almost as soon as it appeared. How could Colin understand when she didn't understand herself? She wasn't being at all fair with him—or logical.

"I was just curious," she whispered. "Did you love any of those women?"

"No."

"Then it was lust?"

He sighed again. "Yes."

"Was it lust with me?"

Or love, she'd wanted to ask. She'd been too afraid to add that word to her question, fearing the answer wouldn't be what she wanted to hear. Oh, God, she wasn't making any sense at all. She knew Colin didn't love her. Why then did she have this consuming need to hear him tell her so?

What in heaven's name was the matter with her?

Colin wanted to put an end to her inquisition. She was prodding him to answer questions he wasn't ready to think about. Hell, yes, it had been lust when he bedded her, he decided. From the moment he'd first seen her, he'd wanted her in his bed.

Yet putting Alesandra into the same category with the other women he'd bedded seemed an atrocity to him. Making love to her had been completely different, and much, much more fulfilling. No other woman had made him burn the way she did; no other woman had made him lose himself so completely.

There was more than lust involved. Colin admitted that much to himself. He cared about Alesandra. She belonged to him now and it was a natural inclination for a husband to want to protect his wife.

But love? Colin honestly didn't know if he loved her or not. He didn't have enough experience to draw upon to know what the hell love was anyway. His gut reaction to the nagging question was that he wasn't capable of letting himself love anyone with real intensity. He remembered the agony his friend and partner, Nathan, had gone through when he'd fallen in love with his wife. Colin blanched over the mere possibility that he wasn't any stronger emotionally than Nathan was. He hadn't believed it was possible for such a tough-skinned giant to fall so hard. Nathan had, however. He'd become damned vulnerable, too.

Colin forced the dour thoughts aside and reached for his wife. She was trying to scoot over to the far side of the bed, away from him. He wasn't about to let her go. He pulled her into his arms, gently pushed her onto her back, and then covered her from head to toes with his body. He propped his weight with his arms and stared down at her. He frowned with concern when he saw the tears in her eyes. "Did I hurt you again, sweetheart? When I'm inside you I go a little crazy. I . . ."

His voice was gruff with emotion. She reached up to stroke the side of his face. "I went a little crazy too," she confessed. "You made me forget all about my tenderness."

"Then why are you upset?"

"I'm not. I was just trying to sort things out in my mind."

"Sort out things like love and lust?"

She nodded. He smiled. "Sweetheart, I've lusted after you for a long, long time. And you've lusted after me," he added with a nod.

He thought his admission would please her. She surprised him with a frown. "Lust is a sin," she whispered. "I will admit I found you very attractive, but I certainly didn't want you in my bed."

"And why the hell not?"

She couldn't believe he was getting pricked over her admission. The man's ego was involved, she supposed, and she'd just inadvertently stomped on it.

"Because I didn't know what would happen there. No one told me how wonderful making love would be. Now do you understand?"

He grinned, looked sheepish.

"Do you know, Colin, I've just worked it all out in my mind," she announced. "I couldn't understand why I was feeling vulnerable but now I know the reason and I'm feeling much better."

"Explain it to me," he ordered.

"It's because this intimacy is new to me, of course. I didn't have a clue it would be so magnificent, and I didn't realize I would become so emotionally involved." She paused to smile up at him. "If I'd had your experience, I probably wouldn't have felt vulnerable at all."

"It isn't a sin for a wife to feel vulnerable," he announced. "It doesn't make any sense in your situation, however."

"Why doesn't it make sense?"

"Because you certainly realize I'm going to take care of you and you therefore have no reason to feel vulnerable at all."

"That's an extremely arrogant thing to say, husband."

He shrugged. "I'm an arrogant man."

"Do husbands ever feel vulnerable?"

"No."

"But, Colin, if . . ."

He didn't let her finish her argument. His mouth covered hers, cutting off all conversation. He thought only to take her mind off the bizarre topic, but she opened her mouth for his tongue and put her arms around his neck and he was suddenly caught up in a burst of passion he didn't feel like squelching.

He made love to her again, tried to be gentle and take it slow and easy, but she waylaid his noble intentions by responding with abandon. Although it didn't seem possible to him, each time was better, even more fulfilling. His own climax almost killed him, and when he felt her tears on his shoulder, he believed he'd really hurt her.

Colin lit the candles and turned back to her. He took her into his arms and soothed her with honeyed words. She promised him he hadn't injured her, but she couldn't explain why she'd started crying.

He didn't prod her into another conversation. Her lusty yawns told him she was exhausted. Odd, but he was wide awake now. The scare that he might have harmed her jarred him and he knew it would take more than just a few minutes to relax again. Her lists drew his attention when he turned to blow out the candles. On the top sheet were two names. Lady Victoria was first, followed by Lady Roberta. Alesandra had placed question marks after each name.

Needless to say, his curiosity was caught. She was just drifting off to sleep when he nudged her.

"What is this all about?"

She didn't open her eyes. Colin read the names to her and asked her to explain.

"Can't we discuss this in the morning?"

He was about to give in to her request when she muttered, "There might be a connection between the two women. Both have disappeared, after all. After I've talked to Lady Roberta's husband, I'll explain everything to you. Good night, Colin."

"You are not going to talk to the viscount."

The tone of his voice cut through her sleepy haze. "I'm not?"

"No, you're not. The man has enough to deal with now. He doesn't need you grilling him with questions."

"Colin, I . . ."

He didn't let her finish. "I forbid it, Alesandra. Give me your word you won't bother him."

She was astonished by his high-handed attitude—angry, too. She wasn't a child who had to gain her parent's permission to pursue an interest or a worry, and Colin had best understand she had a mind of her own and could use it upon occasion.

"Promise me, Alesandra," he demanded again.

"No."

He couldn't believe what he'd just heard. "No?"

Because her face was still tucked under his chin and he couldn't possibly see her expression, she felt it safe to grimace. Lord, he sounded surly. His arm tightened around her. A good wife probably would try to placate her husband, she supposed.

She guessed she didn't have it in her to be a good wife,

however, for no man—not even Colin—was going to direct her actions.

Ask his permission indeed! She pushed herself away from him and sat up. Her hair covered half her face. She brushed it back over her shoulder and matched him glare for glare.

"Marriage is new to you, Colin, and so you will have to take my word when I tell you . . ."

"Correct me if I'm wrong, but haven't we been married the exact length of time?"

"Yes . . ."

"Then marriage is just as new to you too, isn't it?"

She nodded.

"New or old, Alesandra, the vows haven't changed. Wives obey their husbands."

"Ours is not a usual marriage," she countered. "You and I settled upon an agreement of sorts before we spoke our vows. You've obviously forgotten and for that reason I will not take exception to your outrageous command. I will remind you, however, that we both agreed not to hover."

"No we didn't."

"It was an unspoken promise we gave to each other. I told you I didn't want a husband who hovered and you admitted you didn't want a wife who hovered, either."

"What the hell does that have to do with . . ."

"By hover I meant someone who interferes," she told him. "You've made it perfectly clear on several occasions that you don't wish my help or interference in your business affairs and I would now like to take this opportunity to insist you not interfere in my affairs."

She couldn't quite look into his eyes. His incredulous expression made her nervous. She turned her gaze to his chin. "My father would never have forbidden my mother anything. Their marriage was based upon a foundation of mutual trust and respect. In time I hope we can achieve the same kind of arrangement."

"Are you finished?"

She was pleased that he didn't sound angry with her. Colin was going to be reasonable about this after all. He had listened to what she had to say and hadn't allowed his arrogant nature to get in the way.

"Yes, thank you."

"Look at me."

She immediately lifted her gaze to his eyes. He didn't say another word for a long minute. His stare made her worry, though. His expression didn't give her a hint of what he was thinking and his amazing ability to mask his thoughts and his feelings did impress her. She was a little envious, too. She wished she had that much control.

"Did you want to say something to me?" she asked when she couldn't stand the silence a second longer.

He nodded. She smiled.

"You will not talk to the viscount about his wife."

They were right back where they'd started. Colin obviously hadn't heard a word she'd said. She felt like kicking the stubborn man. She didn't, of course, because she was a lady, and her impossible husband was never going to know how furious she was.

God's truth, he could make Mother Superior curse in vexation.

Colin forced himself not to smile. The issue was too important to turn into a laughing matter, but, dear God, her expression was priceless. She looked like she wanted to kill him.

"Give me your promise, wife."

"Oh, all right," she cried out. "You win. I won't bother the viscount."

"This isn't about winning or losing," he countered. "The viscount has enough on his mind. I don't want you adding to his misery."

"You don't trust my judgment at all, do you, Colin?"

"No."

That answer hurt her far more than his high-handed command. She tried to turn away from him, but he reached out and grabbed hold of her chin. "Do you trust my judgment yet?"

He fully expected to hear the same denial. She didn't

know him well enough to give him her complete trust. In time, of course, when they had both learned the other's ways, she would begin to give him her trust.

"Yes, of course I trust your judgment."

He couldn't contain his surprise or his pleasure. He grabbed her by the back of her neck, pulled her toward him, and leaned up at the same time to kiss her hard.

"I'm pleased to know you have instinctively put your faith in me already," he told her.

She leaned back and frowned at him. "It wasn't instinctive," she said. "You had already proven to me that you can upon occasion use sound judgment."

"When was that?"

"When you married me. You used sound judgment then. I understand now, of course, that you knew something I didn't."

"And what did I know?"

"That no one else would have you."

She'd deliberately tried to prick his temper with that remark, for she was still irritated with him, but Colin wasn't at all offended. The slap at his arrogance went unnoticed. He either didn't know she'd just insulted him or he didn't care, she decided when he burst into laughter.

"You please me, Alesandra."

"Of course I please you. I just gave in."

She fluffed her pillow, then got back under the covers to rest on her side. "Marriage is more complicated than I anticipated," she whispered. "Will I always have to be the one to concede?"

God, she sounded forlorn. "No, you won't always have to concede."

Her unladylike snort told him she didn't believe him. "Marriage is a give-and-take arrangement," he speculated.

"With the wife doing all the giving and the husband doing all the taking?"

He didn't answer that question. He turned on his side and pulled her up against him. Her shoulders rested against his chest and her bottom was pressed against his groin. The backs of her thighs, so smooth and silky, covered the tops of his thighs, and, God, how he loved the feel of her against him. He draped one arm over her hip, dropped his chin to rest on top of her head, and closed his eyes.

Long minutes passed in silence. He thought Alesandra had already fallen asleep and was just easing away from her when she whispered, "I dislike the word *obey,* Colin."

"I gathered as much," he told her dryly.

"A princess really shouldn't have to obey anyone."

It was a paltry argument. "But you're my princess," he reminded her. "And you will therefore do what I think is best. We're both going to have to bow to tradition for a while," he added. "Neither one of us has any experience being married. I'm not an ogre, but the fact is you did promise to obey. I specifically remember hearing your pledge when you were reciting your vows."

"I wish you would be more reasonable."

"I'm always reasonable."

"Colin?"

"Yes?"

"Do go to sleep."

He let her have the last word. He waited a long while until he was certain she had fallen asleep before he left her bed and went back to his own chamber.

She felt him leave. She almost called out to him to ask him why he didn't want to sleep with her the rest of the night, but pride stopped her. Tears filled her eyes and she felt as though she had just been rejected by her husband. Her reaction didn't make much sense, especially after the passionate way he'd made love to her, but she was too tired to sort it all out in her mind.

Alesandra's sleep was fitful. She was awakened just an hour later by a scraping sound coming from Colin's bedroom. She immediately got out of bed to investigate. She didn't have any intention of intruding and therefore didn't bother with her robe or her slippers.

She heard a low expletive just as she pulled the door open and peeked inside. Colin stood in front of the fireplace. He'd dragged the footrest over and, while she watched, he put one foot on the cushion and bent over to massage his injured leg with both hands.

He didn't know she was there, watching him. She was certain of that fact because of his expression. It wasn't guarded now, and though she could only see one side of his face, it was enough for her to know he was in agony.

It took all the strength she had not to rush into his room and offer whatever paltry help she could give. His pride was involved, however, and she knew he would be furious with her if he realized she'd been watching him.

Rubbing the injured muscles wasn't easing the pain. Colin straightened up and began to pace back and forth in front of the hearth. He was trying to work out the knot of twisted muscle in what was left of the calf of his left leg. Forcing his full weight on the injured limb caused a spasm of pain to shoot all the way up to his chest. It felt like lightning had just struck every nerve in his body, and it damn near doubled him over. Colin refused to give in to the torment. He clenched his jaw tight, drew a deep breath, and continued walking. He knew from past experience that eventually he would be able to walk the cramp out. Some nights it only took an hour. Other nights it took much, much longer.

Colin walked over to the connecting door to Alesandra's room. He reached for the doorknob, then stopped. He wanted to look in on her, but he didn't want to wake her up and he knew she was a light sleeper. He'd learned that fact when he'd become ill and she slept with him.

Alesandra needed her rest. He turned around and resumed his pacing. His mind was suddenly filled with fragments of their conversation regarding his order and her compliance. He remembered how she had sounded when she'd told him she disliked the word *obey*. Hell, he didn't blame her. He thought it was a bit barbaric for a woman to have to promise to obey her husband for the rest of her life. Such radical opinions would land him in Newgate Prison if the conservatives got wind of his subversive thoughts, and Colin was honest enough to admit that there was a part of him—a very small part—that found the idea of a woman obeying his every command appealing. The appeal wouldn't last long, however. There were paid servants to do his bidding. And perhaps there were wives who would be just as accommodating. Alesandra didn't fit into that group. Thank God for that, he decided. She was feisty and opinionated, and he wouldn't have her any other way. She was so damned passionate about everything.

His princess, he decided, was flawed to perfection.

Alesandra hadn't made a sound when she hurried back to her bed and got under the covers. She couldn't get the picture of Colin's anguished expression out of her mind. Her heart ached for her husband. She hadn't realized until tonight how terrible his pain was, but now that she was aware, she vowed to find a way to help him.

She suddenly had a mission. She lit the candles and made a list of what she needed to do. First she would read whatever literature was available. Second on her list was a visit to the physician, Sir Winters. She would ply him with questions and ask him for suggestions. Alesandra couldn't think of anything else to add to her list now, but she was tired, and surely after some much needed sleep, she would think of other plans of action.

She put the list back on the side table and blew out the candles. Her cheeks were wet from her tears. She used the bed cover to wipe them dry, then closed her eyes and tried to go back to sleep.

A sudden realization rushed into her mind just as she was drifting off. Colin didn't want her to sleep in his bed because of his leg. He didn't want her to know about his agony. Yes, that made sense. His pride was the issue, of course, but he was also probably being thoughtful, too. If he needed to walk every night, he would wake her. That made sense, too. Alesandra let out a loud sigh of relief.

Colin hadn't rejected her after all.

Chapter 11

Colin shook Alesandra awake early the next morning. "Sweetheart, open your eyes. I want to talk to you before I leave."

She struggled to sit up. "Where are you going?"

"To work," he answered.

She started to sink back down under the covers. Colin leaned over the side of the bed and grabbed hold of her shoulders. He couldn't tell if her eyes were open or not, for her curly hair hung over her face, blocking his view. He held on to her with one hand and brushed her hair back over her shoulders with his other. He was both exasperated and amused. "Are you awake yet?"

"I believe I am."

"I want you to stay inside until I return home. I've already given Stefan and Raymond their orders."

"Why do I have to stay inside?"

"Have you already forgotten about the policy in effect for thirty days?"

She let out a loud yawn. She guessed she had forgotten. "Do you mean to tell me I have to stay under lock and key for a full month?"

"We'll take it one day at a time, wife."

"Colin, what time is it?"

"A few minutes past dawn."

"Good God."

"Have you heard my instructions?" he demanded.

She didn't answer him. She got out of bed, put her robe on, and walked into his bedroom. Her husband followed her.

"What are you doing?"

"Getting in your bed."

"Why?"

"I belong here."

She buried herself under his covers and was sound asleep a minute later. He pulled the covers back, leaned down, and kissed her brow.

Flannaghan waited in the hall. Colin went over his instructions with the butler. The town house was going to become a fortress for the next thirty days, and no one other than immediate family was going to be allowed entrance.

"Keeping company out will be easy, milord, but keeping your princess inside is going to be most difficult."

Flannaghan's prediction proved accurate. The battle began late that morning. The butler found his new mistress sitting on the floor in Colin's bedroom. She was surrounded by a stack of her husband's shoes.

"What are you doing, Princess?"

"Colin needs new boots," she replied.

"But he has at least five pairs now he never wears. He's partial to the old Hessians even though the Wellingtons have become more fashionable."

Alesandra was looking at the soles of the boots. "Flannaghan, do you notice the heel on the left boot is barely worn?"

The butler knelt down beside his mistress and looked at the boot she held up for him. "It looks brand-new," he remarked. "But I know he's worn . . ."

"Yes, he has worn these boots," she interrupted. She held up the right-footed boot. "This one's well worn, isn't it?"

"What do you make of it, Princess?"

"We're speaking in confidence now, Flannaghan. I don't want a word of this discussion to reach Colin. He's sensitive about his leg."

"I won't say a word."

She nodded. "It appears Colin's injured leg is just a bit shorter than the other one. I would like a bootmaker to look at these shoes and make a few adjustments."

"Do you mean to make one heel thicker? Colin will notice, Princess."

She shook her head. "I was thinking along the lines of an insert of some kind—perhaps a soft leather pad running the length. Who makes Colin's boots now?"

"Hoby made that pair," Flannaghan answered. "Every fashionable gentleman gives him his business."

"Then he won't do," she countered. "I don't want anyone to know about this experiment. We must find someone else."

"There's Curtis," Flannaghan remarked after a moment's consideration. "He used to make Colin's father's shoes. The man's retired now, but he lives in London and he might be persuaded to help you."

"I shall go and see him at once. I'll take only one pair of Colin's shoes with me. If luck is on our side, my husband won't even notice they're gone."

Flannaghan was vehemently shaking his head at her. "You cannot leave the town house. I would be happy to go on this errand," he added in a rush when she looked like she was about to argue with him. "If you'll write down what you wish Curtis to do . . ."

"Yes," she agreed. "I'll make a list of suggestions. What a fine idea. Could you go this afternoon?"

The butler immediately agreed. Alesandra handed him the pair of boots and then stood up. "If this plan works, I'll have Curtis make a pair of half Wellingtons for Colin. Then he'll have a pair to wear under his trousers. Now then, Flannaghan, I have one more request to ask of you."

"Yes, Princess?"

"Would you please take a note to Sir Winters? I would like him to call late this afternoon."

"Yes, of course," the butler agreed. "May I be bold and ask you why you wish to see the physician?"

"I'm going to be ill this afternoon."

Flannaghan did a double take. "You are? How can you know . . ."

She let out a sigh. "If I give you the full explanation and beg your confidence, you'll have to lie to your employer. We can't have that, now can we?"

"No, of course not."

"So you see, Flannaghan, it's best you not know."

"This has something to do with Colin, doesn't it?"

She smiled. "Perhaps," she replied.

She left Flannaghan to the task of putting the other shoes back in the wardrobe and went back to her room to make her list for the bootmaker. The boots she was sending were made of soft black calfskin and she added in her note the hope that Curtis would be able to stretch the bridge across the top of the boot enough to accommodate the insert she was certain he could make.

Alesandra then sent a note to Sir Winters requesting an audience. She set the time at four o'clock.

The physician was punctual. Stefan escorted him into the salon. He dared to frown at his mistress for insisting he let the man inside. She smiled at the guard.

"Your husband gave us specific orders that no one outside of immediate family be given admittance," he whispered.

"Sir Winters is like family," she countered. "And I'm not feeling at all well, Stefan. I have need of his services."

The guard was immediately contrite. Alesandra felt a bit guilty for telling the blatant lie. She got past the feeling quickly, however, when she reminded herself she only had Colin's best interests at heart.

She closed the guard out by pulling the French doors to the salon closed. Sir Winters stood by her side. He held a brown leather bag under one arm. She ushered him over to the settee.

"If you're indisposed, shouldn't you be in bed, Princess?"

She smiled at the physician. "I'm not that ill," she announced. "I have a little tickle in my throat. That's all."

"Hot tea is just the ticket, then," Sir Winters returned. "A spot of brandy would also do the trick."

Because the white-haired man was being so sincere and looking so concerned, she couldn't continue with the lie any longer. "I had another purpose for asking you to come here," she admitted. "I would like to talk to you about Colin."

Alesandra sat down in the chair across from the physician and folded her hands in her lap. "I used trickery to get you to come here," she admitted. She acted as though she had just confessed a dark sin. "My throat really isn't paining me. 'Tis the truth, the only time it hurts is when I want to shout at my stubborn husband and I know I can't."

Sir Winters smiled. "Colin can be stubborn, can't he?"

"Yes," she whispered.

"He's ill, then?" the physician asked, trying to understand the real motive behind his summons.

She shook her head. "It's his leg," she explained in a whisper. "He won't talk about his injury. He's sensitive about it, you see, but I know he's in terrible pain. I was wondering if something could be done to ease his discomfort."

The physician leaned back against the cushions. The worry on the princess's face told him her concern was genuine. "He hasn't told you how he came by the affliction, has he?"

"No."

"A shark took a bite out of his leg, Princess. I tended him, and there was a time when I considered taking the leg off. Colin's partner, Nathan, wouldn't let me. Your husband, you see, wasn't in any condition to give me his opinion. He blessedly slept through the worst of it."

A knock on the door interrupted their conversation. Flannaghan came inside carrying a silver tray. Neither Alesandra nor Sir Winters said another word until the butler had served both of them cups of hot tea and left the salon again.

Sir Winters pushed his bag out of his way and leaned forward to help himself to the assortment of sweet biscuits from the tray. He popped one into his mouth and then took a long swallow of the tea.

"Colin would be extremely upset if he knew we were discussing his condition," she admitted. "And I do feel guilty because I know he'll be displeased with me."

"Nonsense," Sir Winters countered. "You have his best interests at heart. I won't be telling him about our talk. Now, then, as to your question. How do you help him? I would suggest laudanum or brandy when the pain becomes insistent, but I know Colin won't take either."

"Is pride the reason?" she asked, trying to understand.

Winters shook his head. "Dependency," he countered. "Laudanum is addictive, Princess, and some say spirits can be addictive as well. Regardless, Colin won't take the chance."

"I see," she replied when the physician didn't immediately continue.

"I also suggested a brace of steel be made to fit from the knee to the ankle. Your husband was appalled by that suggestion."

"He's a proud man."

Winters nodded. "He's a sight more clever than I am too," he remarked. "I didn't believe he'd ever walk again without assistance. He's proven me wrong. What muscle is left has strengthened enough to support him. He barely limps now."

"At night, when he's weary, then he limps."

"Hot towels should be applied then. It won't make the leg stronger, of course, but it will ease his discomfort. A soothing massage would also help."

She wondered how in heaven's name Colin would ever allow her to follow those suggestions. That was her problem, however, not Sir Winters', and she would worry about it after he'd left.

"Anything else?" she asked.

"He should get off his feet when the pain intensifies," Sir Winters announced. "He shouldn't wait until it's agonizing."

Alesandra nodded agreement. She was thoroughly discouraged, but she kept her expression serene so the physician wouldn't know how disappointed she was feeling. His suggestions were superficial at best.

"You give me recommendations meant to deal with the symptoms, Sir Winters, but I was hoping you might have an idea or two regarding the cause."

"You're hoping for a miracle," Sir Winters replied. "Nothing can be done to make the leg fit again, Princess." His voice was filled with kindness.

"Yes," she whispered. "I was hoping for a miracle, I suppose. Still, your suggestions will prove helpful. If you think of anything more to add, will you pen me a note? I could use all the advice you can give."

Sir Winters took the last biscuit from the tray. His mind was fully occupied with Colin's condition and he didn't realize he'd eaten all of the treats. Alesandra filled his cup with more tea.

"Are all husbands stubborn?" she asked the physician.

Sir Winters smiled. "It seems to be a trait most husbands share."

He told her several amusing stories concerning titled men who refused to acknowledge they were in need of a physician. His favorite was the tale about the Marquess of Ackerman. The gentleman had been involved in a duel. He'd been shot in the shoulder and wouldn't allow anyone to see to the injury. Winters had been called by his brother to tend to the man.

"We found him at White's at one of the gaming tables," he told her. "It took three of his friends to drag him away. When we got his jacket off, why, there was blood everywhere."

"Did the marquess recover?"

Winters nodded. "He was too stubborn to die," he remarked. "Kept referring to the injury as a paltry nick until he passed out. I advised his wife to tie him to the bed until he recovered."

Alesandra smiled over that picture. "Colin's every bit as stubborn," she announced. She let out a sigh. "I would appreciate it if you would keep this conference secret, please. As I said before, Colin is quite sensitive about his leg."

Sir Winters placed his teacup and saucer back on the tray, picked up his satchel, and stood up to take his leave. "You needn't worry, Princess. I won't say a word about this visitation. You'd be surprised if you knew how many wives seek my advice concerning their husbands' welfare."

The door to the salon opened just as the physician was reaching for the handle. Colin moved out of the way to allow Winters room. He gave the physician a quick nod in greeting and turned to his wife.

"Flannaghan said you were ill."

He didn't give her time to answer but turned to Winters. "What's wrong with her?"

Alesandra didn't want the physician to lie for her. "I had a tickle in my throat, but it's better now. Sir Winters suggested hot tea," she added with a nod.

"Yes, I did," Winters agreed.

Something wasn't quite right, but Colin couldn't put his finger on what was wrong. Alesandra couldn't look him in the eye. He knew her well enough to know she wasn't telling him the truth. She didn't look ill. Her cheeks were high with color, indicating she was embarrassed about something. He decided then he would have to wait until they were alone to find out what was really wrong.

Alesandra stood by Colin's side while he visited with the physician. She happened to glance over her shoulder and found Flannaghan standing just a few feet away. The butler was giving her a sympathetic expression.

She already felt guilty because she'd lied to her husband and Flannaghan's expression made her feel worse.

Her motives were pure, she immediately told herself. She let out a little sigh then. She'd used that very excuse when she'd made the second set of books for the mother superior.

A sin is still a sin, or so the nun had proclaimed when she'd found out about the little deception. Large or little, it didn't matter. God, the mother superior assured her with great authority in her voice, kept an accurate list of each and every sin committed by every man and woman on this earth. Alesandra's list, the nun speculated, was probably long enough to reach the bottom of the ocean.

Alesandra didn't believe she'd sinned that much or that often. She imagined her list was about the length of her shadow by now. She wondered if her Maker had two columns on his sheet of paper for her—one for small infractions and the other for more substantial offenses.

She was pulled back to the present rather abruptly when Sir Winters said, "I was sorry to hear about the loss of the *Diamond,* Colin. Bad piece of luck, that."

"You've lost a diamond?" Alesandra asked, trying to understand.

Colin shook his head. "It's a ship, Alesandra. She went down with a full cargo. Winters, how did you hear about it so soon? I only just found out yesterday."

"A friend of mine had some business dealings at Lloyd's today. One of their agents mentioned it. They insured the loss, didn't they?"

"Yes."

"Is it true it was the second vessel this year you and Nathan have lost?"

Colin nodded.

"Why didn't you tell me?" Alesandra asked.

She tried to keep the hurt out of her voice. It was a difficult task.

"I didn't want you to worry," Colin explained.

She didn't believe he'd given her the full reason. Yes, it was probably true that he didn't want to worry her, but more important, he didn't want to share his burdens with her. She tried not to be offended. Colin had kept his own counsel for a long while and it surely wasn't easy for him to take anyone into his confidence, not even his wife.

She was going to have to be patient, she decided. Colin would have to get used to having her around before he felt comfortable enough to confide in her.

Her husband was still talking to the physician when she excused herself and went upstairs. She went to her room and started her list of suggestions Winters had given her to help ease the pain in Colin's leg, but her mind wasn't on the task.

He should have told her about the ship, damn it. If he was worried, she had every right to be worried too. Husbands and wives were supposed to share their problems, weren't they?

Flannaghan came to fetch her for dinner. On the way downstairs, she asked him for another favor.

"Have you heard about the Viscount of Talbolt's troubles?"

"Oh, yes," Flannaghan replied. "Everyone's talking about it. Lady Roberta left her husband."

"Colin has forbidden me to talk to the viscount and I must go along with his wishes. My husband believes I'll upset the man."

"Why do you want to talk to him?"

"I believe there might be a connection between his wife's sudden disappearance and that of my friend, Lady Victoria. She disappeared, too, Flannaghan. I was wondering if you would mind talking to his servants for me. I want to find out if Lady Roberta received any little presents from an unknown admirer, you see."

"What kinds of gifts, Princess?"

She shrugged. "Flowers—perhaps chocolates," she said. "Wouldn't the maids notice such gifts?"

Flannaghan nodded. "Yes, of course they'd notice. They would talk amongst themselves, too. They won't talk to me, though. Now Cook could learn a thing or two when she goes to market tomorrow. Shall I put the request to her?"

"Yes, please," Alesandra replied.

"What are you two whispering about?"

Colin asked that question from the entrance to the dining room. He smiled over the startle he gave his wife. She jumped a good foot. "You seem a bit nervous tonight," he remarked.

She didn't have a quick answer for that remark. She followed Flannaghan into the dining room. Colin held her chair out for her and then took his place at the head of the table, adjacent to her.

"Am I going to have to stay locked inside for a full month?" she asked.

"Yes."

He was occupied sorting through a stack of correspondence and didn't bother to glance her way when he answered her.

The man couldn't even take time away from his work to eat a proper meal. She wondered if he had digestive problems and almost asked him that personal question. She changed her mind and turned the topic to a more pressing matter.

"What about Catherine's first ball? It's only a week away, Colin. I don't want to miss it."

"I'll tell you all about it."

"You'd go without me?"

She sounded wounded. He smiled. "Yes," he answered. "I have to attend," he added. "And you have to be reasonable about this."

The set of his jaw told her he wasn't going to give in. She drummed her fingertips on the tabletop in agitation.

"It's rude to read your correspondence while at the table."

Colin was so occupied reading the letter from his partner, he didn't hear his wife's rebuke. He finished the long missive, then put the papers on the table.

"Nathan's wife has given him a baby girl. They've named her Joanna. The letter's almost three months old and he mentioned that as soon as Sara is feeling well enough, he's going to bring her and the baby back to London for a brief visit. Jimbo will watch the offices while he's gone."

"Who is Jimbo?" Alesandra asked, smiling over the odd name.

"A very good friend," Colin answered. "He's captain of one of our ships, the *Emerald,* but the vessel is undergoing some much needed repairs so Jimbo has time on his hands."

"This is all good news, Colin," she remarked.

"Yes, of course."

"Then why are you frowning?"

He hadn't realized he was frowning until she asked him why. He leaned back in his chair and gave her his full attention. "Nathan wants to offer ten or twenty shares of stock for sale. I hate the idea and I know that deep down Nathan feels the same way. I understand, however. He has a family now and wants to provide for them. He and Sara have been living in rented rooms, and now that the baby's here he wants more permanent quarters."

"Why are you two so opposed to stockholders?"

"We want to maintain control."

She was exasperated with him. "If only ten or twenty shares are sold, you and Nathan will still be the major stockholders and therefore in complete control."

He didn't seem impressed with her logic, for he continued to frown. She tried another approach. "What if you sold the stock to family members?"

"No."

"Why, in heaven's name, not?"

He let out a sigh. "It would be the same as a loan."

"It would not," she argued. "Caine and your father would make a handsome profit eventually. It would be a sound investment."

"Why did you send for Winters?"

He was deliberately changing the topic on her. She wasn't ready to let him. "Has Nathan given permission for this sale?"

"Yes."

"And when will you decide?"

"I've already decided. I'll have Dreyson handle the transaction. Now, enough about this. Answer my question. Why did you send for Winters?"

"I already explained," she began. "My throat . . ."

"I know," Colin said. "You had a scratch in your throat."

Alesandra was folding and refolding her napkin. "Actually it was a little tickle."

"Yes," he agreed. "Now I want you to tell me the truth. And look at me while you explain."

She dropped the napkin in her lap and finally looked up at him. "It's rude of you to suggest I would lie."

"Did you?"

"Yes."

"Why?"

"Because if I told you the truth, you'd become irritated with me."

"You will not lie to me in future, wife. Give me your word."

"You lied to me."

"When?"

"When you told me you didn't work for Sir Richards any longer. I saw the cash entries in the ledgers, Colin, and I heard him talk to you about a new assignment. Yes, you lied to me. If you give me your promise not to lie in future, I'll be happy to give you my word."

"Alesandra, it isn't at all the same."

"No, it isn't."

She was suddenly furious with her husband. She tossed the napkin down on the table just as Flannaghan came through the swinging door with a tray laden with food in his hands. "I don't take risks, Colin. You do. You don't give a twit about me, do you?"

She didn't give him time to answer her question but rushed on. "You've deliberately involved yourself in danger. I would never do such a thing. Now that we are married, I not only think about my well-being, I think about yours. If something happened to you, I would be devastated. Yet if something happened to me, I believe you would only be mildly inconvenienced. My funeral would force you to put your work aside for a few hours. Do excuse me, sir, before I say something more I know I'll regret."

She didn't wait for his permission to leave the table. She ignored his command to sit back down, too, and ran all the way up to her bedroom. She wanted to vent her frustration by slamming the door shut. She didn't give in to that urge, however, for it wouldn't be dignified.

Thankfully, Colin didn't follow her. Alesandra needed to be alone now so she could get a grip on her own rioting emotions. She was a bit stunned she'd become so angry with Colin so quickly. She wasn't Colin's keeper, she told herself. If he wanted to work for Richards, she couldn't and wouldn't try to talk him into quitting.

But he shouldn't want to take such risks, she decided. If he cared at all about her, he wouldn't deliberately hurt her this way.

Alesandra tried to walk the anger away. She paced back and forth in front of the hearth for a good ten minutes, muttering all the while.

"Mother Superior would never place herself in danger. She knew how I depended upon her and she never would have taken risks. She loved me, damn it."

Even though she wasn't Catholic, Alesandra still made the sign of the cross after muttering that blasphemy.

"I doubt Richards would ask the nun to work for him, Alesandra."

Colin made that comment from the doorway. She had been so intent on her ranting and raving she hadn't heard the door open. She turned around and found her husband lounging against the frame. His arms were casually folded across his chest. He was smiling, but it was the tenderness she saw in his eyes that almost did her in.

"Your amusement displeases me."

"Your behavior displeases me," he countered. "Why didn't you tell me you were upset about all this business with Richards?"

"I didn't know I was."

He raised an eyebrow over that odd admission. "Do you want me to quit?"

She started to nod, then changed her mind and shook her head instead. "I want you to want to quit. There's a difference, Colin. God willing, someday you might understand."

"Help me understand now."

She turned around to face the hearth before she spoke again. "I never would have taken deliberate risks while I lived at the convent—at least, not after the lesson I learned. There was a fire, you see, and I was trapped inside. I got out just as the roof collapsed. Mother Superior was beside herself with worry. She actually wept. She was so thankful I was all right and so furious with me because I'd taken one of the candles out of the holder so I could read Victoria's letter instead of praying like I was supposed to be doing . . . and I felt terrible because I'd caused her so much distress. The fire was an accident, but I made a promise to myself not to act foolish again."

"How did you act foolish if it was an accident?"

"I kept going back inside to save the pictures and the smaller statues the nuns put such store in."

"That was foolish."

"Yes."

"The mother superior loved you like a daughter, didn't she?"

Alesandra nodded.

"And you loved her."

"Yes."

A long minute passed in silence. "With love comes responsibility," she whispered. "I didn't realize that truth until I saw how upset Mother was with me."

"Do you love me, Alesandra?"

He'd cut right to the heart of the matter. She turned around to face him just as he pulled away from the doorway and started walking toward her. She immediately started backing away.

"I do not wish to love you."

The panic in her voice didn't stop him. "Do you love me?" he asked again.

It was a blessing there wasn't a fire burning in the hearth tonight. Her gown would have gone up in flames by now because she'd backed herself up against the stones.

Was she trying to get away from him or from his probing question? Colin wasn't certain. He was relentless, however, in his attempt to make her answer him. He wanted . . . no, he needed to hear her admit the truth.

"Answer me, Alesandra."

She suddenly quit trying to get away from him. She folded her arms in front of her and walked over to stand directly in front of him. Her head was tilted all the way back so she could look into his eyes.

"Yes."

"Yes, what?"

"Yes, I love you."

His satisfied grin said it all. He didn't seem at all surprised, and that thoroughly confused her.

"You already knew I loved you, didn't you?"

He slowly nodded. She shook her head. "How could you know when I didn't?"

He tried to take her into his arms. She quickly backed up a step. "Oh, no you don't. You want to kiss me, don't you? Then I'll forget my every thought. You will answer me first, Colin."

He wouldn't be denied. He pulled her into his arms, nudged her chin up, and kissed her long and hard. His tongue swept inside to rub against her own. She let out a loud sigh when he finally lifted his head. She collapsed against his chest and closed her eyes. His arms were wrapped around her waist. He hugged her tight and let his chin drop to rest on the top of her head.

It felt so damn good to hold her. The end of his workday was now something he looked forward to, because he knew she would be home waiting for him.

It suddenly dawned on Colin that he liked having a wife. Not just any wife, he qualified to himself. Alesandra. He used to dread the evenings, and all because the pain in his leg was usually excruciating by then. His gentle little bride had taken his mind off his aches, however. She exasperated him and she enchanted him, and he was usually so busy reacting to her, there wasn't room in his mind for anything else.

And she loved him.

"Now I'll answer your question," he said in a husky whisper she found wonderfully appealing.

"What question?"

He laughed. "You really do forget your every thought when I touch you, don't you?"

"You needn't sound so happy over that shameful fact. You're above such behavior though, aren't you? Why, I imagine you're full of thoughts while you're kissing me."

"Yes, I am."

"Oh." She sounded crestfallen.

"And every one of them is centered on what I want to do to you with my mouth, my hands, my . . ."

She reached up and clamped her hand over his mouth as a precaution against hearing something indelicate. Her reaction made Colin laugh again.

He pulled her hand away and said, "You wondered when I realized you loved me."

"Yes, I did wonder."

"It was on our wedding night," he explained. "The way you responded to me made it obvious you were in love with me."

She shook her head. "It wasn't obvious to me."

"Sure it was, sweetheart," he replied. "You couldn't hold anything back. Your every reaction was so damn honest. You couldn't have let yourself go that completely unless you loved me."

"Colin?"

"Yes?"

"You really should do something about your arrogance. It's getting out of hand."

"You like my arrogance."

She didn't reply to that outrageous remark. "I won't interfere in your schedule, Colin. I promise you."

"I never thought you would," he replied, smiling because she'd sounded so fervent.

"You haven't changed your plan, have you? You still need five full years before you . . ." She didn't go on.

"Before I what?"

Before you turn your attention to falling in love with your wife, you dolt, she thought to herself. And children, she added. In five years he would probably decide to have one or two. She wondered if she would be too old to have babies by then.

She definitely couldn't have one now. A baby would put too much pressure on Colin. Why, look how his partner, Nathan, had changed. He was now willing to do something he'd found unacceptable before. Selling stock was certainly a last resort, and it was the birth of his daughter that had changed his mind.

"Alesandra, before I what?" Colin asked again. The wistfulness in her voice puzzled him.

"Before you reach your goals," she blurted out.

"Yes," Colin said. "It's still five years."

He made that comment on his way over to the bed. He sat down on the side and bent to take his shoes off. "I didn't realize you were worried about my working for Richards," he said, turning the topic back to that issue. "You should have said something."

He tossed his shoes and socks aside, then turned his attention to his shirt. "And you were right when you said we're both responsible for each other. I haven't taken the time to consider your feelings. I'm sorry about that."

She watched him pull his shirt out of his waistband and work it up over his head. She couldn't take her gaze off him. She hung on his every word, hoping he would tell her how he felt about her. She didn't have enough gumption to ask him if he loved her. Colin hadn't had any problem asking *her,* she thought to herself. But then, he already knew her answer.

She didn't know his.

She had to shake her head over her own fanciful thoughts. Men didn't think about such things as love, or at least she didn't think they did. If Colin hadn't taken the time to consider her feelings regarding his dangerous work for Richards, why in heaven's name would he take the time to think about loving her? His mind was already completely full with his plans to build his company into an empire, and there simply wasn't room for anything else.

Alesandra straightened her shoulders and her resolve. She reminded herself that she found her husband's dedication admirable. She could be patient. Colin would get around to her in five years or so.

He drew her attention away from her thoughts when he said, "I've given my word to Richards I'd pass on a few papers for him." He paused to toss his shirt on the chair and stood up. "As for the other assignment I was offered, I'll let Morgan have it. In truth, I'd already decided against taking on the mission because it would have meant I'd have to be away from London for at least two weeks, possibly even three. Borders could have handled the office, of course, but I didn't want to leave you alone."

She thought that was the sweetest thing Colin had ever said to her. He would have missed her. She decided she wanted to hear him say the words.

"Why didn't you want to leave me alone?"

"Because of the policy, of course."

Her shoulders slumped. "Stefan and Raymond could watch out for me."

"You're my responsibility, Alesandra."

"But I don't wish to be your responsibility," she muttered. "You have enough on your mind. You don't need to add me to your list."

He didn't remark on that little speech. He unbuttoned his pants and stripped out of the rest of his clothes.

Her thoughts became fragments. She couldn't stop staring at her husband. Lord, he was magnificent. He was what she envisioned a warlord from bygone days must have looked like. Colin was all muscle, all power, and he had such sleek, smooth lines.

She followed him with her gaze as he crossed the room and bolted the bedroom door. He walked past her again on his way back to the bed. He pulled the covers back, straightened back up, and crooked his finger at her.

She didn't hesitate. She walked over to stand directly in front of him. Her hands were demurely folded in front of her. She looked serene, composed, but Colin knew better. The pulse in the base of her neck was beating frantically. He noticed when he lifted her hair away from her neck and bent down to kiss her.

She started to undress. Colin gently pushed her hands away from the bodice of her gown. "Let me," he whispered.

Her hands dropped back down to her sides. Colin was much quicker getting her clothes off than she was. He wasn't nearly as careful though. He didn't take the time to fold her garments but tossed them in a heap on top of his shirt. He was anxious to get to her bare skin. He noticed his hands shook when he untied the lace ribbon holding the neckline of her chemise in place and smiled over his lack of discipline.

He was surprised by his own quick response to her. His breathing was already ragged, his heartbeat was slamming inside his chest, and he hadn't even touched her yet—at least, not the way he wanted to touch her. Anticipation made him hard, aching.

Alesandra's thoughts were a little more centered. She was determined to get him to tell her he would have missed her if he'd taken the assignment.

When the last of her clothes had been discarded, she turned her gaze to her husband's chin and whispered his name.

"Colin?"

"Yes?"

"If you'd left London, would you have missed me?"

He lifted her chin up so she would look at him. His smile was filled with tenderness. "Yes."

She was so pleased with his answer, she let out a little sigh. Colin leaned down and brushed his mouth over hers.

"Do you wonder if I would have missed you?"

"No."

"Why not?"

He distracted her by taking her hands and placing them around his neck. Then he began to nibble on her earlobe. "Because I already know you'd miss me. You love me, remember?"

She couldn't fault that reasoning. Her husband certainly didn't have a problem with self-esteem. She thought to tell him so, and just as soon as he quit turning her thoughts into mush with his kisses, she would.

Colin placed wet kisses along the column of her throat. Her pulse was beating frantically now and she was already trembling in his arms. He thought that was a nice start.

He was slowly driving her crazy with his touch, and he knew it. That realization settled in her mind all at once.

Alesandra pushed herself away from him. He let her go, but the look on his face showed his confusion.

"What is it, sweetheart? Why did you push me away? I know you want me, and you sure as hell have to know how much I want you."

Alesandra was determined to turn the tables on her husband. She got into bed, moved to the center, and then knelt on her knees, facing him. She could feel herself blushing, but she absolutely refused to give in to her embarrassment. Colin was her husband and her lover, and she should be able to do anything she wanted with him.

She crooked her finger at him. He was so surprised by her boldness, he laughed. He got into bed and reached for her. She shook her head at him and pushed against his shoulders, telling him without words she wanted him on his back.

"Does my boldness please you?"

"Yes," he answered. "It pleases me."

It wasn't what he'd said as much as how he'd said it that gave Alesandra the courage to continue her game. She trailed her fingers down his chest.

"When you touch me, I go a little crazy," she whispered. "But tonight . . ."

She didn't go on. Her fingertips slowly circled his navel. She smiled over his quick indrawn breath when her hand moved lower.

"Yes?" he asked, his voice rough with need.

"You're going to lose your control before I lose mine. Do you accept my challenge, husband?"

In answer Colin stacked his hands behind his head and closed his eyes. "I'll win, Alesandra. I have far more experience."

She laughed over that boast. Odd, but admitting she loved him had somehow freed her from all restraint. She felt wild, wanton, and she didn't care at all that she wasn't being dignified. She really didn't think it was possible to maintain decorum when she was stark naked.

"Thank you for telling me I love you, Colin."

"You're welcome, sweetheart."

He was tense with anticipation. His voice was gritty when he said, "Are you about finished working up your courage?"

"I'm planning my attack," she countered.

That remark made him smile. She was highly curious about his body. She wanted to learn the taste of him just as he had learned the taste of her. The thought of what she wanted to do to him made her blush intensify, but Colin's eyes were closed so she didn't worry about hiding her embarrassment.

"Colin, is . . . everything permitted or is there something I shouldn't do?"

"Nothing's forbidden," he replied. "Our bodies belong to each other."

"Oh, that's nice."

She leaned back on her heels while she considered where she would like to start. His neck appealed to her, but then so did the rest of his body.

"Sweetheart, I'm going to fall asleep if you don't get started," he announced.

Alesandra decided not to waste time getting to the area that most intrigued her.

He should have kept his eyes open. When he felt her mouth on the tip of his erection, he damn near came off the bed. His groan of pleasure came out as a raw shout.

He came undone. It took every ounce of discipline he possessed not to spill his seed then and there. Perspiration broke out on his brow. Her sweet tongue flicked over his sensitive skin until he was in acute agony to let himself climax.

He couldn't take the torment long. He suddenly let out a low growl as he grabbed hold of her shoulders and lifted her upward. He forced her thighs apart with his knee so that she would straddle his hips, cupped the back of her neck with his hand to bring her mouth down to his, and then sealed her soft lips with his as he thrust inside her with one hard surge. The liquid heat he felt told him she was ready for him. His hands dropped to the sides of her hips and he forced her upward so that he could thrust back inside again. He was beyond reason now, and as soon as he felt her instinctively tighten around him, he was powerless to control his body's reaction. His climax caught him by surprise. He let out another loud groan as he poured his seed into her.

Touching her husband so intimately and watching his own uninhibited response had heightened Alesandra's pleasure. He found his own release before she did, but he didn't stop moving inside her. The ecstasy was almost too much to endure. She whimpered his name when the heat began to uncoil and spread like wildfire through her body. Her head fell back in surrender to the bliss. Colin felt the first tremors of her release and reached down between their joined bodies to stroke her. His touch helped her gain her own fulfillment. She arched against him, rigid with the consuming pleasure cascading down her limbs.

The tremors seemed to go on and on, overwhelming in their intensity, yet she wasn't at all afraid because Colin wrapped his arms around her and pulled her down against his chest. He held her close, keeping her safe until the storm of passion eased.

The beauty of their lovemaking was too much for her. She was so shaken by what had just happened she began to cry great gulping sobs against his neck.

Colin was just as shaken. He stroked her back and whispered honeyed words in a voice as ragged as a winter's wind until she regained a bit of her composure.

"Each time it gets better," she whispered.

"Is that so terrible?" he asked.

"I'll be dead in a week," she countered. "Can't you feel how my heart is hammering away? I'm certain this can't be at all good for me."

"If you die, sweetheart, you'll die happy," he boasted. "You liked being on top, didn't you?"

She slowly nodded. "I won the challenge, didn't I?"

His laughter filled the room. "Yes," he conceded.

She was content. She closed her eyes and snuggled against her husband.

"We forgot to eat our supper," she whispered.

"We'll eat later," he replied. "After I have my turn."

She didn't understand what he meant. "After you have a turn at what?"

Colin rolled her onto her back and covered her with his body. He braced his weight on his elbows and smiled down at her.

When his mouth was just an inch away from hers, he answered her.

"Winning."

Chapter 12

Loving and liking Colin were two different kettles of fish altogether. The man was impossible to reason with but extremely easy to kiss. She knew better than to offer him what was left of her inheritance to put into his company, and she finally had to resort to plain old-fashioned trickery in order to help him. She followed her father's example, and she told herself more than once that God would understand even if Colin didn't. Her husband would eventually get over his stubbornness, but she wasn't willing to let outsiders buy into his company while she waited for him to come to his senses.

The stock went public at ten o'clock on a Wednesday morning. Two minutes later, the transactions were complete and all twenty shares were sold. The price was extremely high.

Colin was stunned by the amount. He was suspicious, too. He demanded to know the names of the new stockholders. Dreyson would only tell him there was a single buyer of all twenty shares, but that he wasn't at liberty to divulge the buyer's name.

"You will answer one question for me," Colin demanded. "I want to know if my wife's name is on the shares as owner."

Dreyson immediately shook his head. "No, Sir Hallbrook," he was able to admit quite honestly. "Princess Alesandra isn't the owner."

Colin was satisfied the broker was telling the truth. A sudden possibility then occurred to him. "And her adviser, the man she calls Uncle Albert? Is he the owner."

"No," Dreyson immediately answered. "I'm certain he would have snapped at the chance but the shares were all sold within a blink of the eye. There wasn't time to notify him."

Colin finally let the matter drop. Alesandra said a prayer of thanksgiving because her husband wasn't going to probe deeper.

She felt extremely guilty because she'd used trickery. She knew it was wrong to manipulate her husband, but she blamed her sin on his stubbornness. She thought she could put the deceit behind her, too, yet found that the longer she went without confessing the truth to her husband, the more miserable she became. She did a lot of muttering to herself. Thankfully, Colin wasn't there to hear her. He was working twelve-hour days at the shipping company. Flannaghan heard her carrying on, of course, but he believed she was just in an irritable mood because of her long confinement.

The month actually did hurry by. Catherine's ball was reported to have been a smashing success, and the event was recounted in vivid detail by both the duchess and her daughter-in-law, Lady Jade. They were sorry Alesandra couldn't attend, of course, but they understood the reason behind Colin's decision to make her stay under lock and key.

Catherine stopped by the following afternoon to add her own descriptions. She announced she was already in love with a marquess and two earls. She was anxiously waiting to receive notes through her father for permission for the gentlemen to call on her.

Because Colin was working such long hours, Alesandra treasured their time together and didn't like bringing up business matters. Still, there were times when it was necessary. The rental agent notified Flannaghan that the owners had decided to stay abroad and wished to sell their town house. Alesandra had become attached to her home and wanted to purchase it. She eased into the topic at the dinner table.

Colin's attitude toward her inheritance hadn't changed. He told her he didn't care what she did with her money.

Then she became more specific. "I would like to purchase this town house," she announced.

She didn't give him time to deny her request right away, but hurried on with her explanation. "Because of your ignorant English law, it's almost impossible for a married woman to make a contract on her own. I wouldn't bother you with this matter, but I need your signature on the papers."

"The reason for that law is simple to understand," he countered. "Husbands are legally responsible for any and all ventures their wives enter into."

"Yes, but the issue under discussion . . ."

"The issue is rather or not I can provide for you," he interrupted. His voice had gone hard. "Do you doubt I'll be able to provide for you?"

"No, of course not," she replied.

He nodded, satisfied. She let out a sigh. He wasn't going to be at all reasonable about this. She briefly considered using her initials and claiming Uncle Albert had purchased the town house for them, then discarded the idea. Colin was bound to pitch a fit. Besides, such trickery would be an out-and-out lie, and she doubted God would forgive her this transgression where her motives were only selfish ones. Using a little bit of deceit to secure the stocks and keep them in the family in order to help Colin and his partner was one thing, but manipulating the purchase of a home just because she'd taken a fancy to it was quite another. Her list of sins had grown by leaps and bounds since she'd married Colin, she supposed, but most of her offenses were surely under God's column of minor transgressions. A blatant lie told to get her own way would definitely come under the heading of more serious sins.

She couldn't deceive him. "As you wish, Colin. I would

like you to note that I believe you're being extremely unreasonable about this."

"So noted," he replied dryly.

He didn't even let her have the last word this time. Yet although he was frequently insensitive to her needs, he was quite the opposite with other people. He could actually be very thoughtful upon occasion. After the month was over and Raymond and Stefan were no longer needed to guard her, Colin offered them employment with his company. The men were eager to work on a ship and travel the world, as they were both young and unattached, and Colin put them under the supervision of his friend, Jimbo, so they would be properly trained.

Colin continued to be a very passionate lover. He spent every night in her bed, and after he made love to her, he held her close until he thought she had fallen asleep. Then he went back to his own room. Alesandra was afraid to make an issue out of the ritual because her husband had made it quite clear he didn't want to talk about his leg. He all but pretended he didn't even have a problem. She didn't understand how his mind worked. Did it make him feel inferior if he acknowledged a human frailty? And if he loved her, wasn't it his duty to share his joys and his sorrows with her?

But Colin didn't love her—at least, not yet, Alesandra reminded herself. She wasn't disheartened, however, because she had complete faith in her husband. He was an intelligent man, after all, and in time she felt certain his attitude would soften and he'd realize what a fine wife she was. If he didn't get around to the realization for five years, that was all right. She could wait. She would keep her promise to him, too. She wouldn't interfere.

The inserts she'd had made for her husband's shoes didn't qualify as interference in her mind, however. She took great delight in the fact that he was now wearing the special pair of Wellingtons almost every day. The bootmaker had made two leather inserts. The first was too thick, or at least she thought it must have been too thick because Colin only wore the boots for a few minutes before taking them off and putting on another pair. The second insert she'd slipped under the lining worked much better. Colin believed he'd broken in the boots and they were now comfortable. She knew better, of course, but she didn't say a word. Neither did Flannaghan. The butler whispered to Alesandra that he'd noticed his employer's limp wasn't quite as pronounced at the end of the day. Alesandra agreed. She was so pleased with the success of her plan she immediately ordered two extra inserts made so that her husband would have comfortable walking shoes and evening dress shoes as well.

To the outside world, Colin appeared to be a man without a care in the world. He always wore a devil-may-care smile, and he was one of the most popular men in London. When he entered a room, he was immediately surrounded by friends. The women wouldn't be left out either. It didn't matter to most of the ladies that he was now married. They continued to flock to his side. Colin was a charmer, yes, but he wasn't a flirt. He usually had hold of Alesandra's hand while he went about the task of mixing business with pleasure. Colin wasn't just intelligent—he was clever, too. Most of the shipping deals were negotiated in the ballrooms. When she realized that fact, she didn't mind the late hours they kept every night.

She did do quite a bit of napping, though. She and Colin attended parties almost every night for two full months, and she was so exhausted she was seized with attacks of nausea.

She was looking forward to tonight's affair, however, because Colin's family was also going to be attending the Earl of Allenborough's bash. The duke and duchess were escorting their daughter Catherine, and Colin's brother, Caine, and his wife were also going to be there.

The earl had rented Harrison House for the ball. The magnificent marble and stone estate was almost as large as the prince regent's palace.

Alesandra wore her ivory-colored gown. The neckline wasn't overly revealing, but Colin still felt compelled to grumble about it. Her only adornment was a beautiful gold and sapphire necklace that fit like a choker around her neck. There was only one sapphire in the center of the looped chain. The precious jewel was at least two carats in size and appeared to be flawless. Colin knew the thing was worth a bloody fortune, and he didn't like the idea of Alesandra wearing it.

"I have a special fondness for this necklace," she remarked once they were settled inside the carriage and on their way to the ball. "But I can tell from your frown you don't care for it. Why is that, Colin?"

"Why do you like it?"

Her fingertips brushed the necklace. "Because it belonged to my mother. Whenever I wear it, I'm reminded of her. The necklace was a gift to her from my father."

Colin's attitude immediately softened. "Then you should wear it."

"But why did it displease you? I saw the way you frowned when you first noticed it."

He shrugged. "I was displeased because I didn't buy it for you."

She didn't know what to make of that remark. She reached behind her neck and started to undo the clasp so she could take the necklace off. Colin stopped her. "I was being foolish. Leave it. The color matches your eyes."

From the look on her husband's face, she concluded he'd just given her a compliment and not a criticism. She folded her hands in her lap, smiled at her husband, and changed the subject. "Shouldn't your partner be home any day now?"

"Yes."

"Will I like him?"

"Eventually."

"Will I like his wife?"

"Yes."

She wasn't upset by his short answers. She could tell from his expression he was in pain. His leg was obviously acting up tonight, she speculated, and when Colin propped his foot up on the cushion next to her, she knew her guess was right.

It took all the self-control she could muster not to reach over and touch his leg. "We don't have to attend the affair tonight," she said. "You look weary to me."

"I'm fine." he said in a clipped, no-nonsense tone of voice. She decided not to argue with him.

She changed the topic again. "It's appropriate for us to give a gift to Nathan and Sara for their baby."

Colin had leaned back against the seat and closed his eyes. She wasn't certain if he was paying attention to what she was saying or not. She lowered her gaze to her lap and began to adjust the folds of her gown. "I didn't think you wanted to be bothered with the chore so I took care of it. Since you and Nathan own a shipping company, I thought it would be nice to have a replica of one of the ships made. What do you think of that idea? When they purchase a home, Sara could put our gift on her mantel."

"I'm sure she'll like it," Colin replied. "Whatever you decide is fine with me."

"There were several drawings of your ships in your library," she said then. "I hope you don't mind that I borrowed one of the *Emerald* to give to the craftsman."

The carriage came to a quick stop in front of Harrison House. Colin had looked half asleep until the door was opened by the coachman. Then his manner changed. He helped Alesandra out, took hold of her arm, and started up the steps. He spotted his brother and his wife walking toward them and immediately smiled.

Colin hadn't made a miraculous recovery. His smile was forced, but Alesandra knew she was the only one who realized how much pain he was in. The physician had told her that Colin should get off his leg when it pained him. Her husband wouldn't listen to such advice, however. He would probably dance the night away just to prove he was all right.

The night air was damp and chilly. Alesandra suddenly felt a bit lightheaded. Her stomach turned queasy, too, and she was thankful she hadn't eaten much of the light supper Cook had prepared. Exhaustion was surely the reason she wasn't feeling well, she told herself.

Jade noticed how pale Alesandra's complexion was and made that mention in front of their husbands. Both Caine and Colin turned to look at her.

"Why didn't you tell me you didn't feel well?" Colin asked.

"I'm just a little weary," she hastily replied. "Do quit frowning at me, Colin. I'm not accustomed to going out every night and that's why I'm a bit fatigued. 'Tis the truth, I would rather stay home every now and then."

"You don't like the parties?"

Her husband looked surprised. She lifted her shoulders in a shrug. "We do what we must," she replied.

"Explain what you mean, sweetheart."

He wasn't going to let the matter drop. "All right then," she said. "No, I don't particularly like the parties . . ."

"Why didn't you say something?"

He was exasperated with her. She shook her head at him. "Because each affair is a business opportunity for you and Nathan," she explained. "You don't like going out either," she added. "And that is why I said that we do what we must. I would have said something eventually."

His wife was an extremely astute woman. She'd understood his motives and known exactly how he'd really felt about all the parties he dragged her to. "Eventually?" he repeated with a grin. "When, exactly, would you have offered a complaint?"

"I would never complain and you should apologize for even suggesting I would," she countered. "Eventually would be exactly five years from now. Then I would mention my preference to stay home."

Caine smiled at Alesandra and said, "Be sure to thank your friend, Albert, for his advice regarding that investment. The stock has already increased threefold."

She nodded.

"What investment?" Colin asked.

Caine answered. "I mentioned I was interested in investment opportunities the last time I was over at your house, and Alesandra told me Albert had recommended shares in Campton Glass. It just went public."

"I thought you were investing in Kent's garment factory," Jade interjected.

"I'm still considering it," Caine replied.

Alesandra shook her head before she could stop herself. "I don't believe that would be a wise investment, Caine. I do hope you'll give the matter careful consideration first."

She could feel Colin's gaze on her but didn't turn to look at him. "Albert was also interested in the garment factory. He had his broker, Dreyson, go and look at the place. Dreyson reported it was a fire trap and ill run. There are hundreds of women and children employed there and conditions are deplorable. Albert wasn't about to make the owner rich or get rich himself on such a venture. Why, he would be profiting from other people's misery—at least, that's what he told me in his last letter."

Caine immediately agreed. The topic was dropped when they entered the foyer of Harrison House. The duke and duchess were waiting in a nearby alcove with Catherine and immediately motioned for Caine and Colin and their wives to join them. Business matters were put aside. Catherine hugged Jade, then turned to hug Alesandra. She noticed the sapphire necklace right away and declared she was about to swoon with envy. Catherine wore a single strand of pearls around her neck. She absentmindedly fingered her necklace as she mentioned that her violet gown would look far more smashing if her father had given her a sapphire to wear.

Alesandra laughed over the not-too-subtle hint. Since no one was observing them, she quickly took off her necklace and handed it to Catherine.

"This belonged to my mother, so you must be very careful with it," Alesandra whispered so Colin wouldn't overhear her. "The clasp is quite secure and as long as you leave it on, you won't lose it."

Catherine gave a halfhearted protest as she unclasped her own necklace and handed it to Alesandra. Jade held on to Catherine's dance card while her sister-in-law put on the necklace, then made her turn around so that she could make certain the clasp was secure.

"You be careful with this," she ordered her.

Colin didn't notice the switch in jewelry for a good hour. Sir Richards came hurrying over to greet the family, and when Caine was occupied answering a question from his father, the director gave Colin the signal that he wanted to speak in private to him. The look on Richards's face indicated the matter was serious.

The opportunity for a quick conference arose when Colin's father requested a dance with Alesandra. As soon as they walked toward the center of the ballroom, Colin went over to the director. Richards stood at the entrance of a triangular alcove, watching the crowd.

The two men stood side by side without speaking for several minutes. Colin noticed Neil Perry across the floor and immediately frowned with displeasure. He hoped Alesandra wouldn't notice the man. She was bound to try to corner him as soon as she spotted him and demand answers about his sister. Neil would turn insulting, of course, and Colin would probably have to smash his face in.

That possibility made Colin smile.

His sister drew his attention then. She was partnered with Morgan. Colin clasped his hands behind his back and watched the pair. Morgan spotted Colin and nodded to him. Colin nodded back.

Sir Richards also nodded to the new recruit. He smiled, too. For that reason Colin was surprised by his angry tone of voice when he spoke. "I shouldn't have given the assignment to Morgan," he whispered. "He made a muck of it. Do you remember Devins?"

Colin nodded. The man Richards referred to was an agent who was occasionally used to transfer information for the government.

"He's dead now. From what I can sort out, he got caught in the middle of what turned into a bloody fight. Morgan said Devins panicked. They were waiting for their contact when Devins's daughter came along. It was a bad piece of luck. The girl was killed in the cross fire. Damn it all, Colin, it should have gone as smooth as ice, but Morgan's eagerness and inexperience turned a simple, uncomplicated mission into a fiasco. Bad luck or not, the man doesn't have the instincts for this line of work," he added with a nod.

"Don't use him again." Colin's voice shook with anger.

"Devins wasn't the type to panic. He had a temper, yes, but he could always be relied on to use sound judgment."

"Yes, under usual circumstances I would agree with your evaluation. However, he was also a protective father, Colin. I can imagine he did panic if he thought she was in danger."

"I would think a father would react in just the opposite manner. He had more reasons not to panic."

Richards nodded. "I've told Morgan he's out. He felt bad about my decision, of course. He was sorry it went sour and admitted he'd overreacted. He blamed you too, son, because you didn't go along and show him the ropes, so to speak."

Colin shook his head. He wasn't buying that excuse. From the look on the director's face, he wasn't buying it either.

"You're right, Richards. He doesn't have the instincts."

"It's a pity," the director remarked. "He's eager to please and he needs the money. I imagine he'll marry well. He's quite a charmer with the ladies."

Colin looked back at the dance floor. He found Morgan right away. He was smiling down at Catherine as he whirled her around the floor. His sister was laughing and obviously having the time of her life.

Colin noticed the necklace Catherine was wearing then. He immediately turned to find Alesandra in the crowd. He spotted his father first, then saw Alesandra. She was now wearing Catherine's pearls. Colin frowned with concern. The switch in jewelry wasn't the cause, however. His wife's complexion had turned as white as her gown. She looked ready to faint.

Colin excused himself from the director and went to his wife. He tapped his father on his shoulder and took Alesandra into his arms. She forced a smile and leaned into her husband's side.

The waltz ended just as Colin turned to take his wife out on the front terrace.

"You're really ill, aren't you, sweetheart?"

Caine was standing with his wife next to the doors leading outside. He took one look at Alesandra's complexion and immediately backed up a step. His sister-in-law's face was turning green. He hoped to God whatever was ailing her wasn't the catching kind.

Alesandra couldn't make up her mind whether she wanted to swoon or throw up. She prayed she wouldn't do either until she was home. The fresh air seemed to help, however, and after a minute or two, her head quit spinning.

"It was all that twirling around and around," she told her husband.

Caine let out a loud sigh of relief and stepped forward to offer his assistance. Colin left Alesandra leaning against his brother while he said their good-byes, then came back to collect her. She hadn't worn a cloak, so he took off his jacket and put it around her shoulders on the way down the steps to their waiting carriage.

Feeling better was short-lived. The rocking motion of the carriage made her stomach start acting up again. She gripped her hands together in her lap and took several deep breaths to calm herself.

Colin reached over and hauled her onto his lap. He tucked her head under his chin and held her tight.

He carried her inside the town house and up to her bedroom. He left her sitting on the side of the bed while he went to fetch a drink of cool water she'd requested.

Alesandra stretched out on top of the covers and closed her eyes. She was sound asleep a minute later.

Colin undressed her. Flannaghan was pacing with worry outside the door, but Colin wasn't about to let him help. He stripped his wife out of her garments and put her under the covers. She really was exhausted, for she slept like a baby now and didn't even open her eyes when he lifted her up so he could pull the blankets back.

He decided to spend the full night with her. If she became ill he wanted to be close by in case she needed his help. And, Lord, he was suddenly feeling exhausted, too. He stripped out of his own clothes and got into bed beside her. She instinctively rolled into his arms. Colin kissed her forehead, wrapped his arms around her, and closed his eyes. He, too, was asleep less than a minute later.

He awakened a little before dawn when his wife rubbed

her backside against him. She was still asleep. Colin was barely awake enough to think about what he was doing. He made love to her, and when they'd both found fulfillment, he fell asleep again still joined to her.

Alesandra was feeling as fit as ever the next day. Catherine arrived on her doorstep at two that afternoon to personally return the necklace. She was full of news, too.

She was having a grand time with her season and wanted to tell Alesandra all about the offers for her hand in marriage her father had already received.

Catherine linked her arm through Alesandra's and pulled her along into the salon.

"Where is my brother on this fine Sunday afternoon?"

"He's working," Alesandra answered. "He should be home by dinner."

Catherine sat down in the chair adjacent to the settee. Flannaghan stood near the entrance, waiting to find out if he was needed.

"I can barely keep all the gentlemen straight in my mind," Catherine exaggerated.

"You must make a list of the gentlemen you're interested in," Alesandra advised. "Then you wouldn't be confused."

Catherine thought that was a sound plan of action. Alesandra immediately asked Flannaghan to fetch her paper and pen.

"I've already asked father to decline several gentlemen and he's been very accommodating. He isn't in any hurry to get me settled."

"You should probably start a list of your rejections, too," Alesandra suggested. "With your reasons by each name, of course, in the event you change your mind or forget why you discarded them."

"Yes, that's a wonderful idea," Catherine claimed. "It's so thoughtful of you to help."

Alesandra was thrilled to be of assistance. "Organization is the key, Catherine," she announced.

"The key to what?"

Alesandra opened her mouth to answer, then realized she

wasn't exactly sure. "To a well-structured, happy life," she decided aloud.

Flannaghan returned with the items she'd requested. Alesandra thanked him and then turned back to Catherine.

"Shall we begin with the rejections?"

"Yes," Catherine agreed. "Put Neil Perry at the top of the list. He offered for me yesterday. I don't like him at all."

Alesandra titled the list, then put Perry's name down. "I don't particularly like him either," she announced. "You've shown sound judgment in rejecting him."

"Thank you," Catherine replied.

"What specific reason should I put next to his name?"

"Disgusting."

Alesandra laughed. "He is that," she remarked. "He's the complete opposite of his sister. Victoria's a dear lady."

Catherine didn't know Victoria and therefore couldn't agree or disagree. She continued with the names of men she found unacceptable. She hurried through the task since she was anxious to concentrate on the appealing candidates. She also had additional news she was dying to share with Alesandra.

"All right, then, let's begin with the second list."

Catherine gave her four names. The last was Morgan. "He hasn't offered for me, of course, and I only just met him last night, but, Alesandra, he's so handsome and charming. When he smiles, I declare, my heart feels like it's going to stop beating. I doubt I'll stand a chance with him, though. He's extremely popular with the ladies. Still, he did mention he was going to ask father if he could call."

"I've met Morgan," Alesandra replied. "And I do agree he's charming. I believe Colin likes him, too."

"He would be a fine catch," Catherine decided. "Still . . . there is one other I would like to consider as well."

"What is his name and I'll add him to your list."

Catherine started blushing. "It's the most romantic thing," she whispered. "But Father wouldn't think so. You must promise not to tell anyone."

"Tell what?"

"Just promise me first, then I'll explain. Put your hand over your heart. That makes your promise more binding."

Alesandra didn't dare laugh. Catherine sounded so sincere. She didn't want to hurt her feelings. She did as she was instructed and placed her hand over her heart while she gave her pledge.

"Now will you explain?"

"I don't know the gentleman's name yet," Catherine said. "He was at the ball last night. I'm certain of it. I'm certain he's wonderful, too."

"How can you know he's wonderful if you've never met him? Or did you meet him? That's it, isn't it? You just don't know his name. Tell me what he looks like. Perhaps I've met the man."

"Oh, I haven't seen him yet."

"You're confusing me."

Catherine laughed. "He has a name we can put on the list for now."

Alesandra dipped her pen into the inkwell. Catherine waited until she'd completed that task, then whispered, "My Secret Admirer."

She let out a long happy sigh after whispering the name. Alesandra gasped at the very same time. She dropped her pen into her lap. Ink blotted her pink dress.

"Good heavens, look what you've done," Catherine cried out. "Your dress . . ."

Alesandra shook her head. "Forget the dress," she countered. Her voice shook with worry. "I want to hear about this secret admirer."

Catherine frowned. "I haven't done anything wrong, Alesandra. Why are you so upset with me?"

"I'm not upset . . . at least not with you," Alesandra said.

"You shouted at me."

"I didn't mean to shout."

She saw the tears in Catherine's eyes then. Her sister-in-law was high-strung, and her feelings were easily hurt. She was still more child than woman, Alesandra realized, and she made up her mind then and there not to tell her about her worries. She would talk to Colin first. He would know what to do about the secret admirer.

"I'm sorry I upset you. Please forgive me." She forced a mild tone of voice when she added, "I'm very interested in hearing all about this secret admirer. Will you explain?"

Catherine blinked away her tears. "There isn't much to explain," she said. "I received a lovely posey this morning with a notecard attached. There wasn't a message—just the signature."

"Which was?"

"Your Secret Admirer. I thought it was very romantic. I don't understand why you're acting so strange."

"Dear God." Alesandra whispered those words and collapsed against the back of the settee. Her mind raced with her fears. Colin would have to listen to her, she decided, even if she had to tie the man up while he slept to get her way.

"You're shivering, Alesandra," Catherine said.

"I'm just a little chilled."

"Mother told Jade she thinks you're carrying."

"I'm what?"

She hadn't meant to shout, of course, but Catherine's blurted-out remark did surprise a near scream out of her.

"They think you might be carrying Colin's baby," Catherine explained. "Are you?"

"No, of course not. It isn't possible. It's too soon."

"You've been married over three months now," Catherine reminded her. "Mother told Jade your nausea could be a symptom. She's going to be disappointed if you're not carrying. Are you sure, Alesandra?"

"Yes, I'm sure."

She wasn't telling Catherine the truth. She really wasn't sure at all. Good Lord, she could be pregnant. It had been quite a long time since her last monthly—over three months ago. She counted back just to be certain. Yes, that was right. She had had cramps two weeks before she got married . . . and none since. Was it possible the stomach upset wasn't due to exhaustion? She'd never napped before, she thought to herself, but now she could barely get through a day without an afternoon rest. Of course, she and Colin had had to go out every night, and she really believed the late hours they were keeping made the afternoon naps necessary.

Her hand dropped to her stomach in a protective gesture. "I would like to have Colin's children," she said. "But he has an important schedule and I promised not to interfere."

"What does a schedule have to do with babies?"

Alesandra tried to pull herself together. She felt as though she were in a daze. She couldn't seem to organize her thoughts. Why hadn't she realized . . . the possibility . . . the only logical answer . . . Oh, yes, she was pregnant.

"Alesandra, do explain," Catherine demanded.

"It's a five-year schedule," Alesandra blurted out. "I'll have children then."

Catherine thought she was jesting with her. She burst into laughter. Alesandra was able to maintain her composure until her sister-in-law took her leave a few minutes later. Then she hurried up to her bedroom, shut the door behind her, and promptly burst into tears.

She was filled with the most conflicting emotions. She was thrilled she was carrying Colin's son or daughter. A precious life growing inside her seemed a true miracle to her and she was fairly overwhelmed with her joy—and her guilt.

Colin might not be happy about the baby at all. Alesandra didn't have any concerns about his ability to be a good father, but wouldn't a child now be an added burden? Oh, God, she wished he loved her. She wished he wasn't so stubborn about her inheritance, too.

She didn't want to feel guilty, and how in heaven's name could she feel so euphoric and frightened at the same time?

Flannaghan came upstairs with a cup of hot tea for his mistress. He was about to knock on her door when he heard her crying. He stood there, uncertain what to do. He wanted to find out what was wrong, of course, so that he could try to help, but she had closed the door, indicating she wanted privacy.

He heard the front door open and immediately turned

back to the steps. He'd reached the landing when Colin walked inside. He wasn't alone. His partner, Nathan, followed behind him. The man was so tall, he had to duck his head under the arch of the doorway.

Flannaghan knew better than to blurt out his worry about his mistress in front of company. He hurried down the steps, bowed to his employer, and then turned to greet his partner.

"We'll go into the salon," Colin said. "Caine and his wife are going to be joining us shortly. Where's Alesandra?"

"Your princess is above the stairs resting," Flannaghan answered. He was trying to act like a dignified man of the house. He had met Nathan before, of course, yet was still a bit intimidated by the man.

"Let her rest until my brother gets here." He turned to his partner and said, "We've had to go out every damn night. Alesandra is exhausted."

"Does she like going out every night?" Nathan asked.

Colin smiled. "No."

A knock sounded at the door just as Colin and his partner walked into the salon. Flannaghan assumed the callers were Colin's family. He hurried to open the door and was in the process of bowing low when he realized it was just a messenger boy standing on the stoop. The messenger held a white gift box tied with a red ribbon. He thrust the package at Flannaghan.

"I've been given a coin to see Princess Alesandra gets this," he announced.

Flannaghan took the box, nodded, and then shut the door. He turned to go up the stairs, smiling now, for he had a good reason to interrupt his princess and hopefully, once he was inside her room, he could nag out of her the reason why she was so upset.

The door knocker sounded again. Flannaghan put the box down on the side table and went back to the front door. Less than a minute had passed and he thought the messenger had returned.

Colin's brother and his wife waited entrance. Lady Jade gave Flannaghan a nice smile. Caine was barely paying attention to the butler, however. He was diligently frowning down at his wife.

"Good afternoon," Flannaghan announced as he pulled the door wide.

Jade hurried inside. She greeted the butler. Caine gave him a nod. He seemed preoccupied.

"We are not finished with this discussion," he told his wife in a hard, no-nonsense tone of voice.

"Yes, we are finished," she countered. "You're being extremely unreasonable, husband. Flannaghan, where are Colin and Nathan?"

"They're waiting for you in the salon, milady."

"I'm going to get to the bottom of this, Jade," Caine muttered. "I don't care how long it takes."

"You're being unreasonably jealous, Caine."

"Damn right I am."

He made that emphatic statement of fact in a loud voice as he followed his wife into the salon.

Both Nathan and Colin immediately stood up when Jade entered the salon. Nathan took his sister into his arms and hugged her tight. He glared at Caine because he had raised his voice to his sister, then added a rebuke.

"A husband shouldn't raise his voice to his wife."

Caine laughed. Colin joined in. "You've done a complete turnaround," Caine remarked. "I seem to remember you were always shouting."

"I'm a changed man," Nathan replied in a calm, matter-of-fact voice. "I'm content."

"I'll wager your Sara's probably doing all the yelling now," Colin said.

Nathan grinned. "The little woman does have a temper," he remarked.

Jade sat down in the chair next to Nathan's. Her brother resumed his seat and turned his attention back to Caine. "Are you two having a difference of opinion?"

"No," Jade replied.

"Yes," Caine answered at the very same moment.

"I don't wish to speak about this now," Jade announced.

She deliberately turned the topic. "I'm dying to see the baby, Nathan. Does she look like you or Sara?"

"She's got my eyes and Sara's feet, thank God," Nathan replied.

"Where are they now?" Colin asked.

"I dropped Sara at her mother's so she could show off the baby."

"Are you staying with her family while you're in London?" Caine asked.

"Hell, no," Nathan answered. There was a true shudder in his voice. "They would drive me daft and I'd probably kill one of them. We're staying with you."

Caine nodded. He smiled, too. How like Nathan to instruct instead of ask. Jade clasped her hands together with joy. She was obviously thrilled with the news.

"Where is your wife?" Nathan asked Colin.

"Flannaghan went upstairs to get her. She'll be down in a minute."

One minute turned into ten. Alesandra had already taken off her ink-stained gown and put on a pretty violet-colored dress. She was sitting at her writing table, absorbed in her fanciful task of making a list of duties for Colin. She would never show the list to her husband, of course, because none of the orders were appropriate. Wives, she was learning, did better to suggest to their husbands. Most, including Colin, didn't like being ordered to do anything.

Still, it was quite all right to pretend, and it did make her feel better to write down her expectations. She put Colin's name at the top of the paper. The list of orders followed.

First, he should listen to his wife explain her concerns about the alarming coincidences involving Victoria and a man who called himself a secret admirer. In brackets she wrote Catherine's name.

Second, Colin should do something about his attitude toward her inheritance. In brackets she added the words *too stubborn.*

Third, Colin shouldn't wait five years to realize he loved her. He should realize it now, and tell her so.

Fourth, he should try to be happy he was going to become a father. He shouldn't blame her for interfering with his schedule.

Alesandra read over her list and let out a loud sigh. She was so thrilled she was going to have Colin's baby and so afraid he would be unhappy, she wanted to weep and shout at the same time.

She let out a long sigh. It wasn't like her to be so disorganized or so emotional.

She added a question to her list: "Can pregnant wives become nuns?"

She wasn't quite finished and added one more sentence: "Mother Superior loves me."

There—that important reminder made her feel a little better. She nodded, calmer now, and lifted the sheet of paper in her hands with the intent of tearing it up.

Flannaghan interrupted her. He knocked on her door and when she bid him enter he rushed inside.

He was relieved to see his princess had quit weeping. Her eyes still looked a bit swollen, but he didn't mention her condition and neither did she.

"Princess, we have . . ."

She didn't let him finish. "Pray forgive me for interrupting, but I don't want to forget my question to you. Has Cook been able to talk to anyone in the viscount's household yet? I know I've been pestering you with this matter and I do apologize, but I have sound reasons for wanting to know my answers, Flannaghan. Please be patient with me."

"She still hasn't run into any of the staff at market," Flannaghan replied. "May I offer a suggestion?"

"Yes, of course."

"Why not send her over to the viscount's town house? If she goes to the back door, the viscount won't know she called. I don't believe the staff would mention it to him."

She immediately nodded agreement. "That's a fine idea," she said in praise. "This is too important to put off any longer. Please ask Cook to go now. She can use our carriage."

"Oh, no, Princess, she wouldn't wish to ride in the

carriage. It wouldn't be proper. The viscount's residence is just a stone's throw away," he exaggerated. "She'll enjoy the brisk walk."

"If you're certain," Alesandra replied. "Now what was it you wanted to speak to be about before I interrupted you?"

"We have company," Flannaghan explained. "Your husband's partner is here. Milord's brother and his wife are with him."

She started to stand up, then changed her mind. "Wait just a minute and I'll follow you down. I've made a fresh list for you."

Flannaghan smiled in anticipation. He'd learned to love her lists, because in his heart he knew she cared about him enough to help him become organized. She always included little bits of praise along with her suggestions for tasks she believed he would wish to complete for the day. His princess was always most appreciative, too, and gracious with her compliments.

He watched as she sorted through her pile. Alesandra finally found the sheet of paper with Flannaghan's name on it and handed it to him.

He tucked the list in his pocket and escorted her down the stairs. He spotted the package on the table in the foyer and only then remembered he was supposed to give it to her.

"That box arrived a few minutes ago," he told her. "Would you like to open it now or wait until later?"

"Later, please," she answered. "I'm most curious to meet Colin's partner first."

Colin was about to get up and go after his wife when she walked into the salon. The men immediately stood up. Alesandra went over to Jade, took hold of her hand, and told her how pleased she was to see her again.

"Damn, but you did all right, Colin."

Nathan whispered that praise. Alesandra didn't hear his remark. She finally gained enough courage to walk over to the huge man and smile up at him.

"Do I bow my head to a princess?" Nathan asked.

"If you do, I'll be able to kiss your cheek in appreciation. I'll need a ladder otherwise."

Nathan laughed. He leaned down, received a kiss on his cheek, and then straightened up again. "Now explain what you meant by appreciation," he ordered.

Lord, he was a handsome devil. Terribly soft-spoken too. "In appreciation for putting up with Colin, of course. I understand how your partnership works so well now. Colin's the stubborn one, and you're surely the peacemaker in the company."

Colin threw back his head and laughed heartily. Nathan looked a little sheepish.

"You've got it backwards, Alesandra," Caine explained. "Nathan's the stubborn one and Colin's the peacemaker."

"She calls me a dragon," Colin announced.

Alesandra frowned at her husband for giving away that secret, then walked over to sit on the settee next to him.

"Caine, quit glaring at your wife," Colin ordered.

"He's extremely upset with me," Jade explained. "And that's ridiculous, of course. I didn't encourage the attraction."

"I never said you did," Caine argued.

Jade turned to Colin. "He threw out the flowers. Can you imagine?"

Colin shrugged. He put his arm around Alesandra's shoulders and stretched out his legs in front of him. "I haven't the faintest idea what you're talking about."

"You had better get this argument settled before I bring Sara and Joanna into your home. Daughters need a peaceful environment."

Nathan made that announcement. Caine and Colin turned to stare at him. They both looked incredulous. Nathan ignored them.

"Were you pleased when you found out you were going to become a father?" Alesandra tried to sound very nonchalant when she asked Nathan that question. She gripped her hands together in her lap.

If Nathan thought her question odd, he didn't remark on it. "Yes, I was very pleased."

"But what about your five-year schedule?" Alesandra asked.

"What about it?" Nathan countered, his confusion obvious.

"Didn't the baby interfere with your company plans?"

"No."

She didn't believe him. Nathan never would have sold company stock if it weren't for the baby. Colin had told her he wanted to purchase a home for his family.

She wasn't about to bring up that tender topic, however. "I see," she said. "You made allowances for such an eventuality in your schedule."

"Colin, what is your wife talking about?"

"When I first met Alesandra, I explained I wasn't going to get married for five years."

"Or have a family," she interjected with a nod.

"Or have a family," he repeated just to please her.

Caine and Jade shared a look. "How organized of you," Caine told his brother.

Alesandra believed Colin's brother had just given a compliment. "Yes, he is very organized," she enthusiastically agreed.

"Plans have a way of changing," Jade said. She was looking at Alesandra when she made that remark. Her expression was filled with sympathy. Alesandra was suddenly looking quite miserable. Jade believed she knew why.

"A baby is a blessing," she blurted out.

"Yes," Nathan agreed. "Jade's correct, too, when she says plans have a way of changing," he added with a nod. "Colin and I were counting on my wife's inheritance from the king to strengthen the company funds, but the prince regent decided to keep the money and we had to turn our minds to finding other solutions."

"Hence the five-year schedule," Colin explained.

Alesandra looked like she was about to burst into tears. Caine felt like throttling his brother. If Colin would only look at her face, he would know something was terribly wrong. His brother obviously didn't have a clue, however, and Caine didn't believe he should interfere . . . yet.

Alesandra was caught up in her own thoughts. She could feel herself getting angry over Nathan's casually given remark. He had made it quite clear that neither he nor Colin had any qualms about using Sara's inheritance. Why, then, was Colin so stubbornly resistant to using some of hers?

Colin drew her attention when he spoke again. "Caine, will you quit scowling at your wife."

"He blames me," Jade announced.

"I do not blame you," Caine argued.

"Blames you for what?" Colin asked.

"I received a bundle of flowers this morning. There wasn't a note, just a signature."

Nathan and Colin frowned in unison.

"You received flowers from another man?" Nathan asked, his astonishment clear.

"Yes."

Nathan turned to glare at his brother-in-law. "You damn well better do something about this, Caine. She's your wife. You can't allow another man to send her flowers. Why the hell haven't you killed the bastard?"

Caine was thankful Nathan had taken his side. "I'm damn well going to kill him just as soon as I find out who he is."

Colin shook his head. "You can't kill anyone," he announced in exasperation. "You're going to have to be reasonable about this, Caine. Sending flowers isn't a crime. He's probably just some young pup caught up in an infatuation."

"It's fine for you to be reasonable, Colin. Jade isn't your wife."

"I would still be reasonable if the flowers had been sent to Alesandra," Colin argued.

Caine shook his head.

"Tell us his name, Jade," Nathan demanded.

No one was paying any attention to Alesandra. She was thankful for their inattention. Her mind raced with speculations. She'd shaken her head when Colin had guessed it was just a young man caught up in an infatuation.

"Yes," Colin asked Jade then. "Who sent them?"

"He signs all his cards Your Secret Admirer," said Alesandra.

Everyone turned in unison to stare at her. Jade's mouth dropped open.

"Isn't that right, Jade?"

Her sister-in-law nodded. "How did you know?"

Nathan leaned back in his chair. "There's more to this than admiration, isn't there?"

No one said a word for a long minute. Alesandra suddenly remembered the package Flannaghan had told her had been delivered. She tried to go and get it. Colin wouldn't let her move. He tightened his hold on her shoulder.

"I believe the man might have sent something to me," she explained. "There's a package in the foyer."

"The hell he did. Flannaghan!"

Colin roared the summons. Alesandra's ears started ringing. Flannaghan came running. He had the package in his hands, indicating he'd been listening to the conversation. He all but tossed the thing to Colin.

Alesandra reached for the package. Colin's glare changed her mind. She leaned back against the settee and folded her hands. Colin leaned forward to attack the box. He ripped the bow off, muttering under his breath, then tore the lid free and looked inside. Alesandra peeked around her husband's shoulder to see what was there. She got a glimpse of the ornately painted fan before Colin slammed the lid back down on the box.

"Son of a bitch!" Colin roared. He repeated the shameful blasphemy a second time. Nathan, Alesandra noticed, nodded each time the foul words were said. Apparently those were his sentiments as well.

Colin held the notecard in his hand and glared at it.

"Aren't you going to be reasonable about this?" Caine challenged.

"Hell, no."

"Exactly," Caine muttered.

"One more and you'll have enough for a lynch mob," Jade announced. "Will you look at our husbands, Alesandra? They're blowing this all out of proportion. Such jealousy is unfounded," she added.

She expected Alesandra's agreement and was therefore surprised when her sister-in-law shook her head.

"Colin and Caine shouldn't be jealous," Alesandra whispered. "But they should be worried."

"How did you know what was signed on the card?" Nathan asked. "Have you received other gifts?"

Colin turned to look at her. His expression was chilling. So was his tone of voice when he said, "You would have told me if you'd received any other gifts. Isn't that right, Alesandra?"

She was thankful she could agree with him. Colin's fury was actually a little frightening. "Yes, I would have told you, and no, I haven't received any other gifts."

Colin nodded. He leaned back, put his arm around her shoulders again, and hauled her up tight against his side. She found his possessiveness a comfort now and didn't mind at all that he was inadvertently squeezing the breath right out of her.

"You know more than you're telling," Nathan announced.

Alesandra nodded. "Yes," she answered. "And I've been trying to get someone to listen to me for a good long while. I even asked Sir Richards for help."

She turned to frown at her husband. "Are you ready to hear what I have to say?"

Colin was a bit surprised by his wife's comments, of course, but he was astonished by her angry tone of voice.

"What have you been trying to tell me?"

"Victoria received letters and gifts from a secret admirer."

Colin was taken aback by that reminder. Alesandra had tried to explain why she was worried about her friend and he hadn't let her. He should have listened, he realized now.

"Who is Victoria?" asked Caine.

Alesandra answered him. She explained how she'd met Victoria. "After she returned to England, she wrote to me at least once a month. I would immediately write back, of course, and I did love hearing from her. She had such an exciting life. In the last few letters, however, she mentioned an admirer who was sending her gifts. She thought it all very romantic. I received her last letter in early September."

"And what did she say in that letter?" Caine asked.

"She had decided to meet the man," Alesandra answered. "I was appalled, of course, and wrote back to her right away. I advised caution and suggested she take her brother with her if she was determined to find out who her admirer was."

Alesandra started to shiver. Colin instinctively hugged her. "I don't know if Victoria received my letter or not. She might have already been gone by then."

"Gone? Gone where?" Jade asked.

"It was reported Victoria ran off to Gretna Green," Colin explained. "Alesandra doesn't believe that."

"There isn't any record of a marriage," Alesandra countered.

"What do you think happened to her?"

Nathan asked her that question, and until that moment she hadn't allowed herself to voice her true fear. She took a calming breath and turned her gaze to her husband's partner.

"I think she was murdered."

He paced the library in a rage. None of it was his fault. None of it. He had stopped. He'd ignored the craving, hadn't given in to the urge. It wasn't his fault. No, it was the bastard who was responsible. He never would have killed again . . . he never would have given in to the urge.

Revenge. He would show him. He would get even. He would destroy him. He would begin by taking away everything he valued. He would make him suffer.

He smiled in anticipation. He would start with the women.

Chapter 13

That statement got an immediate reaction. "Good God," Caine whispered.

"Could it be possible?" Nathan asked.

"I hadn't realized . . ." Jade whispered that remark and placed her hand over her heart.

Colin was the last to react and the most logical in his response. "Explain why you believe this," he commanded.

"Flannaghan, will you please go upstairs and fetch my list for me?"

"You have a list of reasons why you suspect your friend was murdered?" Caine asked.

"She has a list for everything."

Colin made that remark but she was pleased that he didn't sound at all condescending.

"Yes, I do have a list," Alesandra said. "I wanted to organize my thoughts about Victoria's disappearance and try to come up with some sort of plan. I knew something was wrong as soon as I heard she'd eloped. Victoria never would have done such a thing. Appearances were more important to her than love. Besides, I don't think she would have allowed herself to fall in love with someone she believed inferior to her station in life. She was sometimes a little shallow-headed and a bit of a snob as well, but those were her only faults. She was also very kindhearted."

"He has to be someone in society," Nathan decided aloud.

"Yes, I think so, too," Alesandra agreed. "I also think this man begged her to meet him somewhere and that her curiosity led her to forget caution. She was certainly flattered by his attention."

"She must have been terribly naive," Jade remarked.

"So is Catherine."

"Catherine? What does my sister have to do with this?"

"She made me promise not to tell, but her safety is at issue and I must break her confidence. She also received flowers this morning."

"Hell, I need a brandy," Caine muttered.

Flannaghan returned to the salon just then. He handed a pile of papers to Colin to pass along to Alesandra. He'd heard Caine's request and immediately announced he would fetch the brandy.

"Bring the bottle," Caine ordered.

"I hope to God we're all jumping to the wrong conclusion," Nathan said.

"Better that we are," Caine countered. "Three women in our family are being courted by the bastard. Think the worst and plan accordingly," he added with a hard nod.

Colin was sorting through the stack of papers, looking for the list pertinent to their discussion. He was given pause when he saw his name at the top of one sheet.

Alesandra wasn't paying any attention to her husband now. Her gaze was centered on his brother.

"Caine, you don't have sufficient information to assume there are only three," she explained. "This man could have sent dozens of gifts to women all over London."

"She's right about that," Nathan agreed.

Caine shook his head. "My gut feeling is that he's coming after one of ours."

Colin had just finished reading Alesandra's list. It took everything he possessed not to show any reaction. His hand shook when he placed the paper on the bottom of the pile.

He was going to become a father. He was so damn pleased he wanted to take Alesandra into his arms and kiss her.

And what a time to find out, he thought to himself. Colin wouldn't let her know he'd read the list, of course. He would wait until she told him. He'd give her until tonight, when they were in bed together . . .

"Why are you smiling, Colin? It's a damn bizarre reaction to this topic," Caine told him.

"I was thinking about something else."

"Do pay attention," Alesandra requested.

Colin turned to look at her. She saw the warm glint in his eyes and wondered what in heaven's name he'd been thinking about to cause that reaction. Before she could ask him, he leaned down and kissed her.

It was a quick, hard kiss that was over and done with before she could react.

"For God's sake, Colin," Caine muttered.

"We're newly married," Alesandra blurted out, trying to find some excuse for her husband's display of affection.

Flannaghan came in with a tray loaded with goblets and a large decanter of brandy. He placed the tray on the table near Alesandra and leaned over to whisper close to her ear. "Cook's back."

"Does she have news?"

Flannaghan eagerly nodded. Caine poured himself a drink and downed it in one long swallow. Both Nathan and Colin declined the brandy.

"May I have a drink, please?" Alesandra asked. She didn't particularly like the taste of brandy but she thought the warm liquid might take some of the chill out of her. She was feeling queasy, too, and she was certain the distressing talk about murder was the cause.

"Flannaghan, get Alesandra some water," Colin ordered.

"I would rather have brandy," she countered.

"No."

She was clearly astonished by his emphatic denial. "Why not?"

Colin didn't have a quick answer for her question. He

wanted to tell her brandy probably wasn't good for her delicate condition. He couldn't, of course, because she hadn't told him about the baby yet.

"Why are you smiling? I do declare, Colin, you're the most confusing man."

He forced himself back to the matter at hand. "I don't like you drinking," he announced.

"I never drink."

"That's right," Colin agreed. "And you aren't going to start now."

Flannaghan tapped Alesandra on her shoulder, reminding her of his message.

"Will you excuse me for a moment?" she asked. She noticed her lists were in his hands then. "What are you doing with those?"

"I'm holding them for you," he replied. "Would you like me to look through them for the list you made concerning Victoria?"

"No, thank you," she replied. She took the papers, found Victoria's list second from the top, and then started to stand up. Colin shook his head at her and hauled her back.

"You aren't going anywhere."

"I must speak to Cook."

"Flannaghan can answer her questions."

"You don't understand," Alesandra said in a low whisper. "She went on a little errand for me and I wanted to find out the results."

"What errand?" Colin asked.

She debated answering him for a minute or two. "You'll get angry," she whispered.

"No, I won't."

Her expression told him she didn't believe him.

"Alesandra?"

He said her name in that warning tone of voice he was certain would make her wish to answer him with all possible haste, but when she smiled at him he knew she wasn't at all impressed.

"Please tell me," he asked.

He had asked, not ordered, and that made all the difference in her mind. She immediately answered him. "I sent her to the Viscount of Talbolt's town house. Before you get upset over this, Colin, do remember you ordered me not to talk to the viscount. I adhered to your wishes."

He was thoroughly confused. "I still don't understand," he admitted.

"I sent Cook to talk to Lady Roberta's staff. I wanted to find out if she'd received any gifts before she disappeared. Husband, we both know she didn't run away from her husband. Such an excuse is unthinkable."

"She did receive gifts," Flannaghan blurted out. "The viscount pitched a tantrum, too. Staff believes Lady Roberta ran off with the suitor. The viscount isn't talking but his employees believe he thinks his wife ran off, too. The upstairs maid told Cook the viscount has turned to drink to ease his torment and stays locked up in his library day and night."

"What the hell is going on here?" Caine asked. "Could there be a connection between the two women?"

"They both disappeared," Jade reminded her husband. "Isn't that connection enough?"

"That isn't what I meant, sweetheart."

"Maybe he's being random in his selection," Nathan suggested.

"There's always a motive," Colin argued.

"Perhaps with the first one," Nathan agreed.

Alesandra was confused by that comment. "Why a motive with the first and not the second?"

Nathan looked at Colin before answering. Colin nodded. "There was probably a motive behind the first murder," Nathan explained. "But then he got a taste for killing."

"Some do," Caine admitted.

"Dear God," Jade whispered. She visibly shivered. Caine immediately got up and went over to his wife. He pulled her out of the chair, sat down, and then settled her on his lap. She leaned against him.

"Do you mean to tell me he likes killing?" Alesandra asked.

"Could be," Nathan answered.

Alesandra's stomach turned queasy again. She leaned closer into her husband's side in an attempt to gain more of his warmth. She felt safe when she was near him—comforted, too. That was what love was all about, she thought to herself.

"We're going to have to get a lot more information," Caine announced.

"I tried to talk to Victoria's brother, but he wasn't at all helpful," Alesandra said.

"He'll be helpful when I talk to him," Colin snapped.

"I can't imagine why he would cooperate," Alesandra replied. "You threw him out on the pavement the last time you spoke to him."

"What about asking Richards for some help?" Nathan suggested.

Alesandra closed her eyes and listened to the discussion. Colin was rubbing her arm in an absentminded fashion. His touch was wonderfully soothing. The men's voices were low and while they formulated their plans of action, she thought about how nice it was to finally have her husband's cooperation. She knew he would find out what happened to Victoria . . . and why. She didn't have any doubts about Colin's ability to find the culprit, because she was certain she was married to the most intelligent man in all of England. He was probably the most stubborn, too, but that flaw would come in handy now. He wouldn't quit until he had his answers.

"What the hell else do we do?" Caine asked.

Alesandra looked down at her list before she answered him. "You find out who profited from Victoria's death. Colin, you could find out if any policies were taken out. Dreyson would be happy to help you."

All three men smiled in unison. "I thought you were asleep," Colin remarked.

She ignored that comment. "You should also consider all the other motives . . . in the general sense," she explained. "Jealousy and rejection are two motives. Neil mentioned his sister had turned down several proposals. Perhaps one of those men didn't like being told no."

It occurred to Jade that Alesandra was actually very astute. Colin was grinning, suggesting to Jade that he was also aware of his wife's cleverness, but Nathan and Caine hadn't realized it yet.

"Yes, of course, we'll look into every possible motive," Caine said. "I just wish we had a clue or two."

"Oh, but you do," Alesandra replied. "The fact that three women in your family have received gifts is clue enough, Caine. It occurs to me that one of you men or one of us women has offended the man."

Colin nodded. "That thought had already occurred to me," he said. "He's getting careless."

"Or more bold," Nathan interjected.

"Isn't everyone forgetting one important fact?" Jade asked.

"What's that?" Caine asked his wife.

"There aren't any bodies. We really could be jumping in the wrong direction."

"Do you think we are?" Alesandra asked.

Jade thought about it a long minute, then whispered, "No."

Colin took charge then. He gave everyone but Alesandra an assignment. He told Jade to talk to as many of the ladies of the *ton* as possible to find out if anyone else had received a gift. He warned her not to tell the women about the gifts she, Catherine, and Alesandra had received because some of the more foolish women might think this was all some sort of competitive game.

Nathan was given the duty of taking over the offices while Colin concentrated on finding answers.

"Caine, Alesandra's right. Neil won't talk to me. You'll have to deal with him."

"I will," Caine agreed. "I should also talk to Talbolt," he added. "We went to Oxford together and he might be more receptive to hearing me out."

"I'll talk to Father," Colin said then. "He's going to have to keep a watchful eye on Catherine until the bastard is caught."

Alesandra waited to hear what Colin wanted her to do. A few minutes passed before her impatience got the better of her. She nudged her husband to get his attention.

"Haven't you forgotten me?"

"No."

"What is my assignment, Colin? What do you want me to do?"

"Rest, sweetheart."

"Rest?"

She'd sounded incensed. Colin wouldn't let her argue with him. Caine was ready to leave. He lifted his wife off his lap and stood up. Nathan also stood and started for the door.

"Come along, Alesandra. You need a nap," Colin said.

She certainly did not need a nap, she thought to herself, and if she hadn't been so tired she would have told him so. Arguing with her husband required stamina, however, and Alesandra didn't seem to have any left. The dark discussion had taken all of her energy.

Caine was smiling at her. Alesandra didn't want him to think she was a weakling, and she knew he'd heard Colin insist she rest. She shoved the list into his hands. "There are other motives I've written down you might wish to consider," she said.

Before Caine could thank her, she blurted out, "I am a little tired, but only because Colin and I have been keeping such late hours every night. He's weary, too," she added with a nod.

Caine winked at her. She didn't know what to make of that. Colin turned her attention then when he nudged her up the steps. Flannaghan saw their guests out.

"Why are you treating me like an invalid?"

She asked him that question in her bedroom. Colin was unbuttoning her dress for her. "You look worn out," he said. "And I like undressing you."

He was being terribly gentle with her. After she'd been

stripped down to her white silk chemise, he leaned down, lifted the hair away from the back of her neck, and kissed her there.

He pulled the covers back and tucked her in bed. "I'm only going to rest for a few minutes," she said. "I don't dare fall asleep."

He bent over the bed and kissed her brow. "Why not?"

"If I sleep now, I won't be able to sleep tonight."

Colin started for the door. "All right, sweetheart. Just rest."

"Wouldn't you like to rest too?"

He laughed. "No. I have work to do."

"I'm sorry, husband."

He'd just pulled the door open. "What are you sorry about?"

"I always seem to interfere in your work. I'm sorry about that."

He nodded, started out the doorway, then changed his mind. He turned around and walked back to the side of the bed. It was ridiculous for her to apologize for interfering and he wanted to tell her so. She was his wife, after all, not some distant relative making a nuisance of herself.

He didn't say a word. He would have to wait until later to instruct his wife when she would listen to him. She was sound asleep now. He was a little amazed at how quickly she'd fallen asleep and immediately felt a little guilty because he'd kept her out every night. Damn, she looked so delicate and vulnerable to him.

Colin didn't know how long he stood there staring down at Alesandra. His mind was consumed with the need to protect her. He'd never felt this possessive . . . or this blessed, he suddenly realized.

She loved him.

And, Lord, how he loved her. The truth didn't sneak up on him and clobber him over the head, though the picture was fanciful enough to make him smile. He had known for a long time that he loved her, even though he had stubbornly refused to openly acknowledge it. God only knew he had all the symptoms of a man in love. From the moment he'd met her, he'd been acting terribly possessive and protective. He hadn't been able to keep his hands off her and for a long while he believed he was just consumed with a simple case of lust. After a time, he knew better. It wasn't lust at all.

Oh, yes, he'd loved her for a long time. He couldn't imagine why she loved him. Had she been awake, he might have asked her that question then and there. She certainly could have done better with someone else. Someone with a title . . . someone with land and inheritance . . . someone with a sound, healthy body.

Colin didn't think of himself as a romantic. He was a logical, practical man who had learned that he could achieve success if he worked hard enough. In a dark corner of his mind he had harbored the thought that God had turned his back on him. It was an unreasonable belief, and it had taken root right after his leg had been nearly destroyed. He remembered hearing the physician whisper the need to amputate the limb—remembered, too, his friend's vehement refusal. Nathan wouldn't let Sir Winters touch the leg, but Colin had still been so damned afraid to sleep for fear that when he awakened he wouldn't be whole again.

The leg had survived, but the constant pain he now lived with made the victory hollow indeed.

Miracles were for other people, Colin had always believed—until Alesandra came into his life. His princess actually loved him. In his heart he knew there weren't any restrictions or conditions surrounding her love. Had she met a man with only one leg, she would have loved him just as much. He would have gained her sympathy, perhaps, but certainly not her pity. Her every action showed her strength and her determination to take care of him.

She would always be there for him, nagging him and arguing with him—and loving him no matter what.

And that, Colin decided, was definitely a miracle.

God hadn't forgotten him after all.

She wanted to leave him. Alesandra knew she wasn't being reasonable, but she was so upset inside she could barely think what to do. Nathan's casual remark about how he and Colin had both counted on Sara's inheritance to help their shipping company played on her mind until she was ready to weep.

Colin, she decided, had rejected her on every level possible. He didn't want her to help him with his company books, he didn't want her inheritance, and he didn't particularly want—or need—her love. His heart seemed to be surrounded by shields, and Alesandra didn't believe she would ever be able to get him to love her.

She knew she was being pitiful. She didn't care. Mother Superior's letter had arrived that morning, and Alesandra had already read the thing at least a dozen times.

She wanted to go home. She was so horribly homesick for the nuns and the land, she burst into tears. It was quite all right, she decided. She was alone, after all, and Colin was working in his study with the door closed. He wouldn't hear her.

Dear God, she wished she wasn't so emotional these days. She couldn't seem to apply logic to anything. She stood at the window in her robe and gown, looking out, and her mind was so engrossed with her worries she didn't even hear the door open.

"What is it, sweetheart? Don't you feel well?"

Colin's voice was filled with concern. She took a deep, calming breath and turned to look at him.

"I would like to go home."

He hadn't been prepared for that request. He looked quite astonished. He was quick to recover. He shut the door behind him and walked toward her.

"You are home."

She wanted to argue with him. She didn't. "Yes, of course," she agreed. "But I would like your permission to go back to Holy Cross for a visit. The convent is just a walk away from Stone Haven, and I would like to see my parents' home again."

Colin walked over to her writing desk. "What is this really all about?" he asked her. He leaned against the edge of the table while he waited for her to answer him.

"I received a letter from Mother Superior today, and I'm suddenly very homesick."

Colin didn't show any outward reaction to her plea. "I can't take the time right now to . . ."

"Stefan and Raymond would go with me," she interrupted. "I don't expect you to go along. I know how busy you are."

He could feel himself getting angry. The very idea of his wife leaving on such a journey without him at her side appalled him. He stopped himself from immediately denying her request, however, because in truth he had never seen her this upset. It worried the hell out of him, given her delicate condition.

She was out of her mind if she thought he would ever let her go anywhere without him. He didn't tell her that opinion either.

He decided to use reason to make her understand. "Alesandra . . ."

"Colin, you don't need me."

He was taken aback by that absurd comment. "The hell I don't need you," he countered in a near shout.

She shook her head. He nodded. Then she turned her back on him.

"You have never needed me," she whispered.

"Alesandra, sit down."

"I don't wish to sit down."

"I want to talk to you about this . . ." He almost said he wanted to talk to her about her "ridiculous notion," but he caught himself in time.

She ignored him and continued to stare out the window.

He noticed the stack of papers on her desk and suddenly knew what he was going to do. He quickly sorted through her lists until he found the one with his name on the top.

She wasn't paying any attention to him. He folded the sheet in half and tucked it in his pocket. Then he ordered her to sit down again. His voice was harder, more insistent.

She took her time obeying. She mopped the tears away from her face with the backs of her hands and finally walked over to the side of the bed. She sat down, folded her hands in her lap, and bowed her head.

"Have you suddenly stopped loving me?"

He hadn't been able to keep the worry out of his voice. She was so surprised by his question, she looked up at him. "No, of course I haven't stopped loving you."

He nodded, both pleased and relieved to hear her fervent answer. Then he straightened away from the desk and walked over to stand in front of her.

"There isn't any Uncle Albert, is there?"

The switch in topic confused her. "What does Albert have to do with my request to go home?"

"Damn it, this is your home," he countered.

She lowered her head again. He immediately regretted the burst of anger and took a breath to calm himself. "Bear with me for just a moment, Alesandra, and answer my question."

She debated telling him the truth for a long minute. "No, there isn't any Uncle Albert."

"I didn't think so."

"Why didn't you think so?"

"There were never any letters delivered here from the man, yet I heard you tell Caine you'd received a missive. You made him up, and I think I know why."

"I really don't wish to talk about this. I find I'm weary tonight. It's quite late, almost ten."

He wasn't about to let her run away from this discussion. "You had a four-hour nap today," he reminded her.

"I was catching up on my sleep," she announced.

"Dreyson wouldn't take stock orders from a woman, would he? So you invented Albert, a convenient recluse who just happened to have your same initials."

She wasn't going to argue with him. "Yes."

He nodded again. He clasped his hands behind his back and frowned down at her. "You hide your intelligence, don't you, Alesandra? You obviously have a knack for the market, but instead of boasting about your cleverness with investments, you invented another man to take the credit."

She looked up at him so he could see her frown. "Men

listen to other men," she announced. "It isn't acceptable for a woman to have such interests. It isn't considered ladylike. And it isn't a knack, Colin. I read the journals and listen to Dreyson's suggestions. It doesn't take a brilliant mind to be guided by his advice."

"Will you agree you're at least fairly intelligent and can reason most things through logically?"

She wondered where in heaven's name this discussion was leading. Her husband was acting terribly uncomfortable. She couldn't imagine why.

"Yes," she answered. "I will agree I'm fairly intelligent."

"Then why in God's name haven't you been able to reason through all the obvious facts and figure out that I love you?"

Her eyes widened and she leaned back. She opened her mouth to say something to him, but she couldn't remember what it was.

"I love you, Alesandra."

It had been difficult telling her what was in his heart, yet once the words were spoken, he felt incredibly free. He smiled at his wife and said the words again.

She bounded off the bed and frowned up at him. "You do not love me," she announced.

"I sure as hell do," he argued. "If you would apply a little reason . . ."

"I did use reason," she interrupted. "And came to the opposite conclusion."

"Sweetheart . . ."

"Don't you dare 'sweetheart' me," she cried out.

Colin reached for her but she eluded him by sitting down again. "Oh, I reasoned it through and through and through. Shall I tell you my conclusions?"

She didn't give him time to answer her. "You have turned your back on everything I had to give you. It would be illogical for me to assume you love me."

"I've what?" he asked, stunned by the vehemence in her voice.

"You've rejected everything," she whispered.

"Exactly what have I rejected?"

"My title, my position, my castle, my inheritance—even my help with your company."

He finally understood. He pulled her to her feet and wrapped his arms around her. She tried to push herself away from him. They fell onto the bed. Colin protected her from his weight as he stretched out on top of her. He pinned the lower part of her body with his thighs and braced himself on his elbows so he could look down at her.

Her hair spilled out on the pillows and her eyes, cloudy with unshed tears, made her appear more vulnerable to him. Dear God, she was beautiful—even when she was glaring at him. "I love you, Alesandra," he whispered. "And I have taken everything you had to give me."

She started to protest. He wouldn't let her. He clamped his hand over her mouth so she couldn't interrupt him. "I rejected nothing of value. You offered me all a man could ever want. You gave me your love, your trust, your loyalty, your mind, your heart, and your body. None of those offerings is material, sweetheart, and if you lost all the financial trappings that came along with you, it wouldn't matter to me. You're all I have ever wanted. Now do you understand?"

She was overwhelmed by his beautiful words. His eyes were actually misty, and she knew then that it had been difficult for him to tell her how he felt. Colin did love her. She was so filled with joy, she burst into tears.

"Love, don't cry," he pleaded. "It's very upsetting for me to see you so miserable."

She tried to stop crying long enough to explain she wasn't miserable at all. Colin moved his hand away from her mouth and gently wiped her tears away.

"I didn't have anything to give you when I married you," he told her. "And yet . . . on our wedding night I knew you loved me. I had trouble accepting it at first. It seemed so damned unfair to you. I should have remembered a comment you made to me about the prince regent. That reminder would have saved both of us a good deal of worry."

"What comment did I make?"

"I told you I'd heard the prince regent was taken with you," he answered. "Do you remember what you said to me then?"

She did remember. "I told you he was taken with what I am, not who I am."

"Well?" he demanded in a rough whisper.

"Well, what?"

Her smile was radiant. She finally understood.

"I thought you were fairly intelligent," he drawled out.

"You love me."

"Yes."

He leaned down and kissed her. She sighed into his mouth. When he pulled away, she looked properly convinced.

"Have you also worked it out in your mind?" she asked.

He didn't understand what she meant by her question. He was busy unbuttoning the top of her gown. "Worked out what?"

"That I fell in love with who you are, not what you are," she answered. "It was your strength and courage that drew me to you, Colin. I needed both."

He was so pleased with his wife he had to kiss her again. "I needed you," he admitted.

He wanted to kiss her again. She wanted to talk. "Colin, you present yourself to the world as a man struggling to build a company."

"I *am* a man struggling to build a company."

He rolled to his side so he could get her robe and gown off her more quickly.

"You aren't a pauper," she announced. She sat up in bed and started tugging her robe off her shoulders. Colin helped her.

"I had a good look at your books, remember? You've made an amazing profit, but you poured every bit of it back into the operation and the result is very impressive. You've been trying to build an empire, but if you'll only step back and take a good look you'll realize you've already accomplished your goal. Why, you have close to twenty ships now with cargo orders stretching into next year and that must surely convince you that your company is no longer a struggling venture."

He was having trouble listening to what she was telling him. She'd shed her robe and was now inching her gown up over her head. His throat tightened up on him. She finally got rid of the barrier. He immediately reached for her. She shook her head at him. "First, I would like you to answer a question for me, please."

He might have nodded but he couldn't be certain. A fire burned inside him and all he wanted to do was bury himself in her. He was so damn anxious to touch her, he was literally destroying his shirt in his hurry to get the thing off.

"Colin, when is enough enough?"

Her question required concentration. He didn't have any to spare.

"I'll never be able to get enough of you."

"Nor I you," she whispered. "But that isn't what I was asking . . ."

Colin silenced her with his mouth. She couldn't resist him a moment longer. She wrapped her arms around his neck and gave in to the wonder of his passion . . . and his love.

He was demanding, yet incredibly gentle with her at the same time. His touch was magical, and while she was in the throes of her own blissful surrender, he told her again and again how much he loved her.

She would have told him she loved him, too, but Colin had worn her out and she couldn't find the strength to speak. She rolled onto her back, closed her eyes, and listened to her pounding heartbeat while the air cooled her feverish skin.

He rolled to his side, propped his head up on his hand, and grinned down at her. He looked thoroughly satisfied.

He stroked a path from her chin to her belly, and then his hand gently rubbed the flat of her stomach.

"Sweetheart, do you have something you want to tell me?"

She was feeling too content to think about anything other than what had just happened to her.

Colin was going to nag her until she told him about the

baby, but Flannaghan started banging on the bedroom door then, interrupting that intention.

"Milord, your brother's here. I put him in the study."

"I'll be right there," Colin shouted.

He muttered about his brother's bad timing. Alesandra laughed. She didn't bother to open her eyes when she said, "It would have been bad timing ten minutes ago. I would say he was being very considerate."

He agreed with that assessment. He started to leave the bed, then turned back to her. She opened her eyes just in time to watch him lean over her and place a kiss on her navel. She brushed her hand across his shoulder. The hair on the back of his neck curled around her fingers.

Colin was letting his hair grow long again. That sudden realization hit her all at once. She was so pleased she almost started crying again. She didn't, of course, because Colin had told her he found it upsetting to see her weep, and she doubted he would understand anyway. She understood, though, and that was all that mattered. Marriage hadn't turned out to be a prison for her husband.

He was puzzled by the look on her face. "Sweetheart?" he asked.

"You're still free, Colin."

His eyes widened over that remark. "You say the strangest things," he remarked.

"Your brother's waiting."

He nodded. "I want you to think about my question while I talk to Caine. All right, love?"

"What question?"

Colin got out of bed and pulled his pants on. "I asked you if you had anything else to tell me," he reminded her.

He slipped his bare feet into his shoes and started toward his bedroom in search of a fresh shirt. He'd shredded the one he'd been wearing.

"Think about it," he told her. He grabbed his jacket, winked at her, and then left the room.

Caine was sprawled out in the leather chair next to the hearth. Colin nodded and sat down behind his desk. He reached for his pen and paper.

Caine took one look at his brother and broke into a wide grin. "I see I interrupted you. Sorry," he added.

Colin ignored the laughter in his brother's voice. He knew he looked disheveled. He hadn't bothered with a cravat. He hadn't bothered to comb his hair, either.

"Marriage agrees with you, Colin."

Colin didn't pretend indifference. He looked up at his brother and let him see the truth in his expression. The shields were gone.

"I'm a man in love."

Caine laughed. "It took you long enough to realize it."

"No longer than it took you to realize you loved Jade."

Caine agreed with a nod. Colin went back to writing on his paper.

"What are you doing?"

Colin's grin was a bit sheepish when he admitted he was starting a list.

"I seem to have caught my wife's obsession for organization," he said. "Did you talk to the viscount?"

Caine's smile faded. He loosened his cravat while he answered. "Harold's a mess," he said, referring to the viscount. "He's barely coherent. The last time he saw his wife they had an argument and he has spent every minute since tormenting himself over the harsh words he said to her. His anguish is aching to see."

"The poor devil," Colin said. He shook his head, then asked, "Did he tell you what the argument was about?"

"He was certain she'd taken a lover," Caine answered. "She was receiving gifts and Harold jumped to the conclusion she was involved with another man."

"Hell."

"He still hasn't figured it out, Colin. I told him about the gifts our wives received but he was too sotted from drink to understand the ramifications. He kept saying his anger swayed Roberta into running away with her lover."

Colin leaned back in his chair. "Did he have anything helpful to add?"

"No."

The brothers lapsed into silence, each caught up in his

own thoughts. Colin pushed his chair back and bent over to take his shoes off. He tossed off his left shoe, then his right, and was about to straighten up again when he noticed the lining protruding from his left shoe.

"Damn," he muttered to himself. His most comfortable pair of shoes were already wearing out. He picked up the shoe to see if it could be repaired. The thick insert fell into his hands.

He'd never seen anything like it. He immediately picked up the other shoe and examined it. Flannaghan chose that moment to walk into the study with a fresh decanter of brandy so that Caine could have a drink if he was so inclined. He took one look at what Colin was holding in his hand and immediately turned around to leave.

"Come back here, Flannaghan," Colin ordered.

"Did you wish a drink, milord?" Flannaghan asked Caine.

"Yes," Caine answered. "But I want water, not brandy. After seeing Harold tonight, the thought of a hard drink turns my stomach."

"I shall fetch the water at once."

Flannaghan tried to leave again. Colin called him back.

"Did you wish some water?" the butler asked his employer.

Colin held up the insert. "I wish to find out if you know anything about this."

Flannaghan was torn between his loyalties. He was Colin's servant, of course, and was certainly loyal to him, but he had also promised his princess not to say a word about the bootmaker.

Flannaghan's silence was a bit damning. Caine started laughing. "From the look on his face, I would say he knows a great deal about something. What are you holding, Colin?"

He tossed the leather insert to Caine. "I just found this hidden under the lining of my shoe. It's been specifically made for the left foot."

He turned his gaze back to his butler. "Alesandra's behind this, isn't she?"

Flannaghan cleared his throat. "They have become your

favorite shoes, milord," he hastened to point out. "The insert made your shoe fit your heel much better. I pray you won't become too angry over this."

Colin wasn't at all angry, but his butler was too young and too caught up in his worry to realize that fact.

"Our princess realizes that you are a bit . . . sensitive about your leg," Flannaghan continued, "and for that reason she did resort to a little trickery. I do hope you won't berate her."

Colin smiled. Flannaghan's defense of Alesandra was pleasing to him. "Will you ask 'our princess' to come in here? Knock softly on her door, Flannaghan, and if she doesn't immediately answer, assume she's asleep."

Flannaghan hurried out of the study. He realized he was still holding the decanter in his hands and quickly turned back to the study. He put the brandy on the side table and once again left.

Caine tossed the insert back to his brother. "Does the contraption work?"

"Yes," Colin answered. "I didn't realize . . ."

Caine saw the vulnerability in his brother's eyes and was amazed. It wasn't like Colin to let anyone see beyond the smile. He suddenly felt closer to his brother, and all because Colin wasn't shutting him out. He leaned forward in his chair, his elbows braced on his knees.

"What didn't you realize?"

Colin stared at the thick heel of the insert when he answered. "That my left leg was shorter than my right. It makes sense. The loss of muscle . . ."

He forced a shrug. Caine didn't know what to say to him. This was the first time Colin had acknowledged his condition and Caine wasn't certain how to proceed. If he sounded too nonchalant, his brother might assume he didn't care. Yet if he sounded too earnest and prodded him with questions, Colin might slam the door on the subject for another five years.

It was damned awkward. And in the end he didn't say anything. He changed the topic. "Have you talked to Father about Catherine yet?"

"Yes," Colin answered. "He promises to be on his guard. He's alerted his staff, too. If anything else is delivered, Father will see it first."

"Is he going to warn Catherine?"

"He didn't want to worry her," Colin replied. "I insisted. She needs to understand this is a serious matter. Catherine's a bit . . . flighty, isn't she?"

Caine smiled. "She isn't completely grown up yet, Colin. Give her time."

"And protect her until she does grow up."

"Yes."

Alesandra appeared in the doorway with Flannaghan at her side. She wore a dark blue robe that covered her from chin to slippers. She walked inside the study, smiled at Caine, and then turned to her husband. Colin held up the insert for her to see. She immediately lost her smile and started backing out of the room.

She didn't look frightened, just wary. "Alesandra, do you know something about this?"

She couldn't tell from his expression if he was angry or merely irritated with her. She reminded herself that her husband had vowed his love for her just minutes before and took a step forward. "Yes."

"Yes, what?"

"Yes, I know something about the insert. Good evening, Caine. It's good to see you again," she added in a rush.

She was deliberately being obtuse. Colin shook his head at her. "I asked you a question, wife," he said.

"Now I understand your question," she blurted out. She took another step forward. "Just before you left my chamber you asked me if I had something to tell you and now I realize you'd found the insert. All right, then. I'll tell you. I interfered. Yes, I did. I had your best interests at heart, Colin. I'm sorry you're so prickly about your leg, and if you weren't, I could have discussed my idea with you before sending Flannaghan to the bootmaker. I had to force your man to take on the assignment. He's most loyal to you," she hastened to add lest he think Flannaghan had somehow betrayed him.

"No, Princess," Flannaghan argued. "I begged you to let me take on the assignment."

Colin rolled his eyes heavenward. "What made you think of the idea?" he asked.

She looked surprised by his question. "You have a limp . . . at night, when you're tired, you do tend to limp a little. Colin, you are aware you favor your right leg, aren't you?"

He almost laughed. "Yes, I'm aware."

"Do you agree you're a fairly intelligent man?"

She was turning his words back on him. He held his frown. "Yes."

"Then why didn't you try to reason why you were limping?"

He lifted his shoulders in a shrug. "A shark took a bite out of my leg. Call me daft, Alesandra, but I assumed that was the reason I limped."

She shook her head. "That was the reason for the injury," she explained. "I looked at the bottoms of your shoes. The left heel was barely worn on each pair. Then, of course, I knew what to do." She let out a sigh. "I do wish you weren't so sensitive about this issue."

She turned to look at Caine. "He is sensitive, though. Have you, by chance, noticed?"

Caine nodded.

She smiled because she'd gained his agreement. "He won't even talk about it."

"He's talking about it now," Caine told her.

She whirled around to look at her husband. "You are talking about it," she cried out.

She looked thrilled. Colin didn't know what to make of that. "Yes," he agreed.

"Then will you let me sleep in your bed every night?"

Caine laughed. Alesandra ignored him. "I know why you go back to your room. It's because your leg hurts and you need to walk. I'm right, aren't I, Colin?"

He didn't answer her.

"Will you please say something?"

"Thank you."

She was thoroughly confused. "Why are you thanking me?"

"For the insert."

"You aren't angry?"

"No."

She was astonished by his attitude.

He was humbled by her thoughtfulness.

They stared at each other a long minute.

"You aren't angry with Flannaghan, are you?" she asked.

"No."

"Why aren't you angry with me?"

"Because you had my best interests at heart."

"What a nice thing to say."

Colin laughed. She smiled. Flannaghan came running into the study and thrust a glass of water at Caine. His attention was centered on Alesandra. She saw his worried expression and whispered, "He isn't angry."

Caine drew her attention when he announced he was going home. Colin didn't take his gaze off his wife when he bid his brother good night.

"Alesandra, stay here. Flannaghan will see Caine out."

"As you wish, husband."

"God, I love it when you're humble."

"Why?"

"It's so damned rare."

She shrugged. He laughed again. "Is there something else you wanted to tell me?" he asked.

Her shoulders slumped. The man was too cunning by half. "Oh, all right," she muttered. "I talked to Sir Winters about your leg to gain suggestions. We spoke in confidence, of course."

Colin raised an eyebrow. "Suggestions for what?"

"For ways to make it feel better. I made a list of his ideas. Would you like me to fetch it for you?"

"Later," he answered. "Now, then, is there something else you wanted to tell me?"

The question covered a broad range of topics. Colin decided he'd have to remember to ask her that question every other week in future so that he could find out what she'd been up to.

She wasn't about to blurt out another confession until she knew what he was fishing for. "Could you be more specific please?"

Her question told him there were still more secrets. "No," he answered. "You know what I'm asking. Tell me."

She threaded her fingers through her hair and walked over to the side of his desk. "Dreyson told you, didn't he?"

He shook his head. "Then how did you find out?"

"I'll explain how I found out after you tell me," he promised.

"You already know," she countered. "You just want to make me feel guilty, don't you? Well, it won't wash. I didn't cancel the order for the steam vessel and it's too late for you to interfere. Besides, you told me I could do whatever I wanted with my inheritance. I ordered the ship for myself. Yes, I did. I've always wanted one. If, however, you and Nathan would like to use my ship every now and again, I would be happy to share it with you."

"I told Dreyson to cancel the order," he reminded her.

"I told him Albert had decided he wanted it."

"What the hell else have you kept from me?"

"You didn't know?"

"Alesandra . . ."

"You're pricking my temper, Colin. You still don't understand how much you hurt me," she announced. "Can you imagine how I felt when I heard Nathan say that he and you were all set to use Sara's inheritance to build the company? You made such an issue out of turning your back on my inheritance."

Colin pulled her onto his lap. She immediately put her arms around his neck and smiled at him.

He frowned at her. "The money was put aside by the king for both Nathan and Sara," he explained.

"My father put his money away for me and my husband."

She had him there, he thought to himself. She knew it, too. "Your father wonders why he's still in charge of my funds, Colin. It's embarrassing. You should take over the task. I would help."

His smile was filled with tenderness. "How about if I helped you manage it?"

"That would be nice." She leaned against him. "I love you, Colin."

"I love you, too. Sweetheart, isn't there something else you want to tell me?"

She didn't answer him. Colin reached into his pocket and pulled out her list. She snuggled closer to him.

He opened the paper. "I want you to be able to talk to me about anything," he explained. "From this moment on."

She started to pull away from him but he tightened his hold on her. "I made it impossible for you to talk about my leg, didn't I?"

"Yes."

"I'm sorry about that, sweetheart. Now stay still while I answer your questions for you, all right?"

"I don't have any questions?"

"Hush, love," he ordered. He held her close with one hand and lifted the sheet of paper with the other. He silently read her first order and then said, "I have listened to your concerns about Victoria, haven't I?"

"Yes, but why . . ."

Colin squeezed her. "Be patient," he commanded. He read the second order. "I will promise to soften in my attitude toward your inheritance." In brackets Alesandra had written the word *stubborn.* He let out a sigh. "And I won't be mule-headed about it."

The third order made him smile. She had instructed him not to wait five years to realize he loved her.

Since he'd already complied with that command, he moved on to the next order. He should try to be happy he was going to become a father and he shouldn't blame her because she was interfering with his schedule.

Could pregnant wives become nuns? Colin decided to answer the last first.

"Alesandra?"

"Yes?"

He kissed the top of her head. "No," he whispered.

The laughter in his voice confused her. So did his denial. "No, what, husband?"

"Pregnant wives can't become nuns."

She would have jumped off his lap if he'd let her. He held her tight against him until she finally calmed down.

She did a lot of ranting and raving, too. "You knew . . . all the time. . . . Oh, God, it was the list. You found it and that's why you told me you loved me."

Colin forced her chin up and kissed her hard. "I knew I loved you before I read your list," he told her. "You're going to have to trust me, Alesandra. Trust your heart, too."

"But . . ."

His mouth silenced her protest. When he pulled back, she had tears in her eyes. "I'm going to ask you one last time," he said. "Do you have something to tell me?"

She slowly nodded. He looked so arrogantly pleased. Dear God, how she loved him. From the way he was looking at her, she knew he loved her just as much.

Oh, yes, he was happy about the baby. She didn't have any worries about that. His hand had dropped to her stomach and he was gently patting her. She didn't think he was even aware of what he was doing. The action was telling, though. He was caressing his unborn son or daughter.

"Answer me," he commanded in a rough whisper.

He was looking so fiercely intent now. She smiled in reaction. Colin always tried to be so serious, so disciplined. She loved that trait in him, of course, but she found she delighted in making him forget himself every now and again.

She did love to tease him and all because he reacted with such surprise.

Colin couldn't hold on to his patience any longer. "Answer me, Alesandra."

"Yes, Colin. I do have something to tell you. I've decided to become a nun."

He looked like he wanted to throttle her. His glare made her laugh. She wrapped her arms around him again and tucked her head under his chin.

"We're going to have a baby," she whispered. "Have I mentioned that yet?"

Chapter 14

An endless stream of visitors demanded Colin's attention during the following two weeks. Sir Richards was there so often he might as well have had his own bedroom. Caine stopped by every afternoon, and so did Nathan. Alesandra didn't see much of her husband during the daylight hours, but the evenings belonged to her. Colin would catch her up on all the latest developments in his investigation directly after dinner.

Dreyson proved to be very helpful. He found out a policy had been taken out on Victoria's life just four months before her disappearance. The beneficiary named on the contract was her brother, Neil. The policy was underwritten by Morton and Sons.

Through his sources, Colin found out Neil would inherit his sister's sizable dowry, set aside on the day she was born by a distant aunt, if she didn't return to London to claim it.

Sir Richards had joined them at the dinner table. He listened while Colin explained to Alesandra what he'd learned, then interjected a comment of his own.

"Until a body is found he can't collect the insurance money or the inheritance. If he's the culprit and his motive was money, why would he go to such lengths to hide her body?"

"It doesn't make much sense," Colin agreed. "He has a large bank account of his own."

Sir Richards agreed with a nod. "He might think he needed more," he said. "Alesandra did tell us Neil didn't particularly like his sister," he added. "There's another bit of damning evidence wagging its finger in Neil's direction, too, circumstantial though it is. You see, he offered for Roberta six years ago but she turned him down in favor of the viscount. Rumor has it Neil continued to pursue her even after she was married. Some believe she was having an affair with him. And there, you see, is the tie-in between the two women."

"I can't imagine any woman wanting to be with Neil Perry," Alesandra whispered. "He isn't at all . . . charming."

"Have you received any other gifts?" he asked.

She shook her head. "The gift I ordered made for Nathan and Sara arrived this morning. Colin almost destroyed the thing in a rage before he remembered I'd ordered the ship. Thankfully, he only shredded the box."

"You failed to mention you had the gift outlined with strips of gold," Colin said. "It would take five men to destroy it."

Caine interrupted the talk when he came rushing into the dining room.

"They found Victoria's body!"

Colin reached over and covered Alesandra's hand. "Where?" he asked.

"In a field about an hour's ride from here. A cropper happened upon the grave. Wolves had . . ." Caine stopped in midsentence. The look on Alesandra's face showed her anguish. Caine wasn't about to add to her heartache by going into more vivid detail.

"The authorities are certain it's Victoria?" she asked.

Her eyes filled with tears, but she forced herself to remain in control. She could weep for Victoria later—pray for her soul, too—and she would do both . . . after the man who'd hurt her had been caught.

"The jewelry she wore . . . it helped with the identification," Caine explained.

Sir Richards wanted to see where the body was found. He pushed his chair back and started to stand up.

"It's too dark to see anything," Caine told the director. He pulled out the chair next to Alesandra and sat down. "You're going to have to wait until tomorrow."

"Who owns the field where she was found?" Colin asked.

"Neil Perry."

"How convenient," Colin said.

"It's too damned convenient," Caine agreed.

"We take what we're given," Richards announced. "Then we pull it apart to find the truth."

"When will you have your men start digging?" Colin asked.

"Tomorrow at first light."

"Digging?" Alesandra asked. "Victoria's already been found. Why would you . . ."

"We want to see what else we'll find," Richards explained.

"You believe Roberta might also be buried there?"

"I do."

"So do I," Caine interjected.

"Neil wouldn't be so stupid as to bury his victims on his own land," she said.

"We believe he's probably the culprit," Caine said. "We don't believe he's clever."

She grabbed hold of Caine's hand so he would give her his full attention. "But that's just it," she argued. "He's been clever until now, hasn't he? Why would he bury either woman on his own land? It doesn't make sense. You're forgetting something else, too."

"What's that?" Caine asked.

"All of you are assuming there are only two women. There could be more."

"She's got a point, Caine," Colin agreed. "Sweetheart, let go of my brother."

She realized she was squeezing Caine's hand then and quickly let go. She turned her attention to the director. "What are your other plans?"

"Neil will certainly be charged," he announced. "It's just a start, Alesandra. Like you, I'm not completely convinced he's the one. I don't like conveniences."

She was satisfied with his answer. She excused herself from the table. Caine stood up and pulled her chair back for her. She turned to thank him. She was surprised when he put his hands on her shoulders and leaned down. Before she could ask him what he was doing, he kissed her on her forehead.

"Congratulations, Alesandra," he said. "Jade and I are both very happy over the news."

"What news?" Sir Richards asked.

She let Colin tell him. She smiled up at Caine. "We're both very happy, too," she whispered.

Richards was shaking Colin's hand when she started toward the entrance. A sudden thought made her stop. She turned around to look at Colin again. "Don't you still wonder why three women in your family were chosen? You did throw Neil out," she reminded him. "Would that make him angry enough to seek revenge?"

Colin didn't think so. She left him with Caine and Richards to mull over the possibilities and went upstairs. Flannaghan was waiting for her in the study. His younger sister, Megan, was waiting with him.

"Here she is," Flannaghan announced when Alesandra walked inside.

"Princess Alesandra, this is Megan," he announced. "She's eager to see to your needs."

Flannaghan nudged his sister in her side. She immediately stepped forward and made an awkward curtsy. "I would be happy to serve you, milady."

"Not milady," Flannaghan instructed. "Princess."

Megan nodded. She looked very like her brother. She had the same coloring, and her smile was almost identical to Flannaghan's. She looked up at her brother with true adoration, and such devotion warmed Alesandra's heart.

"We're going to get along just fine," she predicted.

"I'll teach her what she needs to know," Flannaghan announced.

Alesandra nodded. "Where is Kate? I thought we had agreed she would start helping me with the correspondence tomorrow?"

"She's still packing up her things," Flannaghan explained. "Have you mentioned my sisters to your husband yet?"

"No," Alesandra answered. "Don't worry so, Flannaghan. He'll be as pleased as I am."

"I've put Megan in the last bedroom along the hallway upstairs," Flannaghan said. "Kate can have the room next to hers if that is all right."

"Yes, of course."

"It's a fine room, milady," Megan blurted out. "And the first I've ever had all to myself."

"Princess, not milady," her brother corrected again.

Alesandra didn't dare laugh. She didn't want to undermine Flannaghan's position.

"We'll start your training tomorrow, Megan. I believe I'll go along to bed now. If you need anything, ask your brother. He'll take good care of you. He certainly takes good care of Colin and me. I don't know what we would do without him."

Flannaghan flushed over her praise. Megan looked properly impressed.

Colin laughed when she told him about the additions to their staff. He was quick to sober, however, upon hearing his ill-paid butler was the sole support of both Megan and Kate. He'd known Flannaghan's parents were both dead—Sterns had told him so when he'd implored Colin to hire his nephew, but he hadn't mentioned the two sisters. No, he hadn't known, and he was thankful Alesandra had taken the sisters in. He increased Flannaghan's salary the following morning.

Flowers arrived for Alesandra that afternoon. Dreyson had sent them with a note filled with sympathy over her tragic loss.

Alesandra was arranging the flowers in a white porcelain vase while Colin scowled over the note. "What's this about?" he asked.

"Albert died."

Colin burst into laughter. She smiled. "I thought you would be pleased."

"It's damned callous of you to laugh, Colin."

Caine stood in the entrance of the dining room, scowling at his brother. He turned to Alesandra to offer his sympathy and only then realized she was smiling.

"Isn't Albert a good friend of yours?"

"Not anymore," Colin drawled out.

Caine shook his head. Colin laughed again. "He never existed," he explained. "Alesandra made him up so Dreyson would take her stock orders."

"But he gave me sound advice. Damn it, I'm going to miss him. I . . ."

"Alesandra gave you *her* sound advice. Ask her in future," Colin suggested.

Caine looked astonished. Alesandra gave her husband an I-told-you-so look before turning back to his brother.

"Dreyson was far more willing to talk to me about investments because he believed I was sending the information on to Albert. Now he'll talk to Colin whenever he hears of good opportunities. He would be very upset if he found out Albert never existed and for that reason I beg you not to say anything."

"Why bother with a middleman?" Caine asked, still not certain if he believed her or not.

"Because men like to talk to men," she patiently explained.

"Why are you here?" Colin asked, switching the topic then. "Do you have more news?"

"Yes," Caine answered, drawn back now to his reason for calling. "They found Lady Roberta's body about fifty yards away from Victoria's grave."

"Dear God," Alesandra whispered.

Colin put his arm around his wife's shoulders. "Were there any others found?"

Caine shook his head. "They haven't found any so far but they're still looking. Neil's being charged with the second murder. He sent a request through his barrister to talk to Alesandra."

"It's out of the question."

"Colin, I think I should talk to him."

"No."

"Please be reasonable," she pleaded. "Don't you want to make certain he's the one?"

Colin let out a sigh. "Then I'll go and talk to him."

"Neil doesn't like you," she reminded her husband.

"I don't give a damn if he likes me or not," Colin replied.

She turned to Caine. "Colin threw him out," she explained. "I can't imagine he would want to talk to him now."

"You'd be surprised how a man changes in Newgate Prison," Caine said. "I imagine he'll talk to anyone he thinks might be able to help him."

"You aren't going, Alesandra," Colin told her. "However," he hastened to add when she tried to argue with him again, "if you write down your questions I'll ask Neil whatever it is you want to know."

"I already have a list," she replied.

"Then go and get it for me."

"Colin, I'm going with you," Caine announced.

Alesandra knew it was useless to continue to argue with her husband. From the look in his eyes she knew he was going to be stubborn about this. She went upstairs to fetch her list, added a few more questions to the sheet of paper, and then hurried downstairs again.

"We'll take my carriage," Caine told his brother.

Colin nodded. He took the list from his wife, put it in his pocket, and kissed her good-bye. "Stay home," he ordered. "I shouldn't be gone long."

"She can't stay home," Caine interjected. "I've forgotten. Nathan's coming by to collect her in about an hour."

"Why?" Colin asked.

"Jade wants your wife to meet Sara," he explained. "Mother and Catherine are at the house, too."

"Nathan will be with Alesandra?" Colin asked.

"Yes."

Alesandra turned and started up the steps. She was in a hurry to change her dress. She wanted to look her best when she met Sara.

"Should I take our gift along?" she called down to her husband.

Colin was starting out the doorway. He told her that was a fine idea, but she could tell from the shrug in his answer he was barely paying attention to her.

Megan helped her change her clothes. Flannaghan's sister was nervous—awkward, too—but her enthusiasm to please her mistress was most apparent.

Nathan came to collect her a short while later. Alesandra carried the gift Flannaghan had rewrapped for her down the stairs. She handed the box to Nathan to carry for her but didn't explain what it was.

Colin's partner seemed preoccupied and barely said a word to her on the way over to Caine's town house.

She finally asked him if something was wrong.

"I've been going over the books," he explained, "and trying to figure out where all the entries came from. Colin's the one with a head for figures," he added. "I'm trying to keep the ledgers current but it's difficult."

"I entered the invoices while Colin was ill," she said. "Perhaps I made a mistake. Are you thinking the balances are wrong?"

Nathan shook his head. "Colin told me you caught him up," he said. He smiled then and stretched his long legs out. She moved her skirts out of his way so he would have more room.

"I couldn't find the invoices for some of the deposits made," he said.

She finally understood what was bothering him. The money Colin had transferred into the company account came from payment for services rendered for the War Department.

"There aren't any receipts for four entries," she remarked.

"Yes, four exactly," Nathan agreed with a nod. "Do you

know where Colin got the money? It doesn't make sense. The income from the ships is accounted for and I know he doesn't have a separate income."

"Have you asked him about it?"

Nathan shook his head. "I just discovered the puzzle this morning."

"Do you and Colin . . . share everything? I mean to ask, does either of you keep secrets?"

"We're partners, Alesandra. If we can't trust each other, who in thunder can we trust?"

He gave her a piercing look. "You know where the money came from, don't you?"

She slowly nodded. "Colin should probably tell you—not me," she reasoned aloud.

"Did the money come from you?"

"No."

"Then who?"

He wasn't going to let it drop. Because Nathan wasn't just Colin's partner but his best friend as well, Alesandra decided it wouldn't be disloyal to tell him.

"You must promise me not to say a word to Caine or anyone else in Colin's family," she began.

Nathan nodded. His curiosity was pricked, of course. "I promise."

"Colin was doing some work on the side to increase the accounts."

Nathan leaned forward. "Who did he work for?"

"Sir Richards."

His roar almost knocked her gift off the seat. Nathan had appeared to be only mildly interested and for that reason his furious reaction was a bit stunning. She visibly jumped. She flinched, too, when he muttered a dark expletive.

Nathan regained his control and apologized for using the foul word. The look in his eyes remained chilling.

"I believe it would be best if you let Colin explain," she stammered out. "He doesn't work for Richards any longer, Nathan."

"You're certain?"

She nodded. "I'm very certain."

Nathan let out a long sigh and leaned back. "Thank you for telling me."

"Colin would have told you, wouldn't he?"

The worry in his voice was very apparent. Nathan thought she was having second thoughts about telling him. He smiled. "Yes, he would have told me. In fact, I'll ask him about the missing invoices tonight."

He deliberately turned the topic so she would quit fretting. They arrived at Caine's town house a few minutes later.

Alesandra met Flannaghan's uncle Sterns when he opened the door for them. He was an extremely dour-faced elderly gentleman, stiff as starch in his manners, but there was a true sparkle in his eyes when he greeted her. Flannaghan, it seemed, had been singing her praises, and Sterns made mention that he'd just heard both Megan and Kate were also in her household now.

The doors to the salon were wide open. Caine's daughter spotted her first and came running into the entrance. The four-year-old grabbed hold of Sterns's hand so she wouldn't tumble when she executed a curtsy. Her ladylike behavior was short-lived. The second she'd finished with the bothersome formality, she let go of Sterns and threw herself at her uncle Nathan's legs. She let out a shriek of joy when he lifted her up and tossed her like a hat into the air.

"Thank God for tall ceilings," Sterns remarked.

Nathan heard the comment and laughed. He settled his niece in his arm and followed Alesandra into the salon.

Jade and Catherine were sitting side by side on the settee. The duchess was seated in the chair across from her daughters. All three women rushed to their feet and surrounded Alesandra.

"We just heard the wonderful news," the duchess announced.

Alesandra laughed.

"I heard it from Catherine," said the duchess.

"I heard it from Jade," Catherine interjected.

"I never . . ." Jade began to protest.

"I heard mother giving you her speculations," Catherine admitted then.

"Where is Sara?" Nathan demanded to know.

"She's feeding Joanna," Jade explained. "She'll be down in a minute or two."

Nathan immediately turned to go to his wife. He tried to put Olivia down, but she tightened her hold on his shoulders and announced she was going with him.

Alesandra put the gift box down on the side table and followed her relatives over to the chairs. She sat down next to her mother-in-law. The duchess was dabbing at her eyes with her linen square.

"I'm beside myself with joy," she announced. "Another grandchild. It's such a blessing."

Alesandra beamed with pleasure. The talk centered on children for several minutes. Catherine quickly became bored. Alesandra noticed and decided to change the topic.

"Are you angry with me for telling Colin about the flowers you received?"

"I was angry at first, but then Father explained everything. Then I became afraid. Now that Neil Perry's been locked away, I'm not at all afraid and Father is going to let me go to all the affairs again. Do you realize the season is almost over. I shall die of boredom when I have to go back to the country."

"You will do no such thing," her mother countered.

"I'm going riding in the park with Morgan Atkins today."

"Catherine, I thought we agreed you would decline the invitation and spend the afternoon with your family," her mother reminded her.

"It's only a short ride and everyone will notice if I don't go. Besides, I can see family anytime."

"Is Morgan coming here to collect you?" Jade asked.

Catherine nodded. "He's so divine. Father likes him, too."

Alesandra was uneasy about Catherine going anywhere. Oh, she knew Morgan was a friend of Colin's and would certainly watch out for Catherine, but she still wished her sister-in-law would stay home. Alesandra wasn't convinced Neil was the culprit. She didn't want to alarm her relatives, though. She wished Colin were here. He would know what to do.

He wouldn't let his sister leave. Alesandra came to that conclusion right away. But Colin was cautious to a fault, she thought to herself.

"Catherine, I believe you should stay here with us," Alesandra blurted out.

"Why?"

Why indeed? Alesandra's mind hunted for a reason. She turned to Jade, silently imploring her help.

Caine's wife was very astute. She caught the worry in Alesandra's eyes and immediately voiced her agreement.

"Yes, you should stay with us," she told Catherine. "Sterns will be happy to send a note to Morgan explaining a family matter has come up and you aren't able to keep your appointment."

"But I wish to keep my appointment," Catherine argued. "Mother, this isn't fair. Michelle Marie is going riding with the Earl of Hampton. Her sisters don't tell her what to do."

"We aren't telling you what to do," Alesandra countered. "We just don't want you to go."

"Why not?"

Catherine's frustration made her voice shrill. Thankfully, Alesandra was saved from having to come up with an answer, for Nathan and his wife walked into the room, drawing everyone's attention.

Alesandra literally bounded to her feet. She hurried across the room to meet Sara.

Nathan's wife was a beautiful woman. She had dark brown hair, a flawless complexion, and eyes the color of a clear blue sky. Her smile was enchanting, too. It was filled with warmth.

Nathan introduced her to his wife. Alesandra wasn't certain if she should formally curtsy or take hold of Sara's hand. Her dilemma didn't last long. The woman was openly affectionate. She immediately walked forward and embraced Alesandra.

It wasn't possible to feel awkward around Sara. She treated Alesandra as though she were a long-lost friend.

"Where is Joanna?" Alesandra asked.

"Olivia's bringing her down," Sara explained.

"With Sterns's assistance," Nathan interjected. He turned to his wife then. "Sweetheart, I'm going back upstairs to finish with the ledgers."

Jade called out to Sara and patted the cushion next to her. Alesandra didn't follow. She chased after Nathan. She caught him halfway up the stairs.

"May I please speak to you in private for just a moment?"

"Certainly," Nathan answered. "Will the study do?"

She nodded. She followed him up the rest of the stairs and into the study. Nathan motioned to a chair, but she declined the invitation to sit.

The room was a clutter of maps and ledgers. Nathan had obviously turned Caine's study into a secondary shipping office. She made that mention to him as he walked across the room.

"Caine's library is downstairs," Nathan explained. "He won't let me inside. He won't come inside this room, either," he added with a grin. "My brother-in-law is a fanatic about order. He can't stand the mess. Have a seat, Alesandra, and tell me what's on your mind."

She again declined the invitation to sit. "This will only take a minute," she explained. "Catherine wishes to go riding with Morgan Atkins. He's coming here to fetch her. I don't think it's a good idea to let her go, Nathan, but I can't come up with a suitable argument why. She's very determined."

"Why don't you want her to go?"

She could have gone into a lengthy and surely confusing explanation that wouldn't make any sense at all, but she decided not to waste Nathan's time.

"I'm just uneasy about it," she said. "And I know Colin wouldn't let her go. Neither one of us is convinced Neil Perry is the guilty man, and until we are convinced we don't want Catherine going anywhere. Colin isn't here to tell his sister no, and her mother won't be able to sway her. Will you please handle this? I don't believe Catherine would dare argue with you."

Nathan started for the door. "So Colin doesn't trust this Atkins?"

"Oh, no, I didn't mean to imply that," she said. "Morgan's a friend of Colin's." She lowered her voice when she added, "He's taken over Colin's position in the department under Sir Richards's supervision."

"But you believe Colin wouldn't wish her to go. All right. I'll take care of it."

"What excuse are you going to give her?" Alesandra asked as she hurried after the giant.

"None," Nathan answered. He smiled then, a rascal's smile to be sure. "I don't need a reason. I'll simply tell her she's staying here."

"And if she argues?"

Nathan laughed. "It isn't what I'm going to say to her, it's how I'll say it. Trust me, Alesandra. She won't argue. There are only two women in this world I can't intimidate. My sister and my wife. Don't worry, I'll take care of it."

"Actually, Nathan, there are three. You can't intimidate Jade, Sara, or me."

She smiled over the look of surprise in his eyes but didn't dare laugh.

The duchess was waiting in the foyer to say good-bye to both Alesandra and Nathan. She had an important dinner party to prepare for, she explained. She kissed Alesandra on her cheek, then made Nathan lean down so she could kiss him, too.

Alesandra assumed Catherine was still inside the salon. She turned to go inside before Nathan so she could pretend she hadn't interfered. Catherine was already a little irritated with her because she'd broken her word to her and Alesandra didn't want to add another sin to her list.

Sara was sitting on the settee. Little Olivia sat next to her and was holding the baby in her lap.

"I do hope Joanna turns out to be as pretty as you are," Sara told Olivia.

"Probably she won't," Olivia replied. "She doesn't have enough hair to be as pretty as me."

Jade rolled her eyes heavenward. Sara smiled. "She's still young," she said. "She might grow more."

"Where's Catherine?" Alesandra asked as she crossed the room. "Nathan wants to have a word with her."

"She left a few minutes ago," Jade answered.

Alesandra immediately jumped to the conclusion that Catherine had left with her mother. She sat down next to Olivia to look at the baby.

"Was she very angry we interfered with her plans? She's probably giving her mother a fit right about now. Oh, Sara, Joanna's beautiful. She's so tiny."

"She'll get bigger," Olivia announced. "Babies do. Mama says so."

"Alesandra, Catherine didn't go home with her mother. She left with Morgan. We did try to make her change her mind, but without a valid reason at hand her mother finally relented. Catherine can cry at the drop of a hat, and I believe her mother didn't want a scene."

The baby started fretting. Sara took her daughter into her arms and stood up. "It's time for her nap," she announced. "I'll be right back down. Sterns will snatch her out of my hands as soon as he can. The man's a wonder with infants, isn't he, Jade?"

"He's a wonder with four-year-old's too," Jade replied. She turned her attention to her daughter. "It's time for your nap, too, Olivia."

Her daughter didn't want to leave. Jade insisted. She took Olivia's hand and pulled her along.

"I'm not a baby, Mama."

"I know you're not, Olivia," Jade answered. "And that's why you only take one nap a day. Joanna takes two."

Alesandra sat down on the settee and watched Jade drag her daughter out of the room. Nathan stood in the doorway.

"Do you want me to go after Catherine?" he asked.

She shook her head. "I'm just a worrier, Nathan. I'm certain it will be all right."

The front door opened just then and both Caine and Colin walked inside. Caine stood in the foyer talking to

Nathan, but Colin immediately went into the salon to his wife. He sat down beside her, hauled her up against him, and kissed her.

"Well?" she demanded when he began to nuzzle on the side of her neck and didn't immediately tell her what happened.

"He's probably guilty," Colin announced.

Caine and Nathan walked inside to join them. Alesandra nudged Colin so he would quit nibbling on her earlobe. Her husband let out a sigh before straightening away from her. He smiled when he saw her blush.

"He had motive and opportunity," Colin remarked then.

Caine heard his brother's comment. "I think we're trying to make this more complicated than it really is. I'll admit it's . . . convenient."

Colin nodded. He pulled out his list. "All right, sweetheart. Here are your answers. First, Neil denies that he went with his sister to meet a man calling himself her admirer. Second, he swears he didn't know anything about an insurance policy. And third, he vehemently denies being involved with Lady Roberta."

"I expected those answers," Alesandra announced.

"He wasn't much of a brother to Victoria," Caine interjected. He sat down and let out a loud yawn.

"What about my other question to Neil?"

"Which one was that?" Colin asked.

"I wanted the names of the suitors Victoria turned down. He mentioned there were three when he visited me and I thought those rejections might be important. Honestly, Colin, did you forget to ask him?"

"No, I didn't forget. There was Burke—he's married now so he wouldn't count—and Mazelton."

"He's getting married soon," Caine interjected.

"And?" Alesandra asked when Colin didn't continue. "Who was the third man?"

"Morgan Atkins," said Caine. Colin nodded. Alesandra glanced over at Nathan. He was frowning. "Colin, isn't Morgan a friend of yours?" he asked.

"Hell, no," Colin answered. "He probably wants to throttle me about now. He blames me for a situation that developed and he messed up."

Nathan leaned forward. "Would he blame you enough to come after your wife?"

Colin's expression changed. He started to shake his head, then stopped himself. "It's a possibility," he admitted. "Remote, but . . . what are you thinking, Nathan?"

His partner turned to look at Alesandra.

They said her name in unison. "Catherine."

Chapter 15

"We did not panic."

"Yes, we did," Alesandra replied. She smiled at her husband while she contradicted him, then turned her attention back to her task.

Both she and her husband were in bed. Colin was stretched out on his back and had pillows propped behind his head. Alesandra knelt at the foot of the bed. She wrung out another long strip of cotton and applied it to her husband's leg. The heat from the water made her fingers red, but the mild discomfort was certainly rewarded by Colin's loud sighs of pleasure.

Her husband had barely grumbled when she had handed him the list of suggestions Sir Winters had made. He refused both pain medication and liquor, but he took the time to explain why. He didn't wish to become dependent on either and so he went without, regardless of how painful the leg became.

The hot cloths helped take the cramp out of his calf, however, and as long as she kept him busy thinking about something else, he forgot to be sensitive or embarrassed about the scars.

He certainly wasn't embarrassed about the rest of his body. He was a bit of an exhibitionist, too. Alesandra wore a prim pink and white high-necked sleeping gown and matching robe. Colin wasn't wearing anything. His hands were stacked behind his head, and when he let out another long sigh, she decided her husband was thoroughly uninhibited with her . . . and just as content.

"I will admit Caine did run around a bit, but only because there was the slightest chance Morgan might somehow be involved."

"Ran around a bit? Surely you jest, Colin. The man picked up his wife and tossed her into his open carriage, then went racing toward the park after Catherine."

Colin grinned over the picture. "All right, he did panic. I didn't, however."

She let out an inelegant snort. "Then I didn't see you leap over the side of their carriage so you wouldn't be left behind?"

"Better safe than sorry, Alesandra."

"And all for nought," she said. "Catherine would have died of mortification if Caine and you had caught up with her. Thank heaven Morgan took her home before her brothers spotted her. This is all my fault, by the way."

"What's all your fault?"

"I got everyone all worked up," she admitted. "I shouldn't have made your relatives so worried."

"They're your relatives, too," he reminded her.

She nodded. "Why do you think Victoria turned Morgan down?"

The switch in topics didn't throw Colin. He was getting used to the way his wife's mind raced from one thought to another. She was an extremely logical woman—damned intelligent, too—and for those reasons he no longer shrugged off any concerns she might have. If she wasn't completely convinced Neil was the culprit, then he wasn't completely convinced either.

"Morgan's up to his neck in debt and could very well lose his estates."

"How do you know that?"

"Richards told me," he answered. "Maybe Victoria thought she could do better."

"Yes," Alesandra agreed. "That is possible, I suppose."

"Sweetheart, let's go to bed."

She scooted off the bed and put the bowl of water on the bench near the window. Then she removed the wet strips from his leg, folded them, and put them next to the bowl.

"Colin, are you feeling guilty because you wouldn't listen to me when I tried to talk to you about Victoria?"

"Hell, yes, I'm feeling guilty. Every time you brought up the topic, I told you to leave it alone."

"Good."

He opened one eye to look at her. "Good? You want me to feel guilty?"

She smiled. "Yes," she answered. She took off her robe, draped it over the edge of the bed, and began unbuttoning her gown. "It's good because I now have the upper hand in negotiating."

He grinned over her choice of words and her expression. She looked so serious. "What exactly do you want to negotiate?"

"Our sleeping arrangement. I'm going to sleep in your bed all night, Colin. It won't do you any good to argue."

Alesandra quit trying to get her sleeping gown off and hurried to get into bed. She thought it would be more difficult for Colin to deny her demand if she was already settled next to him. She pulled the covers over her, fluffed her pillow, and then said, "If guilt doesn't sway you, then I'll have to remind you of my delicate condition. You won't deny the mother of your child anything."

Colin laughed. He rolled to his side and put his arm around his wife. "You're quite the little negotiator," he drawled out. "Love, it isn't that I don't want you to sleep with me, but I get up off and on all night long and I don't want to wake you. You need your rest."

"You won't wake me," she replied. "A nice long letter arrived from Mother Superior today," she said then, turning the topic. "I left it on your desk so you could read it. The roses are in bloom all around Stone Haven now. Perhaps next year, when you take me to see our castle, all the flowers will be in their full glory. It's quite a sight, husband."

"Lord, I really do own a castle, don't I?"

She cuddled closer to his side. "Mother Superior was able to get the funds released from the bankers. I never doubted her ability, of course. She can be very persuasive when she wants to."

Colin was pleased with the news. He didn't want the general to get even a fraction of Alesandra's inheritance. "Dreyson will quit worrying," he remarked. "Once the money is safe in the bank here . . ."

"Good Lord, Colin, you don't believe Mother Superior will send the funds on to us, do you?"

"I did think . . ."

Her laughter stopped him. "What is so amusing?"

"Getting the money away from the general wasn't difficult at all, but trying to get the Mother Superior to release the funds will be quite impossible."

"Why?" he asked, still confused.

"Because she's a nun," she answered. "And nuns solicit funds. They don't give them up. The general wasn't any match for the mother superior, and neither are you, husband. God wants them to have the money," she added. "Besides, it was a gift, remember? And they can certainly put the money to good use. Dreyson will pout for a little while and then he'll forget all about it."

Colin leaned down and kissed her. "I love you, Alesandra."

She'd been waiting to hear that declaration and immediately pounced on it. "Perhaps you do love me just a little, but certainly not as much as Nathan loves Sara."

Her announcement astonished him. He leaned up on one elbow so he could see her expression. She wasn't smiling, but there was a definite sparkle in her eyes. The little woman was up to something, all right.

"Why would you say such a thing?"

She wasn't the least affected by the growl in his voice or the scowl on his face. "I'm negotiating again," she explained.

"What is it you want now?" Colin was having difficulty controlling his frown. He wanted to laugh.

"You and Nathan were going to use Sara's gift from the king, and I ask—nay, I demand—you take the exact amount from my inheritance. It's only fair, Colin."

"Alesandra . . ."

"I don't like being slighted, husband."

"Slighted? Where in God's name did you come up with that notion?"

"I'm really very sleepy now. Think about the fairness in my request and let me know tomorrow. Good night, Colin."

Request? He scoffed over that word. She'd demanded, and that was that. He could tell her mind was set, and she was simply too stubborn for her own good. She wasn't going to let up on the issue, either. From the tone of her voice he knew her feelings had somehow been injured over what she considered a slight.

"I'll think about it," he finally promised.

She didn't hear him. She was already sound asleep. Colin blew out the candles, pulled his wife close, and fell asleep minutes later.

The household hadn't completely settled down for the night. Flannaghan was still downstairs putting the finishing touches on his sister's work. He had given Meg the task of dusting the salon and was now diligently cleaning the spots she'd missed. Flannaghan was a worrier, a perfectionist as well, and until both his sisters learned the routine of the household he would continue to scrutinize their work to make certain it was up to his standards.

It was after one in the morning when he finally finished with the salon and blew out the candles. He'd just reached the foyer when a knock sounded at the front door.

Because of the late hour, Flannaghan didn't open the door to see who was there. He peeked out the side window first, recognized his employer's friend, and then unbolted the latch.

Morgan Atkins rushed inside. Before Flannaghan could explain that both Colin and Alesandra had already retired for the night, Morgan said, "I know it's late, but this is an emergency and I've got to see Colin right away. Sir Richards will be here in a few minutes."

"But milord has already gone to bed," Flannaghan stammered out.

"Wake him," Morgan snapped. He softened his voice when he added, "We have a crisis on our hands. He'll want to know what has happened. Be quick about it, man. Richards will be here any moment now."

Flannaghan didn't argue with the earl. He immediately turned to run up the steps. Morgan followed him. Flannaghan assumed the earl wished to wait in the study. He half turned to ask him to take a seat in the salon.

A blinding light exploded inside his head. The pain was so intense, so consuming, it overwhelmed him. There wasn't time to shout a warning, or enough strength to fight. Flannaghan was whirled into darkness the second the blow was delivered to the back of his head.

He fell backward. Morgan grasped him under his arms so the unconscious man wouldn't make any noise falling down the steps, then propped him against the banister.

He stood there staring down at the butler a long minute to make certain he hadn't just stunned him, then, satisfied he wouldn't wake up anytime soon, he turned his attention to the more important task at hand.

He crept up the stairs. In one pocket was the dagger he planned to use on Alesandra. In the other pocket was the pistol he would use to kill Colin.

His eagerness didn't make him less cautious. He'd replayed his plan over and over again inside his mind to make certain there weren't any flaws.

He was glad now he hadn't given in to his urge and killed her sooner. He'd wanted to . . . oh, yes, he'd wanted to, but he hadn't given in to the urge. Why, he'd even taken out the contract with Morton and Sons, naming Colin as beneficiary of course, so that the husband would be the only one who stood to gain from her death. Oh, yes, he'd been clever about what he was going to do. The princess had intrigued him from the moment he'd met her. Would there be a stronger rush killing royalty?

He smiled in anticipation. In just a few minutes he would have his answer.

He knew which bedroom belonged to Alesandra. He'd found out that interesting fact when he'd called on Colin that first time. He'd met Alesandra in the hallway outside the library, heard her mention she needed to get something from her room, and then watched her hurry down the hallway, past the first doorway and through the second. Oh, he was the clever one, all right. He'd filed that information away for possible future use and now it was going to give him the edge he needed.

He wanted to kill Alesandra first. There was surely a connecting door between the two bedrooms, and if not, then the hallway door would serve him just as well. He wanted to make Alesandra scream with her terror and her pain and watch as Colin rushed into the bedroom to save his beloved wife. Morgan would wait until Colin had taken it all in, had seen the blood pouring from Alesandra's body, and once he'd feasted on the horror and the helplessness in Colin's eyes, then he would kill him with one shot through his heart.

Colin deserved to die a slow, agonizing death, but Morgan didn't dare take such a chance. Colin was a dangerous man, and for that reason alone he would kill him quickly.

Still, the look on his face when he realized his wife was dying would be treasured in Morgan's mind a long, long while. And that would have to be enough, he decided as he slowly made his way down the dark hallway.

He passed the study, then the door to the first chamber, as silent as a cat now, barely breathing at all until he reached the door he'd watched Alesandra open.

He was ready now, composed . . . invincible! And still he waited, more to tease himself with the anticipation of the reward soon to be his than anything else. He listened to the silence for long minutes . . . waiting . . . letting the fever catch hold of him, burn him, strengthen him.

They both deserved to die—Alesandra because she was a woman, of course, and Colin because he had ruined his chances for success with the War Department. Richards didn't trust him anymore, and it was Colin's fault he hadn't succeeded. If Colin had gone along with him on the assignment, he wouldn't have given in to the fever raging inside him when he'd spotted the Frenchman's sister. He wouldn't have thought about how smooth her skin had looked or noticed the innocent vulnerability in her eyes. He would have been able to control the need to touch her with his blade in his hands. . . . But Colin hadn't gone with him, and luck hadn't been on his side that time. The brother returned from town earlier than scheduled and had come upon him while he was sliding his blade in and out, in and out, in his own mating ritual that gave him such a rush of pleasure. The screams had alerted the man—those necessary, thrilling screams that fed his passion—and if Colin had been there both the sister and her brother would still be alive. He would have been able to control himself—yes, yes, he would have—and, oh, God, she'd been so sweet. . . .

Her body had felt like butter against his steel erection, and he knew Alesandra's body would feel just as soft. Her blood would be hot and sticky as it spurted over his hands, as hot and sticky . . .

He didn't dare wait any longer. After Richards told him Colin and he had both come to the conclusion he wasn't suited for their line of work, Morgan had pretended disappointment. Inside he raged with fury. How dare they think him inferior? How dare they?

He'd made up his mind then and there to kill both of them. He'd been so terribly clever with his plans, too. Colin and Richards would both die in tragic accidents, of course, but the plans changed today when he'd taken Colin's sister riding in the park and she'd told him Alesandra had tried to talk her out of going.

The stupid chit told her every thought. Morgan knew then that they were becoming suspicious of him. There wasn't a shred of proof to link him to any of the women . . . was there? No, no, it was wrong of him to think of himself as vulnerable. He was far too cunning to ever give in to self-doubt.

He had immediately changed his plans, however. He'd worked every detail out. He would kill Alesandra for the sheer pleasure involved, then kill Colin, and on his way out he would make certain the butler never awakened.

No one was going to be able to point the finger at him. He had the perfect alibi. He was spending the night with the bitch Lorraine, and she would tell anyone who asked that he had never left her bed. He'd given her a large dose of laudanum mixed in with her drink and slipped out the back window of the whore's cottage. When she awakened from her drug-induced sleep, he would be back by her side.

Oh, yes, he'd thought of everything. He allowed himself to smile with satisfaction. He pulled the dagger out of his pocket and then reached for the doorknob.

Colin heard the squeak of the door as it opened. He was already awake and was just about to get out of bed to walk off the throbbing cramping in his leg when the muffled sound gained his attention.

He didn't waste any time waiting to hear any more noises. His instincts were screaming a warning. Someone was inside Alesandra's bedroom now and he knew it wasn't any of his staff. His servants wouldn't dare enter either bedroom without begging entrance first.

Colin moved with the speed of lightning, yet didn't make a sound. He removed the loaded pistol he kept in the drawer of the nightstand, then turned back to his wife. He clamped one hand over her mouth and dragged her across the bed. His gaze and his pistol stayed centered on the connecting door.

Alesandra came awake with a start. The moonlight filtering through the windows was bright enough for her to see the look on her husband's face. His expression was terrifying. Her mind instantly cleared. Something was terribly wrong. Colin finally removed his hand from her mouth and motioned for her to go across the room. He never looked directly at her. His attention continued to be focused on the door to her chamber.

She tried to walk in front of him. He wouldn't let her. He grabbed hold of her arm and gently pushed her behind him. He followed her across the bedroom, his back to her all the while, then pushed her into the narrow corner between the wall and the heavy wardrobe. He stood in front of her, protecting her from direct attack.

She didn't have any idea how long they stood there. It seemed an eternity to her and yet she guessed only a few minutes actually had passed.

And then the door slowly opened. A shadow spilled across the carpet. A blur followed. The intruder didn't creep into the chamber but ran with a demon's speed and determination.

The low, guttural cry he made sent chills down Alesandra's spine. She squeezed her eyes shut and began to pray.

Morgan held a knife high above his head in one hand and a pistol in his other hand. Because he'd run into the room he'd almost reached the side of the bed before his mind registered the fact that it was empty. The sound he was making, that god-awful mewing, inhuman sound he couldn't seem to control, suddenly turned into an outraged roar very like that of an animal being denied its prey. Morgan knew, even before he started to turn, that Colin was there, waiting for him. He knew without a doubt he had only a second at best to save himself, but he was so very clever, so superior . . . he was certain the second was all he needed.

He was, after all, invincible. In one fluid motion he whirled, his pistol at the ready, his finger caressing the spring . . .

His death was instantaneous. The shot from Colin's pistol entered Morgan's head through his left temple. He collapsed to the floor, his eyes wide open, his weapons still clutched in his hands.

"Don't move, Alesandra."

Colin's command was harsh, clipped. She nodded, then realized his back faced her and he couldn't see her agreement. Her hands started aching. She had been clutching them tight against her bosom. She forced herself to relax.

"Be careful," she whispered in a voice so low she doubted Colin could hear her.

He walked over to the body, kicked the pistol out of Morgan's hand, then knelt down on one knee to make certain he was dead.

He let out a long sigh. His heart was pounding a furious beat. "Bastard," he muttered as he stood up. He turned back to Alesandra and reached out his hand to her. She scooted out of the corner, her gaze locked on Morgan Atkins, and slowly walked over to her husband. Colin pulled her into his arms, blocking her view.

"Don't look at him," he ordered.

"Is he dead?"

"Yes."

"Did you mean to kill him?"

"Hell, yes."

She leaned into his side. Colin could feel her trembling. "It's over now, sweetheart. He can't hurt anyone else."

"You're sure he's dead?" Her voice shivered with worry.

"I'm sure," he answered, his voice still harsh with anger.

"Why do you sound so angry?"

Colin took a deep, cleansing breath before he answered her. "It's just a reaction," he said. "The bastard had some grand plans, Alesandra. If you had been sleeping in your chamber . . ."

He couldn't go on. The thought of what could have happened to her was too terrifying for him to think about.

Alesandra took hold of her husband's hand and led him over to the bed. She gently pushed against his shoulders so he would sit down. "But nothing happened to me because of your instincts. You heard him in the other room, didn't you?"

Her voice was a soothing whisper. Colin had to shake his head. His wife was actually comforting him . . . and, damn it all, he actually needed it.

"Put your robe on, sweetheart," he told her. "I don't want you to get chilled. Are you all right?"

He pulled her onto his lap when he asked her that question. "Yes," she answered. "Are you all right?"

"Alesandra, if anything ever happened to you, I don't know what in God's name I would do. I can't imagine life without you."

"I love you, too, Colin."

Her declaration soothed him. He grunted his pleasure while he lifted her off his lap to sit on the bed beside him.

He took another deep breath, then stood up. "I'm going to wake Flannaghan and send him over to Richards. Sit here until . . ."

He quit his order when she bounded to her feet. "I'm going with you. I don't want to stay here with . . . him."

"All right, love." He draped his arm around her shoulders and started for the door.

She was shivering again. Colin didn't want the fear to catch hold of her again.

"Didn't you say you thought Morgan was a real charmer?"

She let out a gasp. "I certainly did not say such a thing. Catherine thought he was charming. I never thought so."

Colin didn't contradict her. He didn't think now was the time to remind her she'd added Morgan's name to her list of marriage candidates. She'd just get more upset.

He'd made the remark to take her attention away from the dead man they had to walk around to get out of the room. The ploy worked. Alesandra barely spared Morgan a glance. She was fully occupied frowning up at her husband. The color had come back into her face, too.

"I was suspicious of Morgan from the moment I met him," she announced. "Well, almost from the moment I met him," she added when Colin looked incredulous.

He didn't argue with her. They reached the hallway before he realized he wasn't wearing any clothes. He went back inside, put on a pair of pants, then pulled a cover off the top of the wardrobe and tossed it over Morgan. He didn't want Alesandra to see the bastard's face again. He didn't particularly want to look at him either.

Flannaghan wasn't in his room. They found him sprawled out on the steps near the foyer. Alesandra was far more upset over her butler's condition than she had been over Morgan's demise. She burst into tears and clung to Flannaghan's hand until Colin convinced her that the servant had just been knocked into a deep sleep. When Flannaghan let out a low groan, she was able to gain control of herself.

An hour later the town house was filled with visitors. Colin had flagged down a passing hack and sent the driver to fetch Sir Richards, Caine, and Nathan. The three men arrived a scant five minutes apart.

Richards questioned Flannaghan first, then sent him up to bed. Alesandra sat on the settee, flanked by Nathan on one side and Caine on the other. The two men were competing with one another in their bid to comfort her. She thought their concern was terribly sweet and therefore put up with Nathan's awkward, stinging pats and Caine's sporadic words of sympathy that didn't make much sense.

Colin walked into the salon and had to shake his head in vexation when he saw the trio. He could barely find his wife. Caine and Nathan had literally pinned her to the settee with their wide shoulders.

"Nathan, my wife can't breathe. Move. You, too, Caine."

"We're comforting her in her time of need," Caine announced.

"Damn right we are," Nathan agreed.

"It must have been quite a fright for you, Princess."

Sir Richards made that evaluation from the doorway. He hurried across the room and sat down in the chair across from her.

The director was barely put together. He'd obviously been in bed when the summons came, for his hair stood on end and his shirt was only partially tucked into his pants. His shoes didn't match, either. They were both black, but only one had the Wellington tassel. The other was bare.

"Of course it was a fright," Caine announced.

Nathan patted her on her knee again in a bid to soothe her. Alesandra looked at Colin. The sparkle in her eyes told him she was close to laughing. He thought she might be smiling, but couldn't tell, for the lower part of her face was hidden behind Caine's and Nathan's shoulders.

"Get up, Nathan. I want to sit next to my wife."

Nathan gave her one last whack before he moved to another chair. Colin immediately sat down and hauled her close to his side.

"How did you kill him?" Nathan asked then.

Caine motioned to Alesandra and shook his head at his brother-in-law. She missed that action. Since no one else seemed inclined to answer Nathan, she decided to. "One clean shot, directly through the left temple," she said.

"Colin has always been extremely accurate," Sir Richards praised.

"Were you surprised it was Morgan, Sir Richards?" she asked.

The director nodded. "I never would have thought he was capable of such foulness. Lord, I put him to work for my department. The way he bungled the one assignment he was given told me he didn't have the instincts. A sister and brother were killed because of his ineptness."

"Maybe it wasn't ineptness at all," Colin said. "Richards, you told me the sister accidentally got in the way. Now I'm wondering if Morgan deliberately killed her. He did file the report, didn't he?"

Richards leaned forward. "I'll ferret out the truth," he announced. "By God I will. What set him off tonight I wonder? Why did he suddenly come out in the open to get Alesandra. He lured the other women to a secluded spot, but came here to get her. Perhaps he'd just become bolder," he added.

"Catherine is probably the reason he took the risk," Caine interjected. "She must have told Morgan that Alesandra tried to stop her from going riding with him. Catherine does like to tell everything she knows. Perhaps Morgan jumped to the conclusion we were suspicious of him."

Nathan shook his head. "The bastard was demented."

Colin agreed with that assessment. "The sounds he made when he came running into the bedroom makes me think he was out of his mind."

"He'd taken a real liking to it."

Caine made that statement in an emphatic tone of voice.

Alesandra was appalled at the very idea that anyone could gain pleasure from another person's pain.

"We might not have ever found out the truth if he hadn't come after Alesandra tonight," Nathan said. "Neil could have gone to the gallows for two crimes he didn't commit."

"What was Morgan's connection with Lady Roberta? Was he involved with her or was she chosen at random?" Alesandra asked.

No one had a quick answer to her question. Richards decided to speculate. "It was common knowledge the viscount and his wife were having difficulties. Perhaps Morgan pounced on Roberta's vulnerability. Notes and gifts from a secret admirer were probably flattering to her."

"We would have caught Morgan eventually," Caine said. "He would have made more mistakes. He was out of control."

"Catherine thought he was charming."

Nathan made that remark with a dark scowl. Caine nodded.

"Yeah," Colin drawled out. "He was a real lady killer."

Chapter 16

Three months had passed since Morgan's death, and Alesandra still thought about the horrible man at least once a day. The mother superior had taught her to pray for the souls of sinners, for they needed prayers far more than saints did, but Alesandra couldn't quite make herself pray for Morgan yet. She tried to put the horror of that night behind her. She never wanted to forget Victoria, though, and did say a prayer for her soul every night before she went to bed. She prayed for Roberta, too. She wanted to believe that both women had suffered their purgatory while on earth and in Morgan's cruel hands and that they were now at peace with their Maker in heaven.

Nathan and Sara were preparing for their journey back to their island home. Caine had invited Alesandra and Colin over to their town house for a farewell dinner with the rest of the family. The food was elegant but also quite rich, and Jade turned green by the time the second course was served. She suddenly bolted from the table and ran out of the dining room. Caine didn't show much sympathy over his wife's obvious distress. He actually grinned with male arrogance.

It wasn't like Caine to be so insensitive, and when Alesandra asked him why he wasn't a bit more concerned about his wife's health, his grin widened into a full-fledged smile. Jade, he explained, was pregnant again, and while she was thrilled over her condition, she disliked her husband hovering over her while she went through the ritualistic morning and evening sickness.

There was a good deal of pounding done to Caine's shoulders. Toasts were given as well, and then Nathan and Colin, with their wives at their sides, went into the salon.

Sara was called above the stairs by Sterns to feed her impatient daughter. Alesandra sat next to her husband and listened to the talk of business between the partners. The topic of the large entry into the company's banking account came up. Nathan wanted to know where in thunder the money had come from. Colin was surprised by the anger in his friend's tone of voice. Alesandra understood Nathan's reaction. She knew he believed Colin had gone back to work for the director.

Colin explained Alesandra's feelings about her inheritance and how she had felt slighted because they had been willing to use Sara's money but not hers.

"The entry is the exact amount Sara would have received if our greedy ruler hadn't decided to keep it for himself," Colin remarked.

Nathan shook his head. "Alesandra, your gift for Joanna was quite enough," he argued. He glanced up to look at the beautiful golden replica of his favorite ship, the *Emerald,* sitting in the center of the mantel.

Colin also looked up at the treasure. He smiled because Nathan had placed the gift there. "It is beautiful, isn't it?"

"You can quit lusting after it," Nathan countered with a grin. "We're taking it home with us."

"I'm pleased you like it," Alesandra said. She turned to her husband to offer the suggestion that she ask the craftsman to fashion another ship for him, but Nathan interrupted her thought when he told her neither he nor Colin needed any money from her inheritance now. They were financially sound enough.

"Put the money into the town house Colin purchased for you," he suggested.

She shook her head. "My husband used the money he received from the insurance contract for a hefty payment, Nathan, and the castle needs very little work. I wish you could see the inside before you leave. It's only a block away from our rental and it's so large and roomy."

Colin turned his attention back from the ship to look at his wife. "It isn't a castle, sweetheart."

"Oh, but it is," she argued. "It's our home, Colin, and therefore our castle."

He couldn't fault that confusing bit of logic. "So I now have two castles," he said with a laugh. "And a princess."

He stretched his legs out and put his arm around his wife. Nathan wanted to continue to argue about the money, but it didn't take him long to realize Alesandra wasn't going to bend on the issue.

He finally accepted defeat. "Hell," he muttered.

"What now?" Colin asked.

"If I'd known about the gift from your wife's inheritance I never would have suggested we sell stock. Have you found out who owns the shares yet? Maybe we could buy them back."

Colin shook his head. "Dreyson isn't telling," he explained. "He says it would be breaking his client's trust."

"Let me talk to him," Nathan suggested. "Just give me five minutes alone with Dreyson and I promise you he'll tell us."

Alesandra immediately tried to soothe Nathan's temper. "Dreyson's extremely ethical. My father never would have done business with him if he hadn't believed he was honorable. I'm my father's daughter, Nathan, and I therefore follow in his footsteps. I also have complete confidence in his integrity. I would wager every coin I have that you would never be able to get him to break a confidence. You might as well give up."

"Colin and I have a right to know who the owner is," Nathan argued.

Colin closed his eyes and let out a loud yawn while he listened to the conversation. A comment his wife had just made suddenly gained his full attention.

She was her father's daughter. Colin opened his eyes and slowly turned to look at the ship again.

He was reminded of the castle perched on his father's mantel . . . and the bit of trickery Alesandra's father had played when he tucked the notes inside.

And then he knew. She was her father's daughter, all right. The stock certificates were hidden inside the ship. Colin was astonished by the revelation. The expression on his face when he turned to his wife showed his surprise.

"Is something the matter, Colin?"

"You wouldn't lie to me, would you, sweetheart?"

"No, of course not."

"How did you do it?"

"Do what?"

"You don't own the stocks. I asked Dreyson and he told me you weren't the owner. You also told me you didn't own them."

"I don't. Why in heaven's name . . ."

She stopped when Colin pointed to the ship. She knew then her husband had finally guessed the truth.

She was well into her sixth month of confinement and getting more awkward every day, but she was still quick when she needed to be. She hastily stood up and started for the doorway. "I believe I'll see how Sara's doing. I do so love to hold little Joanna. She has the most delightful smile."

"Come back here."

"I'd rather not, Colin."

"I want to talk to you. Now."

"Colin, you shouldn't get your wife upset. She's pregnant, for God's sake."

"Look at her, Nathan. Does she look upset to you? She looks damned guilty to me."

Alesandra let her husband see her exasperation. Nathan winked at her when she walked back to the settee. She folded her hands together and frowned at her husband. "You better not get angry, Colin. Our baby might become upset."

"But you're not upset, are you, sweetheart?"

"No."

He patted the cushion next to him. She sat down and smoothed her gown.

She stared at the floor. He stared at her. "They're inside the ship, aren't they?"

"What's inside the ship?" Nathan asked.

"The stock certificates," Colin answered. "Alesandra, I asked you a question. Please answer me."

"Yes, they're inside the ship."

Relief fairly overwhelmed him. He was so damned happy the certificates hadn't been sold to a stranger he wanted to laugh.

A faint blush crept up Alesandra's face. "How did you do it?" he asked.

"Do what?"

"Are they in my name? I never thought to ask Dreyson that question. Do I own them?"

"No."

"Are they in Nathan's name then?"

"No."

He waited a long minute for her to confess. She remained stubbornly silent. Nathan was thoroughly puzzled.

"I just want to talk to the owner, Alesandra, to see if he might wish to sell the stocks back to us. I won't use intimidation."

"The owner can't talk to you, Nathan, and it really isn't legally possible for you to purchase the stocks—not now anyway."

She turned to look at her husband. "I will admit I did interfere just a bit, husband, but I would remind you that you were being very mule-headed about my inheritance at the time and I had to resort to a bit of trickery."

"Like your father," he countered.

"Yes," she agreed. "Like my father. He wouldn't be angry with me. Are you?" she asked again.

Colin couldn't help but notice that his wife didn't appear to be overly concerned about that possibility. She smiled, a radiant smile that made his breath catch in the back of his throat. She was definitely going to drive him crazy one of these days, and he couldn't imagine anything more wonderful.

He leaned down and kissed her. "Go and say good-bye to Sara. Then you and I are going home to our castle. My leg needs some of your pampering."

"Colin, that's the first time I've ever heard you mention your leg," Nathan interjected.

"He's not nearly as sensitive anymore. The ache in his leg did save our lives, after all. If the throbbing hadn't awakened him, he might not have heard Morgan. Mother Superior told me there was a reason for everything. I believe she was right. Perhaps the shark took a bite out of your leg so you would be able to save me and our son."

"I'm having a son?" Colin asked, smiling over how matter-of-fact Alesandra sounded.

"Oh, yes, I believe so," she answered.

Colin rolled his eyes heavenward. "Have you named him yet?"

The sparkle came back into her eyes. "We should call him Dolphin or Dragon. Both names are appropriate. He is, after all, his father's son."

Alesandra left the room to the sound of her husband's laughter. She patted her swollen middle and whispered, "When you're smiling at me and showing your gentle side, I'll think of you as my dolphin, and when you're angry because you aren't getting your way, I'll know you've turned into my dragon. I'll love you with all my heart."

"What's she whispering about?" Nathan asked Colin.

Both men watched Alesandra until she turned and started up the steps. "She's talking to my son," Colin confessed. "She seems to think he hears her."

Nathan laughed. He'd never heard of anything so absurd.

Colin stood up and went to the mantel. He found the latch cleverly concealed by a trapdoor fashioned into the side of the ship and opened it. The stock certificates were rolled into a tube and tied with a pink ribbon.

Nathan watched him pull the papers out, unroll them, and read the name of the owner.

Then Colin burst into laughter. Nathan bounded to his feet. His curiosity was killing him. "Who owns them, Colin? Give me the name and I'll talk to him."

"Alesandra said the owner wouldn't talk to you," Colin replied. "She was right about that. You're going to have to wait."

"How long?" Nathan demanded.

Colin handed his partner the certificates. "Until your daughter learns how to speak, I imagine. They're all in Joanna's name, Nathan. Neither one of us can buy the stock back. We're both named as joint executors."

Nathan was astonished. "But how did she know? The stock was sold before she even met Sara or Joanna."

"You gave me your daughter's name in your letter," Colin reminded his friend.

Nathan sat down. A slow smile settled on his face. The company was safe from intruders.

"Where are you going, Colin?" he called out when his partner walked out of the room.

"Home to my castle," Colin said. "With my princess."

He started up the steps to collect his wife. The sound of her laughter reached him and he paused to let her joy wash over him.

The princess had tamed the dragon.

But the dragon was still the victor. He'd captured a princess's love.

He was content.

THE LION'S LADY

Prologue

The Black Hills, America, 1797

It was time to seek the vision.

The shaman waited for the Great Spirit to send him a sign. One month passed, then another, and still the gods ignored him. But the shaman was a patient man. He continued his daily prayers without complaint and waited for his humble petition to be heard.

When the moon was covered by a thick mist for four consecutive nights, the holy man knew the time had arrived. The Great Spirit had heard him.

He immediately began his preparations. After gathering his sacred powders, rattle, and drum, he made the slow climb to the top of the mountain. It was an arduous journey, made more difficult by his advanced years and the dense fog the evil spirits had surely sent to test his determination.

As soon as the old man reached the summit, he built a small fire in the center of the ledge overlooking the valley of the bitterroot. He sat down beside the flames with his face turned toward the sun. Then he reached for his powders.

First he sprinkled sage over the fire. The shaman knew all evil spirits hated the bitter smell. The scent would make them stop their mischief and leave the mountain.

The mist left the mountaintop the following morning, a signal to the holy one that the mischief makers had been chased away. He put the remaining sage powder away and began to feed incense to the flames. The scent was made sweet by the addition of sacred buffalo prairie grass. Incense would purify the air and was known to attract benevolent gods.

For three days and nights the shaman stayed close to the fire. He fasted and prayed, and on the fourth morning he reached for his rattle and drum. He then began the chant that would bring the Great Spirit closer.

During the black hours of the fourth night, the shaman's sacrifice was rewarded. The Great Spirit gave him his dream.

While the holy man slept, his mind was suddenly awakened to the vision. The sun appeared in the night sky. He saw a speck of black that grew and took shape, until it was magically transformed into a vast herd of buffalo. The magnificent animals thundered above the clouds towards him. An eagle, gray with white-tipped wings, flew overhead, leading them on.

As the buffalo drew closer, some of their faces became those of the holy man's ancestors who had traveled to the Afterlife. He saw his father and his mother, his brothers, too. The herd parted then, and in the middle stood a proud mountain lion. The animal's coat was as white as lightning, the spirit Thunderbolt's work no doubt, and the Great Spirit had given the lion's eyes the color of the sky.

The herd of buffalo again enclosed the lion before the dream abruptly ended.

The holy man returned to his village the following morning. His sister prepared a meal for him. Once he'd taken his fill, he went to the leader of the Dakota, a mighty warrior named Gray Eagle. He told his leader only that he must continue to guide his people. The holy man kept the rest of his vision to himself, for the full meaning had yet to be revealed to him. And then he returned to his tipi to remember his vision with his dyes. On a soft deerskin hide he painted a circle of buffalo. In the center he drew the mountain lion, making certain the color of the animal's coat was just as white as he could recall, the color of the eyes just as blue as a sky in summer. When the rendering was completed he waited for the dye to dry, then carefully folded the skin and put it away.

The dream continued to haunt the shaman. He'd hoped to be given some comforting message for his leader. Gray Eagle was grieving. The shaman knew his friend wanted to pass leadership on to a younger, more fit warrior. Since his daughter and grandson had been taken from him, the leader's heart hadn't belonged to his people. He was filled with bitterness and anger.

The holy man could offer his friend little comfort. And no matter how he tried, he couldn't ease his anguish.

From anguish came the legend.

Gray Eagle's daughter Merry and her son were returning from the dead. The Dakota woman knew her family believed both she and White Eagle had been killed. Gray Cloud, bastard leader of the tribe's outcasts, had deliberately provoked the battle near the river's edge. He'd left bits of Merry's clothing on the riverbank, too, in hopes Merry's husband would believe his wife and son had been swept away with the others by the swift current.

The tribe would still be in mourning. Though it seemed an eternity to Merry, it had actually only been eleven months since the attack. She'd kept careful count on her reed stick. There were eleven notches now. Two more were needed to complete a full year by the Dakota reckoning.

It was going to be a difficult homecoming. The tribe would welcome White Eagle back into the family. Merry wasn't worried about her son. He was, after all, first grandson of their chief, Gray Eagle. Yes, there'd be much rejoicing with his return to the fold.

The fear, of course, was for Christina.

Merry instinctively tightened her hold on her new daughter. "Soon, Christina," she crooned softly to the baby. "We'll be home soon."

Christina didn't appear to be paying any attention to her mother's promise. The fidgety two-year-old was trying to wiggle out of her mother's lap and off the speckled mount, determined to walk beside her older brother. Merry's six-year-old son was leading the mare down the slope into the valley.

"Be patient, Christina," Merry whispered. She gave her daughter another gentle squeeze to emphasize her order.

"Eagle." The baby wailed her brother's name.

White Eagle turned when his sister cried out to him. He smiled up at her, then slowly shook his head. "Do as our mother orders," he instructed.

Christina ignored her brother's command. She immediately tried to hurl herself out of her mother's lap again. The little one was simply too young to understand caution. Though it was a considerable distance from the top of the horse to the hard ground, Christina didn't appear to be the least intimidated.

"My Eagle," Christina shouted.

"Your brother must lead us down into the village, Christina," Merry said. She kept her voice soft, hoping to calm the fretful child.

Christina suddenly turned and looked up at her mother. The little girl's blue eyes were filled with mischief. Merry couldn't contain her smile when she saw the disgruntled expression on her daughter's face. "My Eagle," the child bellowed.

Merry slowly nodded. "My Eagle," Christina shouted again, frowning up at her mother.

"Your Eagle," Merry acknowledged with a sigh. Oh, how she wished Christina would learn to imitate her soft voice. Thus far, that lesson had failed. Such a little one she was, yet gifted with a voice that could shake the leaves off their branches.

"My mama," Christina bellowed then, jabbing Merry's chest with her chubby fingers.

"Your mama," Merry answered. She kissed her daughter, then brushed her hand across the mop of white-blond curls framing the baby's face. "Your mama," Merry repeated, giving the child a fierce hug.

Comforted by the caress, Christina settled back against her mother's chest and reached for one of Merry's braids. When she'd captured the tip of one braid, she put her thumb in her mouth and closed her eyes, using her other hand to rub Merry's hair across the bridge of her freckled nose. In a matter of minutes, she was sound asleep.

Merry pulled the buffalo hide up over the baby so that her delicate skin would be shielded from the summer's midday sun. Christina was clearly exhausted from their long journey. And she'd been through so much distress in the past three months. It was a wonder to Merry that the child could sleep at all.

Christina had taken to trailing behind White Eagle. She mimicked his every action, though Merry noticed the baby always kept her in sight as well. One mother had left her, and Merry knew Christina was worried she and White Eagle would also disappear. The little girl had become extremely possessive, a trait Merry hoped would lessen in time.

"They watch us from the trees," White Eagle told his mother. The boy stopped, waiting for his mother's reaction.

Merry nodded. "Keep going, son. And remember, stop only when you've reached the tallest tipi."

White Eagle smiled. "I still remember where my grandfather's tipi is," he said. "We've only been away eleven months," he added, pointing to the reed stick.

"I'm pleased you remember," Merry said. "Do you also remember how much you love your father and your grandfather?"

The boy nodded. His expression turned solemn. "It will be difficult for my father, won't it?"

"He's an honorable man," Merry announced. "Yes, it will be difficult for him, but in time he'll see the rightness in it."

White Eagle straightened his shoulders, turned, and continued on down the hill.

He walked like a warrior. The boy's arrogant swagger was almost identical to his father's. Merry's heart ached with pride for her son. White Eagle would become chief of his people when his training was completed. It was his destiny to rule the warriors, just as it had now become her destiny to raise the white-skinned baby girl sleeping so innocently in her arms.

Merry tried to clear her mind of everything but the coming confrontation. She kept her gaze directed on her son's shoulders as he led the mare into the center of the village. Merry silently chanted the prayer her shaman had taught her to chase away her fears.

More than a hundred Dakota stared at Merry and White Eagle. No one said a word. White Eagle walked straight ahead and came to a halt when he'd reached the tipi of his chief.

The older women edged closer until they surrounded Merry's horse. Their faces mirrored their astonishment. Several women reached out to touch Merry's leg, as if the feel of her skin beneath their hands would confirm that what they saw was real.

They petted and sighed. Merry smiled over their show of affection. She glanced up and saw Sunflower, her husband's younger sister. Her good friend was openly weeping.

Thunder suddenly broke the silence. The ground trembled from the pounding of horses being ridden back down into the valley. The warriors had obviously been informed of Merry's return. Black Wolf, Merry's husband, would be leading them.

The flap of the chief's tipi opened just as the braves dismounted. Merry watched her father. Gray Eagle stood at the entrance and stared at her a long while. His leathered face showed his stunned reaction, but his eyes, so warm and kind, soon misted with emotion.

Everyone turned to watch their leader now. They waited for him to give the signal. It was Gray Eagle's duty to be the first to welcome Merry and her son back into his family.

Gray Eagle turned just as Merry's husband walked over to stand by his side. Merry immediately lowered her head in submission. Her hands started trembling, and she thought her heart was pounding loud enough to wake Christina. Merry knew her control would vanish if she looked at her husband now. She would certainly start to cry. That wouldn't be dignified, of course, for such a show of emotion would shame her proud husband.

It wouldn't be honorable either. Merry loved Black Wolf, but the circumstances had drastically changed since she'd last seen him. Her husband would have to make an important decision before he welcomed her back into his arms.

The chief suddenly raised his hands to the Great Spirit above. His palms faced the sun.

The signal was given. A resounding cheer echoed throughout the valley. Chaos erupted as Merry's son was embraced first by his grandfather and then by his father.

Christina stirred in Merry's arms. Though the buffalo skin concealed the baby, there were several startled gasps when the movement was noticed by some of the women.

Black Wolf held his son, but his gaze was directed at his wife. Merry dared a timid look up at him, caught his pleased smile, and tried to smile back.

Gray Eagle nodded several times, showing her his joy and his approval, then slowly made his way over to her side.

The holy man stood outside the purifying tipi, watching the reunion. He understood now why he hadn't seen Merry's face or White Eagle's in his vision. The rest of the dream's meaning continued to elude him. "I am a patient man," he whispered to the spirits. "I will accept one gift at a time."

While the shaman watched, a path was made for the chief. The braves ignored Merry and gathered around Black Wolf and his son. The women swelled forward again, for they wished to hear what their leader would say to his daughter.

Some of the more enthusiastic braves began to shriek with joy. The shrill noise jarred Christina awake.

The baby had little liking for her dark confinement. She pushed the buffalo hide away from her face just as Gray Eagle reached Merry's side.

Merry couldn't decide who looked more surprised. Christina seemed to be quite fascinated by the huge man watching her so intently. She was a bit uncertain, too, for she put her thumb back into her mouth and scooted up against her mother's chest.

Gray Eagle didn't even try to mask his astonishment. He stared at the child a long moment, then turned to look up at his daughter. "There is much for you to tell us, daughter," he announced.

Merry smiled. "There is much I would explain, Father."

Christina caught her mother's smile. She immediately pulled her thumb out of her mouth and looked around her with curiosity. When she found her brother in the crowd of strangers, she reached out with both hands for him. "Eagle," she shouted.

Gray Eagle took a step back, then turned to look at his grandson.

Christina fully expected her brother to come and fetch her. When he didn't immediately obey her order, she tried to squirm out of her mother's lap. "My Eagle, Mama," she bellowed.

Merry ignored her daughter now. She stared at her husband. Black Wolf's expression was hard, impassive. He stood with his legs braced apart and his arms folded across his chest. She knew he'd heard Christina call her mama. The baby spoke the Siouan language as well as any Dakota child and had shouted her claim loud enough for the entire village to hear.

Sunflower rushed over to help her friend dismount. Merry handed Christina to her, thought to caution her friend to keep a firm hold, but it was already too late. Christina easily slipped to the ground, landing on her padded backside. Before Sunflower or Merry could reach for her, the little one grabbed hold of Gray Eagle's legs, pulled herself up, and ran to her brother. The baby's laughter trailed behind her.

No one quite knew what to make of the beautiful white-skinned baby. A few older squaws reached out to touch Christina's golden curls, for their curiosity was too great to contain. The little girl allowed their pawing. She stood beside her brother, barely reaching his knees, mimicking his stance, and clung to his hand.

While Christina didn't mind being touched, she made it quite clear she didn't want anyone near her brother. When the chief tried to embrace his grandson again, Christina tried to push his hands away. "My Eagle," she shouted up at him.

Merry was horrified by her daughter's behavior. She grabbed Christina, managed a weak smile for her father, then whispered to her son, "Go with your father." Merry's husband had abruptly turned and disappeared inside Gray Eagle's tipi.

The moment she was separated from her brother, Christina started crying. Merry lifted the baby into her arms and tried without success to soothe her. Christina hid her face in the crook of her mother's neck and wailed her distress.

Merry's friends surrounded her. No one dared ask about the child until a full accounting had been given to her husband and her chief, but they smiled at the baby and patted her soft skin. Some even crooned the sleeping chant to the little one.

The shaman caught Merry's attention then. She immediately hurried over to stand in front of the holy man, then affected a rather awkward bow.

"Welcome home, my child," the holy man said in greeting.

Merry could barely hear the old man over the screams of her daughter. "I have missed you, Wakan," she said. Christina's wails became ear-piercing, and Merry gently shook her. "Hush, baby," she said. She turned back to the shaman and said, "My daughter roars like a lioness. Perhaps, in time, she will learn. . . ."

The incredulous look on the shaman's face stopped Merry's explanation. "You are ill, Wakan?" she asked, worry sounding in her voice.

The holy man shook his head. Merry noticed that his hands trembled when he reached out to touch Christina. "Her hair is the color of white lightning," he whispered.

Christina suddenly turned to stare at the shaman. She soon forgot her distress and actually smiled at the strange-looking man whose ceremonial feathers seemed to grow out of the top of his head.

Merry heard the shaman gasp. He did seem ill to her. "My new daughter is known by the name Christina, holy one," she said. "If we are allowed to stay, she will need a Dakota name, and your blessing, too."

"She is the lioness," the shaman announced. His face broke into a wide smile. "She will stay, Merry. Do not worry about your child. The buffalo will protect her. The spirits will counsel your father, and your husband as well. Be patient, child. Be patient."

Merry wished she could question the shaman further, but his order to wait couldn't be ignored. His reaction to Christina puzzled her. She wasn't given more time to worry about it, however, for Sunflower took hold of her hand and pulled her toward her home.

"You look exhausted, Merry, and must certainly be hungry. Come into my tipi and we will share our midday meal together."

Merry nodded. She followed her friend across the clearing. Once they were settled on the soft blankets inside Sunflower's home, Merry fed her daughter and then let her explore the tipi.

"I've been away such a long time," Merry whispered. "Yet when I returned, my husband didn't come to me."

"Black Wolf still loves you," Sunflower answered. "My brother has mourned you, Merry."

When Merry didn't comment, Sunflower continued, "It is as though you have returned to us from the dead. After the attack, when no one could find you or White Eagle, some believed you'd been swept away by the river. Black Wolf wouldn't believe that. No, he led the attack against the outcasts, thinking he would find you in their summer village. When he returned without you, he was filled with grief. Now you've come home to us, Merry, yet you bring another man's child with you."

Sunflower turned to look at Christina. "You know how much your husband hates the white man, Merry. I think that is the reason he didn't come to your side. Why have you taken this baby for your own? What happened to her mother?"

"Her mother is dead," Merry answered. "It's a long story, my friend, and you know I must first explain to my husband and my father. I will tell you this much," she added in a firm voice. "If the tribe decides against accepting Christina, then I must leave. She is now my daughter."

"But she has white skin," Sunflower protested, clearly appalled by Merry's fierce announcement.

"I've noticed the color of her skin," Merry answered with a smile.

Sunflower saw the humor in her friend's comment and laughed. The sound was immediately imitated by Christina. "She's such a beautiful child," Sunflower remarked.

"She'll have a pure heart, like her mother," Merry said.

Sunflower turned to reclaim a clay jar Christina had just overturned. Merry helped her scoop up the healing herbs the baby had sprinkled on the ground. "She's a very curious child," Merry commented, apologizing for her daughter.

Sunflower laughed again. The tipi looked as though a strong wind had just passed through. The baby echoed the sound again.

"It isn't possible to dislike such a joyful child," Sunflower remarked. The smile soon faded when she added, "But your husband, Merry. You know he'll never accept her."

Merry didn't argue with her friend. She prayed Sunflower was wrong, though. It was imperative that Black Wolf claim Christina as his daughter. The promise she'd given Christina's mother couldn't truly be fulfilled without her husband's help.

Sunflower couldn't resist the urge to take the baby into her arms. She reached out for Christina, but the little one scooted around her and sat down in Merry's lap.

"I would like to rest for just a few minutes, if you'll watch Christina for me. I warn you," Merry hastily added when

Sunflower nodded eagerly, "My daughter gets into constant mischief. She's too curious to be fearful."

Sunflower left the tipi to gain permission from her husband for Merry and Christina to stay with them. When she returned, she found Merry sound asleep. Christina was curled up against her mother's stomach. Merry's arm was draped over the baby. The little one was also sleeping. Her thumb was in her mouth, and one of Merry's braids rested on her face.

Merry and her daughter slept for several hours. The sun was just setting when Merry carried Christina down to the river to bathe. Sunflower trailed behind with fresh clothing in her arms.

The baby loved the water. The day had been hot and sticky, and the child seemed to delight in splashing in the cool water. She even allowed Merry to wash her hair without making too much fuss.

Merry had just emerged from the water with her daughter when Black Wolf suddenly appeared. He stood on the bank with his hands resting on his hips—a challenging stance, yet Merry could see the tender expression in his eyes.

He confused her, giving her this show of affection now. Merry turned away from her husband to dress herself and Christina.

Black Wolf waited until Merry had finished her task, then motioned for his sister to take the child away. Sunflower had to pry Christina's hands away from her mother. The little girl screamed in distress, but Merry didn't argue with the command. She knew Sunflower would look after her child.

As soon as they were alone, Merry turned to face her husband. Her voice trembled as she told him everything that had happened to her since being taken captive.

"At first I thought their leader, Gray Cloud, wanted to keep us so that he could barter with you. I knew your hatred for each other was fierce, but I didn't think he meant to kill us. We rode for several days—nights, too, when the moon was bright enough—and finally made camp above the brown valley of the white trails. Gray Cloud was the only one who touched us. He boasted to the others that he was going to kill your son and your wife. He blamed you, husband, for his dishonor."

Black Wolf nodded when Merry paused in her recitation, yet didn't offer any comment. Merry took a deep breath before continuing. "He beat our son until he thought he'd killed him. Then he turned on me."

Merry's voice broke. She turned to look at the river. "He used me the way a man uses an unwilling woman," she whispered.

She started to weep then, for her shame was suddenly overwhelming. The memories tore at her heart. Black Wolf reached out to take her into his arms. His touch immediately calmed her. Merry sagged against his chest. She wished she could turn around and cling to her husband, but she knew she needed to tell the rest of her story before she sought his solace.

"An argument broke out among them, for they'd seen the wagons below. Though Gray Cloud was against it, in the end it was agreed by the others that they would attack the whites and take their horses. Gray Cloud stayed behind. He was furious because they went against his decision."

Merry didn't have enough strength to continue. She wept softly. Black Wolf waited several minutes for his wife to go on with her story, then gently forced her to turn around to face him. Her eyes were tightly closed. He wiped the tears away from her cheeks. "Tell me the rest of this," he commanded, his voice as soft as a gentle wind.

Merry nodded. She tried to take a step back, but Black Wolf increased his hold. "Your son awakened and began to moan. He was in terrible pain, husband. Gray Cloud rushed over to our son. He pulled his knife and was about to kill White Eagle. I screamed and edged closer, as close as the rope binding my hands and legs would allow. I cursed Gray Cloud, trying to goad him into turning his anger on me. My plan distracted him. He used his fist to silence me, so fiercely I fell backwards. The blow made me sleep, and when I next opened my eyes I saw a white woman kneeling beside me.

She held White Eagle in her arms. Christina, her baby, was sleeping on the ground next to the woman. Black Wolf, I thought my mind was playing tricks on me until my son opened his eyes and looked at me. He was alive. It was the white woman who saved him, husband. Her knife was in Gray Cloud's back.

"I didn't know where she'd come from until I remembered the wagons trailing below the ridge. I trusted her, too, from the very beginning, because of the way she held our son. I begged her to take White Eagle away before Gray Cloud's followers returned from their raid. The woman wouldn't leave me, no matter how much I protested. She helped me onto her horse, lifted my son into my arms, then led us into the forest, carrying her own child in her arms. The woman didn't speak again until we stopped to rest many hours later."

"The gods favored us that day, for the renegades didn't chase after us. Jessica, the white woman, thought they might have been killed by the people they attacked. We found a cabin high in the hills and wintered there. Jessica took care of us. She spoke the missionary's English, yet all the words sounded very different to me. When I remarked upon this, Jessica explained that she had come from a distant land called England."

"What happened to this woman?" Black Wolf asked, frowning intently.

"When spring arrived, White Eagle was well enough to travel again. Jessica was going to take Christina back down into the valley, and I was going to bring your son home to you. The day before we planned to leave, Jessica went out to collect the traps she'd set the day before. She didn't return. I went searching for her. She was dead," Merry whispered. "A mountain bear had caught her unawares. It was a terrible death. Her body was mangled, barely recognizable. She shouldn't have died in such a way, Black Wolf."

"And this is why you have the white child with you?" Black Wolf asked, though he was already nodding over his own conclusions.

"Jessica and I became sisters in our hearts. She told me all about her past, and I shared my own with her. We made a promise to each other. She gave me her word that if anything happened to me, she'd find a way to bring White Eagle back to you. I also gave her a promise."

"You wish to take the child back to the whites?" Black Wolf asked.

"I must raise Christina first," Merry announced.

Black Wolf looked stunned by his wife's statement. Merry waited a moment before continuing. "Jessica didn't want Christina to go home to this place called England until she was fully grown. We must make Christina strong, husband, so that when she does return to her people, she'll be able to survive."

"I don't understand this promise," Black Wolf confessed, shaking his head.

"I learned all about Jessica's family. She was running away from her mate. She told me this evil man tried to kill her."

"All white men are evil," Black Wolf stated.

Merry nodded. She didn't agree with her husband, yet she wanted to placate him. "Every day Jessica would open a book she called her journal and write inside it. I promised to keep this book for Christina and give it to her when she's ready to go home."

"Why did this man try to kill his wife?"

"I don't know," Merry confessed. "Jessica believed she was a weak woman, though. She spoke of this flaw often, and she begged me to make Christina as strong as a warrior. I told her all about you, but she told me little about her mate. Jessica had the sight, husband. She knew all along she would never see her daughter raised."

"And if I'm against this plan?" Black Wolf asked.

"Then I must leave," Merry answered. "I know you hate the whites, yet it was a white woman who saved your son. My daughter will prove to be just as courageous in spirit."

"Her daughter," Black Wolf corrected, his voice harsh.

Merry shook her head. Black Wolf walked past her to

stand next to the river. He stared out into the night a long while, and when he finally turned back to Merry, his expression was hard. "We will honor this promise," he announced.

Before Merry could show her gratitude, Black Wolf raised his hand. "Sunflower has been wife for three summers now and still hasn't given her husband a child. She will take care of this white-skinned baby. If my sister isn't willing, another will be found."

"No, we must raise her," Merry insisted. "She's my daughter now. And you must also take a hand in this, Black Wolf. I promised to make Christina as strong as a warrior. Without your guidance—"

"I want you back, Merry," Black Wolf said. "But I won't allow this child into my home. No, you ask too much of me."

"So be it," Merry whispered. Her shoulders sagged with defeat.

Black Wolf had lived with Merry long enough to recognize that her stubborn determination was now asserting itself. "What difference will it make if she is raised by you or by another?"

"Jessica died believing you and I would raise her daughter. The child must be taught the skills needed to survive in the white man's world. I bragged to Jessica about your strength, husband, and I—"

"Then we'll never send her back," Black Wolf interjected.

Merry shook her head. "I would never ask you to break your word. How can you ask me to dishonor my pledge now?"

Black Wolf looked furious. Merry started to cry again. "How can you still want me for your wife? I have been used by your enemy. I would have killed myself if I hadn't had White Eagle with me. And now I'm responsible for another child. I can't let anyone else raise her. In your heart, you know I'm right. I think it would be better if I took Christina away. We'll leave tomorrow."

"No." Black Wolf shouted the denial. "I have never

stopped loving you, Merry," he told her. "You will return to me this night."

"And Christina?" Merry asked.

"You'll raise her," he conceded. "You may even call her daughter, but she belongs only to you. I have only one child. White Eagle. I will allow Christina into my tipi because her mother saved my son's life. But this child will have no meaning in my heart, Merry. I will ignore her completely."

Merry didn't know what to make of her husband's decision. She did return to him that night, however, and carried her daughter with her.

Black Wolf was a stubborn man. He proved to be as good as his word, too. He did set out to ignore Christina thoroughly.

It was, however, a task that grew more challenging with each passing day.

Christina always fell asleep next to her brother. Yet each morning, when Black Wolf opened his eyes, he found the baby girl snuggled up between him and his wife. She was always awake before he was, and always staring up at him.

The child simply didn't understand he was ignoring her. Black Wolf would frown when he found her watching him so trustingly. Christina would immediately imitate his expression. If she'd been older, he would have thought she dared to mock him. But she was only a baby. And if she hadn't been white-skinned, he knew he'd find amusement in the way she trailed after his son. Why, he might even have been pleased by the baby's arrogant swagger.

Then Black Wolf would remember Christina didn't exist inside his mind. He'd turn his back on the child and leave his tipi, his mood as black as rain clouds.

The days blended into full weeks as the tribe waited for their chief to call Merry before the council. But Gray Eagle watched his son-in-law, waiting to see if he could accept Christina.

When Black Wolf separated his son from Christina, Merry knew something had to be settled. The baby didn't understand what was happening, of course, and spent most of her waking hours crying. She became extremely fretful and finally quit eating altogether.

Desperate, Merry went to her father and put the problem in his lap. She explained that until he, as chief, openly acknowledged Christina, the women and children would continue to follow Black Wolf's lead and ignore the child.

Gray Eagle saw the wisdom in this argument. He promised to call the council that evening. He then went to the shaman to seek his advice.

The holy man seemed to be just as concerned about Christina's welfare as Merry was. The chief was surprised by this attitude, for the shaman was known to be as hostile towards the whites as Black Wolf was.

"Yes, it is time to call the warriors together. Black Wolf must change his heart towards this child. It would be best if he made the decision alone," he added, "but if he refuses to bend in his attitude, I will tell the council the fullness of my vision."

The shaman shook his head when he saw his leader was about to question him. He walked over to a folded animal skin and handed it to Gray Eagle.

"Do not untie this rope, do not look upon this drawing until the time is right."

"What is this drawing, Wakan?" Gray Eagle asked. His voice had turned to a whisper.

"The vision I was given by the Great Spirit."

"Why have I not seen this before?"

"Because I didn't understand the meaning of all that was revealed to me. I told you only that I'd seen the eagle flying above the herd of buffalo. Do you remember?"

Gray Eagle nodded. "I remember," he said.

"What I didn't tell you is that some of the buffalo were changed into the faces of those who had gone to the Afterlife. Merry and White Eagle weren't among the dead, Gray Eagle. I didn't understand at the time, and didn't want to counsel you until I could solve the riddle in my mind."

"Now we both understand," Gray Eagle announced. "They were not dead."

"But there is more to the vision, my friend. At first I thought the sight of the buffalo meant that hunting would be plentiful. Yes, that is what I thought."

"And now, Wakan?"

The holy man shook his head again. "Do not open the skin until Black Wolf has again stated his position. If he refuses to claim the child, the drawing will sway him. We cannot allow him to go against the spirits."

"And if he decides to call the child his? Will the drawing remain a mystery?"

"No, one and all must see the drawing, but not until Black Wolf has chosen the right path. The recounting will then reaffirm his wisdom."

Gray Eagle nodded. "You must sit beside me this evening, my friend," he announced.

The two men embraced each other. Gray Eagle then returned to his tipi with the animal skin. His curiosity was great, but he forced himself to be patient. There was much to be done before this evening's council. The preparations would take his mind off the skin and what the drawing would reveal.

Merry paced the confines of her tipi until all the warriors had gathered into a circle around their leader's fire. Christina had fallen into a fitful sleep on the pallet she no longer shared with her brother.

When one of the younger braves came to take Merry to the meeting, she left Christina alone, certain the baby was too exhausted to wake before morning.

The men were seated on the ground, with their leader at one end of the long oval. The shaman sat on Gray Eagle's left side, Black Wolf on his right.

Merry slowly walked around the circle, then knelt down in front of her father. She quickly recounted all that had happened to her during the past year, putting great emphasis on the fact that Jessica had saved White Eagle's life.

Gray Eagle showed no outward reaction to this tale. When his daughter finished her recitation, he gave her the formal signal to leave.

Merry was on her way back to Christina when Sunflower intercepted her. The two women stood in the shadows of the clearing, waiting to hear what their leader would decide.

Merry's son was next called to give his version of what had happened. When the boy finished, he went to stand directly behind his father.

All of a sudden, Christina appeared at her brother's side. Merry saw her daughter take hold of White Eagle's hand. She started to go after the child, but Sunflower restrained her. "Wait and see what happens," Sunflower advised. "The warriors will be angry if you interrupt them now. Your son will look after Christina."

Merry saw the wisdom in her friend's advice. She kept her gaze on her son, hoping he'd look her way so that she could motion for him to take Christina back to their tipi.

White Eagle was listening to the fierce argument being given by the majority of the warriors. They all wished to show their loyalty to Black Wolf by supporting his decision to ignore the child.

The chief nodded, then deliberately suggested that an old woman called Laughing Brook take on the duty of raising the child. Black Wolf immediately shook his head, denying the idea.

"Merry's child would suffer at her hand," Black Wolf announced to the warriors. "I could not let this happen. The child is innocent."

Gray Eagle hid his smile. Black Wolf was opposed to giving the child to the crazed old squaw, proving he did in fact care.

The problem would be to make Black Wolf realize the full truth—a difficult challenge, the chief realized, for his son-in-law was a proud, stubborn man.

The chief reached for the animal skin, thinking to put an end to the dispute now, but the shaman stayed the action with a shake of his head.

Gray Eagle let the holy man have his way. He rested his hands on the folded skin and continued to mull over the problem while the warriors argued with one another.

And in the end, it was Christina, with her brother's gentle prodding, who solved the problem for everyone.

Black Wolf's son listened to the harsh debate over Christina's future. Though the boy was only six summers, he'd already shown streaks of his father's arrogant nature. Uncaring what the retributions would be, he suddenly pulled Christina along with him as he edged around to face his father.

Christina hid behind her brother now, though she peeked out at the angry-looking man staring at her brother so ferociously.

The chief was the only one who saw the baby mimick Black Wolf's scowl before she pressed her face against White Eagle's knees.

"Father," White Eagle announced, "a white woman saved my life so that I could return to my people."

The boy's fervent words gained an immediate silence. "Christina is now my sister. I would protect her as well as any brother would protect his sister."

Black Wolf couldn't contain his surprise over the arrogant way his son dared to speak to him. Before he could form a reply, White Eagle turned to where his mother stood. He pointed to her, looked down at Christina, and said, "My mother."

He knew full well what was going to happen. Christina had proved to be quite consistent in her possessiveness. What belonged to White Eagle belonged to her as well. White Eagle only had to repeat the words once before the little girl scooted out to her brother's side. She pulled her thumb out of her mouth long enough to shout, "My mama." Then she smiled up at her brother, waiting for him to continue this new game.

White Eagle nodded. He squeezed her hand to let her know he was pleased with her answer, then turned until he was staring at his father again. He slowly raised his hand

and pointed at Black Wolf. "My father," he announced in a firm voice.

Christina sucked on her thumb while she stared at Black Wolf.

"My papa," White Eagle stated, giving Christina's hand another squeeze.

Christina suddenly pulled her thumb out of her mouth. "My papa," she bellowed, pointing her finger at Black Wolf. She then looked up at her brother to gain his approval.

White Eagle glanced over to look at his grandfather. When the leader nodded, Christina's brother nodded to her.

It was all the approval the little girl needed. She let go of White Eagle's hand, turned, and scooted backwards. Without showing the least bit of fear, she fell into Black Wolf's lap.

Everyone watched the baby settle herself. Black Wolf visibly stiffened when Christina reached up and caught hold of one of his braids. He didn't push her hand away, though, but turned to look at his chief.

Gray Eagle was smiling with satisfaction.

Merry rushed over to kneel down in front of her husband, keeping her head bowed. Black Wolf could see how his wife trembled. He let out a long, controlled sigh of acceptance.

"My children have no place at this council. Take them to our tipi."

Merry immediately reached out to take Christina into her arms. She was prying her daughter's hand away from her husband's braid when the full impact of what he'd just said settled in her mind.

His children.

Merry really did try not to smile, but when she glanced up at her husband, she knew he could see her joy. And certainly her love.

Black Wolf acknowledged both with an arrogant nod.

Gray Eagle waited until Merry had taken the children away. "Do I now have a granddaughter?" he asked Black Wolf, demanding confirmation.

"You do," Black Wolf answered.

"I am pleased," Gray Eagle announced. He turned to the shaman then and asked him to tell the council about his vision.

The holy man stood and recounted his dream to the warriors. He slowly unwound the rope binding the deerskin and held it up for all to see.

There were many startled murmurs. The shaman silenced the group with a dramatic sweep of his hand. "We are the buffalo," he said, pressing his hand to his chest. "The lion does not belong with the buffalo. On this earth, they are enemies, just as the white man is enemy of the Dakota. Yet the gods test us now. They've given us a blue-eyed lioness. We must protect her until the time comes for her to leave us."

Black Wolf was clearly astonished by the shaman's words. He shook his head. "Why didn't you tell me this sooner, Wakan?" he asked.

"Because your heart needed to learn the truth first," the holy man answered. "Your daughter is the lioness, Black Wolf. There can be no mistake. Her hair is the color of white lightning, and her eyes are as blue as the Great Spirit's home in the sky."

Christina's bellow of anger suddenly echoed throughout the village. The shaman paused to smile. "She has the voice of a lioness, too," he remarked.

Black Wolf smiled with the others and nodded.

The holy man raised the skin into the air. "Merry's promise will be fulfilled. The spirits have decreed it."

Christina was formally accepted into the tribe the following evening.

They were a gentle people, the Dakota. Everyone opened their hearts to the blue-eyed lioness and gave her treasures beyond value.

They were intangible gifts that molded her character.

From her grandfather, Christina was given the gift of awareness. The old warrior showed her the beauty, the wonder of her magnificent surroundings. The two became inseparable. Gray Eagle gave Christina his love without restraint, his time without limitation, and his wisdom when she demanded immediate answers to continual little-girl questions of why and why and why. Christina gained patience from her grandfather, but the greatest treasure ofall was the ability to laugh at what couldn't be changed, to weep over what had been lost, and to find joy in the precious gift of life.

From her father, Christina was given courage, and determination to finish any task, to conquer any difficulty. She learned to wield a knife and ride a horse as well as any brave—better, in fact, than most. She was Black Wolf's daughter and learned by observation to strive for perfection in every undertaking. Christina lived to please her father, to receive his nod of approval, to make him proud of her.

From her gentle mother, Christina was given the gift of compassion, understanding, and a sense of justice towards friends and enemies alike. She mimicked her mother's ways until they became a true part of her personality. Merry was openly affectionate with her children and her husband. Though Black Wolf never showed his own feelings in front of others, Christina quickly learned that he'd chosen Merry because of her loving nature. His gruffness with his wife in front of the other warriors was all part of his arrogant manner. Yet in the privacy of their tipi, Black Wolf more than allowed Merry's petting and soft words. He demanded them. His gaze would take on a warm expression, and when he thought his daughter was sound asleep, he'd reach for his wife and give her back all the gentle words of love she'd taught him.

Christina vowed to find a man like Black Wolf when the time came for her to choose a mate. He would be a warrior as proud and arrogant as her father, as demanding and protective of what belonged to him, and with the same fierce capacity to love.

She told her brother she'd never settle for less.

White Eagle was her confidant. He didn't wish to break his sister's innocent determination, but he worried for her. He argued in favor of caution, for he knew, as well as everyone else in their isolated village, that Christina would one day return to the world of the whites.

And in his heart, the truth tormented him. He knew, with a certainty he couldn't deny, that there were no warriors like his father in this place called England.

None at all.

Chapter One

London, England, 1810

Lettie's screams were getting weaker.

Baron Winters, the physician in attendance to the Marchioness of Lyonwood, leaned over his patient and frantically tried to grab hold of her hands. The beautiful woman was writhing in agony. She was clearly out of her head now and seemed determined to tear the skin off her distended abdomen.

"There, there, Lettie," the physician whispered in what he hoped was a soothing tone. "It's going to be all right, my dear. Just a bit longer and you'll have a fine babe to give your husband."

The baron wasn't at all certain Lettie even understood what he was saying to her. Her emerald-green eyes were glazed with pain. She seemed to be staring right through him. "I helped bring your husband into this world. Did you know that, Lettie?"

Another piercing scream interrupted his attempt to calm his patient. Winters closed his eyes and prayed for guidance. His forehead was beaded with perspiration, and his hands were actually shaking. In all his years, he'd never seen such a difficult laboring. It had gone on much too long already. The Marchioness was growing too weak to help.

The door to the bedroom slammed open then, drawing the baron's attention. Alexander Michael Phillips, the Marquess of Lyonwood, filled the doorway. Winters sighed with relief. "Thank God you're home," he called out. "We were worried you wouldn't return in time."

Lyon rushed over to the bed. His face showed his concern. "For God's sake, Winters, it's too early for this to happen yet."

"The baby has decided otherwise," Winters replied.

"Can't you see she's in terrible pain?" he shouted. "Do something!"

"I'm doing everything I can," Winters yelled back before he could control his anger. Another spasm caught Lettie, and her scream turned Winter's attention back to her. The physician's shoulders heaved forward with his effort of restraining her. The Marchioness wasn't a small woman by any means. She was extremely tall and well rounded. She fought the physician's hold on her shoulders with a vengeance.

"She's out of her mind, Lyon. Help me tie her hands to the posts," Winters ordered.

"No," Lyon shouted, clearly appalled by such a command. "I'll hold her still. Just be done with it, Winters. She can't take much more. God, how long has she been this way?"

"Over twelve hours now," Winters confessed. "The midwife sent for me a few hours ago. She ran off in a panic when she realized the baby isn't in the proper position for birthing," he added in a whisper. "We're going to have to wait it out and pray the baby turns for us."

Lyon nodded as he took hold of his wife's hands. "I'm home now, Lettie. Just a little longer, my love. It will be over soon."

Lettie turned toward the familiar voice. Her eyes were dull, lifeless. Lyon continued to whisper encouragement to his wife. When she closed her eyes and he believed she was asleep, he spoke to Winters again. "Is it because the baby is almost two months early that Lettie is having so much difficulty?"

The physician didn't answer him. He turned his back on the Marquess to lift another cloth from the water basin. His motions were controlled, angry, but his touch was gentle when he finally placed the cool cloth on his patient's brow. "God help us if she gets the fever," he muttered to himself.

Lettie's eyes suddenly opened. She stared up at Baron Winters. "James? Is that you, James? Help me, please help me. Your baby is tearing me apart. It's God's punishment for our sins, isn't it, James? Kill the bastard if you have to, but rid me of it. Lyon will never know. Please, James, please."

The damning confession ended with a hysterical whimper.

"She doesn't know what she's saying," Winters blurted once he'd recovered his composure. He wiped the blood away from Lettie's lips before adding, "Your wife is delirious, Lyon. The pain rules her mind. Pay no heed to her rantings."

Baron Winters glanced over to look at the Marquess. When he saw the expression on Lyon's face, he knew his speech hadn't swayed the man. The truth had won out after all.

Winters cleared his throat and said, "Lyon, quit this room. I've work to do here. Go and wait in your study. I'll come for you when it's over."

The Marquess continued to stare at his wife. When he finally lifted his gaze and nodded to the physician, his eyes showed his torment. He shook his head then, a silent denial, perhaps, of what he'd just heard, and abruptly left the room.

His wife's screams for her lover followed him out the door.

It was finished three hours later. Winters found Lyon in the library. "I did everything I could, Lyon. God help me, I lost both of them."

The baron waited several minutes before speaking again. "Did you hear what I said, Lyon?"

"Was the baby two months early?" Lyon asked.

Winters didn't immediately answer. He was slow to recover from the flat, emotionless tone in Lyon's voice. "No, the baby wasn't early," he finally said. "You've been lied to enough, son. I'll not add to their sins."

The baron collapsed in the nearest chair. He watched Lyon calmly pour him a drink, then reached forward to accept the glass. "You've been like a son to me, Lyon. If there is anything I can do to help you through this tragedy, only tell me and I'll do it."

"You've given me the truth, old friend," Lyon answered. "That is enough."

Winters watched Lyon lift his goblet and down the contents in one long swallow.

"Take care of yourself, Lyon. I know how much you loved Lettie."

Lyon shook his head. "I'll recover," he said. "I always do, don't I, Winters?"

"Yes," Winters answered with a weary sigh. "The lessons of brotherhood have no doubt prepared you for any eventuality."

"There is one task I would give you," Lyon said. He reached for the inkwell and pen.

Long minutes passed while Lyon wrote on a sheet of paper. "I'll do anything," Winters said when he couldn't stand the silence any longer.

Lyon finished his note, folded the sheet, and handed it to the physician.

"Take the news to James, Winters. Tell my brother his mistress is dead."

Chapter Two

Your father was such a handsome man, Christina. He could have chosen any woman in England. Yet he wanted me. Me! I couldn't believe my good fortune. I was only pretty enough to be passable by the ton's measure, terribly shy and naive, the complete opposite of your father. He was so sophisticated, so very polished, kind and loving, too. Everyone thought he was the most wonderful man.

But it was all a terrible lie.

Journal entry
August 1, 1795

London, England, 1814

It was going to be a long night.

The Marquess of Lyonwood let out a controlled sigh and leaned against the mantel of Lord Carlson's receiving room. It wasn't a casual stance but one employed for necessity's sake. By shifting his considerable weight, Lyon was able to ease the throbbing in his leg. The injury was still a constant irritant, and the sharp pain radiating up through his kneecap did absolutely nothing to lighten his somber mood.

Lyon was attending the party under duress, having been successfully nagged into doing his duty by escorting his younger sister, Diana, to the event. Needless to say, he wasn't at all happy about his circumstances. He thought he should try to affect a pleasant expression on his face, yet couldn't quite manage that feat. Lyon was simply in too much pain to care if others noticed his sour disposition or not. He settled on a scowl instead, his usual expression these days, then folded his arms across his massive chest in a gesture of true resignation.

The Earl of Rhone, Lyon's good friend since Oxford pranks, stood beside him. Both were considered handsome men. Rhone was dark-haired, fair-skinned, and stood six feet in height. He was built on the lean side, always impeccable in dress and taste, and gifted with a lopsided smile that made the young ladies forget all about his crooked nose. They were simply too mesmerized by his enviable green eyes to notice.

Rhone was definitely a lady's man. Mothers fretted over his reputation, fathers worried about his intentions, while unseasoned daughters ignored their parents' cautions altogether, competing quite brazenly for his attention. Rhone drew women to his side in much the same way honey drew a hungry bear. He was a rascal, true, yet too irresistible to deny.

Lyon, on the other hand, had the dubious distinction of being able to send these same sweetly determined ladies screaming for cover. It was an undisputed fact that the Marquess of Lyonwood could clear a room with just one glacial stare.

Lyon was taller than Rhone by a good three inches. Because he was so muscular in chest, shoulders, and thighs, he gave the appearance of being even larger. His size alone wasn't enough to thoroughly intimidate the stronger-hearted ladies hoping to snatch a title, however. Neither were his features, if you could take them just one at a time. Lyon's hair was a dark golden color, given to curl. The length was left unfashionably longer than society liked. His profile mimicked the statues of Roman soldiers lining

Carlton House. His cheekbones were just as patrician, his nose just as classical, and his mouth just as perfectly sculptured.

The warm color of his hair was Lyon's only soft feature, however. His brown eyes mirrored cold cynicism. Disillusionment had molded his expression into a firm scowl. The scar didn't help matters much, either. A thin, jagged line slashed across his forehead, ending abruptly in the arch of his right eyebrow. The mark gave Lyon a piratical expression.

And so the gossip makers called Rhone a rake and Lyon a pirate, but never, of course, to either gentleman's face. These foolish women didn't realize how their insults would have pleased both men.

A servant approached the Marquess and said, "My lord? Here is the brandy you requested." The elderly man made the announcement with a formal bow as he balanced two large goblets on a silver tray.

Lyon grabbed both glasses, handed one to Rhone, and then surprised the servant by offering his gratitude. The servant bowed again before turning and leaving the gentlemen alone.

Lyon emptied his glass in one long swallow.

Rhone caught the action. "Is your leg bothering you?" he asked, frowning with concern. "Or is it your intention to get sotted?"

"I never get sotted," Lyon remarked. "The leg is healing," he added with a shrug, giving his friend a roundabout answer.

"You came away lucky this time, Lyon," Rhone said. "You're going to be out of commission for a good six months, maybe more. Thank God for that," he added. "Richards would have you back in jeopardy tomorrow if he could have his way. I do believe it was a blessing your ship was destroyed. You can't very well go anywhere until you build another."

"I knew the risks," Lyon answered. "You don't like Richards, do you, Rhone?"

"He never should have sent you on that last little errand, my friend."

"Richards places government business above personal concerns."

"Above *our* personal concerns, you mean to say," Rhone corrected. "You really should have gotten out when I did. If you weren't so vital to—"

"I've quit, Rhone."

His friend couldn't contain his astonishment. Lyon knew he should have waited to give him the news, for there was a real concern Rhone would let out a shout. "Don't look so stunned, Rhone. You've been after me to retire for a good while now."

Rhone shook his head. "I've been after you because I'm your friend and very likely the only one who cares what happens to you," he said. "Your special talents have kept you doing your duty longer than a normal man could stand. God's truth, I wouldn't have had the stomach for it. Do you really mean it? You've actually retired? Have you told Richards?"

Rhone was speaking in a furious whisper. He watched Lyon intently.

"Yes, Richards knows. He isn't too pleased."

"He'll have to get used to it," Rhone muttered. He raised his glass in salutation. "A toast, my friend, to a long life. May you find happiness and peace. You deserve a bit of both, Lyon."

Since Lyon's glass was empty, he didn't share in the toast. He doubted Rhone's fervent wish would come true anyway. Happiness—in sporadic doses, of course—was a true possibility. But peace . . . no, the past would never allow Lyon to find peace. Why, it was as impossible a goal as love. Lyon accepted his lot in life. He had done what he believed was necessary, and part of his mind harbored no guilt. It was only in the dark hours of the night, when he was alone and vulnerable, that the faces from the past came back to haunt him. No, he'd never find peace. The nightmares wouldn't let him.

"You're doing it again," Rhone announced, nudging Lyon's arm to gain his attention.

"Doing what?"

"Frowning all the ladies out of the room."

"It's good to know I've still got the ability," Lyon drawled.

Rhone shook his head. "Well, are you going to frown all night?"

"Probably."

"Your lack of enthusiasm is appalling. I'm in a wonderful mood. The new season always stirs my blood. Your sister must also be eager for all the adventures," he added. "Lord, it's difficult to believe the little brat has finally grown up."

"Diana is excited," Lyon admitted. "She's old enough to start looking for a husband."

"Is she still . . . spontaneous? It's been over a year now since I last saw her."

Lyon smiled over Rhone's inept description of his sister's conduct. "If you mean to ask me if she still charges into situations without showing the least amount of restraint, then yes, she's still spontaneous."

Rhone nodded. He looked around the room, then let out a sigh. "Just think of it. A fresh crop of beautiful ladies waiting to be sampled. In truth, I thought their mamas would have made them stay home, what with Jack and his band of robbers still on the prowl."

"I heard the thieves visited Wellingham last week," Lyon commented.

"Caused quite a stir," Rhone interjected with a true grin. "Lady Wellingham took to her bed after making the vow she wasn't going to get up until her emeralds were recovered. An odd reaction, to my way of thinking, when you consider how much thieving her husband does at the gambling tables. The man's a flagrant cheat."

"I understand Jack only robbed the Wellinghams. Is it true he left the guests alone?"

Rhone nodded. "Yes. The man obviously was in a hurry."

"Seems to me he's aching to get caught," Lyon said.

"I don't agree," Rhone answered. "Thus far, he's only

stolen from those who I think needed a good set down. I actually admire the man."

When Lyon gave him a puzzling look, Rhone hastened to change the topic. "The ladies would approach us if you'd smile. Then you might begin to enjoy yourself."

"I think you've finally lost your mind. How can you pretend to enjoy this farce?"

"There are those who think you've lost *your* mind, Lyon. It's a fact you've been secluded from the ton too long."

"And it's a fact you've endured one too many seasons," Lyon answered. "Your mind has turned to mush."

"Nonsense. My mind turned to mush years ago when we drank sour gin in school together. I really do enjoy myself, though. You would, too, if you'd only remember this is all just a game."

"I don't play games," Lyon said. "And war is a better description for this scene."

Rhone laughed, loud enough to draw curious stares. "Tell me this, friend. Are we pitted against the ladies, then?"

"We are."

"And what is their quest? What do they hope to gain if they conquer us?"

"Marriage, of course."

"Ah," Rhone replied, dragging out the sound. "I suppose they use their bodies as their weapons. Is it their battle plan to make us so glazed with lust we'll offer anything?"

"It's all they have to offer," Lyon answered.

"Good Lord, you are as jaded as everyone says. I worry that your attitude will rub off on me."

Rhone shuddered as he spoke, but the effect was ruined by his grin.

"You don't appear to be too concerned," Lyon remarked dryly.

"These ladies are only after marriage, not our lives," Rhone said. "You don't have to play the game if you don't want to. Besides, I'm only an insignificant earl. You, on the other hand, must certainly marry again if the line is to continue forward."

"You know damn well I'm never going to marry again,"

Lyon answered. His voice had turned as hard as the marble he was leaning against. "Drop this subject, Rhone. I've no sense of humor when it comes to the issue of marriage."

"You've no sense of humor at all," Rhone pronounced in such a cheerful tone of voice Lyon couldn't help but grin.

Rhone was about to continue his list of Lyon's other faults when a rather attractive redheaded lady happened to catch his concentration. He gave her his full attention until he spotted Lyon's little sister making her way over to them.

"Better get rid of your frown," Rhone advised. "Diana's coming over. Lord, she just elbowed the Countess Seringham."

Lyon sighed, then forced a smile.

When Diana came to an abrupt stop in front of her brother, her short-cropped brown curls continued to float around her cherublike face. Her brown eyes sparkled with excitement. "Oh, Lyon, I'm so happy to see you smiling. Why, I do believe you're enjoying yourself."

She didn't wait for her brother to reply to her observation but turned to curtsy in front of Rhone. "It's so good to see you again," she said, sounding quite breathless.

Rhone inclined his head in greeting.

"Isn't it remarkable I was able to plead Lyon into coming this evening? He really doesn't like parties very much, Rhone."

"He doesn't?" Rhone asked, sounding so disbelieving Lyon actually laughed.

"Don't jest with her," Lyon said. "Are you enjoying yourself, Diana?" he asked his sister.

"Oh, yes," Diana answered. "Mama will be pleased. I do hope she's still awake when we get home so I can tell her all about tonight. I've just learned Princess Christina will be making an appearance, too. I confess I'm most curious to meet her. Why, I've heard the most wonderful stories about her."

"Who is Princess Christina?" Lyon asked.

It was Rhone who hastened to answer his question. "You've been secluded too long, Lyon, or you surely would have heard of her. Though I haven't actually met the lady,

I've been told she's very beautiful. There's an air of mystery surrounding her, too. Her father was ruler of some little principality near Austria's border. He was unseated during a rather nasty revolution," Rhone continued. "Lady Christina, if we use the title she gained from her mother, has traveled all over the world. Brummel met her and was immediately infatuated. He was the first to call her Princess. The woman neither accepted nor rejected that title."

"What happened to her mother?" Diana asked.

She looked quite spellbound by the story about the princess. Rhone smiled at her eagerness. "A tragedy, I'm told. The mother was weakheaded, and she—"

"What do you mean by weakheaded?" Diana interrupted to ask.

"Insane," Rhone explained. "When the mother learned she was going to have a child, she ran off. Until three months ago, everyone believed both mother and babe were dead."

"What happened to Princess Christina's father?" Diana asked.

"He left England shortly after his wife disappeared. No one has heard of him since. Probably dead by now," Rhone ended with a shrug.

"Oh, the poor Princess," Diana whispered. "Does she have anyone to call family now, or is she all alone?"

"For God's sake, Diana, you don't even know the woman and you look ready to weep for her," Lyon said.

"Well, it is such a sad story," Diana said, defending herself. She turned back to Rhone and added, "I remember how unbearable it was for all of us when James died. Mother still hasn't recovered. She stays hidden in her room pretending all sorts of ills, when it's truly grief that keeps her there."

Rhone took one look at Lyon's cold expression and immediately hastened to turn the topic around. "Yes, well, we all miss James," he lied, his tone brisk. "I'm anxious to meet Princess Christina, too, Diana. No one has been able to glean a scrap of information about her past. That does make for a mystery to be solved, now doesn't it?"

When Rhone gave Diana a wink, she blushed. Lyon's sister was still such an innocent. She was fetching enough, too, now that Rhone paused to really take a good look at her. Diana had filled out nicely since he'd last seen her. That realization actually irritated Rhone, though for the life of him he couldn't understand why. "Brat," he suddenly blurted out, "you do look pretty tonight." Rhone grimaced over the roughness he'd heard in his own voice.

Diana didn't seem to notice. She smiled over his compliment, affected another curtsy, and said, "Thank you, Rhone. It is kind of you to notice."

Rhone frowned at Lyon. "Her gown is cut entirely too low. What could you have been thinking of to allow her in public this way? You'd better keep a close eye on her."

"If I keep my eye on you, Diana will be safe enough," Lyon answered.

"All the same, I really think . . ." The sentence trailed off, for Rhone had just glanced toward the entrance of the salon. He let out a low whistle. Diana quickly turned around to see what held Rhone so enthralled.

"Princess Christina." Diana whispered the obvious, her voice filled with awe.

Lyon was the last to react. When he saw the vision standing across the room, he literally jerked away from the mantel. His body instinctively assumed a battle stance, his muscles tensed, ready.

He was slow to regain control. He realized his hands were actually fisted at his sides and his legs were braced apart for a fight, and he forced himself to relax. The abrupt movement made his knee start throbbing again. Lyon couldn't do anything about the pain now, or the furious pounding in his chest.

And no matter how valiantly he tried, he couldn't seem to take his gaze away from the Princess.

She really was lovely. She was dressed in silver from head to toe. The color belonged to an angel and highlighted the paler threads of her blond hair.

Without a doubt, she was the most beautiful woman he'd ever seen. Her skin appeared to be flawless, and even from the distance separating them Lyon could see the color of her eyes. They were the most startling shade of blue.

Princess Christina neither smiled nor frowned. Her expression showed only mild curiosity. The woman obviously understood her own appeal, Lyon concluded, hoping his cynical nature would save him from heart failure. He wasn't at all pleased about the way his body continued to respond to her.

"Brummel was right," Rhone announced. "The lady is enchanting."

"Oh, I do hope I'll be able to meet her," Diana said. She whispered as though they were in church. "Just look at everyone, Rhone. They are all taken with her. Do you think the Princess will be agreeable to an introduction?"

"Hush, Diana," Rhone said. "Princess Christina wouldn't dare ignore you. You seem to forget just who your brother is."

Diana gave Rhone a timid nod. "Sweetling, straighten your shoulders and quit wringing your hands. You'll give yourself spots. We'll find someone to give us a proper introduction."

Rhone knew Lyon's little sister hadn't heard the last of his remarks. She'd already picked up her skirts and headed for the entrance. "Now what do we do?" he asked when Lyon grabbed hold of his arm to stop him from chasing after Diana.

"We wait and see," Lyon advised. His voice sounded with irritation.

"Your sister is too impetuous," Rhone muttered, shaking his head. "She's ignoring all her lessons in—"

"It's high time Diana learned the lesson of discretion."

"Let us hope it isn't too painful for her."

Lyon didn't remark on that hope. He continued to give his attention to the beautiful Princess. An elderly couple approached the woman just as Diana came barreling to a halt a bare inch or so in front of them.

Diana almost knocked Christina to her knees. Rhone let out a long groan. The elderly couple didn't even try to hide their displeasure when they were so rudely cut off. Both turned away, staring at each other in obvious embarrassment.

"Oh, God, Diana just cut in front of the Duke and Duchess," Rhone said.

Lyon was infuriated with his sister. He was about to go after her to save her from further humiliation when the Princess took matters into her own hands. Rather nicely, too. She greeted Lyon's sister with what appeared to be a sincere smile, then took hold of Diana's hands when she spoke to her. Lyon thought the Princess was deliberately giving the impression to all those watching that she and Diana were close friends.

He watched the way Christina motioned Diana over to her side so that both could greet the Duke and Duchess of Devenwood. The Princess included Diana in the brief conversation, too, effectively smoothing over the mistake his sister had made.

Rhone sighed with relief. "Well, what do you know? She's still holding Diana's hand, too. A clever ploy to keep Diana from accidentally belting her one, I would imagine."

Lyon rested his shoulder against the mantel again, smiling over Rhone's observation. "Diana does like to use her hands when she speaks," he admitted.

"The Princess has a good heart. God's truth, I believe I'm in love."

"You're always in love," Lyon answered.

He wasn't able to keep the irritation out of his voice. Odd, but for some reason Rhone's jest bothered him. He didn't particularly want Princess Christina added to Rhone's list of future conquests. It was a ridiculous notion, Lyon realized. Why did he care if his friend chased after the woman or not?

He sighed when he realized he didn't have a ready answer. He did care, however. Fiercely so. And that honest admission soured Lyon's mood all the more. Damn, he was too old and too tired for an infatuation.

Christina didn't have any idea of the stir she was causing. She patiently waited in the center of the doorway for her Aunt Patricia to finish her conversation with their host. An eager young lady stood beside her, chattering away at such an incredible pace Christina couldn't quite keep up with her. She pretended interest, smiled when it seemed appropriate, and nodded whenever the lady named Diana paused for breath.

Lady Diana announced she was going to fetch her friends for an introduction. Christina was left alone again. She turned to look at all the people openly gawking at her, a serene smile on her face.

She didn't think she was ever going to get used to them. The English were such a peculiar lot. Though she'd been living in London for almost three months now, she was still perplexed by the odd rituals these whites seemed so determined to endure.

The men were just as foolish as their women. They all looked alike, too, dressed as they were in identical black garb. Their white neck wraps were starched to the point of giving the impression they were being strangled to death, an impression strengthened by their red, ruddy cheeks. No, Christina silently amended, they weren't called neck wraps . . . cravats, she told herself. Yes, that was the proper name for a neck wrap. She mustn't forget again.

There was so much to remember. Christina had studied diligently since arriving on her Aunt Patricia's doorstep in Boston a year ago. She already spoke French and English. The missionary Black Wolf had captured years before had taught her very well.

Her lessons in Boston centered on the behavior expected of a gentle lady. Christina tried to please her aunt, and to ease some of her fears, too. The sour woman was Christina's only link with her mother's family. Later, however, when Christina had conquered the written word well enough to understand the meaning in her mother's diary, her motives had changed. Dramatically. It was now imperative Christina win a temporary place in this bizarre society. She couldn't make any mistakes until her promise was carried out.

"Are you ready, Christina?"

The question was issued by Aunt Patricia. The old woman

came to Christina's side and grabbed hold of her arm in a clawlike grip.

"As ready as I shall ever be," Christina answered. She smiled at her guardian, then turned and walked into the throng of strangers.

Lyon watched her intently. He noticed how protective the princess appeared to be toward the wrinkle-faced woman clinging to her arm; noticed, too, how very correct the beautiful woman was in all her actions. Why, it was almost like a routine of some sort, Lyon thought. The Princess greeted each new introduction with a practiced smile that didn't quite reach her eyes. Next followed a brief conversation, and last, a brisk, efficient dismissal.

Lyon couldn't help but be impressed. The lady was good, all right. No wonder Brummel was so taken with her. The Princess followed all the rules of proper behavior. But Rhone was wrong. She wasn't all that different. No, she appeared to be just as rigid, just as polished, and certainly just as superficial as all the other ladies of the ton. Brummel embraced superficiality with a passion. Lyon detested it.

He wasn't disappointed by his conclusions about the Princess. The opposite was true for he'd felt off balance from the moment he'd first looked at the woman. Now his equilibrium was returning full force. He actually smiled with relief. Then he saw Rhone elbow his way through the crush of guests to get to the Princess. Lyon would have wagered his numerous estates that the woman would pay Rhone far more attention than the other men. Everyone in London knew of Rhone's family, and though he wasn't the most titled gentleman at the party, he was certainly one of the wealthiest.

Lyon would have lost his bet. Rhone didn't fare any better than all the others. A spark of perverse satisfaction forced a reluctant grin onto Lyon's face.

"You're losing your touch," Lyon remarked when Rhone returned to his side.

"What do you mean?" Rhone asked, pretending bewilderment.

Lyon wasn't buying it for a minute. He could see the faint blush on Rhone's face.

He really was starting to enjoy himself, Lyon realized. He decided then to rub salt in Rhone's wounds like any good friend would. "Was it my imagination, or did Princess Christina give you the same treatment she's given every other man in the room? She really didn't seem too impressed with your charms, old boy."

"You won't do any better," Rhone pronounced. "She really is a mystery. I specifically remember asking her several pertinent questions, yet when I walked away—"

"You mean when *she* walked away, don't you?"

Rhone gave Lyon a good frown, then shrugged. "Well, yes, when she walked away I realized I hadn't gotten a single answer out of her. At least I don't think I did."

"You were too interested in her appearance," Lyon answered. "A pretty face always did ruin your concentration."

"Oh?" Rhone said, drawing out the sound. "Well, old boy, let's see how many answers you gain. I'll put a bottle of my finest brandy up against one of yours."

"You're on," Lyon announced. He glanced around the room and found Princess Christina immediately. He had the advantage of being taller than everyone else in the room, and the object of his quest was the only blond-haired woman there.

She was standing next to his father's old friend, Sir Reynolds. Lyon was happy to see that Christina's dour-looking guardian had taken a chair across the room.

When Lyon was finally able to catch Sir Reynolds's attention, he motioned with an arrogant tilt of his head for an immediate introduction.

Sir Reynolds nodded—a little too enthusiastically for Lyon's liking—then leaned down and whispered to the Princess. Christina's back faced Lyon, but he saw her give an almost imperceptible nod. Long minutes elapsed before the heavyset woman speaking to the Princess paused for air. Sir Reynolds seized the opportunity to say goodbye. Lyon concluded his hasty explanation must have included his name, because the woman gave him a frightened look, picked up her skirts, and went scurrying in the opposite direction. She moved like a fat mouse with a cat on her tail.

Lyon's smile widened. His boast to Rhone hadn't been in vain. He really hadn't lost his touch.

He dismissed the silly woman from his mind when Princess Christina came to stand directly in front of him. Sir Reynolds hovered at her side like a nervous guardian angel. Lyon slowly pulled himself away from his lazy repose, patiently waiting for her to execute the perfect little curtsy he'd seen her give everyone else.

Her head was bowed, but even so he could tell she wasn't quite flawless after all. He could see the sprinkle of freckles across the bridge of her nose. The marks made her look less like a porcelain doll and far more touchable.

The woman barely reached his shoulders. She was too delicate-looking and much too thin for his liking, he decided. Then she looked up at him. Her gaze was direct, unwavering, captivating.

Lyon couldn't remember his own name.

He knew he'd eventually thank God for Sir Reynolds's intervention. He could hear the man's voice drone on and on as he listed Lyon's numerous titles. The long list gave Lyon time to recover.

He'd never been this rattled. It was her innocent gaze that held him so spellbound. Her eyes, too, he grudgingly admitted. They were unlike any shade of blue he'd ever seen.

He knew he had to get hold of himself. Lyon deliberately dropped his own gaze, settled on her mouth, and realized his mistake at once. He could feel himself reacting physically again.

Sir Reynolds finally ended his litany by stating, "I believe, my dear, you've already been introduced to the Earl of Rhone."

"Yes," Rhone interjected, smiling at Christina.

"Lyon, may I present Princess Christina to you?" Sir Reynolds said, sounding terribly formal.

Her eyes gave her away. Something said during the

introduction had unsettled her. She quickly recovered, though, and Lyon knew that if he hadn't been watching her so closely, he would have missed the surprise in her gaze.

"I'm honored to meet you, sir," Christina whispered.

Her voice appealed to him. It was soft, sensual. The unusual accent was noticeable, too. Lyon had traveled extensively, yet couldn't put his finger on the origin. That intrigued him almost as much as his senseless urge to grab hold of her, drag her off into the night, and seduce her.

Thank God she couldn't know what was going on inside his mind. She'd go screaming for a safe haven then, no doubt. Lyon didn't want to frighten her, though. Not just yet.

"Rhone has been Lyon's friend for many years," Sir Reynolds interjected into the awkward silence.

"I'm his only friend," Rhone commented with a grin.

Lyon felt Rhone nudge him. "Isn't that true?"

He ignored the question. "And are you a Princess?" he asked Christina.

"It would seem to many that I am," she replied.

She hadn't quite answered his question, Lyon realized. Rhone coughed—a ruse to cover his amusement, Lyon supposed with a frown.

Christina turned to Rhone. "Are you enjoying yourself this evening?"

"Immensely," Rhone announced. He looked at Lyon and said, "Your questions?"

"Questions?" Christina asked, frowning now.

"I was just wondering where you call home," Lyon said.

"With my Aunt Patricia," Christina replied.

"Lyon, surely you remember Lord Alfred Cummings," Sir Reynolds interjected with a great show of enthusiasm. "He was an acquaintance of your father's."

"I do recall the name," Lyon answered. He tried yet couldn't seem to take his gaze away from Christina long enough to spare a glance for Reynolds. It was probably rude, Lyon thought, even as he realized he wasn't going to do anything about it.

"Well, now," Sir Reynolds continued, "Alfred was appointed to the colonies years back. He died in Boston, God rest his soul, just two or three years ago, and the Countess returned home to England with her lovely niece."

"Ah, then you've been in England two years?" Lyon asked.

"No."

It took Lyon a full minute before he realized she wasn't going to expound upon her abrupt answer. "Then you were raised in the colonies." It was a statement, not a question, and Lyon was already nodding.

"No."

"Were you born there?"

"No," Christina answered, staring up at him with a hint of a smile on her face.

"But you lived in Boston?"

"Yes."

"Yes?"

He really hadn't meant to raise his voice, but Princess Christina was proving to be extremely exasperating. Rhone's choked laughter wasn't helping matters much either.

Lyon immediately regretted letting her see his irritation, certain she'd try to bolt at the first opportunity. He knew how intimidating he could be.

"Sir, are you displeased with me because I wasn't born in the colonies?" Christina suddenly asked. "Your frown does suggest as much."

He heard the amusement in her voice. There was a definite sparkle in her eyes, too. It was apparent she wasn't the least bit intimidated. If he hadn't known better, he would have thought she was actually laughing at him.

"Of course I'm not displeased," Lyon announced. "But are you going to answer all my questions with a yes or no?" he inquired.

"It would seem so," Christina said. She gave him a genuine smile and waited for his reaction.

Lyon's irritation vanished. Her bluntness was refreshing, her smile captivating. He didn't try to contain his laughter.

The booming sound ricocheted around the room, drawing startled expressions from some of the guests.

"When you laugh, sir, you sound like a lion," Christina said.

Her comment nudged him off center. It was such an odd remark to make. "And have you heard the roar of lions, Christina?" he asked, dropping her formal title.

"Oh, many times," Christina answered before she thought better of it.

She actually sounded like she meant what she said. That, of course, didn't make any sense at all. "Where would you have heard such a sound?"

The smile abruptly left her face. She'd inadvertently been drawn into revealing more than caution dictated.

Lyon waited for her to answer him. Christina gave him a wary look, then turned to Sir Reynolds. She bid him goodnight, explaining that she and her aunt had promised to make an appearance at another function before quitting the evening. She turned back to Lyon and Rhone and dismissed them both with cool efficiency worthy of a queen.

Lyon wasn't a man used to being dismissed.

Princess Christina was gone before he could mention that fact to her.

She knew she had to get away from him. She could feel her composure faltering. Her guardian was seated in a chair against the wall. Christina forced herself to walk with a dignified stride until she reached her aunt's side.

"I believe we should prepare to leave now," she whispered.

The Countess had lived with her niece long enough to know something was amiss. Her advanced years hadn't affected her keen mind or her physical shape. She all but bounded out of her chair, anchored herself to Christina's arm, and headed for the door.

Lyon stood with Rhone and Sir Reynolds. All three men watched Christina and her aunt make a hasty farewell to their host. "I'll be over tomorrow to get that bottle of brandy," Rhone announced with a nudge to get Lyon's attention.

"Rhone, if you jam your elbow into my ribs one more time, I swear I'll break it," Lyon muttered.

Rhone didn't look worried by the threat. He whacked his friend on the shoulder. "I believe I shall go and guard your sister for you, Lyon. You don't seem capable of the task."

As soon as Rhone left his side, Lyon turned to Sir Reynolds. "What do you know about Patricia Cummings?" he asked. "The truth, if you please, and no fancy fencing."

"You insult me, Lyon," Sir Reynolds announced, grinning a contradiction to his comment.

"You're known for your diplomacy," Lyon answered. "Now, about Christina's guardian. What can you tell me about her? Surely you knew her when you were younger."

"Of course," Reynolds said. "We were always invited to the same functions. I know my comments won't go any further, so I'll give the black truth to you, Lyon. The woman's evil. I didn't like her back then, and I don't like her now. Her beauty used to make up for her . . . attitude," he said. "She married Alfred when his older brother took ill. She believed he'd die at any moment. Patricia was like a vulture, waiting to inherit the estates. Alfred's brother outfoxed her, though. Lived a good ten years beyond everyone's expectations. Alfred was forced to take an appointment to the colonies, else be packed off to debtor's prison."

"What about Patricia's father? Didn't he attempt to settle his son-in-law's debts? I would have thought the embarrassment would have swayed him, unless, of course, he didn't have enough money."

"Oh, he was plenty rich enough," Sir Reynolds announced. "But he'd already washed his hands of his daughter."

"Because she married Alfred, perchance?"

"No, that isn't how the rumor goes," Reynolds said, shaking his head. "Patricia was always an abrasive, greedy woman. She was responsible for many cruelties. One of her little jests ended in tragedy. The young lady made the butt of her joke killed herself. I don't wish to go into further detail, Lyon, but let it suffice to say she doesn't appear to have changed her colors over the years. Did you notice the way she watched her niece? Gave me the shudders."

Lyon was surprised by the vehemence in Sir Reynolds's voice. His father's old friend was known for his calm, easygoing disposition. Yet now he was literally shaking with anger. "Were you the victim of one of her cruelties?" he asked.

"I was," Reynolds admitted. "The niece seems to be such a gentle, vulnerable little flower. She wasn't raised by her aunt. I'm sure of it. I pity the poor child, though. She's going to have a time of it trying to please the old bitch. The Countess will no doubt sell her to the highest bidder."

"I've never heard you speak in such a manner," Lyon said, matching Reynolds's whisper. "One last question, sir, for I can tell this conversation distresses you."

Sir Reynolds nodded.

"You said the Countess's father was a rich man. Who gained his estates?"

"No one knows. The father settled his affections on the younger daughter. Her name was Jessica."

"Jessica was Christina's mother?"

"Yes."

"And was she as demented as everyone believes?"

"I don't know, Lyon. I met Jessica several times. She seemed to be the opposite of her sister. She was sweet-tempered, shy—terribly shy. When she married, her father was extremely pleased. He strutted around like a rooster. His daughter, you see, had captured a king. I can still remember the glorious balls held in their honor. The opulence was staggering. Something blackened, though. No one really knows what happened." The elderly man let out a long sigh. "A mystery, Lyon, that will never be solved, I imagine."

Though he'd promised to curtail his questions, Lyon was too curious to drop the topic just yet. "Did you know Christina's father then? A king, you say, yet I've never heard of him."

"I met him, but I never really got to know him well. His name was Edward," Reynolds remembered with a nod.

"Don't recall his last name. I liked him. Everyone did. He was most considerate. And he didn't hold with pomp. Instead of lording it over us, he insisted everyone call him baron instead of king. He'd lost his kingdom, you see."

Lyon nodded. "It's a riddle, isn't it?" he remarked. "This Jessica does intrigue me."

"Why is that?"

"She married a king and then ran away from him."

"Jessica's reasons went to the grave with her," Sir Reynolds said. "I believe she died shortly after Christina was born. No one knows more than what I've just related to you, Lyon. And after your rather one-sided conversation with the lovely Princess, it would seem evident to me she's going to keep her secrets."

"Only if I allow it," Lyon said, grinning over the arrogance in his remark.

"Ah, then you have taken an interest in the Princess?" Sir Reynolds asked.

"Mild curiosity," Lyon answered with a deliberate shrug.

"Is that the truth, Lyon, or are you giving me fancy fencing now?"

"It is the truth."

"I see," Reynolds said, smiling enough to make Lyon think he didn't really see at all.

"Do you happen to know where Christina and her guardian were going when they left here? I heard Christina tell you they had one more stop to make before finishing the evening."

"Lord Baker's house," Reynolds said. "Do you plan to drop in?" he asked, his voice bland.

"Reynolds, don't make more out of this than it really is," Lyon said. "I merely wish to find out more about the Princess. By morning my curiosity will be appeased."

The briskness in Lyon's voice suggested to Reynolds that he stop his questions. "I haven't greeted your sister yet. I believe I'll go and say hello to her."

"You'll have to be quick about it," Lyon announced. "Diana and I are going to be leaving in just a few minutes."

Lyon followed Reynolds over to the crush of guests. He

allowed Diana several minutes to visit and then announced it was time to leave.

Diana's disappointment was obvious. "Don't look so sad," Sir Reynolds said. "I believe you aren't going home just yet." Sir Reynolds started chuckling.

Lyon wasn't the least amused. "Yes, well, Diana, I had thought to stop by Baker's place before taking you home."

"But Lyon, you declined that invitation," Diana argued. "You said he was such a bore."

"I've changed my mind."

"He isn't a bore?" Diana asked, looking completely bewildered.

"For God's sake, Diana," Lyon muttered, giving Reynolds a glance.

The harshness in Lyon's voice startled Diana. Her worried frown said as much.

"Come on, Diana. We don't want to be late," Lyon advised, softening his tone.

"Late? Lyon, Lord Baker doesn't even know we're going to attend his party. How can we be late?"

When her brother merely shrugged, Diana turned to Sir Reynolds. "Do you know what has come over my brother?" she asked.

"An attack of mild curiosity, my dear," Sir Reynolds answered. He turned to Lyon and said, "If you'll forgive an old man's interference, I would like to suggest that your sister stay here for a bit longer. I would be honored to see her home."

"Oh, yes, Lyon, please, may I stay?" Diana asked.

She sounded like an eager little girl. Lyon wouldn't have been surprised if she started clapping her hands. "Do you have a particular reason to stay?" he asked.

When his sister started blushing, Lyon had his answer. "What is this man's name?" he demanded.

"Lyon," Diana whispered, looking mortified. "Don't embarrass me in front of Sir Reynolds," she admonished.

Lyon sighed in exasperation. His sister had just repeated his opinion that Baker was a bore, and now she had the audacity to tell him he was embarrassing her. He gave her a good frown. "We're going to discuss this later, then," he announced. "Thank you, Reynolds, for keeping a close watch on Diana."

"Lyon, I don't need a keeper," Diana protested.

"You've yet to prove that," Lyon said before he nodded farewell to Sir Reynolds and left the room.

He was suddenly most eager to get to the bore's house.

Chapter Three

We stayed in England longer than Edward really wished so that my father could join in my birthday celebration. Edward was so very thoughtful of my dear papa's feelings.

The day after I turned seventeen, we sailed for my husband's home. I wept, yet remember thinking I was being terribly selfish. I knew I was going to miss my father. My duty was to follow my husband, of course.

After the tears were spent, I became excited about my future. You see, Christina, I thought Edward was taking me to Camelot.

Journal entry
August 10, 1795

Christina was feeling ill. She felt close to suffocating and kept telling herself her panic would dissipate just as soon as the horrible carriage ride was over.

How she hated the closeness inside the wobbly vehicle. The curtains were drawn, the doors bolted, the air dense and thick with her Aunt Patricia's heavy perfume. Christina's hands were fisted at her sides, hidden from her aunt's view by the folds of her gown. Her shoulders were pressed against the padded brown leather backrest.

The Countess didn't realize her niece was having any difficulty. As soon as the door was closed, she started in with her questions, never once allowing her niece time to give answers. The aunt laced each question with sharp, biting remarks about the guests they'd just left at Lord Carlson's townhouse. The Countess seemed to derive great pleasure in defaming others. Her face would twist into a sinister look, her thin lips would pucker, and her eyes would turn as gray as frostbite.

Christina believed the eyes reflected the thoughts of the soul. The Countess certainly proved that truth. She was such an angry, bitter, self-serving woman. Foolish, too, Christina thought, for she didn't even try to hide her flaws from her niece. Such stupidity amazed Christina. To show weakness was to give another power. Aunt Patricia didn't seem to understand that primitive law, however. She actually liked to talk about all the injustices done to her. Constantly.

Christina no longer paid any attention to her guardian's contrary disposition. She'd adopted a protective attitude toward the woman, too. The Countess was family, and while that probably should have been reason enough, there was another motive as well. Her aunt reminded Christina of Laughing Brook, the crazed old squaw who used to chase after all the children with her whipping stick. Laughing Brook couldn't help the way she was, and neither could the Countess.

"Didn't you hear me, Christina?" The Countess snapped, drawing Christina from her thoughts. "I asked you what made you want to leave Carlson's party so suddenly."

"I met a man," Christina said. "He wasn't at all like the others. They call him the Lion."

"You speak of the Marquess of Lyonwood," Patricia said, nodding her head. "And he frightened you, is that it? Well, do not let it bother you. He frightens everyone, even me. He's a rude, impossible man, but then his position does allow for insolence, I suppose. The ugly scar on his forehead gives him a sinister look."

"Oh, no, he didn't frighten me," Christina confessed. "Quite the contrary, Aunt. I was, of course, attracted to his mark, but when I heard Sir Reynolds call him Lion, I was immediately so homesick I could barely think what to say."

"How many times must I tell you those savages should mean nothing to you?" Patricia screeched. "After all I've sacrificed so that you can take your rightful place in society and claim my inheritance . . ."

The Countess caught her blunder. She gave her niece a piercing look to measure her reaction, then said, "You simply must not think about those people. The past must be forgotten."

"Why do they call him Lion?" Christina asked, smoothly changing the topic. She slowly moved her arm away from her aunt's painful grip. "I'm only curious," she explained, "for you did say the English didn't name themselves after animals or—"

"No, of course not, you stupid chit," Aunt Patricia muttered. "The Marquess isn't named after an animal. The spelling isn't the same." The Countess slowly spelled Lyon's name. Her voice lost some of its brittle edge when she continued, "It is in deference to his title that he's called Lyonwood. Closer friends are permitted to shorten the name, of course."

"He won't suit?" Christina asked, frowning.

"He most certainly will not," the Countess answered. "He's too shrewd, too rich. You'll have to stay away from him. Is that understood?"

"Of course."

The Countess nodded. "Why you would be attracted to him is beyond my comprehension. He wouldn't be the least manageable."

"I wasn't truly attracted to him," Christina answered. She lied, of course, but only because she didn't wish to goad her aunt into another burst of anger. And she really couldn't make her aunt understand anyway. How could she reason with a woman who believed a warrior's mark was a detraction? With that feeble mind-set, Christina's aunt would be appalled if she gave her the truth.

Oh, yes, the lion did appeal to her. The golden chips in his dark brown eyes pleased her. His powerful build was that of a warrior, and she was naturally drawn to his strength. There was an aura of authority surrounding him. He was aptly named, for he did remind her of a lion. Christina had noticed his lazy, almost bored attitude, yet she instinctively knew he could move with bold speed if given enough provocation.

Yes, he was attractive. Christina liked looking at him well enough.

But she loved his scent. And what would her aunt think of that admission, Christina wondered with a bit of a smile. Why, she'd probably install another chain on her bedroom door.

No, the Countess wouldn't understand her attraction. The old shaman from her village would understand, though. He'd be very pleased, too.

"We needn't worry that Lyon will show you the least interest," Aunt Patricia announced. "The man only escorts paramours. His latest attraction, according to the whispers I overheard, is a woman called Lady Cecille." The Countess let out an inelegant snort before continuing, "Lady indeed. Whore is the real name for the bitch. She married a man twice and half her age and no doubt began her affairs before the wedding was over."

"Doesn't this woman's husband mind that she—"

"The old goat died," her aunt said. "Not that long ago, I heard. Rumor has it Lady Cecille has her cap set for Lyon as her next husband."

"I don't think he'd marry a woman of ill repute," Christina said, shaking her head for emphasis. "But if she is called Lady, then she must not be a paramour. Isn't that right?" she asked, frowning over the confusion in her mind.

"She's accepted by the ton because of her title. Many of the married women do have affairs. All the husbands certainly keep mistresses," Aunt Patricia said. "The morals disgust me, but men will always follow their baser instincts, won't they?"

Her tone of voice didn't suggest she wanted Christina's opinion. "Yes, Aunt," she answered with a sigh.

"Lyon is rarely seen in public these days," the Countess continued. "Ever since his wife died he has set himself apart."

"Perhaps he still mourns his wife. He seemed vulnerable to me."

"Ha," the aunt sneered. "Lyon has been called many things, but never was the word vulnerable put to his name. I can't imagine any man mourning over the loss of a wife. Why, they're all too busy chasing after their own pleasures to care about anyone else."

The carriage came to a halt in front of the Bakers' residence, forcing an end to the conversation. Christina was acutely relieved when the door to the carriage was finally opened by the footman. She took several deep breaths as she followed her aunt up the steps to the brick-faced townhouse.

A soft, sultry breeze cooled her face. Christina wished she could pull all the pins out of her hair and let the heavy curls down. Her aunt wouldn't allow her to leave it unbound, however. Fashion ordered either short, cropped curls or intricately designed coronets. Since Christina refused to cut her unruly hair, she was forced to put up with the torture of the pins.

"I trust this won't be too much for you," the Countess sarcastically remarked before striking the door.

"I won't fail you," Christina replied, knowing those were the only words her aunt wanted to hear. "You really mustn't worry. I'm strong enough to face anyone, even a lion."

Her jest didn't take. The Countess puckered her lips while she gave her niece a thorough once-over. "Yes, you are strong. It's obvious you haven't inherited any of your mother's odious traits. Thank God for that blessing. Jessica was such a spineless woman."

It was difficult, but Christina held her anger. She couldn't let her aunt know how the foul words about Jessica upset her. Though she'd lived with her aunt for over a year now, she still found it difficult to believe that one sister could be so disloyal to another. The Countess wasn't aware her sister had kept a journal. Christina wasn't going to tell her about the diary—not just yet, anyway—but she wondered what her aunt's reaction would be if she was confronted with the truth. It wouldn't make any difference, Christina decided then. Her aunt's mind was too twisted to accept any changes in her opinions.

The pretense was becoming unbearable. Christina wasn't gifted with a patient nature. Both Merry and Black Wolf had cautioned her to keep a firm hold on her temper. They'd warned her about the whites, too. Her parents knew she'd have to walk the path alone. Black Wolf feared for her safety. Merry feared for her heart. Yet both ignored her pleas to stay with them. There was a promise to be kept, no matter how many lives were lost, no matter how many hearts were broken.

And if she survived, she could go home.

Christina realized she was frowning. She immediately regained her smile just as the door was opened by Lord Baker's butler. The smile stayed firmly in place throughout the lengthy introductions. There were only twenty guests in attendance, most of them elderly, and Christina was given hardly a moment's respite from the seemingly contagious topic of current illnesses until the call for refreshments was given.

The Countess reluctantly left Christina's side when Lord Baker offered her his arm. Christina was able to discourage three well-meaning gentlemen from ushering her into the dining room by pretending an errand in the washroom above the stairs. When she returned to the first floor, she saw that the drawing room was empty of guests. The solitude proved irresistible. Christina glanced over her shoulder to make certain she wasn't being observed, then hurried to the opposite end of the long, narrow room. She'd noticed a balcony beyond a pair of French doors nestled inside an arched alcove. Christina only wanted to steal a few precious minutes of blissful quiet before someone came looking for her.

Her hope was in vain. She'd just made it to the alcove when she suddenly felt someone watching her. Christina stiffened, confused by the feeling of danger that swept over her, then slowly turned around to face the threat.

The Marquess of Lyonwood was standing there, lounging against the entrance, staring at her.

The lion was stalking her. She shook her head, denying her own fanciful notions, yet took an instinctive step back at the same time. The scent of danger was still there, permeating the air, making her wary, confused.

Lyon watched her for a good long while. His expression was intense, almost brooding. Christina felt trapped by his dark gaze. When he suddenly straightened away from the wall and started toward her, she took another cautious step back.

He moved like a predator. He didn't stop when he reached her but forced her with his measured steps to back up through the archway and into the night.

"What are you doing, sir?" Christina whispered, trying to sound appalled and not too worried. "This isn't at all proper, is it?"

"No."

"Why, you've forgotten to make your presence known to our host," Christina stammered. "Did you forget your duty?"

"No."

She tried then to walk around him. Lyon wouldn't let her escape. His big hands settled on her shoulders, and he continued his determined pace. "I know you didn't speak to Lord Baker," Christina said. "Did you?"

"No."

"Oh," Christina replied, sounding quite breathless. "It is a rudeness, that."

"Yes."

"I really must go back inside now, my lord," she said. She was growing alarmed by his abrupt answers. His nearness was driving her to distraction, too. He'd confuse her if she let him, she told herself. Then she'd forget all her training.

"Will you unhand me, sir?" she demanded.

"No."

Christina suddenly understood what he was doing. Though she tried, she couldn't contain her smile. "You're trying to be as abrupt as I was with you, aren't you, Lyon?"

"I am being abrupt," he replied. "Do you like having all your questions answered with a simple yes or no?"

"It is efficient," Christina said, staring intently at his chest.

She'd mispronounced the word "efficient." Her accent had become more noticeable, too. Lyon assumed she was frightened, for he'd also caught the worry in her voice. He slowly forced her chin up, demanding without words that she look at him. "Don't be afraid of me, Christina," he whispered.

She didn't answer him. Lyon stared into her eyes a long minute before the truth settled in his mind. "I don't worry you at all, do I?" he asked.

She thought he sounded disappointed. "No," she admitted with a smile. She tried to shrug his hand away from her chin, and when he wouldn't let go of her she took another step back, only to find a weak railing blocking her.

She was good and trapped, and Lyon smiled over it. "Will you please let me go back inside?" she asked.

"First we're going to have a normal conversation," Lyon announced. "This is how it works, Christina. I'll ask you questions, and you may ask me questions. Neither of us will give abrupt one-word answers."

"Why?"

"So that we may get to know each other better," Lyon said.

He looked determined enough to stay on Lord Baker's balcony for the rest of the night if he needed to. Christina decided she had to gain the upper hand as soon as possible.

"Are you angry because I'm not afraid of you?" she asked.

"No," Lyon answered, giving her a lazy grin. "I'm not angry at all."

"Oh, yes you are," Christina said. "I can feel the anger inside you. And your strength. I think you might be just as strong as a lion."

He shook his head. "You say the oddest things," he remarked. He couldn't seem to stop touching her. His thumb slowly brushed her full lower lip. Her softness fascinated him, beckoned him.

"I don't mean to say odd things," Christina said, frowning now. "It is very difficult to banter with you." She turned her face away from him and whispered, "My Aunt Patricia doesn't want me in your company, Lyon. If she realizes I'm outside with you, she'll be most displeased."

Lyon raised an eyebrow over that announcement. "She's going to have to be displeased then, isn't she?"

"She says you're too shrewd," Christina told him.

"And that is a fault?" Lyon asked, frowning.

"Too wealthy, too," Christina added, nodding her head when he gave her an incredulous look.

"What's wrong with being wealthy?" Lyon asked.

"You wouldn't be manageable." Christina quoted her aunt's opinion.

"Damn right."

"See, you agree with my Aunt Patricia after all," Christina returned. "You aren't like the others, are you, Lyon?"

"What others?"

Christina decided to ignore that question. "I'm not a paramour, sir. Aunt tells me you're only interested in loose women."

"You believe her?" he asked. His hands caressed her shoulders again, and he was starting to have difficulty remembering what they were talking about. He could feel the heat of her through her gown. It was a wonderful distraction.

How he wanted to taste her! She was boldly staring up into his eyes now, with such an innocent look on her face, too. She was trying to make a mockery out of all his beliefs about women, Lyon decided. He, of course, knew better. Yet she intrigued him enough to play the game for just a little longer. There wasn't any harm in that, he told himself.

"No," Christina said, interrupting his thoughts.

"No, what?" Lyon asked, trying to remember what he'd said to her.

"No, I don't believe my aunt was correct. You're obviously attracted to me, Lyon, and I'm not a loose woman."

Lyon laughed softly. The sound was like a caress. Christina could feel her pulse quicken. She understood the danger now. Lyon's appeal could break through all her barriers. She knew, with a certainty that chilled her, he would be able to cut through her pretense. "I really must go back inside now," she blurted out.

"Do you know how much you confuse me?" Lyon asked, ignoring her demand to leave him. "You're very good at your craft, Christina."

"I don't understand."

"Oh, I think you do," Lyon drawled out. "I don't know how you've done it, but you've got me acting like a schoolboy. You've such a mysterious air about you. Deliberate, isn't it? Do you think I'll be less interested in you if I know more about you?"

Less interested? Christina felt like laughing. Why, the man would be appalled if he knew the truth. Yes, her aunt was right after all. The Marquess of Lyonwood was entirely too cunning to fool for long.

"Don't look so worried, my sweet," Lyon whispered.

She could see the amusement in his eyes. "Don't call me that," she said. Her voice shook, but it was only because of the strain of the pretense. "It isn't a proper law," she added, nodding vigorously.

"Proper law?" Lyon didn't know what she was talking about. His frustration turned to irritation. He forced himself to take a deep, calming breath. "Let's start over, Christina. I'll ask you a simple question, and you may give me a direct answer," he announced. "First, however, kindly explain what you mean when you say calling you sweet isn't a proper law."

"You remind me of someone from my past, Lyon. And I'm too homesick to continue this discussion." Her confession came out in a sad, forlorn whisper.

"You were in love with another man?" Lyon asked, unable to keep the anger out of his voice.

"No."

He waited, and when she didn't expound on her answer he let out a long sigh. "Oh, no, you don't," he said. "You will explain," he added, tightening his grip on her shoulders. "Christina, I've known you less than two hours, and you've got me tied in knots already. It isn't an easy admission to make," he added. "Can we not stay on one topic?"

"I don't think we can," Christina answered. "When I'm near you, I forget all the laws."

Lyon thought she sounded as bewildered as he felt. They'd circled back to her laws again, too. She wasn't making any sense. "I'll win, you know," he told her. "I always do. You can push me off center as many times as you like, but I'll always . . ."

He'd lost his train of thought when Christina suddenly reached up and trailed the tips of her fingers across the ragged line of his scar. The gentle touch sent shock waves all the way to his heart.

"You have the mark of a warrior, Lyon."

His hands dropped to his sides. He took a step back, thinking to put some distance between them so he could cool the fire rushing through his veins. From the innocent look in her eyes, he knew she didn't have any idea of the effect she was having on him.

It had happened so suddenly, so overwhelmingly. Lyon hadn't realized desire could explode so quickly.

Christina took advantage of the separation. She bowed her head and edged her way around him. "We must never touch each other again," she said before turning her back on him and walking away.

She had reached the alcove when his voice stopped her. "And do you find warriors with scars unappealing?"

Christina turned, so swiftly her skirt swirled around her ankles. She looked astonished by his question.

"Unappealing? Surely you jest with me," she said.

"I never jest," Lyon answered. His voice sounded bored, but the look in his eyes told her of his vulnerability.

She knew she must reveal this one truth. "I find you almost too appealing to deny."

She couldn't quite look into his eyes when she made her

confession, overcome by shyness because of her bold admission. She thought she might be blushing, too, and that thought irritated her enough to turn her back on Lyon once again.

He moved with the speed of a lion. One minute he was standing across the balcony, and the next he had her pinned against the brick wall adjacent to the alcove. His body kept her right where he wanted her. The lower half of Christina's body was trapped by his legs, and his hands were anchored on her shoulders. When he suddenly reached over to shut the doors, his thighs brushed intimately against hers. The touch unsettled both of them. Christina pushed herself up against the wall, trying to break the contact. Lyon's reaction was just the opposite. He leaned closer, wanting the touch again.

Lyon knew he was embarrassing her. He could see her blush, even in the soft moonlit night. "You're like a fragile little flower," he whispered while his hands caressed her shoulders, her neck. "Your skin feels like hot silk."

Her blush deepened. Lyon smiled over it. "Open your eyes, Christina. Look at me," he commanded in a voice as gentle as the breeze.

His tender words sent shivers down her arms. Love words, almost identical in meaning to the words Black Wolf always gave Merry when he thought they were alone. Lyon was trying to gentle her in much the same way. Did that mean he wanted to mate with her? Christina almost blurted out that question, then realized she shouldn't. Lyon was an Englishman, she reminded herself. The laws weren't the same.

Heaven help her, she mustn't forget. "I would never flirt with a lion," she blurted. "It would be dangerous."

Lyon's hands circled her neck. He wasn't sure if he wanted to kiss her or strangle her. The woman certainly did confuse him with her ridiculous comments. He could feel the frantic pulse of her heartbeat under his fingers. "Your eyes don't show any fear, but your heart tells the truth. Are you afraid of your attraction to me?"

"What an arrogant man you are," Christina said. "Why,

I'm so frightened I believe I might swoon if you don't unhand me this very minute."

Lyon laughed, letting her know he didn't believe her lie. He leaned down until his mouth was just a breath away from hers. "Didn't you tell me I was too irresistible to deny, Christina?"

"No," she whispered. "I said you were almost too irresistible to deny, Lyon. Almost. There is a difference."

She tried to smile yet failed the task completely. Christina was simply too occupied fighting the nearly overwhelming urge to melt against him, to hold him tightly, to learn his touch, his taste. She wanted his scent to mate with her own.

She knew it was a forbidden, dangerous longing. It was one thing to tease a cub and quite another to play with a fully grown lion. The dark look in Lyon's eyes told her he'd be just as determined as a hungry lion, too. He'd consume her if she didn't protect herself.

"Lyon," she whispered, torn between desire and the need for caution. "You really must help fight this attraction. I'll forget everything if you don't cooperate."

He didn't know what she was talking about. What did she think she'd forget? Perhaps he hadn't heard her correctly. Her accent had become so pronounced it was difficult to be certain. "I'm going to kiss you, Christina," he said, catching hold of her chin when she started to shake her head.

"One kiss," he promised. He nuzzled his chin against the top of her head, inhaled her sweet scent, and let out a soft, satisfied sigh. Then he took hold of her hands and slipped them around his neck.

God, she was soft. His hands slid down her arms, causing goosebumps he could feel. Pleased with her reaction to his touch, he settled his hands possessively on her hips and pulled her closer.

He was taking entirely too long getting on with it. Christina couldn't fight her attraction any longer. One small touch would certainly satisfy her curiosity. Then she'd go back inside and force herself to forget all about Lyon.

Christina leaned up on her tiptoes and quickly brushed

her mouth against his chin. She placed a chaste kiss on his mouth next, felt him stiffen in reaction. Christina drew back, saw him smile, and knew her boldness had pleased him.

His smile abruptly faded when she traced his lower lip with the tip of her tongue. Lyon reacted as though he'd just been hit by lightning. He dragged her up against him until her thighs were flattened against his own. He didn't care if his arousal frightened her or not. His arms circled her in a determined grip that didn't allow any leverage. Christina wasn't going to bolt until he let her.

She suddenly tried to turn her head away, and the tremor he felt rush through her made him think she might be having second thoughts. "Lyon, please, we will—"

His mouth found her, effectively silencing her protests. He teased and tantalized, coaching her to open her mouth for him. Christina responded to his gentle prodding. Her fingers slid into his hair as a passionate tremor coursed through his body. Lyon groaned into her mouth, then thrust his tongue deeply inside, demanding with his husky growl that she mate with him.

Christina forgot caution. Her hands clung to Lyon's shoulders. Her hips moved instinctively until she was cuddling his heat with her own. A whimper of pleasure escaped her when Lyon began to move against her hips. Christina used her tongue to explore the wonderful textures of Lyon's warm mouth, mimicking him.

A fire raged in his loins. Lyon's mouth slanted over hers once again in a hot, wild kiss that held nothing back. Christina's uninhibited response was a blissful torment he wanted never to end. The way she kissed him made him think she wasn't innocent of men after all. Lyon told himself he didn't care. The desire to bed her at the first possible moment overrode all other considerations.

Lyon had never experienced such raw desire. Christina made a soft moan deep in her throat. The sound nearly drove him beyond common sense. He knew he was about to lose all control and abruptly ended the kiss. "This isn't the time or the place, love," he told her in a ragged whisper.

He took a deep breath and tried desperately not to stare at her mouth. So soft, so exciting. She looked as though she'd just been thoroughly kissed, which of course she had, and Lyon could tell she was having as much difficulty regaining control as he was.

That fact pleased him immensely. He had to peel her hands away from his shoulders, too, for Christina didn't seem capable of doing more than staring up at him. Her eyes had turned a deep indigo blue. Passion's color, Lyon thought as he kissed her fingertips and then let go of her hands.

"I'm going to learn all of your secrets, Christina," Lyon whispered, thinking of the pleasure they could give each other in bed.

His promise penetrated with the swiftness of a dagger. Christina believed he'd just promised to find out about her past. "Leave me alone, Lyon," she whispered. She scooted around him, walked inside the archway, and then turned to look at him again. "Your curiosity could get you killed."

"Killed?"

She shook her head to let him know she wasn't going to expound upon that comment. "We satisfied each other by sharing one kiss. It was enough."

"Enough?"

His bellow followed her inside the drawing room. Christina grimaced at the anger she'd heard in his voice. Her heart was pounding, and she thanked the gods that the guests were still in the dining room. There was an empty chair next to her aunt. Christina immediately sat down and tried to concentrate on the boring conversation the Countess was having with their host and hostess.

Minutes later Lyon appeared in the entrance. Lord Baker was beside himself with excitement. It was obvious that he and everyone else in the dining room believed the Marquess of Lyonwood had only just arrived.

Christina acknowledged Lyon with a curt nod, then turned her back on him. The rude gesture delighted the Countess. The old woman actually reached out to pat

Christina's hand. It was the first show of affection she'd ever given her niece.

Lyon ignored Christina just as thoroughly. He was, of course, the center of attention, for his title and his wealth set him above the others. The men immediately surrounded him. Most of the women also left their chairs. They stood together like a covey of quail, bobbing their heads and eyelashes in unison whenever Lyon happened to glance their way.

When Christina couldn't stand the disgusting display any longer, she returned to the drawing room.

Lyon was trapped by their eager host into a discussion about crop rotation. He listened rather than advised, using the time to regain control of his temper. Though nothing showed on his face, inside he was shaking with fury.

Hell, she'd dismissed him again. Twice in one evening. Had to be some sort of record in that feat, he told himself. She was good, too. Why, she'd made him believe she was as hot as he was. Quite a little temptress, he decided.

Lyon was feeling as though he'd just been tossed into a snowbank. Christina was right, too. She had satisfied his curiosity. The problem, he grudgingly admitted, was the taste of her. Hot, wild honey. He hadn't gotten enough. And while Lord Baker enthusiastically spoke about the merits of barley, Lyon heard again the soft whimpers Christina had given him. It was all surely an act on her part, but the memory still made his blood run heavy.

Christina's aunt had followed her into the drawing room. The Countess stayed right by her niece's side, making snide remarks about the ill-tasting food of which she'd just eaten a horrendously large portion. Christina thought she was safe enough until Lyon happened to walk into the room at the very moment the Countess left to go upstairs to the washroom to repair her appearance.

Christina was suddenly vulnerable again. Lyon was striding toward her, and though he smiled at the other guests, she could certainly see the anger in his eyes. She immediately hurried over to Lord Baker and spoke to him, warily watching Lyon out of the corner of her eye.

"You have such a lovely home," Christina blurted out to the host.

"Thank you, my dear. It is comfortable for my needs," Lord Baker stated, his chest puffing out with new importance. He began to explain where he'd picked up various pieces of art littering the shelves in the room. Christina tried to pay attention to what he was telling her. She noticed Lyon hesitate, and she smiled over it.

"My wife actually made most of the selections. She has a keen eye for quality," Lord Baker commented.

"What?" Christina asked, puzzled by the way Lord Baker was staring at her. He did seem to expect some sort of answer. It was unfortunate, for she didn't have the faintest idea what they were talking about.

Lyon was getting closer. Christina blamed her lack of concentration solely on him, of course. She knew she'd make a fool of herself in front of her host if she didn't try to pay attention. She deliberately turned her back on Lyon and smiled again at her host. "Where did you find that lovely pink vase you've placed on your mantel?" she asked.

Lord Baker puffed up again. Christina thought he looked like a fat rabbit. "The most valuable piece in my collection," he announced. "And the only one I picked out on my own. Cost more than all my wife's jewels put together," he whispered with a nod. "Had to be firm with Martha, too. My wife declared it simply didn't work."

"Oh, I think it's very beautiful," Christina said.

"Baker, I'd like to speak to Princess Christina for a moment. In privacy, if you wouldn't mind." Lyon spoke right behind her. Christina knew if she took a step back she'd touch his chest. The thought was so unsettling she couldn't seem to come up with a quick denial.

"Certainly," Lord Baker announced. He gave Lyon a speculative look. Matching in his mind, Lyon decided. The rumor that he'd taken an interest in Christina would certainly be all over London by noon tomorrow. Odd, but that realization didn't bother Lyon too much. If it kept all the other dandies at bay, then perhaps the rumor would work to his advantage.

"Certainly not," Christina suddenly blurted out. She smiled at Lord Baker to soften her denial while she prayed he'd come to her rescue.

It was an empty prayer. Lord Baker looked startled and confused until Lyon interjected in a smooth, lying voice, "Christina does have the most wonderful sense of humor. When you get to know her better, I'm sure you'll agree, Baker."

Their host was fooled by Lyon's chuckle. Christina wasn't. Lyon's unbreakable hold on her hand told her he wasn't really amused at all.

He was determined to win. Christina thought he'd probably cause a scene if she tried to deny his request again. The man didn't seem to care what others thought of him. It was a trait she couldn't help but admire.

Lyon didn't have to use pretense, she reminded herself. His title assured compliance. Why, he was as arrogant and as confident as the chief of the Dakotas.

Christina tried to disengage herself from his hold when she turned to confront him. Lyon was smiling at Lord Baker, yet increasing the pressure in his grip at the same time. He was telling her without words not to argue, she supposed. Then he turned and started to pull her with him.

She didn't struggle but straightened her shoulders and followed him. Everyone was staring at them, and for that reason she forced herself to smile and to act as though it was nothing at all to be dragged across the room by a man she'd only just met. When she heard one woman whisper in a loud voice that she and the Marquess made a striking couple, she lost her smile. Yes, she did feel like hitting Lyon, but it was certainly uncomplimentary of the woman to make such a remark. She knew Lyon had also heard the comment. His arrogant grin said as much. Did that mean he wanted to strike her?

Lyon stopped when they reached the alcove. Christina was so relieved he hadn't dragged her outside, she began to relax. They were still in full view of the other guests—a blessing, because Christina knew Lyon wouldn't try to kiss her senseless with an audience watching his every move. No, tender embraces and soft words belonged to moments of privacy, when a man and woman were alone.

After nodding to several gentlemen, Lyon turned back to Christina. He stood close enough to touch if she took just one step forward. Though he'd let go of her hand, his head was inclined toward hers. Christina deliberately kept her head bowed, refusing to look up into his eyes. She thought she probably appeared to be very humble and submissive. It was an appearance she wished to give her audience, yet it irritated her all the same.

Another lie, another pretense. How her brother, White Eagle, would laugh if he could see her now. He knew, as well as everyone else back home, that there wasn't a submissive bone in Christina's body.

Lyon seemed patient enough to stare at her all evening. Christina decided he wasn't going to speak to her until she gave him her full attention. She captured her tranquil smile and finally looked up at him.

He was angry with her, all right. The gold chips were missing. "Your eyes have turned as black as a Crow's," she blurted out.

He didn't even blink over her bizarre comment. "Not this time, Christina," he said in a furious whisper. "Compliments won't get me off balance again, my little temptress. I swear to God, if you ever again dismiss me so casually, I'm going to—"

"Oh, it wasn't a compliment," Christina interrupted, letting him see her irritation. "How presumptuous of you to think that it was. The Crow is our enemy."

Heaven help her, she'd done it again. Lyon could so easily make her forget herself. Christina fought the urge to pick up her skirts and run for the front door. But she suddenly realized he couldn't possibly understand her comment. The confused look on his face told her she'd swayed his attention, too.

"Birds are your enemies?" he asked in a voice that sounded incredulous.

Christina smiled. "Whatever are you talking about?" she asked, feigning innocence. "Did you wish to speak to me about birds?"

"Christina." He'd growled her name. "You could make a saint lose his temper."

She thought he looked ready to pounce on her, so she took a protective step back and then said, "But you aren't a saint, are you, Lyon?"

A sudden shout drew Lyon's full attention. Christina also heard the sound, yet when she tried to turn around, Lyon grabbed hold of her and roughly pushed her behind his back. His strength amazed her. He'd moved so quickly Christina hadn't even guessed his intent until the deed was accomplished.

His broad shoulders blocked her view. Christina could tell by his rigid stance that there was danger. And if she hadn't known better, she would have thought he was trying to protect her.

She was highly curious. She hadn't sensed any threat, yet when she peeked out from Lyon's side she could see armed men standing in the entrance. Her eyes widened with surprise. The evening had certainly taken another bizarre twist. First she'd encountered a lion, and now it appeared that they were about to be robbed by bandits. Why, it was turning out to be an extremely interesting evening after all.

Christina wanted to get a better look at the mischief makers. Lyon, however, had other ideas. As soon as she moved to his side he pushed her behind him again.

He was protecting her. A warm feeling swept over Christina. She was pleased with his determination and actually smiled over it. She decided to let him have his way, then stood on her tiptoes, braced her hands against Lyon's back, and peeked over his shoulder so she could see what was going on.

There were five of them. Four held knives. Poor workmanship, Christina noted with a shake of her head. The fifth man held a pistol in his right hand. All wore masks that covered the lower portion of their faces. The man with the pistol—obviously the leader in Christina's judgment—shouted orders from the entrance. His voice was strained into a deep, guttural tone. Christina immediately assumed he was known by some of the guests. He wouldn't have disguised his voice unless he thought he'd be recognized. And while he was dressed like the others in peasant garb and an ill-fitting hat, his boots weren't the same at all. They were old and scruffy, like the boots the others wore, but the quality of the leather was apparent to Christina.

And then the leader turned and looked across the room. His eyes widened in surprise. Christina let out an involuntary gasp. Good Lord, she'd just met the man not an hour past.

Lyon heard her indrawn breath. The scowl increased on his face, for he immediately assumed Christina was terrified. He backed up a space, pushing Christina further into the shadows. His intent was to block her inside the alcove, and if the danger increased, he'd shove her out the doorway.

Lord Baker's wife swooned when one of the bandits demanded her diamond necklace. She conveniently landed on the settee. Christina was desperately trying not to laugh. Swooning was such a delightful pretense.

All of a sudden, Christina's aunt walked into the middle of the commotion. The Countess didn't seem to comprehend the fact that there was a robbery going on. When the leader turned and aimed his pistol in her direction, Christina immediately retaliated.

Crazed or not, Aunt Patricia was family. No one was going to harm her.

It happened too quickly for anyone to react. Lyon heard the whistle of the knife seconds before the bandit's howl of pain. He'd seen the glint of metal fly by his right shoulder. He turned, trying to protect Christina from the new threat, but didn't see anyone standing behind her. Whoever had thrown the weapon had vanished out the doorway to the balcony, he concluded.

Poor Christina. She tried to look dignified. Her hands were demurely folded together, and she gave him only a curious look. She even looked behind her when Lyon did, yet she didn't seem to understand there might be jeopardy there, lurking in the shadows.

Lyon quickly pushed her into the corner so that the wall protected her back. When he was satisfied no one could get to her from behind, he turned back to face the bandits. His shoulders pressed Christina against the wall.

She didn't argue over the confinement. She knew what he was doing. Lyon was still protecting her and was making sure no one was going to come back in through the archway. A noble consideration, Christina thought.

There wasn't any need, of course, for there had never been anyone behind her. She couldn't very well tell Lyon that, however, and his concern for her safety did please her immensely.

The leader had disappeared out the front door. The other bandits threatened the guests by waving their knives in front of them as they backed out of the room.

Both pistol and knife lay on the floor.

Lyon turned to Christina. "Are you all right?" he demanded.

He sounded so concerned. Christina decided to look frightened. She nodded, and when Lyon placed his hands on her shoulders and pulled her toward him she could feel the anger in him.

"Are you angry with me?" she asked.

He was surprised by her question. "No," he announced. His voice was so harsh, he thought he might not have convinced her. "Of course I'm not angry with you, love."

Christina smiled over the forced gentleness in his tone. "Then you may quit squeezing my shoulders," she told him.

He immediately let go of her. "You're angry because you couldn't fight the mischief makers, aren't you, Lyon?"

"Mischief makers? My dear, their intent was a little more serious," Lyon said.

"But you did want to fight them, didn't you?"

"Yes," he admitted with a grin. "I was aching to get in the middle of it. Some habits die hard," he added.

"You'll always be a warrior, Lyon."

"What?"

Oh dear, he was looking confused again. Christina hastened to say, "There are too many old people here. It wouldn't have been safe for you to interfere. Someone might have been hurt."

"Is your concern only for the old men and women?" he asked.

"Yes."

Lyon frowned over her answer. Then she realized he wanted her to be concerned for his safety, too. Didn't he realize it would have been an insult for her to show concern for him? Why, that would mean she didn't have enough faith in his ability! Still, he was English, she reminded herself. And they were a strange breed.

"I wouldn't worry for you, Lyon. You would have held your own."

"You have that much faith in me, do you?"

She smiled over the arrogance in his tone. "Oh, yes," she whispered, giving him the praise he seemed to need. She was about to add a bit more when a loud wail interrupted her.

"Our hostess is coming out of her swoon," Lyon announced. "Stay here, Christina. I'll be back in a minute."

She did as he ordered, though she kept her attention directed on him. Her heart started pounding when Lyon knelt down and picked up her knife. She took a deep breath, held it, and then sighed with relief when he put the knife on the table and turned his attention to the pistol.

The chaos surrounding her was confusing. Everyone was suddenly talking at the same time. Perhaps she should try to swoon after all, Christina considered. No, the settee was already taken, and the floor didn't look all that appealing. She settled on wringing her hands. It was the best she could do to look upset.

Two gentlemen were in deep discussion. One motioned Lyon over to join them. As soon as he moved toward the dining room Christina edged her way over to the table. She made certain no one was paying her any attention, then she cleaned and sheathed her knife.

She hurried over to stand beside her aunt. The Countess

was administering blistering advice to the distressed woman draped on the settee.

"I believe we've had enough excitement for one evening," Christina told her guardian when she was finally able to catch her attention.

"Yes," the Countess answered. "We'd better be on our way."

Lyon was blocked in the dining room, listening to absurd suggestions as to how two ancient gentlemen thought to trap Jack and his band.

After ten minutes or so, he'd had his fill. His attention kept returning to the unusual dagger he'd held in his hands. He'd never seen the like before. The weapon was crudely made, yet toned to needle-point sharpness. The handle was flat. Whoever owned the knife certainly hadn't purchased it in England.

Lyon decided to take the weapon with him. He was highly curious and determined to find the man who'd thrown it.

"I'll leave you gentlemen to think your plans through," Lyon announced. "I believe I'll see Princess Christina and her guardian safely home. If you'll excuse me?"

He didn't give them time to start in again but turned and hurried back inside the drawing room. He remembered telling Christina to wait for him until he returned. He shouldn't have left her alone, assuming she was still frightened enough to need his comfort. He sincerely hoped she was, for the thought of offering her solace was very appealing.

Lyon was already planning how he'd get Christina away from her guardian. He just wanted to steal a few minutes so he could kiss her once more.

"Well, hell." Lyon muttered the obscenity when he realized Christina had vanished. He glanced over at the table where he'd left the knife, then let out another foul expletive.

The knife had vanished, too. Lyon's mood blackened. He considered questioning the guests, but they were all still occupied rehashing their reactions to the robbery. He decided not to bother.

Lyon turned to look again at the alcove where he and

Christina had stood together during the robbery. A sudden revelation popped into his mind. No, he told himself. It wasn't possible.

Then he strolled over to the alcove and continued on until he was standing next to the balcony railing.

A good twenty feet separated the balcony from the sloping terrace below. Impossible to scale. The railing was shaky, too weak to hold rope and man.

His mind immediately jumped to a ludicrous conclusion.

Lyon shook his head. "Impossible," he muttered out loud. He decided to put that puzzle aside and concentrate on the real worry now.

Lyon left Baker's house in a black mood. He was too angry to speak just yet. He determined to wait until tomorrow.

Then he was going to have a long, hard talk with Rhone.

Chapter Four

Edward always wore white. Colors displeased him. He preferred me to wear long, flowing Grecian-styled gowns of white also. The palace walls were whitewashed once a month, and all the furnishings were devoid of even a splash of color. While Edward's peculiarity amused me, I did comply with his wishes. He was so good to me. I could have anything I wanted and wasn't allowed to lift a finger in labor. He only bound me to one rule. Edward made me promise never to leave the pristine palace grounds, explaining it was for my protection.

I kept my promise for almost six months. Then I began to hear rumors about the conditions outside my walls. I believed Edward's enemies spread the rumors of brutality solely to cause unrest.

My maid and I changed into peasant clothing and set out on foot for the nearest village. I looked upon the outing as an adventure.

God help me, I walked into purgatory.

Journal entry
August 15, 1795

The solicitors in care of the Earl of Acton's estate called upon Countess Patricia Cummings Tuesday morning at ten o'clock. Misters Henderson and Borton were prompt to the minute.

The Countess could barely contain her enthusiasm. She ushered both gray-haired gentlemen into her study, shut the door behind her, and took her place behind the scarred desk.

"You'll have to forgive such shabby furnishings," she said. She paused to give both men a brittle smile before continuing. "I was forced to use the last of my reserves to dress my niece, Christina, for the season ahead of us, and there just wasn't anything left over. Why, I've had to turn down many requests for visitations with my niece—too embarrassed, you understand, to let anyone see the way we're living. Christina has caused a sensation. I'll marry her well."

The Countess suddenly realized she was rambling. She gave a dainty little cough to cover her embarrassment. "Yes, well, I'm certain you both know this townhouse is only on loan to us for another month. You did receive the bid for purchase, did you not?"

Henderson and Borton nodded in unison. Borton turned to his associate and gave him an odd, uncomfortable look. He poked at his cravat. The Countess narrowed her eyes over the rudeness. "When will my money be transferred into my hands?" she demanded. "I can't go on much longer without proper funds."

"But it isn't your money, Countess," Borton announced after receiving a nod from his associate. "Surely you realize that fact."

Borton blanched over the horrid frown the Countess gave him. He couldn't continue to look at her. "Will you explain, Henderson?" he asked, staring at the floor.

"Certainly," Henderson said. "Countess, if we might have a word in privacy with your niece, I'm certain this misunderstanding will be cleared up."

Henderson obviously wasn't intimidated by the Countess's visible anger. His voice was as smooth as good gin. He continued to smile all through the foul woman's tantrum. Borton was impressed.

Patricia slammed her fists down on the desk. "What does Christina have to do with this meeting? I am her guardian, and therefore I control her funds. Isn't that the truth?" she screeched.

Before Henderson could answer, Patricia slapped the desk again. "I do control the money, don't I?"

"No, madam. You do not."

Christina heard her aunt's bellow all the way upstairs. She immediately left her bedroom and hurried down the steps to see what had caused the Countess such an upset. Christina had learned the difference between her aunt's screams long ago. This one resembled the protest of a trapped owl, telling Christina her Aunt Patricia wasn't frightened. Just furious.

She reached the library door before she realized she was barefoot. Lord, that would certainly push her aunt into a tither, Christina thought. She hurried back upstairs, found her impractical shoes, and quickly put them on.

Christina counted five more shrieks before she was once again downstairs. She didn't bother to knock on the library door, knowing her aunt's shouts would drown out the sound. She threw the door open and hurried inside.

"Is there something I can do to help, Aunt?" Christina asked.

"This is your niece?" Henderson asked as he hurried out of his chair.

"Christina, go back to your room. I'll deal with these scoundrels."

"We'll not speak to you of the conditions set down in writing by your father, Countess," Borton said. "It is you who must leave us alone with your niece. Those were your father's wishes as spelled out in his will."

"How could such a condition exist?" the Countess shouted. "My father didn't even know Jessica was carrying a child. He couldn't have known about her. I made certain."

"Your sister wrote to your father, madam, and told him about his grandchild. I believe she sent the letter when she was staying with you. And she'd also left a message for him. The Earl found it a year after her disappearance."

"Jessica couldn't have written to him," Patricia announced with an inelegant snort. "You're lying. I would have known. I looked through each letter."

"You mean you destroyed each letter, don't you, Countess?" Henderson asked, matching Patricia's glare. "You didn't want your father to know about his heir, did you?"

Aunt Patricia's face turned as red as fire. "You can't know that," she muttered.

Christina was concerned about her aunt's extreme anger. She walked over to her side and put her hand on the old woman's shoulder. "It doesn't matter how my grandfather learned about me. The past is behind us, gentlemen. Let it rest."

Both men hastily nodded. "A sensible request, my dear," Henderson commented. "Now, according to the conditions of the will, we must explain the finances to you in privacy."

Christina increased her grip on her aunt's shoulder when she saw she was about to object. "If I request that the Countess remain, will you agree?" she asked.

"Of course," Borton said after receiving another nod from his partner.

"Then kindly sit down and begin your explanation," Christina instructed. She felt the tension leave her Aunt Patricia and slowly let go of her.

"A man by name of Captain Hammershield delivered your mother's letter to the Earl of Acton," Henderson began. "We have the letter in our file, and the one Jessica left behind in our files, if you wish to challenge this, Countess," the solicitor added. "I need not go into the other details of the letters, for as you say, Princess Christina, the past is behind us. Your grandfather fashioned a new will immediately. He had turned his back on you, Countess, and was so infuriated with his other daughter's behavior that he decided to put his fortune in holding for his only grandchild."

Borton leaned forward to interject, "He didn't know if you were going to be a boy or girl. There are conditions in both events, of course, but we will only explain the conditions for a granddaughter, you see."

"What did my mother do to cause her father to change his mind about her? I thought they were very close to each other," Christina said.

"Yes, whatever did my sainted sister do to turn Father against her?" Patricia asked, a sneer in her voice.

"Jessica humiliated her father when she left her husband. Princess Christina, your grandfather was most upset. He liked his son-in-law and thought his daughter was acting . . . out of sorts," he ended with a shrug to cover his embarrassment.

"What you're sniffing around and refusing to say is that my father at last realized Jessica was crazy," the Countess announced.

"That is the sad truth," Borton said. He gave Christina a sympathetic look.

"So the money goes directly to Christina?" the Countess asked.

Henderson saw the shrewd look that came into the woman's eyes. He almost laughed. The Earl of Acton had been right about this daughter, the solicitor decided. Henderson decided to rush through the rest of the stipulations, concerned that the old woman would ruin his midday meal if he had to look at her much longer.

"The funds were placed in abeyance until your nineteenth birthday, Princess Christina. If you marry before that day, the funds will be given to your husband."

"That is less than two months away," the Countess remarked. "She will not marry so soon. And so, as guardian—"

"Please listen to the rest of the stipulations," Henderson requested in a hard voice. "While the Earl liked his son-in-law, he decided to proceed with caution, in the event that his daughter's accusations about her husband turned out to have a drop of credibility."

"Yes, yes," Borton eagerly interjected. "The Earl was a most cautious man. For that reason, he added further controls to the distribution of his vast fortune."

"Will you get on with it?" the Countess demanded. "Spell out the damned conditions before you make me as demented as Jessica was."

The Countess was getting all worked up again. Christina supported her demand, though in a much softer tone of voice. "I would also like to hear the rest of this, if you will please continue."

"Certainly," Henderson agreed. He deliberately avoided looking at the Princess now, certain he'd lose his train of thought if he paused to appreciate the lovely shade of her blue eyes. He found it amazing that the two women were actually related to each other. The Countess was an ugly old bitch, in looks and manners, yet the lovely young woman standing next to her was as pretty as an angel and seemed to be just as sweet-tempered.

Henderson focused his attention on the desktop and continued. "In the event you reach nineteen and are unmarried, your father will oversee your inheritance. Princess Christina, your father was informed of the conditions of the will before he left England in search of your mother. He understood he wouldn't have access to the money until—"

"He can't still be alive," the Countess exclaimed. "No one's heard of him in years."

"Oh, but he is alive," Borton said. "We received a missive from him just a week past. He's currently living in the north of France and plans to return to claim the money on the day of his daughter's nineteenth birthday."

"Does he know Christina is alive? That she's here, in London?" the Countess asked. Her voice shook with anger.

"No, and we didn't feel the need to so inform him," Henderson said. "Princess Christina's birthday is less than two months off now. Of course, if you wish us to try to notify your father, Princess, before—"

"No." Christina controlled her voice. She felt like shouting the denial, however, and could barely catch her breath over the tightness in her chest. "It will be a happy surprise for him, don't you agree, gentlemen?" she added with a smile.

Both men smiled back in agreement. "Gentlemen, we

have tired my aunt," Christina announced. "As I understand this will, I can never control my own money. If I marry, my husband will direct the funds, and if I do not, then my father will have free hand with the inheritance."

"Yes," Borton answered. "Your grandfather would not allow a woman to have such power over his money."

"All this time I believed I would . . ." The Countess crumbled against her chair. "My father has won."

Christina thought her aunt might start weeping. She dismissed the two gentlemen a few minutes later. In a magnanimous gesture, Henderson told Christina he'd release a sum of money to tide her over until her father returned to gain guardianship.

Christina was humble in her gratitude. She saw the solicitors out the front door, then returned to the library to speak to her aunt.

The Countess didn't realize how upset her niece was. "I've lost everything," she wailed as soon as Christina rushed back into the room. "Damn my father's soul to hell," she shouted.

"Please don't get upset again," Christina said. "It cannot be at all good for your health."

"I've lost everything, and you dare to tell me not to get upset?" the Countess screeched. "You're going to have to plead on my behalf to your father, Christina. He'll give me money if you ask. Edward didn't like me. I should have been nicer to him, I suppose, but I was so jealous of Jessica's good fortune in capturing him I could barely be civil to the man. Why he chose her over me still doesn't make any sense. Jessica was such a mouse. I was far better-looking."

Christina didn't answer her aunt's mutterings. She started to pace in front of the desk, her mind filled with the problem ahead of her.

"Were you surprised to learn that your father is still alive?" the Countess asked.

"No," Christina answered. "I never believed he'd died."

"You're going to have to take care of me, Christina," the aunt whined. "Whatever will I do if your father doesn't support me? How will I get along? I shall be the laugh of the *ton*," she cried.

"I've promised to take care of you, Aunt," Christina said. "Remember how I gave you my word before we left Boston? I shall see my promise carried through."

"Your father might not agree with your noble intentions, Christina. He'll have control of *my* money, the bastard, and I'm sure he'll refuse to give me a single shilling."

Christina came to an abrupt halt in front of her aunt. "Giving my father control of the money does not suit my purposes," she announced. "I'll not let it happen."

Patricia Cummings had never seen her niece look so angry. She nodded, then smiled, for she assumed the stupid chit was infuriated on her behalf. "You're a dear girl to be so concerned about my welfare. Of course, your concern isn't misplaced. A grave injustice was done to me by my father, and I did use the last of my own accounts to see you properly attired. It was all for nought," the Countess added. "I should have stayed in the Godforsaken colonies."

Christina was irritated by the self-pity she heard in her aunt's voice. She took a deep breath, hoping to regain her patience, and said, "All is not lost. The solution to our problem is obvious to me. I will marry before my father returns to England."

Christina's calmly stated announcement gained her aunt's full attention. The old woman's eyes widened, and she actually straightened in her chair. "We don't know when Edward will arrive. He could walk into this very room as early as tomorrow," she said.

Christina shook her head. "No, I don't think so. Remember, he must surely believe I didn't survive. Everyone else seemed very surprised to see me. And I plan to marry as soon as possible."

"How could we make the arrangements in time? We don't even have a suitable man in mind."

"Make a list of those I must consider," Christina advised.

"This isn't at all proper," the Countess protested.

Christina was going to argue when she noticed the gleam

settle in her aunt's gaze. She knew then that she was giving the idea consideration. Christina goaded her into complete agreement. "We must move quickly if we are to be successful."

"Why? Why would you sacrifice yourself this way?" Patricia gave her niece a suspicious look. "And why would you rather have the money in your husband's hands instead of your father's?"

"Aunt, as I said before, it doesn't suit my purposes to let my father have any money. Now, what other objections must you raise before you see the wisdom of my plan?"

"Your father might have gained a new fortune by now. He may not even want the money."

"You know better," Christina said. "I doubt that he's rich. Why would he keep in correspondence with the solicitors if he was so wealthy? Oh, he'll come back to England, Aunt Patricia."

"If you claim Edward will want the inheritance, I won't argue with you," the Countess said.

"Good," Christina said. "I think you are one of the most clever women I've ever known," she praised. "Surely you can come up with a plausible reason for my hasty marriage."

"Yes," the Countess agreed. "I am clever." Her shoulders straightened until her spine looked ready to snap. "Just how will your marriage help me?" she demanded.

"We will ask the man I marry to sign over a large amount to you. He must sign the papers before we are wed."

"Then it will have to be someone manageable," the Countess muttered. "There are plenty of that kind around. I'll have to think of a good reason for the rush. Leave me now, Christina, while I make a list of possible husbands for you. With your looks, we can get just about anyone to agree to my conditions."

"I would like the Marquess of Lyonwood placed at the top of your list," Christina announced, bracing herself for her aunt's displeasure.

"You can't be serious," the Countess stammered. "He's rich, doesn't need the money, and simply isn't the type to cooperate with my plans."

"If I can get him to sign your papers, then will it be all right for me to wed with him for the short time I'm in England?"

"To wed with him isn't proper English, Christina. Oh, very well, since you're willing to make this necessary sacrifice, I'll allow you to approach the disgusting man. He won't agree, of course, but you have my permission to try."

"Thank you," Christina said.

"You're still set on returning to those savages?"

"They are not savages," Christina whispered. "And I will return to my family. Once you have the money in your hands, it shouldn't matter to you."

"Well, you certainly shouldn't mention that fact to the man we choose to marry you. It would surely set him against you, Christina."

"Yes, Aunt," Christina answered.

"Get out of here and change that gown," the Countess snapped. "You look positively ugly in that color of yellow. Your hair needs tending, too. Do something about it at once."

Christina immediately left the library, ignoring the ridiculous criticisms of her appearance.

By the time she shut the bedroom door behind her she'd shed the pretense. Christina was visibly shaking. Her stomach felt as though it was twisted into knots, and her head was pounding.

Though it was difficult to admit, Christina was honest enough to realize she was really frightened. She didn't like the strange feeling at all.

She understood the reason. The jackal was returning to England. He'd try to kill her. Christina didn't doubt her father's determination. Jackals didn't change their nature over the years.

Christina was going to give Edward a second chance to murder her. God willing, she'd kill him first.

Chapter Five

There really are demons living on this earth, Christina. I didn't know such evil men existed until I saw innocent children who'd been tortured, mutilated, destroyed, just to gain their parents' obedience. An army of enforcers slaughtered defenseless peasants. My husband was a dictator; anyone believed to have a subversive thought was murdered. The dead, the dying littered the alleys. Carts would come to collect the bodies every night. The stench that would make us close our doors in the palace each sunset wasn't due to excess garbage . . . no, no, the odor came from the burial fires.

The people were kept hungry so they would be too weak to rebel. Even the water was rationed. I was so sickened by the atrocities I couldn't think clearly. Mylala, my faithful maid, cautioned me against confronting Edward. She feared for my safety.

I should have listened to her, child. Yes, I acted the part of a naive fool, for I went to challenge my husband.

Learn from my mistakes, Christina. It's the only way you'll survive.

Journal entry
October 12, 1795

Lyon was slouched behind his desk, a full goblet of brandy in his hand and a hot container of water balanced on his knee.

Odd, but the injury hadn't given him any notice until this evening. It was well past four o'clock in the morning now. The nagging pain—and the dreams, of course—had forced him back to his study to work on the problems of his estates. He wouldn't retire until dawn was well upon the city of London . . . when his mind was too fatigued to remember.

He was feeling out of sorts. An old warrior, he thought with a smile. Wasn't that what Christina had called him? Warrior, yes, he remembered her calling him that . . . old, no, he didn't recall that mention.

The past had caught up with the Marquess. His years working for his country had taken a toll. He was a man who was feared still—had become legend, in fact, in many disreputable circles of French society. Lyon had always been given the most difficult, delicate missions. He was never called until the atrocity had been done, the evidence judged. His duty was solitary, his reputation unblemished by failure. The Marquess of Lyonwood was considered to be the most dangerous man in England. Some claimed the world.

No matter where the traitor hid, Lyon could ferret him out and dispatch him with quiet, deadly efficiency.

He'd never failed in his duty. Never.

The results of his loyalty were twofold. Lyon was given knighthood for his courage, nightmares for his sins. It was an easy enough retirement to accept. Since he lived alone, no one ever knew his torment. When the nightmares visited, and he once again saw the faces of those he'd eliminated, no one was there to witness his agony.

Lyon rarely thought about James or Lettie anymore, though he continued to shake his head over the irony of it all. While he was abroad defending his homeland against betrayers, his brother was home in England betraying him.

No, he didn't think about James much, and since meeting

Princess Christina his mind had been in such a turmoil he could barely think with much reason at all.

He was a man given to intrigue. A good puzzle held his attention until he'd resolved it. Christina, however, still proved too elusive to understand. He didn't know what her game was . . . yet. When she didn't openly flirt with him—or Rhone either, for that matter—his interest had picked up. Lyon kept mulling over the strange conversation he'd had with the lady, but after a while he gave up. He'd have to see her again, he told himself. She still hadn't given him enough clues to satisfy him.

And where in God's name would she have heard the roar of lions?

Lyon knew he was becoming obsessed with finding out about her past. His determination didn't make much sense to him. Christina was affecting him in ways he'd thought impossible. He'd never felt so overwhelmed by a woman before. The admission bothered him far more than the nagging pain in his knee.

He would learn all her secrets. She was sure to have them—every woman did—and then his curiosity would be satisfied. Yes, then he'd dismiss her.

The obsession would end.

With that decision reached, Lyon dispatched notes to the gossip leaders of the ton. He was, of course, discreet in his requests for information about the Princess, using his sister Diana and her introduction into society as his main reason for wanting to know the ins and outs of "business."

He wasn't the least concerned about his deceitful endeavor. And in the end, when all the letters had been answered, Lyon was more frustrated than ever. According to all those in the know, Princess Christina didn't have a past.

The woman hadn't even existed until two months ago.

Lyon wasn't about to accept such a conclusion. His patience was running thin. He wanted real answers . . . and he wanted to see Christina again. He had thought to corner her at Creston's ball the following Saturday, then decided against waiting.

Ignoring good manners altogether, he called upon No. 6

Baker Street at the unholy hour of nine o'clock in the morning. Lyon hadn't bothered to send a note begging an audience, certain the ill-tempered Countess would have denied him entrance if she'd been given advance warning.

Luck was on Lyon's side. An extremely feeble old man with a mop of stark yellow hair opened the door for him. His clothing indicated that he was the butler, and his manner resembled that of an uncivil pontiff.

"The Countess has just left for an appointment, sir, and won't return home for a good hour or more."

Lyon held his grin. "I don't want to see the Countess," he told the butler.

"Then who exactly did you want to see?" the servant asked in a haughty tone of voice.

Lyon let his exasperation show. The old man guarded the entrance like a gargoyle. Lyon brushed past him before he could issue a protest, calling over his shoulder, "I wish to speak to Princess Christina." He deliberately used his most intimidating voice to gain compliance. "Now."

A sudden grin transformed the servant's dour expression into wrinkles of delight. "The Countess ain't going to like it," he announced as he shuffled ahead of Lyon to the double doors on the left of the entryway. "She'll be displeased, she will."

"You don't seem too disturbed by that eventuality," Lyon remarked dryly when the butler let out a loud cackle.

"I won't be telling her about your visit, sir," the butler said. He drew himself up and turned toward the staircase. "You can wait in there," he said with a wave of his hand. "I'll go and inform the Princess of your wish to speak to her."

"Perhaps it would be better if you don't tell your mistress who her caller is," Lyon instructed, thinking Christina just might decide against seeing him. "I'd like to surprise her," he added.

"Since you ain't given me your name, it'll be easy enough to comply with your wishes."

It seemed to Lyon that it took an eternity for the butler to make it across the hallway. He leaned against the door frame and watched the old man. A sudden question made him call out, "If you don't know who I am, how can you be so sure the Countess will be displeased?"

The butler let out another crackle of laughter that sounded very like a long nail being dragged across a chalkboard. The effort nearly toppled him to the floor. He grabbed hold of the bannister before giving Lyon an answer. "It doesn't matter who you be, sir. The Countess don't like anyone. Nothing ever makes the old bat happy." The butler continued up the stairs in his slow, sluggish stride.

Lyon would have sworn it took the old man ten minutes to gain three steps.

"I take it the Countess wasn't the one who employed you," Lyon remarked.

"No, sir," the servant answered between wheezes. "It was Princess Christina who found me in the gutter, so to speak. She picked me up, dusted me off, and fixed me up real nice in new clothes. I was a butler many years ago, afore hard times caught me." The old man took a deep breath, then added, "The Princess don't like me calling her aunt an old bat, though. Says it ain't dignified."

"It might not be dignified, my good man, but old bat really does describe the Countess rather well."

The butler nodded, then grabbed hold of the bannister again. He stayed in that position a long moment. Lyon thought the man was trying to catch his breath. He was wrong in that conclusion, however. The butler finally let go of the railing, then cupped his hands to the sides of his mouth and literally bellowed his announcement up the stairwell. "You got yourself a visitor, Princess. I put him in the drawing room."

Lyon couldn't believe what he'd just witnessed. When the servant repeated the scream, he started laughing.

The butler turned back to explain to Lyon. "She don't want me overdoing," he said. "Got to save me strength for the old bat's orders."

Lyon nodded. The butler shouted to his mistress again.

Christina suddenly appeared at the top of the steps,

drawing Lyon's full attention. He wasn't ever going to get used to looking at her, he decided. She kept getting prettier. Her hair wasn't pinned atop her head today. Glorious. It was the only word that came to mind, for the thick, silvery mass of curls framing the angelic face defied any other description.

When she started down the steps, Lyon saw that the length of hair ended against the swell of her slender hips.

She was dressed in a pale pink gown. The scoop neckline showed only a hint of the swell of her bosom. There was something a little unusual about the modest ensemble, but Lyon was too distracted watching her smile at her butler to decide what seemed out of place to him.

She hadn't seen him yet. "Thank you, Elbert. Now go and sit down. The Countess will be home soon, and you'll have to be on your feet again."

"You're too good to me," Elbert whispered.

"It is good of you to think so," she said before continuing on down the steps. She spotted Lyon leaning against the entrance to the salon.

He knew she was surprised. Her eyes widened. "Oh, dear, the Countess is going to be—"

"Displeased," Lyon finished her comment with an exasperated sigh.

Elbert had obviously heard the remark. His scratchy laughter followed Christina into the drawing room. Lyon followed her, pausing long enough to shut the door behind him. "Believe it or not, Christina, I'm considered pleasing enough by the rest of the town. Why your aunt takes exception to me is beyond my comprehension."

Christina smiled over the irritation she'd caught in Lyon's voice. He sounded like a little boy in need of assurance. She sat down in the center of the gold brocade settee so Lyon couldn't sit beside her, motioned for him to take the chair adjacent to her, and then said, "Of course you're pleasing. Do not let my aunt's opinions upset you. Though it is rude of me to admit, your feelings are surely at stake, and so I will confess that my aunt doesn't really like too many people."

"You mistake my comment," Lyon drawled out. "I don't give a damn what your aunt thinks of me. I just find it puzzling that I . . ."

She was giving him a wary look, and he paused in his reply to change the topic. "Are you unhappy I called?" he asked, frowning over his own question.

Christina shook her head. "Good day to you," she suddenly blurted, trying to remember her manners. It was a problem for her, of course, because Lyon was looking wonderfully handsome again. He was dressed in buckskin riding pants that were the color of a young deer. The material clung to his powerful thighs. His shirt was white, probably made of silk, Christina thought, and partially covered by a forest-in-autumn-colored brown jacket that nicely matched the color of his shiny Hessian boots.

She realized she was staring at him, yet decided to excuse her ill conduct because he was looking at her with much the same intensity.

"I like looking at you."

"I like looking at you, too," Lyon answered with a chuckle.

Christina folded her hands in her lap. "Was there a specific reason for your sporadic visitation?" she asked.

"Sporadic? I don't understand . . ."

"Spontaneous," Christina said hastily.

"I see."

"Well, sir? Was there a specific reason?"

"I don't remember," Lyon answered, grinning at her.

She gave him a hesitant smile back. "Would you care for refreshment?"

"No, thank you," Lyon answered.

"Well, then, kindly explain what it is you don't remember," she instructed.

She gave him an expectant look, as if what she'd just requested was the most logical thing in the world. "How can I explain what it is I don't remember?" he asked. "You're back to making little sense again, aren't you?"

His smile could melt snow. Christina was having difficulty sitting still. All she wanted to think about was the way Lyon had kissed her, and all she wanted to do was find a way to get him to kiss her again.

It was, of course, an unladylike thought. "The weather has turned warm, hasn't it? Some people say it's the warmest autumn in many years," she added, staring intently down at her hands.

Lyon smiled over her obvious nervousness. He slowly stretched out his long legs, settling in for a confrontation. It was going to be easy work finding out his answers if Christina remained this ill at ease.

The tips of Lyon's boots touched the hem of her gown. She immediately scooted back against the settee, glanced down at the floor, and let out a small gasp. "Would you care for refreshments?" she asked in a surprisingly loud voice, jerking her gaze back to him. She wiggled to the edge of the settee again.

She was as skittish as an abandoned kitten. "You've already asked me that question," Lyon reminded her. "No, I don't care for refreshments. Do I make you uncomfortable?" he added, grinning enough to let her know he'd be happy if he did.

"Why would you think that?" Christina asked.

"You're sitting on the edge of the cushion, looking ready to run at any second, my sweet."

"My name is Christina, not sweet," she said. "And of course I'm uncomfortable. You'd make a buffalo nervous."

"A buffalo?"

"You'd make anyone nervous when you frown," Christina explained with a dainty shrug.

"Good."

"Good? Why, Lyon, you do say the oddest things."

"I say . . ." Lyon shouted with laughter. "Christina, you haven't made any sense since the moment I met you. Every time I see you I promise myself I'll get a normal conversation out of you, and then—"

"Lyon, you're being fanciful," Christina interrupted. "This is only the second—no, the third time I've seen you, if you count two times in one evening—"

"You're doing it again," Lyon said.

"Doing what?"

"Trying to push me off center."

"I couldn't push you anywhere. You're too big. I know my strengths, Lyon."

"Do you take everything in literal meaning?"

"I don't know. Do I?"

"Yes."

"Perhaps you're the one who has trouble making sense. Yes," Christina added with a quick nod. "You see, Lyon, you don't ask logical questions."

She laughed when he glared. "Why are you here?" she asked again.

She was back to staring at her hands again. A faint blush covered her cheeks. She was suddenly embarrassed about something.

He didn't have any idea what or why. That didn't surprise him, though. The unusual was becoming commonplace where Christina was concerned. Lyon thought he was ready for just about anything now. He was confident he'd have her game found out before the end of their visit.

"I really do know why you came to see me," Christina whispered timidly.

"Oh?" Lyon asked. "What is that reason?"

"You like being with me," she answered, daring a quick look up to see his reaction. When he didn't seem irritated by her honesty, she warmed to her topic.

"Lyon? Do you believe in destiny?"

Oh, dear, he was looking confused again. Christina let out a long sigh. "Well, you do admit you like being with me, don't you?" she coached.

"Yes, but God only knows why," Lyon confessed. He leaned forward and rested his elbows on his knees.

"Yes, the Great Spirit does know why."

"Great Spirit?" Lyon shook his head. "Lord, I'm starting to sound like an echo. All right, I'll ask. Who is this Great Spirit?"

"God, of course. Different cultures have their own names for the All Powerful, Lyon. Surely you know that. You aren't a heathen, are you?" She sounded quite appalled at that possibility.

"No, I'm not a heathen."

"Well, you needn't get irritated with me. I only asked."

He stared at her a long, silent minute. Then he stood up. Before Christina knew what he was going to do, he'd pulled her up into his arms. He hugged her to him and rested his chin against the top of her head. "I'm either going to strangle you or kiss you," he announced. "The choice is yours."

Christina sighed. "I would prefer that you kiss me. But first, please answer my question, Lyon. It's important to me."

"What question?"

"I asked you if you believed in destiny," she said. She pulled away from him and looked up at his face. "You really do have trouble holding a thought, don't you?"

She had the gall to sound disgruntled. "I don't have any trouble holding a thought," he muttered.

Christina didn't look like she believed him. She was a witch, trying to cast her magical spell on him. Lyon felt as besotted as a silly, worthless fop and as puny as an infant when her gaze was directed on him so enchantingly.

"Well?"

"Well what?" Lyon asked. He shook his head over his ridiculous reaction to the nymph glaring up at him. A lock of hair fell forward, concealing a part of his scar. Christina quit trying to pull away from him and reached up to smooth the lock back in place. The gentle touch jarred him back to her question.

"No, I don't believe in destiny."

"That's a pity."

She acted as though he'd just confessed a grave, unforgivable sin. "All right," he announced. "I know better than to ask, but God help me, I'm going to anyway. Why is it a pity?"

"Dare you laugh at me?" she asked when she saw his smile.

"Never," he lied.

"Well, I guess it really doesn't matter."

"That I laugh at you?"

"No, it doesn't matter if you believe in destiny," Christina answered.

"Why doesn't it matter?"

"Because what will happen will happen whether you believe or not. See how simple it is?"

"Ah," Lyon said, drawing the sound out. "You're a philosopher, I see."

She stiffened in his arms and glared at him again. The change in her mood happened so swiftly that Lyon was thrown off center. "Did I just say something to upset you?" he asked.

"I'm not a flirt. How can you so easily slander me? Why, I've been honest with you all during this conversation. I came right out and said I liked looking at you, and that I'd like you to kiss me. A philosopher, indeed."

The woman was making him daft. "Christina, a philosopher is a man who devotes his mind to the study of various beliefs. It was not slander for me to call you such."

"Spell this word, please," she said, looking extremely suspicious.

Lyon did as she requested. "Oh, I see now," she said. "I believe I've confused philanderer with this man who studies. Yes, that's what I've done. Don't look so confused, Lyon. It was an easy mistake to make."

"Easy?" He told himself not to ask. Curiosity won out again. "Why is it easy?"

"Because the words are close in spelling," she answered.

She sounded as though she was instructing a simple-minded child. He took immediate exception to her manner. "That is without a doubt the most illogical explanation I've ever heard. Unless of course . . . you've only just learned to speak English, haven't you, Christina?"

Because he seemed so pleased by his conclusion, Christina really didn't have the heart to tell him no, she hadn't just learned English. She'd been speaking the difficult language for several years now.

"Yes, Lyon," she lied. "I speak many languages and sometimes confuse my words. I'm not at all a bluenose, though. And I only seem to forget the laws when I'm with you. I do prefer to speak French. It's a much easier language, you see."

It all fell into place in Lyon's head. He'd solved the puzzle. "No wonder I had difficulty understanding you, Christina. It's because you've just learned our language, isn't that so?"

He was so happy he'd reasoned it all out, he'd just repeated his statement.

Christina shook her head. "I don't think so, Lyon. No one else seems to have the least bit of trouble understanding me. Have you been speaking English long?"

He hugged her again and laughed over the outrageous way she'd just turned the tables on him. In the corner of his mind was the thought that he could be content standing in the center of her salon holding her for the rest of the morning.

"Lyon? Would it make you unhappy if I really was a bluestocking? Aunt says it's not at all fashionable to even admit to reading. For that reason I must also pretend to be uninformed."

"Must also pretend?" Lyon asked, homing in on that odd remark.

"I really do like to read," Christina confessed, ignoring his question. "My favorite is the story of your King Arthur. Have you read it, by chance?"

"Yes, love, I have. Sir Thomas Mallory wrote it," Lyon said. "Now I know where you get your fantasies. Knights, warriors—both are the same. You have a very romantic nature, Christina."

"I do?" Christina asked, smiling. "That's good to know," she added when Lyon nodded. "Being romantic is a nice quality for a gentle lady to have, isn't it, Lyon?"

"Yes, it is," he drawled.

"Of course, we mustn't let Aunt Patricia know of this inclination, for it would surely—"

"Let me guess," Lyon interrupted. "It would displease her, right?"

"Yes, I fear it would. You'd better go home now. When you remember what it was you wanted to speak to me about, you may call again."

Lyon wasn't going anywhere. He told himself he couldn't take much more of her conversation, though. He decided to kiss her just to gain a moment's peace. Then he'd have her submissive enough to answer a few pertinent questions, providing of course that he could remember what those questions were. He'd already gained quite a bit of information about her. Christina had obviously been raised in France, or in a French-speaking neighborhood. Now he wanted to find out why she guarded that simple truth so ferociously. Was she ashamed, embarrassed? Perhaps the war was the reason for her reticence.

Lyon caressed her back to distract her from dismissing him again. Then he leaned down and tenderly nuzzled her lips while his hands continued to stroke her, gentle her. Christina moved into his embrace again. Her hands slowly found their way up around his neck.

She obviously liked the distraction. When Lyon finally quit teasing her and claimed her mouth completely, she was leaning up on her tiptoes. Her fingers threaded through his hair, sending a shudder through him. Lyon lifted her off the floor, bringing her mouth level with his own.

It was a strange sensation to be held in such a way, though not nearly as strange as the way Lyon was affecting her senses. His scent drove her wild. It was so masculine, so earthy. Desire swept through her in waves of heat when Lyon's tongue slid inside her mouth to deepen the intimacy.

It didn't take Christina any time at all to become as bold as Lyon was. Her tongue mated with his, timidly at first, and then with growing ardor. She knew he liked her boldness, for his mouth slanted almost savagely over hers and she could hear his groan of pleasure.

Christina was the most responsive woman Lyon had ever encountered. Her wild enthusiasm stunned him. He was a man conditioned to the game of innocence most women played. Christina, however, was refreshingly honest with her desire. She aroused him quickly, too. Lyon was actually shaking when he dragged his mouth away. His breath was choppy, uneven.

She didn't want to let go of him. Christina wrapped her arms around his waist and gave him a suprisingly strong hug. "You do like kissing me, don't you, Lyon?"

How could she dare to sound timid now, after the way she'd just kissed him? Hell, her tongue had been wilder than his. "You know damn well I like kissing you," he growled against her ear. "Is this part of the charade, Christina? You needn't be coy with me. I honestly don't care how many men you've taken to your bed. I still want you."

Christina slowly lifted her gaze to stare into his eyes. She could see the passion there, the possessiveness. Her throat was suddenly so constricted she could barely speak. Lyon was being just as forceful as a warrior.

God help her, she could easily fall in love with the Englishman.

Lyon reacted to the fear in her eyes. He assumed she was frightened because he'd guessed the truth. He captured a handful of her hair, twisted it around his fist, and then pulled her back up against his chest until her breasts were flattened against him. Then he gently forced her head further back. He leaned down, and when his mouth was just a breath away he said, "It doesn't matter to me. I give you this promise, Christina. When you're in my bed, you won't be thinking about anyone but me."

He kissed her again, sealing his vow. The kiss was unashamedly erotic. Ravenous. Entirely too short-lived. Just when she began to respond, Lyon pulled away.

His gaze immediately captured her full attention. "All I've been able to think about is how good we're going to be together. You've thought about it, too, haven't you, Christina?" Lyon asked, his voice husky with arousal.

He was already prepared for her denial. He was expecting the ordinary. That was his mistake, he realized, and certainly the reason he was so stunned when she answered him. "Oh, yes, I have thought about mating with you. It would be wonderful, wouldn't it?"

Before he could reply, Christina moved out of his arms.

She slowly walked across the room. Her stride was every bit as sassy as the smile she gave him over her shoulder when she tossed her hair behind her. When she'd opened the doors to the foyer, she turned back to him. "You have to go home now, Lyon. Good day."

It was happening again. Damn if she wasn't dismissing him. "Christina," Lyon growled, "come back here. I'm not finished with you yet. I want to ask you something."

"Ask me what?" Christina responded, edging out of the room.

"Quit looking so suspicious," Lyon muttered. He folded his arms across his chest and frowned at her. "First I would like to ask you if you'd like to go to the opera next—"

Christina stopped him by shaking her head. "The Countess would forbid your escort."

She had the audacity to smile over her denial. Lyon sighed in reaction.

"You're like a chameleon, do you know that? One second you're frowning and the next you're smiling. Do you think you'll ever make sense to me?" Lyon asked.

"I believe you've just insulted me."

"I have not insulted you," Lyon muttered, ignoring the amusement he heard in her voice. Lord, she was giving him such an innocent look now. It was enough to set his teeth grinding. "You're deliberately trying to make me daft, aren't you?"

"If you think calling me a lizard will win my affections, you're sadly mistaken."

He ignored that comment. "Will you go riding with me in the park tomorrow?"

"Oh, I don't ride."

"You don't?" he asked. "Have you never learned? I'd be happy to offer you instruction, Christina. With a gentle mount . . . *now* what have I said? You dare to laugh?"

Christina struggled to contain her amusement. "Oh, I'm not laughing at you," she lied. "I just don't like to ride."

"Why is that?" Lyon asked.

"The saddle is too much of a distraction," Christina confessed. She turned and hurried across the foyer. Lyon rushed after her, but Christina was already halfway up the steps before he'd reached the bannister.

"The saddle is a distraction?" he called after her, certain he hadn't heard her correctly.

"Yes, Lyon."

God's truth, he didn't have an easy argument for that ridiculous statement.

He gave up. Christina had just won this battle.

The war, however, was still to be decided.

Lyon stood there, shaking his head. He decided to be content watching the gentle sway of her hips, and it wasn't until she was out of sight that he suddenly realized what it was that had bothered him when he first saw her.

Princess Christina was barefoot.

The Countess Patricia was in high spirits when she returned home from her appointment. Calling upon a possible suitor for her niece had been an improper undertaking, yes, but the outcome had been so satisfying, the Countess snickered away any worry of being found out.

Emmett Splickler was everything the Countess had hoped he'd be. She'd prayed Emmett had inherited his father's nasty disposition. Patricia hadn't been disappointed. Emmett was a spineless halfwit, pint-sized in stature and greed. Very like his father, Emmett's crotch controlled his mind. His lust to bed Christina was soon obvious. Why, the man positively drooled when the Countess explained the reason for her visit. From the moment she'd mentioned marriage to Christina, the stupid man became jelly in her hands. He agreed to sign over anything and everything in order to get his prize.

The Countess knew Christina wasn't going to take to Emmett. The man was too much of a weakling. To placate her niece, Patricia had made a list of possible candidates. She'd even put the odious Marquess of Lyonwood at the top of the lines. It was all a farce, of course, but the Countess wanted Christina docile and unsuspecting for what was to come.

The Countess wasn't about to leave anything to chance.

Under no circumstances would she allow her niece to wed someone as honorable as Lyon.

The reason was very simple. Patricia didn't want just a substantial portion of her father's estate. She meant to have it all.

The plan she laid out for Splickler was shameful, even by a serpent's measure. Emmett had blanched when she calmly told him he'd have to kidnap her niece, haul her off to Gretna Green, and force her to marry him there. He could or could not rape the girl before or after the marriage certificate was signed. It made no matter to the Countess.

Emmett was more frightened of being found out than she was. When she told him to include two or three other men to help restrain Christina, the stupid man quit his complaining and grasped the plan wholeheartedly. She'd noticed the bulge grow between his legs, knew his mind had returned to the picture of bedding her niece, assumed then he'd be desperate enough to do what was required.

The worries exhausted the Countess. There was always the remote possibility that Emmett's cowardice was greater than his lust to bed Christina. The plan could fail if there was any interference.

For that reason, Patricia knew she was going to have to get rid of Christina's filthy Indian family. If her niece didn't marry Emmett, and she ended up with someone as strong-willed as Lyon, the union couldn't possibly last long. Christina's upbringing was bound to come out sooner or later. She wouldn't be able to hide her savage instincts forever. And what normal husband would put up with her disgusting ideas about love and honor? He'd be horrified by her true nature, of course. Though it wouldn't be possible for him to set her aside, for divorce was an unheard-of undertaking, he certainly would turn his back on her and turn to another woman for his needs.

Such rejection might well send Christina scurrying back to the savages who'd raised her. The stupid chit still insisted on returning home. The Countess couldn't let that happen. Christina had become her means of getting back into the ton. Even those who remembered her past indiscretions were so taken with Christina that they forced themselves to include the Countess again.

Last of all her worries was Edward. Christina's father wasn't going to take it kindly that she'd outwitted him. As goodnatured as she remembered him to be, Edward would probably still try to get his hands on a share of the fortune. Christina would certainly be able to control her father, the Countess believed.

Oh, yes, it was imperative that the little bitch remain in England until the Countess was finished with her. Imperative indeed.

Chapter Six

Edward kept his private quarters in a separate building adjacent to the main wing of the palace. I decided not to wait to tell him what his men were doing. You see, child, I couldn't believe my husband was responsible. I wanted to place the blame on his officers.

When I entered Edward's office by the side door, I was too stunned by what I saw to make my presence known. My husband was with his lover. They'd shed their clothes and were cavorting like animals on the floor. His mistress's name was Nicolle. She rode Edward like a stallion. My husband was shouting crude words of encouragement, his eyes tightly closed in ecstasy.

The woman must have sensed my presence. She suddenly turned her head to look at me. I was sure she'd cry out my presence to Edward. She didn't. No, Nicolle continued her obscene gyrations, but she was smiling at me all the while. I thought it was a smile of victory.

I don't remember how long I stood there. When I returned to my own rooms, I began to plan my escape.

Journal entry
August 20, 1795

Lyon, whatever is the matter with you? Why, you actually smiled at Matthews. Didn't I hear you ask after his mother, too? You aren't feeling well, are you?"

The questions were issued by Lyon's sister, Lady Diana, who was now chasing her brother up the stairs to the bedrooms.

Lyon paused to turn back to Diana. "You aren't happy when I'm frowning, and now you seem upset because I'm smiling. Make up your mind on the matter of my disposition and I shall try to accommodate you."

Diana's eyes widened over the teasing tone in her brother's voice. "You are sick, aren't you? Is your knee paining you again? Don't look at me as though I've grown another head. It isn't at all usual for you to smile, especially when you come to visit Mama. I know how tiring she can be. Remember, brother, I live with her. You only have to visit her once a week. I know Mama can't help the way she is, but there are times I wish you'd let me move into your townhouse. Is that shameful of me to admit?"

"Being honest with your brother is not shameful. You've had a time of it since James died, haven't you?"

The sympathy in Lyon's voice made Diana's eyes fill with tears. Lyon hid his exasperation. His sister was such an emotional whirlwind when it came to matters of family. Lyon was quite the opposite. It was difficult for him to show outward affection. He briefly considered putting his arm around his sister's shoulders to offer her sympathy, then pushed the awkward notion aside. She'd probably be so astonished by the gesture she'd break down into full-blown weeping.

Lyon wasn't up to tears today. It was quite enough he was going to endure another god-awful visit with his mother.

"I really thought Mama was going to get better when you made her servants open her townhouse for my season, Lyon, but she hasn't left her room since the day we arrived in London."

He merely nodded, then continued toward his destination. "Mama isn't the least bit better," Diana whispered. She trailed behind her brother's shadow. "I try to talk to her about the parties I've attended. She doesn't listen, though. She only wants to talk about James."

"Go back downstairs and wait for me, Diana. There's something I wish to discuss with you. And quit looking so worried," he added with a wink. "I promise I won't upset our mother. I'll be on my best behavior."

"You will?" Diana's voice squeaked. "You aren't feeling well, are you?"

Lyon started laughing. "God, have I really been such an ogre?"

Before Diana could think of a tactful answer that wouldn't be an outright lie, Lyon opened the door to his mother's quarters. He used the heel of his boot to close the door, then proceeded across the dark, stuffy room.

The Marchioness was reclining on top of her black satin covers. She was, as usual, dressed in black, from the silk cap covering her gray hair to the cotton stockings covering her feet. Lyon wouldn't have been able to find her if it weren't for her pasty white complexion glaring out from the shroud of black.

It was a fact that the Marchioness mourned with true dedication. Lyon thought she took to the task with as much intensity as a spoiled child took to tantrums. God only knew the woman had done it long enough to have become a master.

It was enough to make a dead man sit up and take notice. James had been gone for over three years now, but his mother continued to act as though the freakish accident had just taken place the day before.

"Good afternoon, Mother." Lyon gave his standard greeting, then sat down in the chair adjacent to the bed.

"Good afternoon, Lyon."

The visit was now over. They wouldn't speak again until Lyon took his leave. The reason was simple. Lyon refused to talk about James, and his mother refused to talk about any other topic. The silence would be maintained during the half hour Lyon stayed. To pass the time, he struck light to the candles and read *The Morning Herald.*

The ritual never varied.

He was usually in a foul mood when the ordeal was over. Today, however, he wasn't too irritated by his mother's shameful behavior.

Diana was waiting in the foyer. When she saw the smile was still on her brother's face, her worry about his health intensified. Why, he was acting so strangely!

Her mind leapt from one horrid conclusion to another. "You're going to send Mama and me back to the country, aren't you, Lyon? Oh, please, do reconsider," Diana wailed. "I know Uncle Milton has been a disappointment, but he can't help being bedridden with his liver again. And I do so want to go to Creston's ball."

"Diana, I shall be honored to take you to Creston's bash. And I never considered sending you home, sweet. You've had your presentation, and you'll certainly have the rest of the season. Have I ever gone back on my word?"

"Well . . . no," Diana admitted. "But you've never smiled this much either. Oh, I don't know what to think. You're always in a terrible mood after you've seen Mama. Was she more agreeable today, Lyon?"

"No," Lyon said. "And that's what I wanted to discuss with you, Diana. You need someone here to show you the way to go around. Since Milton isn't able and his wife won't go anywhere without him, I've decided to send for Aunt Harriett. Does that meet with your—"

"Oh, yes, Lyon," Diana interrupted. She clasped her hands together. "You know how much I love Father's sister. She has such a wonderful sense of humor. Will she agree, Lyon?"

"Of course," Lyon answered. "I'll send for her immediately. Now then, I'd like a favor."

"Anything, Lyon. I'll—"

"Send a note to Princess Christina inviting her here for tea. Make it for the day after tomorrow."

Diana broke into giggles. "Now I understand your strange behavior. You're smitten with the Princess, aren't you?"

"Smitten? What a stupid word," Lyon answered. His voice sounded with irritation. "No, I'm not smitten."

"I shall be pleased to invite the Princess. I can't help but wonder why you don't just send a note requesting an audience, though."

"Christina's aunt doesn't find me suitable," Lyon announced.

"The Marquess of Lyonwood isn't suitable?" Diana looked horrified. "Lyon, you have more titles than most men in England. You can't be serious."

"By the way, don't tell Christina I'll be here. Let her think it will be just the two of you."

"What if she requests that I come to her home instead?"

"She won't," Lyon advised.

"You seem very certain."

"I don't think she has enough money to entertain," Lyon said. "Keep this a secret, Diana, but I believe the Princess is in dire financial straits. The townhouse is a bit shabby—so are the furnishings—and I've heard the Countess had denied everyone who has requested entrance."

"Oh, the poor dear," Diana announced, shaking her head. "But why don't you want her to know you'll be here?"

"Never mind."

"I see," Diana said.

Lyon could tell from her expression she didn't see at all.

"I do like the Princess," Diana gushed when Lyon glared at her.

"You didn't come away confused?"

"I don't understand," Diana said. "Whatever do you mean?"

"When you spoke to her," Lyon explained. "Did she make sense with her answers?"

"Well, of course she made sense."

Lyon hid his exasperation. It had been a foolish question to put to someone as scatterbrained as his little sister. Diana's disposition had always been as flighty as the wind. He loved her, yet knew he'd go to his grave without having any understanding of what went on inside her mind. "I imagine you two will become fast friends," Lyon predicted.

"Would that upset you?"

"Of course not," Lyon answered. He gave Diana a curt nod, then started out the door.

"Well, why are you frowning again?" Diana called after him.

Lyon didn't bother to answer his sister. He mounted his black steed and went riding in the countryside. The brisk exercise was just what he needed to clear his mind. He was usually able to dispatch all unnecessary information and target in on the pertinent facts. Once he'd thrown out the insignificant, he was certain he'd be able to figure out his attraction to the most unusual woman in all of England. He was going to use cold reason to come to terms with his unreasonable affliction.

And it was an affliction, Lyon decided. To let Christina affect his every thought, his every action, was simply unacceptable. Confusing, too.

As confusing as being told he made her as nervous as a buffalo.

And where in God's name had she seen buffaloes?

The Earl of Rhone paced the carpet in front of his desk. His library was in shambles, but Rhone wouldn't let any of the servants inside to clean. Since being wounded, he'd been in too much discomfort to think about such mundane matters as household chores.

The injury was healing. Rhone had poured hot water over the opening, then wrapped his wrist in clean white gauze. Even though he wore an oversized jacket from his father's closet so that he could conceal the bandage, he was determined to stay hidden inside his townhouse until the wound was completely healed. He wasn't about to take any chances of being found out. There was too much work still to be done.

Rhone's primary concern was Princess Christina. He thought she might have recognized him. The way she'd stared at him and the funny, surprised look on her face did suggest she had known who was behind the mask.

Did Lyon know? Rhone mulled over that worry a long

while, then concluded his friend had been too occupied with protecting the little Princess to take a good look at him.

And just who in God's name had thrown the knife at him? Why, he'd been so surprised, he'd dropped his pistol. Whoever it was had a lousy aim, Rhone decided, and he'd thank God for that small blessing. Damn, he could have been killed.

He was going to have to be more careful. Rhone had no intention of quitting his activity. There were four names on his list, and every one of them was going to be tormented. It was the least he could do to ease his father's humiliation.

A servant's hesitant knock on the door broke Rhone's pacing. "Yes?" he bellowed, letting his irritation carry through the door. He had specifically ordered his staff not to interrupt him.

"The Marquess of Lyonwood is here to see you, my lord."

Rhone rushed over to take his seat behind the desk. He rested his good arm on a stack of papers, hid his injured hand in his lap, then called out in a surly voice, "Send him in."

Lyon strolled into the room with a bottle of brandy tucked under his arm. He placed the gift on the desk, then sat down in a leather chair in front of Rhone. After casually propping his feet on the desktop, he said, "You look like hell."

Rhone shrugged. "You never were a diplomat," he remarked. "What's the brandy for?"

"Our wager," Lyon reminded him.

"Oh, yes. Princess Christina," Rhone grinned. "She never did answer any of your questions, did she?"

"It doesn't matter. I've already found out quite enough about her. She was raised somewhere in France, or thereabouts," he stated. "There are a few little nagging inconsistences, but I'll have them worked out in short time."

"Why the interest, Lyon?"

"I'm not sure anymore. In the beginning I thought it was just curiosity, but now—"

"In the beginning. Lyon, you sound as though you'd known the woman for months."

Lyon shrugged. He reached over to the sideboard, extracted two glasses, and poured each of them a drink. Lyon waited until Rhone was in the process of swallowing a hefty portion before asking his question. "How's the hand, Jack?"

Needless to say, Lyon was immensely satisfied with his friend's reaction. Rhone started choking and coughing and trying to effect a denial all at the same time. It was laughable. Damning, too, Lyon thought with a sigh.

He waited until his friend had regained some control before speaking again. "Why didn't you tell me you were in such financial trouble? Why didn't you come to me?"

"Financial trouble? I don't know what you're talking about," Rhone protested. It was a weak lie. "Hell," he muttered. "It's always been impossible to lie to you."

"Have you lost your mind? Do you have a passion to live in Newgate prison, Rhone? You know it's only a matter of time before you're found out."

"Lyon, let me explain," Rhone stammered. "My father has lost everything. I've used my own estates, put them up as promise against the rest of the notes, but . . ."

"You and your father are free of debt as of yesterday eve," Lyon said. "Get angry and then get over it, Rhone," Lyon demanded, his voice edged with steel. "I paid off the moneylenders. In your name, by the way."

"How dare you involve—" Rhone bellowed. His face was flushed a bright red.

"Someone sure as hell had to intervene," Lyon announced. "Your father means as much to me as he does to you, Rhone. God only knows the number of times he put himself in front of my father to protect me when I was young."

Rhone nodded. Some of the fight went out of him. "I'll pay you back, Lyon, just as soon—"

"You will not pay me back," Lyon roared. He was suddenly furious with his friend. He took a deep, settling breath before continuing. "Do you remember what I was like when Lettie died?" he asked.

Rhone was surprised by the change in topic. He slowly nodded. "I remember."

"You stood by me then, Rhone. You're the only one who

knows about James. Have I ever asked to pay you back for your friendship?"

"Of course not. I would have been insulted."

A long moment stretched between the two men. Then Rhone actually grinned. "May I at least tell my father that you—"

"No," Lyon interrupted, his voice soft. "I don't want him to realize I know what happened to him. Let him think his son is the only one who knows, that you came to his assistance."

"But Lyon, surely—"

"Let it rest, Rhone. Your father is a proud man. Don't take that away from him."

Rhone nodded again. "Tell me what you know about my father's problems."

"I recognized you at Baker's, of course," Lyon began, smiling over the start that statement gave his friend. "It was foolish of you to—"

"You weren't supposed to be there," Rhone muttered. "Why did you attend his party? You can't stand Baker any more than I can."

Lyon chuckled. "The most carefully laid plans," he drawled. "For all his good points, your father is still a little naive, isn't he, Rhone? Baker and his cohorts took advantage, of course. Baker would have been the one to set up the games. Let's see if I have this straight. He would have included Buckley, Stanton, and Wellingham in the farce, too. They're all bastards. Did I get all the names, Rhone?"

His friend was astonished. "How did you learn all this?"

"Do you honestly think I wouldn't know about their little club? Your father isn't the only one to fall victim to their scheme."

"Does everyone know?"

"No," Lyon answered. "There isn't a hint of a scandal about your father. I would have heard of it."

"You've been out of circulation, Lyon. How can you be so sure?"

Lyon gave Rhone a look of exasperation. "With my line of work, you can seriously ask me that question?"

Rhone grinned. "I thought you might have gotten a little rusty," he said. "Father is still hiding in his country home. He's so ashamed of his own gullibility he won't show his face. He'll be relieved to learn no one is the wiser."

"Yes, he can come out of hiding now. And you can give up this foolish plan of yours. You'll eventually get caught."

"You'd never turn me in." Rhone's voice was filled with conviction.

"No, I wouldn't," Lyon acknowledged. "How was it done, Rhone? Did Baker mark the cards?"

"Yes. They are all blatant cheats, which of course is all the more humiliating for my father. He's feeling duped."

"He *was* duped," Lyon said. "Will you give it up, Rhone?"

Rhone let out a harsh groan. "Damn it all, Lyon. I'm itching to get even."

Lyon took a drink of his brandy. "Ah," he drawled. "Now you've touched on my area of expertise. Perhaps, Rhone, a game of chance is what is needed."

Lyon grinned when Rhone finally caught his meaning. "You mean to give them a dose of their own medicine, to cheat the cheaters?"

"It would be easy enough to accomplish."

Rhone slapped his hand on the tabletop, then let out a groan. "I keep forgetting about this injury," he excused. "Count me in, Lyon. I'll leave the details to you. As you just admitted, you're better versed in trickery than I am."

Lyon laughed. "I'll take that as a compliment."

Another knock sounded at the door, interrupting their conversation. "Now what is it?" Rhone shouted.

"I'm sorry to disturb you, my lord, but Princess Christina is here to see you," the servant shouted back.

The announcement gave Rhone a start. Lyon didn't look too happy with the news either. He glared at Rhone. "Have you been after Christina, Rhone? Did you invite her here?"

"No," Rhone answered. "My charms must have impressed her after all, Lyon." He grinned when Lyon's scowl increased. "So it is as I guessed. You're more than mildly interested in our little Princess."

"She isn't our little Princess," Lyon snapped. "She belongs to me. Understood?"

Rhone nodded. "I was only jesting," he said with a sigh. "Send her in," he bellowed to his servant.

Lyon didn't move from his position. Christina hurried into the library as soon as the door was opened for her. She spotted Lyon immediately and came to an abrupt stop. "Oh, I didn't mean to interrupt your conference, sir. I shall come back later, Rhone."

Christina frowned at Lyon, turned, and started back out the door.

Lyon let out a long, controlled sigh. He carefully put his glass down on the desk, then stood up. Christina saw him out of the corner of her eye. She ignored Rhone's pleas for her to stay and continued to move toward the front door.

Lyon trapped her just as she reached for the handle. His hands settled on the door on either side of Christina's face. Her back touched his chest. Lyon smiled when he saw how rigid her shoulders became. "I really must insist you stay," he whispered against her ear.

A tremor of warmth shook Christina. She slowly edged around until she was facing Lyon. "And I really must insist upon leaving, sir," she whispered.

She pushed one hand against his chest, hoping to dislodge him.

He didn't budge. He gave her a rascal's grin, then leaned down and kissed her.

Rhone's deep chuckle interrupted his desire to continue.

Christina immediately blushed over the intimacy. Didn't the man realize he wasn't supposed to show affection in front of others? She guessed he didn't. Lyon winked at her before grabbing hold of her hand and dragging her back inside the library.

She was wearing a light blue gown. Lyon deliberately checked to see if she'd remembered to put her shoes on. He wasn't disappointed to see she had.

Rhone hurried back to his chair. He hid his bandaged arm in his lap.

Christina refused to sit down. She stood beside Lyon,

trying to ignore him altogether. He put his booted feet back up on the edge of Rhone's desk and reached for his glass. She gave him a disgruntled look. If the man was any more relaxed, he'd fall asleep.

It soon became awkward. Rhone was looking at her expectantly. Christina clutched the blue receptacle in her left hand and kept trying to pull her other hand out of Lyon's hold. He'd forgotten to let go of her.

"Was there something in particular you wished to speak to me about?" Rhone prodded gently. He tried to put Christina at ease. The poor woman looked terribly worried.

"I'd hoped to find you alone," Christina announced. She gave Lyon a meaningful look. "Were you about to take your leave, Lyon?"

"No."

His abrupt answer was given in such a cheerful voice, Christina smiled. "I would like to speak to Rhone in private, if you don't mind."

"Ah, sweet, but I do mind," Lyon drawled out. He increased his grip on her hand, then suddenly jerked her off balance.

She landed right where he wanted her. Christina immediately started to struggle out of his lap. Lyon circled her waist with one arm, anchoring her to him.

Rhone was amazed. He'd never seen Lyon act in such a spontaneous manner. To show such open possessiveness was certainly out of character. "Princess Christina? You may speak freely in front of Lyon," Rhone advised.

"I may?" Christina asked. "Then he knows?"

When Christina hesitated, Rhone announced, "Lyon is privy to all my secrets, my dear. Now what is it you wanted to say to me?"

"Well, I was wondering, sir, how you're feeling."

Rhone blinked several times. "Why, I'm feeling very well," he replied awkwardly. "That is all you wanted to ask me?"

The two of them were dancing around the real issue, to Lyon's way of thinking. "Rhone, Christina wants to know how your injury is doing. Isn't that right, Christina?"

"Oh, then you do know?" Christina asked, turning to look at Lyon.

"You know?" Rhone's voice cracked.

"She knows," Lyon confirmed, chuckling over the flabbergasted look on Rhone's face.

"Well, hell, who *doesn't* know?"

"You sound pathetic," Lyon told his friend.

"It was the color of your eyes, Rhone," Christina explained, giving him her attention again. "They're an unusual shade of green, and very easy to remember." She paused to give him a sympathetic look. "And you did look right at me. I really didn't mean to recognize you. It just happened," she ended with a delicate shrug.

"Are we putting all our cards on the table?" Rhone asked, leaning forward to give Christina an intent look.

"I don't understand," Christina said. "I don't have any cards with me."

"Christina takes everything you say in its literal sense, Rhone. It's a trait guaranteed to make you daft. Believe me, I know."

"That is most uncharitable of you, Lyon," Christina announced, glaring at him. "I don't know what you mean when you say I'm literal. Is it yet another insult I should take exception to, perchance?"

"Rhone is asking you if he may speak freely," Lyon told Christina. "Hell, I feel like an interpreter."

"Of course you may speak freely to me," Christina announced. "No one's holding a knife to your neck, Rhone. I've some medicine with me. I'd like to tend your injury, Rhone. You probably haven't had proper care."

"I couldn't very well call upon my physician, now could I?" Rhone said.

"Oh, no, you'd be found out," Christina said. She scooted off Lyon's lap and went to Rhone's side. Rhone didn't protest when she began to unwrap his badly fashioned bandage.

Both men watched as Christina opened a small jar of horrid-smelling salve. "My God, what's in there? Dead leaves?"

"Yes," Christina answered. "Among other things."

"I was jesting," Rhone said.

"I wasn't."

"The smell will keep me hidden," Rhone muttered. "What else is in there?" he asked, taking another sniff of the foul medicine.

"You don't want to know," Christina answered.

"It's best not to ask Christina questions, Rhone. The answers will only confuse you."

Rhone took Lyon's advice. He watched Christina pat a large amount of the brown-colored salve on the cut, then rewrap the arm. "You have a nice scent, Rhone. Of course, the salve will soon remove it."

"I have a nice scent?" Rhone looked as though he'd just been handed England's crown. He thought he should return her compliment. "You smell like flowers," he told her, then promptly laughed over saying such a thing. It was the truth, but certainly ungentlemanly of him to comment upon. "You're the one with the unusual eyes, Christina. They're the most wonderful color of blue."

"That's quite enough," Lyon interjected. "Christina, hurry up and finish your task."

"Why?" Christina asked.

"He doesn't want you standing so close to me," Rhone explained.

"Give it up, Rhone." Lyon's voice had turned hard. "You aren't going to pursue Christina, so you can save your charms for someone else."

"Lady Diana would like your charms very much, Rhone," Christina interjected. She smiled at the reaction her comment caused in both men. Rhone looked perplexed. Lyon looked appalled. "Lyon, you don't own me. It is therefore unreasonable of you to dictate to other gentlemen. If I wanted Rhone's attention, I would let him know it."

"Why do you suggest Lyon's sister would like my attention?" Rhone asked. He was highly curious about her strange remark.

Christina replaced the jar in her receptacle before answering. "You English are so narrow-minded in your thinking sometimes. It's obvious Lady Diana is taken with you, Rhone. You only have to look at her to see the adoration in her eyes. And if you count the way you look after her, why, you'd realize you were meant for each other."

"Oh, God." It was Lyon who groaned out the words.

Both Christina and Rhone ignored him. "How can you be so certain?" Rhone asked. "You only met her once, and you couldn't have spent more than fifteen minutes with her. No, I think you're imagining this infatuation. Diana's just a child, Christina."

"Believe what you will," Christina answered. "What will happen will happen."

"I beg your pardon?"

Rhone looked confused again. Lyon shook his head. It was good to know he wasn't the only one dimwitted around Christina. "Destiny, Rhone," Lyon interjected.

"I really must leave now. Aunt Patricia believes I'm resting in my room," she confessed. "You will have to share my confidence, Rhone. Or should I call you Jack now?"

"No."

"I was only jesting, sir. Do not be so distressed," Christina said.

Rhone sighed. He reached out to take hold of Christina's hand, thinking to keep her by his side while he thanked her properly for tending his injury.

Christina moved so quickly Rhone was left reaching for air. Before he could blink, she was standing next to Lyon's chair again.

Lyon was just as surprised. He was arrogantly pleased, too, for even though Christina probably wasn't aware of what she'd done, she had instinctively moved back to him. There was some kind of little victory in that choice, wasn't there?

"Christina, if you recognized me, why didn't you tell Baker and the others?" Rhone asked.

She took exception to his question. "They'll have to find out on their own," she said. "I would never break a confidence, Rhone."

"But I didn't ask you to keep this confidence," Rhone stammered.

"Don't try to understand her, Rhone. It will be your undoing," Lyon advised with a grin.

"Then please answer me this," Rhone asked. "Did you see who threw the knife at me?"

"No, Rhone. In truth, I was too frightened to look behind me. If Lyon hadn't been there to protect me, I think I would have swooned."

Lyon patted her hand. "The pistol wasn't loaded," Rhone protested. "Did you think I'd actually hurt someone?"

Lyon prayed for patience. "I cannot believe you set out to rob Baker with an empty pistol."

"Why would you use an empty weapon?" Christina asked.

"I wanted to scare them, not kill them," Rhone muttered. "Will you two quit looking at me like that? The plan did work, I might remind you."

"You just did remind us," Christina announced.

"Lyon, will you be able to find out who injured me?" Rhone asked.

"Eventually."

Christina frowned. Lyon sounded too certain. "Why does it matter?"

"Lyon likes a good puzzle," Rhone announced. "As I recall, Baker's balcony is a good fifty feet from the terrace below. Whoever it was had to be—"

"Twenty feet, Rhone," Lyon interjected. "And the balcony couldn't be scaled. The railing was too weak."

"Then whoever it was must have been hiding behind you . . . somewhere," Rhone said with a shrug. "No, that doesn't make sense. Well, thank God he had a lousy aim."

"Why do you say that?" Christina asked.

"Because he didn't kill me."

"Oh, I think his aim was quite on target," she announced. "If he'd wanted to kill you, I think he might have. Perhaps he meant to make you drop your weapon."

Christina suddenly realized she was sounding too sure of herself. Lyon was staring at her with a strange, intent expression on his face. "It was just a possibility I was giving you," she added quickly. "I could be wrong, of course. His aim could have been faulty."

"Why did you come over here to tend Rhone's injury?" Lyon asked.

"Yes, why did you?" Rhone asked also.

"Now I am insulted," Christina announced. "You were hurt, and I only thought to help you."

"That was your only motive?" Lyon asked.

"Well, there was another reason as well," Christina admitted. She walked over to the door before explaining. "Didn't you tell me you were Lyon's only friend?"

"I might have made that remark," Rhone admitted.

"You did," Christina said. "I never forget anything," she boasted. "And it seemed to me that Lyon is a man in need of friends. I shall continue to keep your secret, Rhone, and you must promise not to tell anyone I came to see you. The Countess would be upset."

"He doesn't suit either?" Lyon asked, sounding vastly amused.

"I don't suit?" Rhone asked. "Suit what?"

Christina ignored the question and started out the doorway.

"Christina."

Lyon's soft voice stopped her. "Yes, Lyon?"

"I didn't promise."

"You didn't?"

"No."

"Oh, but you'd never . . . you don't even like the Countess. You wouldn't bother to tell her . . ."

"I'm seeing you home, love."

"I'm not your love."

"Yes, you are."

"I really prefer to walk."

"Rhone, what do you think the Countess will say when I inform her that her niece is strolling around town, paying calls on—"

"You don't fight with an ounce of dignity, Lyon. It's a sorry trait."

"I've never fought fair."

Her sigh of defeat echoed throughout the library. "I shall wait for you in the hall, you despicable man." Christina slammed the door shut to emphasize her irritation.

"She isn't at all what she appears to be," Rhone remarked. "She called us English, Lyon, as if we were foreigners. Doesn't make sense, does it?"

"Nothing Christina says makes sense, unless you remember she wasn't raised here." He stood up, stretched to his full height, and started for the door. "Enjoy the brandy, Rhone, while I go back into battle."

"Battle? What are you talking about?"

"Not what, Rhone. Who. Christina, to be exact."

Rhone's laughter followed Lyon out the door. Christina was standing next to the front door. Her arms were folded across her chest. She wasn't trying to hide her irritation.

"Ready, Christina?"

"No. I hate carriages, Lyon. Please let me walk home. It's only a few short streets away from here."

"Of course you hate carriages," Lyon said. His voice was filled with amusement. "Now, why didn't I realize that sooner, I wonder?" he asked as he took hold of her elbow. He half led, half dragged Christina to his vehicle. Once they were seated across from each other, Lyon asked, "Are carriages as much a distraction as saddles, perchance?"

"Oh, no," Christina answered. "I don't like being confined like this. It's suffocating. You weren't going to tell the Countess I left without permission, were you, Lyon?"

"No," he admitted. "Are you afraid of the Countess, Christina?"

"I'm not afraid of her," Christina said. "It's just that she is my only family now, and I don't like to upset her."

"Were you born in France, Christina?" Lyon asked. He leaned forward to take hold of her hands.

His voice coached, his smile soothed. Christina wasn't fooled for a moment. She knew he thought to catch her off guard. "When your mind is set on finding something out, you really don't give up, do you, Lyon?"

"That's about right, my dear."

"You're shameful," Christina confessed. "Quit smiling. I've insulted you, haven't I?"

"Were you born in France?"

"Yes," she lied. "Now, are you satisfied? Will you quit your endless questions, please?"

"Why does it bother you to be questioned about your past?" Lyon asked.

"I merely try to protect my privacy," she answered.

"Did you live with your mother?"

He was like a dog after a meaty bone, Christina decided. And he wasn't going to let up. It was time to soothe his curiosity. "A very kind couple by the name of Summerton raised me. They were English but enjoyed traveling. I've been all over the world, Lyon. Mr. Summerton preferred to speak French, and I'm more comfortable with that language."

The tension slowly ebbed away from her shoulders. She could tell by Lyon's sympathetic expression that he believed her. "The Countess can be difficult, as you well know. She had a falling out with the Summertons and refuses to let me speak of them. She wants everyone to think I was raised by her, I suppose. Lying is very difficult for me," she added with a straight face. "Since Aunt Patricia won't let me tell the truth, and I'm not any good telling lies, I decided it would be best to say nothing at all about my past. There, are you satisfied?"

Lyon leaned back against the upholstery. He nodded, obviously satisfied with her confession. "How did you meet up with these Summertons?"

"They were dear friends of my mother," Christina said. She gave him another smile. "When I turned two years of age, my mother took ill. She gave me to the Summertons because she trusted them, you see. My mother didn't want her sister, the Countess, to become my guardian. And the Summertons weren't able to have children."

"Your mother was a shrewd woman," Lyon remarked. "The old bat would have ruined you, Christina."

"Oh, my, did Elbert call my aunt an old bat in front of

you? I really must have another firm talk with him. He seems to have taken an extreme dislike to her."

"Love, everyone dislikes your aunt."

"Are you finished with your questions now?" Christina asked.

"Where did you hear the sound of lions, Christina, and where did you see buffaloes?"

The man had the memory of a child given the promise of candy. He didn't forget anything. "I did spend a good deal of time in France, because of Mr. Summerton's work, but he was very devoted to his wife—and to me, for he did think of me as his daughter. And so he took both of us with him when he went on his trips. Lyon, I really don't want to answer any more of your questions."

"Just one more, Christina. Will you let me escort you to Creston's ball on Saturday? It will be very proper. Diana will be with us."

"You know my aunt won't allow it," Christina protested.

The carriage came to a halt in front of Christina's home. Lyon opened the door, dismounted, and turned to lift Christina to the ground. He held her a bit longer than necessary, but Christina didn't take exception. "Simply tell your aunt that arrangements have already been made. I'll call for you at nine."

"I do suppose it will be all right. Aunt Patricia need never know. She's going to the country to visit a sick friend. If I don't mention the ball, I really won't have to lie. It isn't quite the same if the Countess believes I mean to stay home, is it? Or is it still a lie by deliberate silence, I wonder."

Lyon smiled. "You really do have trouble telling a lie, don't you, sweet? It is a noble trait," he added.

Heaven help her, she really mustn't laugh. Lyon would certainly grow suspicious then. "Yes, it is difficult for me," she confessed.

"You don't know how it pleases me to find a woman with such high standards, Christina."

"Thank you, Lyon. May I put a question to you now?"

Elbert opened the door just then. Christina became

distracted. She smiled at the butler, then waved him inside. "I shall see the door closed, Elbert. Thank you."

Lyon patiently waited until Christina turned back to him. "Your question?" he gently prodded.

"Oh, yes," Christina said. "First of all, I would like to ask you if you will be attending Sir Hunt's party Thursday evening."

"Are you going?"

"Yes."

"Then I shall be there."

"There is one more question, please."

"Yes?" Lyon asked, smiling. Christina was acting terribly shy all of a sudden. A faint blush covered her cheeks, and she couldn't quite meet his gaze.

"Will you marry me, Lyon? For just a little while?"

"What?"

He really hadn't meant to shout, but the woman did say the damnedest things. He couldn't have heard her correctly. Marriage? For just a while? No, he had misunderstood. "What did you say?" he asked again, calming his voice.

"Will you marry me? Think about it, Lyon, and do let me know. Good day, sir."

The door closed before the Marquess of Lyonwood could summon a reaction.

Chapter Seven

It took over three weeks before Mylala was able to find a captain willing to take the risk of helping us escape. I don't know what I would have done without my loyal maid. She put her family and her friends in jeopardy to aid me. I listened to her advice, for she had been in my husband's household for several years and knew his ways.

I had to act as though nothing had changed. Yes, I played the loving wife, but every night I prayed for Edward's death. Mylala suggested that I not take any possessions with me. When the call came for me to go, I would simply walk away with only the clothes on my back.

Two nights before word came from the captain, I went to see Edward in his quarters. I entered by the side door again, very quietly, as a precaution against finding Nicolle with him again. Edward was alone. He was sitting at his desk, holding a large, sparkling sapphire in his hands. On the desk top were over twenty other gems. Edward was fondling them in much the same way he fondled Nicolle. I stood there, in the shadows, watching him. The madman actually spoke to the jewels. After another few minutes, he wrapped the gems in a cloth and put them back in a small black lacquered box.

There was a false panel built into the wall. Edward slid the box into the dark crevice.

I went back to my rooms and related what I'd seen to my maid. She told me she'd heard a rumor that the treasury was barren. We came to the conclusion that the revolution was closer to reality than we'd believed. My husband had converted the coins into jewels, for they would be much easier to carry with him when he left his country.

I vowed to steal the jewels. I wanted to hurt Edward in any way that I could. Mylala cautioned me against such a plan, but I was past caring. The jewels belonged to the people. I promised myself that one day I'd find a way to give the jewels back.

God, I was so noble, but so very, very naive. I really thought I would get away with it.

Journal entry
September 1, 1795

The early morning hours belonged to Christina. It was a peaceful, quiet time of day, for the Countess rarely made an appearance or a demand before noon. Christina's aunt preferred to take her morning meal of biscuits and tea in bed, and only broke that ritual when an important visitation couldn't be rescheduled.

Christina was usually dressed and finished with her duties before the full light of dawn warmed the city. She and her aunt shared a lady's maid between them, but Beatrice had quite enough to do filling the Countess's orders. For that reason, Christina took care of her clothes and her bedroom. In truth, she was happy with the arrangement. She didn't have to keep up a pretense when she was alone in her room. Since Beatrice rarely interrupted her, Christina didn't have to wrinkle the covers on her bed every morning to give the appearance she'd actually slept there.

Once she bolted the door against intruders, she could let

her defenses slide. Every night she carried her blanket across the room to sleep on the floor in front of the double windows.

She didn't have to be strong when she was alone. She could cry, just as long as she was quiet about it. It was a weakness to shed tears, yet since no one was there to witness her distress, Christina felt little shame.

The tiny garden hidden behind the kitchens was Christina's other private domain. She usually spent most of the morning hours there. She blocked out the noise of the city and the stench of discarded garbage, slipped off her shoes, and wiggled her toes in the rich brown dirt. When the droplets of dew had been snatched away by the sun, Christina would return to the erupting chaos inside the house.

The precious reunion with the sun helped her endure the rest of the day. She could usually worry through any perplexing problem in such a tranquil setting too. However, since meeting the Marquess of Lyonwood, Christina hadn't been able to concentrate on much of anything. Her every thought belonged to him.

She'd been attracted to him from the moment of their meeting. When Sir Reynolds had called him Lyon, she'd been nudged into awareness. Then she'd looked up into his eyes, and her heart had been captured. The vulnerability she'd seen there, in his dark gaze, had made her want to reach out to him.

He was a man in need of attention. Christina thought he might be just as lonely as she was. She didn't understand why she'd come away with that impression, however. Lyon was surrounded by his family, embraced by the ton, envied, and somewhat feared. Yes, the ton bowed to him because of his title and his wealth. They were superficial reasons, to Christina's way of viewing matters, but Lyon had been raised in such a fashion.

He was different, though. She'd noticed he didn't bend to any of their laws. No, Lyon seemed determined to make his own.

Christina knew it hadn't been proper to ask him to marry her. According to the laws, it was the man's place to offer for his woman, not the other way around. She'd given the matter considerable thought, then reached the decision that she'd simply have to break this one law in order to be wed before her father returned to England.

Still, her timing might not have been perfect. She knew she'd stunned him with her hastily blurted question. The astonished look on his face worried her. She couldn't make up her mind if he was getting ready to shout with laughter or explode with anger.

Once he'd gotten over his initial reaction, however, Christina was certain he'd say yes. Why, he'd already admitted how much he liked being with her, how much he liked touching her. Life in this strange country would be so much more bearable with Lyon by her side.

And it would only be for a little while . . . he wouldn't have to be saddled with her forever, as the Countess liked to say.

Besides, she told herself, he really wouldn't be given a choice, would he?

She was the lioness of the Dakota. Lyon simply had to marry her.

It was his destiny.

Thursday evening didn't arrive soon enough to suit the Marquess of Lyonwood. By the time he entered Sir Hunt's townhouse, he was fighting mad.

Lyon had alternated between absolute fury and total disappointment whenever he thought about Christina's outrageous proposal. Well, he sure as hell had her game now, didn't he? She was after marriage, all right—marriage and money, just like every other woman in the kingdom.

He was just as angry with himself. His instincts had certainly been sleeping. He should have known what she was up to from the very beginning. God's truth, he'd done exactly what he accused Rhone of doing—he'd fallen victim to a pretty face and a clever flirtation.

Lyon was disgusted enough to want to bellow. And he was

going to set Christina straight at the first opportunity. He wasn't about to get married again. Once had been enough. Oh, he meant to have Christina, but on his terms, and certainly without benefit of clergy to muck up the waters. All women changed once wedded. Experience had taught him that much.

It was unfortunate that the first person he ran into when he entered Hunt's salon was his sister, Diana. She spotted him immediately, picked up her skirts, and charged over to curtsy in front of him.

Hell, he was going to have to be civil.

"Lyon, thank you for asking Sir Reynolds to escort me. He is such a kind man. Aunt Harriett will be arriving Monday next, and you won't have to be bothered with the duty any longer. Do you like my new gown?" she asked, straightening the folds of her yellow skirt.

"You look very pretty," Lyon announced, barely giving her a glance.

There was such a crowd, Lyon was having difficulty finding Christina. Though he was much taller than the other guests, he still hadn't been able to spot the golden crown of curls he was looking for.

"Green is a nice color for me, isn't it, Lyon?"

"Yes."

Diana laughed, drawing Lyon's attention. "My gown is yellow, Lyon. I knew you weren't paying me the least notice."

"I'm in no mood for games, Diana. Go and circulate through the crush like a good girl."

"She isn't here, Lyon."

"She isn't?" Lyon asked, sounding distracted.

Diana's giggles increased. "Princess Christina hasn't arrived yet. I had the most wonderful visit with her yesterday."

"Where did you see her?" Lyon asked. His voice was a bit sharper than he intended.

Diana didn't take exception. "For tea. Mother didn't join us, of course. Neither did you, by the way. Did you actually forget you asked me to invite her, Lyon?"

Lyon shook his head. "I decided against intruding," he lied. He really had forgotten the appointment, but he placed the blame for his ill discipline on Christina's shoulders. Since receiving her proposal of marriage, he hadn't been able to think about anything else.

Diana gave her brother a puzzled look. "It isn't like you to forget anything," she announced. When he didn't comment on that fact, she said, "Well, I was happy to have the time alone with her. Princess Christina is a fascinating woman. Do you believe in destiny, Lyon?"

"Oh, God."

"You needn't groan," Diana chided.

"I do not believe in destiny."

"Now you're shouting. Lyon, everyone is giving us worried looks. Do force a smile. I believe in destiny."

"Of course you do."

"Now why would that displease you?" Diana asked. She continued on before her brother could form an answer. "The princess makes such refreshing observations about people. She never says anything unkind, either. She's such a delicate, dainty woman. Why, I feel very protective around her. She's so gentle, so—"

"Was the old bat with her?" Lyon interrupted impatiently. He wasn't in the mood to hear about Christina's qualities. No, he was still too angry with her.

"I beg your pardon?" Diana asked.

"The Countess," Lyon explained. "Did she join you?"

Diana tried not to laugh. "No, she wasn't with Christina. I made an unkind remark about her aunt, though of course I didn't call her an old bat, and my comment was quite by accident. Christina was very gracious when she told me it was impolite to speak of the elderly in such a fashion. I was humbled by her gentle rebuke, Lyon, and then found myself telling her all about Mama and how she still grieves for our James."

"Family matters shouldn't be discussed with outsiders," Lyon said. "I really would appreciate it if you'd—"

"She says it's all your fault about Mama being—"

"What?" Lyon asked.

"Please let me finish before you sanction me," Diana advised. "Christina said the strangest thing. Yes, she did."

"Of course she did," Lyon returned with a long sigh.

Lord, it was contagious. One afternoon with Princess Christina had turned Diana completely senseless.

"I didn't understand what she meant, but she did say—rather firmly, too—that it was all your fault, and that it was up to you to direct Mama into returning to her family. Those were her very words."

Diana could tell by Lyon's expression he was just as puzzled as she was. "I tell you, Lyon, it was as though she was repeating a rule from her memory. I didn't want her to think me unschooled, so I didn't question her further. But I didn't understand what she was telling me. Princess Christina acted like her advice made perfect sense. . . ."

"Nothing the woman says or does makes any sense," Lyon announced. "Diana, go back to Sir Reynolds's side. He'll introduce you around. I've still to speak to our host."

"Lady Cecille is here, Lyon," Diana whispered. "You can't miss her. She's dressed in bright, shameful red."

"Shameful red?" Lyon grinned over the absurd description.

"You aren't still involved with the woman, are you, Lyon? Princess Christina would surely be put off if she thought you were seeing a woman of such stained reputation."

"No, I'm not involved with Cecille," Lyon muttered. "And how did you find out—"

"I listen to the rumors, just like everyone else," Diana admitted with a blush. "I'll leave you to your grumpy mood, Lyon. You may lecture me later." She started to turn away from him, then paused. "Lyon? Is Rhone going to be here tonight?"

He caught the eagerness in her voice. "It shouldn't matter to you if Rhone shows up or not, Diana. He's too old for you."

"Old? Lyon, he's your age exactly, and you're only nine years my senior."

"Don't argue with me, Diana."

She dared to frown at her brother before giving in to his advice. When Diana finally left him alone, Lyon leaned against the bannister in the foyer, waiting for Christina.

His host found him and dragged him across the salon and into a heated debate about government issues. Lyon patiently listened, though he kept glancing toward the entrance.

Christina finally arrived. She walked into the salon, flanked by their hostess and the Countess, just as Lady Cecille touched Lyon's arm.

"Darling, it is wonderful to see you again."

Lyon felt like growling. He slowly turned around to acknowledge his former mistress.

What in God's name had he ever seen in the woman? The difference between Cecille and Christina was stunning. Lyon felt like taking a step back.

Cecille was a tall woman, somewhat stately, and terribly vulgar. She wore her dark brown hair piled high atop her head. Her cheeks were tinged with pink paint, as were her full, pouting lips.

Christina never pouted. She didn't pretend coyness either, Lyon decided. His disgust with Cecille was a sour taste in his mouth. Cecille was trying to be provocative now. She deliberately lowered her eyelashes to half mast. "I've sent you notes asking you to call, Lyon," she whispered as she increased her hold on his arm. "It's been such an unbearably long while since we shared a night together. I've missed you."

Lyon was thankful the men he was speaking to had walked away. He slowly removed Cecille's hand. "We've had this discussion, Cecille. It's over. Accept it and find someone else."

Cecille ignored the harshness in Lyon's voice. "I don't believe you, Lyon. It was good between us. You're only being stubborn."

Lyon dismissed Cecille from his mind. He didn't want to waste his anger on her. No, he told himself, he was saving all of it for Princess Christina. He turned to find the woman he sought to reject and spotted her immediately. She was standing next to their host, smiling sweetly up at him. She looked entirely too pretty tonight. Her gown was the color of blue ice. The neckline was low-cut, showing a generous amount of her full, creamy-looking bosom. The gown wasn't as indecently fashioned as Cecille's, but Lyon still didn't like it. Hunt was giving Christina's chest lecherous looks. Lyon thought he just might kill him.

There were too many dandies at the party, too. Lyon looked around the room, glaring at all the men openly coveting his Christina. He knew he wasn't making any sense. He wasn't going to marry Christina, but he wasn't willing to let anyone else have her, either. No, he wasn't making any sense at all. It was Christina's fault, of course. The woman had made him crazy.

Cecille stood beside Lyon, watching him. It didn't take her long to realize he was mesmerized by the Princess. Cecille was irritated. She wasn't about to let anyone compete for Lyon's attention. No one was going to interfere with her plan to marry him. Lyon was a stubborn man, but Cecille was certain enough of her own considerable charms to believe she'd eventually get her way. She always did. Yes, Lyon would come around, provided she didn't prod too obviously.

From the way Lyon kept his gaze directed on the beautiful woman, Cecille knew she'd better act quickly. The little Princess could cause trouble. Cecille made up her mind to have a talk with the chit as soon as possible.

She had to wait a good hour before she gained a proper introduction. During that time she heard several comments about Lyon's preoccupation with the woman. There was actual speculation that Lyon was going to offer for her. Cecille turned from irritated to incensed. It was obviously far more serious than she'd first guessed.

She waited for her opportunity. When Christina finally stood alone, Cecille nudged her arm and begged for a private audience in their host's library to discuss an issue of high importance.

The innocent little Princess looked confused by her request. Cecille smiled as sweetly as she could manage. She felt like gloating. In just a few minutes she'd have the silly girl terrified enough to do anything she suggested.

The library was located in the back of the main floor. They entered the chamber from the hallway.

Three high-backed chairs were angled in front of a long desk. Christina sat down, folded her arms in her lap, and smiled up at Lady Cecille expectantly.

Cecille didn't sit down. She wanted the advantage of towering over her adversary.

"What is it you wish to say to me?" Christina asked, her voice soft.

"The Marquess of Lyonwood," Cecille announced. The sweetness was missing from her voice now. "Lyon belongs to me, Princess. Leave him alone."

Lyon had just opened the side door to the library in time to overhear Cecille's demand. It wasn't by accident that he happened upon the conversation, nor was it coincidence he'd chosen to go around to the door connecting the kitchens to the study. Lyon remembered from past meetings with Sir Hunt that there were two doors leading to the library. And he'd kept his attention on Christina since the minute she'd entered the townhouse. When Cecille had taken hold of Christina's arm and led her down the hallway, Lyon was right behind her.

Neither Christina nor Cecille noticed him. Lyon knew it was bad form to listen in on their private conversation, yet he believed his motives were pure enough. He knew what Cecille was capable of. She could make mutton out of a gentle little lamb. Gentle Christina wasn't up to handling anyone as cunning, as vicious as Cecille. Lyon only wanted to protect Christina. The beautiful woman was simply too naive for her own good.

"Has Lyon offered for you, then?" Christina suddenly asked.

"No," Cecille snapped out. "Don't give me that innocent look, Princess. You know he hasn't offered for me yet. But he will," she added with a sneer. "We're intimate friends. Do you know what that means? He comes to my bed almost every night. Do you get my meaning?" she asked in a malicious voice.

"Oh, yes," Christina answered. "You're his paramour."

Cecille gasped. She folded her arms across her chest and glared down at her prey. "I'm going to marry him."

"No, I don't think you are, Lady Cecille," Christina answered. "Was that all you wanted to say to me? And you really don't have to raise your voice. My hearing is sound."

"You still don't understand, do you? You're either stupid or a real bitch, do you know that? I'm going to ruin you if you get in my way," Cecille announced.

Lyon was puzzled. He'd thought to intervene the moment Cecille started her insults, but the look on Christina's face kept him from moving.

Christina seemed to be totally unaffected by the discussion. She actually smiled up at Cecille, then asked in an extremely casual voice, "How could you ruin me?"

"I'll make up stories about you. It won't matter if they're true or not. Yes," Cecille rushed on, "I'll tell everyone you've slept with several men. Your reputation will be in tatters when I'm done with you. Give Lyon up, Christina. He'd tire of you soon anyway. Your looks are nothing in comparison to mine. Lyon will always come back to me. My beauty captivates him. You will immediately let him know you aren't interested in him. Then ignore him completely. Otherwise—"

"Say what you will," Christina said. "I don't care what your people think of me."

Cecille was infuriated by the amusement in Christina's voice. "You are a stupid woman," she shouted.

"Please don't get so bothered, Lady Cecille. It's upsetting your complexion. Why, your face is full of splotches."

"You . . . you . . ." Cecille paused to take a deep, calming breath. "You're lying. You have to care what others think. And your aunt will certainly care, I can promise you that. She can't be as ignorant as you are. Ah, I see I've finally gotten your attention. Yes, the Countess will be ruined by the scandal I'm going to weave."

Christina straightened in her chair. She frowned up at Cecille. "Are you saying your made-up stories will upset my aunt?"

"God, you really are a simple one, aren't you? Of course she'll be upset. When I'm finished, she won't be able to show her face in public. Just you wait and see."

Cecille could smell victory. She turned her back on Christina to circle the chair as she began to detail the vile lies she would spread.

Lyon had heard enough. He turned to pull the door wide open, determined to walk into the library and end Cecille's terror tactics at once.

It was time to protect his angel from the serpent.

She must have moved with incredible speed. Lyon had only taken his gaze off Christina for a second or two, but when he glanced back, the scene he witnessed so astonished him that he couldn't move.

He had trouble believing what he was seeing. Christina had Cecille pinned up against the wall. His former mistress wasn't making a sound of protest over the violation. She couldn't. Christina's left hand was anchored around the woman's neck, holding her in place. From the way Cecille's eyes were beginning to bulge, Lyon thought Christina just might be strangling her to death.

Cecille outweighed Christina by a good twenty pounds. She was much taller, too, yet Christina acted as though she was holding up a trinket for closer observation.

The little angel Lyon wanted to protect used only one hand to secure Cecille. She held a dagger in her other hand. The tip of the blade rested against Cecille's cheek.

The victim had just turned victor.

Christina slowly increased her hold on Cecille's neck, then let her see the tip of her knife. "Do you know what my people do to vain, deceitful women?" she asked in a soft whisper. "They carve marks all over their faces, Cecille."

Cecille started whimpering. Christina pricked her skin

with the tip of the knife. A drop of blood appeared on her cheek. Christina nodded with satisfaction. She had Lady Cecille's full attention now. The woman looked terrified. "If you tell one lie, I'll hear about it. Then I'm going to hunt you down, Cecille. There isn't a rock large enough for you to crawl under, nor enough men in England to see to your protection. I'll come to you during the night, when you're sleeping. And when you open your eyes, you'll see this blade again. Oh, yes, I'll get to you, I promise. And when I do," Christina added, pausing to dramatically drag the flat of her blade across the woman's face, "I'm going to cut your skin into ribbons. Do you understand me?"

Christina let up on her hold only long enough for Cecille to gulp air and nod. Then she squeezed her up against the wall again. "The Countess is my family. No one upsets her. And no one is going to believe you if you think to tell them I just threatened you. Now get out of here and go home. Though it is unkind of me to say so, you really do look a fright."

With those words of dismissal, Christina moved away from the disgusting woman.

Lady Cecille didn't possess an ounce of dignity. She was weeping all over her gown. She had obviously believed every word of Christina's threats.

Lord, she was a silly woman. Christina had difficulty maintaining her stern expression. She wanted to laugh. She couldn't, of course, and she kept her gaze locked on the terrified woman a long moment before she took pity on her. Lady Cecille couldn't seem to move. "You may leave now," Christina announced.

Cecille nodded. She slowly backed away from Christina until she reached the exit. Her hands shook when she lifted her skirt all the way up to her knobby knees, then she flung the door wide and ran with enough speed to suggest she thought demons were chasing her.

Christina let out a long, weary sigh. She replaced the dagger in the sheath above her ankle, straightened the folds of her gown, then daintily patted her hair into place. "Such a silly woman," she whispered to herself before walking out of the room.

Lyon had to sit down. He waited until Christina was out of sight before he went over to Hunt's desk and leaned against it. He tried to pour himself a drink of his host's whiskey from the cart to the side of the desk, but he quickly discarded that idea. God help him, he was laughing too hard to get the deed done.

So much for his conclusion that Christina was just like every other woman. She certainly wasn't raised in France, either. Lyon shook his head. She gave the appearance of being helpless . . . or had he drawn that conclusion on his own, he wondered. It was an easy mistake to make, he realized. Christina was so feminine, so dainty, so damned innocent-looking . . . and she wore a knife strapped to her leg.

It was identical to the knife he'd held in his hands the night of Baker's party, the knife that had wounded Rhone. What a cunning little liar she was. Lyon remembered how he'd turned to see who'd thrown the weapon. Christina had looked so frightened. Hell, the woman had turned around to look behind her, too. She'd gone right along with his thought that someone lurked behind them in the shadows. Then, when he was locked in conversation with the gentlemen, she'd quietly snatched her weapon back.

Lyon's instincts were wide awake now. His temper began to simmer, too. Hadn't she told him the night of the robbery she was so frightened she thought she might swoon?

No wonder she'd gone to Rhone to take care of his injury. Guilt, Lyon decided.

He wasn't laughing now. Lyon thought he just might throttle the woman.

"Has trouble telling a lie, does she?" he muttered to himself. Oh, yes, she'd looked him right in the eye when she told him that story. It was very difficult for her . . . yes, she'd said that, too.

He *was* going to throttle her. But first he was going to have a long talk with her . . . his little warrior had a large amount of explaining to do.

Lyon slammed his empty glass down on the tray and went in search of Christina.

"Are you enjoying yourself?"

Christina visibly jumped. She whirled around to confront Lyon. "Where did you just come from?" she asked, sounding highly suspicious. She glanced around him to look at the library door.

Lyon knew exactly what she was thinking. She looked worried. He forced himself to look calm. "In the library."

"No, I just came from the library, Lyon. You couldn't have been in there," she announced, shaking her head.

He almost said that he wasn't the one who lied, then caught himself. "Oh, but I was in the library, my sweet."

His announcement gave her a start. "Was there anyone else in there?" she asked, trying to sound only mildly curious.

Lyon knew she was testing him.

"I mean to ask, sir, that is, did you happen to notice if anyone else was in the library?"

He took his sweet time nodding. Christina decided he looked just like a mischievous devil. He was dressed like one, too. Lyon's formal attire was all of black, save for the white cravat, of course. The clothing fit him well. The man was too handsome for her peace of mind.

She was certain Lyon hadn't seen or heard anything. He was looking down at her with such a tender expression in his eyes. Christina felt safe enough. Lyon wasn't acting the least appalled. But why had he lied to her? Christina decided he must have seen her go inside the study with Lady Cecille. The poor man was probably worried that his paramour had told Christina something he didn't want repeated. Yes, she told herself, he was just prodding for information.

It was a plausible explanation. Still, one did need to be absolutely certain. Christina lowered her gaze to stare at his waistcoat. She forced a casual voice and asked, "You didn't perchance overlisten to my conversation with Lady Cecille, did you?"

"The word is eavesdropping, Christina, not overlistening."

His voice was strained. She thought he might be trying not to laugh at her. Christina didn't know if it was her question or her mispronunciation that had caused the change. She was too irritated with him for lying to her to take great exception, however. "Thank you, Lyon, for instructing me. Eavesdropping, yes, I do recall that word."

Lyon wouldn't have been surprised if she'd started wringing her hands. She was upset, all right, for she'd just spoken to him in French. He doubted she was even aware she'd slipped into the foreign language.

He decided to answer her in kind. "I am always happy to instruct you, love."

She didn't notice. "But you didn't eavesdrop, did you?"

"Why, Christina, what an unkind question to put to me. Of course not."

She tried not to let her relief show.

"And you know I'd never lie to you, my sweet. You've always been so open, so honest with me, haven't you?"

"Yes, I have," Christina returned, giving him a quick smile. "It is the only way to be with each other, Lyon. Surely you realize that."

Lyon clasped his hands behind his back so he wouldn't be able to give in to his urge to grab her by her throat. She seemed very relaxed with him now, very sure of herself. "Did you learn the value of honesty from the Summertons?" he asked.

"Who?"

His grip on his control intensified. "The Summertons," Lyon repeated, trying to control his anger. "Remember, love, the people who raised you?"

She couldn't quite look him in the eye when she answered him. He was such a good, trusting man. It was becoming a little bit of a strain to lie to him. "Yes, the Summertons did teach me to be honest in all endeavors," she announced. "I simply can't help myself. I'm not any good at fabrications."

He was going to strangle her.

"Did I hear you say you were in the study with Lady Cecille?"

Her guess had been right all along. Lyon was worried about the conversation. He had seen her go inside the library with Lady Cecille. Christina decided to put his fears to rest. "I was," she said. "Lady Cecille seems to be a dear woman, Lyon. She had some rather pleasing remarks to make about you."

No, he wasn't going to strangle her. He thought he'd beat her first. "I'm pleased to hear it," Lyon said. His voice was as smooth as a soft wind. The effort made his throat ache. "What exactly did she say?"

"Oh, this and that."

"What specific this and that?" Lyon insisted. His hands had moved to rest on Christina's shoulders, and it was all he could do not to shake the sincerity right out of her.

"Well, she did mention that we made a lovely couple," Christina said.

She was back to staring at his waistcoat again. While she appreciated the fact that the English tended to be somewhat naive, she was beginning to feel ashamed of herself for lying so blatantly to Lyon.

"Did she mention destiny, perchance?" Lyon asked.

She hadn't noticed the edge in his voice. "No, I don't recall Lady Cecille mentioning destiny. That does remind me, though, of my question. Have you given my proposal consideration?"

"I have."

"Lyon, why are you speaking French to me? We're in England, and you really should speak the language of your own people."

"It seemed appropriate," Lyon muttered.

"Oh," Christina said. She tried to shrug his hands away from her shoulders. They were still alone in the hallway, but there was always the chance someone could come along and see them. "Are you going to mate with . . . I mean, are you going to marry me?"

"Yes, I'm going to mate with you. As for marriage, I fear I will have to decline your proposal."

Christina wasn't given time to react to Lyon's announcement. Sir Reynolds called out, interrupting them. Lyon let go of her shoulders, then pulled her around and up against his side. He trapped her with one hand wrapped around her waist.

"Lyon, I've been looking all over this house for you. Do you approve of my taking your sister over to Kimble's do? We'd stay here until dinner hour is over, of course."

"Certainly," Lyon said. "And I appreciate your taking Diana under your wing, sir."

"Glad to do it," Reynolds said. "Good evening, Princess Christina. I trust you are well?"

"Yes, thank you," Christina answered. She tried to curtsy, but Lyon wouldn't let up on his hold. She settled on a smile instead. It was a puny half effort at best, for Lyon's answer had just settled in her mind.

Though she told herself it didn't matter, that she'd surely find someone else to marry, she knew she was lying to herself. It did matter. Lord, she felt close to weeping.

"My dear," Sir Reynolds said, addressing Christina, "I've agreed to see you home. Your aunt pleaded fatigue and has taken your carriage. She explained she was leaving for the countryside tomorrow. I was given to understand you won't be going with her."

"Yes, that is correct," Christina answered. "My aunt is going to visit a friend who has taken ill. She prefers that I stay in London. I will have to wait for another opportunity to see your lovely countryside."

"I forget you've only been here a very short while," Sir Reynolds said. "But you're surely not on your own for an entire week, are you? Do you wish me to lend my arm Saturday eve? You do intend to go to Creston's ball, of course. Or do you already have an escort?"

"I shall not be going," Christina interjected, her voice firm.

"Yes, you will," Lyon said. He squeezed her waist before adding, "You promised."

"I've changed my mind. Sir Reynolds, I'm also fatigued. I'd be pleased if you'd—"

"I'll take you home." Lyon's voice was hard with anger.

Sir Reynolds could feel the tension between the two. They'd obviously had a falling out, he decided. From the way Princess Christina was trying to get out of his embrace, and the determined way Lyon wasn't letting her, it was very apparent. Why, he could almost see the sparks between them.

Determined to douse the argument and aid Lyon at the same time, he asked him, "Are you sure you wish to see Princess Christina home?"

"Yes," Lyon snapped. "When must she get there, Reynolds? Did the Countess set the hour?"

"No, she assumed Christina would accompany your sister and me to Kimble's. You've at least two hours before the Countess takes notice," he added with a grin.

"Please don't discuss me as if I were not present," Christina said. "I really am tired now and would prefer—"

"That we leave immediately." Lyon finished the sentence for her, increasing his hold on her waist until she could barely catch her breath.

"Perhaps you might consider leaving by the back door," Sir Reynolds suggested in a conspiratorial whisper. "I shall make certain everyone believes Princess Christina left with her aunt, you see, and will of course offer your regrets to our host as well."

"A good idea," Lyon announced with a grin. "Of course, Reynolds, we must keep this deception between the three of us. Christina has such difficulty telling a lie. As long as she doesn't have to fabricate a story to her aunt, her honor will remain unblemished. Isn't that right, love?"

She gave him a good long frown. And she really wished he'd quit dragging up the issue of her honesty. It was making her terribly uncomfortable. Lyon looked sincere enough for her to believe he actually admired her.

It no longer signified what he thought, she told herself when Lyon started dragging her toward the back of the house. He'd just rejected her offer of marriage. No, it didn't matter what he thought of her anymore.

She wouldn't see him again after this evening. Heaven help her, her eyes were filling with tears. "You've just broken another law," she muttered into his back. She tried to sound angry instead of desolate. "My aunt will be outraged if she hears of this trickery."

"Speak English, sweetheart."

"What?"

Lyon didn't say another word until he had Christina settled inside his carriage. He sat down next to her, then stretched his long legs out in front of him.

The carriage was much bigger than the one Aunt Patricia had rented, and much more elegant in detail.

Christina still hated it. Large or small, elegant or not, it made no difference to her. "Don't you have any of those open carriages like the ones I've seen in Hyde Park, Lyon? And please quit trying to crush me. Do move over."

"Yes, I have an open carriage. It's called a phaeton. One doesn't use a phaeton after dark, however," he explained with exasperation. His patience was wearing thin. Lyon was itching to get the truth out of her, not discuss such mundane matters as carriages.

"One should," Christina muttered. "Oh, God, I shouldn't admit this to you, but I won't be seeing you again, so it really doesn't matter. I can't stand the darkness. May we open the drapes covering the windows, please? I can't seem to catch my breath."

The panic in her voice turned his attention. His anger quickly dissipated when he felt her tremble against his side.

Lyon immediately pulled the drapes back, then put his arm around her shoulders.

"I've just handed you a weapon to use against me, haven't I?"

He didn't know what she was talking about. The light filtering in through the windows was sufficient for him to see the fear in her eyes, though. He noticed that her hands were fisted in her lap.

"You really are frightened, aren't you?" he asked as he pulled her up against him.

Christina reacted to the gentleness in his voice. "It isn't really fear," she whispered. "I just get a tightness here, in my chest," she explained. She took hold of his hand and placed it against her heart. "Can you feel how my heart is pounding?"

He could have answered her if he'd been able to find his voice. The simple touch had sent his senses reeling.

"I'll try to take your mind off your worry, love," he whispered when he could speak again. He leaned down and kissed her. The intimacy was slow, languid, consuming, until Christina reached up to brush her fingertips across his cheek.

A shudder rushed through him. His heart was pounding now. "Do you know what a witch you are?" he asked when he pulled away. "Do you have any idea what I want to do to you, Christina?" His fingers slid just inside the top of her gown to gently caress her softness.

He whispered erotic, forbidden longings into her ear. "I can't wait much longer, my love. I want you under me. Naked. Begging. God, I want to be inside you. You want me just as much, don't you, Christina?"

He didn't wait for her answer but claimed her soft lips for another deep kiss. His mouth moved hungrily over hers, his tongue delving inside, deeper and deeper with each new penetration, until she was reaching for his tongue with her own whenever he deliberately withdrew.

Christina didn't know how it happened, but she suddenly realized she was sitting on his lap with her arms wrapped around his neck. "Lyon, you mustn't say such things to me." Her protest sounded like a ragged moan. "We cannot share the same blankets unless we're wed," she added before she cupped the sides of his face and kissed him again.

She forgot all about the closeness inside the carriage, forgot all her worries and his rejection of her proposal. His kisses were robbing her of all thoughts.

Her breasts ached for more of his touch. She moved, restlessly, erotically, against his arousal. Lyon trailed wet kisses down the side of her neck, pausing to tease her earlobe with his warm breath, his velvet tongue. His knuckles brushed against her nipples, once, twice, and then again, until a fever began to burn inside her.

She tried to stop him when he pushed the top of her gown down, exposing her breasts. "No, Lyon, we mustn't—"

"Let me, Christina," Lyon demanded, his voice harsh with need. His mouth found her breasts before she could protest again, and then she was too weak, too overwhelmed by what he was doing to her to protest at all.

"I love the taste of you," he whispered. "God, you're so soft." His tongue caressed the nipple of one breast while his hand stroked the other. Christina clung to him, her eyes tightly closed. A soft whimper escaped when he took the nipple into his mouth and began to suckle. An aching tightness made her move against Lyon again. He groaned, telling her how much pleasure her instinctive motion had given him.

Christina never wanted the sweet torture to end.

It was Lyon's driver who saved her from disgrace. His shout that they'd gained their destination penetrated her sensual haze. "Dear God, we are home!" Her announcement came out in a strained voice.

Lyon wasn't as quick to recover. It took a moment for her announcement to settle in his mind. His breathing was harsh, ragged. He leaned back against the cushion and took a deep breath while he fought to regain some semblance of control.

Christina had adjusted her gown to cover her breasts and moved to sit beside him. She dropped her hand on his thigh. Lyon reacted as though she'd just stabbed him. He pushed her hand away. "Are you angry with me?" she whispered.

His eyes were closed now. The muscle was flexing in the side of his cheek, though, and she thought he really was angry with her. She clasped her hands together in her lap, trying to stop herself from trembling. "Please don't be angry with me."

"Damn it, Christina. Give me a minute to calm down," Lyon snapped.

Christina bowed her head in shame. "I'm so sorry, Lyon. I didn't mean for our kisses to go so far, but you made me weak and I forgot all about stopping."

"It was my fault, not yours." Lyon muttered his roundabout apology. He finally opened his eyes and glanced down at her. Hell, she looked so dejected. Lyon tried to put his arm around her again, but she scooted over into the corner. "Sweetheart, it's all right." He forced a smile when she looked up at him. "Do you want me to come inside with you?"

She shook her head. "No, the Countess is a light sleeper. She'd know," Christina whispered.

Lyon didn't want to leave her. Not yet . . . not like this. He was feeling extremely guilty because she was looking so ashamed. If she started to cry, he didn't know how he'd be able to comfort her.

"Hell," he muttered to himself. Every time he touched her he went a little crazy. If he tried to offer her solace, he'd probably make it worse.

Lyon threw open the door and helped Christina to the ground. "When will I see you again?" he asked her. They were in the midst of a struggle, and he wasn't certain she heard him. Christina was trying to push his hands away, and he was trying to hug her. "Christina, when will I see you again?"

She refused to answer him until he let go of her.

Lyon refused to let go of her until she answered him. "We'll stand here all night," he told her when she kept pushing against his shoulders.

Christina suddenly threw her arms around his neck and hugged him. "I blame myself, Lyon. It was wrong of me to ask you to marry with me. I was being very selfish."

Her words so surprised him, he let go of her. Christina kept her head bowed so he couldn't see her distress, yet was powerless to keep her voice from trembling. "Please forgive me."

"Let me explain," Lyon whispered. He tried to pull her

back into his arms. Christina evaded him again by taking a quick step back. "Marriage changes a person. It isn't a rejection of you, Christina, but I—"

She shook her head. "Do not say another word. You might have fallen in love with me, Lyon. When the time came for me to go home, you would have had a broken heart. It is better for me to choose someone else, someone I don't care about."

"Christina, you *are* home. You aren't going anywhere," Lyon said. "Why can't we go along the way we—"

"You're very like Rhone, do you know that?"

Her question confused him. Christina hurried up the steps to her townhouse. When she turned back to look at Lyon, he could see how upset she was. Tears streamed down her cheeks. "Your friend only steals jewels, Lyon. Your sin is greater. If I let you, you'd steal my heart. I cannot allow that to happen. Goodbye, Lyon. I must never see you again."

With those parting words, Christina went inside the house. The door closed softly behind her.

Lyon was left standing on the stoop. "The hell you will forget me," he bellowed.

Lyon was furious. He thought he had to be the most frustrated man in England. How in God's name had he ever allowed himself to get involved with such a confusing woman?

She'd had the audacity to tell him he might fall in love with her.

Lyon knew the truth. Heaven help him, he was already in love with her.

Needless to say, that admission didn't sit well. Lyon almost ripped the door off the carriage when he climbed back inside. He shouted the order to his driver to take him home, then began to list all the reasons he should stay away from Christina.

The woman was a blatant liar.

He despised liars.

God only knew how many hearts she'd broken.

Destiny . . . he decided he hated that word.

By the time he arrived home, he'd accepted the fact that none of his reasonable arguments made any difference. He was stuck with Christina whether he wanted to be or not.

Chapter Eight

Mylala wouldn't leave her homeland. She wouldn't leave her family. While I understood her reasons, I was afraid for her. She promised me she'd take every precaution. My maid planned to hide in the hills until Edward was unseated from power or fled the country. Her family would look after her. I gave her all my own treasury, though it was a pittance by England's standards. We wept together before we parted, like true sisters who knew they'd never see each other again.

Yes, she was my sister, in spirit and heart. I'd never had a confidant. My own sister, Patricia, could never be trusted. Be warned, child. If Patricia is still alive when you've grown up, and you meet up with her one day, protect yourself. Don't put your faith in her, Christina. My sister loves deception. She feeds on others' pain.

Do you know, she really should have married Edward. They would have been very compatible. They are so very much alike.

Journal entry
September 3, 1795

Lyon spent most of Friday afternoon sitting in the Bleak Bryan tavern, located in a particularly seedy section of the city. Lyon wasn't there to drink, of course, but to glean information from the captains and shipmates who favored the tavern.

He moved easily in and out of such a setting. Though dressed in quality buckskins and riding jacket, he didn't need to worry about being set upon. Lyon was always given a wide berth. Everyone in this area knew his reputation well. They feared him, yet respected him, and entered into conversation only when he motioned to them for an audience.

Lyon sat with his back against the wall. Bryan, a retired shipmate from the moment he lost his hand in a knife fight, sat beside him. Lyon had purchased the tavern and set Bryan up in business as a reward for past loyalty.

He questioned one man after another, refusing to become impatient when the hours stretched or the shipmates lied in order to get another free glass of ale. A newcomer strutted over to the table and demanded his share of the bounty. The big man lifted the seaman Lyon was questioning by his neck and carelessly threw him to the side.

Bryan smiled. He still enjoyed a good fight. "Have you never met the Marquess of Lyonwood, then?" he asked the stranger.

The seaman shook his head, took his seat, and then reached for the pitcher of ale. "Don't give a belch who he be," the man muttered menacingly. "I'm wanting my due."

Bryan's eyes sparkled with amusement. He turned to Lyon and said, "He's wanting his due."

Lyon shrugged. He knew what was expected of him. Every face in the tavern was looking at him. There were appearances to keep up, and if he wanted a peaceful afternoon, he'd have to take care of this little matter.

He waited until the seaman had put the pitcher back on the table, then slammed the heel of his boot into the man's groin.

It happened too quickly for the seaman to protect himself. Before he could scream in pain, Lyon had him by the throat. He squeezed hard, then flung the big man backwards.

The crowd roared their approval. Lyon ignored them. He tilted his chair back against the wall, never taking his gaze off the man writhing in agony on the floor.

"You got your due, you horse's arse. Now crawl on out of here. I run a respectable tavern," Bryan bellowed between bouts of laughter.

A thin, jittery man drew Lyon's attention then. "Sir, I hear you're wanting information about ships from the colonies," he stammered out.

"Take a seat, Mick," Bryan instructed. "He's a good, honest man, Lyon," Bryan continued, nodding at his friend.

Lyon waited while the seaman exchanged news with Bryan. He continued to watch the man he'd just injured until the door slammed shut behind him.

Then his thoughts returned to Christina and his mission.

Lyon had decided to start over. He was finished forming his own conclusions based on logical assumptions. Logic didn't work where Christina was concerned. He threw out all her explanations about her past. The only fact he knew to be truthful was that the Countess had returned to England approximately three months ago.

Someone had to remember the old bat. The woman was foul enough to have drawn attention to herself by complaining about something to someone. She wouldn't have been an appreciative passenger.

Mick, as it turned out, remembered the woman. Rather well. "Captain Curtiss weren't a fair man with me, sir. I would have chosen to slop the decks or empty the pots rather than fetch and carry for the Cummings woman. Gawd, she kept me legs running day and night."

"Was she traveling alone?" Lyon asked. He didn't let Mick know how excited he was to finally have real information, thinking the man might lace his answers in order to please him into giving him more ale.

"Of a sort," Mick announced.

"Of a sort? That don't make sense, Mick. Tell the man straight," Bryan advised.

"I mean to say, sir, she came on board with a gentleman and a pretty little lady. I only got a quick glance at the lovey, though. She wore a cape with the hood over her head, but before the Countess pushed her below deck she looked right at me and smiled. Yes, sir, she did."

"Did you happen to notice the color of her eyes?" Lyon asked.

"Blue they were, as blue as my ocean."

"Tell me what you remember about the man traveling with the Countess," Lyon instructed. He motioned for Bryan to refill Mick's glass.

"He weren't family," Mick explained after taking a swig of ale. "A missionary, he told some of the men. Sounded Frenchy to me, but he told us he lived in a wilderness past the colonies. He was going back to France to see his relatives. Even though he was French, I liked him. Because of the way he protected the little lass. He was old enough to be her father—treated her like he was, too. Since the Cummings woman stayed below most of the voyage, the missionary man would take the pretty for a stroll on the decks."

Mick paused to wipe his mouth with the back of his hand. "The old woman was a strange bird. She didn't have nothing to do with the other two. Even demanded to have an extra chain put on the inside of her door. Captain Curtiss tried to calm her fears by telling her none of us would touch her. Gawd almighty, we couldn't stomach to look at her, and why she'd be thinking we'd want to bother her didn't make a spit of sense. It took a while, sir, but some of us did finally figure out her scheme. She was bolting her door against the little miss. Yes, sir, she was. The missionary man was overheard telling the little lady not to feel sad 'cause her aunt was afraid of her. Don't that beat all?"

Lyon smiled at Mick. It was all the encouragement the seaman needed to continue. "She was such a sweet little thing. 'Course, she did throw Louie overboard. Flipped him right over her shoulder, she did. Couldn't believe it—no, sir, couldn't believe it. Louie had it coming, though. Why, he snuck up behind her and grabbed her. That's when I seen the color of her hair. Real light yellow. She'd always been wearing that hood, even in the heat of the afternoons. Must have been mighty uncomfortable."

"She threw a man overboard?" Bryan asked the question. He knew he shouldn't interfere in Lyon's questions, but he was too astonished by Mick's casually given remark to keep silent. "Enough about the hood, man, tell me more about this girl."

"Well, it were a good thing for Louie the wind weren't up. We fished him out of the water without too much backache. He left the miss alone after that surprise. Come to think on it, most o' the men did."

"When will Captain Curtiss be returning to London?" Lyon asked.

"Not for another month or two," Mick said. "Would you be wanting to speak to the missionary man, too?"

"I would," Lyon answered, keeping his expression impassive. He sounded almost bored.

"He's coming back to London real soon. He told us he was only going to stay in France a short while, then planned on giving the little miss a nice visit before going back to the colonies. He was real protective toward the girl. Worried about her, too. Don't blame him none. That old . . ."

"Bat?" Lyon supplied.

"Yes, she was an old bat," Mick said with a snicker.

"Do you remember the missionary's name, Mick? There's an extra pound for you if you can give me his name."

"It's right on the tip of me tongue," Mick said, frowning intently. "When it comes to me, I'll tell you, Bryan. You'll keep the coins safe for me, won't you?"

"Question some of your shipmates," Bryan suggested. "Surely one of them will recall the man's name."

Mick was in such a hurry to gain his reward, he immediately left the tavern to go search for his companions.

"Is this government business?" Bryan asked when they were once again alone.

"No," Lyon answered. "A personal concern."

"It's the lady, isn't it? Don't need to pretend with me, Lyon. I'd be interested in her, too, if I were young enough."

Lyon smiled. "You've never even seen her," he reminded his friend.

"Makes no matter. Mick said she was a slip of a girl with blue eyes and yellow hair. Sounds pretty enough for my tastes, but that isn't the true reason I'd chase after her skirts. Have you ever met Louie?"

"No."

"He's as big as I am, though he weighs a few stones more. Any lady who could toss him overboard has to be mighty interesting. Lord, I wish I'd been there to see it. Never could like Louie. There's a rank smell coming from him. His mind's as sour as his body. Damn, I wish I'd seen him hit the water."

Lyon spent a few more minutes exchanging bits of news with Bryan, then stood to take his leave. "You know where to find me, Bryan."

The tavern owner walked Lyon to the curb. "How's Rhone getting on?" he asked. "Up to his usual antics?"

"Afraid so," Lyon drawled. "That reminds me, Bryan. Would you have the back room ready for Friday after next? Rhone and I are setting up a card game. I'll give you the details later."

Bryan gave Lyon a speculative look. "Always trying to outguess me, aren't you, Bryan?" Lyon asked.

"My thoughts are always on my face," Bryan answered, with a grin. "It's why I'd never make it in your line of work," he added.

Bryan held the door of the carriage open for Lyon. He waited until the Marquess was about to close the door behind him before calling out his ritual farewell. "Guard your back, my friend." On the spur of the moment, he included another caution. "And your heart, Lyon. Don't let any pretties throw you overboard."

That suggestion had come a little too late, to Lyon's way of thinking. Christina had already caught him off guard. He'd vowed long ago not to get emotionally involved with another woman for as long as he lived. He was going to keep his relationships short and sweet.

So much for that vow, Lyon thought with a sigh. He couldn't guard his heart now. It already belonged to her.

His mind returned to the puzzle of Christina's bizarre remarks. He remembered she'd told him that his curiosity could get him killed. Was she lying or was she serious? Lyon couldn't decide.

Christina had been truthful when she announced she wasn't going to stay in London long, that she meant to return home. At least she looked like she was telling the truth.

He wasn't about to let her go anywhere. Christina was going to belong to him. But he wasn't taking any chances. If she did manage to get away from him, his job of hunting her down would be much easier if he knew exactly where her home was.

"She isn't going anywhere," Lyon muttered to himself. No, he wasn't going to let her out of his sight.

With a growl of new frustration, Lyon accepted the truth. There was only one way he could keep Christina by his side.

Hell, he was going to have to marry her.

"Where in God's name have you been? I've been sitting in your library for hours."

Rhone bellowed the question as soon as Lyon strode into the foyer of his townhouse. "I have messengers searching the town for you, Lyon."

"I wasn't aware I had to account to you, Rhone," Lyon answered. He threw off his jacket and walked into the study. "Shut the door, Rhone. What do you think you're doing? You shouldn't be out in public. Someone might notice the bandage. You took a needless chance. Your man would have found me soon enough."

"Well, where have you been? It's almost dark outside," Rhone muttered. He collapsed in the first available chair.

"You're beginning to sound like a nagging wife," Lyon said with a chuckle. "What's the problem? Is your father having more difficulties?"

"No, and you sure as hell won't be laughing when I tell you why I've been looking all over London for you. Better put your jacket back on, my friend. You've work to do."

The seriousness in Rhone's tone gained Lyon's complete attention. He leaned against the desk top, folded his arms across his chest, and said, "Explain yourself."

"It's Christina, Lyon. She's in trouble."

Lyon reacted as though he'd just been hit by lightning. He bounded away from the desk and had Rhone by his shoulders before his friend could take a new breath. "There's still plenty of time, Lyon. I was just worried you might have taken off for your country home. We've got until midnight before they come after her . . . for God's sake, man, unhand me."

Lyon immediately let Rhone fall back into his chair. "Who are they?" he demanded.

His expression had turned deadly. Rhone was immensely thankful Lyon was his friend and not his enemy. "Splickler and some men he hired."

Lyon gave Rhone a brisk nod, then walked back out into the foyer. He shouted for his carriage to be brought around front again.

Rhone followed Lyon out the front door. "Wouldn't your steed get you there quicker?"

"I'll need the carriage later."

"What for?"

"Splickler."

The way he'd said the bastard's name told Rhone all he needed or wanted to know. He waited until they were both settled inside the conveyance to give his full explanation. "One of my men—or rather one of Jack's men—was offered a sizable amount to help take Christina to Gretna Green. Splickler thinks to force a marriage, you see. I went to meet with my men to tell them there wasn't going to be another raid. One of them is a decent enough fellow—for a bandit—by the name of Ben. He told me he'd been asked by Splickler and agreed to go along. Ben thought it was a rather amusing way to make some easy money."

The look on Lyon's face was chilling.

"Splickler hired Ben and three others. I paid Ben so he'd pretend to be in on the scheme. He won't help Splickler, if we can count on his word."

"You're certain it's set for midnight?" Lyon asked.

"Yes," Rhone answered with a nod. "There's still plenty of time, Lyon." He let out a long sigh. "I do feel relieved you're going to take care of the matter," he admitted.

"Oh, yes, I'll take care of the matter."

Lyon's voice was whisper-soft. It sent a chill down Rhone's spine. "You know, Lyon, I always thought Splickler was a snake, but I didn't think he had enough rattle in him to do something this obscene. If anyone finds out about this plot of his, Christina's reputation might very well suffer."

"No one's going to find out. I'll see to it."

Rhone nodded again. "Could someone have put Splickler up to this, Lyon? The man isn't smart enough to make change."

"Oh, yes, someone put him up to it, all right. The Countess. I'd stake my life on it."

"Good God, Lyon, she's Christina's aunt. You can't believe—"

"I do believe it," Lyon muttered. "She left Christina all alone. A little too convenient, wouldn't you agree?"

"Do you have an extra pistol for me?" Rhone asked.

"Never use them."

"Why not?" Rhone asked, appalled.

"Too much noise," Lyon answered. "Besides, there are only four of them, if we can believe your friend's count."

"But there are five."

"Splickler doesn't count. He'll run at the first sign of trouble. I'll find him later."

"I don't doubt that," Rhone answered.

"Rhone, when we reach Christina's townhouse, I'll have my man take you home. I don't want my carriage sitting out front. Splickler would see it. We don't want him to change his plans. I'll have my driver return for me an hour after midnight."

"I insist on lending a hand," Rhone muttered.

"You've only got one good hand to lend," Lyon answered, smiling.

"How can you be so glib?"

"The word is controlled, Rhone. Controlled."

Lyon was out of the carriage giving fresh instructions to his driver before the vehicle had rocked to a full stop. "Damn it, Lyon. I could be of help," Rhone shouted.

"You'd be more of a hindrance than a help. Go home. I'll send word to you when it's over."

Lord, he acted so unaffected by what was taking place. Rhone knew better, though. He almost felt a little sorry for the stupid, greedy men who'd joined with Splickler. The poor fools were about to find out just how the Marquess of Lyonwood had earned his reputation.

Damn, he really hated to miss the action. "I'm sure as certain not going to," Rhone muttered to himself. He waited for his opportunity. When the carriage slowed to round the corner, Rhone jumped to the street. He landed on his knees, cursed himself for his clumsiness, then brushed himself off and started walking towards Christina's house.

Lyon was going to get his good hand whether he wanted it or not.

The Marquess was shaking mad. He knew he'd calm down as soon as he saw Christina and knew she was all right. She was taking her sweet time opening the door for him. His nerves were at the snapping point. Lyon was about to break the lock with one of the special tools he always carried with him for just such an eventuality when he heard the sound of chain being slipped from the bar.

Though he'd held his temper in front of Rhone, the minute Christina opened the door he exploded with anger. "What in God's name do you think you're doing opening the door with just a robe on? Hell, you didn't even find out who it was, Christina!"

Christina clutched the lapels of her robe together and backed out of Lyon's way. The man literally charged into the foyer like a crazed stallion.

"What are you doing here?" she asked.

"Why didn't Elbert answer the door?" Lyon demanded. He stared at the top of her head, knowing full well that the sight of her dressed in such scanty attire, with her hair unbound in lovely disarray, would make him lose his train of thought.

"Elbert's visiting his mother," Christina explained. "Lyon, isn't it terribly late to be paying a call?"

"His what?" Lyon's anger suddenly evaporated.

"His mama. And just why is that so amusing, I wonder?" she asked. "You're the lizard, Lyon. You shout at me, then turn to laughing in the blink of an eye."

"Chameleon, Christina, not lizard," Lyon instructed. "Elbert has to be at least eighty if he's a day. How can his mother still be alive?"

"Oh, I've met her, Lyon. She's a dear woman. Looks just like Elbert, too. Well, are you going to tell me why you're here?"

"Go upstairs and get dressed. I can't think with you strutting around like that."

"I'm not strutting," Christina protested. "I'm standing perfectly still."

"We're going to have company in a little while."

"We are?" Christina shook her head. "I didn't invite anyone. I'm really not in the mood to entertain, Lyon. I had only just begun to mourn you, and now here you are—"

"Mourn me?" Lyon repeated, matching her frown. "What the hell are you mourning me for?"

"Never mind," Christina said. "And quit losing your temper. Who is coming to pay a call?"

Lyon had to take a deep breath to regain his control. He then explained all about Splickler and his men. He deliberately left out mention of the Countess's involvement, for he didn't want Christina too upset. He decided to wait, thinking to take care of one problem at a time.

"What is it you want me to do?" Christina asked. She bolted the front door and walked over to stand directly in front of him.

Lyon inhaled the scent of flowers. He reached out to take her into his arms. "You smell good," he told her.

His hands cupped the sides of her angelic face. Lord, she was staring up at him with such trust in her eyes.

"You must tell me what to do," Christina whispered again.

"Kiss me," Lyon commanded. He lowered his head to steal a quick kiss.

"I was talking about the mischief makers," Christina said when he'd pulled away. "You really can't hold a thought for more than a minute, can you, Lyon? Does the flaw run in your family?"

Lyon shook his head. "Of course I can hold a thought. I've been thinking about getting you into my arms since the moment you opened the door. You don't have anything on underneath this flimsy little robe, do you?"

She would have shaken her head if he hadn't been holding her so securely. "I just finished my bath," she explained, smiling over the fact that he'd just admitted wanting to touch her.

He was such an honest man. Christina leaned up on her tiptoes to give him what he wanted. She thought only to imitate the same quick kiss he'd given her. Lyon had other notions. His thumb nudged her chin down just enough for his tongue to thrust inside her mouth in search of hers.

Christina held onto the lapels of his jacket, fearing her knees were about to buckle. When she was certain she wouldn't disgrace herself by falling down, she returned his kiss with equal fervor.

The way she responded to him made him half-crazed. His mouth slanted over hers, powerfully, possessively. Christina wasn't able to hold back. That fact aroused Lyon almost as much as her whispered moans, her soft lips, her wild tongue.

Yes, he was thoroughly satisfied with her response. He was fast coming to the conclusion that it was the only time she was honest with him.

Lyon reluctantly pulled away from her. "You've made my hands tremble," Christina said. "I won't be much help to you if they knock on my door now."

"Too bad you aren't talented with a knife," Lyon remarked.

He waited for the lie, knowing full well she couldn't admit to such training.

"Yes, it is too bad," Christina answered. "But knives are for men. Women would harm themselves. I don't have a pistol, either. Perhaps you're disappointed I'm so poorly educated?"

He could tell by the way she'd asked the question she was hoping for agreement.

"Not at all, sweet," Lyon answered, his voice smooth. He draped his arm around her shoulder and started up the steps. "It's a man's duty to protect his little woman."

"Yes, that's the way in most cultures," Christina returned. Her voice turned hesitant, almost shy, when she added, "Still, you wouldn't take great exception if this same little woman did know how to defend herself. Would you? I mean to say, you wouldn't think it was unladylike . . . or would you?"

"Is this your room?" Lyon asked, deliberately evading her question. He pushed the door of the first bedroom open, took in the dark colors and the rank odor of old perfume, and knew before Christina answered him that he'd breached the Countess's quarters.

The room was dark enough to please a spider. Or an old bat, Lyon thought with a frown.

"This is my aunt's room," Christina said. She peeked inside. "It's awfully gloomy, isn't it?"

"You seem surprised. Haven't you ever been inside?"

"No."

Lyon was pulling the door closed when he saw the number of bolts and chains attached to the inside. "Your aunt must be an uneasy sleeper," he remarked. "Against whom does she lock her door, Christina?"

He knew the answer and was already getting angry. Lyon remembered the seaman's remark about the Countess being frightened of the pretty little miss.

The locks were on the wrong side of the door, as far as Lyon was concerned. Christina should be protecting herself against the Countess, and not the other way around.

What kind of life had Christina been forced to live since

returning to her family and her homeland? She must surely be lonely. And what kind of woman would shun her only relative?

"My aunt doesn't like to be disturbed when she sleeps," Christina explained.

Lyon reacted to the sadness in her voice by hugging her close to him. "You haven't had an easy time of it since coming home, have you, love?"

He could feel her shrug against him. "My room is at the end of the hall. Is that what you're looking for?"

"Yes," he answered. "But I want to check all the windows, too."

"I have two windows in my room," Christina said. She pulled away from him, took hold of his hand, and hurried into her room.

Lyon took in everything in one quick glance. The bedroom was sparse by most women's standards, immensely appealing by his own. Trinkets didn't litter the two chest tops. No, there wasn't any clutter. A single chair, angled in the corner, a privacy screen behind it, a canopy bed with a bright white coverlet, and two small chests were the only pieces of furniture in the large square room.

Christina obviously liked order. The room was spotless, save for the single blanket someone had dropped on the floor by the window.

"The garden's right below my windows," Christina said. "The wall would be easy to scale. The greenery reaches the ledge. I think the vines are sturdy enough to hold a man."

"I'd rather they didn't come in through the windows," Lyon remarked, almost absentmindedly. He tested the frames, then looked down at the garden. He wished the moon wasn't so accommodating this evening. There was too much light.

Lyon glanced over at Christina. His expression and his attitude had changed. Drastically.

Christina felt like smiling. He really was a warrior. His face was just as impassive as a brave's. She couldn't tell what he was thinking now, and the rigidity of his bearing indicated to her he was preparing for battle.

"The drawing room only has two front windows, as I recall. Is there another entrance besides the one from the foyer?"

"No," Christina answered.

"Good. Get dressed, Christina. You can wait in there until this is over. I'll make it safe enough."

"How?"

"By blocking the windows and the doors," Lyon explained.

"No. I mean, I don't wish to be locked inside anywhere, Lyon."

The vehemence in her tone surprised him. Then he remembered how uncomfortable she'd been inside the closed carriage. His heart went out to her. "If I fashion a lock on the inside of the door so you'll know you could get out if you—"

"Oh, yes, that would do nicely," Christina interrupted with a brisk nod. She looked very relieved. "Thank you for understanding."

"Now why are you frowning?" Lyon asked, clearly exasperated.

"I've just realized you have another weapon to use against me if you become angry with me," she admitted. "I've just shown you a weakness," she added with a shrug.

"No, you've just insulted me," Lyon returned. "I don't know too many men, or women either, who would like to be locked in a room, Christina. Now quit trying to distract me. Get dressed."

She hurried to do his bidding. "I don't think I want to wait in the drawing room at all," she muttered to herself as she grabbed the first gown she could lay her hands on and moved behind the screen to change. She realized what a poor selection she'd made after she'd shed her robe and put the royal blue dress on.

"Lyon? The fastenings are in the back," she called out. "I can't do them up properly."

Lyon turned from the window to find Christina holding the front of her dress against her chest.

When she turned to give him her back, the first thing he noticed was her flawless skin. In the candlelight she looked too enticing for his peace of mind.

The second thing he took notice of was that she wasn't wearing a damn thing underneath. He wasn't unaffected either. His hands shook when he bent to the task of securing her gown, his fingers awkward because he wanted to caress her smooth skin.

"Where's your maid, Christina?" he asked, hoping conversation would pull him away from the ungentlemanly thought of carrying her over to the bed and seducing her.

"I'm alone for the week. I let Beatrice have the time away."

Her casually spoken comment irritated him. "For God's sake, no gentle lady stays all by herself," he muttered.

"I do well enough for myself. I'm most self-serving."

"Self-sufficient," Lyon said with a sigh. He was having difficulty catching the last button. Her silky hair kept getting in his way.

"I beg your pardon?"

Lyon lifted her hair and draped it over her shoulder. He smiled when he saw the goosebumps on her skin. "Self-sufficient, my sweet, not self-serving."

"There is a difference?" she asked, trying to turn around to look at him.

"Stand still," Lyon ordered. "Yes, there is a difference. Your aunt is self-serving. You're self-sufficient."

"Do you know I never make mistakes except when I'm with you, Lyon? It is therefore all your fault I get confused."

He didn't want to waste time arguing with her. "Come along," he ordered after he'd finished fastening her gown. He took hold of her hand and pulled her behind him.

Christina had to run to keep up with him. "I haven't braided my hair," she said quickly. "I really must, Lyon. It could be used against me. Surely you realize that."

He didn't realize, knew he shouldn't ask, but did anyway. "Why is your hair a weapon?"

"The men could catch hold of me if they grabbed my hair,

unless of course I'm as quick as a panther, as fearless as a wolf, as cunning as a bear."

The woman was getting carried away. Lyon let her see his exasperation when they'd reached the drawing room.

"Will you be all right sitting in the dark?" Lyon asked. He walked over to the front windows, pulled the braided cord from one side of the drape, and handed it to Christina.

"I'm not afraid of the dark," she answered, looking disgruntled. "What a silly question to put to me."

"Tie this rope around the door handles, Christina. Make it good and tight. If anyone tries to break in, I'll hear the noise. All right?"

Lyon checked the windows. Age had sealed them tight. "Yes, Lyon, I'll not let you down," Christina said from behind him.

"Now listen well, my little warrior," Lyon said in a hard voice. He took hold of her shoulders to give her a squeeze. "You're going to wait inside this room until the danger is over. Do you understand me?"

His voice had been harsh, angry. It didn't seem to worry Christina, though. She was still smiling up at him. "I really would like to help you, Lyon. After all, I would remind you that they are my attackers. Surely you will allow me to do my part."

"Surely I will not," Lyon roared. "You'd just get in my way, Christina," he added in a softer voice.

"Very well," Christina said. She turned to the small oval mirror hanging on the wall adjacent to the windows and began the task of braiding her hair. She looked so graceful, so feminine. When she lifted her arms, her gown edged up above her ankles.

"You've forgotten to put your shoes on," Lyon said, a smile in his voice. "Again."

"Again? Whatever do you mean?" Christina asked, turning back to him.

He shook his head. "Never mind. You might as well leave your hair alone. You aren't going to get involved."

Her smile reeked of sincerity. Lyon was immediately suspicious. "Give me your word, Christina. Now."

"What word?" she asked, feigning innocence. She turned away from his glare and started braiding her hair again.

Lyon held his patience. The little innocent didn't realize he could see her reflection in the mirror. She wasn't looking sincere now, only very, very determined.

He would gain her promise, even if he had to shake it out of her. Her safety was his primary concern, of course. Lyon wasn't about to let anything happen to her. But there was another reason as well. Though it was insignificant in comparison with the first, it still worried him. In truth, he didn't want her to watch him. There was a real possibility Christina would become more frightened of him than of Splickler and his men by the time the night was over.

Lyon didn't fight fair, or honorably either. Christina couldn't have heard about his past. Now that he realized how much he cared about her, he wanted to protect her from the world in general, bastards like Splickler in particular . . . but protect her from knowing about his dark side, too. He didn't want to disillusion her. She believed he was simply the Marquess of Lyonwood, nothing more, nothing less. God help him, he meant to keep her innocent.

He thought he'd lose her if she knew the truth.

"I promise I won't interfere until you ask me to," Christina said, interrupting his dour thoughts. "Mrs. Smitherson did show me how to defend myself," she hastened to add when he gave her a dark look. "I would know what to do."

"Summerton," Lyon answered on a long, drawn-out sigh. "The people who raised you were called Summerton."

His mood was just like the wind, Christina decided. Completely unpredictable. He wasn't smiling now but looking as though he was contemplating murder.

"You act as though we have all the time in the world before our visitors arrive," Christina remarked. "Won't they be here soon?" she asked, hoping to turn his attention away from whatever sinister thought had him glaring so.

"Not for a while yet," Lyon answered. "Stay here while I have a look around."

Christina nodded. The minute he was out of sight she ran

upstairs to fetch a ribbon for her hair. And her knife, of course. Lyon was going to get her help whether he wanted it or not.

She was back inside the drawing room, sitting demurely on the worn settee, her knife hidden under the cushion, when Lyon returned.

"I've decided to make it easy for Splickler."

"How?"

"Left the back door unlatched."

"That was most accommodating of you."

Lyon smiled over the praise in her voice. He walked over to stand directly in front of her. His big hands rested on his hips, his legs were braced apart, and Christina was given the disadvantage of having to tilt her head back as far as she could just to see his face. Since he was smiling again, she assumed his mood had lightened. "If you're sure they'll come through the garden, why let them inside the house at all? Why not greet them outside?"

"Greet them?" Lyon shook his head. "Christina, they aren't coming here to speak to you. There might very well be a fight."

He hated to worry her but knew she needed to understand. "Well, of course there will be a fight," Christina answered. "That's the reason I prefer you to meet them outside, Lyon. I'm the one who'll have to clean up the mess, after all."

He hadn't thought of that. And when he realized she thoroughly understood what was going to happen, he was immensely relieved. "You're very brave," he told her. "The moon, however, gives too much light. I memorized every detail of the room they'll enter before I put out the candles. They'll have the disadvantage."

"They'll also have to come through one at a time," Christina interjected. "A very cunning idea, Lyon. But what if they climb the vines instead of trying the door?"

"They won't, sweetheart."

He seemed so certain, Christina decided not to worry about it. She watched him walk over to the doors. "Time to put out the candles, love. Tie the rope around the doorknobs first, all right? You aren't frightened, are you? I'll take care of you. I promise."

"I trust you, Lyon."

Her answer warmed him. "And I trust you to stay here."

"Lyon?"

"Yes, Christina?"

"Be careful."

"I will."

"Oh, and Lyon?"

"Yes?"

"You'll try not to make too much of a mess, won't you?"

"I'll try."

He winked at her before closing the door behind him. Christina tied the rope around the two door handles, forming a tight double knot. She blew out the candles and settled down to wait.

The minutes dragged by at a turtle's pace. Christina kept straining to hear sounds from the back of the house. For that reason, she was quite unprepared to hear a scraping sound coming from the front windows.

They weren't suppose to come through the front of the house. Lyon was going to be disappointed. Christina felt like instructing the villains to go around back, then realized how foolish that suggestion would have been. She decided she'd just have to wait it out in hopes they'd give up trying to breach the windows and eventually try the back door.

"Christina?"

Her name was called out in a soft whisper, but she recognized the voice all the same. The Earl of Rhone was trying to get her attention.

She pulled the drape back and found Rhone hanging on the ledge, grinning up at her. The smile didn't stay long—nor did Rhone, for that matter. He suddenly lost his grip on the ledge and disappeared. A soft thud came next, followed by several indecent curses telling Christina the poor man hadn't landed on his feet.

She was going to have to fetch him out of the hedges, she decided. He was making such a commotion he was sure to alert the mischief makers.

Rhone met her at the front door. He looked a sight, for his jacket was ripped away from his sleeve, his cravat was soiled and undone, and he was favoring one leg.

He was such a clumsy man, she thought, yet her heart warmed to him all the same. Lyon must have confided in him. Christina believed he'd ventured out to give his friend assistance. It was the only answer for such an unexpected visit. "You look as though you've already lost one fight. Rhone, behind you!"

A crash echoing from the back of the house nearly drowned out her voice. Rhone caught her warning, however. He reacted with good speed, wasted little time by turning around to face the threat, and used his right shoulder to shove the door into the face of a wiry-looking man trying to barrel through the opening. His legs were buckled to the task, his face red with exertion.

When it became evident he wasn't going to get the door closed without her help, Christina added her own strength.

"Lyon!"

Rhone's shout made her ears ring. "Go and hide someplace," Rhone gasped out to Christina, his voice strained.

"Christina. Go back inside the salon."

Lyon's voice came from behind her. Christina thought only to glance over her shoulder to explain that her weight was needed to get the door closed, but the sight that met her pushed her explanation out of her mind.

She slowly turned around and took a tentative step forward. She was too dazed to move more quickly.

The transformation in the Marquess held her spellbound. He didn't even resemble an Englishman now. His jacket was gone, his shirt torn to the waist. Blood trickled down his chin from a cut on the side of his mouth. It wasn't a significant wound, and it didn't frighten her. Neither did the splatter of blood on his sleeve, for she instinctively knew the blood wasn't his . . . no, she wasn't frightened of his appearance.

The look in his eyes was another matter. He looked ready to kill. Lyon appeared to be quite calm. His arms were folded across his chest, and his expression was almost bored. It was all a lie, of course. The truth was there, in his eyes.

"*Now!*"

His bellow shook her from her daze. Christina didn't even spare a backward glance for Rhone as she ran toward the drawing room.

"Get out of the way, Rhone."

Rhone didn't hesitate to follow Lyon's order. As soon as he jumped back, three men the size of giants lunged inside. They fell, one atop another. Rhone stood in the corner, hoping Lyon would ask for his help.

Lyon stood in the center of the foyer patiently waiting for the three cutthroats to get back on their feet. Rhone thought that was just a bit too accommodating of his friend.

He was outnumbered, outweighed, outweaponed. The men now crouched in front of him all held knives in their hands. One of the bastards clutched a dagger in each hand.

Someone started to snicker. Rhone smiled. The poor fool obviously didn't realize Lyon still had the advantage.

The fat man in the center suddenly lashed out at Lyon with his blade. Lyon's boot caught him under his chin. The force of the blow lifted the man high enough in the air for Lyon to slam his fists into the man's groin. The attacker blacked out before he hit the floor.

The other two attacked in unison just as another man came charging up the front steps. Rhone heard him coming, reached out, and kicked the door shut. The howl of pain radiating through the door told Rhone his timing had been excellent.

Rhone never took his gaze off Lyon. Though he'd seen him in battles before, Lyon's strength continued to impress him. Lyon used his elbow to crack one man's jaw while he anchored the other man's arm away from him. He dealt with him next, and when Rhone heard the snap of bone he knew Lyon had broken the man's wrist.

Bodies littered the entrance when Lyon was done. "Open the door, Rhone."

"Hell, you're not even out of breath," Rhone muttered. He got the door open, then moved out of the way as Lyon, showing not the least amount of effort, lifted each man and threw him out into the street.

"We work well together," Rhone commented.

"We?"

"I watch, you work," Rhone explained.

"I see."

"What happened to Splickler? Did he come in through the back door, or did he run away?"

Lyon grinned at Rhone, then nodded toward the pyramid of bodies at the bottom of the steps. "Splickler's on the bottom. I think you probably broke his nose when you slammed the door in his face."

"Then I did do my part," Rhone announced, puffing up like a cloud.

Lyon began to laugh. He whacked Rhone on the shoulder, then turned to find Christina standing in the center of the doorway.

She looked like she'd just seen a ghost. The color was gone from her cheeks, and her eyes were wide with fright. Lyon's heart lurched. God, she must have seen the fight. He took a step toward her but stopped when she took a step back.

He felt defeated. She was afraid of him. Lord, he'd meant to protect her, not terrify her.

Christina suddenly ran to him. She threw herself into his arms, very nearly knocking both of them to the floor. Lyon didn't understand what had caused the change in her attitude, yet he was thankful all the same. Relief washed the rigidity from his stance. He put his arms around her, rested his chin on the top of her head, and let out a long sigh. "I'm never going to understand you, am I?"

"I'm so happy you aren't angry with me."

Her voice was muffled against his chest, but he understood her. "Why would I be angry with you?"

"Because I broke my promise," Christina reminded him. "I left the salon to let Rhone in the front door."

Lyon looked over at his friend. "I specifically remember

telling you to go home." He frowned at his friend, then suddenly noticed his appearance. "What happened to you? I don't recall you getting in the fight."

"A little mishap," Rhone said.

"He fell in the hedge," Christina explained, smiling over the embarrassment she could see in Rhone's face. Why, the man was actually blushing.

"The hedge?" Lyon sounded incredulous.

"I think I'll walk home. Your carriage is probably waiting in front of my townhouse, Lyon. I'll have your driver bring it along for you. Good evening, Princess Christina."

"No, you really mustn't walk. Lyon, you should—"

"Let him walk. It's only a short distance away," Lyon interjected.

Christina didn't argue further. Someone was going to have to fetch the carriage, and she preferred that Rhone took care of the matter so that she could spend a few minutes alone with Lyon.

"Thank you for your assistance, Rhone. Lyon, what are you going to do about those men cluttering my walkway? And am I mistaken, or are there one or two in the back of the house as well?"

"There are two," Lyon said. "I threw them out back."

"They'll wake up and crawl home," Rhone advised. "Unless, of course, you—"

"I didn't," Lyon said.

"Didn't what?" Christina asked.

"Kill them," Rhone said.

"Rhone, don't frighten her," Lyon said.

"Goodness, I hope not. Think of the mess." Christina sounded appalled, but for all the wrong reasons. Both Lyon and Rhone started laughing.

"Shouldn't you be crying or something?" Rhone asked.

"Should I?"

"No, Christina, you shouldn't," Lyon said. "Now quit frowning."

"You aren't wearing any shoes, Christina," Rhone suddenly blurted out.

"Do be careful walking home," Christina answered, ignoring his comment about her bare feet. "Don't let anyone see your bandage. They might begin to wonder."

As soon as the door was bolted shut, Christina turned back to Lyon, only to find that he was already halfway up the stairs, taking them two at a time. "Where are you going?"

"To wash," Lyon called back. "Wasn't there a pitcher of water in your room, Christina?"

He was out of sight before she could give him a proper answer. Christina hurried up the steps after him.

When she caught up with him she wished she'd waited below the stairs. Lyon had already stripped out of his shirt. He was bent over the basin, splashing water on his face and arms.

Christina was suddenly overwhelmed by his size. She could see the sinewy strength in his upper arms, his shoulders; a pelt of golden hair covered his chest, narrowed to a line above the flat of his stomach, then disappeared below the waistband of his pants. She'd never seen the like. She was fascinated and wondered what it would be like to be held in his arms now.

He reached for the cloth. Christina took the strip of linen from his hands and began to pat his face dry. "Your skin is so dark, Lyon. Have you been working in the sun without your shirt on?" she asked.

"When I was on my ship I used to," Lyon answered.

"You have a ship?" Christina answered, sounding quite pleased.

"Had a ship," Lyon corrected. "Fire destroyed it, but I plan to build another."

"With your own hands, Lyon?"

Lyon smiled down at her. "No, love. I'll hire others to do the work."

"I liked the ship I was on when I came to England. I didn't like it much below the deck though. It was too confining," she admitted with a shrug.

Her voice trembled. So did her hands when she started to dry his shoulders. There were several glorious marks on him, and the sight of such handsome scars made her heartbeat quicken.

For the first time in his life, Lyon was actually feeling a little awkward. Christina was such a beautiful woman, while he was covered with marks. They were reminders of his black past, Lyon thought, but the ugly scars hadn't bothered him until this moment.

"I promise to take you on my new ship," he heard himself say.

"I would like that, Lyon," Christina answered. The towel dropped to the floor when she gently traced the long, curved scar on Lyon's chest. "You are so handsome," she whispered.

"I'm covered with flaws," Lyon whispered back. His voice sounded hoarse to him.

"Oh, no, they are marks of valor. They are beautiful."

She was looking up at him, staring into his eyes, and Lyon thought he'd never get used to her beauty.

"We should go back downstairs." Even as he said the words, he was pulling her into his arms. God help him, he couldn't stop himself. The realization that he was alone with her, that they were in fact in her bedroom, rocked all the gentlemanly thoughts out of his mind.

"Will you kiss me before we go downstairs?" she asked.

Lyon thought she looked as though she'd already been kissed. A faint blush covered her cheeks, and her eyes had turned a deep blue again.

The woman obviously didn't understand her own jeopardy. And if she only knew the wild thoughts rambling through his mind, her face would turn as white as the sheets.

She trusted him. She wouldn't have asked him to kiss her if she didn't trust him. Lyon was going to have to control his baser instincts. Yes, he was going to be a gentleman.

One kiss surely wouldn't hurt. He'd wanted to take her into his arms the moment the fight had ended. The anger had been flowing like lava through his veins. Oh, he'd wanted her then, with a primitive passion that had shaken him.

And then she'd backed away from him. The sudden remembrance gave him a start.

"Christina, are you afraid of me?"

She could tell he was serious. The worry in his gaze said he was. The question was puzzling. "Why would you think I'd be afraid of you?" she asked, trying not to laugh. He did look terribly concerned.

"After the fight, when you backed away from me . . ."

She did smile then, couldn't help herself. "Lyon, the little skirmish I witnessed couldn't possibly be called a fight . . . and you actually thought I was afraid?"

He was so surprised by her comment, he immediately defended himself. "Well, I'll admit that I didn't think it was much of a fight either, but when you stared at me with such a frightened look on your face I naturally assumed you were upset. Hell, Christina, most women would have been hysterical."

By the time he'd finished his statement, he'd gone from sounding very matter-of-fact to muttering with irritation.

"Was it my duty to weep, Lyon? I apologize if I've displeased you, but I've still to understand all your laws."

"You could make a duck daft," Lyon announced.

Because he was grinning down at her, Christina decided not to let her exasperation show. "You're the most confusing man," she remarked. "I have to keep reminding myself that you're English."

The temptation was too compelling. Before she could stop her inclination, she reached out to touch his chest. The heat in his skin felt good against her fingertips, the mat of hair crisp yet soft.

"I wasn't afraid of you, Lyon," Christina whispered, avoiding his eyes now. "I've never been afraid of you. How could I be? You're such a gentle, kind man."

He didn't know how to answer her. She sounded almost in awe of him. She was wrong, of course. He'd never been kind or gentle. A man could change, though. Lyon determined to be anything and everything Christina wanted him to be. By God, if she thought him gentle, then gentle he'd be.

"You really are a warrior, aren't you, Lyon?"

"Do you want me to be?" he asked, sounding confused.

"Oh, yes," Christina answered, daring a quick look up.

"Warriors aren't gentle," he reminded her.

She didn't want to press the issue because she knew he wouldn't understand. He was wrong, but it would be rude of her to set him straight. Her hands slipped around his neck, her fingers entwining in his soft, curly hair.

She felt him shudder; his muscles tightened.

Lyon would have spoken to her, but he was certain his voice would betray him. Her touch was driving him to distraction.

Gentle, he cautioned himself, I have to be gentle with her. He placed a kiss on her forehead. Christina closed her eyes and sighed, encouraging him. He kissed her on the bridge of her freckled nose next and finally reached her soft lips.

It was a very gentle kiss. Sweet. Undemanding.

Until her tongue touched his. The hunger inside him seemed to ignite. The feeling was so intoxicating, so overpowering, he forgot all about gentleness. His tongue penetrated her warmth, tasting, probing, taking.

When Christina pulled him closer, his demand increased until all he could think about was filling her . . . completely.

She wasn't resisting. No, her soft moans told him she didn't want him to stop. Her hips cuddled his arousal. He knew her action was instinctive, yet the way she slowly arched against him made him wild. She felt so good, so right.

Lyon dragged his mouth away from hers with a harsh groan. "I want to make love to you, Christina," he whispered against her ear. "If we're going to stop, it has to be now."

Christina's head fell back as Lyon rained wet kisses along the column of her throat. Her hands, still entwined in his hair, clenched, pulled, begged.

He knew he'd soon be past the caring point. Lyon tried to separate himself from the torment. "God, Christina, walk away from me. Now."

Walk away? Dear Lord, she could barely stand up. Every part of her body responded to his touch. She could hear the anger in his voice, could feel the tension in his powerful hold. Her mind tried to make sense out of the confusion of his reaction. "I don't want to stop, Lyon."

She knew he'd heard her. Lyon clasped her shoulders, squeezed until it was painful. Christina looked into his eyes, saw the desire there. The force of his passion overwhelmed her, robbed her of her own strength to think logically.

"Do you know what you're saying to me?"

She answered him the only way she knew how. Christina used her body to give him permission. She deliberately arched against him again, then pulled his head down toward her.

She kissed him with a passion that sent his senses reeling. Lyon was at first too stunned to do more than react to her boldness, but he soon became the aggressor again.

He wanted to pleasure her so completely that any memory of other men would be washed away. She would belong to him, now and forever.

Lyon fumbled with the fastenings at the back of her gown, his mouth fastened on hers. Christina heard the sound of material being ripped away. He suddenly pulled her hands away from him, then tore the gown completely free. The dress fell to the floor.

There were no undergarments to hinder his gaze. When he took a step back, Christina stood before him, her hands at her sides.

Her body belonged to him. He was her lion. Christina accepted the truth, repeated it again and again inside her mind, trying to overcome her shyness, her fear.

She couldn't shield her body from him . . . or her heart.

Both belonged to Lyon.

Lyon's gaze was ravenous as it swept over her. She was so perfectly formed, so very, very beautiful. Her skin was smooth, creamy-looking in the soft candlelight. Her breasts were high, full, taut. The nipples were erect, waiting for his touch. Her waist was so narrow, her stomach flat, her hips slender.

She was irresistible.

And she belonged to him.

Lyon's hands shook when he reached for her, drew her back into his arms.

Christina gasped from the initial contact of her bare breasts against his chest. His hair tickled her, his skin warmed her, and the way he controlled his strength as he held her close to him made her forget all her fears. She was innocent of men, yes, yet she knew with a certainty that made tears come to her eyes that Lyon would be gentle with her.

She kissed his throat where she could see the throbbing of his pulse, then rested her head in the crook of his shoulder, inhaling his wonderful masculine scent, waiting for him to show her what to do.

Lyon slowly untied the ribbon from the bottom of Christina's braid, then unwound the silky curls until a blanket of sunlight covered her back. He lifted her into his arms and carried her over to the bed, pausing only to pull the covers back before placing her in the center.

Christina tried to protest, to tell him it was her duty to undress him, but Lyon had already taken his shoes and socks off. Her voice became locked in her throat when he stripped out of the rest of his clothes, and all she could do was stare at him in wonder.

He was the most magnificent warrior she'd ever seen. The power was there, in his arms and legs. His thighs were muscular, strong, beautiful. His arousal was full, hard, and when he came to lie on top of her Christina instinctively opened herself to him. He settled himself between her thighs. Christina had barely accepted his weight before he captured her mouth for another searing kiss.

Christina wrapped her arms around his waist. His mouth had never felt so wonderful, his tongue never so exciting. His hands were never still, stroking, caressing, giving her shivers of pleasure. Their legs entwined, and when Lyon moved to take her breast into his mouth her toes brushed against his legs. Her moans of pleasure drove him wild. His hands fondled her breasts while his tongue swirled around one nipple and then the other. When he finally began to suckle, a white-hot knot of need started to burn inside her.

Christina's hips moved restlessly, rubbing against his arousal. She wanted to touch him, to worship his body the way he was worshipping hers, but the sensations coursing through her body were too new, too raw. She could only cling to him and beg him with her whimpers.

His hands settled between her thighs to tease her sensitive skin. His fingers soon made her wild with need, caressing the nub protected by her soft curls until she was moist with desire. His fingers penetrated her tight sheath just as his tongue thrust into her mouth.

Lyon could feel the incredible heat of her. He was nearly out of control now, for Christina was so unashamedly responsive to his touch. He couldn't wait much longer, knew he'd soon lose his control. He cautioned himself against hurrying her even as his thigh pushed her legs further apart.

"From this moment on you belong to me, Christina. Now and forever."

He entered her with a swift, determined thrust, lifting her hips with his hands to penetrate her completely.

She was a virgin. The realization came late. Lyon was fully embedded inside her now. He took a deep breath and tried not to move. The effort nearly killed him. Christina was so hot, so tight; she fit him perfectly.

His heart was slamming against his chest. His breath was harsh, choppy. "Why didn't you tell me?" he finally asked her. He propped himself up on his elbows to look down into her face. God, she hadn't made a sound. Had he hurt her? "Why didn't you tell me you haven't been with a man before?" he asked again, capturing her face with his hands.

"Please, Lyon, don't be angry," Christina whispered.

She knew she was going to start weeping. The fierce light in his eyes frightened her. Her body was throbbing with pain from his invasion, and every muscle was tense, tingling. "I'm sorry if I disappointed you," she apologized in a ragged voice. "But I didn't want you to stop. Could you be disappointed later, please?"

"I'm not disappointed," Lyon answered. "I'm very pleased." He was trying to keep his voice soft, gentle. It was an excruciating task, because his arousal was begging for release, and all he wanted to do was spill his seed into her.

He was going to make certain she found complete satisfaction first. "I'll try not to hurt you, Christina."

"You already did."

"Oh, God, I'm sorry. I'll stop," he promised, knowing full well he wouldn't.

"No," Christina protested. Her nails dug into his shoulders, keeping him inside her. "It will be better now, won't it?"

Lyon moved, groaning over the pleasure he gained. "Do you like that?" he asked.

"Oh, yes," Christina answered. She arched her hips up against him, pulling him higher inside her. "Do you like that?"

He might have nodded. She was too consumed by the waves of heat to notice. His mouth slanted over hers then, claiming her full attention.

Lyon tried to be tender, but she was making it an impossible quest. She kept moving against him restlessly, demandingly, urgently. Lyon's discipline deserted him.

"Easy, love, don't let me hurt you."

"Lyon!"

"Christina, why did you let me think you'd been with other men?"

Lyon was stretched out on his back, his hands behind his head. Christina was cuddled up against his side, one shapely leg draped over his thigh. Her face rested on his chest. "Let you think?" she asked him.

"You know my meaning," Lyon said, ignoring the laughter he'd heard in her voice.

"It seemed unimportant to argue with you. Your mind was set on the matter. Besides, you probably wouldn't have believed the truth anyway."

"I might have believed you," he protested. He knew he was lying. No, he wouldn't have believed her.

"Why did you think I'd—"

"It's the way you kissed me," Lyon explained, grinning.

"What is the matter with the way I kiss you? I was only imitating you."

"Oh, nothing's the matter, love. I like your . . . enthusiasm."

"Thank you, Lyon," Christina said, after she'd given him a good look to see if he was jesting with her or not. "I like the way you kiss, too."

"What else do you imitate?" Lyon asked.

Because he was teasing her, he was unprepared for her answer. "Oh, everything. I'm quite good at it, you know, especially if I like what I'm imitating."

"I'm sorry I hurt you, Christina," Lyon whispered. "If you'd told me you were a virgin before, I could have made it easier for you."

Lyon was feeling a bit guilty, but terribly arrogant, too.

She belonged to him. He hadn't realized just how possessive he could be. Lyon wanted to believe Christina wouldn't have given herself to him unless she loved him.

He knew she'd reached fulfillment. Lord, she'd cried out his name loud enough for the streetwalkers to hear. A smile settled on his face. She hadn't been the delicate little flower he'd thought she was. When she let go, she let go. Wild. Totally uncontrolled. And loud, Lyon admitted. His ears were still ringing from her lusty shouts. Lyon didn't think he could ever be happier. No, Christina hadn't held back. He had the scratches to prove it.

Now all he wanted to hear from her was the truth inside her heart. He wanted her to tell him how much she loved him.

Lyon let out a long sigh. He was acting just like a virgin on his wedding night. Uncertain. Vulnerable.

"Lyon, do all Englishmen have such hair on their bodies?"

Her question nudged him away from his thoughts. "Some do, others don't," he answered with a shrug that nearly pushed her off his chest. "Haven't you ever seen Mr. Summerton without his shirt on, love?" he teased.

"Who?"

He wasn't going to remind her again. If the woman couldn't keep her lies straight, he certainly wasn't going to help. Lyon was immediately irritated. He knew it was his own fault for bringing up the lie, but that didn't seem to matter. "Christina, now that we've become so intimate, you don't have to fabricate stories any longer. I want to know everything about you," he added, his voice a little more intense than he wished. "No matter what your childhood was like, I'll still care for you."

Christina didn't want to answer his questions. She didn't want to have to lie to him again . . . not now. A warm glow still surrounded her heart. Lyon had been such a tender lover. "Did I please you, Lyon?" she asked, trailing her fingers down his chest to distract him.

"Very much," he answered. He captured her hand when she'd reached his navel. "Honey, tell me about—"

"Aren't you going to ask me if you pleased me?" she asked, pulling her hand free of his grasp.

"No."

"Why not?"

Lyon took a deep breath. He could feel himself getting hard again. "Because I know I pleased you," he ground out. "Christina, stop that. It's too soon for you. We can't make love again."

Her hand touched his arousal, stealing the breath out of his protest. Lyon let out a low groan. His hand dropped to his side when she began to place wet kisses on the flat of his indrawn stomach. She moved lower to taste more of him.

"No more," Lyon commanded.

He pulled her by her hair, twisting the curls to get her attention. "If you want to tease, you'd better wait until tomorrow," he warned. "A man can only take so much, Christina."

"How much?" she whispered. Her mouth was getting closer to his hard shaft.

Lyon jerked her back up to his chest. "We only have this one night," Christina protested.

"No, Christina," Lyon said. "We have a lifetime."

She didn't answer him, but she knew he was wrong. Her

eyes filled with tears when she turned her face away from him. Christina was almost desperate to touch him again, to taste all of him. The memory of her Lyon would have to stay with her . . . forever.

She lowered her head to his stomach again. She kissed him there, moved to his thighs next, and finally between them.

His scent was just as intoxicating as the taste of him. She was only given a few minutes to learn his secrets, however, before Lyon dragged her up on top of him.

He kissed her hungrily as he rolled her to his side. Christina moved her leg over his thigh and begged him with her mouth and her hands to come to her.

She was more than ready for him. Lyon was shaken when he touched the sweet wetness between her thighs. He slowly penetrated her warmth, holding her hips in a fierce grip, determined not to let her hurt herself by pushing up against him too quickly.

She bit him on his shoulder in retaliation. Lyon was driving her mad. He slowly penetrated her, then withdrew just as slowly. It was agonizing. Maddening.

He had the patience and the endurance of a warrior. She thought she could withstand the sweet torment for the rest of her life. But Lyon was far more adept at the ways of loving than she was. When his hand slipped between them and he touched the heat of her in such a knowing way, her control completely vanished.

Her climax was unimaginable, consuming her. Christina clung to him, her face pillowed against the side of his neck, her eyes tightly closed against the hot sensations shooting through her body.

Lyon was no longer controlled. His thrusts became powerful. When she instinctively arched against him, tightened herself around him, he found his release. The force of his climax stunned him. Lyon felt it in the very depths of his soul.

He was at peace.

Several long minutes elapsed before he could slow his

racing heart or his ragged breath. He was too content to move.

Christina was crying. Lyon suddenly felt the wetness of her tears on his shoulder. The realization jarred him out of his haze. "Christina?" he whispered, hugging her close to him. "Did I hurt you again?"

"No."

"You're all right?"

She nodded against his chin.

"Then why are you crying?"

If he hadn't sounded so caring, she might have been able to restrain herself. There wasn't any need to be quiet about it now, since he knew she was weeping, and she was soon wailing, loud and undignified as a crazed old squaw.

Lyon was horrified. He rolled Christina on her back, brushed her hair out of her face, and gently wiped her tears away. "Tell me, love. What is it?"

"Nothing."

It was a ludicrous answer, of course, but Lyon held his patience. "I really didn't hurt you?" he asked, unable to keep fear out of his voice. "Please, Christina. Quit crying and tell me what's the matter."

"No."

His sigh was strong enough to dry the tears from her cheeks. Lyon cupped the sides of her face, his thumbs rubbing the soft skin below her chin. "I'm not going to move until you tell me what's bothering you, Christina. Your aunt will find us in just this position when she comes home next week."

She knew he meant what he said. He had a stubborn look on his face. The muscle in the side of his jaw flexed. "I've never felt the way you make me feel, Lyon. It frightened me," she admitted.

She started crying again. Dear God, how could she ever leave him? The full truth was unbearable. Shameful. Lyon probably loved her. No, she admitted, shaking her head. He loved a princess.

"Christina, you were a virgin. Of course you were frightened," he said. "Next time it won't be so terrifying for you. I promise you, my sweet."

"But there can't be a next time," Christina wailed. She pushed against Lyon's shoulders. He immediately shifted his weight, then rolled to his side.

"Of course there's going to be another time," he said. "We'll be married first, just as soon as possible. *Now* what have I said?"

He had to shout his question. Christina was making so much noise he knew she wouldn't have been able to hear him if he'd spoken in a normal tone of voice.

"You said you wouldn't marry me."

Ah, so that was the reason. "I've changed my mind," Lyon announced. He smiled, for he understood her real anxiety now. He was also very pleased with himself. Lord, he'd just said the word marriage without blanching. Even more amazing was the fact that he really wanted to marry her.

The turnabout stunned him.

Christina struggled to sit up. She threw her hair over her shoulder when she turned to look at Lyon. She stared at him a long while and tried to form an explanation that wouldn't sound confusing. Christina finally decided to say as little as possible. "I've changed my mind, too. I can't marry you."

She jumped off the bed before Lyon could stop her, then hurried over to her chest to get her robe. "At first I thought I could, because I knew you'd be able to make my stay in England so much more bearable, but that was when I thought I'd be able to leave you."

"Damn it, Christina, if this is some kind of game you're playing, I would advise you to stop."

"It isn't a game," Christina protested. She tied the belt around her waist, pausing to wipe the fresh tears away from her face, then walked back over to stand at the foot of the bed. Her head was bowed. "You want to marry Princess Christina," she said. "Not me."

"You're not making any sense," Lyon muttered. He got out of bed and walked over to stand behind her.

He hadn't the faintest idea what was going through her mind, and he told himself it didn't matter.

"You can tell me all the lies you want to, but the way you just gave yourself to me was honest enough. You want me as much as I want you."

He was about to pull her up against him when her next comment gave him pause. "It doesn't matter."

The sadness in her voice tore at him. "This isn't a game, is it? You really think you aren't going to marry me."

"I can't."

Her simple answer made him livid. "The hell you can't. We're getting married, Christina, just as soon as I can make the arrangements. God's truth, if you shake your head at me one more time I'm going to beat you."

"You needn't shout at me," Christina said. "It's almost dawn, Lyon. We are both too tired for this discussion."

"Why did you ask me to marry you," he asked, "and then change your mind?"

"I thought I'd be able to marry you for just a little while and then—"

"Marriage is forever, Christina."

"According to your laws, not mine," she answered. She took a step away from him. "I'm too upset to speak of this tonight, and I'm afraid you'll never understand anyway—"

Lyon reached out to pull her up against his chest. His hands circled her waist. "Did you know before we made love that you weren't going to marry me?"

Christina closed her eyes against the anger in his voice. "You had already declined my proposal," she said. "And yes, I knew I wouldn't marry you."

"Then why did you give yourself to me?" he asked, sounding incredulous.

"You fought for my honor. You protected me," she answered.

He was infuriated over her perplexed tone of voice. She acted as though he should have understood. "Then it's damned fortunate someone else didn't—"

"No, I wouldn't have slept with any other Englishman. Our destiny is—"

"Your destiny is to become my wife, understand, Christina?" he shouted.

Christina pulled away from him, somewhat surprised he'd let her go. "I hate England, do you understand me?" she shouted back at him. "I couldn't survive here. The people are so strange. They run from one tiny little box to another. And there are so many of them, a person has no room to breathe. I couldn't—"

"What little boxes?" Lyon asked.

"The houses, Lyon. No one ever stays outside. They scurry like mice from one place to another. I couldn't live like that. I couldn't breathe. And I don't like the English people, either. What say you to that full truth, Lyon? Do you think me daft? Perhaps I'm as crazy as everyone here believes my mother was."

"Why don't you like the people?" he asked. His voice had turned soft, soothing. Christina thought he really might be thinking she'd just lost her mind.

"I don't like the way they act," she announced. "The women take lovers after they've pledged themselves to a mate. They treat their old like discarded garbage. That is their most appalling flaw," Christina said. "The old should be honored, not ignored. And their children, Lyon. I hear about the little ones, but I've yet to see one. The mothers lock their children away in their schoolrooms. Don't they understand the children are the heartbeat of the family? No, Lyon, I could not survive here."

She paused to take a deep breath, then suddenly realized Lyon didn't look very upset about her comments. "Why aren't you angry?" she asked.

He grabbed her when she tried to step away from him again, wrapped his arms around her, and held her close to him. "First of all, I agree with most of what you've just said. Second, all during your irate protest you kept saying 'they,' not 'you.' You didn't include me with the others, and as long as it's the other English you dislike, that's quite all right with me. You told me once you thought I was different. It's why you've been drawn to me, isn't it? It doesn't really matter," he added with a sigh. "You and I are both English. You can't change that fact, Christina, just as you can't change the fact that you belong to me now."

"I'm not English where it matters most, Lyon."

"And where might that be?" Lyon asked.

"In my heart."

He smiled. She sounded like a small child in need of comfort. She happened to pull away from him just at that moment, saw his smile, and was infuriated. "How dare you laugh at me when I tell you what is in my heart?" she shouted.

"I dare, all right," Lyon shouted back. "I dare because this is the first time you've ever been completely honest with me. I dare because I'm trying to understand you, Christina," he added, taking a menacing step toward her. "I dare because I happen to care about you. God only knows why, but I do care."

Christina turned her back on him. "I'll not continue this discussion," she announced. She picked up his pants and threw them at him. "Get dressed and go home. I'm afraid you'll just have to walk, because I don't have a servant available to fetch your carriage for you."

She glanced back at him, took in his startled expression. A sudden thought made her gasp. "Your carriage isn't waiting out front, is it?"

"Oh, hell," he muttered. He had his pants on in quick time, then strode out of the bedroom, barechested and barefooted, still muttering under his breath.

Christina ran after him. "If anyone sees your carriage . . . well, I can certainly count on someone telling my aunt, can't I?"

"You don't care what the English think, remember?" Lyon shouted back. He threw the front door open, then turned to give her a good glare. "You would have to live on the main street," he said, sounding as if her choice of townhouses had been a deliberate provocation somehow.

Lyon turned to yell instructions to his driver after making that accusation. "Go and wake up the servants, man. Bring half the number over here. They'll stay with Princess Christina until her aunt returns from the country."

He'd been forced by circumstances to bellow his orders. His driver wouldn't have heard him otherwise. No, the parade of carriages coming down the street was making too much of a clatter.

He knew he should have felt a shred of shame for what he was deliberately doing. When he spotted the first carriage rounding the corner, the very least he could have done was wave his driver away and shut the door.

"Thompson's party must have just let out," he remarked in a casual voice to the horrified woman hovering behind his back.

Lyon actually smiled when he heard her gasp, pleased she understood the ramifications well enough. Then he leaned against the door frame and waved at the startled occupants of the first carriage.

"Good eve, Hudson, Lady Margaret," he shouted, totally unconcerned that his pants were only partially buttoned.

Over his shoulder he told Christina, "Lady Margaret looks like she's about to fall out of the carriage, love. She's hanging halfway out the window."

"Lyon, how could you?" Christina asked, clearly appalled by his conduct.

"Destiny, my dear."

"What?"

He waved to three more carriages before he finally closed the door. "That ought to do it," he remarked, more to himself than to the outraged woman looking ready to kill him. "Now, what were you saying about not marrying me, my sweet?"

"You are a man without shame," she shouted when she could find her voice.

"No, Christina. I've just sealed your fate, so to speak. You still do believe in destiny, don't you?"

"I'm not going to marry you, no matter what scandal you weave."

If she hadn't been so infuriated, she might have tried to explain again. But Lyon was grinning at her with such a victorious, arrogant look on his face, she decided to keep the full truth to herself.

He drained the anger right out of her. Lyon suddenly pulled her into his arms and kissed her soundly. When he finally let go of her, she was too weak to protest.

"You will marry me."

He started back up the stairs in search of his shoes.

Christina held on to the bannister, watching him. "Do you think ruining my reputation will matter, Lyon?"

"It's a nice start," Lyon called back. "Remember, what will be is going to be. Your words, Christina, not mine."

"I'll tell you what's going to be," she shouted. "I won't be in England long enough to care about my reputation. Don't you understand, Lyon? I have to go home."

She knew he'd heard her. She'd shouted loud enough to rattle the walls. Lyon disappeared around the corner, but Christina patiently waited for him to come back downstairs. She wasn't about to go chasing after him again. No, she knew she'd end up back in bed with him if she went up the stairs. God help her, she'd probably be the one to suggest it. Lyon was simply too appealing, and she was too weak-hearted to fight him.

Besides, she told herself, she hated him. The man had the morals of a rattlesnake.

He was dressed when he came downstairs. He was ignoring her, too. Lyon didn't speak another word until his carriage had returned with two big men and one heavyset maid. Then he spoke to his staff, giving them his orders.

Christina was infuriated with his high-handed manner. When he instructed the men to see to her protection, to let no one enter her home without his permission, she decided to protest.

The look he gave her made her reconsider. She was seeing a different side of Lyon's character now. He was very like Black Wolf when he was addressing his warriors. Lyon was just as cold, as rigid, as commanding. Christina instinctively knew it would be better not to argue with him now.

She decided to ignore him just as thoroughly as he was ignoring her. That decision was short-lived, however. Christina was staring into the fireplace, trying to pretend the man didn't even exist, when she heard a rather descriptive curse. She turned just in time to see Lyon jump up from the settee.

He'd sat on her knife.

"Serves you justice," she muttered when he held the blade up and glared at it.

She tried to snatch her weapon away from him, but Lyon wouldn't let her have it. "It belongs to me," she announced.

"And you belong to me, you little warrior," Lyon snapped out. "Admit it, Christina, now, or I swear to the Great Spirit I'll show you how a real warrior uses a knife."

Their gazes held a long, ponderous moment. "You really don't know what you're trying to catch, do you? Very well, Lyon. For now—until you change your mind, that is—I will belong to you. Does that satisfy you?"

Lyon dropped the knife and pulled Christina into his arms. He then proceeded to show her just how immensely satisfied he really was.

Chapter Nine

Edward had left to put down a resistance in the West. When the captain of my ship came for me, I made him wait outside my husband's office while I went inside to steal the jewels. I briefly considered leaving a note for Edward, then decided against it.

We set sail immediately, but I didn't begin to feel safe until we were two days out to sea. I stayed below in my cabin most of the time, for I was terribly ill. I couldn't hold any food in my stomach, and I believed it was the weather that was the cause.

It wasn't until a week had passed that the truth settled in my mind. I was carrying Edward's child.

God forgive me, Christina, but I prayed for your death.

Journal entry
September 7, 1795

Monday was a trial of endurance for Christina. Although she protested vehemently, Lyon's servants had her possessions packed up and transferred to his mother's townhouse by noon.

Christina kept insisting that she wasn't going anywhere, that the Countess would be home Monday next, and that she would take care of herself until that time. No one paid her the least attention. They followed the instructions from their employer, of course, and though they were friendly enough, one and all suggested she mention her distress to the Marquess of Lyonwood.

Although Christina had not seen Lyon since Friday evening, his presence was certainly felt. He hadn't allowed her to attend Creston's ball, or to go anywhere else, for that matter. Christina thought he kept her closeted inside her townhouse so she wouldn't be able to run away.

There was also the possibility that he was trying to protect her feelings, Christina realized. He might not want her to hear any of the whispers circling the ton about her liaison with Lyon. It was a scandal, to be sure, but a scandal Lyon had personally caused.

Perhaps Lyon thought she'd be upset about the slurs against her character. She was unmarried, Lyon had been undressed, and half the ton had witnessed the scene. Oh, there was a scandal floating about; Christina had heard Colette, the lady's maid Lyon had thrust upon her, tell one of the other servants a juicy bit of gossip she'd overheard when she'd gone to do the marketing with the cook.

Christina had a splitting headache by midafternoon. It came upon her all at once when she happened to notice the wedding announcement in the newspapers. Lyon had had the gall to post his intention to marry Princess Christina the following Saturday.

Colette caught her tearing up the paper. "Oh, my lady, isn't it romantic the way the Marquess flaunts tradition? Why, he's doing everything to his liking and doesn't care what others will say."

Christina didn't think it was romantic at all. She felt like screaming. She went upstairs to her bedroom, thinking to find a few minutes' peace, but she'd barely closed the door behind her when she was once again interrupted.

A visitor was waiting for her in the drawing room. Since Lyon had ordered that no one was to be allowed entrance, Christina naturally assumed he was the one waiting for her.

She was fighting mad when she stormed into the salon. "If you think you can . . ."

Her shout tapered off as soon as she saw the elderly woman sitting in the gold wing-back chair. "If I think what, my dear?" the woman asked, looking perplexed.

Christina was embarrassed by her outburst. The woman smiled at her then. Some of the awkwardness left her. Christina could tell the stranger was kind. There were laugh wrinkles around her eyes and her mouth. The top of her gray-haired bun was level with the top of the chair, indicating she was an extremely tall woman. She wasn't very attractive. Her hooked nose took up a good portion of her face, and she had a slight yet noticeable line of hair above her thin upper lip. She was a heavy-bosomed woman with wide shoulders.

She seemed to be about the Countess's age. "I do apologize for shouting at you, madam, but I believed you were Lyon," Christina explained after making a low curtsy.

"How very bold of you, child."

"Bold? I don't understand," Christina said.

"To raise your voice to my nephew. Proves you've got spirit," the woman announced with a brisk nod. She motioned for Christina to sit down. "I've known Lyon since he was a little boy, and I've never had the courage to shout at him. Now, allow me to introduce myself," she continued. "I'm Lyon's aunt. Aunt Harriett, to be correct. I'm his father's younger sister, you see, and since you'll soon be the new Marchionness of Lyonwood, you might as well call me Aunt Harriett from the beginning. Are you ready to come home with me now, Christina, or do you need a little more time to prepare? I shall be happy to wait in here, if you could order me a spot of tea. My, it has gone warm again today, hasn't it?" she asked.

Christina didn't know how to answer her. She watched her take a small fluted fan from her lap, open it with a quick flip of her wrist, and begin to wave it a bit violently in front of her face.

Because of the woman's advanced years, Christina naturally took a submissive attitude. The elders were to be respected and—whenever possible—obeyed without a word of protest. It was the way of the Dakota, the way Christina was raised.

Christina bowed her head and said, "I am honored to meet you, Aunt Harriett. If you have the patience to listen to me, I would like to explain that there seems to be a misunderstanding."

"Misunderstanding?" Harriett asked. Her voice sounded with amusement. She pointed her fan at Christina. "My dear, may I be open with you? Lyon has ordered me to see you settled in his mother's townhouse. We both know he'll have his way, regardless of your feelings. Don't look so crestfallen, child. He only has your best interests at heart."

"Yes, madam."

"Do you want to marry Lyon?"

Her blunt question demanded an answer. She was staring intently at Christina. Very much like a hawk, Christina thought.

"Well, child?"

Christina tried to think of a way to soften the truth. "What I would like to do and what I must do are two separate issues. I'm trying to protect Lyon from making a terrible mistake, madam."

"Marriage would be a mistake, you say?" Aunt Harriett asked.

"If he marries me, yes," Christina admitted.

"I've always been known for my bluntness, Christina, so I'm going to ask you right out. Do you love my nephew?"

Christina could feel herself blushing. She looked up at Aunt Harriett for a long moment.

"You don't need to answer me, child. I can see you do."

"I am trying not to love him," Christina whispered.

Aunt Harriett started fanning herself again. "I certainly don't understand that remark. No, I don't. Lyon did tell me you've only just learned the English language, and that you might not make sense all the time. Now, don't get red in the face, Christina, he meant no criticism. Do you have any idea how remarkable it is that this union will be based on love?"

"When I first met Lyon, I believed we were meant to be together . . . for a short time. Yes," she added when Aunt Harriett gave her a puzzled look. "I believed it was our destiny."

"Destiny?" Aunt Harriett smiled. "What a romantic notion, Christina. I believe you're just what my nephew needs. He's such an intense, angry man most of the time. Now please explain what you meant by saying it would be for only a short while. Do you believe you'd fall out of love so quickly? That is a bit of a shallow constitution, isn't it?"

Christina wasn't sure what the woman meant by her remark. "Lyon would like to marry a princess. I would like to go home. It is really very simple."

The look on Aunt Harriett's face indicated she didn't think it was simple at all.

"Then Lyon will have to go home with you," Aunt Harriett announced. "I'm sure he'd insist upon visiting your homeland."

The absurd suggestion made Christina smile.

"See? I've lightened your worry already," Aunt Harriett said. "Why, of course, Lyon will take you home for a visitation."

Christina knew it was pointless to argue with the kind woman's expectations, and it would have been rude to disagree openly with her. After ordering refreshments, Christina spent the next hour listening to Aunt Harriett tell amusing stories about her family.

She learned that Lyon's father had died in his sleep. Lyon was away at school when the tragedy happened, and Christina thought it sad indeed that he hadn't been by his father's side. She also learned that Lyon's wife, Lettie, had died in childbirth. The story was so sad, Christina had to fight back her tears.

And when the hour was up, Christina went with Aunt Harriett to Lyon's mother's home.

She'd been inside the beautiful townhouse once before, when she'd visited Lady Diana by request, and for that reason the sight of such luxury didn't quite take her breath away.

The entrance blazed with candlelight. The receiving room was on the left. It was a good three times the size of all the others Christina had seen. The dining room was on the right. A long, narrow table took up most of the room, polished to such a sheen one could actually see his face in the reflection. There were sixteen chairs lining each side.

Christina assumed there were that many relatives living with Lyon's mother. Lyon had provided well for his family. There were servants rushing around, fetching and carrying. Aunt Harriett had told her that Lyon paid for it all.

Lady Diana rushed down the steps to greet Christina. "Lyon is waiting for you upstairs in the library," she announced, tugging on Christina's arm. "Oh, you do look lovely in pink, Christina. It's such a soft color," she added. "Do you know, I wish I were as delicate in stature as you are. Why, I feel like an elephant when I'm standing next to you."

Diana continued her chatter, so Christina assumed she wasn't supposed to comment on that observation.

Lady Diana led her up the stairs and into the library. It was a bright, airy room, but that was all Christina noticed when she walked inside. Lyon captured her full attention. He was standing by the windows, his back to her. A surge of anger washed over her. Christina was suddenly infuriated with Lyon's high-handed manner in taking over her life. She knew she was going to shout at him. The urge was making her throat ache.

She kept her intention hidden from his sister, even managed a weak smile when she said, "Lady Diana? May I have a few minutes alone with your brother?"

"Oh, I really don't know if that's a good idea. Aunt Harriett says you can't be unchaperoned for a single minute. She'd heard the rumors, you see," Diana whispered to Christina. "Still, she's downstairs now, and if you give me your promise that it will only be for a few minutes, no one will—"

"Diana, close the door behind you."

Lyon had turned around. He was staring at Christina when he gave the order to his sister.

Christina held his gaze. She wasn't going to be intimidated by him. And she certainly wasn't going to take any time at all to notice how ruggedly handsome he looked today. He was wearing a dark blue riding jacket. The fit made his shoulders look bigger than she'd remembered them to be.

Christina suddenly realized he was frowning at her. Why, he was actually angry with her. The observation didn't sit well. Christina was at first so astonished she could barely speak. How dare he be angry? He was the one causing all the mischief.

"I understand you accepted Baron Thorp's request to accompany you to Westley's affair, Christina. Is that true?"

"How did you hear that?" Christina asked.

"Is it true?"

He hadn't raised his voice, but the harshness was there in his tone.

"Yes, Lyon, I did agree to the baron's request. He asked me last week. We're going to this Westley's lawn party, whatever in heaven's name that is, and I don't particularly care if you're angry or not. It would be rude of me to cancel his escort now. I did give my word."

"You aren't going anywhere unless you're by my side, Christina," Lyon said. He took a deep breath before continuing. "One does not accompany other men when one is about to be married. It's becoming obvious to me that you don't grasp the situation, love. We are getting married Saturday, and I'll be damned if you'll have another escort the day before."

Lyon had tried to hold his temper, but by the time he ended his comments he was shouting.

"I shall not marry you," Christina shouted, matching his tone. "No, we shouldn't get married. Can't you see I'm trying to protect you? You don't know anything about me. You want a princess, for God's sake."

"Christina, if you don't start making sense . . ."

Lyon suddenly moved and had her in his arms before she could take a step back. Christina didn't try to struggle. "If you weren't so stubborn, Lyon, you'd realize I was right. I should find someone else. If Thorp doesn't agree to my proposal, I could ask someone else, even Splickler."

He had to force himself to take another deep breath. "Listen carefully, Christina. No one's going to touch you but me. Splickler's not going to be able to walk for a month, and I forsee a long voyage coming Thorp's way. Believe me when I tell you that every man you settle on will meet with a few unpleasant surprises."

"You wouldn't dare. You're a Marquess. You can't just go around frightening people. Why can't Splickler walk?" she suddenly asked. "I remember quite specifically that Rhone shut the door on his nose. You're exaggerating. You wouldn't—"

"Oh, but I would."

"Dare you smile at me while you make such obscene remarks?"

"I dare to do whatever I want to do, Christina." He rubbed his thumb across her mouth. Christina felt like biting him.

Then her shoulders sagged in defeat. All the man had to do was touch her, and her rational thoughts went flying out the window. God help her, she could feel the shivers gathering in her stomach now.

She let him kiss her, even opened her mouth for his tongue, then let him coach all the anger out of her.

Lyon didn't let up on his tender assault until Christina was responding to him with equal ardor. He ended the intimacy only after she'd put her arms around his shoulders and was clinging to him.

"The only time you're honest with me is when you kiss me, Christina. For now, that's quite enough."

Christina rested her head against his chest. "I will not give my heart to you, Lyon. I will not love you."

He rubbed his chin against the top of her head. "Yes, you will, my sweet."

"You're very sure of yourself," she muttered.

"You gave yourself to me, Christina. Of course I'm sure."

A loud knock on the door interrupted them. "Lyon, unhand that maiden immediately. Do you hear me?"

The question was unnecessary. Aunt Harriett had shouted loud enough for the neighbors to hear.

"How did she know you were holding me, Lyon? Does she have the sight?" Christina asked, her voice filled with awe.

"The what?" Lyon asked.

"Open this door. Now."

"The sight," Christina whispered between Aunt Harriett's bellows. "She can see through the door, Lyon."

Lyon laughed. The booming sound made her ears tingle. "No, my love. My Aunt Harriett just knows me very well. She assumed I'd be holding you."

She looked disappointed. When Aunt Harriett shouted again, Christina turned to go to the door. "If you give me one or two promises, I'll wed you Saturday," she said.

Lyon shook his head. The little innocent still didn't understand. Promises or not, he was going to marry her.

"Well?" she asked.

"What promises?"

Christina turned and found Lyon standing with his arms folded across his chest, waiting. His manner seemed condescending to her. "One, you must promise to let me go home when my task is done here. Two, you must promise not to fall in love with me."

"One, Christina, you aren't going anywhere. Marriage is forever. Get that little fact in your head. Two, I don't have the faintest idea why you wouldn't want me to love you, but I'll try to accommodate you."

"I knew you'd be difficult. I just knew it," Christina muttered.

The door suddenly opened behind her. "Well, why didn't you tell me it wasn't latched?" Aunt Harriett demanded. "Did you get this misunderstanding straightened out, Christina?" she asked.

"I have decided to marry Lyon for a little while."

"A long while," Lyon muttered.

The woman was as dense as fog. Lyon felt like shaking her.

"Good. Now come along with me, Christina, and I'll show you your room. It's next to my bedroom," she added, with a long, meaningful look in Lyon's direction. "There will be no private meetings during the night while I'm about."

"She'll be there in just a minute," Lyon said. "Christina, answer me one question before you leave."

"I shall wait right outside this door," Aunt Harriett announced before pulling the door closed.

"What is your question?" Christina asked.

"Are you going to change your mind before Saturday? Do I have to keep you guarded inside the townhouse until then?"

"You're smiling as though you'd like to do just that," Christina announced. "No, I won't change my mind. You're going to be very sorry, Lyon," she added in a sympathetic voice. "I'm not at all what you think I am."

"I know exactly what I'm getting," Lyon said, trying not to laugh. She was giving him a forlorn look, telling him without words that she felt sorry for him.

"You're marrying me because you realize how good it was when we slept together," he announced.

It was an arrogant statement, and he really didn't think she'd bother to answer him.

"No."

Christina opened the door, smiled at Aunt Harriett, then turned to give Lyon her full answer. "The full truth, Lyon?"

"That would be nice for a change," Lyon answered with a drawl.

"In front of your dear Aunt Harriett?" she qualified, giving the perplexed woman a quick smile.

Aunt Harriett let out a sigh, then pulled the door closed again. Christina could hear her muttering something about not needing her fan what with the door flapping back and forth in her face, but she didn't understand what the older lady meant.

"Answer me, Christina, with your full truth."

His sudden impatience irritated her. "Very well. I'm marrying you because of the way you fought the mischief makers."

"What does that have to do with marriage?" he asked.

"Oh, everything."

"Christina, will you make sense for once in your life?" Lyon demanded.

She realized then she should simply have lied to him again. The truth was often more upsetting, more complex than a simple fabrication. Still, it was a little too late to fashion another lie now. Lyon looked as if he wanted to shout. "I'm trying to make sense, Lyon. You see, even though the battle wasn't much to boast about, you did fight like a warrior."

"And?"

"Well, it's perfectly clear to me."

"Christina." His voice was low, angry.

"You aren't going to be an easy man to kill. There, now you have the full truth. Does it satisfy you?"

Lyon nodded, giving her the impression he understood what she was talking about. He knew in that moment that nothing the woman ever said to him in the future would confuse him. No, he'd just reached his limit. A man could only take so many surprises, he told himself.

Then he tried to concentrate on the new puzzle she'd handed him. "Are you telling me you'll try to kill me once we're wed, but because I can defend myself, you might not be able to accomplish the deed? And that is why you're marrying me?"

He had to shake his head when he'd finished his illogical conclusions.

"Of course not," Christina answered. "How shameful of you to think I'd want to harm you. You've a devious mind, Lyon."

"All right," he said, clasping his hands behind his back. "I apologize for jumping to such unsavory conclusions."

Christina looked suspicious. "Well, I would hope so," she muttered. "I shall accept your apology," she added grudgingly. "You look contrite enough to make me believe you're sincere."

Lyon vowed he wasn't going to lose his patience. He wasn't as certain about his mind, however. Christina was making mincemeat out of all his thoughts. God help him, he was going to get a clear answer out of her, no matter how long it took. "Christina," he began, keeping his voice soothing enough to lull an infant, "since you've decided I'm not an easy man to kill—and I do appreciate your faith in me, by the way—do you happen to know who's going to try?"

"Try what?"

"To kill me."

The man really needed to learn how to control his temper. Christina had just opened the door again. She smiled at Aunt Harriett, saw the poor woman was about to speak, but shut the door in her face before she could get a word out. She didn't want the woman to overhear her answer.

"My father. He's coming back to England. He'll try to kill me. I promise to protect you, Lyon, for as long as I'm here. When I go away again, he'll leave you alone."

"Christina, if he's going to try to kill you, why do you think to protect me?"

"Oh, he'll have to kill you first. It's the only way he'll be able to get to me," she reasoned. "You're a very possessive man, Lyon. Yes, you are," she added when she thought he was about to protest. "You'll guard me."

Lyon was suddenly feeling extremely pleased but didn't have the faintest idea why. Had she just given him a compliment? He couldn't be sure.

He decided to make certain. "Then you trust me," he announced.

She looked astonished. "Trust a white man? Never."

Christina jerked the door open and set about smoothing the bluster out of Aunt Harriett. It was a difficult undertaking, for her mind was still occupied with Lyon's outrageous conclusion. Trust him? Where in God's name had he come by that ridiculous notion?

"It's about time, young lady. A woman could grow old waiting for you."

"Aunt Harriett, I appreciate your patience. And you were so right. A good talk with Lyon has resolved all my worries. Will you show me to my room now? I would like to help the maid unpack my gowns. Do you think there's enough room here for my aunt when she returns to London next week? The Countess will be displeased when she learns I've moved away."

Her ploy worked. Aunt Harriett immediately lost her puzzled expression. The urge to take charge overrode all other considerations. "Of course I was right. Now come along with me. Did you know Diana has invited several people over for the afternoon? Quite a number have already arrived. They're all very anxious to meet you, Christina."

The door clicked shut on Aunt Harriett's enthusiastic remarks.

Lyon walked back over to the windows. He saw the gathering in the garden below, then dismissed the guests from his mind.

The puzzle was taking shape. Lyon concentrated on the new item he believed to be true. Christina did think her father was going to come back to England.

To kill her.

The frightened look in her eyes, the way her voice had trembled, told him she was, for once, giving him the truth. She knew far more than she was telling, however. Lyon guessed the only reason she'd admitted that much to him was to put him on his guard.

She was trying to protect him. He didn't know if he should feel insulted or happy. She had taken on his duty. But she was right. He was possessive. Christina belonged to him, and he wasn't about to let anyone harm her. They'd have to kill him first in order to get to her.

How had she ever come by such conclusions about her father? Lyon remembered how emphatic Sir Reynolds had been when he told him Christina had never even met her father.

None of it made sense, unless Christina's mother had lived longer than anyone believed and had handed down her fears to her daughter . . . or possibly left the fears with someone else.

Who had raised Christina? It surely wasn't the

Summertons, Lyon thought with a smile. What a little liar she was. Though he should have been furious with her for deceiving him, he was actually amused. He sensed she'd fabricated the story just to placate him.

How simple it would be if only she'd tell him the whole truth. Christina wouldn't, of course, but at least now he understood her reason. She didn't trust him.

No, he corrected himself, she didn't trust white men.

She'd meant to say Englishmen . . . or had she?

The key to the riddle rested in the missionary's hands. Lyon knew he'd have to be patient. Bryan had sent him a note telling him that Mick had remembered the man's name. He was called Claude Deavenrue.

Lyon had immediately dispatched two of his loyal men in search of Deavenrue. Although he knew the missionary had told Mick he was going to stop in England on his way back from France to pay Christina a visit, Lyon wasn't about to put his faith in that possibility. There was always the chance Deavenrue might change his mind, or that Mick had been wrong in what he'd heard.

No, Lyon wasn't taking any risks. It had suddenly become imperative that he speak to the missionary as soon as possible. His reasons for finding out about Christina's past had changed, however. A feeling of unease had settled in his mind. She was in danger. He wasn't certain if her father was the true threat, but all his instincts were telling him to beware. The urge to protect Christina fairly overwhelmed him. Lyon had learned long ago to trust his instincts. The scar on his forehead had been the result of one of those foolish instances when he hadn't heeded their warning.

Lyon hoped the missionary would be able to shed some light on the mystery, to tell him enough about Christina's past to help him protect her. Lyon had already drawn his own conclusions. From all her comments, he decided she was probably raised by one of those courageous frontier families he'd heard about. He even pictured Christina inside a small log cabin somewhere in the wilderness beyond the colonies. That would explain the facts that she liked to go barefooted, loved the outdoors, had heard the sounds of mountain lions, and had possibly seen a buffalo or two.

Yes, that explanation made good sense to Lyon, but he wasn't going to hold firm to that easy conclusion until he had confirmation from Deavenrue.

Lyon let out a long, weary sigh. He was satisfied that he was doing all he could for the moment. Then his mind turned to another troubling thought. Christina kept insisting she was going to go home.

Lyon vowed to find a reason to make her want to stay.

A loud knock on the door interrupted Lyon's thoughts. "Have time for us, Lyon?" Rhone asked from the doorway. "Lord, you're scowling like a devil," he remarked in a cheerful voice. "Don't let it put you off, Andrew," he told the young man standing beside him. "Lyon is always in a foul mood. Had another recent conversation with Christina, perchance?" he asked, his voice as bland as the color of his beige jacket. When Lyon nodded, Rhone started chuckling. "Andrew has yet to meet your intended, Lyon. I thought you would like to do the introductions."

"Good to see you again, Andrew," Lyon said, trying to sound as if he meant it. He hadn't wanted to be interrupted; he didn't want to be civil, and he glared just that message to Rhone.

His friend was tugging on the sleeve of his jacket, probably trying to keep his bandage concealed, Lyon thought. The man had no business being out and about yet. Lyon would have pointed out that fact if they'd been alone. Then he decided Rhone had deliberately dragged Andrew with him up to the library to avoid an argument.

"The ladies are outside in the garden," Rhone said, ignoring the black look his friend was giving him. He strolled over to the windows where Lyon stood, then motioned for Andrew to follow.

Rhone's companion made a wide berth around Lyon to

stand beside Rhone. His face was red, his manner timid. "Perhaps I should wait downstairs," Andrew remarked with a noticeable stammer. "We have intruded upon the Marquess," he ended in a whisper to Rhone.

"There's Christina, Andrew," Rhone announced, pretending he hadn't heard his complaint. "She's standing between two other ladies, in front of the hedges. I don't recognize the pretty one speaking to her now," Rhone continued. "Do you know who the other blonde is, Lyon?"

Lyon looked down at the flutter of activity below. His sister had obviously invited half the ton to her afternoon party, he decided.

He found Christina almost immediately. He thought she looked confused by all the attention she was getting. The women all appeared to be talking to her at the same time.

Then one of the gentlemen began to sing a ballad. Everyone immediately turned toward the sound. The doors to the music room had been opened, and someone was playing the spinet in the background.

Christina liked music. The fact was obvious to Lyon. The way her gown floated around her ankles indicated she was enjoying the song. Her hips were keeping gentle rhythm.

She was so enchanting. Her smile of pleasure made Lyon feel at peace again. Christina looked quite mesmerized. Lyon watched as she reached out and tore a leaf from the hedge, then began to twirl it between her fingers as she continued to sway to the music.

He thought she didn't even realize what she was doing. Her gaze was directed on the gentleman singing the song, her manner relaxed, unguarded.

Lyon knew she wasn't aware she was being watched, either. She wouldn't have eaten the leaf otherwise, or reached for another.

"Sir, which one is Princess Christina?" Andrew asked Lyon, just as Rhone started in choking on his laughter.

Rhone had obviously been watching Christina, too.

"Sir?"

"The blond-headed one," Lyon muttered, shaking his head. He watched in growing disbelief as Christina daintily popped another leaf into her mouth.

"Which blond-headed one?" Andrew persisted.

"The one eating the shrubs."

Chapter Ten

Father was overjoyed to see me. He thought Edward had approved of my visit, and I didn't tell him the truth for several days. I was too exhausted from my journey, and knew I had to regain my strength before explaining all that had happened to me.

Father was driving me mad. He'd come into my room, sit on the side of my bed, and talk of nothing but Edward. He seemed convinced that I didn't yet realize how fortunate I was to have married such a fine man.

When I could listen no more, I began to sob. The story poured out of me in incoherent snatches. I remember I screamed at my father, too. He thought I'd lost my mind to make up such lies about my husband.

I did try to speak to him again. But his mind was set in Edward's favor. Then I heard from one of the servants that he'd sent a message to my husband to come and fetch me home.

In desperation, I wrote the full story down on paper, including the fact that I was carrying his grandchild. I hid the letter in my father's winter chest, hoping he wouldn't find it until long months had passed.

Christina, he would have believed my delicate condition was the reason for what he referred to as my nervous disposition.

I began to make my plans to go to my sister, Patricia. She was living with her husband in the colonies. I didn't dare take the gems with me. Patricia was like a hound; she'd find them. She had such an inquisitive nature. For as long as I could remember, she'd read all my letters. No, I couldn't risk taking the jewels with me. They were too important. I'd taken them with the sole intent of seeing them returned to the poor in Edward's kingdom. He'd robbed them, and I was going to see justice done.

I hid the jewels in a box, then waited until the dead of night to go into the back garden. I buried the box in the flower bed, Christina.

Look for the blood roses. You'll find the box there.

Journal entry
October 1, 1795

The bride was nervous throughout the long wedding ceremony. Lyon stood by her side, holding her hand in a grip that didn't allow for any movement—or escape.

He was smiling enough to make her think he'd lost his mind. Yes, he was thoroughly enjoying himself. If Christina had been gifted with a suspicious nature, she might have concluded that her frightened state was the true reason for his happiness.

His mood did darken when she refused to repeat the vow "until death do we part," however. When she realized the holy man with the pointed velvet cap on his head wasn't going to continue along until he'd had his way, and Lyon started squeezing her hand until she thought the bones were going to snap, she finally whispered the required words.

She let Lyon see her displeasure for having to lie to a holy man, but he didn't appear to be bothered by her frown. He gave her a slow wink and a lazy grin. No, he hadn't been bothered much at all.

The man was simply too busy gloating.

Warriors did like to get their way, Christina knew. This one more than most, of course. He was a lion, after all, and he had just captured his lioness.

When they left the church, Christina clung to his arm for support. She was worried about her wedding gown, concerned that any abrupt movement would tear the delicate lace sewn into the neckline and the sleeves. Aunt Harriett had supervised the making of the gown, standing over three maids to see the task done to her satisfaction.

It was a beautiful dress, yet impractical. Lady Diana had told Christina she would only wear the garment once and must then put it aside.

It seemed such a waste. When she remarked on that fact to her new husband, he laughed, gave her another good squeeze, and told her not to be concerned. He had enough coins to keep her in new dresses every day for the rest of her life.

"Why is everyone shouting at us?" Christina asked. She stood next to Lyon on the top step outside the chapel. They faced a large crowd of people she'd never seen before, and they were making such a commotion she could barely hear Lyon's answer.

"They're cheering, love, not shouting." He leaned down and kissed her on her forehead. The cheers immediately intensified. "They're happy for us."

Christina looked up at him, thinking to tell him that it made little sense to her that complete strangers would be happy for them, but the tender expression in his eyes made her forget all about her protest, the crowd, the noise. She instinctively leaned into his side. Lyon put his arm around her waist. He seemed to know how much she needed his touch at that moment.

She quit trembling.

"My, it was a splendid ceremony." Aunt Harriett made her announcement from directly behind Christina. "Lyon, get her into the carriage. Christina, do be sure to wave to all the well-wishers. Your wedding is going to be the talk of the season. Smile, Christina. You're the new Marchioness of Lyonwood."

Lyon reluctantly let go of his bride. Aunt Harriett had taken hold of Christina's arm and was trying to direct her down the steps. Lyon knew his aunt would have her way, even if it meant a tug of war.

Christina was looking bewildered again. Little wonder, Lyon thought. His aunt was fluttering around them like a rather large bird of prey. She was dressed like one, too, in bright canary yellow, and kept flapping her lemon-colored fan in Christina's face while she barked her orders.

Diana stood behind Christina trying to undo the long folds in the wedding gown. Christina glanced behind her, smiled at Lyon's little sister, and then turned back to the crowd.

Lyon took hold of her hand and led her to the open carriage. Christina remembered to do what Aunt Harriett had instructed. She waved at all the strangers lining the streets.

"It's a pity your mama couldn't attend the ceremony," she whispered to Lyon when they were on their way. "And my Aunt Patricia is going to be angry," she added. "We really should have waited for her return from the country, Lyon."

"Angry because she missed the wedding or angry because you married me?" Lyon asked, his voice laced with amusement.

"Both, I fear," Christina answered. "Lyon, I do hope you'll get along with her when she comes to live with us."

"Are you out of your mind? The Countess will not be living with us, Christina," he said. His tone had taken on a hard edge. He took a deep breath, then started again. "We'll discuss your aunt later. All right?"

"As you wish," Christina answered. She was confused by his abrupt change in disposition, yet didn't question him. Later would be soon enough.

The reception had been hastily planned, but the result was

more than satisfactory. Candles blazed throughout the rooms, flowers lined the tables, and servants dressed in formal black scooted through the large crowd with silver trays laden with drinks. The guests spilled out into the gardens behind Lyon's mother's home, and the crush, as Aunt Harriett called it, proved that the party was a success.

Lyon took Christina upstairs to meet his mother. It wasn't a very pleasing first meeting. Lyon's mother didn't even look at her. She gave Lyon her blessing, then began to talk about her other son, James. Lyon dragged Christina out of the dark room during the middle of one of his mother's reminiscences. He was frowning, but once the door was shut behind them the smile slowly returned to his face.

Christina decided to speak to Lyon about his mama at the first possible opportunity. He'd been remiss in his duty, she thought, and then excused his conduct by telling herself he simply didn't understand what his duty was. Yes, she'd speak to him and set him straight.

"Don't frown so, Christina," Lyon said as they walked down the stairs again. "My mother is content."

"She'll be more content when she comes to live with us," Christina remarked. "I shall see to it."

"What?"

His incredulous shout drew several stares. Christina smiled up at her husband. "We shall speak of this matter later, Lyon," she instructed. "It is our wedding day, after all, and we really must be getting along. Oh, see how Rhone stands next to your sister? Do you notice the way he glares at the young men trying to get her attention?"

"You see only what you want to see," Lyon said. He pulled her up against his side when they reached the entrance, guarding her just like a warrior when they were once again surrounded by their guests.

"No, Lyon," Christina argued between introductions. "You're the one who sees only what you want to see," she explained. "You wanted to marry a princess, didn't you?"

Now what in heaven's name did she mean by that remark? Lyon thought to query her when her next question turned his attention. "Who is that shy man hovering in the doorway, Lyon? He can't seem to make up his mind if he should come inside or not."

Lyon turned to see Bryan, his friend. He caught his attention and motioned him over. "Bryan, I'm pleased you could make it. This is my wife, Christina," he added. "My dear, I'd like you to meet Bryan. He owns the Bleak Bryan tavern in another part of town."

Christina bowed, then reached out to take the timid man's hand. He offered her his left hand, thinking to save her embarrassment when she noticed his right hand was missing, but Christina clasped her hands around his scarred wrist and smiled so enchantingly that Bryan could barely get his breath. "I am honored to meet you, Bleak Bryan," she announced. "I've heard so much about you, sir. The tales of your boldness are quite wonderful."

Lyon was immediately puzzled. "My dear, I didn't speak of Bryan to you," he commented.

Bryan was blushing. He'd never had a lady of such quality pay him so much attention. He tugged his cravat, making a mess of the knot he had spent hours trying to perfect.

"I would certainly like to know where you've heard my name," he said.

"Oh, Rhone told me all about you," she answered with a smile. "He also said you would be giving your back room to Lyon next Friday eve for a game of chance."

Bryan nodded. Lyon frowned. "Rhone talks too much," he muttered.

"Is this the lady Mick told the story about, Lyon?" Bryan asked his friend. "No, she cannot be the same. Why, she doesn't look like she'd have the strength to throw a man . . ."

Bryan finally noticed Lyon was shaking his head.

"Who is Mick?" Christina asked.

"A shipmate who frequents my establishment," Bryan answered. His leathery face wrinkled into another smile. "He told the most remarkable story about—"

"Bryan, go and get something to eat," Lyon interjected.

"Ah, here comes Rhone now. Rhone? Take Bryan into the dining room."

Christina waited until she was once again alone with Lyon, then asked him why he'd suddenly become irritated. "Did I say something to upset you?"

Lyon shook his head. "I can't take much more of this crowd. Let's leave. I want to be alone with you."

"Now?"

"Now," he announced. To show her he meant exactly what he'd said, he took hold of her hand and started pulling her out the front doorway.

Aunt Harriett cut them off at the bottom step.

Christina had the good grace to look contrite. Lyon looked exasperated.

Aunt Harriett didn't budge from her position. She reminded Lyon of a centurion, for her hands were settled on her hips and her bosom was heaving forward like a solid plate of armor.

A smile suddenly softened her rigid stance. "I've put Christina's satchel inside your carriage, Lyon. You've lasted a good hour longer than I imagined you would."

Aunt Harriett wrapped Christina in a suffocatingly affectionate hug, then released her.

"Be gentle this night," she instructed Lyon.

"I shall."

It was Christina who gave the promise. Both Lyon and his aunt looked at her. "She means me, Christina," Lyon said dryly.

"You have only to remember that Lyon is your husband now, my dear," Aunt Harriett announced with a true blush. "Then all your fears will be put to rest."

Christina didn't have any idea what the woman was trying to tell her. She kept giving Christina knowing nods, and an intense hawklike stare as well.

Lyon suddenly swept her up into his arms and settled her on his lap inside the carriage. Christina wrapped her arms around her husband's neck, rested the side of her face against his shoulder, and sighed with pleasure.

He smiled against the top of her head.

Neither said a word for quite a while, content to hold each other and enjoy the blissful solitude.

Christina didn't know where he was taking her, and she didn't particularly care. They were finally alone, and that was all that mattered to her.

"Christina, you don't seem frightened of the closed quarters today," Lyon remarked. He trailed his chin across the top of her forehead in an affectionate caress. "Have you conquered this dislike?"

"I don't think I have," Christina answered. "But when you're holding me so close to you, and when I close my eyes, I do forget my worry."

It was because she trusted him, Lyon told himself. "I like it when you're honest with me, Christina," Lyon said. "And now that we're married, you must always tell me the truth," he added, thinking to ease into the topics of love and trust.

"Haven't I always told you the truth?" Christina asked. She leaned away from him to look up at his face. "Why are you looking so out of sorts? When have I ever lied to you?"

"The Summertons for one," Lyon drawled.

"Who?"

"Exactly," Lyon answered. "You told me the Summertons raised you, and we both know that was a lie."

"A fabrication," Christina corrected.

"There's a difference?"

"Sort of."

"That's not an answer, Christina," Lyon said. "It's an evasion."

"Oh."

"Well?"

"Well, what?" Christina asked. She tickled the back of his neck with her fingertips, trying to turn his attention. It was their wedding night, and she really didn't want to have to lie to him again.

"Are you going to tell me the truth about your past now? Since the Summertons don't exist . . ."

"You really are persistent," Christina muttered. She softened her rebuke with a quick smile. "Very well, Lyon. Since I am your wife, I do suppose I should tell you the full truth."

"Thank you."

"You're welcome, Lyon."

She settled herself against his shoulder again and closed her eyes. Lyon waited several long minutes before he realized she thought the discussion was over.

"Christina?" he asked, letting his exasperation show. "Who took care of you when you were a little girl?"

"The sisters."

"What sisters?"

Christina ignored the impatience in his voice. Her mind raced for a new fabrication. "Sister Vivien and Sister Jennifer mostly," she said. "I lived in a convent, you see, in France. It was a very secluded area. I don't remember who took me there. I was very young. The sisters were like mothers to me, Lyon. Each night they'd tell me wonderful stories about the places they'd seen."

"Buffalo stories?" Lyon asked, smiling over the sincerity in her voice.

"Why, as a matter of fact, yes," Christina answered, warming to her story. She made the decision not to feel guilty about deceiving her husband. Her motives were pure enough. Lyon would only be upset by the truth.

He was English, after all.

"Sister Frances drew a picture of a buffalo for me. Have you ever seen one, Lyon?"

"No," he answered. "Now tell me more about this convent," Lyon persisted. His hands caressed her back in a soothing motion.

"Well, as I said, it was in a very isolated spot. A giant wall surrounded the buildings. I was allowed to run barefoot most of the time, for we never had visitors. I was terribly spoiled, but I was still a sweet-tempered child. Sister Mary told me she knew my mother, and that is why they took me in. I was the only child there, of course."

"How did you learn to defend yourself?" he asked, his voice mild.

"Sister Vivien believed that a woman should know how to protect herself. There weren't any men around to protect us. It was a reasonable decision."

Christina's explanation made good sense. She'd answered his question about her confusion with the English laws, the reason she preferred to go shoeless, and where she'd seen a buffalo. Oh, yes, the explanation tied up some of the dangling strings all right. It was convincing and logical.

He wasn't buying it for a minute.

Lyon leaned back against the upholstery and smiled. He accepted the fact that time was needed for Christina to learn to trust him with the truth. He'd probably know all there was to know about her before she finally got around to telling him, of course.

Lyon realized the irony. He was determined that Christina would never find out about his past activities. He meant to keep his sins from her, yet he persisted, like a hound after a meaty rabbit, in prodding her into telling him all about herself.

He wasn't, however, the one insisting he was going home. She was. And Lyon knew full well the mythical convent wasn't her real destination.

She wasn't going anywhere.

"Lyon, you're squeezing the breath right out of me," Christina protested.

He immediately softened his hold.

They arrived at their destination. Lyon carried her up the steps to his townhouse, through the empty foyer, and up the winding staircase. Christina barely opened her eyes to look around.

His bedroom had been made ready for them. Several candles burned with soft light on the bedside tables. The covers had been drawn back on the huge bed. A fire blazed in the hearth across the room, taking the chill out of the night air.

Lyon placed her on the bed and stood there smiling at her for the longest time. "I've sent my staff on ahead to open the country home, Christina. We're all alone," he explained as he knelt down and reached for her shoes.

"It's our wedding night," Christina said. "I must undress you first. It is the way it should be done, Lyon."

She flipped her shoes off, then stood beside her husband. After she'd untied the knot of his cravat, she stood back to help him with his jacket.

When his shirt had been removed and her fingers slipped into the waistband of his pants, Lyon couldn't stand still any longer. Christina smiled when she noticed how his stomach muscles reacted to her touch. She would have continued undressing him, but Lyon wrapped his arms around her waist, pulled her up against his chest, and claimed her mouth in a hot, sensual kiss.

For long sweet minutes they teased each other with their hands, their tongues, their whispered words of pleasure.

Lyon had vowed to go slowly this night, to give Christina pleasure first, and he knew that if he didn't pull away and help her get undressed soon he'd end up ripping another gown off her.

She was trembling when he dragged his mouth away from hers. Her voice had deserted her, and she had to nudge him toward the side of the bed. When he sat down, she pulled off his shoes and socks.

She stood on the platform between Lyon's legs and slowly worked the fastenings free on her sleeves. It was an awkward task because she couldn't seem to take her gaze away from Lyon to watch what she was doing.

"You'll have to help me with the back of my gown," she said, smiling because her voice sounded so strained to her.

When she turned around, Lyon pulled her down onto his lap. She fought the urge to lean against him, impatient now to get her scratchy gown out of the way. Her hands reached to her coronet, but she'd only pulled one pin free before Lyon pushed her hands away and took over the task. "Let me," he said, his voice husky.

The heavy curls unwound until the rich, sun-kissed locks fell to her waist. Christina sighed with pleasure. Lyon's fingers were making her shiver. He slowly lifted the mass to drape it over her shoulder, paused to kiss the back of her neck, and then began the arduous task of unhooking the tiny fastenings.

His heart was slamming against his chest. The scent of her was so appealing, so wonderfully feminine. He wanted to bury his face in her golden curls; he would have given in to his urge if she hadn't moved against his arousal so impatiently, so enticingly.

Lyon was finally able to get her gown open to her waist. She was wearing a white chemise, but the silk material easily tore free when he slipped his hands inside. He found her breasts and cupped their fullness as he pulled her forcefully back against his chest.

Christina arched against him. His thumbs slid over her nipples, making her breath catch in her throat. Her skin tingled when she rubbed her back against the warm pelt of hair on his chest.

"You feel so good, my love," Lyon whispered into her ear. He nuzzled her earlobe as he tugged on her gown, lifting her away from him only long enough to push the garment down over her hips.

Christina was too weak to help. Her hips moved against him. Lyon thought her motions were excruciatingly blissful. He kissed the side of her neck, then her shoulder. "Your skin is so smooth, so soft," he told her.

Christina tried to speak to him, to tell him how very much he pleased her, but his hand slid between her thighs, making her forget her own thoughts. His thumb teased her sensitive nub again and again until the sweet torture threatened to consume her. She called his name with a ragged moan when his fingers penetrated her, then tried to push his hand away. Lyon wouldn't cease his torment, and she was soon lost to the sensations coursing through her, unable to think much at all. She could only react to the incredible heat. "Lyon, I can't stop."

"Don't fight it, Christina," Lyon whispered. He increased his pressure until she found her release. Christina arched against him, called his name again.

He could feel the tremors flowing through her. Lyon

didn't remember taking the rest of his clothes off, didn't know if he'd been gentle or rough when he moved her from his lap to the center of the bed.

Her hair fanned out on top of the pillows, shining almost silver in the candlelight. She was so beautiful. She was still wearing her white stockings. He might have smiled, but the surge of white-hot desire consumed him and he couldn't be sure.

He came to her then, settling himself between her thighs, wrapping his arms around her. He captured her mouth in a searing kiss and thrust into her tight, moist heat just as his tongue thrust inside her mouth to mate with hers.

Christina put her legs around him, pulling him deeper inside. She met each thrust completely, forcefully, arching with demand when he withdrew.

They both found their release at the same moment.

"I love you, Christina."

Christina couldn't answer him. The sweet ecstasy overwhelmed her. She felt like liquid in his strong arms, could only hold onto him until the storm had passed.

Reality was slow to return to Lyon. He wanted never to move. His breathing was harsh, erratic. "Am I crushing you, love?" he asked when she tried to move.

"No," Christina answered. "But the bed seems to be swallowing me up."

Lyon leaned up on his elbows to take most of his weight off her. His legs were tangled with hers, and he shifted his thighs to ease the pressure.

His gaze was tender. "Say the words, Christina. I want to hear them."

Because he fully expected to hear her tell him that she loved him, he wasn't at all prepared for her tears. "My sweet?" he asked, catching the first drops that fell from her thick lashes with his fingertips. "Are you going to cry every time we make love?"

"I cannot seem to help myself," Christina whispered between sobs. "You make me feel so wonderful."

Lyon kissed her again. "You sound like you're confessing

a grave sin," he said. "Is it so terrible to feel wonderful?"

"No."

"I love you. In time you'll give me the words I want. You're very stubborn, do you know that?"

"You don't love me," Christina whispered. "You love—"

His hand covered her mouth. "If you tell me I love a princess, I'll—"

"You'll what?" Christina asked when he moved his hand away from her mouth.

"Be displeased," Lyon announced, giving her a lopsided grin.

Christina smiled at her husband. Lyon rolled to his side, then pulled her up against him. "Lyon?"

"Yes?"

"Will I always feel as though my soul has merged with yours?"

"I hope so," Lyon answered. "Very few people are able to share what we've—"

"It's destiny," Christina said. She wiped her tears away with the back of her hand. "You may laugh at me if you want, but it was our destiny to be with each other. Besides, no other woman would have you."

Lyon chuckled. "Is that so?" he asked.

"Oh, yes. You're a scoundrel. Why, you ruined my reputation just to get your way."

"But you don't care what others say about you, do you, Christina?"

"Sometimes I do," she confessed. "It's a sorry trait, isn't it? I care what you think of me."

"I'm glad," Lyon answered.

Christina closed her eyes with a sigh. The last thing she remembered was Lyon pulling the covers up over them.

Lyon thought she looked like a contented kitten, curled up against him. He knew he wouldn't be able to sleep for very long, and the familiar tension settled in the pit of his stomach. The nightmares would certainly visit him again. He hadn't missed a night in over two years. His worry was for Christina, of course. He didn't want to frighten her. No, he knew he'd have to go downstairs and meet his past there, in the privacy of his library.

He closed his eyes for a moment, wanting to savor her warmth just a little longer.

It was his last thought until morning light.

Chapter Eleven

The voyage to the colonies was very difficult. The ocean in winter was angry with giant swells. The bitterness of the frigid air kept me inside my cabin most of the time. I tied myself to my bed with rope the captain had supplied, for I would have been tossed around the room if I hadn't taken that precaution.

I wasn't sick in the mornings any longer, and my heart had softened toward you, Christina. I actually thought I'd be able to make a new beginning in the colonies.

I felt so free, so safe. Another ocean would soon separate me from Edward. You see, I didn't realize he'd come after me.

Journal entry
October 3, 1795

Morning sun flooded the bedroom before Lyon awakened. His first thought was an astonishing one. For the first time in over two years, he'd actually slept through the night. The pleasant realization didn't last long, however. Lyon rolled to his side to take his wife into his arms, and only then he realized she wasn't there.

He bolted out of the bed, then thanked God and his quick reflexes, for he'd just missed stepping on her.

She'd obviously fallen out of bed, and in her sound sleep she hadn't awakened enough to climb back in.

Lyon knelt down next to Christina. He must have slept like an innocent, too, he decided, because he hadn't heard her fall. She'd dragged one of the blankets with her, and she did look comfortable. Her breathing was deep, even. No, he didn't think the fall had harmed her.

He gently eased her into his arms. When he stood up, she instinctively cuddled against his chest.

You trust me when you're sleeping, he thought with a grin as her hands slipped around his waist and he caught her contented sigh.

Lyon stood there holding her for long, peaceful minutes, then placed her in the center of his bed. Her breathing hadn't changed, and he really didn't think he'd awakened her, but when he tried to move her hands away from his waist her grip increased.

Christina suddenly opened her eyes and smiled at him.

He smiled back a bit sheepishly, for the way she was watching him made him feel as though he'd just been caught in the act of doing something forbidden.

"You fell out of bed, sweetheart," he told her.

She thought his comment was vastly amusing. When he questioned her about her laughter, she shook her head, told him he probably wouldn't understand, and asked why he didn't just make love to her again and quit frowning so ferociously.

Lyon fell into her arms, and into her plan wholeheartedly.

Christina proved to be just as uninhibited in the morning light as she was during the dark hours of the night. And he was just as satisfied.

He stayed in bed with his hands behind his head, watching his wife as she straightened the room and got dressed. He was amazed by her lack of shyness. She didn't seem to be the least embarrassed by her nudity. She was dressed all too soon for his liking, in a pretty violet-colored walking gown, and when she began to brush the tangles from her hair, Lyon noticed the length didn't reach her hips now. No, her hair was waist-length.

"Christina, did you cut your hair?"

"Yes."

"Why? I like it long," Lyon said.

"You do?"

She turned from the mirror to smile at him. "Don't pin it up on top of your head, either," Lyon ordered. "I like it down."

"It isn't fashionable," Christina quoted. "But I shall bend to my husband's dictates," she added with a mock curtsy. "Lyon, are we leaving for your country home today?"

"Yes."

Christina tied a ribbon around her hair at the back of her neck, a frown of concentration on her face. "How long will it take us?" she asked.

"About three hours, a little longer perhaps," Lyon answered.

Then came a sound of someone banging on the front door. "Now who do you suppose that could be?" Christina asked.

"Someone with bad manners," Lyon muttered. He reluctantly got out of bed, reached for his clothing, then quickened his actions when his wife hurried out of the room. "Christina, don't you open that door until you know who it is," he bellowed after her.

He stumbled on a piece of sharp metal, let out a curse over his awkwardness, then glanced down to see the handle of Christina's knife protruding from the edge of the blanket she'd pulled to the floor with her. Now what in heaven's name was her knife doing there? Lyon shook his head. He determined to question her just as soon as he got rid of their unwanted visitors.

Christina had requested names as Lyon instructed before she unlocked the chains and opened the door.

Misters Borton and Henderson, her grandfather's solicitors, stood on the front stoop. They both looked terribly uncomfortable. Aunt Patricia was standing between the two men. She looked furious.

Christina wasn't given time to greet her guests properly or to get out of her aunt's way. The Countess slapped Christina across her face so forcefully that Christina stumbled backwards.

She would have fallen if Mr. Borton hadn't grabbed hold of her arm to steady her. Both solicitors were shouting at the Countess, and Henderson endeavored to restrain the wily old woman when she tried to strike Christina again.

"You filthy whore," the Countess screeched. "Did you think I wouldn't hear the stories of the vile things you did while I was away? And now you've gone and married the bastard!"

"Silence!"

Lyon's roar shook the walls. Borton and Henderson both took hesitant steps back. The Countess was too angry to show similar caution, however. She turned to glare up at the man who had ruined all her plans.

Christina also turned to look at her husband. The left side of her face was throbbing with pain, but she tried to smile at her husband, to tell him it was really all right.

Lyon was down the stairs and pulling Christina into his arms before she could begin her explanation. He tilted her face up for his scrutiny, then asked her in a voice chilled with his rage, "Who did this to you?"

She didn't have to answer. The solicitors interrupted each other as they hastened to explain that the Countess had struck her niece.

Lyon turned to Christina's aunt. "If you ever touch her again, you won't live to boast of it. Do you understand me?"

The aunt's eyes turned to slits, and her voice was filled with venom when she answered Lyon. "I know all about you. Yes, you would kill a defenseless woman, wouldn't you? Christina's going home with me now. This marriage will be annulled."

"It will not," Lyon answered.

"I'll go to the authorities," the Countess shouted, so forcefully that the veins stood out in the sides of her neck.

"Do that," Lyon answered, his voice soft. "And after you've spoken to them, I'll send your friend Splickler to tell them the rest of the story."

The Countess let out a shrill gasp. "You cannot prove—"

"Oh, but I already have," Lyon interjected. A smile that didn't quite reach his eyes changed his expression. "Splickler has conveniently written everything down on paper, Countess. If you want to make trouble, go right ahead."

"You can't believe I had anything to do with Splickler," the Countess said to Christina. "Why, I was visiting my friend in the country."

"You were staying all by yourself at the Platte Inn," Lyon answered.

"You had me followed?"

"I knew you'd lied to Christina," Lyon announced. "It's a fact you don't have any friends, Countess. I was immediately suspicious."

"Then you're the one who caused all the mishaps when I tried to return to London before the wedding. I would have stopped it. You knew that, didn't you, you—"

"Get out of here," Lyon commanded. "Say goodbye to your niece, Countess. You're never going to see her again. I'll see to it."

"Lyon," Christina whispered. She was about to soothe his anger. He gave her a gentle squeeze, however, and she assumed he didn't want her interference.

Christina wished he wouldn't get so upset on her behalf. It really wasn't necessary. She understood her aunt far better than Lyon did. She knew how greed motivated her aunt's every action.

"Christina, do you know you've married a cold-blooded murderer? Oh, yes," the Countess sneered. "England knighted him for his cold-blooded—"

"Madam, hold your tongue," Mr. Henderson said in a harsh whisper. "It was wartime," he added, with a sympathetic look at Christina.

Christina could feel the rage in her husband. His hold on her was rigid. She tried to think of a way to calm him and rid them of their uninvited guests. She slipped her hand under his jacket and began to stroke his back, trying to tell him without words that the angry comments didn't matter to her.

"Mr. Borton? Have you carried along the papers for me to sign?" she asked in a whisper.

"It is your husband who must sign the papers, my dear," Mr. Henderson answered. "My lord? If you would only give us a few minutes of your time, the funds will be handed over to you without further delay."

"Funds? What funds?" Lyon asked, shaking his head.

The Countess stomped on the floor. "Christina, if he doesn't give me my money, I'll make certain he never wants to touch you again. Yes, I'll tell him everything. Do you understand me?"

Christina's soothing strokes on Lyon's back weren't helping. She could feel his new fury. She gave him a squeeze.

Lyon had never harmed a woman, but he didn't think it was an odious thought to murder the evil woman defaming his wife. He was aching to throw her out the door.

"Did this woman come with you or does she have her own carriage?" Lyon asked the two gentlemen.

"Her conveyance is out front," Henderson answered with a nod.

Lyon turned back to the Countess. "If you aren't out of here in exactly thirty seconds, I'm going to throw you out."

"This isn't over," the Countess shouted at the Marquess. She glared at Christina. "No, this isn't over," she muttered again as she strode out the doorway.

Mr. Borton shut the door and sagged against the frame. Henderson poked at his collar. He held a satchel in his other hand. Suddenly he seemed to remember what his duty was, and he said, "Sir, I do apologize for rushing in on you this way, but the Countess was set on disrupting you."

"Who in God's name are you, man?" Lyon asked, his patience at an end.

"He is Mr. Henderson, Lyon, and the man holding up the door is Mr. Borton. They are my grandfather's solicitors. Let us get this over and done with, please, Lyon? If you'll take the gentlemen into the library, I shall fetch some soothing tea. My, it has been quite a morning, hasn't it, husband?"

Lyon stared down at his wife with an incredulous look on

his face. She acted as though nothing upsetting had taken place. Then he decided her calm manner was deliberate. "Are you trying to placate me?" he asked.

"Soothing your temper," Christina corrected. She smiled at her husband, then grimaced against the sting of her swelling skin.

Lyon noticed her discomfort. His grip tightened around her waist. She felt his anger again, had to sigh over it. "I shall go and make the tea now."

It wasn't as easy for Lyon to let go of his anger. He was abrupt when he motioned the men into his study, then took great pleasure in slamming the door shut behind him. "This had better be worth the interruption," he told the men.

Christina deliberately took her time so that Lyon would hear the facts of her grandfather's will before she interrupted.

She could tell, when Mr. Borton opened the door to her knock and took the tray from her, that the meeting hadn't gone well. No, he was looking very nervous. Christina glanced over to look at her husband and immediately understood Borton's worry. Lyon was scowling.

"Why didn't you tell me, Christina? Damn, you have more money than I do."

"And that displeases you?" she asked. She poured the tea, handed him the first cup, then continued her task until the solicitors had both been served.

"I don't believe your wife understood the exact amount left to her by her grandfather," Mr. Henderson said.

"Is it important, Lyon? It all belongs to you now, doesn't it? That is what you said earlier, Mr. Borton," Christina said. "Of course, we must make an allowance for Aunt Patricia. It must be substantial, too."

Lyon leaned back in his chair. He closed his eyes and prayed for patience. "Do you really think I'm going to provide for that . . . that . . ."

"She cannot help what she is," Christina interjected. "She's old, Lyon, and for that reason alone we must provide for her. It isn't necessary that you like her."

Christina smiled at their visitors. "At first I believed that my aunt could come and live with us, but I see that wouldn't work. No, she would never get along with Lyon. Of course, if my husband doesn't agree to finance her, then I suppose she'll have to stay with us."

He knew exactly what she was doing. A slow smile pushed his frown away. His gentle little wife had a pure heart, and a mind worthy of a diplomat. She was manipulating him now, hinting at the ridiculous possibility that the Countess would have to live with them if he didn't provide for her.

At that moment though, with her smiling so innocently at him, he decided he didn't want to deny her anything.

"Henderson, if you've the stomach for it, I would like to put you and Borton in charge of the Countess's account. Let me know what is needed to keep Christina's aunt content enough to leave us alone."

While Christina patiently waited, the details were worked out. She then saw the gentlemen out the door and hurried back into the library.

"Thank you, husband, for being so understanding," she said as she walked over to stand beside him.

Lyon pulled her down into his lap. "You knew damn well I'd do anything to keep that old bat away from you. God's truth, I'd even quit the country if I had to."

"Thank you for not calling my aunt an old bat in front of our guests," Christina said.

"I was about to," Lyon answered, grinning. "You knew that, of course. It's the reason you interrupted me, wasn't it?"

Christina wrapped her arms around Lyon's neck. "Yes," she whispered. She leaned forward to nuzzle the base of his throat. "You are such a shrewd man."

Lyon's hand rested on her thigh. His other hand was busy pulling the ribbon out of her hair. "Christina, what weapon does the Countess hold over you?"

The softly spoken question caught her unprepared. "I don't understand your meaning, Lyon. My aunt doesn't have any weapons."

"Christina, I saw the fear in your eyes when the Countess said she'd tell me everything. What did she mean?"

He felt the sudden tension in her, knew then she understood exactly what the threat was. "You're going to have to tell me the truth, Christina. I can't protect you unless I know whatever secrets there are."

"I don't want to talk about it now, Lyon," she announced. She started to nibble on her husband's ear, hoping to distract him. "We are newly married, after all, and I'd rather be kissing you."

He told himself he wouldn't let her waylay his topic, tried to ignore the surge of desire hardening his loins when Christina moved against his arousal, but when she boldly whispered into his ear how much she wanted him to touch her he decided to give in to her demand before asking her any more questions.

His mouth had never felt as wonderful to Christina. The fear of his rejection when he learned all her secrets made her feel almost desperate to take and to give as much as she could now, before the truth was turned against her.

His kiss was magical, soon robbing her of all her frightening thoughts. Yes, it was magic, for Lyon made her feel so desirable, so loved.

The kiss exploded into raw passion. His breathing was harsh when he pulled away from her. "Let's go back upstairs," he rasped.

"Why?"

"Because I want to make love to you," Lyon answered, trying to smile over her innocent question. He was literally shaking with his need for her.

"I want to make love to you, too," Christina whispered between fervent kisses along his jaw. "Do we have to go back upstairs? I don't want to wait that long."

His laughter confused her until he lifted her off his lap and started undressing her. Then she decided he was pleased by her idea.

They came together in wild abandon, fell to the floor in one fluid motion.

Christina was stretched out on top of Lyon, her legs tangled with his. Her hair fell to the floor, on the sides of Lyon's profile, acting as a shield against the outside world.

She was content to stare into her husband's eyes for a long moment, to savor the anticipation of the splendor only he could give her. Lyon's hands stroked shivers down her spine. The heat of his arousal warmed her belly, and the hairs on his chest tickled her nipples into hardening.

"I'm shameless, for I can't seem to get enough of you," she whispered.

Lyon cupped her soft, rounded bottom in his hands. "I wouldn't want you any other way," he told her. "Kiss me, wife. Christina, all you have to do is look at me and I start throbbing."

Christina kissed his chin while she slowly, deliberately rubbed her breasts and her thighs against him.

He groaned with pleasure. His hands moved to the back of her head. He forced her mouth upward to seal it with his own. His tongue plunged hungrily inside to taste again the intoxicating sweetness she offered him.

Christina was more impatient than he was. She moved to straddle him, then slowly lowered herself until he was completely inside her. She leaned back, tossing her hair over her shoulder in an utterly wanton motion. Lyon pulled his legs up until his knees pressed against her smooth back. His hands fell to cup the sides of her hips. "Don't let me hurt you," he ground out. "Slow down, love. I won't be able to stop."

He quit his protests when he felt her tighten around him, knew she was about to find her own release. His hand slid into the silky triangle of curls nestled against him. His fingers stroked her there until the fire consumed her and she turned into liquid gold in his arms.

He spilled his seed into her with a harsh groan of blissful surrender, then pulled her down to cover his chest, to hold her close, to share the rapture.

It had never been this good. It kept getting better, too, Lyon realized when his mind could form a logical thought again. "You're a wild tigress," he whispered to Christina in a voice that sounded thoroughly satisfied.

Christina propped her chin on her hands and stared down at her husband. "No, I am your lioness," she whispered.

He didn't dare laugh. Christina had sounded so terribly serious, as if what she'd just told him was of high importance. He nodded, giving her his agreement while his fingers combed through the tumble of luxuriant curls covering her back. He lifted and then rearranged the strands in an absentminded fashion as he stared into his wife's magnificent blue eyes.

"Do you know, when you look at me like that I immediately lose my concentration," he told her.

"I'll take that as a compliment," Christina announced. She leaned down to kiss him again. "You feel so good inside me," she whispered against his mouth. "And now you must give me the soft words, Lyon."

He wasn't sure what she meant by soft words, but she looked serious again. She'd stacked her hands under her chin and was staring down at him with an expectant look on her face.

"What are soft words, Christina? Tell me and I'll give them to you."

"You must tell me what is inside your heart," she instructed.

"Ah," Lyon drawled. His eyes took on a tender look when he added, "I love you, Christina."

"And?"

"And what?" Lyon asked, exasperated. "Christina, I never thought I'd be able to love again. And to actually get married . . . you've made me change all my old ways. I do not tell you I love you on a whim, Christina."

"But I already know you love me," Christina answered. "I didn't want you to, but I do admit it still pleases me. Now you must praise me, Lyon. It's the way it's done."

"I don't understand," Lyon said. "That doesn't surprise me," he added with a wink. He looked around the room and saw the chaos their hastily discarded clothing had made. The fact that he was stretched out on the carpet in his library with his uninhibited wife draped over him, trying to have a logical conversation, vastly amused him. "Do you think you're always going to be so shameless, my sweet?"

"Do not change this topic, Lyon. You must tell me I'm as

beautiful as a flower in spring, as soft and delicate as a flower's petal. And why is that amusing to you? A woman must feel as desirable after loving as before, Lyon."

He quit smiling when he realized she was about to cry.

Lyon understood what she needed now. He could see the vulnerability in her eyes. He cupped the sides of her face and leaned up to kiss her. It was a soft, tender caress meant to remove her worry, her tears.

And then he wrapped his arms around her waist and gave her all the soft words she longed to hear.

Chapter Twelve

It wasn't a very joyful reunion with my sister. Patricia acted just like Father. She was happy to see me until she realized Edward wasn't with me. Patricia's husband, Alfred, was as kind as I remembered, and he made my stay as pleasant as he could. Patricia told me they'd broken all their engagements to stay home with me, but after a while I realized they didn't have any friends at all. Patricia hated the people of Boston, and I believed the feeling was reciprocated.

My sister longed to go back to England. She fashioned a ridiculous plan. Once she was convinced I meant to stay in the colonies and never return to my husband, she announced that I must give her my baby. She would pass the child off as her own.

She tried to make me believe she wanted to be a mother, that her life wouldn't be filled until she had a child to call her own. I knew the truth, of course. Patricia hadn't changed over the time we'd been separated. No, she wanted a grandchild to give our father. An heir. Father would forgive her transgressions; he'd want to provide well for his only grandchild.

I was vehemently against this deception, Christina. I knew greed was my sister's only reason. I told her I'd never give my child away. Patricia ignored my protests. I saw her destroy a letter I'd given her husband to post to London for me. I was able to get one letter past her scrutiny, though, and I was also secure in the knowledge that my father would find the missive I'd left behind in his winter chest.

Albert kept me supplied with the daily papers to keep my mind occupied while I awaited your birth, and it was quite by chance that I came upon an article about the frontier people.

Journal entry
October 5, 1795

Lyon and Christina set out for his country manor shortly after a picnic luncheon Christina had insisted upon. They ate crusty bread, cheese, sliced mutton, and plump apple tarts. The fare was spread out on a soft blanket Christina had dragged down from upstairs. Lyon had instinctively reached for his pants, thinking to get dressed first, but his wife had laughed at his modesty, and he'd been easily convinced there really wasn't any need to be in such a hurry.

They were both covered with a layer of dust by the time they arrived at their destination, thanks to Christina's plea to ride in an open carriage and Lyon's agreement to let her have her way.

During the journey he tried to bring up the subject of her father several times, but Christina easily evaded his questions. And once they'd put the city behind them, the beauty of the surrounding wilderness kept Christina fully occupied. Her amazement was obvious. It didn't take Lyon long to realize she had believed all of England was like London.

"Why would you ever want to go into the city when you could stay in such splendor?" Christina asked him.

Splendor? Lyon hadn't thought of the countryside in such a way. Yet the pleasure he could see in his wife's expression made him open his mind to the raw beauty around him.

"We take for granted what is familiar to us," Lyon excused.

"Look around you, Lyon. See God's gifts," Christina instructed.

"Will you promise me something, Christina?" Lyon asked.

"If I am able," she answered.

"Never change," he whispered.

He'd meant it as a compliment and was therefore confused by her reaction. Christina clasped her hands in her lap and bowed her head for a long minute. When she finally looked up at him again, she was frowning.

"My dear, I haven't asked you how to settle England's debts," Lyon remarked. "And my question was irrelevant anyway. I'll make certain you don't change."

"How will you do that?" Christina asked.

"Remove all temptations," Lyon announced with a nod.

"Temptations?"

"Never mind, my sweet. Quit frowning. It will be all right."

"Did Lettie change?"

She knew he didn't like her question. That irritated her, of course, for it was the very first question about his past she'd ever put to him. "Did you love your wife very much, Lyon?" she asked.

"Lettie's dead, Christina. You're all that matters to me now."

"Why is it quite all right for you to prod me about my past and not acceptable for me to ask you questions? Your scowl won't work with me, Lyon. Please answer me. Did you love Lettie?"

"It was a long time ago," Lyon said. "I thought I did . . . in the beginning . . ."

"Before she changed," Christina whispered. "She wasn't what you thought she should be, isn't that the way of it?"

"No, she wasn't." His voice had taken on the familiar chill.

"You still haven't forgiven her, have you, Lyon? Whatever did she do to hurt you so?"

"You're being fanciful," Lyon announced. "How in God's name did we get on this topic?"

"I'm trying to understand," Christina answered. "Your sister told me you loved Lettie. Is it so painful you cannot even speak her name?"

"Christina, would you prefer that I act like my mother? All she'll talk of is James," he added.

"Lyon, I'd like our time together to be filled with joy. If I knew how Lettie changed, perhaps I wouldn't make the same mistakes."

"I love you just the way you are. And I'm damned tired of hearing our marriage is only for a short duration. Get this through your head, woman. We're married until death separates us."

"Or until I change like Lettie did," Christina answered. Her voice was just as loud, just as angry as his had been.

"You aren't going to change."

Lyon suddenly realized he was shouting at her. "This is a ridiculous conversation. I love you."

"You love a princess."

"I don't give a damn if you're a princess or not. I love you."

"Ha."

"What in God's name is that supposed to mean?" Lyon reached out to pull her into his arms. "I cannot believe we're yelling at each other like this."

"Lyon, I'm not a princess."

She'd whispered the confession against his shoulder. Lord, she sounded so forlorn. Lyon's anger evaporated. "Good," he whispered.

"Why is it good?" Christina asked.

"Because now you can't tell me I love a princess," he reasoned with a smile in his voice. "I didn't marry you because of your title."

"Then why? You've told me I'm not at all sensible, that I try to make you daft—"

"Your money."

"What?" Christina pulled out of his arms to look into his face. There was a definite sparkle in his eyes. "You're jesting with me. You didn't know I had any money until after we'd wed."

"How astute of you to remember," Lyon said. He kissed the frown away from her face, then draped his arm around her shoulder.

Christina rested against his shoulder. The continuous clip of the horses and the rocking motion of the carriage made her sleepy and content.

"Lyon? You haven't asked me why I married you," she whispered several minutes later.

"I already know why you married me, love."

She smiled over his arrogant comment. "Then explain it to me, please. I still haven't come to understand it."

He gave her a squeeze to let her know he wasn't amused by her announcement. "First, there are the scars. You happen to love my flawed body."

"And how would you know that?" she asked, pretending outrage.

"You can't keep your hands off me," he told her. "Second, I remind you of a warrior."

Christina shook her head. "You haven't any humility," she told him. "And you *are* a warrior, Lyon. A vain one, yes, but a warrior all the same."

"Ah, vanity," Lyon drawled. "Does that mean you might have to use your knife on me?"

"What are you talking about?"

"Lady Cecille. You did threaten to—"

"So you *were* listening to our conversation in the library." Christina sounded stunned. "You lied to me. That is shameful."

"*I* lied to *you*?" Lyon's voice was incredulous. "You, of course, have always been honest with me."

"You will have to cast Lady Cecille aside," Christina announced, flipping the subject to avoid another argument. "I won't be wed to a roamer."

"A what?"

"A man who chases other women," Christina explained. "I shall be true to you, and you must be true to me. Even though it is fashionable in England to take a lover, you aren't going to have one. And that's that."

He was surprised by the vehemence in her tone. He hadn't

known she had such an assertive manner. In truth, her demand pleased him immensely. "You're a bossy bit of goods, do you know that?" he whispered. He kissed her again in a leisurely fashion.

Christina realized he hadn't given her his promise, but she decided not to press the issue. Later would be soon enough.

She was about to fall asleep when they reached Lyonwood. Lyon nudged her out of her sleepy state. "We're home, Christina."

The carriage rounded the curve in the road. The wilderness suddenly disappeared.

The land had been transformed into a lush, well-manicured lawn. There were sculptured bushes lining the circle drive of gravel, with wildflowers of bold colors woven between the trees. At the top of the gently sloping hill stood Lyon's magnificent home.

Christina thought it looked like a palace. The house was made of gray and brown stone, double storied, with windows one above the other all across the front of the house. Bright green ivy splattered the stones.

"Lyonwood is as handsome as its master," Christina whispered. "I shall never remember how to get around."

"You get around me well enough," Lyon remarked. "I'm sure you'll conquer your new home just as swiftly."

Christina smiled at his teasing manner. "How many of your family members live here with you? Will I meet all of your relatives today, do you suppose?"

"I suppose not," Lyon answered. "I live by myself." He laughed when he saw her astonished reaction. "Now, of course, my gentle little wife will live with me."

"How many bedchambers are there?"

"Just twelve," Lyon answered with a shrug. The carriage stopped in the center of the circle just as the front door opened. Lyon's butler, a stout, dark-haired young man by the name of Brown, led the parade of servants down the four steps. The staff lined up behind their leader. Their uniforms were starched, as well as their stance, and though they kept their expressions contained, every gaze was directed upon their new mistress.

Lyon refused assistance in helping his wife out of the carriage. Her hands were cold and her nose pink from the brisk, windy ride. He thought she might be a bit nervous meeting his servants for the first time, and so he kept her hand clasped in his.

It didn't take him long to realize she wasn't the least bit nervous. Her manner was worthy of a queen . . . or a princess, Lyon thought with a grin. There was an air of quiet dignity in her bearing. She was gracious as she greeted each one, attentive when she listened to their explanations of what their duties were.

She captivated them, of course, just as she'd captivated him. Even Brown, his dour-faced butler, was affected. When Christina took hold of his hand and announced that it was obvious to her he'd done his duty well, the man's face broke into a spontaneous smile.

"I shall not give you interference, Mr. Brown," she explained.

Brown looked relieved at that announcement. He turned then to address his employer. "My lord, we have prepared both your chamber and the adjoining one for the Marchioness."

Christina looked up at her husband, fully expecting him to set the man straight. When Lyon simply nodded and took hold of her elbow to walk up the steps, she forced a smile for the watching servants while she whispered her displeasure to her husband.

"I shall not have my own room, Lyon. I am your wife now. I must share your blankets. And I really don't want a lady's maid." Looking around, she added, "Heavens, Lyon, this entryway is larger than your whole townhouse."

Christina wouldn't have been surprised if she'd heard an echo. The entrance was gigantic. The floors were polished to a gleam. There was a large sitting room on the left, another of equal proportions on the right. A hallway began to the left of the circular staircase. Lyon explained that the dining room was adjacent to the sitting room, with the gardens behind. The kitchens, he added, were on the opposite side.

Their bedrooms were linked by a door. "I'll have your

clothes moved in here," Lyon told Christina when she gave him a good frown. He motioned to his bed with a raised eyebrow and asked her if she'd like to see if it was comfortable enough.

"You look just like a rascal," Christina laughed. "I should like a bath, Lyon, and then I would like to see your stables. You do keep horses here, don't you?"

"But you don't like to ride," Lyon reminded her.

"Never mind that," Christina answered.

"Christina, if you don't think you'll be happy with Kathleen, I will assign the task of lady's maid to another."

"Oh, Kathleen seems very capable," Christina answered. "I just don't want any maids."

"Well, you're having one," Lyon announced. "I won't always be here to fasten your gowns, love, so quit scowling at me."

Christina sauntered over to the windows. "You're a bossy bit of goods, do you know that, Lyon?" she announced.

Lyon grabbed her from behind. He placed a wet kiss on the column of her throat. "I really insist that you try the bed."

"Now?"

Christina turned to watch Lyon walk over to the door. When he turned the lock and faced her again she could see he wasn't jesting. He gave her his most intimidating look, then motioned her over with an arrogant nod of his head.

"I'm covered with dust."

"So am I."

She was already breathless, and he hadn't even touched her yet.

Christina kicked off her shoes and walked over to the bed. "Will you always be this demanding with your wife?" she asked him.

"Yes," Lyon answered. He discarded his jacket and his shoes, then went to Christina. "Will my wife always be this submissive?" he asked as he pulled her into his arms.

"It's the wife's duty, isn't it, to be submissive to her husband?" Christina asked.

"It is," Lyon answered. His hands moved to the fastenings on her dress. "Oh, yes, it definitely is."

"Then I shall be submissive, Lyon," Christina announced. "When it suits me."

"A man can't ask for more than that," Lyon said with a grin.

Christina threw her arms around his neck and kissed him passionately. She wasn't submissive now. Her tongue darted inside his mouth to rub against his. She knew he liked her aggressiveness. His hold tightened around her waist and he growled his pleasure.

"My love, I think I'm going to tear another gown," he whispered.

He didn't sound overly contrite. And his wife's soft laughter told him it really didn't matter to her.

The following two weeks were as wonderful and magical to Christina as the early pages of Sir Thomas Mallory's story of Camelot. The weather accommodated her fantasy, for it only rained during the black night hours.

Christina and Lyon spent most of the sun-filled days exploring the vast wilderness surrounding his home.

She was amazed that one man could own so much land.

He was astonished that one woman could know so much about it.

Christina gave him the gift of awareness and a new appreciation for the wonders of nature.

Lyon began to realize how important her freedom was to her. She was happiest when they were outside. Her joy was contagious. Lyon found himself laughing with just as much joy as he tramped through the jungle of bushes in pursuit of his wife.

They always ended their days in front of a peaceful stream they'd chanced upon quite by accident their first day out, and usually soaked their feet in the cool water while they ate the meal the cook had thoughtfully prepared for them.

On one such afternoon, Lyon decided to tease his wife. He plucked a leaf from the nearest shrub and pretended that he was going to eat it. Christina wasn't amused. She slapped the leaf out of his hand, admonished him for his ignorance, and then explained that the leaf was poisonous and that he shouldn't be putting plants in his mouth anyway. If he was that hungry, she'd be more than happy to give him her portion of their meal.

Friday morning arrived too soon for Lyon's liking. He had to return to London to meet with Rhone and their unknowing victims for a game of cards.

Lyon was extremely reluctant to leave his gentle little wife even for one evening.

Lyon awakened early to find his wife sound asleep on the floor again. He immediately lifted her into his arms and put her back in his bed. Her skin felt cold to him, and he used his hands and his mouth to warm her.

He was hard and throbbing when Christina finally opened her eyes. His mouth was fastened on her breast, his tongue like rough velvet as it brushed against her nipple. He began to suckle while his hands stoked the growing fire inside her.

He knew just where to touch, just how to drive her wild. His fingers slipped inside her, drawing a breathless moan from her, then withdrew to tease and torment, and then thrust inside again.

Christina wanted to touch him. "Lyon." She could barely get his name out. His mouth had moved to her stomach to place wet, hot kisses there while his fingers continued their magic.

She couldn't catch her breath. "Tell me you want this," Lyon demanded, his voice hoarse now. His head was slowly moving toward the junction of her legs. "Tell me, Christina," he whispered. His breath was warm against her sensitive skin. His fingers plunged deep and then withdrew to be replaced by his mouth, his tongue.

What he was doing to her made her forget to breathe. Her eyes were tightly closed and her hands clutched the sheets. The pressure grew inside her until it consumed her. Emotion swept through her like a blaze out of control.

"Lyon!"

"Do you like this, love?"

"Yes. Oh, God, yes . . . Lyon, I'm going to—"

"Let it happen, Christina," he demanded in a rough, husky voice.

He wouldn't let her hold on to her control. The tension was unbearable as the fire rushed through her body.

Christina arched against him, cried out his name in a soft gasp. The splendor still captivated her when Lyon plunged inside her.

He was too greedy to hold back. His breathing was ragged against her ear.

"You like this, don't you, love?" he demanded.

"Yes, Lyon," she whispered.

"Put your legs around me, take me . . ." The order ended on an intense groan. Christina had wrapped her arms and her legs around him, pulling him high inside her. Her nails raked his shoulders, her grip tight and sweet, as tight and sweet and hot as her sheath.

He grunted his satisfaction. Christina slowly moved her hips. "Do you like that, Lyon?" she whispered as she pushed up against him again.

He couldn't answer her. But his body showed her how very much he did like it. And when he spilled his seed into her, he thought he'd died and gone to heaven.

An hour later, Lyon walked with Christina down the steps, his arm draped around her shoulders possessively.

Brown was waiting at the bottom of the steps. After announcing that the stablemaster had Lyon's mount ready and waiting out front, the butler discreetly withdrew so that the Marquess could have another minute alone with his wife to give her a proper farewell.

"Christina, when you get over your fear of horses we'll go riding every—"

"I'm not afraid of horses," Christina interrupted. Her voice sounded outraged. "We've had this discussion before, Lyon. I fear the saddles, not the animals. There is a difference."

"You're not going to ride without a saddle," Lyon announced. "And that's that."

"You're too stubborn for my own good," she muttered.

"I don't want you to fall and break your pretty little neck."

Lyon opened the front door, grabbed hold of Christina's hand, and dragged her outside.

Christina was frowning. She thought he might have insulted her again. Then she reasoned he couldn't know how skilled she was with a good mount. Perhaps he hadn't slandered her after all but was truly concerned for her safety or, as he'd just put it, her pretty little neck.

She wondered what he'd think if he found out she went out riding most mornings. He'd be upset with her, she supposed. She had to sigh over that little deception, then cast her guilt aside. She was always back in his bed before he awakened and really wasn't worried he'd find out. Wendell, the stablemaster, wouldn't say anything to Lyon. No, Wendell was a man of few words. Besides, he thought she'd gained Lyon's permission.

"Christina, I'll be back home by noon tomorrow," Lyon said, interrupting her thoughts. He tilted her chin up and kissed her soundly.

When he started down the steps, Christina hurried after him. "I still don't understand why I can't go with you. I would like to see your sister, and your mama, too, Lyon."

"Next time, sweetheart. Diana will be going to Martin's party tonight."

"Will Aunt Harriett also be going?"

"Probably," Lyon answered.

"I could go with them," Christina suggested.

"I thought you liked it here in the country," Lyon returned. "You do, don't you?"

"Yes, very much. But I'm your wife, Lyon. I should do my duty with your relatives. Do you know, it's rather odd of me to admit, but I did enjoy some of the parties. There were some very nice people I would like to see again."

"No."

His voice was so firm, Christina was immediately perplexed. "Why don't you want me to go with you? Have I done something to displease you?"

Lyon reacted to the worry in her voice. He paused to look down at her, then gave in to his sudden urge to kiss her again. "Nothing you could ever do would displease me. If you want to attend some of the parties, you'll wait until I can go with you."

"May I play cards with you and the mischief makers?" she asked. "I've never played before, but I'm certain it wouldn't be too difficult to master."

Lyon hid his amusement. His wife was obviously serious in her request. The sincerity in her voice said as much. "I'll teach you another time, Christina. If you wish, I'll wait while you write a note to Diana and Aunt Harriett."

Christina could tell by his manner that he wasn't going to give in to her plea to go along. "I've already written to everyone, even Elbert and my Aunt Patricia," she informed him. "Brown sent a messenger with my letters yesterday."

They walked on, hand in hand. When they reached his mount, he turned. "I have to leave now, my sweet."

"I know."

She hadn't meant to sound so pitiful. The fact that Lyon was leaving was distressing, yes, but not nearly as much as his casual, dismissive attitude. She didn't think he was going to mind the separation at all. She, on the other hand, minded very much.

It wasn't like her to be so clinging. She couldn't seem to let go of his hand. What in heaven's name was the matter with her? Lord, she felt like crying. He was only going to be away for one night, she told herself, not an eternity.

Lyon kissed her on her forehead. "Do you have anything you wish to say to me before I leave, Christina?"

His voice coaxed a response. Christina dropped his hand. "No."

Lyon let out a long sigh. He took hold of her hand again and dragged her off to the side of the path so that the stablemaster wouldn't overhear him. "I'll miss you," he said.

His voice wasn't coaxing now, but brisk.

Christina smiled.

"Damn it, wife, I want the soft words," he muttered. He

immediately felt like a fool for making such a ridiculous confession.

"Damn it, Lyon, I want to go to London with you."

"Christina, you're staying here," Lyon bellowed. He drew a deep breath, then added in a furious whisper, "I love you, Christina. Now tell me you love me. I've waited all week to hear you admit it."

She gave him a disgruntled look. Lyon wasn't waylaid. "I'm waiting, Christina."

"Have a safe journey, Lyon."

Lyon hadn't realized how important it was for him to hear her tell him she loved him until his demand was so thoroughly ignored. He stood there feeling angry and defeated, his gaze brooding as he watched Christina walk away from him.

"Hell," he muttered to himself. He mounted his steed, accepted the reins from Wendell, yet seemed incapable of nudging his stallion into moving. He couldn't even tear his gaze off the stubborn woman strolling to the front door.

Christina couldn't dismiss him this time. Her hand shook when she took hold of the brass door handle. He was so horribly stubborn. He constantly prodded and nagged. He wouldn't let her shield her feelings from him. But he didn't understand the significance of what he was asking of her. Once she'd given him the words, there could be no going back.

No, she'd never be able to go home.

A half smile changed her expression. The truth was both painful and joyful. She'd never really been given a choice in the matter, had she? From the moment she'd met Lyon, her heart had known the truth. Why had it taken her mind so long to accept?

Christina looked over her shoulder. Tears clouded her vision. "Hurry home, Lyon. I will be waiting for you."

"Say the words, Christina." He'd shouted this time, and the look on his face showed his anger.

"I love you."

Several heartbeats passed before he acknowledged her admission. And then he gave her a curt nod. Oh, he was arrogant. But his expression was tender, caring, so very loving.

It was quite enough. Christina hid her smile. A feeling of contentment and joy filled her. She suddenly felt as light as the wind.

The truth had set her free.

Christina opened the door and started to walk inside when her husband's bellow stopped her. "Wife?"

"Yes, husband?"

"Tell me you trust me as well."

She turned around again. Her hands settled on her hips. She hoped he could see her exasperation. "Don't push me, Lyon. Savor one victory at a time, like any noble warrior would."

Lyon shouted with laughter. "Yes, Christina, one victory at a time. I've got you now, haven't I?" he asked, his voice and his eyes filled with merriment.

The man was gloating again.

Christina strolled over to the top step. "Yes, Lyon, you've got me. And when you come home from London, you're going to find out just exactly what you've gotten. No more pretenses, husband. No more lies."

"I couldn't be happier," Lyon remarked.

"Enjoy the feeling, Lyon. I fear it will not last long."

She'd called the warning over her shoulder. The front door slammed shut before Lyon could question her further.

Lyon felt as though a weight had been lifted from his shoulders—and from his heart. She loved him. "The rest will come, wife," he whispered to himself. "I'll see to it."

He'd never felt so confident, so very, very peaceful.

The feeling wasn't going to last long.

Chapter Thirteen

You were only three months old when I bundled you up and set out on another adventure. I left in the dead of night so that Patricia wouldn't be able to stop me. I didn't leave a note for her, for I believed she'd send men after me.

You were such a precious infant. Upon reflection, I think the journey was far more difficult for me than for you. You'd just begun to smile, and you were such a sweet-tempered little one.

I had made arrangements to travel with Jacob and Emily Jackson. I'd met them through Sunday church, you see, and took to them at once. They were a newly wedded couple who had sold their wedding gifts so that they'd have enough coins to go in search of a new life. They were very appreciative of my contributions. Emily took to you, too, Christina. She'd sing to you and rock you to sleep while I saw to the night meals.

Jacob was a man bitten by wanderlust. Every evening he'd tell us the most wonderful stories about the courageous people living in the Black Hills. His brother had already taken his family there and had sent Jacob word that he was prospering as a gentleman farmer.

Jacob's fever was contagious. I soon became as excited as he was. Emily told me there were many unattached men working the raw land, that I would surely find a good man to marry. I led them to believe my husband had recently died, I admit to you, and I felt great shame for lying to them.

I told myself over and over that the lie didn't count. Edward would never find me in this vast wilderness.

We joined another wagon train when we reached what I believed was the end of the earth. I fought my exhaustion. Emily was always so cheerful. And then, on a bleak, rainy afternoon, we finally reached the valley below the most magnificent mountains I'd ever seen.

I remember that it was a bitterly cold day. It didn't matter, though. We were free, Christina. Free. No one could hurt us now.

Journal entry
October 11, 1795

Lyon had been gone for over an hour when two letters arrived. Both were addressed to Christina, and both required her immediate attention.

After instructing Kathleen to take the messenger into the kitchens for refreshments, Christina took her letters into Lyon's study.

The first missive came from her Aunt Patricia. It was a hateful note, filled with defaming remarks about Lyon. The Countess told Christina she'd learned the truth about the Marquess and felt it was her duty to warn her niece that she was married to a murderer.

The Countess then demanded that Christina return to London immediately so that she could accompany her aunt to the various functions of the ton. She whined about the disgraceful fact that she hadn't received a single invitation since Christina's outrageous marriage.

Christina shook her head. It had been less than a month since the wedding, but her aunt was carrying on as though a full year had passed.

The Countess ended her list of complaints with the

statement that she was sending along a letter she'd received from the missionary Deavenrue.

She hoped Christina didn't find ill news.

Christina was immediately suspicious. It wasn't like her aunt to offer such a good-hearted remark. She thought the Countess might be up to her usual tricks. She was familiar with her former teacher's handwriting, however, and the flourishing style of his script on the envelope indicated that he had in fact written the letter. The seal on the back of the envelope hadn't been tampered with, either.

Convinced that the letter was really from her dear friend, Christina finally opened it.

Brown was the first to react to the heart-wrenching scream coming from the library. He rushed into the room and nearly lost his composure altogether when he saw his mistress had collapsed on the floor.

He shouted orders over his shoulder as he knelt down beside the Marchioness. Kathleen, Christina's maid, came running next. When she saw her mistress, she gave a yell. "Did she swoon? What made her cry out, Brown? Is she hurt?"

"Cease your questions, woman," Brown snapped. He carefully lifted his mistress into his arms, then noticed that she clutched a letter in her hands. He decided that whatever news she'd just received had caused her to faint. "Go and prepare your lady's bed, Kathleen," he whispered. "She doesn't weigh more than a feather. God help us all if she's ill."

Most of the staff had assembled, and they trailed silently behind Brown as he carried Christina up the winding staircase. Kathleen had hurried on ahead to turn down the bed, but Brown walked right past Christina's bedroom and continued on into his master's quarters.

"She'll find comfort here when she wakes up," he whispered to the cook. "They are a very close couple. She sleeps in here every night."

"Do we send for the Marquess?" Kathleen asked between sobs.

"Get Sophie," Brown ordered. "She'll know what to do about the swoon. Is the messenger still here?"

When Kathleen nodded, Brown said, "I shall send a message to the Marquess with him. Lewis," he commanded the gardener, "go and delay him."

Christina opened her eyes just as Brown was awkwardly pulling the covers over her. "Do not make a fuss over me, Brown."

"Are you in pain, milady?" Brown asked, his voice ragged with worry. "I've sent for Sophie. She'll know what to do," he added, trying to force the tremor out of his voice.

Christina struggled to sit up just as a large gray-headed woman came rushing into the room. She grabbed two pillows and tucked them behind Christina's back.

"What do you think it is, Sophie?" Kathleen asked. "She let out a horrible scream and then fainted dead away."

"I heard her," Sophie announced. She slapped the back of her hand against Christina's forehead. Her manner was brisk, her frown intense. "Best send for Winters, Brown. She feels fevered to me. Winters is your husband's physician," Sophie explained to Christina.

"I'm not ill," Christina protested. She was surprised her voice sounded so weak to her. "Brown, do not send for a physician. I'm quite all right now. But I must go to London immediately. Please bring the carriage around front for me. Kathleen, would you see to packing a few of my gowns for me?"

"Milady, you cannot leave this bed. You are ill whether you know it or not," Sophie exclaimed. "You're as pale as a cloud. Yes, you are."

"I must go to my husband," Christina argued. "He will know what to do."

"It was the letter that caused your swoon, wasn't it?" Kathleen asked, wringing her hands.

Brown turned to glare at the maid. Kathleen was immediately contrite. "I'm sorry for prying, milady, but we are all so concerned. You gave us all a scare, and we've come to care about you."

Christina tried to smile. "And I care about all of you," she said. "Yes, Kathleen, it was the letter."

"Was it bad news?" Kathleen asked.

"Of course it was bad news, you silly chit," Brown muttered. "Anyone with half a mind can see that it was," he added. "Milady, is there anything I can do to ease your distress?"

"Yes, Brown," Christina answered. "Don't fight me when I tell you I must leave for London at once. Please help me, Brown. I beg of you."

"I would do anything for you," Brown blurted out in a fervent voice. He blushed and added, "The Marquess will be upset by this change in orders, but if you are truly set on going, I shall send four strong men to accompany you. Kathleen, hurry and do your lady's bidding."

"Will I be going with you?" Kathleen asked her mistress.

"You will," Brown announced before Christina could dissuade her eager maid.

"I would like a few minutes alone," Christina whispered. "I must grieve in privacy."

They understood then. Someone close to their mistress had passed away.

Brown immediately ushered the servants out of the bedroom. He hesitated after closing the door behind him, then stood there, feeling impotent and unworthy, as he listened to his mistress's tormented sobs.

He didn't know how to help her. Brown straightened his shoulders and hurried down the hall. The welfare of his mistress rested on his shoulders now. He wasn't going to take any chances. He decided to send six men along instead of four to protect the Marchioness.

And though it was highly unusual for a butler to leave his post as guardian of the household, Brown didn't care. He wasn't going to leave his mistress's side until she was safely in her husband's arms. Yes, he would go along with the assembly. And if he could remember how to hang onto a mount, he just might lead them.

Christina had no idea of the worry she was causing her

staff. She huddled under the covers, hugging Lyon's pillow to her bosom, weeping softly.

When her tears were spent, she slowly climbed out of the bed and went in search of her scissors. She would cut her hair and begin the mourning ritual.

As of this moment, her Aunt Patricia was dead. Christina would never again acknowledge her existence.

The task of cutting several inches off the length of curls took little time. Kathleen rushed into the room with a pale green gown draped over her arm. Her eyes widened when she saw what her mistress had done to her hair, but she held her silence and assisted her mistress in changing her clothing.

"We will be ready to leave in ten minutes' time," Kathleen whispered to Christina before leaving her alone again.

Christina walked over to the windows to stare out at the land. She thought about her family. How Merry would love this country. Black Wolf would be impressed, too, though he'd never acknowledge it, of course. He was too arrogant to make such an admission. He'd be perplexed, too, if he knew that Lyon owned so much land.

White Eagle would be more impressed with Lyon's stables. The horses had been bred for strength and endurance, and the new foals, so feisty, so magnificent, were proof of Lyon's careful selection.

"They are not dead." Christina's voice was filled with anger.

She started to cry again. No, they weren't dead. The letter was a lie. She would have known, in her heart, if anything had harmed her family.

"I would have known," she whispered.

Yes, it was trickery. Christina didn't know how her aunt had accomplished the foul deed, but she was behind the deception. The evil woman wanted Christina to believe that her Indian family was dead.

Christina didn't understand the Countess's reasons.

Lyon would be able to explain. He was a cunning warrior who knew all the ways of the jackals in this world.

She felt a desperate need to get to her husband.

Christina would demand that he take her into his arms and tell her how much he loved her. And then she would make him kiss her. His touch would take the pain and the sorrow away.

She would demand and Lyon would give. It was his duty.

When Lyon arrived at his townhouse in London proper, Sir Fenton Richards was waiting on his doorstoop.

Richards wasn't smiling.

Lyon was immediately on his guard. "You've put on weight," he announced in lieu of a greeting.

"I have put on weight," Richards admitted with a grin. He patted his belly to emphasize just where the extra pounds had settled.

Lyon began to relax. His friend's manner told him all he needed to know. There had to be a problem, for Richards wouldn't have waited for him just to pay a social call. Yet his casual manner indicated it wasn't a terribly important problem.

Richards turned to bang on the door. It was immediately opened by a servant. Lyon motioned to his man to take the reins and see to his mount, then led his friend inside to the library.

Richards lumbered in behind him. He was a large man with a bushy beard and silver-tipped hair. He was softspoken, stoop-shouldered, and usually guarded in his expressions. Except when he was in Lyon's company. The older man could relax then, because his trust in his young friend was absolute.

"All hell has broken loose, and with a vengeance."

Lyon raised an eyebrow over the mildly given remark.

"Rhone is under house arrest," Richards announced. He settled himself in one of the two leather-backed chairs in front of Lyon's desk before adding, "I tried to intervene, but the charges had already been filed by Wellingham. It's up to you to take care of the matter now."

"How was he found out?" Lyon asked. He sat down

behind his desk and began to sift through the stack of letters and invitations piled in the center.

Richards chuckled. "You're taking our friend's demise well," he remarked.

"As you said, it's up to me now. I'll take care of the matter. Tell me what happened. How—"

"Wellingham noticed the bandage on Rhone's wrist. One guess led to another after that. Rhone takes too many chances," Richards announced. "It seems he ran into Wellingham on his way home from your wedding. I was sorry I missed the celebration, by the way," he added. "Couldn't be helped. I just got back to London the day before yesterday."

"It was a small affair," Lyon said. "You'll have to come to Lyonwood to meet my Christina," he added. "How's Rhone taking the situation?" he asked, turning the subject back to the immediate problem.

"With his usual flair for nonsense," Richards commented dryly. "Since he can't get out, he's had a party at his townhouse every night. There's another one scheduled for this eve, as a matter of fact. I thought I'd drop in."

Richards paused to give Lyon a long, meaningful look.

Lyon grinned. "I'll be there," he told his friend. "Don't bring any valuables with you, Richards. You wouldn't want to be robbed by Jack, would you?"

"Ah, then Jack will be making an appearance?"

"You may wager on it."

"Won't Rhone be amused?" Richards commented. He straightened in his chair, his manner suddenly brisk. "Now that Rhone's problem is taken care of, I'll move on to my other reason for coming to see you. Your wife's father, to be exact."

Richards had just captured Lyon's full attention. He pushed the letters aside and leaned forward.

"Did you know your wife's father is on his way to London?"

Lyon shook his head. "How would you know him?" he asked.

"His name is Edward Stalinsky, but of course you would know that," Richards said.

Lyon nodded. He did know his father-in-law's full name, but only because he'd watched Christina sign the marriage certificate. "Yes, Baron Stalinsky," he said, urging Richards along.

"He did a favor for us a very long time ago. The Brisbane affair. Do you remember hearing about that mishap?"

Mishap? Lyon shook his head. "I remember you called the Battle of Waterloo Napoleon's mishap," he said. "Tell me about this Brisbane business. I have no memory of it in my mind."

"You were a young lad. Still, I thought you might have heard of the matter sooner or later," Richards said, his voice whisper-soft. "I forget I'm a good twenty years your senior. I suppose I should let the younger ones take charge," he added with a sigh.

"You've tried to resign several times since I've worked for you," Lyon answered.

He was eager to hear Richards recount the happening to him and learn all he could about Christina's father, but he knew his friend well enough to understand he would take his usual slow time getting to it.

"I'm like an old hound," Richards said. "The scent of trouble still captures my mind. Brisbane was an Englishman," he continued, finally getting to the heart of the matter. "You might say he was our Benedict Arnold. He turned traitor, sold a few secrets, then his family began to worry his conscience. He had a wife and four little girls. He came to us and confessed his transgressions. We, or rather my predecessors, worked a promise with the man. We were after bigger fish, you see. With Brisbane's full cooperation, we set a trap to catch his superiors. Baron Stalinsky acted as our intermediary. I don't remember how he got involved," he added with a shrug. "The baron did all he could—took every precaution, I'm told—but the plan failed miserably all the same."

"How?" Lyon asked.

"Brisbane's wife and children were murdered. Their

throats were cut. The atrocity was made to look as if Brisbane had killed them and then turned the blade on himself."

"You don't believe that's what really happened, do you?" Lyon asked.

"No, of course not. I think one of Brisbane's superiors found out about the trap," Richards answered. "Either by chance or by payment."

"What about Baron Stalinsky? Did he continue to work with the government?"

"No. He married shortly after the Brisbane business and returned to his home. He was outraged by the horror he'd witnessed. He was the first to find the bodies, you see, and he refused to lend England a hand after that. Can't fault the man. I wasn't there, but I can imagine the nightmare Stalinsky walked into."

"Have you kept in touch with the Baron since that time?"

"None of us have," Richards said. "But several of his old friends have received notice from him that he'll be arriving in England soon."

"I wonder if he knows he has a daughter now."

"Good God. You mean to tell me he didn't know?" Richards asked.

"Father and daughter have never met. I believe the baron thought his wife and child had died years ago. For that matter, everyone I talked to thought the Baron had passed away, too. Sir Reynolds was one to make that speculation."

"Yes, there was surprise when the letters arrived," Richards said.

"I wonder what the baron has been up to all these years."

"I heard that a year or so later Stalinsky lost his kingdom. Then he vanished. We never had reason to keep track of the man," Richards added. A frown marred his expression. "Something's bothering you. What is it?"

"Do you have any reason at all to distrust the baron?"

"Ah, so that's the itch, is it?"

"Tell me everything you know about the man," Lyon ordered. "Everything you can remember. I realize it was a long time ago," he added.

"There's very little to tell. I was young and impressionable back then, but I do remember being in awe of the man. He wasn't much older than I was. He had a commanding presence. I envied him. Lyon, damn it all, you've got my guts churning. Now you tell me what you know about the baron," he ordered.

"I don't have any information to give you. I've never met him. Christina hasn't either, but she's afraid of him. When you meet my wife, you'll understand the full force of that comment. Christina isn't a woman who frightens easily."

"I already know that much about her," Richards said.

"How?"

"She married you, didn't she?"

Lyon grinned. "Yes, she did," he said. "Not very willingly, but . . ."

Richards snorted with laughter. "Perhaps she's afraid of her father because of the unusual circumstances," he said after a moment's pause. "Not to know one's father and then finally to meet him . . ."

"No," Lyon said, shaking his head. "Her fear is based on something else. She called him a jackal. Keep your guard up when you're with the baron, Richards. My instincts and Christina's fears are enough to sway my mind."

"You're that uneasy?"

"I am."

"Why hasn't Christina explained the real reasons for her fears, then?"

"She's very stubborn," Lyon announced with a smile that told Richards he thought that was a noble quality. "And she is just beginning to trust me. It's a fragile bond, Richards. For that reason, I'm not going to prod her. Christina will tell me when she's ready, and not a minute before."

"But you trust her judgment?" Richards asked. "You trust her?"

"I do." His answer was given without hesitation, his voice emphatic.

And then the full realization settled in his mind . . . and in his heart. He did trust her. Completely. "In all matters,"

Lyon acknowledged in a soft voice. "God only knows why, but I do," he told his friend before he started to laugh.

"And that's amusing?"

"Oh, yes. My little wife and I have been playing a game with each other," Lyon confessed. "It's amusing, you see, because neither one of us has realized it."

"I don't understand," Richards confessed.

"I'm only just beginning to understand," Lyon said. "Christina hides her past from me . . . just as I've been hiding my past from her. I think she believes I'll find her inferior in some way," he added. "I wouldn't, of course, but she needs to learn to trust me enough to believe it in her heart."

"I would be happy to investigate your wife's past for you," Richards volunteered.

"No. I sent men to France to make inquiries, but I'm going to call them home. I will not look into her past, and I don't want you to either, Richards. In time she'll tell me what she wants me to know."

"And will you tell her your secrets?" Richards asked. His voice was whisper-soft. "You have no cause to worry, Lyon. I've never been able to trust a man the way I trust you. Your loyalty to your country has always been absolute. That is why you were always given the most difficult assignments."

Lyon was surprised by the vehemence in his friend's voice. Richards wasn't a man given to compliments. In all their years working together, Lyon had never heard such praise.

"Now you've got me worried about Stalinsky," Richards continued. "I'll start looking into his affairs immediately. There's another problem, however," he added. He scratched his beard in an absentminded fashion. "The department had hopes that you'd give a reception honoring your father-in-law when he arrives. Heaven help us, there's already talk of knighthood. Some of the older gentlemen remember with exaggerated recall the noble deeds Baron Stalinsky accomplished for the good of England. I'm going to look into those deeds as well," he added with a brisk nod.

"A reception isn't going to sit well with Christina," Lyon said.

Richards gave a discreet cough, then said, "Lyon, I certainly don't want to be the one to tell you how to manage your marriage, but it would seem to me that you must simply question your wife about her father at the first opportunity. Order her to explain her fears to you. Make her answer your questions, son."

Question her? Lyon felt like laughing. Since the minute he'd met Christina he'd done nothing but question her. "There will be no questions. She'll tell me—"

"I know, I know," Richards interrupted with a long sigh. "In her own time."

"That's about it," Lyon answered. "Until then, it's my duty to keep her safe."

"Safe?"

"Christina believes her father will try to kill her."

"Oh, Lord."

"Exactly. And you can see how offended we both would be if the baron is knighted."

"Lyon, I insist that you question your wife. If there is danger—"

"I will deal with it. I will not question her again."

Richards ignored the irritation in his friend's tone. "I'm not one to judge, but I believe you have a very unusual marriage."

"I have a very unusual wife. You'll like her, Richards."

A sudden noise coming from the foyer interrupted the conversation. Lyon glanced up just as the library doors were thrown open.

Brown, his loyal butler, came rushing into the room.

Lyon bounded out of his chair. His heart started slamming against his chest and he felt as though the breath was being squeezed out of him.

Something had happened to Christina. She'd been hurt . . . taken . . .

The feeling of panic slowly dissipated. When Christina came flying into the room, her golden hair floating around her shoulders, Lyon literally fell back into his chair.

She was all right. Oh, her eyes were clouded with unshed tears, and her expression showed how troubled she was. She was upset, yes, but she hadn't been injured.

He started breathing again.

"Lyon, you just tell me how it was done," Christina demanded. She rushed right past Richards, didn't even seem to notice that anyone else was in the room, reached her husband's side, and thrust two envelopes into his hands. "I recognized his handwriting, and at first I thought it might be true. But in my heart I didn't feel it was so. I would have known if something had happened to them. I would have known."

Lyon grabbed hold of Christina's hands. "Sweetheart, calm down and start at the beginning."

"Read this letter first," Christina said. She pulled her hand away and motioned to the Countess's envelope. "Then you'll understand why I know it's trickery."

"The Marchioness fainted dead away, my lord," Brown called out.

Lyon turned his attention to his butler. Brown was still standing in the doorway.

"She what?" Lyon roared.

"She swooned," Brown said, nodding vigorously.

"Then why did you bring her to London?"

Lyon was suddenly infuriated. He glared at his butler, then turned to Christina. "You should be home in bed," he shouted.

"Don't yell at me," Christina ordered. Her voice was every bit as loud as Lyon's had been. "Brown knew better than to argue with me. I was determined to come to you, Lyon. Please read the letters. I know it is all a lie."

Lyon forced himself to calm down. Christina had started crying. He decided to get to the matter of her health after he'd dealt with her problem.

Lyon read the Countess's letter first. By the time he was finished with it his hands were shaking.

God help him, she'd learned the truth about him. The Countess had found out about his past and had recounted several damning details in her letter to her niece.

Now Christina wanted his denial. She'd come all the way to London to confront him, to hear him tell her that they were lies.

He wasn't going to lie to her. But the truth could destroy her.

No more lies, no more pretenses . . . hadn't she given him that promise just this morning?

She deserved equal measure. "Christina," Lyon began. He slowly lifted his gaze to hers, "We do what we must do when there is a threat, and I . . ."

He couldn't seem to finish his explanation.

Christina could see his pain, his anguish. The need to comfort him overrode all other considerations. She instinctively reached out to him.

And then the confusion of it all hit her. Her hand stilled in the air between them. "What are you talking about?"

"What?"

"Why are you looking at me like that?"

"I'm trying to explain," Lyon muttered. He turned to glare at Brown. The butler caught the message and immediately closed the door.

Lyon's gaze then settled on Richards. His friend rudely ignored the silent order and stayed right where he was.

"Lyon, answer me," Christina demanded.

"Christina, it's very difficult to explain with an audience listening," he said. He took a deep breath. "It's true. All of it. I did exactly what your aunt has told you. My motives were a hell of a lot cleaner, however, and I would . . ."

She finally understood. Christina closed her eyes and prayed for guidance. She knew she probably wasn't being a good wife now, that Lyon obviously felt the need to unburden himself of his secrets. He'd picked a strange time to share his worries with her, she thought. Although it was selfish of her to feel this way, she really wished he'd help her with her problem first.

When Christina closed her eyes, Lyon felt as though a knife had just been plunged into his heart. "My dear, I was a soldier. I did what I had to . . ."

She finally looked at him. Her gaze was direct and filled with tenderness.

He was too stunned to say another word.

"You are a warrior, Lyon. But you are also a gentle, loving man. You wouldn't have killed anyone who hadn't challenged you. No, you hunt only jackals."

He seemed to have trouble taking it all in. "Then why did you come to London to—"

"I knew you'd help me find the truth," Christina said.

"I'm trying to tell you the truth."

He was shouting again. Christina shook her head. "How can you tell me that when you haven't even read the other letter?"

"If you two will forgive an old man's interference," Richards interjected.

"What is it?" Lyon snapped.

"Who is that man?" Christina asked Lyon.

"Fenton Richards," Lyon said.

Christina recognized the name. She frowned at Lyon's guest and then said, "Lyon cannot come back to work for you. His leg still has not healed to my satisfaction. It may be long years before he mends completely," she added.

"Christina, how do you know about Richards?"

"Rhone," she answered. "And you do talk in your sleep some nights," she added. "I hadn't thought to mention that flaw to you in front of an outsider, but . . ."

"Oh, hell," Lyon muttered.

"Oh, my God," Richards whispered.

"Don't be concerned, sir," Christina told Richards. "I will keep his secrets safe."

Richards stared at her a long minute and then slowly nodded. "I believe you will," he acknowledged.

"How did you know about my leg?" Lyon asked, drawing Christina's attention again. "I haven't complained. It has healed, damn it. Did Rhone—"

"The first night I met you I could tell you were in pain. I could see it in your eyes. You kept leaning against the mantel, too. That was another sign. Later I did question

Rhone, and he confessed that you'd injured your knee. And it hasn't healed," she added with a hasty glance in Richards's direction.

Richards hid his smile. Lyon's wife was a charmer. "The two of you seem to be at cross purposes," he remarked. "Lyon, I don't think your wife is upset about the news in her aunt's letter. It's something else, isn't it, my dear?"

"Yes," Christina answered. "The Countess enclosed a letter from my good friend. The writing on his envelope is by his hand, I'm certain of it, and the writing on the paper looks the same, but—"

"You don't think it is. That's the trickery you're referring to?" Lyon asked.

She nodded. "See how the Countess ends her letter, Lyon? She tells me she hopes my friend hasn't sent ill news."

Her eyes filled with tears again. Lyon quickly read the letter from Deavenrue. He then held the envelope up next to the paper to compare the writing style. Christina held her breath and waited.

It didn't take him long to see the differences. "It's similar, but it isn't the same. Richards, you want to have a look at this?" Lyon asked. "Another opinion would make Christina rest easy."

Richards leapt out of his chair, his curiosity nearly out of control, and snatched the envelope and the letter. He soon saw the discrepancies. "Oh, yes. The letter was written by another hand. It is a deception."

He then read the contents. His gaze was sympathetic when he looked at Christina again. "These people in the wilderness . . . they were like family to you?"

Christina nodded. "What is spotted fever?" she asked, frowning. "The letter says they died of—"

"God only knows," Lyon said.

"Who is responsible for this?" Richards asked. "What kind of monster would do such a thing?"

"Christina's aunt." Lyon's voice sounded his anger.

Richards dropped the letter on the desk. "Forgive me for saying this, Christina, but I believe your aunt is a—"

"Think it but don't say it," Lyon interrupted before Richards could finish his sentence.

Christina sagged against Lyon's chair. Lyon put his arm around her waist. "I still don't understand how it was done. The seal wasn't disturbed."

Richards was the one who explained how easy it was to use steam to open an envelope. "An expert would have been able to tell, my dear," he said.

Richards left minutes later. As soon as the door closed behind him, Christina burst into tears. Lyon pulled her onto his lap. He hugged her close to him.

He didn't try to quiet her. She had a good store of tears, and it was quite a while before her racking sobs slowed down.

"I've gotten your shirt all wet," Christina whispered between hiccups.

She obviously wasn't ready to do anything about it. Christina cuddled up against his chest, tucked her head under his chin, and let out a weary sigh.

She didn't move again for a long time. Lyon thought she might have fallen asleep. He didn't mind. He'd hold her close for the rest of the afternoon, if that was what she needed. In truth, he thought it might take him that long to rid himself of his anger.

Richards had meant to call the Countess a bitch, Lyon decided. The old bat was that, all right, and more.

Christina's mind must have been following the same path, for she suddenly whispered, "Do you know that I used to believe all the English were like my aunt?"

He didn't answer her. But his breath caught in his throat, and he prayed his silence would encourage her to tell him more.

His patience was rewarded minutes later.

"My father hated the whites. And when I lived with the Countess in Boston, my only friend was Mr. Deavenrue. He is the one who took me to my aunt, and he would come every day to tutor me. I wasn't permitted to go outdoors. The Countess kept telling me she was ashamed of me. I was very confused. I didn't understand why she believed I was so unworthy."

"You aren't, my love," Lyon said emphatically. "You are very, very worthy."

Christina nodded. "It is good of you to notice," she said.

He smiled over the sincerity in her voice.

And then he waited for her to tell him more.

It seemed an eternity had passed before she spoke again. "She used to lock me in my room at night. I tried not to hate her for that."

Lyon closed his eyes and drew a shaky breath. He could feel her anguish. It washed over him like hot lava until his eyes smarted with tears.

"I couldn't stand being locked in like that. I finally put a stop to it."

"How, sweetheart?"

"I took the hinges off the door," Christina confessed. "The Countess started bolting her bedroom door then. She was afraid of me. I didn't mind that. She's old, Lyon, and for that reason I tried to respect her. It is what my mother would have wanted."

"Jessica?"

"No, I never knew Jessica."

"Then who?"

"Merry."

Lyon couldn't stop himself from asking her another question. "And does she also hate the whites?"

"Oh, no, Merry doesn't hate anyone."

"But the man you call Father does?"

He didn't think she was going to answer him. The silence stretched between them for long minutes.

He shouldn't have prodded her, he told himself. Damn, he'd only just vowed never to ask her any more questions.

"Yes, he does," Christina whispered. "But not me, of course. My father loves me with all his heart."

Christina waited for his reaction. Her heart pounded furiously.

Lyon didn't say a word. Christina decided then that he hadn't understood.

"I have a brother."

Nothing. Not a word, not a sigh, not even a mutter. "His name is White Eagle."

A slow smile settled on Lyon's face.

"Do you understand what I'm telling you, Lyon?" she asked.

He kissed the top of her head. "I understand," he whispered. He cupped the sides of her face and gently forced her mouth upward. He kissed her tenderly.

And then he soothed her fears away. "I understand that I am the most fortunate man in all the world. I never believed I'd find anyone I could love the way I love you, Christina. I owe your family a great debt, sweetheart. They kept you safe for me."

"You don't know them, and yet you sound as if you care about them," Christina whispered. Her voice shook with emotion.

"Of course I care," Lyon said. "Your mother must be a gentle, loving woman, and your father . . ."

"A proud warrior," Christina supplied. "As proud as you, Lyon."

"I love you, Christina. Did you really believe that your background would make me think you were less than—"

"I have never felt unworthy. Never. I am a lioness. In truth, I thought the English were unworthy . . . until I met you."

Lyon smiled. "You have gained some of your father's arrogance," he noted. "That pleases me."

"It isn't going to be easy for you, Lyon. I have different habits. I don't want to have to pretend any longer. At least not when we are alone . . ."

"Good. I don't want you to pretend whatever it is you pretend either," Lyon announced. He laughed then, for he didn't have the faintest idea what he'd just said.

"I love you, Lyon," Christina whispered. Her fingers caressed the nape of his neck. "Lyon? I want . . ."

"I do too," Lyon growled. He kissed her again, hungrily this time. His tongue plunged inside to taste, to stroke. Christina curled her arms around his neck. She'd meant to tell him she wanted to go home to Lyonwood, but his kiss soon pushed that thought aside. His mouth slanted over hers, again and again, until her breath was little more that a soft pant.

"Let's go upstairs, Lyon," she whispered between passionate kisses.

"There isn't time, Christina."

"Lyon!"

He tried to smile over the demand in her voice, but he was too occupied trying to hold onto his control. Christina was rubbing against his arousal, nipping his earlobe with her teeth, and stroking him wild with her hands.

He couldn't have made it up the stairs if his life had depended upon it.

Chapter Fourteen

He came during the night, while everyone was sleeping. The Jacksons had made their beds outside. It was bitterly cold, but Jacob wanted privacy, and for that reason he'd made a small tent.

I heard a strange sound, and when I looked outside the wagon I saw a man bent over Emily and Jacob. I called out to the man, still not realizing the danger. In my mind I thought it was Jacob's turn to take the watch.

The man stood and turned into the moonlight. The scream was trapped in my throat. Edward had come after me. He held a bloody knife in his hand.

I was so stunned and so terrified I could barely move. You were the one who forced me into action, Christina. Yes, for when you awakened and started to whimper, I came out of my stupor. I wasn't going to let Edward kill you.

I grabbed Jacob's hunting knife just as Edward climbed into the wagon. I screamed and thrust the blade in his face. Edward snarled in pain. The tip of the knife cut the edge of his eye. "Give me the jewels," he demanded as he knocked the weapon out of my hands.

The camp awakened to my screams. Edward heard the shouts of confusion behind him. He told me he'd come back to kill me. He looked over at the basket you slept in, Christina, then turned back to me. "I'll kill her first. You should have let Patricia have her," he added with a sneer before he slithered out of the wagon.

The Jacksons were dead. Their throats had been slashed. I told the wagonmaster I'd heard a sound and had seen a man leaning over Jacob and Emily.

A search was made of the camp. The light was poor, and Edward wasn't found.

Several hours later the camp again settled down. Three times the number of guards were posted as a precaution, and it had been decided that the burial for the Jacksons would take place at daybreak.

I waited, then bundled you up and calmly rode out of the camp. I didn't know where I was going, didn't care.

I had failed you, Christina. It was over. It was only a matter of time before Edward hunted us down.

Journal entry
October 20, 1795

It was early afternoon when Lyon kissed Christina good-bye. She assumed he was going to meet Rhone for their scheduled card game. Lyon, in his haste to make the necessary arrangements for Jack's arrival at Rhone's house, didn't take the time to set his wife straight. He told her only that the card game had been delayed and that he had important business to see to.

Christina had just changed into a deep blue dress when Kathleen announced that Lady Diana was downstairs waiting to see her.

"She's terribly upset about something," Kathleen told her mistress. "The poor dear is crying."

Christina hurried down the winding staircase. When Diana saw her, she blurted out the news about Rhone.

Christina led her sister-in-law into the drawing room, then sat down beside her and patted her hand while she poured out the full story.

"The poor man is innocent," Diana sobbed. "He's trying to be so noble, too. Did you know he is even having parties every night? Oh, if only Lyon will come home soon so that I can tell him what has happened. He will know what to do."

"I'm sure he'll find out very soon," Christina said. "This is all my fault," she added.

"How can it be your fault?" Diana asked.

Christina didn't answer her. She felt responsible for Rhone's problem. She was the one who'd wounded him, after all, and the guilt belonged on her shoulders.

"I must think of a way to . . . Diana, did you say Rhone is having a party tonight?"

"Yes. Aunt Harriett won't let me attend," Diana said. "We are already promised to another affair, but I would much rather go to Rhone's."

Christina hid her smile. "Of course you would," she said, patting Diana's hand again. "It's all going to be over by tomorrow," she added in a mock whisper.

"How could that be?" Diana whispered back. "Do you know something you aren't telling me?" she asked.

"Yes," Christina answered. She deliberately paused, then cast a glance over her shoulder. When she turned back to Diana, she said, "I have it on good authority that the real Jack is going out hunting tonight."

Diana's gasp told Christina she believed her. "You mustn't say a word to anyone, Diana, else Jack might find out and decide against going out."

Diana clasped her hands together. "I won't tell, I promise you," she said. "But how did you learn—"

"There isn't time to go into the details," Christina announced. "And I have an important errand to see to. May I ride with you back to your home and then borrow your carriage for a short spell?"

"Yes, of course," Diana responded. "I could go with you on your errand," she volunteered.

Christina shook her head. "Hurry, Diana. There's much to be done."

"There is?"

"Never mind. Now dry your eyes and come along."

Christina pulled Lyon's sister behind her. She turned Diana's attention away from the matter of Jack by asking several questions about her family.

"Was Lyon close to his brother James?" she asked.

"For a time. They were very competitive," Diana said. "Lyon would always best James—in riding, sword fighting, and . . . well, even with women," she added with a shrug. "James seemed obsessed with winning. He took chances."

"How did he die?"

"Fell from his mount. He didn't linger. His death was quick. Baron Winters, our family physician, said it was painless. I think he might have said that to ease Mama's mind."

"About your mother," Christina began, her voice hesitant. "Diana, I know you must be very close to her, but I hope you won't argue with my plan."

"What plan?" Diana asked, frowning.

"I would like to take your mother with me tomorrow when I return to Lyonwood."

"Are you serious? Does Lyon know of this intention?"

"Quit looking so suspicious," Christina admonished with a small smile. "I do have your mama's best interests at heart. You have a season to see to, or I'd ask you to come along. I know the separation will be difficult for you. She is your mama, after all," she told her as she continued on.

Diana lowered her gaze to stare at her hands. She was ashamed of the acute relief she was feeling. Someone was finally going to take charge of her mama. "It is dreadful for me to admit this to you, but you are my sister now, and so I will confess I will not miss Mama at all."

Christina didn't know what to say. She opened the door of the carriage for her sister-in-law, then said, "Your mother has been a bit . . . difficult, then?"

"You've met her," Diana whispered. "All she wants to talk about is James. She doesn't care about me or Lyon.

James was her firstborn. Oh, I know you think less of me now. I shouldn't have told you that I—"

Christina reached out to take Diana's hands in hers. "You must always tell me the truth. It's the only way to go along, you see. Diana, I know you love your mama. You wouldn't be so angry with her if you didn't."

Diana's eyes widened. "I am angry," she announced.

"You must go inside now. I have to see to my errand," Christina said, changing the subject. "Please have the servants pack up your mother's things. I shall come and fetch her tomorrow morning."

Diana suddenly lunged at Christina, capturing her in an awkward hug. "I am so happy Lyon married you."

"I'm also happy that I married him," Christina told her.

Diana let go of Christina. She climbed out of the carriage, then turned to plead once more to go along on the mysterious errand. Christina again denied her request, then waited until she'd gone inside the townhouse before turning to the driver and giving him her destination.

"Do you know where the Bleak Bryan is located?" the driver responded. His eyes were bulging out of his face, and he swallowed several times.

"No, I don't know exactly where it's located. Do you, sir?"

"Well, yes, madam, I do," the driver stammered.

"Then that is all that matters, isn't it? Please take me there at once."

Christina got back inside the carriage and shut the door. The driver's pale face suddenly appeared at the open window. "You cannot be serious, madam. The Bleak Bryan is in the most unsavory part of London. Cutthroats and—"

"Bryan is a special friend of mine. I must go to him now, sir. What is your name?" she asked.

"Everet," the driver announced.

"Everet," Christina repeated. She gave him a smile meant to dazzle him, then said, "It is a very good name. Now then, Everet, I must tell you that I will be very unhappy if you don't do as I've requested. Yes, I will," she added in a firm voice.

Everet paused to scratch the bald spot on the top of his head before answering. "That's the rub of it, madam. You'll be unhappy if I don't take you to the Bleak Bryan tavern, but your husband, when he hears of it, will kill me. I'll be getting it no matter what I do. That's the rub, all right."

"Oh, I understand your hesitation now. You don't realize my husband has specifically requested that I make this visitation to Mr. Bryan. Put your fears aside, my good man. Lyon knows all about this."

Everet did look relieved. The Marchioness's sincerity was apparent to him. She was such an innocent little thing, Everet thought. Why, she wouldn't even know how to be devious.

The driver stammered out his apology, requested that Christina bolt her doors from the inside, and then hastened back up on his perch.

He drove the carriage at breakneck pace. Christina thought the man might be a little frightened.

Her conclusions were proven correct when they finally arrived at the tavern. When Everet helped her from the carriage, his hands were shaking. He kept glancing over his shoulder. "Please, madam, be quick with your business in there. I'll be waiting inside your carriage, if you don't mind," he whispered.

"Oh, you don't have to wait for me. I don't know how long my business will take. Go along home now, Everet. Mr. Bryan will see that I get home."

"But madam," Everet stammered out. "What if he ain't inside? What if he went on an errand of his own?"

"Then I shall have to wait for him," Christina announced. She started toward the door, calling her gratitude over her shoulder, and before Everet could get his wits about him to think what to do the Marchioness had disappeared inside the tavern.

She hadn't come unprepared. No, she wasn't as foolish as Everet's look suggested. Christina hid a small knife in her hand; her regular one was strapped above her ankle. She was far more comfortable with the larger knife, but she couldn't very well carry it in her hand. Why, she'd be giving the impression she wanted a confrontation.

From past experience, Christina had learned that most mischief makers were an ignorant breed. One had to be firm from the outset.

She stood inside the doorway for a long minute as she looked around the crowded area in search of the owner. There were at least twenty men sitting at the wooden tables and another few leaning against the warped bar that ran the length of the right side of the large room.

A man was standing behind the bar, staring gape-mouthed at her. Christina assumed the gentleman worked for the owner and immediately started over to him.

She didn't get more than halfway there before the first oaf tried to deter her. The man was rank with the smell of ale, his motion awkward when he tried to grab her.

Christina slapped his hand away with her blade. The man immediately let out a howl of pain. Everyone inside the tavern watched the big man lift his hand and stare at it in astonishment.

"You cut me!"

His bellow shook the rafters. "You cut me," he roared again as he started to lunge toward Christina.

Christina hadn't moved. She flashed the knife in front of his eyes. "Sit down or I shall have to hurt you again."

She really didn't have time for this, she told herself. There was so much to be seen to before Rhone's party.

"You cut me, you—"

"You tried to touch me," Christina answered. The tip of her knife rested against the befuddled man's throat. "And if you try again, you'll be drinking your ale from the hole I shall fashion in your neck."

She heard the snickers and turned her gaze to find the offender. "I have business to attend to with Mr. Bleak Bryan."

"Are you his lovey, then?" someone shouted out.

Christina let out a sigh of frustration. The mischief maker sitting next to her immediately thought to attack again.

She never even looked down at him as she pricked a narrow, shallow cut in his neck.

He howled again. Christina turned her gaze to the ceiling, praying for patience.

Yes, the mischief makers of the world were all the same. Ignorant.

"I'm the Marquess of Lyonwood's lovey," she told the group of men. "My husband's friend is the owner of this tavern. I have immediate business with the man, and my patience is wearing thin." She paused to scowl at the man holding his neck. "It is a paltry cut, sir, but if you do not cease this foolishness, I promise the next will be more painful."

Though Christina didn't realize it, the news that she was Lyon's wife had changed every man's opinion. "Leave her be, Arthur, if you want to live. She's the mistress of Lyonwood."

"Your name is Arthur?" Christina asked.

The man she'd just questioned was too terrified to answer her.

"Arthur is an appealing name, sir. Do you know the story of Camelot? No?" she asked when the man continued to stare at her stupidly. "Your mama must have read the tale then and named you after King Arthur," she decided for him.

Arthur wasn't listening to her. His mind was far away, captured by the nightmare of what the Marquess of Lyonwood was going to do to him when he heard of this foul incident. "I didn't mean nothing by trying to snatch you. I'm good as dead," he whined. "I didn't know—"

"That I was a married lady?" Christina asked. She let out a sigh. "Well, I suppose you couldn't have known I wasn't available, but it was rude of you to try to snatch a lady without gaining her permission first," she instructed. "But you're not going to die because of your ill manners, Arthur," she added in a gentle voice.

She turned to address her audience. "Does anyone else want to try to snatch me?"

Every single man inside the tavern shouted his denial. And they kept shaking their heads in unison.

It was an amusing sight, but Christina hid her smile. She didn't want them to think she was laughing at them.

"Is your promise true?" she demanded, just to make certain it was safe to put her knife away.

Christina did smile then. She couldn't help herself. The men's vigorous nods were too amusing a sight.

"Arthur, go and wash your cuts now," Christina instructed over her shoulder as she walked over to the bar to wait for the attendant. "I shall send medicine to soothe the sting just as soon as I'm finished here. Does anyone happen to know where Mr. Bleak Bryan is?" she asked the silent men.

"Connor went to fetch him, miss," a man called out.

Christina smiled at the thin little man. She noticed then that he was holding cards in his hand. "Are you having a game of chance?" she called out, biding her time until Bryan arrived and trying at the same time to ease the tension in the room. "I'm sorry if I interrupted you, sir."

"No, no," the man replied. "I couldn't get no one to play."

"Why is that?"

"Nitty is too lucky, miss," another shouted out.

"Are you a patient man, Nitty?" Christina asked.

"Don't rightly know, your grace," Nitty answered.

Christina decided against explaining that she shouldn't be addressed as "your grace." The man looked very nervous to her.

"Shall we find out?" Christina asked. Her husky laughter warmed smiles onto the men's faces. "I would like to learn to play cards, sir, and if you have the time and the inclination, now would be fine with me. I must wait to speak to the owner . . ."

"I would be honored to teach you the ways," Nitty announced. His shoulders straightened. "Poppy, clear a space for the lady," he ordered. "Get her a clean seat, Preston. What game were you wanting to learn, miss?" he asked.

"What game do men like to play?"

"Well now, your husband's game is poker, miss, but of course you wouldn't be wanting to learn—"

"Oh, but I would," Christina announced.

"Here, miss," another shouted. "I'll stake you to a few coins when you've caught on."

"Coins?"

"To bet with," another eager man said.

Christina couldn't believe how helpful the men were. The man named Poppy made a dramatic flourish with his arm as he bowed. "Your chair awaits, my lady," he announced. "Spit's dry now. It's clean as can be."

After taking her seat at the round table, Christina nodded to Nitty. "Do you know my husband, then?" she asked as she watched him flip the cards together. "You said poker was his game," she added as explanation for her question.

"We all know of him, miss," Poppy announced over her shoulder.

"Oh, that is nice," Christina said. "Now then, Nitty. Explain this game to me. Thank you for your coins, sir, and you as well, and . . . oh, I don't believe I need this much money, gentlemen," she added when the coins mounted into a heap in front of her. "You are all so very generous. My husband is fortunate to have such good friends."

Christina's husband was thinking much the same thought as he finished giving his orders to five seedy-looking but very loyal men behind the tavern. Bryan stood by his side, wishing with all his heart he could take part in the charade.

"Damn it all, Lyon, I wish I could be there to see Rhone's expression. Remember, lad," he told the man who was going to imitate Jack, "to stay in the background. Your eyes aren't as green as Rhone's are. Someone might notice."

"Bryan, you got to come back inside," the bartender nagged for the third time. "I'm telling you a fight is brewing. Didn't you hear the screams?"

"I only hear men having a good time, Connor. Whoever sparked the fight must have changed his mind. Now get back inside before I'm robbed blind."

Bryan scowled Connor inside, then stayed beside Lyon, listening to him advise the men.

A sudden roar of laughter caught his attention. Bryan nodded to Lyon and then strolled back inside the tavern to see what everyone was cheering about. He immediately noticed the crowd had gathered around the corner table, and he started forward just as several men shifted their positions. He was able to see the occupants of the table then. After a long disbelieving minute, Bryan turned tail and ran out the back door.

"Lyon, are you finished yet?"

"I was just leaving," Lyon answered. "Why? Do you have a problem?" he asked. The tone in Bryan's voice had put him on his guard. His friend sounded like he was strangling.

"It isn't my problem, it's yours," Bryan answered.

When Lyon tried to walk inside, Bryan blocked the entrance with his arm. "Are you still a betting man, Lyon?"

Lyon let Bryan see his exasperation. "I am."

"Then I'll wager you're about to get the surprise of your life," Bryan said. He moved to the side, then crooked his thumb. "Your surprise is waiting inside."

Lyon didn't have time for foolishness. He hurried inside, believing Bryan wanted him to disarm a man or two.

The crowd of men blocked his view of the table. "There's no danger here," he told Bryan. "What's the attraction, I wonder," he added. "Does Nitty have a new victim for his card tricks?"

"Oh, it's a card game all right," Bryan drawled out. "Frankie, how's the game going?"

"The little miss just bested Nitty with a paltry pair of tens," someone called out from the crowd.

"Ain't my fault," Nitty bellowed goodnaturedly. "She's got a quick mind. Why, she took to the game the way crabs takes—"

"Watch your mouth, Nitty," another man shouted. "The Marquess of Lyonwood's woman is respectable, you stupid little sod. Talk clean in front of her."

The Marquess of Lyonwood's woman.

He couldn't have heard what he thought he'd just heard. No, it couldn't be . . .

Lyon turned to Bryan. His friend was slowly nodding. Lyon still had trouble believing. He walked over to the crowd. Some of the more anxious men moved out of his way.

The cheering abruptly stopped. Christina wasn't aware of the tension in the atmosphere, or the fact that her husband was standing directly behind Nitty, staring at her.

She was concentrating on her hand, her frown intense. Nitty, on the other hand, was afraid to look behind him. He could see the expressions on the faces of the men who stood behind Christina. None of them looked too happy. "I believe I'll fold, miss."

Christina didn't look up, but she drummed her fingertips on the tabletop and stared at the five cards she held in her other hand. "No, Nitty, you can't fold now. You told me I had to put up or fold." She pushed the pile of coins into the center, then glanced up to smile at her new friend. "I shall see you."

Nitty dropped his cards on the table. "Uh, miss, you didn't have to put all the coins in the pot. I've got you beat with my three kings, you see, but you can have the coins back. It's only a teaching game."

The men nodded. Some grumbled their approval while others cast fearful glances in Lyon's direction.

Christina didn't dare look up from her hand. Nitty had warned her that the expressions on players' faces often revealed what they held in their hands. Since Nitty had already shown her his cards, she wasn't sure if that law still applied, but she wasn't about to take any chances . . . not with the wonderful cards she'd been dealt.

"Fair is fair, Nitty. Winner takes all. Didn't you say that?"

"I did, miss," Nitty stammered out.

Christina placed two sevens down on the table. She'd deliberately withheld the other three cards. "Gentlemen," she told the men hovering around her, "Prepare to collect your winnings."

"But miss, you've got to best my . . ."

Nitty stopped his explanation when Christina flipped over the other cards.

"Good God, she's got three aces," Nitty whispered. His voice was filled with relief. Lyon's woman had won the hand.

Christina's husky laughter wasn't echoed by her audience. They all watched the Marquess of Lyonwood, awaiting his judgment. He didn't look too happy. If the powerful Marquess wasn't amused, then neither were they.

Christina was busy stacking the coins in several piles. "Nitty? While we continue to wait for Mr. Bleak's return, I would like you to show me how to cheat. Then, you see, I'll know how it's done and won't be easily tricked."

Nitty didn't answer her request. Christina glanced up at her teacher.

The man looked terrified. The silence finally registered in her mind. She didn't understand until she looked up and found her husband staring down at her.

Her reaction was immediate, her surprise obvious. "Lyon, what are you doing here?"

Her sweet, welcoming smile infuriated him beyond measure. The woman appeared to be pleased to see him.

Christina's smile did falter as her husband continued to stand there staring at her without giving her a greeting.

A tremor of apprehension slowly straightened her shoulders. The truth finally settled in her mind. Lyon was furious. Christina frowned in confusion. "Lyon?" she asked, her voice hesitant. "Is something the matter?"

Lyon ignored her question. His cold gaze swept over the crowd of men.

"Out."

He cleared the tavern with one word. His voice had cracked like a whip. While Christina watched, the men rushed to do his bidding. Nitty tripped over his chair in his hurry to leave the tavern.

"You've forgotten your coins," Christina called after the men.

"Do not say another word."

Lyon had roared his command to her. Christina's eyes

widened in disbelief. She stood up to face her husband. "You dare to raise your voice to me in front of strangers? In front of our friend, Bleak Bryan?"

"I damn well do dare," Lyon bellowed.

The chilling rebuke stunned her. She turned to look at his friend, caught his sympathetic expression, and was suddenly so ashamed she wanted to weep.

"You are humiliating me in front of another warrior." Her voice trembled and she clasped her hands together.

He believed she was afraid of him. Her forlorn expression cut through his haze of anger. Lyon's expression slowly changed until he looked almost in control.

"Tell me what you're doing here," Lyon demanded. His voice was still harsh with his suppressed anger. Lyon considered that a victory of sorts over his temper, for he still felt the need to shout.

She hadn't understood the danger. Lyon kept repeating that statement inside his head until it became a litany. No, she hadn't realized what could have happened to her . . .

He was all too aware of the horrors awaiting a gentle lady in this part of London. Lyon forced himself to block the black possibilities from his thoughts, knowing he'd never regain control if he didn't.

Christina couldn't look at her husband. She stood with her head bowed, staring at the tabletop.

"Lyon, your wife must have had a terribly important reason for coming here," Bryan stated, trying to ease the tension between husband and wife.

Christina's head jerked up to look at Bryan. "My husband is angry because I came here?" she asked, her voice incredulous.

Bryan didn't know what to say to that absurd question. He decided to ask one of his own. "You didn't know what a sorry area this is?"

She had to take a deep breath before she spoke again. Her hands were fisted at her sides. "I will go wherever I wish to go . . . whenever I want."

Oh, hell, Bryan thought to himself, she's done it now. He gave Lyon a quick glance before looking back at Christina.

The sweet innocent didn't know her husband very well yet. Why, she'd just waved a red flag in front of his face.

Lyon wasn't over his initial anger. It helped little to prod him the way Christina was doing. Bryan rushed to intervene before Lyon had time to react to his wife's ill-chosen remark. "Why don't you both sit down? I'll leave you to your privacy . . ."

"Why? He already humiliated me in front of you," Christina whispered.

"Christina, we're going home. Now."

Lyon's voice had turned into a soft whisper. Bryan hoped Christina would realize that wasn't a good sign.

No, she hadn't realized. She turned to glare at her husband. Bryan had to shake his head over her indiscretion.

Lyon moved with the speed of lightning. Christina suddenly found herself pinned up against the back wall, her sides blocked by his hands. His face was only inches away from hers, and the heat of his anger was hot enough to burn.

"This is how it works in England, Christina. The wife does as her husband orders. She goes only where the husband allows her to go, only when he allows it. Got that?"

Bryan was pacing behind Lyon's back. His heart went out to the delicate flower Lyon had wed. The poor dear had to be terrified. Why, even he was a bit nervous. Lyon's temper still had the power to frighten him.

When Christina answered her husband, Bryan realized she wasn't frightened at all. "You have shamed me. Where I come from, that is sufficient reason for a wife to cut her hair, Lyon."

He was trying to calm down, but her absurd remark made him crazy. "What the hell does that mean?"

She didn't want to take the time to explain. No, Christina could feel her anger burning inside her. She wanted to scream at him. But she wanted to weep, too. That made little sense to her, but she was too upset to reason the contrary emotions clear. "When a woman cuts her hair, it is because she has lost someone. A wife cuts her hair when her husband dies . . . or when she casts him aside."

"That is the most ridiculous notion I've ever heard of,"

Lyon muttered. "Do you realize what you're implying? You're speaking of divorce."

The enormity of her folly and her outrageous remarks suddenly hit him full force. Lyon dropped his forehead on top of hers, closed his eyes, and started to laugh. Her blessed arrogance had pushed his anger away.

"I knew you'd change when you knew my past, you inferior Englishman," she raged against him. "You're nothing but a . . . stupid little sod," she announced, remembering one of the men's earlier comments to another.

"You and I are going to have a long talk," Lyon drawled. "Come along," he ordered as he grabbed hold of her hand and started to pull her after him.

"I have still to speak to Mr. Bleak," Christina said. "Unhand me, Lyon," she added, trying to jerk her hand away.

"Perhaps you didn't get it after all," Lyon remarked over his shoulder. "I just told you that a wife goes where her husband—"

"Lyon? I'm ready to kill with curiosity," Bryan interposed. He'd caught the irritation in his friend's voice and was trying to intervene before another conflict started. "I would like to know why your wife came here," he added with an embarrassed stammer.

Lyon paused at the door. "Tell him," he ordered Christina.

She wished she could deny his command so that he would realize she'd meant every word of what she'd said to him, but Rhone's well-being was at issue, so she put her pride aside. "Rhone is having a party tonight," she began. "I wanted to ask you if you could find some good men to act as mischief makers and—"

Christina never finished her explanation. Lyon dragged her out the door in the middle of her sentence. They walked halfway around the block before his carriage came into view. No wonder she hadn't known he was visiting Bryan, she thought to herself. The man had hidden his vehicle a good distance away.

She didn't understand his reason, yet she wasn't about to

question him. Her voice might betray her. Christina knew she was close to weeping. She didn't think she'd ever been this angry in all her life.

Neither said a word to the other until they were home. Lyon used the time to try to calm down. It was a difficult endeavor. He couldn't quit thinking about what could have happened to Christina. The unwanted images fueled his temper. God help him, his knees had nearly buckled under him when he'd first spotted Christina in the tavern.

She was playing cards with the worst thugs in London. She hadn't realized her jeopardy, of course; she couldn't have. She wouldn't have looked so pleased with herself if she had. And she had smiled at him. Lyon didn't think he'd ever been so furious . . . or so frightened.

"You're too damned innocent for your own good," he muttered after he'd jerked the door to the carriage open.

Christina wouldn't look at him. She kept her gaze directed on her lap, and when he made his unkind remark she merely shrugged her shoulders in indifference.

He offered her his hand when she climbed out of the vehicle. She ignored it.

It wasn't until she'd raced on ahead of him that he realized she'd cut a portion of her hair. The curls ended in the middle of her back now.

Brown met them at the door. After giving his butler instructions to watch over his wife, he chased after Christina. She was halfway up the staircase when he stopped her. "When I'm not too angry to speak of this matter, I will explain to you why—"

"I don't wish to hear your reasons," Christina interrupted.

Lyon closed his eyes and took a deep breath. "Don't you dare venture out again until tomorrow morning," he told her. "I have to go to Rhone's now."

"I see."

"No, I don't think you do see," Lyon muttered. "Christina, you went to Bryan to ask his help in finding men to masquerade as Jack and his friends, didn't you?"

She nodded.

"Wife, you have little faith in me," Lyon whispered, shaking his head.

Christina believed his comment was ridiculous. "Faith has nothing to do with my errand. I didn't know you'd been informed of Rhone's terror."

"Terror?"

"He's been barred inside his house," Christina explained. "Since he is your friend, I thought of a most cunning plan. You ruined it," she added.

"No, *you* would have ruined it," Lyon announced. "I've already taken care of the problem, Christina. Now give me your word that you'll stay inside."

"I have no other errands to take care of," Christina answered.

When he let go of her arm, Christina turned and rushed up the rest of the steps. Lyon was just walking out the front door when she called out to him.

"Lyon?"

"Yes."

"You're going to have to apologize. Will you do it now or when you return from Rhone's house?"

"Apologize?"

He'd shouted the word at her. Christina concluded he wasn't contrite. "Then you're going to have to start all over," she shouted back.

"What are you talking about? I don't have time for riddles," Lyon announced. "If anyone's going to apologize . . ."

He didn't bother to finish his demand, for his wife had turned her back on him and disappeared down the hallway.

She'd just dismissed him again. Lyon didn't think he was ever going to get used to that action.

He wasn't ever going to understand her, either. She had a devious mind. She'd come up with the same plan he had to help Rhone. He couldn't help being impressed.

Lord, the task ahead of him would certainly prove exhausting. He was going to have to go to great lengths to keep Christina safe. She'd get into quick trouble if he wasn't always by her side, watching over her. Christina didn't seem to understand caution. Hell, she didn't even know enough to be afraid of him when his temper exploded.

No woman had ever raised her voice to him . . . nor had many men, Lyon realized. Yet Christina certainly had. When he shouted at her, he got equal measure in return.

She was his equal in all things. Her passion matched his own, and in his heart, he knew she loved him just as much.

Yes, the next twenty years, God willing, were going to be exhausting.

And very, very satisfying.

Chapter Fifteen

I didn't want any more innocent people to die because of me. Edward would come after us. I knew I'd only been given a temporary stay of execution.

When dawn arrived, I'd only made it to the first peak. The wagon train was waking up. Would they send searchers out to find me?

I saw the Indians pouring down the hill then and thought to scream a warning, but I knew they wouldn't be able to hear me. Then another scream came from behind me. It was a woman's voice. Edward! He was there, I believed. Another innocent would die because of me. I grabbed the knife Jacob kept in his saddle pocket and ran toward the sound.

The sight that met me when I rushed through the trees broke through my cowardice, my fear. I saw a little boy, so battered, so bloody, crumbled like a fallen leaf on the ground. The woman who'd screamed was silent now. Her hands and feet had been bound.

Mother and child . . . like you and me, Christina . . . the attacker became Edward in my mind. I don't remember putting you down on the ground, don't know if I made a sound as I ran forward and plunged my knife into his back.

The knife must have pierced his heart, for the attacker didn't struggle.

I made certain he was dead, then turned to help the little boy. His whimpers of agony tore at me. I gently lifted the child into my arms to give him what little comfort I could. When I began to croon to him, his breathing deepened.

I suddenly felt someone watching me. I turned and saw that the Indian woman was staring at me.

Her name was Merry.

Journal entry
November 1, 1795

Lyon didn't return to his townhouse until the early hours of the morning. It had been a thoroughly satisfying evening all around. The look on Rhone's face when he was being robbed by the man pretending to be Jack would live in Lyon's memory a good long while.

Yes, it had all been worth his efforts. The charges against Rhone would be dropped by tomorrow at the latest. Everyone now believed Rhone's story that he'd injured his wrist by accident when he'd fallen on a piece of jagged glass.

Wellingham had been made to look like a fool. That thought pleased Lyon. He wasn't through with that bastard—or the other three, for that matter—but Lyon knew he'd have to wait before making their lives as miserable as he had planned. Rhone's father would be avenged. The four thieves were going to regret the day they'd decided to make Rhone's family their target. Lyon would see to it.

Christina was sound asleep on the floor next to his side of the bed. Lyon undressed quickly, then lifted his wife into his arms, careful to avoid being pricked by the knife under her blanket. Put her where she belonged—in his bed. He wrapped his arms around her until she was snuggled against his chest.

He'd have to do something about the soft mattresses, he

supposed. He smiled as he remembered Christina telling him on their wedding night that the bed was trying to swallow her up.

She hadn't fallen out of bed. No wonder she'd laughed when he'd announced that she had. Lyon fervently hoped she'd get used to the bed. He didn't relish the idea of bedding down on the ground, but he would do it, he realized with a sigh, if it was the only way he could hold her.

Compromise. The word whispered through his mind. It was a foreign concept to him. Until Christina. Perhaps now, he decided, it was time to practice it.

Lyon was eager for morning to come. After explaining his reason for being so angry with her when he'd found her at Bryan's tavern, he'd ease into the issue of her safety. He'd make her understand he only had her best interests at heart, and that she couldn't go flitting about town without proper escort.

And she would learn to compromise.

Lyon wasn't able to lecture his wife the following morning. She wasn't there to listen to him.

He didn't wake up until noon—an amazing fact, for he rarely slept more than three hours at a stretch. He felt rested, ready to take on the world. More exactly, he was ready to take on his wife, and he hurried in his dress so that he could go downstairs to begin her instruction.

Lyon had jumped to the erroneous conclusion that Christina would actually be waiting for him.

"What do you mean? She can't be gone!"

His bellow frightened the timid servant. "The Marchioness left several hours ago, my lord," he stammered out. "With Brown and the other men. Have you forgotten your orders to your wife? I heard the Marchioness tell Brown you had insisted she return to Lyonwood immediately."

"Yes, I did forget," Lyon muttered. He lied to his servant, of course. He hadn't given any such instructions. Yet he wasn't about to let a member of his staff know Christina wasn't telling the truth. It wasn't *her* character he was protecting but his own. Lyon didn't want anyone to know the lack of control he had over her.

It was humiliating. Lyon grumbled about that sorry fact until a sudden thought made him cheer up a bit. Christina must have been nervous to leave so quickly. Perhaps she'd realized the significance of her actions yesterday.

Lyon at first thought to go to Lyonwood immediately, then decided to let Christina stew in her own worries for most of the day. By the time he arrived home she might even be contrite.

Yes, time and silence were his allies. He hoped he'd have her apology by nightfall.

Lyon spent an hour going over estate details, then decided to stop by his mother's townhouse to tell Diana about Rhone.

He was given a surprise when he barged into the drawing room and found Rhone sitting on the settee with his arm draped around Diana.

"Am I interrupting?" he drawled.

His entrance didn't seem to bother either one of them. Diana's head continued to rest on Rhone's shoulder, and his friend didn't even glance up.

"Here's Lyon now, sweetling. Quit crying. He'll know what's to be done."

Lyon barked orders as he strode over to the fireplace. "Rhone, get your arm off my sister. Diana, sit up and behave with a little decorum, for God's sake. What are you crying about?"

His sister tried to comply with his command, but as soon as she straightened up Rhone pulled her back, forcing the side of her cheek onto his shoulder again.

"You stay right there. I'm comforting her, damn it, Lyon, and that's that."

Lyon decided he'd have to deal with his friend later. "Tell me why you're crying, Diana. Now. I'm in a hurry," he added.

"You don't need to raise your voice to her, Lyon." Rhone glared at his friend. "She's had an upset."

"Will one of you please tell me what the hell the upset was?"

"Mama." Diana wailed. She pulled away from Rhone to

dab at her eyes with her lace handkerchief. "Christina took her."

"She what?" Lyon asked, shaking his head in confusion.

"Your wife took your mother to Lyonwood with her," Rhone said.

"And that's why Diana's crying?" Lyon asked, trying to get to the bottom of the matter.

Rhone was trying not to laugh. His eyes sparkled with merriment. "It is," he said as he patted Diana's shoulder.

Lyon sat down across from his sister and waited for her to get hold of herself. She looked like a butterfly, he thought, dressed in a yellow gown with brown trim. Her tears were making a mess of the gown.

"Diana," he said in what he hoped was a soothing voice, "You needn't be afraid that I'm angry because my wife took our mother with her. That's why you're crying, isn't it?"

"No."

"You wanted Mother to stay here?"

When she shook her head and continued to sob, Lyon's patience wore out. "Well?"

"Mama didn't want to go," Diana cried. "Rhone, you tell him. You saw what happened. I just don't know what to think. And Aunt Harriett laughing like a loon the whole time. Oh, I didn't know what—"

"Rhone, do you care about Diana?"

"I do. Very much."

"Then I suggest you quiet her down before I strangle her. Diana, stop that snorting."

"I'll explain, my sweet," Rhone told Diana in a tender, soothing voice.

Lyon hid his exasperation. Rhone was acting like a lovesick puppy.

"Your mama denied Christina's request to go along with her to Lyonwood, you see. And that's when the fireworks began."

Rhone couldn't control his smile. Diana was weeping into his jacket now, so he felt safe grinning. "Your wife was very determined to take your mother with her. So determined, in fact, that she . . . well, she dragged your mother out of bed."

"You're jesting."

"Mama didn't want to go."

"Obviously," Lyon drawled. "Did Christina explain her reasons for being so forceful?"

A smile pulled at the corners of his mouth, but his sister was watching him intently, and he didn't want to upset her further by letting her see his amusement.

Rhone didn't help his determination to shield his sister's feelings. "You should have seen it, Lyon. Your mother is a strong woman. I never realized that fact. I thought she'd been languishing these past years, but she did put up quite a fight. Of course, that was only after . . ."

"After what?" Lyon asked, thoroughly puzzled by his wife's conduct.

"Mama told Christina she wanted to stay where she was. She had people coming to call, and she wanted to talk to them about James, of course," Diana said to Lyon.

"Yes, well, that's when Christina asked your mother if her heart had died."

"I don't understand," Lyon announced, shaking his head.

"I didn't either," Rhone answered. "Anyway, your mother said that since James had died, her heart was also dead . . . whatever in God's name that means."

Lyon smiled then. He couldn't help himself. "My mother is a professional mourner, Rhone. You know that well enough."

"Was," Rhone drawled out. "Christina had gotten your mother down into the entryway by this time. Your aunt, Diana, and I were standing there, watching the two ladies, wondering what was going on. Then Christina explained it all to us."

"She's going to kill Mama."

"Now, Diana, that isn't what she said," Rhone said. He patted her shoulder, then turned to grin at Lyon again.

"Rhone, will you get on with it?"

"Christina told your mother that where she came from—and God only knows where that is—an old warrior who was broken in spirit and in heart would go into the wilderness."

"What for?" Lyon asked.

"Why, to find a nice, secluded spot in which to die, of course. Needless to say, your mother didn't take kindly to being called an old warrior."

Lyon stared at the ceiling a long minute before daring to look at his friend again. He was dangerously close to laughing. "No, I don't suppose she would," he whispered.

"Well, part of it is Mama's own fault," Diana interjected. "If she hadn't agreed that her heart was broken, Christina wouldn't have insisted on taking her with her. She told Mama she'd help her find a lovely spot."

"That was good of her," Lyon said.

"Lyon, Mama hadn't had her chocolate yet. She hadn't had her maids pack any of her possessions, either. Christina told her it didn't matter. One didn't have to pack when one was going to die. Those were her very words."

"Your mother started shouting then," Rhone announced.

"Rhone wouldn't let me interfere," Diana whispered, "and Aunt Harriett was laughing."

"Not until your mother was inside the carriage," Rhone commented.

"Was she shouting James's name?" Lyon asked.

"Well . . . no, of course not," Diana muttered. "What has that got to do with anything?"

Neither Rhone nor Lyon could answer her. They were too busy laughing.

It took Lyon several minutes before he could speak again. "I guess I'd better get back to Lyonwood."

"What if Christina hides Mama somewhere in the countryside and won't tell you where?"

"Do you really believe Christina would harm your mama?" Rhone asked.

"No," Diana whispered. "But she sounded as though it was the most natural thing for . . . an old warrior to do." Diana let out a loud sigh. "Christina has some unusual notions, doesn't she?"

"She's bluffing, Diana. She's pretending to give our mother what she wants."

"Lyon, would you like me to ride along with you to Lyonwood?" Rhone asked.

Lyon could tell by the gleam in his friend's green eyes that he was up to mischief. "Why do you offer?" he asked.

"I could help you search the estate," Rhone drawled.

"Very amusing," Lyon snapped. "Now see what you've done? Diana's crying again. You deal with it, Rhone. I don't have time. Come down to Lyonwood this weekend with Aunt Harriett and Diana."

Lyon strolled over to the doorway, then called over his shoulder, "If I haven't found your mother by then, Diana, you can help search."

Rhone contained his smile. "He's only jesting, sweetheart. Now, now, let me hold you, love. You can cry on my shoulder."

Lyon closed the door on Rhone's soothing voice. He shook his head in vexation. He'd been so wrapped up in his own life, he hadn't realized Rhone was falling in love with Diana.

Rhone was a good friend . . . but a brother-in-law . . . Lyon would have to adjust to that possibility.

Christina wouldn't be surprised by the attraction. No, she'd been the one to instruct Rhone on his destiny, Lyon recalled with a smile.

Ah, destiny. He decided it was now his destiny to go home and kiss his wife.

The desire to take Christina into his arms, to make slow, sweet love to her, made the journey back to Lyonwood seem much longer than usual.

The sun was just setting when Lyon rode toward the circle drive in front of his house. He squinted against the sunlight, trying to make out the sight he thought he was seeing.

As he rode closer, he recognized the man dragging his shoes down the steps. It was Elbert. What was he doing there? And what in God's name was he doing with Lyon's boots? Lyon was close enough to see his dozens of shoes and boots lined up on the steps, the walkway.

Lyon dismounted, slapped his horse on the hindquarters as a signal to take to the stables, then called out to Christina's former butler. "Elbert? What are you doing with my shoes?"

"The madam's orders, my lord," Elbert answered. "Didn't know a man could own so many boots," he added. "Been at this task near an hour now. Up the stairs and down the stairs, then up—"

"Elbert? Give me the reason why," Lyon interrupted, his voice irritated. "And what are you doing at Lyonwood? Did Christina invite you to visit?"

"Hired me, sir," Elbert announced. "I'm to be Brown's assistant. Did you know how worried she was about me? She knew I wouldn't last with the old bat. Your misses has a good heart. I'll do my part, my lord. I won't be shirking me responsibilities to you."

Christina did have a good heart. His gentle wife knew Elbert wouldn't be able to find work with anyone else. He was simply too old, too feeble. "I'm sure you'll do fine, Elbert," Lyon said. "Glad to have you on staff."

"Thank you, my lord," Elbert returned.

Lyon noticed Brown standing in the open doorway then. His butler looked upset. "Good afternoon, my lord," Brown called out. "It is so very good to have you back," he added. His voice sounded strained to Lyon, relieved as well. "Did you see your shoes, sir?"

"I'm not blind, man. Of course I saw them. Would you care to explain what in thunderation is going on?"

"Your wife's orders," Brown announced.

"Past wife," Elbert interjected with a cackle.

Lyon took a deep breath. "What are you talking about?" He addressed his question to Brown, believing his young butler would make more sense than the old man snickering with laughter behind him.

"You're being divorced, my lord."

"I'm what?"

Brown's shoulders sagged. He knew his lord wasn't going to take the news well. "Divorced."

"Cast out, my lord, pushed aside, forgotten, dead in her heart—"

"I get your meaning, Elbert," Lyon muttered in exasperation. "I'm aware of what the word divorce means."

Lyon continued into the house. The old servant shuffled

after him. "Those were her very words. My mistress is divorcing you the way her people do. She said it was quite all right to get rid of a husband. You have to find someplace else to live."

"I what?" Lyon asked, certain he hadn't heard correctly.

Brown's insistent nod indicated he had.

"You're cast out, pushed aside—"

"For God's sake, Elbert, cease your litany," Lyon demanded. He turned back to Brown. "What is the significance of the shoes?"

"They signify your departure, my lord," Brown said.

The butler tried not to stare at the incredulous look on his master's face. He was in jeopardy of losing his control. He stared at the floor instead.

"Let me get this straight in my mind," Lyon muttered. "My wife believes the house belongs to her?"

"And your mother, of course," Brown blurted out. "She's keeping her."

Brown was biting his lower lip. Lyon thought he might be trying not to laugh.

"Of course," Lyon drawled.

Elbert tried to be helpful once again. "It's the way her people do," he interjected, his voice gratingly cheerful.

"Where is my wife?" Lyon asked, ignoring Elbert's comments.

He didn't wait for his servants to answer him but took the steps two at a time to reach the bedrooms. A sudden thought made him pause. "Did she cut her hair?" he called out.

"She did," Elbert shouted before Brown could open his mouth. "It's the way of it," Elbert insisted. "Once the hair's cut—well, then you're as good as dead to her. You're set aside, cast—"

"I've gotten her message," Lyon shouted. "Brown, bring my shoes inside. Elbert, go sit somewhere."

"My lord?" Brown called out.

"Yes?"

"Do the French really follow these laws?"

Lyon contained his smile. "Did my wife say it was the law?" he asked.

"Yes, my lord."

"And she told you she was from France?" he asked his butler.

Brown nodded.

"Then it must be true," Lyon announced. "I would like a bath, Brown. Leave the shoes until later," he added before turning back to his destination.

Lyon smiled. There were times when he forgot just how young and inexperienced Brown was. Of course, he'd been lied to by someone who radiated innocence and sincerity. Christina.

His wife wasn't waiting for him in their bedroom. He really hadn't expected her to be there. The sun still gave sufficient light for her to stay outdoors. Lyon doubted she'd return to the house until darkness forced her to do so.

Lyon walked over to the windows to look out at the setting sun. It was a magnificent sight, and one he'd never taken the time to notice until he'd married Christina. She had opened his eyes to the wonders of life.

And the wonder of love. Yes, he did love her, so ferociously it almost frightened him. If anything happened to her, Lyon didn't know how he'd be able to go on.

That odious thought wouldn't have intruded on his peace of mind if he hadn't been so concerned about Christina's reunion with her father. Lyon was more than uneasy.

She believed he'd try to kill her. Richards hadn't been able to tell Lyon much about Christina's father, but the fact that Stalinsky had been involved in the Brisbane affair, with such shameful results, worried Lyon.

How simple it would be if Christina would trust him, confide in him. Lord, he felt as if he was being asked to fence with an enemy with a blindfold tied around his eyes.

Equal measure. Wasn't that what he wanted from Christina?

The truth hit him like a blow. He'd demanded from his wife what he'd been unwilling to give her. Trust. Yes, he wanted her absolute trust, yet he hadn't let her know how much he trusted her. No, he told himself with a shake of his head, his sin was worse. He hadn't opened his heart to her.

Christina had only questioned him once about his past. When they were on their way to Lyonwood, she'd asked him to tell her about his first wife, Lettie.

His answers had been abrupt. He'd let her know the subject wasn't one he would discuss.

She hadn't asked him again.

Yes, he was getting equal measure.

The door opened behind him. Lyon glanced over his shoulder and saw the servants carrying the tub and pails of steaming water into the room.

He turned back to the landscape and was in the process of drawing off his jacket when he saw Christina.

His breath caught in his throat. The sight was more magnificent than the sunset. Christina was riding bareback. The gray stallion she'd chosen was racing across the grounds with such speed his legs were a blur.

She rode like the wind. Her golden hair flew out behind her. Her back was as straight as a lance, and when she directed her mount over the hedge that separated the wilderness from the immediate grounds, Lyon started breathing again.

Christina was far more skilled than he was. That fact became obvious as he continued to watch her. He was arrogantly pleased, as if her skill somehow reflected on him. "She's my lioness," he whispered, excusing his reaction.

She was so incredibly graceful . . . and he had offered to teach her how to ride.

Another incorrect assumption, Lyon realized. As incorrect as believing he would actually gain an apology from her for yesterday's folly.

Lyon was chuckling to himself as he stripped off his clothes. He ignored his servants' worried glances. He knew they weren't used to hearing him laugh. Then he stretched out in the long tub, his shoulders propped against the back. Brown was occupied getting fresh clothing ready for him.

"I'll take care of that," Lyon told his butler. "You may leave now."

Brown started for the door, then hesitated. When he

turned around to look at his employer, his expression showed his concern.

"What is it?" Lyon asked.

"My lord, I would never presume to intrude upon your private affairs, but I was wondering if you'll be honoring your wife's decision."

Lyon had to remind himself that Brown was very young and hadn't been in his household long enough to know his lord's ways well. He'd never have asked such a ridiculous question otherwise. "Why, of course, Brown," Lyon drawled out.

"Then you'll let her divorce you?" Brown blurted out, clearly stunned.

"I believe she already did divorce me," Lyon answered with a grin.

The butler wasn't at all happy with that announcement. "I shall miss you, my lord."

"She's keeping you, too?" Lyon asked.

Brown nodded. He looked miserable. "My lady explained that we are part of her family now."

"We?"

"She's keeping the full staff, my lord."

Lyon started laughing. "I really wish you'd stay," Brown blurted out.

"Quit worrying, Brown. I'm not going anywhere," Lyon announced. "As soon as my wife walks into the house, send her to me. If she can divorce me so easily, then there must be a quick way to remarry again. This little problem will be resolved by nightfall, I promise you."

"Thank God," Brown whispered. He hurried out of the room, closing the door behind him.

Brown could hear his lord's laughter all the way down the hall.

Christina met the butler at the bottom of the steps. When he informed her that the Marquess was upstairs and wished an audience with her, she gave him a disgruntled look before giving in to his request.

When she walked into the bedroom, she came to a sudden stop.

"Close the door, sweetheart."

Christina did as he asked, but only because she wished privacy for their confrontation.

"Did you enjoy your ride?" Lyon asked.

The mildness in his tone confused her. Christina was ready for a fight. Lyon didn't seem to be in an accommodating mood. "Lyon," she began, deliberately avoiding his gaze, "I don't think you realize what I've done."

"Of course I do, my dear," Lyon answered, in such a cheerful voice that Christina was more confused than ever.

"You're going to have to start all over. You'll have to court me, though now that you are aware of my . . . unusual upbringing, I doubt you'll—"

"All right."

Christina looked at him. "All right? That is all you have to say to me?" She shook her head, let out a long sigh, and then whispered, "You don't understand."

"Yes, I do. You've just cast me aside. Elbert explained."

"You aren't upset?"

"No."

"Well, why not? You told me you loved me," Christina said. She moved a step closer to Lyon. "Your words were false, weren't they? Now that you know—"

"They weren't false," Lyon answered. He leaned back and closed his eyes. "God, this feels good. I tell you, Christina, the ride from London gets longer every time."

She couldn't believe his casual attitude. Christina felt like weeping. "You cannot humiliate me and then act as though nothing has happened. A warrior would kill another for such an offense," she told him.

"Ah, but you aren't a warrior, Christina. You're my wife."

"Was."

He didn't even open his eyes to look at her when he asked, "Exactly what did I do?"

"You don't know?" She had to take a deep breath before she could go on. "You shouted at me in front of a witness. You shamed me. You disgraced me."

"Who was the witness?" Lyon asked, in such a soft voice that she had to move a bit closer to hear him.

"Bryan," Christina announced.

"Didn't I yell at you in front of Richards, too? I seem to remember—"

"That was different."

"Why?"

"You were shouting because I fainted. You weren't angry with me. Surely you can see the difference."

"I do now," Lyon admitted. "Do you wonder why I shouted at you in front of Bryan?"

"No."

Lyon opened his eyes. His irritation was obvious. "You scared the hell out of me," he announced. Each word was clipped, hard.

"I what?"

"Don't look so surprised, Christina. When I walked inside that tavern and found you sitting so peacefully in the midst of the worse scum in England, my mind could barely take it in. Then you had the gall to smile at me, as if you were happy to see me."

He had to stop talking. The memory was making him angry again.

"I *was* happy to see you. Did you doubt that I was?" she asked.

Her hands rested on her hips. She tossed her hair over her shoulder and continued to frown at him. "Well?" she demanded.

"Did you cut your hair again?"

"I did. It is all part of the ritual of mourning," Christina announced.

"Christina, if you cut your hair every time you're unhappy with me, you'll be bald in a month's time. I promise you."

Lyon drew a long breath, then said, "Let me get this straight inside my mind. I'm never to raise my voice to you in future? Christina, it won't work. There will be times when I shout at you."

"I don't care if you raise your voice to me," Christina muttered. "I shall also let my temper show on occasion," she admitted. "But I would never, ever let an outsider see my displeasure. That was the humiliation, Lyon."

"Oh? Then I should have dragged you into the back room to shout at you in privacy?" he asked.

"Yes, you should have," Christina agreed.

"You took a foolish risk, Christina. You were in danger, whether you realized it or not. I want your apology and your promise never to take such a risk again."

"I shall have to think about it," she said. Now that she was forced to consider what he was saying to her, she realized she had been in a bit of danger. There were too many men in Bryan's tavern for her to subdue . . . if they'd all decided to challenge her at the same time. She'd thought she'd gained the upper hand, though, after the single challenger had backed down . . . and after she'd mentioned her husband was the Marquess of Lyonwood. "Yes," she repeated, "I shall have to think about these promises you want from me."

She could tell from Lyon's ferocious expression that he didn't care for her honest answer. "I warned you that it wouldn't be easy for you," she whispered.

"That's what this is really all about, isn't it?"

"I've just said—"

"You're testing me, aren't you, Christina?"

She made the mistake of getting too close to the tub, realizing her error a second too late. Lyon grabbed her and pulled her down into his lap. Water sloshed over the sides of the tub.

"You've ruined my gown," Christina gasped.

"I've ruined others," Lyon told her when she quit struggling. He cupped the sides of her face and made her look at him. "I love you."

Her eyes filled with tears. "You humiliated me."

"I love you," Lyon repeated in a harsh whisper. "I'm sorry you felt humiliated," he added.

"You're sorry?"

A single tear slid down her cheek. Lyon wiped it away with his thumb.

"I'm sorry I frightened you," she whispered. "I shall try not to do it again."

"Tell me you love me," Lyon demanded.

"I love you."

"Should I believe you?" he asked. His voice was husky, coaxing.

"Yes," Christina answered. She tried to push his hands away when she realized he was actually insulting her. "Of course you should believe me."

"But you don't believe me when I tell you I love you," Lyon said. "You have it in your head that it's only a temporary condition, don't you?" He kissed her slowly, tenderly, hoping to take the sting out of his gentle rebuke. "When you learn to trust me completely, you'll know I won't change my mind. My love is forever, Christina."

Lyon didn't give her time to argue over that fact. He kissed her again. His tongue flicked over her soft lips until they parted for him.

And then he began to ravage her mouth.

Christina tried to protest. "Lyon, I must—"

"Get your clothes off," Lyon interrupted. He was already pulling apart the fastenings on the back of her gown.

No, she hadn't meant to say that. But her thoughts got confused inside her mind. Lyon had pulled her gown down to her waist. His hands cupped her breasts, his thumbs rubbed her nipples, forced her response. His mouth had never seemed so warm, so inviting.

There was more water on the floor than in the tub. Lyon didn't seem to mind. He was determined, and he had Christina stripped out of her soggy clothes in little time.

Christina didn't want to struggle. She put her arms around his neck and let out a soft sigh. "The water isn't very hot," she whispered against his ear.

"I am."

"What?"

"Hot."

"Lyon? I want—"

"Me, inside you," Lyon whispered. His mouth feasted on the side of her neck. His warm breath sent shivers down her spine. "You want to feel me inside you," he rasped out. "Hard. Hot. I'll try to go slow, but you'll want me harder, faster, until I'm touching your womb and you're begging me for release."

Christina's head fell back so that Lyon could kiss more of her throat. His dark promise of what was to come made her throat tighten and her heartbeat quicken. "I'll stay inside you until I'm hard again, won't I, Christina? And then I'll pleasure you again."

His mouth settled on hers for another long, drugging kiss. "That's what you want, isn't it, my sweet?"

"Yes," Christina answered. She sighed against his mouth. "It's what I want."

"Then marry me. Now," Lyon demanded. He kissed her again as a precaution against any protest. "Hurry, Christina. I want to . . . Christina, don't move like that," Lyon ground out. "It's torture."

"You like it."

She whispered the truth against his shoulder, then nipped his skin with her teeth, her nails. She moved again to straddle his hips, rubbing her breasts against his chest.

Yet when she tried to take Lyon inside her, he wouldn't allow it. His hands settled on the sides of her hips, holding her away from his arousal.

"Not yet, Christina," he groaned. "Are we still divorced inside your head?"

"Lyon, please," Christina begged.

He drew her up against him until her heat rested on the flat of his stomach. His fingers found her, slowly penetrated her. "Do you want me to stop?" he asked with a growl.

"No, don't stop."

"Are we married?"

Christina gave in. "Yes, Lyon. You were supposed to court me first." She moaned when he increased the pressure. She bit his bottom lip, then opened her mouth for him again.

"Compromise," Lyon whispered as he slowly pushed her downward and began to penetrate her.

She didn't understand what he was saying to her, thought to at least try to question him, but Lyon suddenly shifted.

His movement was forceful, deliberate. Christina couldn't speak, couldn't think. Lyon was pulling her into the sun. Soon, when she could bear the scorching heat no longer, he would give her sweet release.

Christina clung to her warrior in blissful surrender.

"We should have gone downstairs for dinner. I don't want your mother to think she can hide in her bedroom. She must eat all her meals with us in future, husband."

Lyon ignored his wife's comments. He pulled her up against his side, draped the bed covers over her legs when he noticed she was trembling, then began to tickle her shoulder with his fingers.

"Christina? Didn't your father ever yell at you when you were a little girl?"

She turned and rested her chin on his chest before she answered him. "That's an odd question to put to me. Yes, Father did yell."

"But never in front of others?" Lyon asked.

"Well, there was one time when he lost his temper," she admitted. "I was too little to remember the incident, but my mother and the shaman liked to tell the story."

"Shaman?"

"Our holy man," Christina explained. "Like the one who married us. My shaman doesn't ever wear a cone on his head, though." She ended her comment with a dainty shrug.

"What was the reason for your father to lose his temper?" Lyon asked.

"You'll not laugh?"

"I won't laugh."

Christina turned her gaze to stare at his chest so that his golden eyes wouldn't break her concentration. "My brother carried home a beautiful snake. Father was very pleased."

"He was?"

"It was a fine snake, Lyon."

"I see."

She could hear the smile in his voice but didn't take exception. "Mother was also pleased. I must have watched the way my brother held his prize, and the shaman said I was envious of the attention given my brother, too, for I went out to capture a snake of my own. No one could find me for several hours. I was very little and in constant mischief."

"Ah, so that is why your father lost his temper," Lyon announced. "Your disappearance must have—"

"No, that isn't the reason," Christina interjected. "Though of course he was unhappy that I'd left the safety of the village."

"Well, then?" Lyon prodded when she didn't immediately continue with her story.

"Everyone was frantically searching for me when I strutted back into the village. Mama said I always strutted because I tried to imitate my brother's swagger. White Eagle walked like a proud warrior, you see."

The memory of the story she'd heard so many times during her growing years made her smile. "And did you have a snake with you when you strutted back into the village?" Lyon asked.

"Oh, yes," she answered. "The shaman recounted that I held it just as my brother had held his snake. Father was standing on the far side of the fires. Mother stood beside him. Neither showed any outward reaction to my prize. They didn't want to frighten me into dropping the snake, I was told later. Anyway," she added with a sigh, "Father walked over to me. He took the snake out of my hand, killed it, and then began to shout at me. Mother knew I didn't understand. Father had praised my brother, you see, yet he was yelling at me."

"Why do you think that was?" Lyon asked, already dreading her answer.

"My brother's snake wasn't poisonous."

"Oh, God."

The tremble in her husband's voice made her laugh. "Father was soon over his anger. The shaman announced that the spirits had protected me. I was their lioness, you see. Mama said Father was also sorry for making me cry. He took me riding with him that afternoon and let me sit on his lap during the evening meal."

The parallel was too good to pass up. "Your father was frightened," Lyon announced. "He loved you, Christina—so much so that when he saw the danger you were in, his discipline deserted him. Just like my discipline deserted me when I saw the danger you were in yesterday."

He dragged her up on top of him so he could look into her eyes. "It was his duty to keep my lioness safe for me."

Christina slowly nodded. "I think you would like my father. You're very like him in many ways. You're just as arrogant. Oh, don't frown, Lyon. I give you a compliment when I say you're arrogant. You're full of bluster, too."

She sounded too sincere for Lyon to take insult. "What is your father's name?" he asked.

"Black Wolf."

"Will he like me?"

"No."

He wasn't insulted by her abrupt answer. In truth, he was close to laughing. "Care to tell me why not?"

"He hates the whites. Doesn't trust them."

"That's why you have such a suspicious nature, isn't it?"

"Perhaps."

She rested the side of her face against Lyon's shoulder.

"You're still a little suspicious of me, too, aren't you?"

"I don't know," she admitted with a sigh.

"I trust you, my sweet. Completely."

She didn't show any reaction.

"Christina, I want equal measure. I will have your trust. And not just for a day or two. Those are my terms."

She slowly lifted her head to stare at Lyon. "And if I'm unable to meet your terms?" she asked.

He saw the worry in her eyes. "You tell me," he whispered.

"You'll set me aside," she whispered.

He shook his head. "No."

"No? Then what?"

He wanted to kiss her frown away. "I'll wait. I'll still love you. In your heart you really don't believe me, do you? You think you'll do something to displease me and I'll quit loving you. It won't happen, Christina."

She was humbled by his fervent words. "I worry." Her confession was whispered in a forlorn voice. "There are times when I don't think I shall ever fit in. I'm like a circle trying to squeeze into a square."

"Everyone feels like that at times," Lyon told her, smiling over her absurd analogy. "You're vulnerable. Are there times when you still want to go home?"

His hands caressed her shoulders while he waited for her answer. "I couldn't leave you," she answered. "And I couldn't take you back with me. You're my family now, Lyon." Her frown intensified. "It really isn't going to be easy for you, living with me."

"Marriage is never easy in the beginning," he answered. "We both have to learn to compromise. In time we'll understand each other's needs."

"Your family and your staff will think me odd."

"They already do."

Her frown was forced now, and a sparkle appeared in her eyes. "That was unkind of you to say," she told him.

"No, it was an honest admission. They think I'm odd, too. Do you care so much what others think of you, Christina?"

She shook her head. "Only you, Lyon. I care what you think."

He showed her how pleased he was to hear her admission by kissing her.

"I also care what you think," Lyon whispered. "Will my shoes be lining the steps outside again?"

"The old ways are familiar to me," Christina explained. "I was so angry with you. It was all I could think to do to make you realize how unhappy you'd made me."

"Thank God you didn't try to leave me."

"Try?"

"You know I'd chase you down and drag you back where you belong."

"Yes, I knew you would. You are a warrior, after all."

Lyon moved Christina to his side, determined to finish their conversation before making love to her again. Her hand moved to his thigh. It was a distraction. Lyon captured both her hands and gave her a gentle squeeze. "Christina?

Did you ever love another man? Was there someone back home who captured your heart?"

Her head was tucked under his chin. Christina smiled, knowing Lyon couldn't see her reaction. He'd tensed against her after he'd asked the question. He hadn't been able to keep the worry out of his voice.

He was letting her see his vulnerability. "When I was very young, I thought I'd grow up and marry White Eagle. Then, when I was seven summers or so, I put those silly thoughts aside. He was my brother, after all."

"Was there anyone else?"

"No. Father wouldn't let any of the warriors walk with me. He knew I had to return to the whites. My destiny had already been decided."

"Who decided your destiny?" Lyon asked.

"The dream."

Christina waited for his next question, but after a minute or two, when she realized he wasn't going to ask her to explain, she decided to tell him anyway.

She wanted him to understand.

The story of the shaman's journey to the top of the mountain to seek his vision captured Lyon's full attention.

The dream made him smile. "If your mother hadn't called you a lioness, would the shaman ever have—"

"He would have sorted it all out," Christina interrupted. "I had white-blond hair and blue eyes, just like the lion in his dream. Yes, he would have sorted it out. Do you understand now how confused I was when Sir Reynolds called you Lyon? I knew in that moment that I had found my mate."

The logical part of Lyon's mind saw all the flaws in the dream, the superstitions of the rituals. Yet he easily pushed reason aside. He didn't care if it didn't make sense. "I knew in that moment, too, that you'd belong to me."

"Both of us fought it, didn't we, Lyon?"

"That we did, love."

Christina laughed. "You never stood a fair chance, husband. Your fate had already been decided."

Lyon nodded. "Now it's your turn to ask me questions. Would you like me to tell you about Lettie?"

Christina tried to look up at Lyon, but he wouldn't let her move. "Do you want to tell me about her?" she asked, her voice hesitant.

"Yes, I do. Now ask me your questions," he commanded, his voice soft.

"Did you love her?"

"Not in the same way I love you. I was never . . . content. I was too young for marriage. I realize that now."

"What was she like?"

"The complete opposite of you," Lyon answered. "Lettie enjoyed the social whirl of the ton. She hated this house, the countryside. Lettie loved intrigue. I was working with Richards then. The war was coming, and I was away from home quite a lot. My brother, James, escorted Lettie to various events. While I was away, he took her to his bed."

Her indrawn breath told him she understood. Lyon had wanted to tell Christina about his first wife so that she would see how much he trusted her. Yet now that the telling had begun, the anger he'd held inside him for so long began to fade. That realization surprised him. His explanation wasn't hesitant now. "Lettie died in childbirth. The babe also. It wasn't my child, Christina. James was the father. I remember how I sat next to my wife, trying to give her comfort. God, she was in terrible pain. I pray you'll never have to endure it. Lettie wasn't aware that I was there. She kept screaming for her lover."

Christina felt like weeping. The pain of his brother's betrayal must have been unbearable. She didn't understand. How could a wife shame her husband in such a way?

She hugged Lyon but decided against offering him additional sympathy. He was a proud man. "Were you and your brother close to each other before his betrayal?" she asked.

"No."

Christina scooted away from Lyon so she could see his expression. His gaze showed only his puzzlement over her question. Lettie's sin no longer affected him, she decided.

"You never gave Lettie your heart," she announced. "It's your brother you've yet to forgive, isn't it, Lyon?"

He was amazed by her perception. "Were you close to James?" she asked again.

"No. We were very competitive when we were younger. I grew out of that nonsense, but my brother obviously didn't."

"I wonder if James wasn't like Lancelot," she whispered, "from the story of Camelot."

"And Lettie was my Guinevere?" he asked, his smile gentle.

"Perhaps," Christina answered. "Would it make his deception easier to bear if you believed it wasn't a deliberate sin?"

"It wouldn't be the truth. James wasn't Lancelot. My brother took what he wanted, when he wanted it, regardless of the consequences. He never really grew up," Lyon ended.

She ignored the harshness in his voice. "Perhaps your mama wouldn't let him," she said.

"Speaking of my mother," Lyon began with a sigh, "you have a plan to keep her here?"

"I do."

"Hell. How long?"

"Quit frowning. She'll stay with us until she wishes to leave. Of course, we have to make her want to stay first," she qualified. "I have a plan to help her, Lyon. Together we'll draw her back into the family. Your mama feels responsible for your brother's death."

"Why do you say that?" Lyon asked.

"She kept him tied to her skirts," Christina answered. "Diana said your mother protected both of you from your father's cruel temper."

"How could Diana know? She was only a baby when Father died."

"Aunt Harriett told her," Christina explained. "I questioned both your sister and your aunt, Lyon. I wanted to know all about your mama so that I could help her."

"How long will this take? I don't have the patience to sit through meals listening to her talk of James."

"We aren't going to let her speak of James," Christina said. "Your mama's very determined." She kissed Lyon on his chin, then said, "But I'm far more determined. Do I have your complete support in this undertaking?"

"Will you be taking her out into the wilderness to find a place for her to die?" he asked. He chuckled over the picture of Christina dragging his mother outdoors before adding, "Diana's worried you really will do just that."

Christina sighed in exasperation. "Your sister is very naive. I was only bluffing. Would you like for me to explain my plans for your mama?"

"No."

"Why not?"

"I'd rather be surprised," Lyon answered. "I just thought of another question to ask you."

"That doesn't surprise me. You're full of questions."

He ignored her rebuke and her disgruntled expression. "Do you realize you sometimes lapse into speaking French? Especially when you're upset. Is that the language your family spoke?"

Twin dimples appeared in her cheeks. Lyon thought she looked like an angel. She wasn't acting much like one, however, for her hand suddenly reached down to capture his arousal.

Lyon groaned, then pulled her hand away. "Answer me first," he commanded in a husky voice.

She let him see her disappointment before she answered him. "Father captured Mr. Deavenrue to teach me the language of the whites. If Mother had been allowed to speak to the man, she would have told him that I was going to return to England. Father didn't think that was significant. He didn't understand that there were different white languages. Deavenrue told me later, when we became friends, that he was very frightened of my father. I remember being amused by that fact," she added. "It was an unkind reaction, but I was only ten or eleven then, so I can excuse my attitude. Deavenrue was very young, too. He taught me the language of the whites . . . his whites."

Lyon's laughter interrupted her story. She waited until

he'd calmed down before continuing. "For two long years I suffered through that language. Day in and day out. Mother was never allowed near Deavenrue. He was a handsome man, for a white," she qualified. "In fact, everyone stayed away from him. He was there to complete a task, not to befriend."

"Then it was only the two of you working together?" Lyon asked.

"Of course not. I wasn't allowed to be alone with him either. There were always at least two old women with me. In time, however, I really came to like Deavenrue, and I was able to persuade my father into being a little friendlier to him."

"When did Deavenrue realize he wasn't teaching you the correct language? And how did he converse with your father?"

"Deavenrue spoke our language," Christina answered. "When my mother was finally allowed to visit Deavenrue's tipi, and she heard me reciting my lessons, she knew immediately that it wasn't the same language she'd been taught when she was a little girl."

"Was there an uproar?" Lyon asked, trying not to laugh again.

"Oh, yes. Mother caught Father alone and let him see her displeasure. If he hadn't been so stubborn in keeping her away from the missionary, two years wouldn't have been wasted. Father was just as angry. He wanted to kill Deavenrue, but Mother wouldn't let him."

Lyon laughed. "Why didn't your mother teach you?"

"Her English wasn't very good. She decided Deavenrue's English was better."

"Why do you prefer to speak French?"

"It's easier at times."

"Tell me you love me in your family's language."

"I love you."

"That's English."

"The language of my family now," Christina said. She then repeated her vow of love in the language of the Dakota.

Lyon thought the sound was lyrical.

"Now I will show you how much I love you," Christina whispered. Her hands slid down his chest. She thought to stroke him into wanting her but found that he was already throbbing with desire.

"No, I'm going to show you first," Lyon commanded.

He rolled his wife onto her back and proceeded to do just that.

A long while later husband and wife fell asleep, wrapped in each other's arms. They were both exhausted, and both thoroughly content.

Lyon awakened during the night. He immediately reached for his wife. As soon as he realized she wasn't in bed with him, he rolled to his side and looked on the floor.

Christina wasn't there either. Lyon's mind immediately cleared of sleep. He started to get out of bed to go in search of his wife when he realized the candles were burning on the bedside table. He remembered quite specifically that he'd put out all three flames.

It didn't make sense until he saw the black book in the center of the light.

The leather binding was scarred with age. When Lyon picked up the book and opened it, a musty smell permeated the air around him. The pages were brittle. He used infinite care as he slowly lifted the first pages of the gift Christina had given him.

He didn't know how long he sat there, his head bent to the light as he read Jessica's diary. An hour might have passed, perhaps two. When he finished the account of Jessica's nightmare, his hands shook.

Lyon stood up, stretched his muscles awake, then walked over to the hearth. He was chilled but didn't know if it was the temperature in the room or Jessica's diary that was the cause.

He was adding a second log to the fire he'd just started when he heard the door open behind him. Lyon finished his task before he turned around. He knelt on one knee, his arms braced on the other, and stared at his lovely wife a long minute.

She was dressed in a long white robe. Her hair was tousled, her cheeks flushed. He could tell she was nervous. Christina held a tray in her hands. The glasses were clattering.

"I thought you might be hungry. I went—"

"Come here, Christina."

His voice was whisper-soft. Christina hurried to do his bidding. She put the tray down on the bed, then rushed over to stand in front of her husband.

"Did you read it?" she asked.

Lyon stood up before he answered her. His hands settled on her shoulders. "You wanted me to, didn't you?"

"Yes."

"Tell me why you wanted me to read it."

"Equal measure, Lyon. Your words, husband. You opened your heart to me when you told me about James and Lettie. I could do no less."

"Thank you, Christina." His voice shook with emotion.

Christina's eyes widened. "Why do you thank me?"

"For trusting me," Lyon answered. He kissed the wrinkle in her brow. "When you gave me your mother's diary, you were also giving me your trust."

"I was?"

Lyon smiled. "You were," he announced. He kissed her again, tenderly, then suggested that they share their midnight meal in front of the fire.

"And we will talk?" Christina asked. "I want to tell you so many things. There's so much we must decide upon, Lyon."

"Yes, love, we'll talk," Lyon promised.

As soon as she turned to fetch the tray, Lyon grabbed one of the blankets draped over the chair and unfolded it on the floor.

Christina knelt down and placed the tray in the center of the blanket. "Do you want me to get your robe for you?" she asked.

"No," Lyon answered, grinning. "Do you want me to take yours off?"

Lyon stretched out on his side, leaned up on one elbow,

and reached for a piece of cheese. He tore off a portion and handed it to Christina.

"Do you think Jessica was crazy?" she asked.

"No."

"I don't either," Christina said. "Some of her entries are very confusing, aren't they? Could you feel her agony, Lyon, the way I did when I read her journal?"

"She was terrified," Lyon said. "And yes, I could feel her pain."

"I didn't want to read her thoughts at first. Merry made me take the book with me. She told me that in time I'd change my heart. She was right."

"She kept her promise to your mother," Lyon interjected. "She raised you, loved you as her own, and made you strong. Those were Jessica's wishes, weren't they?"

Christina nodded. "I'm not always strong, Lyon. Until tonight I was afraid of him."

"Your father?"

"I don't like to call him my father," Christina whispered. "It makes me ill to think his blood is part of mine."

"Why aren't you afraid now?" He asked.

"Because now you know. I worried you'd think Jessica's mind was . . . weak."

"Christina, when you walked into the library and I was talking to Richards, we had just finished a discussion about your father. Richards told me about an incident called the Brisbane affair. Did you hear any of it?"

"No. I would never overlisten," Christina answered.

Lyon nodded. He quickly told her the sequence of events leading up to the murders of the Brisbane family.

"Those poor children," Christina whispered. "Who would kill innocent little ones?"

"You won't like the answer," Lyon said. "I wouldn't have related this story to you if it wasn't important. Brisbane's wife and children were all killed in the same way."

"How?"

"Their throats were slashed."

"I don't want to picture it," Christina whispered.

"In Jessica's diary she talks about a couple she traveled with to the Black Hills. Do you remember?"

"Yes. Their names were Emily and Jacob. The jackal killed them."

"How?"

"Their throats . . . oh, Lyon, their throats were slashed. Do you mean to say—"

"The same method," Lyon answered. "A coincidence, perhaps, but my instincts tell me the baron murdered the Brisbane family."

"Can't you challenge him?"

"Not in the way you'd like me to," Lyon answered. "We will force his hand, Christina. I give you my word. Will you leave the method to me?"

"Yes."

"Why?"

"Why what?" she hedged.

She was deliberately staring at the floor now, avoiding his gaze. Lyon reached over and tugged a strand of her hair. "I want to hear you say the words, wife."

Christina moved over to Lyon's side. Her hand slowly reached out to his. When her fingers were entwined with his, she answered his demand.

"I trust you, Lyon, with all my heart."

Chapter Sixteen

Merry and I made a promise to each other. She gave me her pledge to take care of you if anything happened to me, and I gave my word to find a way to get White Eagle back to his family if anything happened to her.

From that moment on, my fears were gone. Her promise gave me peace. She would keep you safe. You already had her love, Christina. I could see the way she'd hold you, cuddled up tenderly against her chest until you fell asleep.

She would be a better mother to you.

Journal entry
November 3, 1795

Lyon was trying to keep his temper under control. He kept telling himself that breakfast would be over soon, that Richards should be arriving at any moment, and that he was pleasing his wife by being patient with his mother. The effort cost him his appetite, however, a fact everyone at the table seemed compelled to comment upon.

He was surrounded by family and considered that a most unfortunate circumstance. His Aunt Harriett had arrived the previous afternoon with Diana. The Earl of Rhone had just happened to show up an hour later.

The coincidence was forced, of course. Diana had pretended surprise when Rhone strolled into the house. His sister was as transparent as water. Lyon wasn't fooled for a minute. He had had the necessary talk with his friend last evening. Rhone had asked for Diana's hand. Lyon was happy to give him all of her. He kept that thought to himself, for Rhone was in the middle of his obviously prepared dissertation on the seriousness of his pledge to love and protect Diana. When Rhone finally slowed down, Lyon gave him his blessing. He didn't bother to advise his friend on the merits of fidelity, knowing that Rhone would honor his commitment once he'd spoken the vows.

Lyon was seated at the head of the table, with Rhone on his left and Christina on his right. His mother faced him from her position at the opposite end of the table. Aunt Harriett and Diana took turns trying to draw the elderly Marchioness into conversation. Their efforts were wasted, though. The only time Lyon's mother glanced up from her plate was when she wanted to make a comment about her James.

Lyon was soon clenching his jaw.

"For heaven's sake, Diana, unhand Rhone," Aunt Harriett blurted out. "The boy will starve to death if you don't let him at his food, child."

"James always had a very healthy appetite," Lyon's mother interjected.

"I'm certain he did, Mother," Christina said. "Do you like your room?" she asked, changing the topic.

"I do not like it at all. It's too bright. And while we're on the subject of my dislikes, please tell me why you insist that I not wear black. James preferred that color, you know."

"Mama, will you please stop talking about James?" Diana begged.

Christina shook her head at Diana. "Lyon?" she asked, turning to smile at him. "When do you think Richards will arrive? I'm eager to get started."

Lyon frowned at his wife. "You aren't going anywhere. We discussed this, Christina," he reminded her.

"James was always on the go," his mother commented.

Everyone but Christina turned to frown at the gray-haired woman.

"When are we going to discuss the marriage arrangements?" Aunt Harriett asked, trying to cover the awkward silence.

"I really don't wish to wait a long time," Diana said. She blushed before adding, "I want to be married right away, like Lyon and Christina."

"Our circumstances were different," Lyon said. He winked at Christina. "You aren't going to be as fortunate as I was. You'll wait and have a proper wedding."

"James wanted to marry. He simply couldn't find anyone worthy enough," Mama interjected.

Lyon scowled. Christina placed her hand on top of his fisted one. "You look very handsome this morning," she told him. "You must always wear blue."

Lyon looked into his wife's eyes and saw the sparkle there. He knew what she was doing. Yes, she was trying to take his mind off his mother. And even though he understood her intent, it still worked. He was suddenly smiling. "You always look beautiful," he told her. He leaned down to whisper, "I still prefer you without any clothes on, however."

Christina blushed with pleasure.

Rhone smiled at the happy couple, then turned to speak to Lyon's aunt. "Do you still believe Diana and I are mismatched? I would like your approval," he added.

Aunt Harriett picked up her fan. She waved it in front of her face while she considered her answer. "I will give you my approval, but I don't believe the two of you will be as compatible as Lyon and Christina. You can see how well they get along."

"Oh, we are also mismatched," Christina interjected. "Rhone and Diana are really much more suited to each other. They were raised in the same fashion," she explained.

Aunt Harriett gave Christina a piercing look. "Now that you're part of this family, would you mind telling me just where you were raised, child?"

"In the Black Hills," Christina answered. She turned to Lyon then. "The Countess will certainly tell, and I really should prepare your family, don't you think?"

"The Countess wouldn't say a word," Lyon answered. "As long as the money keeps pouring in, she'll keep your secrets safe until you're ready to tell them."

"Tell what secrets?" Diana asked, frowning.

"She's entitled to her privacy," Rhone interjected, winking at Christina.

Aunt Harriett let out an inelegant snort. "Nonsense. We're family. There shouldn't be any secrets, unless you've done something you're ashamed of, Christina, and I'm certain that isn't the case. You're a good-hearted child," she added. She paused to prove her point by tilting her head toward the elderly Marchioness.

"James was such a good-hearted man," she blurted out.

Everyone ignored that comment.

"Well?" Diana prodded Christina.

"I was raised by the Dakotas."

Christina really believed her statement would gain an immediate reaction. Everyone just stared at her with expectant looks on their faces. She turned to Lyon.

"I don't believe they understand, my sweet," he whispered.

"Who are the Dakotas?" Aunt Harriett asked. "I don't remember meeting anyone by that name. They must not be English," she concluded with another wave of her fan.

"No, they aren't English," Lyon said, smiling.

"A large family?" Aunt Harriett asked, trying to understand why Lyon was smiling and Christina was blushing.

"Very large," Lyon drawled.

"Well, why haven't I heard of them?" his aunt demanded.

"They're Indians." Christina made the announcement, then waited for a true reaction.

It wasn't long in coming. "No wonder I haven't heard . . . good Lord, do you mean savages?" she gasped.

Christina was about to explain that she didn't care for the word savages—the Countess had often preferred that description—and that the Dakotas were gentle, caring people, but Aunt Harriett's and Diana's bold laughter interrupted her bid to defend.

Aunt Harriett was the first to regain control. She'd noticed that Rhone, Lyon, and Christina hadn't joined in. "You aren't jesting with us, are you, Christina?" she asked. She felt lightheaded but kept her voice soft.

"No, I'm not jesting," Christina answered. "Rhone? You don't seem too surprised."

"I was better prepared for such news," Rhone explained.

"Are the Black Hills in France, then?" Diana asked, trying to sort it out in her mind.

Lyon chuckled over that question.

"James loved to go to France," the mother announced. "He had many friends there."

Aunt Harriett reached over to take hold of Christina's hand. "My dear, I'm so sorry I laughed. You must think me terribly undisciplined. It was such a surprise. I pray you do not believe I now think you inferior in any way."

Christina hadn't been upset with their reaction, but she assumed Aunt Harriett thought she had. She smiled at the dear woman, then said, "I pray you do not believe I think you are inferior in any way, Aunt Harriett. In truth, I have come to realize that my people are far more civilized than the English. It is a confession I'm very proud to make."

"James was always civil to everyone he met," the mother announced.

Aunt Harriett patted Christina's hand, then turned to glare at her relative.

"Millicent," she muttered, using the elderly Marchioness's given name, "will you let up, for God's sake? I'm trying to have a serious conversation with Christina here."

Aunt Harriett turned to smile at Christina again. "I eagerly await your stories about your childhood, Christina. Will you share them with me?"

"I would be happy to," Christina answered.

"Now, I would advise you not to tell anyone outside this

family. Outsiders wouldn't understand. The ton is a shallow group of twits," she added with a vigorous nod. "And I'll not have you subjected to malicious gossip."

"Did you have strange habits when you lived with—"

"For God's sake, Diana," Lyon roared.

"It's all right," Christina interjected. "She is only curious."

"Let's change the topic for now," Rhone advised. He frowned at Diana, then contradicted his displeasure by taking hold of her hand.

Aunt Harriett didn't like the peculiar way Diana was staring at Christina. Her mouth was hanging open. The silly girl was looking quite fascinated.

Concerned about Christina's feelings, the aunt hastened to turn Diana's attention. "Lyon? Diana insisted on bringing that ill-disciplined pup Rhone gave her. She's tied up in the back," Aunt Harriett explained. "Diana was hoping you'd keep the dog while we're in London. Isn't that right, Diana?"

Rhone had to nudge Diana before she answered. "Oh, yes. It would be cruel to keep her tied up in the townhouse. Christina, did you have a puppy when you were a little girl? Were their dogs in your . . . town?"

"It was called a village, not a town," Christina answered, wishing Diana would stop staring at her so intently.

"But were there dogs there?" Diana persisted.

"Yes, there were dogs," Christina answered. She turned to wink at her husband when she felt his hand tense under hers, then turned back to look at her sister-in-law. "They weren't considered pets, though," she lied. "And, of course, they never stayed long."

"James always loved animals. He had a beautiful speckled dog he named Faithful."

"An inappropriate name, if you ask me," Lyon commented. "Wouldn't you agree, Christina?" he asked, duplicating her wink.

Brown appeared in the doorway at that moment and announced that Sir Fenton Richards had just arrived. Both Christina and Lyon stood up to take their leave.

"I'd like to ride along with you and Richards," Rhone called out.

Lyon glanced down at Christina, received her nod, then told Rhone he'd be glad for his help.

Christina was halfway across the dining room when Diana called out to her.

"Christina? Why didn't the dogs stay long?"

She was going to ignore that question until she realized Diana was still gaping at her. Lyon's sister was looking at her as though she'd just grown another head or two. "What happened to the dogs?"

"We ate them," Christina called out, trying to tell her lie without laughing.

Aunt Harriett dropped her fan. Diana let out a gasp. Lyon never even blinked until his mother's determined voice called out, "James never ate his dog. He . . . oh, God, what have I just said?"

Everyone joined in laughing. The elderly Marchioness even cracked a smile. It was a small one, but a smile all the same.

Christina thought it was a nice beginning. Lyon's hug told her he thought so, too.

"Diana, I was only jesting with you. We didn't eat our pets. You needn't worry about your pup. I won't have her for dinner. You have my word."

"She never breaks her word," Lyon advised his sister. "Unless, of course, she gets very hungry," he added before he pulled his wife out of the room.

Richards was highly puzzled when Lyon and Christina came strolling into the library, smiling as though neither had a care in the world. Their manner was certainly at odds with the mysterious note he'd received the day before.

"Has your problem been resolved, then?" Richards asked Lyon in lieu of greeting.

"No, we still need your help," Lyon announced. He sobered quickly. "How tired are you, Richards? Feel up to taking another ride?"

"Where?"

"The Earl of Acton's former estate," Lyon answered.

"That's a good four hours' ride, isn't it?"

"From London," Lyon reminded him. "Only two from here."

"Who's living there now?"

"No one. My inquiries tell me the house is boarded up."

Richards turned to Christina. "I could use a spot of tea, my dear. I'm rather parched," he added. "I set out at dawn and didn't take time to breakfast."

"I shall see to serving you a full meal at once," Christina said. "You'll need your strength for the task ahead of you," she added before she hurried out of the library.

Richards shut the door, then turned to Lyon. "I sent your wife on a false errand so I could speak to you in private."

"I don't have any secrets from Christina," Lyon returned.

"You misunderstand," Richards said. "It isn't a secret I'm about to tell you. But your wife will become upset. You might wish to wait until our return from this mysterious journey before telling her. Baron Stalinsky is back. He arrived yesterday. He wanted to come to meet his daughter immediately. When I heard his intent, I waylaid his plan with the lie that you and Christina were off visiting distant relatives in the North. I told him you would both be returning to London day after tomorrow. I hope that was the right thing to do, Lyon. It was a spur-of-the-moment fabrication."

"It was good thinking," Lyon answered. "Where is the Baron staying?"

"With the Porters. They are hosting a party for him Wednesday evening. The Baron expects to see his daughter there."

Lyon let out a long sigh. "It can't be put off," he muttered.

"Does Christina still believe her father will try to kill her?"

"She planned to bait him into trying," Lyon said.

"When are you going to explain it all to me?" Richards demanded.

"On the way to Acton's place," Lyon promised. "Rhone's coming with us. It should be quick work with the three of us at it," he added.

"What is this mission?" Richards asked.

"We're going to dig up the roses."

Lyon, Richards, and Rhone didn't return to Lyonwood until late afternoon. Their moods were as foul as the weather.

Christina had just walked inside the back of the house when the trio of soggy men rushed inside the front door.

They met in the hallway. Lyon was drenched to the skin. When he saw Christina in the same condition, he shook his head with displeasure. Droplets of rain flew from his hair.

"You look like a drowned cat," Lyon muttered to Christina. He was struggling to get out of his sodden jacket, glaring at his wife all the while. Her burgundy-colored gown was indecently molded to her body. Clumps of hair hung over her eyes.

Richards and Rhone were being ushered up the steps by Brown. Lyon blocked their view of his wife.

When his friends had disappeared upstairs, Lyon confronted his wife. "What in God's name were you doing outside?"

"You needn't yell at me," Christina shouted. "Did you find—"

"Do you have any idea how many damn rosebushes there were? No?" he bellowed when she shook her head. "Your grandfather must have had an obsession for the things. There were hundreds of them."

"Oh, dear," Christina cried. "Then you weren't successful? I told you I should have gone with you. I could have helped."

"Christina, you're shouting at me," Lyon announced. "I found the box. You can calm down."

"I'm not shouting at you," Christina said. She lifted her wet locks and threw them over her shoulder. "I can't be very sympathetic over the difficulty you had. I've lost the damned dog."

"What?"

"I've lost the damned dog," Christina repeated. She forced herself to calm down. "It appears that both of us have had a pitiful day. Give me a kiss, Lyon. Then please put your jacket back on. You must help me look for Diana's puppy."

"Are you crazy? You're not going back outside in this downpour, and that's that."

Christina grabbed hold of Lyon's soggy shirt, kissed him on his hard mouth, then turned around and started walking toward the back of the house. "I have to find the dog. Diana's upstairs trying desperately to believe I didn't eat the stupid animal," she muttered.

Lyon's laughter stopped her. She turned around to glare at him.

"Sweetheart, she can't really believe you'd do such a thing."

"I never should have made that jest," Christina admitted. "I told her I was only teasing. I don't think she believes me, though. I was the last person seen with the pup. I heard her mention that sorry fact to Aunt Harriett several times. Lyon, I only wanted to let the puppy run for a while. The poor little thing looked miserable all tied up. Then she took off after a rabbit, and I've spent the rest of the day looking for her."

Rhone came sloshing down the stairs. His soft curses caught Christina's attention. Without pausing to speak to either Lyon or Christina, Rhone opened the front door and went outside.

They could hear him whistling for the dog through the door. "See? Rhone's helping to look for the pup," Christina stated.

"He has to," Lyon told his wife. "He wants to make Diana happy. And the only reason I'm going to give into your request is because I want to make you happy. Got that?" he muttered before slamming out the front door.

Christina didn't laugh until he'd left, knowing that if he heard her, his bluster would turn into real anger.

Her husband found the undisciplined puppy about an hour later. The dog was curled up under the overhang behind the stables.

Once Lyon was warm and dry again, his mood improved.

After a pleasant dinner he, Rhone, and Richards all retired to the library to share a bottle of brandy. Christina was thankful for the privacy. She wasn't feeling well. She'd been unable to keep down the rich meal she'd just eaten, and her stomach was still upset.

Lyon came upstairs around midnight. Christina was curled up in the center of their bed, waiting for him.

"I thought you'd be asleep," Lyon said. He began to strip out of his clothes.

Christina smiled at him. "And miss the chance to see my handsome husband disrobe? Never. Lyon, I don't think I shall ever get used to looking at you."

She could tell by his arrogant grin that he liked her praise. "I shall show you something even more handsome," Lyon teased. He walked over to the mantel, lifted a black lacquered box from the center, and carried it over to the bed. "I transferred the jewels from the old box to this one. It's more sound," he added.

Christina waited until Lyon was settled in bed beside her before she opened the box. A small square cloth covered the gems. She seemed hesitant to remove the covering and look at the jewels.

Lyon didn't understand her reticence. He took the cloth, unfolded it, and poured the assortment of precious jewels in the middle.

They were the colors of the rainbow, the sapphires and rubies and diamonds. They numbered twenty, and their value by anyone's standards would have kept a gluttonous man well fed for a very long while.

Lyon was puzzled, for Christina continued to show no outward reaction.

"Sweetheart, do you have any idea of the price these gems will bring?"

"Oh, yes, I understand, Lyon," Christina whispered. "The price was my mother's life. Please put them away now. I don't want to look at them. I think they're very ugly."

Lyon kissed her before he complied with her wish. When he got back into their bed he pulled her into his arms. He briefly considered telling her that Baron Stalinsky was in London, then decided that tomorrow would be soon enough to give her that ill news.

He knew Christina thought they had more time before setting their plan into motion. Her birthday had passed two weeks before, and she'd made up her mind that her father must have had other business to keep him away from England.

Lyon blew out the candles and closed his eyes. He couldn't remember when last he'd been this tired. He was just about to drift off to sleep when Christina nudged him.

"Lyon? Will you promise me something?"

"Anything, love."

"Never give me jewels."

He sighed over the vehemence in her voice. "I promise."

"Thank you, Lyon."

"Christina?"

"Yes?"

"Promise me you'll love me forever."

"I promise."

He caught the smile in her voice and suddenly realized he wasn't nearly as tired as he thought he was. "Tell me you love me," he commanded.

"My Lyon, I love you, and I shall continue to love you forever."

"A man can't ask for more than that," Lyon drawled as he nudged her around to face him.

He thought he'd make slow, sweet love to his wife, but in the end it was a wild, undisciplined mating, and thoroughly satisfying.

The blankets and pillows were on the floor. Christina fell asleep with Lyon as her cover. He was so content he didn't want to sleep just yet. He wanted to savor the moment, for in the back of his mind was the thought that this night could well be the calm before the storm.

Chapter Seventeen

Forgive me for not writing in this journal for such a length of time. I have been content and haven't wanted to remember the past. But we are now preparing to leave our safe haven. I shall not be able to speak to you again through this journal for long months, until we are both settled. My plan is to catch up with another wagon train. The way west is crowded with newcomers. The valley below is the only way the wagons can go to get into the mountains. Surely someone will take pity on us and offer us assistance.

Is it a fantasy for me to think that you and I might survive?

I will finish this entry with one request, Christina. I would beg a promise from you, dear child. If you do survive and one day chance upon this diary, have a kind thought for me.

And remember, Christina, always remember how very much I loved you.

Journal entry
May 20, 1796

The time had come to face the jackal.

Christina was nervous, though not nearly as nervous as her husband. Lyon's expression was grim. The ride from their London townhouse to Porter's home was silent. Yet once they'd reached their destination, Lyon seemed disinclined to let Christina out of the carriage.

"Sweetheart, you're sure you're all right?"

Christina smiled up at her husband. "I'm fine, really."

"God, I wish there had been a way to keep you out of this," he whispered. "You look pale to me."

"You should be complimenting me on my new gown, Lyon. You chose the fabric, remember?" she asked. Christina pushed open the door of the carriage.

"I've already told you how beautiful you look," Lyon murmured.

He finally got out of the carriage and turned to help his wife. He thought she looked quite beautiful. The royal blue velvet gown was modestly scoop-necked. Her hair was curled into a cluster with a thin blue velvet ribbon threaded through the silky mass.

Christina reached up to brush a speck of link off Lyon's black jacket. "You also look beautiful," she told him.

Lyon shook his head. He pulled her matched blue cloak over her shoulders. "You're doing this deliberately. Quit trying to ease my worry. It won't work."

"You like to worry, husband?" she asked.

Lyon didn't bother to answer her. "Give me your promise again," he demanded.

"I'll not leave your side." She repeated the vow she'd already given him at least a dozen times. "No matter what, I'll stand next to you."

Lyon nodded. He took her hand and started up the steps. "You really aren't frightened, are you, love?"

"A little," Christina whispered. "Richards has given me his assurance that justice in England is equal to that of the Dakotas. He'd better be right, Lyon, or we shall have to take matters into our own hands." Her voice had turned hard. "Strike the door, husband. Let's get this pretense of joyful reunion over and done with."

Richards was waiting for them in the foyer. Christina was surprised by his enthusiastic reception. Lyon had lost his grim expression, too. He acted as though he hadn't seen his friend in a long while, which was exactly what they wanted everyone to believe.

After greeting their host, a dour-faced man with a portly figure, Christina asked if Baron Stalinsky was in the receiving room.

"I can imagine how eager you must be to meet your father," Porter announced, his voice filled with excitement. "He's still upstairs, but he will certainly be joining us in a moment or two. I've kept the list of guests to a minimum, my dear, so that you may have time for a lengthy visit with your father. You must certainly have a book's worth of news to exchange."

Lyon removed Christina's wrap, handed it to the butler waiting beside them, then told Porter he'd take his wife into the drawing room to await the Baron.

Her hand was cold when he clasped it in his own. He could feel her trembling. The smile never left his face, but the urge to take Christina back home and return to face her father alone nearly overwhelmed him.

The Dakotas had the right idea, Lyon decided. According to Christina, verbal slander was all that was needed for an open challenge. What followed next was a battle to the death. Justice was swift. The system might have been a bit barbaric, yet Lyon liked its simplicity.

There were only eighteen guests in the drawing room. Lyon counted them while Christina had a long conversation with their hostess. Although his wife stood next to him, he paid little attention to what the two women were discussing. Richards had walked over to join him, and he was trying to listen to his friend advise him on the merits of the changing weather.

When their hostess left, Christina turned to Richards. "Are you aware that our host previously worked for your government in the same manner as you?"

"I am."

She waited for him to say more, then let him see her displeasure when he failed to comment further. "Lyon, Mrs. Porter surely exaggerated her mate's position, but she did mention a fact I found most enlightening."

"What was that, love?" Lyon asked. He draped his arm around her shoulders and pulled her closer to him.

"She's a gossip," Christina began. "When she saw the way Richards greeted you, she boasted that her husband held the same favor when he was a younger man. I asked her why he'd retired, and she told me she didn't know all the facts but that his last assignment had soured him. It seemed he handled a project that caused a good friend of his some discomfort. Yes, she actually used that word. Discomfort."

"Discomfort? I don't understand. Do you, Richards?" Lyon asked.

Richards was staring at Christina. "You would do well to work for us, Christina. You have ferreted out what took me hours of research to ascertain."

"Lyon, can you guess the name of Porter's good friend?"

"Stalinsky," Lyon said in answer to Christina's question.

"Porter wasn't guilty of error, Christina. His only mistake was in befriending the Baron. He trusted him—still does, for that matter. The baron is a guest in his home, remember. God's truth, I think you'll understand what an easy man the Baron is to trust when you finally meet him."

"By England's standards, perhaps," Christian replied. "Not by mine. Appearances and manners often cloak a black soul. Are you still unconvinced that Lyon and I are right about the Baron, then?"

"I'm convinced. The court might not see it our way, however, and for that reason we're bypassing our own legal system. There are those who believe Jessica had lost her mind. The argument that your mother had imagined—"

"Did she imagine the mark she gave the baron in his right eye when he tried to kill her? Did she imagine that her friends' throats were slashed? Did she imagine she stole the jewels and hid them under the roses? You've seen the gems, Richards. Did you only imagine you saw them?"

Richards smiled at Christina. "You really should work for me," he said in answer to her challenges. "Now, to refute your arguments. One, the baron could have others testify for him, telling a different story of how he came by the scar. Two, Jessica was the only one who saw the baron kill the husband and wife on that wagon train. No one else saw anyone, according to the writing in her journal. It would be next to impossible to track any of those people down to determine how the couple was killed. We have only Jessica's diary to tell us what happened. In a court of law that wouldn't be enough. Three, there wouldn't be any argument about the jewels. But," he added in a whisper, "we have only Jessica's account to say that her husband had acquired the gems by foul means. He was a king, remember, and the jewels were but a part of his treasury. The fact that he was a ruthless dictator is the last of the rebuttals I will give you. If that is dragged out in court, it will mean little. The Baron would simply retaliate by bringing witness after witness who would testify to his kindness toward his subjects."

"He will admit his sins to me," Christina whispered.

"And your husband and I will gain justice for you with or without your father's admission."

"Christina, your father has just walked into the room." Lyon made the announcement with a wide smile, but his hold on his wife tightened.

The moment had arrived. With it came a fresh surge of anger. Christina forced a smile onto her face, turned from her husband, and began to walk toward the man waiting for her just inside the entrance.

She understood his physical appeal as soon as she looked at him. Baron Stalinsky was a man who commanded attention. He'd aged well. His hair wasn't white, but silver-tipped. The years hadn't made him stoop-shouldered or pot-bellied, either. No, he was still tall, lance-thin, regal in his bearing. It was the color of his eyes that attracted attention, though. They were a piercing blue. Christina was sorry they shared so many physical attributes.

The Baron was smiling at her. His eyes were filled with unshed tears, and surely everyone in the room could see the dimple in his left cheek.

Christina concentrated on the scar beneath his right eye.

She stopped when she was just a foot away, then made a formal curtsy. And all the while she prayed her voice wouldn't betray her.

She knew she'd have to let him embrace her. The thought made her skin crawl. All the guests in the room had focused their attention on this reunion. She never took her gaze off the jackal and was sickened by the fact that everyone was probably smiling over the sweetly emotional reunion.

It seemed to Christina that they stared at each other for a long while before either spoke a word. She could feel Lyon by her side, and when he suddenly took hold of her hand, she recovered her composure.

Lyon was trying to give her his strength, she thought. "Good evening, Father. It is a pleasure to meet you at last."

Baron Stalinsky seemed to come out of his stupor then. He reached out to clasp Christina's shoulders. "I'm overjoyed to meet you, Christina. I can barely think what to say to you. All these precious years wasted," he whispered. A tear escaped from his thick lashes. Christina pulled her hand away from Lyon's grasp and reached up to brush the tear from her father's cheek. The touch was witnessed by the guests, and Christina could hear their sighs of pleasure.

She let him embrace her. "I thought you were dead, daughter," he admitted. "Do you know how happy I am to have you back, child?"

Christina kept smiling. The effort made her stomach hurt. She slowly pulled away from her father and moved next to Lyon again. "I'm a married woman now, Father," she announced. She quickly introduced Lyon, then prayed he'd take up the conversation for a minute or two. She needed to catch her breath.

"You cannot imagine our surprise to learn you were still alive, Baron," Lyon interjected. His voice was as enthusiastic as a schoolboy's. He kept up the idle chatter until the other guests, led by the Porters, rushed over to express their congratulations.

Christina played the pretense well. She smiled and laughed whenever it was appropriate.

It was bearable only because Lyon stood by her side. An hour passed and then another before Christina and her husband were given a few moments' privacy with Stalinsky.

"Father, how did you come by that scar below your eye?" Christina asked, pretending only mild interest.

"A boyhood accident," the Baron replied, smiling. "I fell from my mount."

"You were lucky," Lyon interjected. "You could have lost your eye."

The baron nodded. "I was thinking quite the same thing about your scar, Lyon. How did that happen?"

"A fight in a tavern," Lyon said. "My first outing as a man," he added with a grin.

One lie for another, Christina thought.

Lyon gave Christina's shoulder a gentle squeeze. She recognized the signal. "Father, I have so many questions to ask you, and I'm certain you have as many to ask me. Does your schedule permit you to lunch with us tomorrow?"

"I would love to, daughter," the Baron replied. "Daughter! It's a joyful word to me now."

"Will you be staying in London long, Baron?" Lyon asked.

"I have no other plans," the Baron answered.

"I'm pleased to hear that," Christina interjected. She prayed her voice sounded enthusiastic. "I've already sent word to my stepfather. When he receives my message and returns from Scotland, you must sit down with him and put his fears to rest."

"Stepfather?" the Baron asked. "The Countess didn't mention a stepfather, Christina. She led me to believe . . ." The Baron cleared his throat before continuing. "It was a bizarre story, and one look at you would certainly make a mockery out of what she actually suggested . . . tell me about this stepfather. What fears does the man harbor, and why?"

"Father, first you must appease my curiosity," Christina said. There was laughter in her voice. "Whatever did the horrid old woman tell you?"

"Yes," the Baron sighed, "she is a horrid woman." He made the remark almost absentmindedly.

"Do I detect a blush?" Christina asked.

"I fear you do, daughter. You see, I have only just realized how gullible I was. Why, I did believe her story to be true."

"You've pricked my curiosity as well," Lyon said. "The Countess is very upset with Christina. She was against our marriage because of the matter of my wife's inheritance. The Countess seemed to think she'd control the money," Lyon explained. "Now tell us what fabrication she gave you."

"I've been played for a fool," the Baron returned, shaking his head. "She told me Christina was raised by savages."

"Savages?" Christina asked, trying to look perplexed.

"Indians of the Americas," the Baron qualified.

Christina and Lyon looked at each other. They turned in unison to stare at the Baron. Then they both burst into laughter.

The Baron joined in. "I really was naive to believe her fool's story," he said between chuckles. "But I had heard from the Countess—years ago, you understand—that Jessica had left with a newborn baby girl to join a wagon train headed through the wilderness."

"She did do that," Christina acknowledged. "And it was on the way that she met Terrance MacFinley. He became her protector. Terrance," she added with a soft smile, "didn't know my mother was still married. She told him you'd died. My mother's mind wasn't very . . . strong." Christina paused after making that comment, furious inside when the Baron nodded agreement. "Terrance was a good man. He told me about my mother."

"But what did you mean when you said I could put your stepfather's fears to rest?"

"Oh, it's a small matter," Christina stalled. "Jessica died when I was just a baby," she continued. "Terrance kept me with him. In one of my mother's sane moments, she made him promise to take care of me until I was old enough to be returned to England."

"How did she die?" the Baron asked. His voice was low and filled with emotion. Tears had gathered in his eyes again. "I loved your mother. I blame myself for her death. I should have recognized the signs of her condition."

"Signs?" Christina asked.

"Of her mind's deterioration," he explained. "She was frightened of everything. When she realized she was going to have a child, I think it was all that was needed to push her completely over the edge. She ran away from me."

"Did you go after her, Father?"

"Not right away," the Baron admitted. "There were business matters to attend to. I had a kingdom to run, you see. I abdicated three weeks later, then went back to England. I fully expected to find my wife with her father. Yet when I reached the Earl of Acton's home, I found out Jessica had fled again. She was headed for the colonies. I, of course, made the assumption she was going to her sister's home in Boston and posted passage on a ship to follow her."

"Mother died of the fever," Christina said.

"I hope she didn't have too much pain," the Baron commented.

"It must have been terrible for you, searching in vain for the woman you loved," Lyon stated.

"Yes, it was a bad time," the Baron acknowledged. "The past is behind us, Christina. I look forward to speaking to this Terrance. How long did he stay with your mother before she died?" he asked.

"I'm not certain of the exact length of time," Christina said. "One night, when the wagon train rested in the valley below the Black Hills, Jessica was awakened by a thief," Christina said. "The couple she was sharing her quarters with were both killed by the villain. Jessica got it into her head that it was you, Father, chasing after her."

Christina paused to shake her head. "She packed me up and ran into the hills. MacFinley saw her leave. He went after her, of course, for he loved her fiercely. I'll be completely honest with you, Father. I don't understand how Terrance could have loved my mother. From what he told me about her, I would think he should have pitied her."

"MacFinley sounds like an honorable man," the Baron said. "I'm eager to meet him to give him my thanks. At least he made Jessica's last hours more comfortable. He did, didn't he?"

Christina nodded. "Yes, but I don't think she really knew he was there with her. Terrance told me he actually spent most of his time protecting me from her. She was so crazed she didn't even remember she had a child. All she talked about was the sin she'd snatched out of some wall."

She paused again, watching for a reaction. The Baron only looked perplexed.

After a long minute he said, "That certainly doesn't make sense. A sin out of a wall?"

"It didn't make any sense to Terrance either. He told me he kept trying to get through to my mother, but all she would talk about was taking the sin and burying it. A tragic ending, wouldn't you agree?"

"Let's not talk about this any longer," Lyon interjected. "Tonight should be a happy reunion," he added.

"Yes, husband, you're right. Father, you must tell me all about the past years and what you've been—"

"Wait!" The Baron's voice had a sharp edge to it. He immediately softened his tone and gave Christina a wide smile. "My curiosity is still to be appeased," he explained. "Did your mother happen to tell Terrance where she buried this sin?"

"Under the blood roses of her father's country home," Christina answered with a deliberate shrug. "Blood roses, indeed. Poor woman. I pray for her soul every night, and I do hope she has found peace."

"I also pray for my Jessica," the Baron said.

"Terrance happened to see the man sneaking toward Jessica's wagon."

Lyon let the lie settle and waited for a reaction. It wasn't long in coming. "You mean the thief?" the Baron asked.

He hadn't blinked an eye. Christina was a little disappointed not to have rattled him. "Yes," she said. "He blames himself for thinking it was only one of the night watchmen. Terrance was late in joining the wagon and didn't know all the people yet. He vows he'll never forget the man's face." Christina quickly described the clothing the thief was wearing from the description in Jessica's diary.

And still there was no outward reaction from the Baron.

"Even though he knows my mother was crazed, there's always been a quiet fear in the back of his mind that it might have been you. And so you see what I mean when I tell you that once he has met you, his fears will be put to rest."

"Tomorrow you both can catch up on all of the past," Lyon said. He could feel Christina trembling and knew he had to get her away from the Baron soon.

Lord, he was proud of her. She had played her part well this night. She had faced the jackal without showing the least amount of fear.

"Shall we go and find some refreshments?" Lyon suggested.

"Yes," the Baron agreed.

Christina, flanked by her husband and her father, walked into the dining room. She sat between them at the long table, sipping from her glass of punch. She didn't want to eat anything, but her father was watching her closely, so she forced herself to swallow the food Lyon placed before her.

"Where did you receive your schooling, Christina? Your manners are impeccable," the Baron announced. "I cannot believe this Terrance MacFinley was responsible," he added with a teasing smile.

"Thank you for your compliment," Christina returned. She was smiling at her father, but her left hand was squeezing Lyon's thigh under the table.

"MacFinley and his close friend, Deavenrue, kept me until I was seven years of age. Then I was placed in a convent in the south of France. The sisters taught me my manners," she added.

"So there was a Deavenrue after all," the Baron said. "The Countess said he was a missionary who'd stayed with you in the village of the Indians."

"He was a missionary for a short while, and an excellent teacher as well. While I was in Boston Deavenrue came to my aunt's house quite often to see me. The Countess didn't like Deavenrue. Perhaps the rascal told my aunt I'd been with the savages just to provoke her," Christina added. She laughed. "It would be just like Deavenrue. He has the most bizarre sense of humor."

Lyon put his hand on top of Christina's. Her nails were digging into his thigh. His fingers laced with hers, and he gave her a squeeze of encouragement. He was anxious to get Christina out of Porter's house, yet he knew he had to wait until the last lie had been given.

Christina couldn't stand the pretense any longer. "Father, the excitement of the evening has exhausted me. I hope you won't be too disappointed if I go home now. Tomorrow I'll have Cook prepare a special meal just for the three of us. We'll have all afternoon to visit with each other. And, of course, MacFinley will be here in two, three days' time at the most. Then we must have another get-together."

"As soon as two days?" the Baron asked. He looked pleased with that possibility.

"Yes," Lyon answered for Christina. "Terrance lives just beyond the border," he explained. "He surely has Christina's request by now. Why, he is probably on his way to London even as we speak."

"Lyon, Terrance can't travel by night," Christina said. "Are you ready to take me home, husband? I'm terribly fatigued," she added with a flutter of her lashes.

They said their farewells moments later. Christina suffered through another embrace by the Baron.

Lyon pulled her onto his lap when they were once again inside his carriage. He was going to tell her how much he loved her, how very courageous she had been, but the carriage had barely rounded the corner when Christina bolted out of his lap and begged him to have the vehicle stopped.

Lyon didn't understand until Christina started to gag. He shouted to the driver, then got the door open just in the nick of time. He felt completely helpless as he held his wife by her shoulders. She threw up her meal, sobbing without control between her soul-wrenching heaves.

And when she had finished he wrapped her in his arms again. He held her close to him and tried to soothe her with soft words of love.

Lyon didn't speak of her father. Christina had been through enough torment for one evening.

God help her, there was still more to come.

Baron Stalinsky left the Porter residence a few minutes before dawn. Lyon was informed of his departure less than fifteen minutes later. Richards had placed a watch on Porter's house, for he was just as convinced as Lyon was that the Baron wouldn't waste any time running to the Earl of Acton's country home to dig up his treasure.

Christina had told her lies well. Lyon was proud of her, though he laced his praise with the fervent hope that once this deception was over, she'd never have to lie again.

Baron Stalinsky was very good at his deadly game. Neither Christina nor Lyon had noticed any visible change in his expression when MacFinley was mentioned. And when Christina said that MacFinley had seen the man who'd killed Jessica's friends, the Baron hadn't even blinked.

There wasn't any MacFinley, of course, but the smooth way Christina had told the story, added to the sincerity in her voice, must have convinced the Baron. He believed the story all right, to the point of rushing out at dawn to regain the jewels.

The morning after the reception Lyon had sent a note to the Baron pleading to reschedule their luncheon for three days hence, explaining that Christina was indisposed. The Baron had sent his note back with Lyon's messenger, stating that he hoped his daughter would soon recover, and that he would be pleased to honor the later date.

That evening Richards called on Lyon to tell him that the Baron had booked passage on a seafaring vessel bound for the West Indies. His departure was in two days.

He had no intention of ever seeing his daughter again. So much for fatherly love, Lyon thought.

Lyon hurriedly dressed in the dark. He waited until the last possible minute before waking Christina.

When his leaving couldn't be put off any longer, he leaned

over the side of the bed, let out a reluctant sigh, and then nudged his wife awake.

"Sweetheart, wake up and kiss me goodbye. I'm leaving now," he whispered between quick kisses on her brow.

Christina came awake with a start. "You must wait for me," she demanded, her voice husky with sleep.

She bolted up in bed, then fell back with a groan of distress. Nausea swept over her like a thick wave. She could feel the bile rising from her stomach. "Oh, God, I'm going to be sick again, Lyon."

"Roll over on your side, sweetheart. It helped last night," Lyon reminded her. His voice was filled with sympathy. "Take deep breaths," he instructed while he rubbed her shoulders.

"It's better now," Christina whispered a minute or two later.

Lyon sat down on the edge of the bed. "Exactly."

"Exactly what?" Christina asked. She didn't dare raise her voice above a whisper, fearing the effort would bring back her nausea.

"Exactly why you're staying here, Christina," Lyon announced. "Seeing your father has made you ill. You've been sick twice a day since the reception."

"It's this stupid bed that makes me sick," she lied.

Lyon stared at the ceiling in exasperation. "You told me the wooden slats made the mattress more accommodating," he reminded her. "You aren't going anywhere, my love, except back to sleep."

"You promised I could go with you," she cried.

"I lied."

"Lyon, I trusted you."

Lyon smiled over the way his wife wailed her confession. She sounded quite pitiful. "You still do trust me, wife. I'll get his confession, I promise you."

"My sore stomach is just an excuse you're using, isn't it, Lyon? You never meant for me to go along. Isn't that the truth of it?"

"Yes," he confessed. "I was never going to let you go

along." His voice turned gruff when he added, "Do you think I would ever put you in such jeopardy? Christina, if anything every happened to you, my life would be over. You're the better half of me, sweetheart."

Christina turned her head so that he could see her frown. Lyon realized then that his soft words hadn't swayed her, knew he was going to have to take another tack. "Does a Dakota warrior take his mate along to help him fight his battles? Did Black Wolf take Merry with him?"

"Yes."

"Now you're lying," Lyon stated. He frowned to let her see his displeasure.

Christina smiled. "If the injury had been done to Merry's family, Black Wolf would have taken her with him to see justice done, husband. Lyon, I made a promise to my father and my mother."

"To Black Wolf and Merry?"

Christina nodded. She slowly sat up in bed and was pleased to find that her stomach was cooperating with the movement. Ignoring Lyon's protest, she swung her legs to the side and stood up.

"Damn it, Christina, you're my mate now. Your promises became mine the moment we were wed. You do belong to me, don't you?"

The challenge in his voice couldn't be ignored. Christina nodded. "You're beginning to sound a bit too much like a warrior for my liking," she muttered. "I would like you to bring me a cup of tea before you leave. It is the least you could do for me," she added.

Lyon smiled, believing he'd won. "I shall fix it myself," he announced.

Christina waited until he'd left the room. She dressed in record time, taking deep, gulping breaths to keep her stomach controlled.

When Lyon returned to their bedroom, he found his wife dressed in a black riding outfit. He let out a soft curse, then sighed with acceptance.

"I must do this for Jessica, Lyon. Please understand."

Lyon nodded. His expression was grim. "Will you do exactly what I tell you to do, when I tell you to do it?" he barked.

"I will."

"Promise!"

"I promise."

"Damn!"

She ignored his muttering. "I'm taking my knife with me. It's under the pillow," she said as she walked back over to the bed.

"I know where it is," Lyon said with another drawn-out sigh. "I really wish you wouldn't insist on sleeping with it. The table's close enough."

"I'll think about your suggestion," Christina answered. "Now you must give me your word, Lyon. You won't take any chances, will you? Don't turn your back on him, not even for a second. Don't leave your fate in Richards's hands, either. I trust him, but I have far more faith in your instincts."

She would have continued her litany of demands if Lyon hadn't stopped her by pulling her into his arms and kissing her. "I love you, Christina."

"I love you, too, Lyon. Here, you carry this. It's fitting that you have it, for it was fashioned by a warrior whom I also love. My brother would want you to have it."

Lyon took the weapon and slipped it inside his right boot. Christina nodded with satisfaction, then started out the door. "Lyon?" she called over her shoulder.

"What now?" he grumbled.

"We must make him say the words."

"We will, Christina. We will."

Richards was waiting outside the front door for him. Lyon's friend was already mounted and holding the reins of Lyon's stallion. A few minutes were spent waiting for Christina's horse to be readied.

Lyon paced the walkway while he waited. "We have plenty of time," Richards announced when he took in Lyon's grim expression. "Remember, even if he took men along to help, there are still over a hundred of those prickly rose bushes to be dug up again."

Lyon forced a smile."I don't think Stalinsky took anyone with him," he remarked as he helped Christina mount her steed. He then climbed atop his own horse with one fluid motion. "How many men do you have posted there?"

"Four of my best," Richards answered. "Benson is in charge. The Baron won't know they're there, and they won't interfere unless he tries to leave," he added. "My dear, are you sure you're up to this outing?"

"I'm sure."

Richards gave Christina a long look, then nodded. "Come along, children. Let's get this done. The captain of Percy's ship is waiting for his passengers."

"Passengers?"

"I've decided to go along. I promised your wife justice would be served. Though we're gaining it through the back door, so to speak, I'm going to be there to make certain. Do you understand my meaning?"

Lyon gave a brisk nod. "I do."

"I don't," Christina admitted.

"I'll explain it later, sweet."

They were the last words spoken until they reached their destination some four hours later. After they dismounted, Richards handed Lyon the moldy box they'd retrieved from the ground on their last visit to Acton's estate.

"I've replaced the real gems with glass replicas. Wait until I get into position before you confront him."

Lyon shook his head. He handed the box to Christina. "She's going to confront him," he told Richards.

One of Richards's men came over to lead their horses away. He spoke to his superior before pulling the mounts into the forest surrounding them. "You were right, Lyon. Stalinsky came alone."

They separated then. Richards went up the front path and turned to circle the right side of the house. Lyon and Christina moved to the left. He paused before rounding the corner, opened the box his wife held in her hands, and lifted two pieces of cut glass. At first glance they did look like the real thing. They were good enough to fool the Baron, Lyon decided, for the brief minute he wanted him fooled.

He then explained what Christina was going to do.

Baron Stalinsky was kneeling on the ground, his shoulders bent to his task. He was muttering obscenities as he struggled to pull the stem of one fat bush out of the ground. He wore black gloves to protect his hands and worked with determined speed. A narrow shovel rested on the ground beside him.

"Looking for something, Father?"

The Baron whirled around on his knees to confront Christina. Dirt streaked his sweaty forehead and angular cheeks.

He didn't look very commanding now. No, he was a jackal to be sure. The sneer on his face reminded Christina of an angry animal baring his teeth. The look sickened her, and she thought she wouldn't have been surprised if he'd started growling.

Christina faced her father alone. She stood a good twenty feet away from him. She had his full attention, of course, and when she thought he was just about to spring forward, she lifted the box and took out a handful of the fake gems. She casually tossed some of the jewels into the air. "Are these what you're looking for, Father?"

Baron Stalinsky slowly came to his feet. His eyes darted to the left and then to the right. She decided to answer his unspoken thought. "Lyon? I believe my father is looking for you."

Lyon walked over to stand next to Christina. He took the box from her, then motioned her to move away. Christina backed up several paces immediately.

"This fight is between the two of us, Baron."

"Fight? I'm an old man, Lyon. The odds wouldn't be fair. Besides, I have no quarrel with you or my daughter. Those jewels belong to me," he added with a wave of his hand toward the box. "Jessica stole them. In court I'll be able to prove they're mine."

Lyon didn't take his gaze off the Baron. "There isn't going

to be a day in an English court, Baron. In fact, as soon as you've answered a single question for Christina and a few more for me, you can be on your way. It's going to be simple for you. I won't have my wife involved in a scandal," he lied.

"Scandal? I don't know what you're talking about," the Baron replied. His voice reeked with authority.

"The murder trial would be upsetting for Christina. I won't have her humiliated." Lyon paused in his explanation to throw a bright red ruby over his shoulder. "It will take you days to find all of these. I'll toss the rest into the creek behind the bluff, Baron, if you don't agree to answer my questions. The current's swift."

"No!" the Baron shouted. "Don't you realize what they're worth? You're holding a fortune in your hands!" His voice had turned coaxing, eager.

Lyon noticed that the Baron's right hand was slowly moving to his back. Reacting with incredible speed, he drew a pistol from his waistcoat, took aim, and fired just as Stalinsky was bringing the hidden pistol around to the front.

The shot lodged in the Baron's hand. His pistol fell to the ground. Lyon threw the box on the ground, retrieved Christina's knife from his boot, and had the Baron by his throat before he'd finished his first howl of pain.

"Christina wants you to speak the truth. She knows Jessica wasn't crazy and wants to hear you say it." Lyon increased his pressure around the Baron's neck as he threatened, then suddenly threw the Baron backwards. He stood over his prey and waited for him to look up. "After you've answered my questions you can pick up your precious gems and leave. You've booked passage for the West Indies, but I've convinced the captain to leave today. He's waiting for you and the next tide, Baron."

The Baron's eyes narrowed. He stared at the box for a long minute, then turned to Lyon. The tip of his tongue ran over his lower lip. "I don't have to answer your questions. Everyone knows Jessica was out of her mind. When I go to the authorities—"

"Lyon," Christina called out. "I don't think he quite grasps the situation."

"Then let me make it simple for him," Lyon said. "Baron, if you don't tell me what I want to know, you won't be going anywhere. I'll slit your throat. A fitting end, wouldn't you agree, after all the throats you've cut?"

"What are you talking about?" the Baron asked, feigning confusion. He clasped his injured hand to his chest.

"Come now, Baron. You know what I'm talking about," Lyon answered. "You've gotten away with your murders all these years. Haven't you ever wanted to boast of your skill? You couldn't, of course, until now. Is your ego so inflated you haven't any need to admit something you know you'll never be hanged for?"

Stalinsky pretended to struggle to his feet. Lyon saw him reach into his boot and extract a small pistol of the sort a woman would carry. He lunged at Lyon as he pulled the pistol forward. Lyon kicked the weapon out of his hand, then lashed out again with the side of his boot to hit the Baron's injured hand.

The screech of pain echoed throughout the countryside. "This is your last chance, Baron. My patience has run out." He flipped the knife from one hand to the other. "Was Jessica crazy?"

"Christina," the Baron shouted. "How can you let him terrorize me this way? I'm your father, for God's sake. Have you no mercy? Do you really want him to slit my throat?"

"No, Father," Christina denied. "I don't want him to slit your throat. I'd rather he cut your heart out, but Lyon does have his preferences, and I must let him have his way."

The Baron glared at his daughter. He stood up. A gleam appeared in his eyes, and he actually started to laugh. "No, Jessica wasn't crazy." He laughed again, a grating sound that chilled Christina. "But it's too late to do anything now, Lyon."

"Terrance MacFinley would have recognized that it was you sneaking around the wagon train. Isn't that right?" Lyon challenged.

"Your deductions are most amazing," the Baron said with a chuckle. "Yes, Terrance would have noticed me."

Lyon pushed the box towards Stalinsky with the tip of his

boot. "One last question and then you may leave. Were you behind the Brisbane murders?"

The Baron's eyes widened. "How did you—"

"You outsmarted our War Department, didn't you?" Lyon asked, trying to sound impressed and not sickened. He was deliberately playing upon the Baron's vanity, hoping the bastard would feel safe enough to admit the truth.

"I did outsmart them, didn't I? I lived off the money Brisbane had received for the secrets he'd sold, too. Oh, yes, Lyon, I was smarter than all of them."

"Was Porter involved in your scheme, or did you act alone?" Lyon asked.

"Porter? He was as stupid as the rest of them. I always acted alone, Lyon. It's the reason I've survived these many years, the reason I've been such a wealthy man."

Lyon didn't think he could stand to look at the man much longer. He motioned to the box, the backed up several paces. "Pick it up and get out of here. If I ever see you again, I'll kill you."

The baron scurried over to the box. He flipped it open, barely glanced at the contents, then slammed it shut with a snort of pleasure.

"Are you finished, Lyon?"

Richards, surrounded by his men, strolled out from their hiding places.

"Did you hear?"

"All of it," Richards announced. He touched Lyon's shoulder before walking over to the Baron.

"Damn your . . ." the Baron shouted. He stopped himself, then glared at Lyon. "I'll make certain your wife's humiliation is complete. I promise I'll say things in court about her mother that will—"

"Close your mouth," Richards bellowed. "We're taking you to the harbor, Baron. In fact, Benson and I shall be your travel companions on your trip back to your homeland. I believe you'll get a nice reception. The new government will undoubtedly be happy to let you stand trial."

Lyon didn't stay to listen to the Baron's demands to be given a trial in England. He took hold of Christina's hand without saying a word and started walking toward their mounts.

Richards was right. They were using the back door to gain justice. Baron Stalinsky would be returned to his homeland, where he would be judged by his former subjects. It would mean a death sentence. And if, by some chance, the new government proved to be just as corrupt, then Richards and Benson were prepared to take care of the Baron.

By the time he and Christina returned to their London townhouse, she was looking terribly pale.

He ignored her protests and carried her up to their bedroom. "You're going back to bed now," he told her as he helped her get out of her clothes.

"I will be better now," Christina told him. "It is finished."

"Yes, love. It is finished."

"I never believed Jessica was crazy," Christina told Lyon. She put on her silk robe, then wrapped her arms around her husband's waist. "I never believed that."

The sadness in her voice pulled at his heart. "I know you didn't," Lyon soothed. "Jessica can rest in peace now."

"Yes. In peace. I like to believe that her soul lingers with the Dakotas now. Maybe she waits for Merry to come and join her."

"I don't think Black Wolf would care for that hope of yours," Lyon said.

"Oh, he would join them, too, of course," Christina replied.

She sighed into his jacket, then kissed him on the base of his throat. "It's his destiny to meet Jessica in the Afterlife," she announced.

"Yes, destiny," Lyon said. "Now it's your destiny to quit being sick every morning and night, my love. You've kept your promise to your mother. The treasure is being returned to the rightful owners. Richards is going to see to the sale of the gems and the distribution of the money. We're going home to Lyonwood, and you'll get fat and sassy. I command it."

Christina really did try to comply with her husband's commands. The sickness eventually left her. She gained weight, too—so much, in fact, that she thought she waddled like a duck. She wasn't very sassy, however, for she spent most of her confinement trying to soothe her husband's worries.

She denied being with child until it became ludicrous. Poor Lyon was terrified of the birthing. Christina understood his fear. He'd watched Lettie go through terrible pain. She'd died a horrible death, with the babe trapped inside her.

Christina used denial and then reason. She told Lyon she was strong, that it was a very natural condition for a woman to be in, and that she was Dakota in her heart and knew exactly what to do to make the birthing easier. Dakota women rarely died in childbirth.

Lyon had a rebuttal for each of her arguments. He told her she was too small for such a mighty task, that it wasn't at all natural for such a gentle woman to have to go through such terrible agony, and that she was English, not Dakota, where it most counted—in her womb, for God's sake, not her heart.

Ironically, it was Lyon's mother who softened Lyon's fears somewhat. The elderly woman was slowly returning to her family. She reminded her son that she was just as small in stature as Christina was, and that she had given her husband three fine babies without making a single whimper.

Christina was thankful for her mother-in-law's help. She didn't have to threaten to drag her new confidante outside into the forest to choose a burial site any longer. Lyon's mother finally admitted she wasn't quite ready to die yet. The woman still liked to talk about James, but she interlaced her remarks with stories about Lyon and Diana, too.

Deavenrue came to visit Christina. He stayed a month's time, then left with six fine horses Lyon had chosen as gifts for the Dakotas. Three men eager for the adventure went along to help Deavenrue.

The missionary helped to ease Lyon's mind about Christina, but once he'd left, Lyon was back to scowling and snapping at everyone.

Baron Winters, the family's physician, moved into their

house two weeks before Christina went into labor. She had no intention of letting the physician help her, of course, yet she had the good sense to keep that determination to herself. His presence calmed Lyon, and Christina was thankful for that.

The pains began after dinner, then continued into the night. Christina didn't wake her husband until the last possible minute. Lyon had time only to wake up and do as Christina instructed. He was holding his infant son in his arms minutes later.

Christina was too exhausted to weep, so Lyon wept for both of them while their magnificent little warrior bellowed his indignation.

He wanted to name his son Alexander Daniel.

She was having none of that. She wanted to name him Screaming Black Eagle.

Lyon was having none of that.

In the end, they compromised. The future Marquess of Lyonwood was christened Dakota Alexander.

The following is a preview of *Heartbreaker*...

It was hotter than hell inside the confessional. A thick black curtain, dusty with age and neglect, covered the narrow opening from the ceiling of the box to the scarred hardwood floor, blocking out both the daylight and the air.

It was like being inside a coffin someone had absent-mindedly left propped up against the wall, and Father Thomas Madden thanked God he wasn't claustrophobic. He was rapidly becoming miserable though. The air was heavy and ripe with mildew, making his breathing as labored as when he was back at Penn State running that last yard to the goalposts with the football tucked neatly in his arm. He hadn't minded the pain in his lungs then, and he certainly didn't mind it now. It was all simply part of the job.

The old priests would tell him to offer his discomfort up to God for the poor souls in purgatory. Tom didn't see any harm in doing that, even though he wondered how his own misery was going to relieve anyone else's.

He shifted position on the hard oak chair, fidgeting like a choirboy at Sunday practice. He could feel the sweat dripping down the sides of his face and neck into his cassock. The long black robe was soaked through with perspiration, and he sincerely doubted he smelled at all like the hint of Irish Spring soap he'd used in the shower this morning.

The temperature outside hovered between ninety-four and ninety-five in the shade of the rectory porch where the thermostat was nailed to the whitewashed stone wall. The humidity made the heat so oppressive, those unfortunate souls who were forced to leave their air-conditioned homes and venture outside did so with a slow shuffle and a quick temper.

It was a lousy day for the compressor to bite the dust. There were windows in the church, of course, but the ones that could have been opened had been sealed shut long ago in a futile attempt to keep vandals out. The two others were high up in the gold, domed ceiling. They were stained glass depictions of the archangels Gabriel and Michael holding gleaming swords in their fists. Gabriel was looking up toward heaven, a beatified expression on his face, while Michael scowled at the snakes he held pinned down at his bare feet. The colored windows were considered priceless, prayer-inspiring works of art by the congregation, but they were useless in combating the heat. They had been added for decoration, not ventilation.

Tom was a big, strapping man with a seventeen-and-a-half-inch neck left over from his glory days, but he was cursed with baby sensitive skin. The heat was giving him a prickly rash. He hiked the cassock up to his thighs, revealing the yellow and black happy-face boxer shorts his sister, Laurant, had given him, kicked off his paint-splattered Wal-Mart rubber thongs, and popped a piece of Dubble Bubble into his mouth.

An act of kindness had landed him in the sweatbox. While waiting for the test results that would determine if he needed another round of chemotherapy at Kansas University Medical Center, he was a guest of Monsignor McKindry, pastor of Our Lady of Mercy Church. The parish was located in the forgotten sector of Kansas City, several hundred miles south of Holy Oaks, Iowa, where Tom was stationed. The neighborhood had been officially designated by a former mayor's task force as the gang zone. Monsignor always took Saturday afternoon confession, but because of the blistering heat, his advanced age, the broken air conditioner, and a conflict in his schedule—the pastor was busy preparing for his reunion with two friends from his seminary days at Assumption Abbey—Tom had volunteered for the duty. He had assumed he'd sit face-to-face with his penitent in a room with a couple of windows open for fresh air. McKindry, however, bowed to the preferences of his faithful parishioners, who stubbornly clung to the old-fashioned way of hearing confessions, a fact Tom learned only after he'd offered his services, and Lewis, the parish handyman, had directed him to the oven he would sit in for the next ninety minutes.

In appreciation Monsignor had loaned him a thoroughly inadequate, battery-operated fan that one of his flock had put in the collection basket. The thing was no bigger than the size of a man's hand. Tom adjusted the angle of the fan so that the air would blow directly on his face, leaned back against the wall, and began to read the *Holy Oaks Gazette* he'd brought along to Kansas City with him.

He turned to the society page on the back first, because he got such a kick out of it. He glanced over the usual club news and the smattering of announcements—two births, three engagements, and a wedding—and then he found his favorite column, called "About Town." The headline was always the same: the bingo game. The number of people who attended the community center bingo night was reported along with the names of the winners of the twenty-five-dollar jackpots. Interviews with the lucky recipients followed, telling what each of them planned to do with his or her windfall. And there was always a comment from Rabbi David Spears, who organized the weekly event, about what a good time everyone had. Tom was suspicious that the society editor, Lorna Hamburg, secretly had a crush on Rabbi Dave, a widower, and that was why the bingo game was so prominently featured in the paper. The rabbi said the same thing every week, and Tom invariably ribbed him about that when they played golf together on Wednesday afternoons. Since Dave usually beat the socks off him, he didn't mind the teasing, but he did accuse Tom of trying to divert attention from his appalling game.

The rest of the column was dedicated to letting everyone in town know who was entertaining company and what they were feeding them. If the news that week was hard to come by, Lorna filled in the space with popular recipes.

There weren't any secrets in Holy Oaks. The front

page was full of news about the proposed town square development and the upcoming one-hundred-year celebration at Assumption Abbey. And there was a nice mention about his sister helping out at the abbey. The reporter called her a tireless and cheerful volunteer and went into some detail describing all the projects she had taken on. Not only was she going to organize all the clutter in the attic for a garage sale, but she was also going to transfer all the information from the old dusty files onto the newly donated computer, and when she had a few minutes to spare, she would be translating the French journals of Father Henri VanKirk, a priest who had died recently. Tom chuckled to himself as he finished reading the glowing testimonial to his sister. Laurant hadn't actually volunteered for any of the jobs. She just happened to be walking past the abbot at the moment he came up with the ideas, and gracious to a fault, she hadn't refused.

By the time Tom finished reading the rest of the *Gazette,* his soaked collar was sticking to his neck. He put the paper on the seat next to him, mopped his brow again, and contemplated closing shop fifteen minutes early.

He gave up the idea almost as soon as it entered his mind. He knew that if he left the confessional early, he'd catch hell from Monsignor, and after the hard day of manual labor he'd put in, he simply wasn't up to a lecture. On the first Wednesday of every third month—Ash Wednesday he silently called it—Tom moved in with Monsignor McKindry, an old, broken-nosed, crackled-skinned Irishman who never missed an opportunity to get as much physical labor as he could possibly squeeze out of his houseguest in seven days. McKindry was crusty and gruff, but he had a heart of gold and a compassionate nature that wasn't compromised by sentimentality. He firmly believed that idle hands were the devil's workshop, especially when the rectory was in dire need of a fresh coat of paint. Hard work, he pontificated, would cure anything, even cancer.

Some days Tom had a hard time remembering why he liked the monsignor so much or felt a kinship with him. Maybe it was because they both had a bit of Irish in them. Or maybe it was because the old man's philosophy, that only a fool cried over spilled milk, had sustained him through more hardships than Job. Tom's battle was child's play compared to McKindry's life.

He would do whatever he could to help lighten McKindry's burdens. Monsignor was looking forward to visiting with his old friends again. One of them was Abbot James Rockhill, Tom's superior at Assumption Abbey, and the other, Vincent Moreno, was a priest Tom had never met. Neither Rockhill nor Moreno would be staying at Mercy house with McKindry and Tom, for they much preferred the luxuries provided by the staff at Holy Trinity parish, luxuries like hot water that lasted longer than five minutes and central air-conditioning. Trinity was located in the heart of a bedroom community on the other side of the state line separating Missouri from Kansas. McKindry jokingly referred to it as "Our Lady of the Lexus," and from the number of designer cars parked in the church's lot on Sunday mornings, the label was right on the mark. Most of the parishioners at Mercy didn't own cars. They walked to church.

Tom's stomach began to rumble. He was hot and

sticky and thirsty. He needed another shower, and he wanted a cold Bud Light. There hadn't been a single taker in all the while he'd been sitting there roasting like a turkey. He didn't think anyone else was even inside the church now, except maybe Lewis, who liked to hide in the cloakroom behind the vestibule and sneak sips of rot whiskey from the bottle in his toolbox. Tom checked his watch, saw he only had a couple of minutes left, and decided he'd had enough. He switched off the light above the confessional and was reaching for the curtain when he heard the swoosh of air the leather kneeler expelled when weight was placed upon it. The sound was followed by a discreet cough from the confessor's cell next to him.

Tom immediately straightened in his chair, took the gum out of his mouth and put it back in the wrapper, then bowed his head in prayer and slid the wooden panel up.

"In the name of the Father and of the Son . . . ," he began in a low voice as he made the sign of the cross.

Several seconds passed in silence. The penitent was either gathering his thoughts or his courage before he confessed his transgressions. Tom adjusted the stole around his neck and patiently continued to wait.

The scent of Calvin Klein's Obsession came floating through the grille that separated them. It was a distinct, heavy, sweet fragrance Tom recognized because his housekeeper in Rome had given him a bottle of the cologne on his last birthday. A little of the stuff went a long way, and the penitent had gone overboard. The confessional reeked. The scent, combined with the smell of mildew and sweat, made Tom feel as though he were trying to breathe through a plastic bag. His stomach lurched and he forced himself not to gag.

"Are you there, Father?"

"I'm here," Tom whispered. "When you're ready to confess your sins, you may begin."

"This is . . . difficult for me. My last confession was a year ago. I wasn't given absolution then. Will you absolve me now?"

There was an odd, singsong quality to the voice and a mocking tone that put Tom on his guard. Was the stranger simply nervous because it had been such a long time since his last confession, or was he being deliberately irreverent?

"You weren't given absolution?"

"No, I wasn't, Father. I angered the priest. I'll make you angry too. What I have to confess will . . . shock you. Then you'll become angry like the other priest."

"Nothing you say will shock or anger me," Tom assured him.

"You've heard it all before? Is that it, Father?"

Before Tom could answer, the penitent whispered, "Hate the sin, not the sinner."

The mocking had intensified. Tom stiffened. "Would you like to begin?"

"Yes," the stranger replied. "Bless me, Father, for I will sin."

Confused by what he'd heard, Tom leaned closer to the grille and asked the man to start over.

"Bless me, Father, for I will sin."

"You want to confess a sin you're going to commit?"

"I do."

"Is this some sort of a game or a—"

"No, no, not a game," the man said. "I'm deadly serious. Are you getting angry yet?"

A burst of laughter, as jarring as the sound of gunfire in the middle of the night, shot through the grille.

Tom was careful to keep his voice neutral when he answered. "No, I'm not angry, but I am confused. Surely you realize you can't be given absolution for sins you're contemplating. Forgiveness is for those who have realized their mistakes and are truly contrite. They're willing to make restitution for their sins."

"Ah, but Father, you don't know what the sins are yet. How can you deny me absolution?"

"Naming the sins doesn't change anything."

"Oh, but it does. A year ago I told another priest exactly what I was going to do, but he didn't believe me until it was too late. Don't make the same mistake."

"How do you know the priest didn't believe you?"

"He didn't try to stop me. That's how I know."

"How long have you been a Catholic?"

"All my life."

"Then you know that a priest cannot acknowledge the sin or the sinner outside of the confessional. The seal of silence is sacred. Exactly how could this other priest have stopped you?"

"He could have found a way. I was . . . practicing then, and I was cautious. It would have been very easy for him to stop me, so it's his fault, not mine. It won't be easy now."

Tom was desperately trying to make sense out of what the man was saying. Practice? Practice what? And what was the sin the priest could have prevented?

"I thought I could control it," the man said.

"Control what?"

"The craving."

"What was the sin you confessed?"

"Her name was Millicent. A nice, old-fashioned name, don't you think? Her friends called her Millie, but I didn't. I much preferred Millicent. Of course, I wasn't what you would call a friend."

Another burst of laughter pierced the dead air. Tom's forehead was beaded with perspiration, but he suddenly felt cold. This wasn't a prankster. He dreaded what he was going to hear, yet he was compelled to ask.

"What happened to Millicent?"

"I broke her heart."

"I don't understand . . ."

"What do you think happened to her?" the man demanded, his impatience clear now. "I killed her. It was messy; there was blood everywhere, all over me. I was terribly inexperienced back then. I hadn't perfected my technique. When I went to confession, I hadn't killed her yet. I was still in the planning stage and the priest could have stopped me, but he didn't. I told him what I was going to do."

"Tell me, how could he have stopped you?"

"Prayer," he answered, a shrug in his voice. "I told him to pray for me, but he didn't pray hard enough, now did he? I still killed her. It's a pity, really. She was such a pretty little thing . . . much prettier than the others."

Dear God, there were other women? How many others?

"How many crimes have you—"

The stranger interrupted him. "Sins, Father," he said.

"I committed sins, but I might have been able to resist if the priest had helped me. He wouldn't give me what I needed."

"What did you need?"

"Absolution and acceptance. I was denied both."

The stranger suddenly slammed his fist into the grille. Rage that must have been simmering just below the surface erupted full force as he spewed out in grotesque detail exactly what he had done to the poor innocent Millicent.

Tom was overwhelmed and sickened by the horror of it all. Dear God, what should he do?

"Well, Father, aren't you going to ask me if I'm sorry for my sins?" he taunted.

"No, you aren't contrite."

A suffocating silence filled the confessional. And then, in a serpent's hiss, the voice returned.

"The craving's come back."